THEY RACED TO GLORY . . . AND TO LOVE

ANNIE—When it came to love and horses, she'd learn that the rules don't apply to the mob or to the rich. When it comes to winning, anything goes . . . seduction, manipulation, and very dirty tricks.

SAM—He'd conquered Annie's body and heart, but when he hurt her as only a lover could, he found out that the dark side of desire is revenge.

PHIL—He'd chosen the underworld's quick riches and sudden violence, and he'd destroy a woman, no matter how beautiful, who threatened his manhood or his mob ties.

FRANK—He'd trained high-strung thoroughbreds to be champions, but his own passions were not in control . . . and he might kill either the horse or the woman he loved.

BASE BLOOD—He was Annie's dream and obsession, a defiant, troublemaking colt with an unyielding heart that drove him to cross the finish line first or die trying.

"FOR THOSE WITH AN INTEREST IN HORSE RACING AND THOSE WHO ENJOY STRONG CHARACTERS AND GOOD FICTION, *BRED TO WIN* SHOULD BE AN ACROSS-THE-BOARD FAVORITE." —*Star News*

WILLIAM KINSOLVING

Bred to Win

A NOVEL

A Dell Book

Published by
Dell Publishing
a division of
Bantam Doubleday Dell Publishing Group, Inc.
666 Fifth Avenue, New York, New York 10103

All of the characters in this book are fictitious, and any resemblance to actual persons, living or dead, is purely coincidental.

ISBN: 0-440-20962-5

Reprinted by arrangement with Doubleday, New York, New York

Printed in the United States of America

Published simultaneously in Canada

October 1991

10 9 8 7 6 5 4 3 2 1
OPM

For Eliza

ACKNOWLEDGMENTS

FOR THEIR ENTHUSIASM and expertise, my deepest gratitude goes to Tom and Marguerite Whitney. Andrew Beyer and Whitney Tower were kind enough to vet the manuscript and offer their advice. I took most of it; therefore, if any mistakes remain, they are mine.

For time and counsel, my thanks are due to Cot and Anne Campbell, John and Betty Hettinger, Rt. Hon. Earl of Harrington, Christian de Lagarde, Evelyn de Rothschild, Criquette Head, Hamish Scott-Dalgleish, Alfred Gwynne Vanderbilt, Henry D. White, Mary Lou Whitney, Robert Barry, Jonathan Irwin, Del Carroll, Nina Hahn, "Jello" Hall, The Lady Camrose, the Bell family of Jonabel Farm, John and Lee Carroll, Merry Farrington, and the late Liz Tippett.

The public relations directors of three tracks were most hospitable: Karl Schmidt of Churchill Downs, Jim Peden of Hollywood Park, and particularly Steven Schwartz of the New York Racing Association at Saratoga. Louis Romanet kindly arranged access to the racing venues in France.

Out of a lengthy bibliography, two books deserve special mention, Steven Crist's *The Horse Traders* and Jocelyn de Moubray's *The Thoroughbred Business.*

For helping to turn these pages into a book, my deep appreciation goes to my editor, Nan A. Talese, who placed her bet early and held on for the finish. Frances Apt, my copy editor, is a wizard to any author lucky enough to have her services. To my literary agent, Helen Brann, who understands both horses and writers, I owe much, including the spur to start writing this book.

Eileen FitzGerald my researcher, Robert J. Baumann, and Susan Kinsolving were instrumental in its creation. Finally, my assistant, Susan York, gave this book hundreds of devoted hours.

CONTENTS

PART ONE

Certainty

1955–1960

ONE

COMING UP FROM THE SOUTH along the Big Sandy River, the night breeze was a temperate one, a relief from the frigid northern winds that had blown down the Ohio throughout the winter. The two rivers intersected a few miles from where Annie stood outside her family's shack. Holding herself for warmth, she shivered. Under her flannel pajama top, she pressed her hands over her breasts. For the first time that year, the air was pungent with a scent of pine. She inhaled deeply as she heard a diesel's air horn moan five miles away. A train was passing through Ashland and starting down the Kentucky bank of the Ohio River.

At fifteen, she was taller than most of the boys at Catlettsburg High School. Her breasts had developed over the winter. She tried to hide them by wearing loose sweaters. Nevertheless, the boys looked at her differently, although they still avoided talking to her. The girls still talked to her, saying more mean things than usual about her hair and clothes. Annie took another deep breath and shook her head.

The kids at school called her Ratsnest because her amber-colored hair was so thick and tangled. She reached up and ran her fingers through it. There was no hot water tank in the shack; to wash her hair, she had to heat water in pots on the coal stove. Her hair was still damp from the bath she had managed to take that night. Shivering again, she started walking down the dirt road to the railroad tracks that ran along the Ohio.

Through the winters, Annie's two older brothers, Jimmy Lee and Fungo, slept beside her in the double bed next to the coal stove. They hogged the covers, breathed noisily through their mouths, and stank from winter sweats, which they would not wash off until the river was warm enough for swimming. Jimmy Lee had tried to get into her earlier in the night, but she had kicked him. When he started punching her in the back and pulling her hair, Annie jumped out of bed, jammed on her Keds, and ran outside. Always prepared, she wore her flannel pajama top and her jeans to bed.

The shack was no more than a shelter made of planks and tar paper. Annie had lived there all her life. The floorboards were set on the ground, which froze in the winter, leaked up mud in the spring, dried to dust in the summer, and gathered in the corners when the wind came off the river in the fall. There were three rooms, but only the big one had the coal stove. Annie measured the seasons not only by the condition of the dirt on the floor, but by how many bodies slept with her in the bed beside the stove. Walking along the road, Annie wished she had grabbed a sweater. It was almost dawn and she felt snow coming in the spring air.

She flinched when she thought about what had happened the previous day. The blood rose in her cheeks from the shame. On Tuesday, a nice woman from the Baptist church in Catlettsburg had delivered another package of used clothes to the shack. They were always so clean, cleaner than anything Annie had, and on this occasion, there was a pretty dress that actually fit her. It had yellow and white stripes. She had never been excited about her clothes before, usually because they looked worn and seldom fit her gangling body. The yellow striped dress had a line of buttons from the white-collared scoop neckline down to the hem. They buttoned over her breasts and waist in a tight fit, as if the dress had been made for her. The skirt flared out and the sleeves came down exactly to her wrists with more buttons to close the white cuffs.

She was determined to wear it to school the next day. That night, she tried to wash her hair, but her brothers would not leave her alone. They were both dropouts from school, and Tuesday was their night off from the roadhouse where they washed dishes. Annie never took a bath when they were around.

The next morning, she tied her hair back in a ponytail. Years before, she had received a pair of white patent leather shoes in another church bundle. They were badly cracked and did not fit well anymore, but Annie wore them with no socks. She took pleasure in buttoning each button of the yellow striped dress, and just before she left to catch the bus for school, dared to look in the mirror over the kitchen sink. She thought she had never looked so pretty.

Running up to the county road, she caught the school bus. She kept her secret covered with her old pea jacket, but she imagined the reaction of the other students when she revealed her dress, and tried to think up what to say to their compliments.

After Annie put her coat in her locker, Mary Lou Mc-Casslin, the richest, most popular girl in school, who had never spoken to Annie before, yelled down the hall, "Where'd you get that? That's my dress!" She started to laugh. "My momma made me throw it out because it was so old. Well, come on, Ratsnest, what are you doing in *my* dress?"

Remembering her humiliation, Annie stopped on the road and stood still in the dark. "I ain't ever going back to school," she said aloud. She did not go regularly. Her father often caused her to miss the school bus, and running the six miles of county road into Catlettsburg when there was snow on the ground was impossible. She liked learning and was good at it, but she was planning on leaving home.

When she was five, her mother had died; when she was ten, her father had broken her arm. It was 1955; she was three times five, so she believed that something was bound to happen. There were only a couple of weeks left, though. She had a birthday coming soon.

As she walked on, Annie remembered the book her English teacher had given her. He had heard Mary Lou McCasslin yelling in the hall. A nice old man who had never seemed to pay much attention to Annie, he had put the book on her desk just before the bell and told her she could take it home. "You'll enjoy it, Annie," he said. Its title was *Great Expectations.* He had never given anyone else a book. At the time, Annie wanted no more attention and barely thanked him.

The air horn blasted again, two miles away at the signal bridge, where her father waited to switch the rails back for the local trains. Annie ran down to the tracks to watch the train go by, a ritual she had performed ever since she was a little girl.

The train that was coming was a "streamliner," her father's old-fashioned word but one Annie liked. It sounded right for what it described, a gleaming, fast projectile of private comfort and public ease, of dining cars, club cars, sleepers, and compartment cars. Annie had known the schedules of the passing trains for as long as she could remember. This one, the George Washington, shot through the dawn three mornings a week and streaked past on its way into a new day. It came from Chicago and Cincinnati, picked up cars in Ashland from the Toledo and Louisville-Lexington spurs, and a few minutes after going by, it crossed over the Big Sandy River from Kentucky to West Virginia, taking its privileged passengers in their luxurious compartments on to Charleston, Washington, D.C., Philadelphia, and then New York. Ever since she could remember, Annie had collected her glimpses through the windows of the streamliners as they passed. To her, the images were a substitute for a camera. She remembered a man in a maroon smoking jacket with slicked-back hair holding a long cigarette holder, and, startlingly, a naked woman staring out into the early light. There was once a boy Annie's age who stuck out his tongue; another time a man with a sheepdog; a woman with gold coins around her neck. During the Korean

War, soldiers filled the luxurious Pullman cars; one played a trumpet, which she could not hear. Once an officer with many medals peed off the back platform of the club car. Annie kept the images like an album in her mind.

She hurried to be at the tracks when the train came by. "Momma, I miss you so bad," she whispered as she heard the low roar of the approaching streamliner. "I swear to you, Momma, I'll get away from here on one of those."

It began to snow, a spring snow of big fluffy flakes. Her brothers and father had always said that her mother's death was Annie's fault, because her mother never recovered fully after Annie was born. Remembering how they had treated her mother in the years of her illness, Annie never accepted the death or the blame. When she was hurt or afraid, she talked to her mother. Jimmy Lee and Fungo said she was crazy for doing that.

She reached the service road, which ran beside the tracks, and thought again of the yellow striped dress hanging over a chair inside the shack. "Please get God to do something real bad to Mary Lou McCasslin."

Then Annie heard brakes shriek and air horns bellow. Steel grated against steel. She started running up the service road toward the noise. Metal screamed and buckled, glass shattered, couplings tore out, pressure hoses exploded, wheel rims shrieked against collapsing rails, their spikes pulling out of the ties with reports like gunshots. There was a one-second pause as if the metal had given up resisting and taken a last breath, then the concussive blast of the diesel engine exploding. As she ran around a turn and stopped, Annie already knew her father had caused the crash. She saw the diesel engine burning; behind it, the silver cars had accordioned, smashing into themselves. Some had turned over; some remained upright. The last two had lurched off the tracks and slid down the embankment to the river's edge. Annie heard the passengers' screams and, farther away, shrill shrieks from what sounded like horses. She stood transfixed, watching the conflagration as if it were safely on a movie screen instead of fifty yards in front of her. Then, as adrenaline hit and dissolved her shock, she started running to find her father.

The snow melted high above the diesel fire. Yelling for help, people were climbing out of smashed windows, staggering around in their nightclothes, holding themselves, bleeding, groaning, and screaming.

Annie kept running, determined to get beyond the wreck to her father a mile up the tracks toward Ashland. She hated him, but if she could find him, she might rid him of that night's bottle of white lightning, drag him into the river, and sober him up. Then maybe she could get to whatever switch he had thrown wrong, and fix it.

A gunshot from one of the cars at the end of the train stopped her again. She heard horses' death whinnies and their hoofs pounding in panic against the siding. Jumping onto the tracks, she saw the last two cars at the foot of the embankment, lying on their sides by the river's edge. Looking down on them, Annie noticed that one car had fancy curtains on the windows, small chandeliers inside on the ceiling, polished wood, and velvet upholstery. The other looked like a boxcar with huge sliding doors and several windows. Annie watched as two women wearing fancy nightclothes under fur coats crawled out through a window of their overturned car. The old one had pallid skin and gray-blue hair in tight curls like steel wool. The other one, younger, pale, pretty, blond, was bleeding from her chin onto the white fur. She helped the older woman walk. They were silent, seeming to know exactly where they must go, as if even in a train crash a place were already reserved for them.

As two men climbed out after them from the private car's window, the thrashing of horses' hoofs against the side of the boxcar became so rapid that it sounded to Annie like a machine gun. Then a real shot blasted through the other noises. The thrashing hoofs stopped abruptly. An intense bleating from other terrified horses began.

The sliding door rolled open on the upper side of the boxcar. Holding a gun, a bare-chested man lifted himself out and looked around. The older woman had found a place to sit on a log of driftwood from the river. She yelled at one of the men, as if she were sitting on a throne, "My purse! Go find my purse!" One man obediently hurried back to the overturned railroad car. The other man, with gray hair falling in front of his eyes, limped toward the two women, but a shout came from the boxcar.

A horse leaped straight through the boxcar's open door and, stumbling onto its side, thrashed its legs in the air. The bare-chested man dropped his gun and grabbed the horse's halter, trying to hold the animal down on the boxcar. They both fell to the ground, the man on top. Once on its feet, the horse shook the man off and reared, beating its hoofs in the air. Then it started up the embankment directly toward Annie.

The man quickly stood and looked up at her. To Annie, the horse was huge, and as it got closer, she saw that its eyes were wild and its teeth were bared. It let out a deep roar of breath with the effort of each struggling leap up the embankment. Scared of being trampled, Annie scrambled out of its path.

"Get that colt!" the man yelled as the gasping animal plunged by her. Across the tracks the colt broke into a gallop as he hit the dirt service road. Stumbling, he recovered and veered into a growth of scrub pines on the other side.

Annie took off after the colt. Though she was familiar with the ground, she knew she could not overtake him. Following the hoofprints in the new snow, she ran into the stand of scrub pine. If the colt reached the county road, he could run forever. She had to head him off.

Unable to see him, Annie heard him break blindly through the low-branched trees. Suddenly it was quiet ahead. Annie slowed down and tried to avoid making any noise. To her right, she heard him whinny. At the same time, over to her left, she heard sirens. Fire trucks were coming up the incline of the county road.

Protecting her face, Annie ran through the low branches and stumbled over a fallen log. Using her hands to keep from falling, she rushed on even as she heard somewhere to her right the colt plunging nearer. Running out of the woods onto the county road, she saw a hook and ladder gather momentum as it sped down the incline toward her. Annie turned to look for the colt. She heard him and started up the road, waving her arms. The fire engine blasted its horn above the sirens and flashed its bright lights. It started braking as the colt charged

9

out of the woods. He hesitated at the shoulder, allowing Annie to get in front of him, then reared as the fire engine started to skid on the fresh wet snow, its sirens shrieking. Terrified, the colt turned and charged back into the woods. Annie leaped away as the fire engine skidded toward her, the cab jackknifing and just missing her.

She landed hard on the side of the road. Looking for the colt, she stood up, only then realizing she could not breathe. Nothing else hurt. Firemen were already off the truck, running toward her and yelling, but she did not wait to hear whether it was with anger or concern. Barely able to say, "I'm real sorry, mister," Annie ran, following the hoofprints back into the woods.

At first, she could not force enough air into her lungs, but gradually her speed increased. The colt was a long way ahead of her, but at least he was headed away from the road. Sweat fell into her eyes and she wiped it away. Seeing blood as well as sweat on her hand, she rubbed it off on her jeans and kept running. She had seen the whites of the colt's eyes when he reared, a look of pure terror. She knew about that kind of fear, and ran faster.

For two hours, Annie tracked the colt through woods, up and down rock croppings, across open meadows. The snow stopped and the day began to brighten. Three times he halted to watch her. Each time she tried not to scare him, and once she spoke a few words before he bolted again.

Then she decided to drive him into the river; surely a horse could not swim as fast as he could run. She herded him toward the cliff face of Murlowe Hill, forcing him to choose the rocky rise to the clearing on top of Cowell's Bluff. Following him, Annie felt that her legs were like limp licorice strings.

In the bluff's clearing, the colt trotted back and forth at the edge, blowing, whinnying, looking for an escape. He saw the twenty-five-foot drop to the river. Annie watched him and sank to her knees to rest. The colt abruptly stopped and watched her. She did not know what to do. Around his head was a leather halter, but even if she could grab it, she doubted that she would be able to control him. He was too big, too powerful.

The colt took a tentative step forward. Annie did not move, although she realized that she was losing circulation in her legs from kneeling. His ears twitched around nervously. Knowing he could bolt at any second, Annie slowly reached out her hand. The colt hesitated, then came forward and sniffed it. Terrified that he would bite her, she noticed that the halter had a gold nameplate on the side strap. Dropping her hand slowly to the ground, she pulled up some scrub weeds and offered them. He could have stepped on her hand. She noticed that his ankles were a little larger than her wrist and wondered how such a huge animal could run on such small support. As the colt began to chew on the weeds, Annie slowly reached with her other hand up to the halter and took hold of it. The name on the plate was CERTAINTY.

The colt jerked, felt the restraint, and, neighing loudly, rose up and turned. Annie was lifted from her knees, but she held on to the halter. As the colt picked up speed, she tried to run with him and was carried in huge flying steps until her legs fell away under her. She started to be dragged, but swiftly was in midair, out over the bluff, still holding on to the halter. She saw the water coming, let go of the halter, and tried to push away from the colt. She thought she was going to die.

The colt hit the river just before Annie did. She did not go deep, but the ice-cold water again made it hard to breathe. She heard the colt thrashing and whinnying, and swam away from him. Treading water, choking from the cold, she turned and saw him ten yards away, lunging up from the water, his neck straining to keep his head above the surface, then plunging back down. Annie swam as close as she dared.

"Certainty!"

The colt turned to look, thus finding an equilibrium. His legs continued to thrash, causing him to surge forward, sink back, and surge again, but his head remained above water.

"That's the way, Certainty. You keep on swimming just like that." Annie swam to keep up with him, staying at a careful distance so that he could see and hear her. Her legs were numb with cold below the knees. She was, however, a strong swimmer; she always beat Fungo, but not Jimmy Lee.

Annie knew the river; the current would carry them back to the train wreck, and she could yell for help. She swam closer to the colt, talking to him, urging him. "It ain't far; you keep going, you're doing real good, Certainty." She took a chance and reached over to grab hold of his mane. Letting herself float onto his back, she kept talking, allowing the colt to pull her through the water.

As they came around the bend in the river, Annie saw the site of the train crash several hundred yards downstream. Red lights flashed from dozens of fire engines, police cars, and ambulances. A huge derrick was lifting one of the smashed railroad cars above the tracks. Holding on to the colt's mane with one hand, Annie tried to use the other arm to swim, but she could not lift it. From the bank of the river came a loud, urgent whinny, which Certainty heard and answered. Floating over the colt's back as it plunged ahead with greater urgency toward the river's bank, she saw the two railroad cars at the end of the train still on their sides. At the top of the embankment on the service road was a huge silvery van and a large gray limousine. Annie yelled as she saw figures start to run down to the edge of the river.

She kept yelling as the colt's mane began to slip through her frozen fingers. Certainty swam out from under her while she tried to keep afloat. Her head went under. As she fought her way to the surface again, she glimpsed the man who had yelled at her to get the colt. The last thing she saw was him diving into the water.

TWO

ANNIE OPENED HER EYES. She saw sunlight refracted through square cut-glass bottles and six small glasses held in a case of highly polished wood. It was three feet in front of her. A motor was running; without moving, she looked around. Covered with a fur blanket, she was lying across the back seat of a car unlike any she had ever seen.

She heard men talking outside. Exhausted, she began to remember the train crash, Certainty, the bluff, the river. Then she remembered seeing the gray limousine and the man . . .

The door opened and Annie looked up. The man she had seen diving into the river was gazing down at her. He was wearing a coat and tie and said, "Hello, Long-Legs, how're you feeling?" Then he smiled.

Annie was unable to answer. She had watched handsome men in movies but never had seen one so close. With dark lashes and eyebrows, his eyes were a light shade of blue that

Annie had seen only on birds' eggshells. His head seemed large and his wavy black hair was the color of newly poured tar. Deeply suntanned, the skin of his face set off the whiteness of his teeth. His brilliant crooked smile caused Annie to stare with honest wonder. "What's your name, Long-Legs?"

"Annie—" She choked up some water and lurched forward to let it fall on the floor. Mortified, she kept her head down.

"Don't worry about that. After what you did for us, you can throw up the whole Ohio River in here if you have to. Here's the doctor, Annie. He just wants to look you over." His accent did not sound to Annie as if he came from anywhere nearby. She thought he must be a Yankee.

The seat pressed down as a man sat next to her. "Well, young lady, let me take another look at you, if I may."

Without facing the doctor, Annie sat up and nodded. She flinched, not from the cold metal stethoscope placed on her back, but from thinking about having thrown up on the floor rug of the limousine. At least it was just water.

"Take some deep breaths for me, please."

As she did so, Annie looked out the window. The snow had melted. The black-haired man was talking to a policeman. Behind them were the two men Annie had seen climbing out of the private railroad car. Both men wore suits and ties. Annie noticed how neat they looked, how shiny their shoes were. There was no sign of the two women.

"Do you feel any pain, miss? Any bones broken?"

"No, sir."

"Let's listen to your heart, then. Seems you've survived pretty well."

She suddenly wondered what had happened to her father and where her brothers were.

"Let me just check your ears. That water's awful cold."

"How come the train crashed?"

"Trainman forgot to close a switch. No wonder, either. They found him upline, dead drunk and ready to fight anyone for bothering him . . . You stay warm in here until we figure a way to get you home," the doctor said as he got out of the back seat.

Before Annie had time to hope it would happen, the black-haired man took the doctor's place next to her and closed the door. He smiled again; she tried to return the smile, then quickly looked away. Outside was the man who had been sent to get the woman's purse and another man in a black suit and a chauffeur's cap carrying matched leather luggage up the river embankment.

"The doctor thinks you're in amazing shape for what you did, Annie. What we all want to know is how you came out of nowhere to save our colt like that?"

She turned toward him. She could not believe how good-looking he was. Without warning, she began to shake, hard.

Assuming she might be going into shock, he grabbed a bottle from the polished wooden rack, unstoppered it, and poured the amber liquid into one of the glasses. He handed it to her and said, "Sip this, very slowly." Annie shook her head. *"Sip it."* It was a command, and she obeyed. Annie thought the liquid felt like syrup and tasted like kerosene.

"My name's Sam Cumberland. My father and I, that's him out there, we want you to know how very grateful we are to you for running down that colt. I had to put down two fillies; I'd have hated to lose him, too. You must have gone all over hell and gone to get him back here."

Annie stared into the glass. "That's okay."

"It's more than okay, Annie. Here's a small token of our gratitude." Glancing over at the envelope he was holding out to her, Annie took it, noting the thickness of the paper.

"How's Certainty?" she asked, still looking at the envelope.

"He's fine," he answered. "Probably resting in a stall right now. The insurance company's vet was out here; said he ought to rest a couple of days before we ship him . . . Where'd you get that dimple?"

He was looking at her. She reached up to touch the familiar spot on her left cheek, and responded with a shrug.

There was a long pause. She did not want him to go, and urgently tried to think of something to say.

"Who got me out of the river?"

"I did, and let me tell you, I *hate* cold water." He laughed. Annie liked the sound; it was a deep, cracking laugh. She wondered how he had carried her, whether he had laid her down on the back seat, whether her ripped pajama top had covered her. But she could not ask that. She had to ask something else. Anything.

"What kind of car is this?"

"It's a Rolls-Royce."

"Oh . . . how'd it get here so fast?" She turned to see if he was still smiling. He was, but something in his eyes made Annie feel suddenly inferior.

"Our driver was taking it from Lexington back to Long Island," he said, gazing distractedly out the window, "and happened to be spending the night in Grayson. The state police were kind enough to locate him, and here we are." He turned back to Annie and smiled quickly. She did not turn away, sensing their time together was about to end. She watched him, wide-eyed, which disconcerted him.

"Annie, we have to get started. The policeman out there will give you a ride home, with sirens if you want."

He reached out his hand to shake hers. Awkwardly, Annie put the glass in the rack, changed the envelope from one hand to the other, and took his hand.

He said, "I bred that colt. I really love him. Thank you."

Annie looked up at him just as he glanced idly down at her breasts. Mortified by what he might be able to see through the torn flannel of her pajama top, she took her hand away to cross her arms.

"Come on out this side, Annie. I want you to meet my father."

Annie stuffed the envelope in her pants pocket and stepped out of the car. The father looked at her appraisingly without a smile and said, "Walker, find the young lady's shoes."

As the man searched, introductions were made. Annie gave a false last name; McCasslin was the first one that came to her mind. The elder Cumberland expressed his deep gratitude to Annie while looking slightly over her head, speaking as if he were looking at the scenery. "You see, my dear, in that colt's veins mingles the blood of Phalarus and Nearco from his sire, almost the same pedigree as Nashua, probably the finest colt of the year. But Certainty's dam is by Man O' War! That's as close to royal blood as America gets, my dear. To have lost that colt would have been a tragedy, not only to the sport of racing but to the generations that will follow."

He spoke with passion, but Annie did not know what he was talking about. She felt dumb, the same way she often did in school after missing several days. Mr. Cumberland glanced down at her face, saw her lack of comprehension, then looked off toward the crash site. Annie noticed the similarity between father and son in the intense light blue, deep-set eyes and particularly the straight long nose.

"This horrible tragedy," Mr. Cumberland said; "two such fillies as those . . . *gone.*" On the last word, his voice quavered deep in his throat.

"Six *people* died, too, Father," Sam said. Although his voice was serious, he included Annie in a quick, mocking glance.

"Horrible, horrible," the older man replied, shaking his head. Annie's stomach grabbed. She saw that the policeman was looking at her.

"Ah, the young woman's shoes," Mr. Cumberland noted as the chauffeur appeared, holding the Keds by one lace apiece, as if they were two fish on a line. "Come along, Sam, we must join the ladies. You took care of her, ah, *pourboire?*" He moved toward the Rolls-Royce without any doubt that someone would be there to open the door for him, which the chauffeur accomplished just in time.

Annie took her shoes, wondering what a *pourboire* was, and sat down on the service road to loosen the still wet laces.

"Well, Annie Long-Legs, thanks again."

He was standing next to her, and she noticed that the laces in his shoes went straight across instead of being crisscrossed. She tried to think of some way to make him stay. "Where're you going now?"

"On down to Huntington," he replied. "A plane's coming so Mother can get back to her special pack of New York doctors." He laughed softly to himself and shook his head.

A crowd of railroad workers suddenly started yelling at the crash site. The policeman left their group and ran toward the derrick, where one of the railroad cars suspended by cables was swaying about ten feet above the ground. Annie saw first Jimmy Lee, then Fungo appear at the car's open doorway.

Each was holding fur coats and handfuls of jewelry. They were yelling at each other, arguing about jumping. Finally, after throwing everything out of the car, Jimmy Lee leaped out and fell to the ground. Fungo watched his brother land and roll, spring up and start running, only to be caught by four policemen, two with shotguns. Other policemen were shouting at Fungo not to move; they too had shotguns. The railroad workers started throwing rocks at Fungo, who dodged them after he let the coats and jewelry fall to the ground.

"Good Christ, looters," Sam said with disgust.

"Come along, Sam," Mr. Cumberland called from the limousine's open door; "we'll keep the ladies waiting." Sam hurried to the Rolls-Royce and the chauffeur shut the door behind him.

Hoping for a wave or a smile, Annie stood and watched as the limousine drove away. In case he could see her, she waved but then felt silly doing so. She gazed after the car until it disappeared.

The noise around the derrick grew louder. Rather than watch what was happening, Annie moved inconspicuously across the service road and up a rise into the woods. When she reached its edge, she turned to see if anyone had noticed her. The railroad car was being lowered to the ground and a crowd was waiting for Fungo. Another crowd had gathered around Jimmy Lee. She caught a glimpse of his face being pushed into the dirt and a hand holding on to his blond curls. Annie slipped into the woods. She did not want any policeman taking her home and finding out she was related to those "looters."

She crouched on a layer of pine needles behind a fallen log. From there, she could look down on the scene of the wreck. Jimmy Lee and Fungo had been dragged to a police car. They were spread-eagled against it, being searched, both with shotguns jammed into the back of their heads. Annie wondered how scared they were. She knew that Fungo was probably babbling excuses to anyone who would listen. That was what he usually did when he was scared and could not beat up someone. Jimmy Lee would stay very quiet and take what came. Then he would smile as sweetly as an angel, and go right for the eyes or the crotch. That was what he had done the night two men followed the brothers home from the road-house. Alone in the shack, Annie had watched through the window. Jimmy Lee stayed clear as they beat up Fungo for a while, then offered them a bottle of his father's white lightning as a peace offering. While they were drinking, Jimmy Lee pulled a knife out of his boot, stabbed one of them between the legs, grabbed the bottle, and smashed it into the other one's face.

The derrick swung the railroad car slowly around to a flat-bed car that had been moved up on the tracks from the opposite direction. From another of the wrecked cars, an emergency rescue team succeeded in prying a body loose. It was loaded onto a waiting stretcher. As the dead woman was laid down, a man standing next to her quickly pulled the night-gown down over her legs, then awkwardly took her hand. Annie could see that the man was talking to the body, and as rescue and railroad workers hurried around them, he knelt down and began to cry.

Annie felt her own tears. "Momma," she said, "tell God He's made another terrible mistake."

She rolled over, let her head rest on the log, and closed her eyes.

Just then, she heard sirens. She turned in time to see two state highway patrol cars speeding away on the service road. Slowly she stood up. They had taken her father; now her two brothers were gone. The shack would be empty. She started through the woods.

Annie knew how quickly the social workers would come, as they had the last time her father had gone to jail. He had wrecked the only car that Annie ever remembered them own-ing. The highway patrol found him pinned in his car at the bottom of a culvert, raging drunk. The judge had given her father thirty days and the railroad company put him on proba-tion. As soon as he was taken away, her brothers stole a car, went to Cincinnati, and worked in a bowling alley. The same day, when Annie came home from school, two social workers were waiting for her. She spent ten weeks in a foster home.

It had been the most embarrassing time in her life. She was

thirteen, at her most awkward. On the first day, she managed to stumble against the mirrored table on which the woman's collection of elaborately decorated blown-out eggs was assembled. Three of them were broken, causing a yelling rage. Annie was unable to speak to the couple. She remained in her cellar room except when she went to school or ate. The meals they gave her were made up of their leftovers.

Then one night Annie woke up lying in a thick fluid. She was terrified, and tried to wash the sheets in the cellar laundry sink. She spent the rest of the night cleaning her room and herself. When she went to school the next morning, she bound herself up with a towel and prayed that her damp sheets, which she had put back on the bed, would not be discovered. At school, the nurse had explained what no one in her family had thought to mention. The sheets were discovered, however, and for the rest of her stay, Annie slept without them.

Coming out of the woods, she reached the dirt road that ran in front of the shack. Hurrying to the front door, she went in and slammed it shut. She knew she had to leave before she could think about it. She could not wait, or she would be sent away again.

Grabbing a paper sack from behind the open garbage can near the sink, Annie hurried to the wooden box by the bathtub where her clothes were stacked. Without thinking of what she would need, she picked her favorite things: a pale green blouse, a plastic bracelet, her heavy blue sweater, and a clean pair of jeans. Her toothbrush hung on a nail by the kitchen sink.

Under the bed, she saw the book her teacher had given her. It was heavy, but she put it in the bag anyway. Then she turned and saw two things in the same glance: the yellow striped dress and the can of kerosene they used to start the stove. The urge to pour it all over the dark wooden boards of the shack was strong. In her mind, she saw the place burning, leaving nothing standing except the outhouse in back.

She shook her head. The shack was railroad property. Burning it down would cause trouble. They would come after her, and she did not want anyone to have a reason to do that. She wanted to disappear.

Taking off her jeans to change into the dress, she heard the envelope crunch in her pocket. She opened the thick paper carefully and pulled out five bills. At first, they looked like play money, very new, very clean. The numbers seemed crowded on the paper. Each had the number 100 on it. Annie had never seen anything bigger than a twenty-dollar bill. Staring at the unfamiliar portrait engraved on the money, she slowly realized that she had five hundred dollars.

"Five *hundred* dollars. *Five hundred dollars,*" she repeated, folding the bills and opening them up again. At last, she put them back into the envelope and ran her finger over the engraved address on its flap: 10 East Seventieth Street, New York 21, New York.

So this was a *pourboire,* she thought, and those people travel with their own letter paper. She put the envelope on the bed beside her and took off her Keds, jeans, and flannel top. She let them lay where they fell. As she slipped into her underwear, socks, her shoes, the yellow striped dress, and her pea jacket, she looked around the shack for what she hoped would be the last time.

The small window beside the sink framed the view of the outhouse and the pile of rusting junk nearby. A tire swing hung by a rusted chain from a tree; she remembered her brothers pushing her on it, the forts the three of them had made, their snowball attacks on passing trains before the boys had turned mean.

The sink was filled with dirty dishes. The faucet dripped, as always, with the rhythm to which Annie fell asleep. In the middle of the room, the coal stove stood massively with the bed crowded between it and the wall. Nearby was the worn rag rug on which Annie had slept when her mother was dying. There was a wobbly table with its four unmatched chairs where the family ate. Annie thought of the fifth chair her father had smashed and used for kindling after her mother died. Two doorways led to the other rooms where her brothers slept in warm weather, and where her father slept in the daytime because he worked at night.

The wall opposite the sink was covered with her brothers' girlie pictures, women with huge breasts and skewed smiles on their pretty faces. To one side was a strip of molding Annie had carved with slots to hold the silverware. She had seen a picture somewhere of that kind of arrangement, and thought it would help keep spoons, forks, and knives clean.

She went over to the rack and straightened a fork. From her bed, she often had stared at the neat line of utensils held solidly in their places, catching the moonlight, their order giving her calm. Nearby on the wall was a series of knots in the wood which she had always believed were the six eyes of a horrible monster that came in the night. She looked at them, then turned back to the bed. She took the money out of the envelope and folded the bills in half, putting three of them in her left shoe and two in her right. She put the envelope in the paper bag and started to pick it up.

Just then, she caught a glimpse of herself in the mirror above the sink. She walked over and lifted the mirror off the wall. The sun came in the window and made her hair shine reddish gold, almost the color of the liquid Sam Cumberland had poured from the cut-glass bottle. She was glad she had washed her hair the night before, that her brothers had not been there to bother her. She remembered the time when Fungo held the mirror in her face so that she could see Jimmy Lee on top of her, saying, "You think you're so smart. Well, looka here how smart you are." Jimmy Lee had seen the reflection and made Fungo hold the mirror every time from then on. Annie raised it above her head and smashed it down on the sink. The shards fell into the puddles of murky water, covering the plates, mugs, and pans. Stepping back, Annie picked up the paper bag and, without closing the door behind her, ran out of the shack and into the woods.

Not until Annie was out of sight of the shack did she realize that she had no idea where she was going. She kept walking, figured out how to reach Ashland, and before she knew how or why, she thought of herself getting on a streamliner headed for New York City.

THREE

████████████████████████████████████

████████████████████████████████████

SIX MONTHS LATER, Annie was dreaming that she had missed her train and was running down the track after it when the policeman's billy club poked into her ribs. Before she was awake, she jerked her arms over her head for protection.

"Come on now, get up," the voice said. "The wagon's waiting."

Annie sat up, still cringing, and glimpsed policemen shooing other men and women off the dark wooden benches of the Pennsylvania Station waiting room. Their voices echoed through the immense vaulted space that a slanted shaft of sunlight from a high window cut neatly into irregular halves.

"I'm a passenger," Annie said, still groggy with sleep.

"Where's your ticket, then?" the policeman asked.

"I haven't bought it yet."

"I'm sure of that. All right, come along."

"Wait," she said urgently and leaned down to take off her left shoe. From it, she produced a twenty-dollar bill.

Unmollified, the policeman said, "The ticket window's right over there."

Annie stood and walked across the dimly lit room. She was momentarily blinded as she passed through the shaft of sunlight. At the ticket window, she looked back at the policeman. He was watching her carefully as he pulled a man off one of the benches. Feeling the cold, she pulled her pea jacket tight around her and felt the seam under the left arm tear open.

"Where to?"

"The Belmont Special."

"Round trip?"

Annie hesitated. "No, one way." She pushed the bill under the glass. It was the last of the Cumberland *pourboire.* She stuffed the change into her pocket, turned, and held up the ticket for the policeman to see. He saw it but did not acknowledge it.

"Excuse me, sir," she said, turning back to the ticket window. "Could you tell me when the—"

"I sell tickets. You want information, it's in the main waiting room."

Reacting to what she had learned, over the past half year, was typical New York courtesy, Annie smiled and said, "Thank you, sir," and walked to the information booth.

The first train to Belmont Park was at ten-thirty. She had a four-hour wait. The ladies' room was empty but filthy. Having spent the last four nights in the station, she knew the maintenance people came at seven-thirty. She would not use any of the toilets, but she found a relatively clean sink and washed herself under her clothes with paper towels. Besides the pea jacket, she was wearing two sweaters. She unbuttoned her jeans to wash, but left her shoes and socks on. She did not look in the mirror.

Returning to the same bench on which she had slept, she sat down to wait. As she watched the shaft of sunlight gradually become vertical and finally disappear, she smelled first coffee, then toast from the station's coffee shops. She had not eaten the previous night as a defiant gesture against spending the last twenty dollars, but now she realized how hungry she was, and tried to think of something else.

Belmont Park. Nervousness jolted through her. She knew that the Cumberlands raced their horses there. In the newspapers that customers left in the various places where she had waited tables, she had read of the Cumberlands. The *Journal-American* was the most useful, with its endless number of society gossip columns, and a man named Breslin who wrote well about horse racing. There had been photographs of the Cumberlands in their Belmont box, in the winner's circle, and at their barn. Annie had hoped to go to Belmont one day when she was successful, to say hello, to find out about Certainty, perhaps to talk to Samuel Barkeley Cumberland III again. Instead, she was going to beg for a job. She pressed her lips together to keep them from trembling.

Looking down at her jacket, she saw that the lining was hanging out and quickly tried to tear it off so that it would not show. All she accomplished was to pull more of the lining loose. She stuffed it inside the sleeve.

She had slept in the same clothes for four nights. The sweaters were the two she had bought in Ashland, Kentucky, along with a cardboard suitcase, before boarding the first train for New York. The rest of her clothes were in the fifth-floor walkup in Greenwich Village that she rented for thirty-three dollars a month. Her landlord had locked it and refused to let her in until she paid the two months' back rent she owed him.

Her Cumberland money had gone quickly; saving the last twenty-dollar bill was a kind of superstition. Annie believed that if she spent it, there was no hope. In the six months she had been in New York, she had worked at fourteen jobs, mostly as a waitress, mostly in bars. Few employers cared about her age unless they received a complaint from an irate customer who had propositioned Annie and been turned down, or until a zealous cop spotted her serving alcohol. The money she made was negligible; she never could save enough to pay the rent or buy any new clothes. Sitting on the wooden bench, holding her ticket to Belmont Park, she felt a familiar panic. She fought against it by trying to hope for a job. As people began to hurry by from the commuting trains, Annie took quick glances at their faces. She considered holding out her hand and asking for money, but she could not do it. Not yet.

During the four hours, she moved only once, to go to the bathroom after it was cleaned. She drank a great deal of water, but in spite of the smells that wafted by her, she did not buy food. Instead, she tried to convince herself that breaking the twenty-dollar bill was now good luck. In the light-headedness caused by her hunger, she allowed herself to daydream again about the Cumberlands.

Several weeks before, Annie had walked by 10 East Seventieth Street on her night off. There was a party. She remembered that a piano played; candlelight flickered on a dark oak ceiling behind carelessly closed draperies. Laughter floated across Seventieth Street as limousines waited to pick up the suntanned men and women in dinner jackets and long dresses.

Number 10, as Annie thought of it, seemed like a castle peculiar to New York. She had passed it several times. Double the width of the other houses on the block, the mansion had a facade of carved stone. On the second floor were six long French windows, which opened from the floor to the ceiling onto a narrow iron balcony. Through their heavy scalloped draperies could be seen walls covered in dark green velvet on which hung paintings with lamps on their elaborate gold frames. The ceilings were of carved oak. The floor above had windows with heavily draped curtains all hanging in the same fashion. The top floor had gabled windows projecting from the slanted green coppered roof.

Behind the seven-foot-high black iron fence and gate was a double front door of dark shining wood and glistening brass hardware. On each side of the entrance were gas lamps that burned day and night. Bright marigolds, small chrysanthemums, and daisies grew in concrete tubs along the sidewalk and front walk. On all four floors, each window had a window box overflowing with the same bright blossoms. Annie had wanted to pick a daisy from one of the tubs, but did not dare.

The Belmont Special was called. When she stood up, Annie felt dizzy and almost fell, but, finding her balance, she hurried to the gate, climbed slowly down the tunnel stairs, and looked

for a seat next to the window. It was a weekday; the train was
not crowded. The men who boarded sat down and quickly
unfolded the *Morning Telegraph.* She had retrieved a copy of
the daily racing paper occasionally in a bar where she worked,
but was confused by the numbers, symbols, and tiny print. She
was looking for news about the Cumberlands. The past performance charts described the racing records of every horse running in each race at five or six tracks throughout the East. The
only words she recognized were "Caernarvon Farms," listed
as "owner" of horses running at Belmont. The Cumberlands
owned Caernarvon Farms.

As the train moved out of the tunnel into the bright October light, Annie's head slumped forward into the palm of her
hand. The headache she had tried to ignore became a sharp
gouge of pain behind her eyes. She wondered how cold it was
outside and if her jacket would be warm enough. Suddenly
panic gripped her; she had no idea of how she would go about
finding the Cumberlands to ask for a job. Looking urgently
out the window, she saw her half reflection and closed her
eyes. She wondered where Certainty was, then thought of
Sam.

With no money to spend in her free time, Annie had often
sat in her apartment reading over and over again the collection
of articles about the Cumberlands from newspapers, Sunday
supplements, and by luck an old magazine. She had read that
Sam was ten years older than she was. He was gradually taking
over the responsibility of Caernarvon Farms from his father, J.
Cardell Cumberland. The family stable included the three-
hundred-acre Long Island estate near Stony Brook, the twelve-
hundred-acre Kentucky stud farm outside Lexington, and the
wintering and training facility on the four-thousand-acre Cumberland plantation near Aiken, South Carolina. There were
also the Caernarvon stud farms in Newmarket, England, and
County Limerick in Ireland.

In a Fifth Avenue apartment just around the corner from
Number 10, Sam lived with his wife, Belinda. They had a
Swiss cook, two Norwegian maids, an English butler, and a
French nanny. Annie leaned back in her seat. Their baby, a

girl, was born in September and was christened Alycia by an Episcopal bishop.

According to the society columns, the Cumberlands' life was well ordered, and Annie had memorized it. On every January 2, the Cumberlands' private railroad car, named Gwydian, was hooked up to an Atlantic Coast Line train for the Cumberlands' trip to Palm Beach. The family stayed in Florida through March, spent April either at the farm in Lexington or traveling in Europe. No matter where they were, they always returned to Lexington for their party on the eve of the Kentucky Derby, which was run on the first Saturday in May. The crimson, gold, and royal blue silks of Caernarvon Farms had won the race four times since the turn of the century. After the Derby, the Gwydian was attached to the Chesapeake and Ohio's train for the Cumberlands' return to New York. The previous April, the Cumberlands were involved in a train wreck. Two Caernarvon fillies had to be destroyed, and the Gwydian was damaged beyond repair.

"Six *people* died, too," Annie muttered, imitating what Sam had said. She stared out the train window, remembering her moment in their life.

For the rest of the spring and into early summer, the Cumberland family stayed in town or on Long Island. Visiting their cousins, they commuted back and forth to Newport in July, sometimes by private plane, sometimes on the family's hundred-and-twenty-foot square-rigged schooner, *Merlin,* named for King Arthur's Welsh sorcerer. Mrs. Cumberland was prone to seasickness and avoided the boat. Then, in August, they went by rail up to their "camp," a huge stone lodge on Saranac Lake in the Adirondacks, two hours north of the track in Saratoga Springs where Caernarvon horses had run for the last forty-five years.

Created by Sam's grandfather in 1910, Caernarvon Farms had been named for the town in Wales from which the original Cumberlands had emigrated to America in 1756. The stables had been the passion of the last three Cumberland generations, all of whom regarded their responsibility to the thoroughbred breed as sacrosanct. As an only child, Samuel Barkeley Cumberland III (his uncle and great-grandfather having been the first and second) had been raised to carry on this heritage. In the Cumberland Foundation offices on Park Avenue, he was the titular president; his mother, Cornelia Talasker Cumberland, however, determined the recipients of the foundation's largess. An oil company heiress in her own right, she had put in half the foundation's principal.

Sam had his own pony at five, went to Saratoga at six, and played polo while he was at Princeton. A year after graduating, he had married Belinda Hasquith Clayton, the daughter of one of Kentucky's oldest families. The Claytons owned Sweetwater Farm, the eighteen-hundred-acre thoroughbred stable contiguous to Caernarvon in Kentucky. Belinda, after attending Chatham Hall and Sweet Briar, was introduced to society at the Black and White Ball in New York and the International Debutante Cotillion at the Palace of Versailles. She had known Sam Cumberland all her life. Their romance had not started until she returned to Lexington after two years of show jumping in Europe, where she learned to speak Italian and French.

Annie wondered if Belinda Hasquith Clayton Cumberland had ever had a worry in her life. Even in the train wreck, she had seemed to be so serene. Annie thought of the picture she had found in the magazine, of Sam and Belinda standing beside a new barn at Caernarvon Farm in Kentucky. They were holding hands, laughing at something. She wore a light sweater, a string of pearls, breeches, and dark riding boots. A crop hung idly in her other hand. She was thin, very blond, with smoky suggestive eyes and a determined, confident mouth.

In the same picture, Sam wore old jeans, a sweaty work shirt, a raveled straw hat, and dirty clod-kicker boots. His smile was the same crooked one that had caused Annie to look away when they met. The only item that indicated he was something more than another stable hand was his molded silver belt buckle which attached the letter C to the letter F. Annie had cut out the picture and kept it folded between pages of *Great Expectations* in her apartment. She had looked at it so often that it fell apart on the crease through their hands, neatly severing Belinda from Sam.

• • •

Annie did not notice the train's approach to Belmont Park; she was sitting on the wrong side of the car. The conductor yelled the destination, and Annie waited for the other passengers to get off. When she stood, she had to wait for the dizziness to pass before going to the door. Stepping down from the train, she was instantly aware of the cold. She stopped, surprised that the train had pulled in so near the track's massive stands. A hundred yards from where she stood, the structure seemed to be a high wall with no entrances. In front of it were several one-story buildings and a series of hedges leading to a stand of trees. The other passengers appeared to know where to go, so she followed them. The sun was shining and there was no wind; she thought her jacket would keep her warm.

As she approached the stands, she saw first a tunnel going through them, then numerous entrances, all behind a chain-link fence interspersed with ticket booths. A sign of arrows pointed one way for GRANDSTAND, the other way for CLUB-HOUSE. She did not know where to go.

A uniformed guard stood on the other side of the fence. When Annie smiled at him, his blank look narrowed into a hostile sneer.

"Hi," Annie said. Openness could sometimes disarm New York people by causing them a moment's confusion.

"What d'ya want?" he said.

"Nothing. I was wondering where they keep the horses."

"Not in here, honey. This here's for people. Where'd you get that coat, at the Salvation Army?"

Annie saw that the lining was hanging down in full view. She stuffed it back into her sleeve and walked on, not giving him the pleasure of seeing his effect on her. She had learned that New Yorkers needed little time if they were going to be nasty; back home in Kentucky, malice took longer.

She walked toward a ticket booth. The sign read CLUB-HOUSE $2. Two dollars was three meals in New York.

"Hey, beautiful, you wanna make a bet?"

A man holding open the *Morning Telegraph* was leaning against the pole of an awning that ran from the ticket booth to one of the clubhouse entrances. He spoke with a thick New

York accent; a toothpick danced across his mouth until he grinned, which pinned the pick under his tongue.

She tried to look directly at him but could not. Ordinarily, she would not have responded, but she thought he might help her get inside the fence so that she could find the barns.

"What on?" she asked.

"The license plate of the next car that drives up here. A hundred bucks says it's an even number." He spoke softly, just loud enough to be heard. Annie watched as, tucking the newspaper under his arm, he pulled out a roll of bills, flicked off a hundred, and held it up between his fingers. He grinned again and tongued the toothpick across his mouth.

Annie's mouth was dry, but she forced herself to respond. "I'm sorry. I don't have a hundred dollars with me."

He shrugged the problem away. "How much you got?"

"Not too much."

"How much?"

"Five." If she lost, she would have $9.65 left.

"Cool. I'll give you twenty-to-one odds. Odd or even?"

"Wait. Why are you doing this?"

"I like it. Odd or even?"

"Even."

"Here it comes." He pointed toward the road behind her, which led away through two high hedges. A black limousine was approaching.

He walked over to the fence next to her, watching the car. Annie watched him. He was thin, almost skinny, with a pompadour and a ducktail of black hair. His blue flannel overcoat hung open to reveal a jacket, slacks, and a vest, each made of a different material. A naked woman was hand-painted on his tie. His elastic-sided boots and his belt, which showed under the short vest, were matching white patent leather. A menacing frown was cut into his forehead. His skin was creamy and smooth, shaved to perfection. When she looked at the hand that still held the bill, Annie noticed that his fingers seemed unusually long, with the cleanest, shiniest nails she had ever seen.

"Ain't you the lucky one, beautiful! That last number is an eight. Here you go . . ." and he folded the bill lengthwise and pushed it through the fence. "Double or nothing on that next one?"

"No! I can't take your—"

"Sure you can. You won it fair and square."

"I don't even know who you are, or—"

"Well, that's an easy problem to solve, ain't it?"

He grinned at her again, still holding the bill through the fence. His toothpick was motionless as he stared directly into her eyes. Since she arrived in the city, a lot of men had tried to get close, but none was as smooth as he was. Annie was scared, but he was on the other side of the fence. She reached up and took the hundred-dollar bill.

"With an accent like that," he said pleasantly, "you gotta be from Georgia, or someplace real south like that."

"Catlettsburg, Kentucky."

"Looking for a job?"

She felt her face go hot. "Does it show that bad?"

"In my line of work, you get an instinct. I'd say you been sleeping in your clothes, but that don't hide what *you* are. Come on in, beautiful. It's almost lunchtime. I'll buy."

She had her two months' rent and more. It was a public place. She was very hungry and she wanted a job. She reached into her pocket, took out two dollars, and went down to the entrance booth. He met her as she pushed herself through the turnstiles with the hundred-dollar bill held tight in her fist.

"You're very smart," he said, still smiling.

"How do you know?"

"Well, you're looking for a job, probably close to broke, but you came to the clubhouse. You could've saved a buck going over there to the grandstand with the rest of the crowd. But you never go with the crowd, do ya?"

He took her arm, lightly, and directed her into the club-house entrance. "I don't know what you mean."

"You ever been to the track before?"

"No."

He nodded as if his private assessment had been proved right. "Every track has a grandstand and a clubhouse. The clubhouse costs more to get in, and you don't get much for your money—a few potted plants around, a couple of coats of paint. But it's a different world. People have boxes here; the Jockey Club has private dining privileges; you run into people who've owned horses for generations . . ."

Annie stopped. It was not where she wanted to be. She looked around nervously. They were standing in a huge hall with a line of barred windows along one wall like the ticket windows at Pennsylvania Station. They were not open yet; nevertheless, people wandered around the hall, most reading the *Morning Telegraph* or marking it with a pencil.

"What's the matter?" he asked.

"Looks pretty crowded in here."

He grinned, impressed. "Yeah. They oughta raise the price of admission, keep the hoi polloi out."

She looked at him and liked him. When she smiled, he took the toothpick out of his mouth and looked at her with serious appraisal, saying, "See, you always go against the crowd, or you don't get no odds."

"What's that mean?"

He smiled, pleased to share his knowledge.

"In a horse race, the crowd always bets on the favorite. If it wins, the crummy odds gets them a nickel on their two-buck bet, and they stand in line all day to collect. Hey, big deal, dig? Favorites win a third of the time. That's the best odds the crowd can ever find. The rest of their lives, they're losers. I'd bet twenty-to-one you got better odds than that going for you. I mean, look! You just met me, didn't ya?" He put the toothpick back in his mouth and took her arm again. "Come on, I'll show you around."

"How come you know so much about the track?" Annie asked as they moved to some steps opposite the wall of betting windows.

"This is where I earn a living."

She looked at him, surprised. Then they reached the top of the stairs and the track spread out before her.

"Like it?" he asked.

"It's so huge. So . . . beautiful." She meant more than that, but could not explain it. From the shadowed surround of the stands on each side of her, the blocks of color—sand, green, and blue—seemed to burn. Never had the sky seemed such an intense covering. There was a hint of a sweet smell in the cold air. To Annie, the broad surface of the dirt track looked combed as it curved gracefully in a huge oval. Just inside it, another track of vivid green had been mowed with careful precision. The two tracks surrounded a hilly area of grass and lakes. They were outlined by the mile and a half of bright white rails accented at intervals by striped and colored posts. Just below the spot where Annie was standing was an old-fashioned weight scale with a large clocklike face. Beyond it, stretched high over the track, was a wire. The stanchion that held it was marked FINISH. Four tractors came down the dirt track in staggered order, furrowing the surface. A group of men moved over the grass replacing torn-up pieces of sod. In the distance beyond the two tracks were neat rows of barns. The entire scene was one of serenity and order. Annie took a deep breath and made a contented sound.

"It looks all right now," he said. "When it rains, it ain't so pretty. Come on down to my office."

He led her through the rows of boxes, most of which were still empty. Formed by pipe railings, each box had room for eight chairs in two rows with a small shelf along the front. Attached to the outside rail of each box was a small plaque with a name on it. Annie followed as the man passed several ushers and greeted them by name; they called him Phil.

"Gil, how ya doin'?" Phil said to an usher, who responded with an expectant smile. Phil peeled off a five-dollar bill from his roll and gave it to him. "You wanna get food for me and the lady?"

"Sure thing, Phil," the usher said. "The usual?"

"Bring her something. What do you want to drink—coffee, beer . . . milk?"

"Milk, please." The usher hustled away.

Phil stepped into a box that had no plaque. It was on the first row of a balcony. Below them was a concrete apron with rows of benches on it. He moved one of the metal chairs for Annie. As she sat down, she watched people filing in, finding their boxes, and greeting one another.

"What are those little signs for? With the names on them?" she asked.

"That's who owns the box."

"Owns it?"

"They buy it for the season, but once they got it, they got it till they die. Then they leave it to their kids." He looked off toward the boxes near the finish line. "When one of them boxes comes free, closer to the finish line than the box they got, there's a Wasp stampede," he said. "A lot of blue blood pours all over the Jockey Club, lemme tell you."

Annie did not understand what he meant. Taking the tooth-pick out of his mouth, he flicked it over the edge of the balcony with his long fingers.

"You know how to drive?" he asked.

"No."

"Okay. What about horses? You ever been around a horse?"

"Yes."

"Yeah? That's great. Then I think I know about a job for you."

Before she could ask about it, the usher arrived with two hot dogs, french fries, and milk. The smell made her stomach cramp and saliva spurt into her mouth. She stayed still as the usher put the paper holders on the shelf. Then she ate, swallowing without chewing.

"Hey, take it easy. When's the last time you ate, anyway?"

She shrugged and smiled, but did not answer. He picked up one of the programs the usher had delivered and read it as she finished. She wanted more food, but did not ask for it.

"You think you could get out here to the backstretch every morning at five?" he asked, still reading.

"What's the backstretch?"

He looked at her and grinned, unbelieving. "You don't know nothing, do ya? Lucky I'm a good teacher."

She returned his smile.

"It's right over there," he said, gesturing to the opposite side of the track. "One backstretch is the straight part of the track farthest away from the stands. You got the clubhouse turn right down there, which is the first turn after the start of the race, then the backstretch, then way over there is the final turn, and then there's the stretch, the top of the stretch, and then the final stretch, which is up to the finish line. D'ya get that?''

Annie made a slow tracing in the air following the grand oval. "Clubhouse turn, backstretch, final turn, and stretch, top and final, then the finish line."

He nodded. "Like I said, you're smart."

"You're a good teacher."

Her headache was gone and she was finally warm. She took another deep breath and felt fine.

"You'll be my prize student. The backstretch I'm talking about is where all the barns are, over there. It's called the backstretch because that's where it is at most tracks. Some people call it the backside. It's where all the horses are stabled while they're racing at that track. They always need people to work over there, and I know some trainers who I'll talk to if you think you could get up that early, seven days a week. Horses don't understand about weekends and holidays."

"I used to get up that early all the time back home. What would I be doing?"

He looked up to the sky and then he glanced at his wristwatch. Annie noticed that it had jewels on the face where the numbers should be.

"Come on," he said, "I'll take you over there."

He talked as they walked up the aisle toward the exit. "There are four levels of people that work on the backstretch. There's hotwalkers, who do nothing but lead horses around in a circle for a half hour or so after they work in the morning, one horse after another for three or four hours. Then there are grooms, who look after three or four horses each, feed them, wash them, brush them, wrap their ankles, and muck out their stalls . . ."

They approached the boxes near the finish line. The plaques began to appear and Annie read them quickly, casually, as if glancing out at the track. Many of the names she read were those of different farms or stables. As she approached the boxes nearest the finish line, however, she saw names she had read about in the *Journal-American:* Whitney, Vanderbilt, Belmont. There were some others—Widener, Guest, Chenery, Phipps, Mellon—that Jimmy Breslin had mentioned in his racing column. And then she saw "Mr. and Mrs. J. Cardell Cumberland," four boxes away from the finish line.

As she and Phil walked by, Annie quickly glanced around to see if any of the Cumberlands were coming, then looked back at the box. The chairs had detachable cushions tied to the seats; a fancy shield was woven into the cushions in crimson, gold, and royal blue with the letters C and F worked into it exactly like Sam's silver buckle in the picture Annie had. The screws that held the plaque in place on the rail were rusted.

"Then you got the exercise boys," Phil continued, "who take the horses out on the track to work them every morning. These guys are usually retired jockeys, or people who hope to catch a trainer's eye and become a jockey, but usually they're too tall or too heavy. Anyway, they don't do nothing but ride . . . Hey, what're you waiting for?"

Annie walked away from the Cumberland box and hurried up the steps. She stopped at the top and turned back to look at the view again.

"I love this place," she said. "Thanks for bringing me in here."

"Wait'll you see the races. Come on."

As they went through the hall, Annie noticed that lines had formed at some of the windows. They were marked $2 WIN or $10 WIN. Two at the end were marked $50 WIN. Interspersed between the WIN windows were similar denominations for PLACE and SHOW.

Phil anticipated her question. "Place is when a horse comes in second; show is third."

Annie turned and laughed. "Win, place, show, hotwalker, groom, and exercise boy. What's a trainer, Professor?"

He took her arm and asked, "What's your name?"

"Annie Grebauer," she answered hesitantly.

"No," he said.

"What? No?"

"No. Not Grebauer. It's Annie, let's see, Annie . . . Brown! Right? Annie Brown. I like that. Very simple. Tasteful, you know what I mean? I'm very good at names. Try it."

"Annie Brown," she said and smiled doubtfully.

"You'll love it when you get used to it. All right, listen. The trainer is the boss on the backstretch, runs the whole show for the horses that owners give him to train. He has to know everything about the horse, how far to work him, if he's off his feed, if he's sore, when he's ready to run, how to point him to a race. There are private trainers who work for a single owner, and public trainers who take on the best horses they can get. Some trainers have two horse stalls; the big ones have up to thirty at one track, and maybe fifty more in training or running somewhere else. They're given stall space in the barns by the track, which wants the best trainers with the best horses to run in their races. Here at Belmont, that's what they get. I mean, this is the best track in the county." He said it with pride.

"Must be a nice place to work. What do you do here?"

"I gamble."

They were at the turnstiles. A man stamped their hands with invisible ink. Phil took her arm again and directed her toward the parking lot. Annie remained quiet. Where she came from, gamblers were disreputable characters, not to be trusted. This one was getting her a job and had lost a bet to her. She reached in her pocket and felt the hundred-dollar bill.

They arrived at a black car, and Phil opened the door for her. It was spotlessly clean. Annie hesitated.

Phil saw it and said, "I ain't into rape, if that's what's bothering you. I just don't want to walk all the way back there."

Annie nodded and got in. The seat still gave off the smell of leather. She read the name Oldsmobile on the glove compartment. Hearing the trunk open, she turned to see Phil take out a traffic cone, which, after they had pulled out of the parking space, he placed in the center of it.

They drove out of the parking lot and turned onto the road that ran by the track's perimeter fence.

"Listen, Annie, after we finish over here, I want you to come back and meet my partner. He might have something else for you to do, make working out here worth your time."

"Is he a gambler, too?"

"Yeah, nice guy, retired, you'll love him."

"Why are you doing all this?"

He glanced over at her, then back at the road. "My life is

about making bets, Annie. I get real good odds on doing favors."

He turned into an entrance through a chain-link fence, and two guards in uniform signaled for him to slow down. He did and pointed to something on his front bumper. The guards waved him through, and, driving slowly, he started through the line of barns.

"Favors are blind bets, though," he said as Annie watched out her window. "You never know when the payoff will come or what it'll be. But with people in my business, favors are a better investment than you can find on Wall Street. Here, lemme show you something."

He pulled the Oldsmobile off the road, and they got out. He guided her between the barns, each with thirty stalls facing one another across an open space. The top halves of the stall doors were open, and most of the horses were looking out. "This is where the Belair Stud, owned by the Woodward family, keeps its horses. And that big bay horse there, with the white star on his forehead"—he was whispering with respect —"that's the greatest race horse in the world today. Nashua."

Annie remembered the name. Mr. Cumberland had mentioned it as some connection to Certainty. Annie stared at the animal, but saw little difference between him and any other horse standing in a stall. What impressed her was how neat the barn looked. Each stall had a box hanging on the wall, a webbing across the opening, and a tub painted green and pink. The dirt in front of the barn was raked, and at every fifth stall was a half barrel of flowers. Nothing looked out of place. Barns she had seen in Kentucky usually were falling down, with tools, equipment, and machinery lying wherever they had been dumped.

"That horse won a hundred thousand dollars in a match race last summer against Swaps. I won a thousand on him, so I stop by and say thank you."

"What's a match race?" Annie asked.

He looked at her hopelessly, his respectful reverie broken. "Whew! You don't know nothing! Come on, we can walk to where we're going. All right, there are four kinds of races you should know about. A match race is special, only two horses running for all the purse money, put up by the track or the owners, usually for two famous horses. The races you'll see every day are claimers. All the horses run with the same price tag on them, which anyone can pay before the race and own the horse after its run, even if the horse is dead by then. An allowance race has each horse given extra weight to carry, depending on the conditions of that particular race. A handicap race is when the guy called the handicapper, who works for the track, adds weight to each horse—little bars of lead stuck into pockets on the saddle—with the idea that each horse will be equal and all of them will come in a dead heat for first place. It ain't ever happened. Then the stakes race is one where the purse is made up of fees from the horses' owners, usually with a big kicker from the track. The best horses run in stakes races. You understand?"

"Oh, sure!" She laughed at herself. "Well, at least I can name them: claimers, allowance, handicap, and stakes. A match race is something special for two horses."

He lifted a hand in appreciation. "You'll be running the place in no time. Here we are."

They had walked past two barns and now came to a door in the middle of one of them. Phil opened the door and went in first, letting Annie follow. Riding equipment hung from every bit of space on the walls of the room. Sitting at a table was a balding, jowly man who wore glasses and had a cigar in his mouth. When he saw Phil, he scowled and said, "Owners aren't allowed in my tack room unless asked."

"Hey, Johnny, I'm not an owner; I'm only a friend of an owner. I want you to meet Annie Brown. She's from Kentucky, grew up with horses, been around 'em all her life. She's very smart and looking for a job hotwalking your horses."

Annie started to object but had no chance. The man glared contemptuously at Phil and said, "I don't have any 'horses' here; they're fillies and colts. They don't become 'horses' until they're five. Why the hell can't you learn that? And you don't have to bullshit me about her talent. She could be an ape from the North Pole if she'll do the job." He turned to Annie. "To be a hotwalker, all she has to be able to do is walk, and get here at five sharp in the morning. How about it, sweetheart?"

"I can do that," she said quietly. "What does it pay?"

"Twenty dollars a week."

"I'll be here tomorrow morning, if you want."

FOUR

PHIL LEFT ANNIE on the backstretch to look around and went to pick up his partner. Following his instructions, she returned to the clubhouse in time for the first race. As she approached the box where she had been sitting, Annie saw Phil talking with three other men. One had white hair under an old hat, rimless glasses, and a rumpled black overcoat with a plaid muffler. Another was very large; his neck and wrists put considerable strain on his leather jacket, and his stomach bulged over his belt. He wore a tweed cap. The third man was fat with long, greasy brown hair. A gray raincoat billowed over him. The skin of his little fingers was bunched around the rings he wore. The bridge of his wire-rimmed glasses sank into the flesh of his nose.

At the box entrance, she hesitated, wondering which of the three men was Phil's partner. The white-haired man in the hat and the thick man looked at her and ended their conversation.

Only the fat man kept talking, until he noticed their distraction. On seeing Annie, he exclaimed in a high-pitched voice, "Holy Christ, look at that gorgeous hair!"

Phil glanced at Annie indifferently, then said to the fat man, "Anything for you, Blimpie. Meet Annie Brown."

The fat man said, "Hiya, honey," and stared at her without smiling.

From his chair, Phil went on with the introductions. "This here's Teddy Lapps." The thick man nodded. "And Charlie, this is Annie Brown. Annie, meet Mr. Charlie Dell."

The white-haired man stood up, lifted his hat, and smiled. "Hello, Miss Brown," he said courteously and offered her a chair in the front row.

Annie sat down between Phil and Charlie Dell. She noticed that Phil had changed; he seemed suddenly remote and indifferent to her. The men continued to converse, each picking up his program and working over a copy of the *Morning Telegraph.* Sometimes Phil or Charlie Dell would comment, without looking up. "Look at the odds they give the number two filly in the second, and her last work was a bomb." "Since when did Billy Dixter lose his bug?" "Who do you want in the double?"

Annie understood none of it. The fat man did not succeed in concealing his glances at her over his newspaper. He shifted in his chair, as if about to start talking to her, but then went back to his paper. She wondered what to do. Charlie Dell offered her a pair of binoculars.

"Care to use these?"

Annie took them awkwardly. "Thank you," she said.

"You look through them that way, and adjust them with that thing, there."

She smiled, grateful for his consideration. He returned the smile, nodding. He had a kind face, with sharp gray eyes surrounded by deep wrinkles, which gave him a look of sad understanding. Lifting the binoculars, she focused them on the flagpole, then looked beyond the track to the backstretch. Refocusing, she turned and watched the clubhouse boxes nearest the finish line. A number of them were occupied by well-dressed people waving and calling to one another. The Cumberland box was empty.

"Hey, Annie, how'd you like to go down to the paddock?" It was the fat man.

"I don't know what that is," she responded without lowering the binoculars.

She heard Phil say, "What'd I tell you." She looked at him, but he did not acknowledge her.

"It's where they saddle the horses before the race," Charlie Dell explained pleasantly. "The trainers tell the jockeys how to run the race, and the owners stand around trying to look as if they mattered."

The other men laughed knowingly, but Charlie Dell smiled only at her. "Miss Brown," he continued softly, "I have some business to talk over with Phil. You'll enjoy the paddock. Blimpie will look after you. And on your way back, would you put this down to win on the number two horse in the first race?" He reached into his suit pocket and counted out ten hundred-dollar bills. "The horse's name is Valencia."

"Ain't you goin' to wheel for the double, Charlie?" Phil asked.

"No," the older man replied patiently. "The second race has a couple of good horses. You only wheel a wide-open race."

"You better let someone else go," Annie replied, staring at the bills. "I don't know what to do."

"No, you can do it," Charlie Dell insisted. "I have a feeling you're lucky." Charlie put the bills in her hand.

Annie took the money, stood up, and walked out of the box. She heard the fat man hurry after her. "It's this way, Annie," he said. At the top of the stairs, he was breathing hard behind her. She saw an arrowed sign reading TO THE PADDOCK and went quickly down the stairs. Just outside the stands was a wide-board white fence surrounding a broad oval over which tree branches spread a dappled shade. People were lining the fence as a half-dozen horses were led around in a circle under the trees. At the back of the paddock was a shed with numbered stalls where several horses were being saddled.

Annie found a place at the fence as a man led past a horse

that was the same shimmering red-brown color as Certainty. She remembered the beauty of the colt, her excitement as well as her fear at being so close to it, and thought of Sam saying, "I bred that colt. I really love him." She smiled. She would not have to ask him for a job. One day, she thought, maybe they would run into each other. The thought made her eyes open wide.

As other horses were led into the paddock, elegant people entered from another direction, casually greeting one another. Some drifted along under the huge old trees, some moved gracefully toward the line of stalls where men in neckties and work boots were supervising the horses as saddles were put on their backs. Then the jockeys came into the paddock, all wearing jackets and caps in combinations of brilliant color with patterns of stripes, dots, diamonds, and triangles. Each went to a group of people around a horse, where the jockey's minute size became startlingly apparent. There were hands to shake, and Annie observed some intense exchanges between jockeys and other men. The women smiled; to Annie, their composure seemed as intimidating as their clothing. Then a man in a red jacket shouted, "Riders up!" and the jockeys mounted their horses, formed a line, and circled the ring again. By then, there were twelve horses; some of them jumped or pranced sideways, needing control from their jockeys. Other horses were utterly calm, moving with a graceful sense of purpose.

"That one's the winner," Blimpie said, close enough behind Annie for her to whiff his rotten breath.

Edging away, Annie replied, "How do you know?"

"Number two, see? That's who you're supposed to bet on, and Uncle Charlie always wins." He smiled proudly.

"Where'm I supposed to bet all this money?" Annie asked.

"Oh, I'll show you. Hey, I just love that cute accent of yours. You mind me calling you Annie?" he asked eagerly.

Annie smiled weakly but did not answer. She watched as the men and women inside the paddock returned to the clubhouse. Never before had she seen so much beautiful clothing and jewelry, so many carefully groomed people. Everything about them, from shoes to hats, hemlines to haircuts, looked perfect and polished. Leisurely, they followed the horses and glided past the guards through a special entrance to the club-house boxes. Annie stopped for a moment to observe them.

"Come on," Blimpie urged, "you'll get shut out at the windows if you don't hurry."

They climbed the steep, crowded stairs to the hall with the betting windows, and found long lines of tense, unsmiling people. Many of them studied the *Telegraph,* a track program, or a colored piece of paper listing horses' names.

"Oh, Lord, I'll never get up there," Annie said.

"Come over here, Annie, here," Blimpie said, putting his hand on her shoulder to guide her around a corner.

Annie let him. He steered her to a window marked $50 WIN. There were only three people in front of her.

"What do I say?"

"Number two, a thousand to win."

Annie repeated the phrase to herself several times before placing the bet. When she received the win tickets, she started back to the box, trying to ignore Blimpie.

"Annie, can we talk?" he said as she passed by, then followed, saying, "Just a minute, I want to . . . *Annie . . .*" Without warning, she felt a grip on her arm and was jerked around to face him. His face was damp, and she could see saliva whitening at the corners of his mouth.

"Listen, I don't *have* to be nice," he said, the words forcing themselves through pursed lips. His eyes bulged as he let go of her arm.

"Just don't touch me anymore, okay?" Annie said quietly, trying to reason with him, feeling frightened in spite of the crowd. Then she turned and walked down the steps through the box section. She did not hear him following, only what he hissed in her ear: "Don't touch you? Couldn't I just run my hands through that gorgeous hair?"

Annie moved faster, and finally he gave up as she hurried up another aisle. She stopped and stood, trembling. An usher approached; she did not want to go back to the box. She moved away quickly, returning to the hall with the betting windows. Wandering around, she heard the loudspeaker announce post time. The betting windows closed; there was a groan from those still waiting to bet; and the lines quickly dispersed.

In the empty hall, Annie paced back and forth as a voice announced the race. The public address system echoed badly. She realized she was shaking and tried to stop. Then she heard the track announcer say, "Valencia coming on third on the outside."

Annie walked over to stand at the back of the box seat section and looked for the horses. She could barely see them as they went into the far turn. The horses and the jockeys' outfits blended into a blur of color. Over the swelling reaction of the crowd came the track announcer's voice: ". . . at third, but coming up fast is Valencia . . ."

Without thinking, Annie started to yell, "Run, Valencia! Run faster!" Several people turned briefly to smile at her as she kept yelling. The crowd grew louder and the announcer no longer could be heard. Suddenly down the stretch Annie could see the numeral 2 on the horse that was running second. It was going faster than the horse who was first. Annie started jumping up and clapping.

"Run! Run, Valencia!" The number two horse swept past the fading front runner and Annie screamed as Valencia sped first across the finish line. In a few strides, the horse passed in front of the section where she stood. Several other standees nearby turned and yelled to her, holding up their tickets, establishing the instant camaraderie of winners. Annie laughed back, nodding in agreement. Then a mass of people pressed past her, urgently hurrying back to the betting windows.

Still too excited to leave, Annie watched the track as Valencia completed his run around the clubhouse turn to the backstretch. Then he was pulled up by his jockey.

"Where the hell you been?" Phil was behind her, and he was angry. "Did you place Charlie's bet?" he demanded.

"Sure did." She handed him the tickets.

His face relaxed. "Goddamn horse came in at six-to-one. You're in the money, Annie. Charlie rounds his wins off to the nearest five hundred and gives his runner the rest." Relieved, he guided her back to the fifty-dollar window. They joined the short line.

"Phil, tell me about Blimpie."

"What about him? And by the way, you made an impression. Charlie's going to offer you a job."

"Wait! What's a runner? What's six-to-one mean? Who *is* Charlie Dell, anyway?"

He looked at her impatiently; then he grinned and shook his head. "He's my partner. He needs somebody to drive him and Teddy Lapps over here." He took her arm gently and spoke to her in the intimate way he had used earlier in the day. "A runner's somebody that a big money gambler uses to place his bets so he doesn't have to stand in line, and his face don't get too familiar at the betting windows. Six-to-one means that for every dollar you put down, you get six and a little change back. Charlie just made more than six grand; you'll pick up a coupla hundred and change."

He looked at Annie. She stood wide-eyed. Phil grinned.

"Blimpie is Charlie's nephew, his widowed sister's only kid. Charlie can't stand him, but he's family."

"Is Blimpie crazy?"

Phil looked at her inquisitively. "Oh, yeah, especially about little girls." Then he laughed.

They were getting close to the window. "Okay, cash the tickets and *count the money* before you leave the window," Phil said as he hurried away.

Annie collected $6260 at the window. When she returned to the box, Charlie Dell gave her $260 and started explaining how to read the *Morning Telegraph*'s past performance charts. By the end of the eighth race, she had collected $240 more for running two smaller bets.

Blimpie did not return to the box, and Annie said nothing more about him. She was having too good a time to worry. Teddy Lapps said little but seemed friendly. Phil was silent except when addressed.

"So, Miss Brown, how'd you like to learn how to drive?" Charlie Dell asked as they waited for the ninth race. Annie glanced at Phil, but he did not look up from his *Telegraph*. Charlie Dell saw the glance and smiled at her reassuringly. "Phil told me you didn't know how, but it doesn't take long to learn."

"Would you mind just calling me Annie?"

Charlie Dell's eyes crinkled behind his glasses when he smiled. He seemed very kind. "Let me explain my problem," he said. "I own a few horses out here, which Johnny Phillips trains for me. I like to come out two or three mornings a week and watch them work. Helps me keep up with what's going on. Then, in the afternoon, I come to the races. Teddy here used to drive me, but he has a bad leg; old war wound makes it painful for him to drive. I thought you could bring us out in the morning on your way to your job with Johnny, drive us home when you're finished, then bring us back for post time, stay around, and run some bets for me if you like. You might enjoy it. You seem to like the horses." He smiled at her again. "How long did they say the driving school took, Phil?"

Glancing over at Phil, Annie realized that Charlie was not Phil's partner, but his boss.

"Three weeks. She could do it in two."

"See, Annie," Charlie Dell explained, "Phil's been driving for a week and he hates getting up so early. So he'd be very happy if you took this on." He and Teddy Lapps chuckled; Phil shrugged.

"So what do you say, Annie?" Charlie asked.

"Yes, sir, that'll be just fine."

"Good," Charlie said as he stood up. Teddy Lapps also rose. "Phil, set up the driving lessons for tomorrow. She can use the Olds after you take us home from the morning works. I'm going to wash my hands. We'll meet you in the parking lot. See you tomorrow, Annie."

"Thank you, Mr. Dell," Annie said.

"It's Charlie," he said, and he and Teddy Lapps walked away. Annie noticed Teddy's limp as the big man lumbered after Charlie Dell.

"So Annie Grebauer becomes Annie Brown and goes home with six hundred bucks her first day. Not bad." Phil was grinning at her. "Can you get back out here tomorrow morning all right? Where do you live, anyway?"

"In New York."

"Not anymore," he said as he stood up. "You'll have to find someplace out here. You're gonna be too busy to commute.

But listen, don't sign any leases. Go to a motel in Elmont. Charlie's gonna offer you an apartment over his garage if all this works out. It's a nice place in Garden City . . . Hey, what's the matter?''

Annie had put her hands on her head. With a gasp of astonishment, she said, "I can't believe all this is happening."

"You will tomorrow morning. Dress warm. You have a hat? Here's mine. Wear it. And don't be late." He reached out and ran the tips of his fingers over her cheek. "I'm glad I found you, Annie."

"How long have you been looking for someone?"

"Since the day I had to get up at four-thirty."

"How come you picked me?"

"I got an eye," he said, pointing to one. "I can spot class in two things in this world: women and horses. I'm better at horses, but you were an easy pick. See ya."

Annie returned to New York, paid her landlord, and took a long, hot bath. After consuming the most expensive steak dinner she had ever eaten, she packed up the few clothes and articles she owned in the cardboard suitcase. Too excited to sleep, she rode the milk train to Mineola, took a cab, and found a motel a half mile away from the track. She arrived at Belmont's backstretch gate at four-thirty and showed the pass that Johnny Phillips, the trainer, had given her the previous day.

Wearing Phil's hat and every bit of clothing she could put on, she stood and waited outside the barn's tack room. Phillips arrived, along with his grooms, exercise riders, and other hotwalkers. They drifted out of the dark and, after perfunctory greetings to one another, started their work. Other than a few glances, no notice was taken of her. Phillips started writing with chalk on a blackboard, and the grooms went to work in the stalls. The cold night air was still, and the smell of manure and leather was strong.

"What's your name?" a man said as he handed her a leather strap with a foot-long section of chain at the end.

"Annie," she answered.

"You can start walking Tonyblue. He ain't working today," he ordered and started to walk away.

"Which one is it?"

"Number five stall," he said impatiently as he continued on his way.

Annie hustled to the stall where a groom was just leading out a colt. "All yours," the groom, a black man, said without looking at her.

"Excuse me, but what do I do?"

He stopped and stared at her, disgusted. Then he said aloud, "Green on the backside," which was repeated by several others who heard it. He took the leather strap from her and began to attach it to the colt's halter. "This is a *shank*, or a *lead*. You pass the chain through the *left* halter ring; then you attach the swivel snap to the *right* halter ring and over the colt's nose. The horse acts up, you pull on the shank. You understand?" Annie nodded. "Good. Now, you know how to walk?" She nodded again and took the lead. Stepping out in front of the colt, Annie gave him a tug, but he refused to move. She turned back and looked at the immensity of the animal. Out of the corner of her eye, she saw the groom watching her. Gripping the lead, she yanked it and said quietly but hard, "You come on, hear?"

The colt jerked up his head and started walking so quickly that Annie had to back up to keep out of his way. Another colt was being led around an oval path between the two barns. Hesitantly, Annie followed, looking back at her colt with every other step. Even in the cold morning, she had begun to sweat with fear. She felt as if she were being pursued by a giant.

The routine continued as the first light of day filtered through clouds into the sky. Every breath of horse and human condensed into vapor in the cold October air. The exercise riders arrived with containers of coffee and congregated around the blackboard. In their riding boots, leather chaps, and denim jackets, they were not as small as jockeys, but just as lean and hard. Suddenly, at the end of the barn, there appeared a woman who had a long platinum ponytail and was dressed in a leather jacket and chaps with lizard-skin cowboy boots.

"Watch out, Belmont, here comes Vera!" she said in a voice that sounded to Annie like a truck motor on a cold morning. The grooms groaned in recognition and the other exercise riders welcomed her at the blackboard.

"Graycloud?" she said when she saw the list. "He puts my poor tired ass on that bony spine the first set?"

Johnny Phillips came along on an old fat horse and said, "That ass has ridden a lot worse, Vera. So let's all go for a ride."

The five exercise riders went to the mounts that the grooms had saddled, and each lifted a leg backward. A groom took hold of the leg, hoisted the rider up, and the boots slid easily into the stirrups. A line was formed, and the set followed Johnny Phillips to the track. Vera passed by Annie on Graycloud and watched her.

"My God, they're hiring babies now!" Vera said.

"Pretty baby," a groom sang.

Annie looked down at the ground and kept walking.

Phillips looked after fifteen runners at Belmont, four of which, as Annie learned, belonged to Charlie Dell. There was one groom to care for every three horses; five exercise riders worked the sets, and five hotwalkers, including Annie, were on hand to cool the horses out when they were returned to the barn. Theirs was the worst, lowest job on the backstretch, but one that was vital. "If you let a horse stand after a work, it'd catch pneumonia," one of the grooms told her when she asked. "It'd be dead in hours. That's a fact."

The second colt Annie walked was a frisky two-year-old who followed quietly at first. Then, without any warning, he moved up and tried to nibble at Annie's jeans. She jumped, afraid of his teeth. This brought silent observation from Annie's fellow hotwalkers, as well as from the other personnel working around the Phillips barn. She tried not to let it bother her, but after several nudging repetitions by the colt, she began to hear laughter.

As she continued around the ring, she watched the grooms move into the empty stalls to gather up the manure with the soiled straw and carry it away to a pit at the far end of the barn. Comments continued about Annie's struggle, but not loud enough for her to hear. Guffaws and idle smiles followed, just the kind of attention Annie did not want. She kept walking the colt, looking back over her shoulder to watch out for him. Nevertheless, he managed to nip at her again.

Suddenly one of the fillies reared; her rider jumped off to hold her reins and let her calm down. At the moment everyone was distracted, Annie felt someone jam something in her back pocket. It was a handkerchief; Vera had leaned down from her mount and put it there. As attention shifted from the calmed filly back to Annie, her colt nickered behind her, then followed her without further incident. Vera moved her horse back into line. There was no more laughter and everyone went on with his own work.

The grooms worked quickly in the empty stalls, raking them out and filling them with clean straw. At one point, Annie absentmindedly tucked the handkerchief down into her pocket. Within seconds, her colt came up and nipped at her for it. She turned around and looked into his eyes; his face seemed to acknowledge a joke. Annie smiled and led him on, pulling out the handkerchief and hearing his nickering. They played the game for the rest of the walk.

When she led the colt to the wash buckets and sponges his groom had assembled, Annie reached up to pat the colt's head. He shied away, whinnying in alarm, and the groom had to grab hard at his halter. "Listen, green girl," the groom drawled when the colt was calmed, "y'don't put your hand up in the air toward a horse. They got a little bone running between their ears, called the poll bone. Nothing much protects it, so something hits it, they're dead, and every horse knows it. Something moves anywhere near it, they get scared. You bring your hand up from underneath, let 'em smell it, see it. Go on, try it."

Annie did, and the colt sniffed at her hand deeply, after which he let her pat his cheek while he looked imperiously toward his stall door.

"Thanks," Annie said, holding the colt's lead as the groom started washing him with a sponge, spreading the warm, soapy water over his hindquarters. "Can I come back and watch what you're doing when I'm done walking?"

"I'll probably put you to work," he warned without looking up from the circular motion of his sponge.

"That's okay with me," Annie said.

As the groom finished washing the colt, Annie heard the last set returning from the track. Carrying her shank over her shoulder, as she had seen the other hotwalkers do, she went over to find her next horse.

A groom was waiting for her with a filly. Snapping her shank onto the filly's halter, Annie started walking. When she looked down the shedrow, she could see the activity going on at the other barns between her and the track. There she saw horse after horse dashing by, their riders crouched or standing in the stirrups. The early sun made a misty light, diffusing the stands and flags in the distance. Annie suddenly felt buoyant. She believed she had found one of the better jobs in the world. She liked everything—the dawn air, the sense of purpose, the beauty and instinct of the animals, the calm order of the barn.

"All right, everyone," Vera called out as she walked over toward Annie, "don't forget tonight in the bar of your choice that I'm running for Miss Rheingold again. Fill out your ballots . . ." Another collective groan came from just about everyone. "Listen, just remember, when I win, I'll never forget you little people, and I don't mean the jockeys." She fell into step with Annie and said quietly, "When you finish, come over to the kitchen. I'll buy you coffee." Without waiting for an answer, she walked away, calling out, "Can any of you guys figure out how to spell Vera? V-E-R-A. Help each other."

Annie had to ask the groom where the kitchen was. When she arrived at the old clapboard-and-shingle hut, Vera was sitting at a crowded table, making the others laugh. She saw Annie, excused herself, and came over to her.

"What'd Johnny make you do, walk that horse to Brooklyn and back?"

She wore violet eye shadow and deep red lipstick. Her face was very pretty, with a turned-up button nose, strong cheekbones, and a wide mouth that seemed permanently cocked to smile. Her forehead and eyebrows were always lifted, as if waiting for an answer. She was shorter than Annie; the skin of her face and hands was weathered. Her body was compact, thin, and seemed as solid as stone.

"Mary Mother of Jesus, ain't you a beauty," she said, appraising Annie. "What's your name?"

"Annie . . . Brown."

"*Ha!*" Vera bellowed. "Phil give you that?"

Surprised, Annie nodded.

"Oh boy," Vera muttered and started for the cafeteria line. "Come on over and get some breakfast. Your face is gorgeous. And that hair under your cap is really some color. What do you call it? Amber? Yeah, amber, and your body's almost as good as mine was at your age. Oh, God, when was that? When dinosaurs *roamed* the *land!*"

They went through the line and Annie ordered a full breakfast of eggs and bacon. They even had grits, which she had not seen since she left Kentucky. The air in the kitchen was heavy with greasy heat and cigarette smoke. The decor featured worn linoleum, wooden tables, metal chairs, and a scene of Mount Rushmore on a calendar. They found a corner table and sat down, Vera with only a cup of coffee.

"I asked Johnny where you came from," Vera said. "That's how I knew about Phil."

"Is he a friend of yours?"

"Phil? Oh, no," Vera answered through a rumbling laugh. "Call him an acquaintance that I know too well. What do you know about him?"

"Nothing. He got me the hotwalking job."

"Did you meet Charlie Dell? And Teddy Lapps?"

Annie nodded and started to eat, hoping to slow down the questions.

"So you're going to drive them and move into Charlie's garage."

Annie put down her knife and fork and gazed at Vera for a moment. "How do you know that?"

"Charlie offered me the job a week ago, hinting that the old body here might want to get out of the saddle and into a driver's seat. I told him to go to hell." She smiled affectionately at the story. "Listen, Annie, you're a kid and I don't know where you've come from, but you ought to know what you're getting into"—she drank some coffee—"if you want."

Annie picked up her knife and fork again. "Yes, please," she said and nervously started eating. She thought everything was about to fall apart.

"Don't worry," Vera offered, noticing her apprehension. "Charlie Dell is the nicest guy in the world. If he likes you, he'll always be there. He's quite something. When he was fourteen, he came over from some place called Calabria. In Italy. In the twenties, he started selling junk on a cart. From junkyards, he went into the construction business on the New York waterfront. World War Two made him rich, and after V-J Day he retired to buy real estate and play the horses. But that's not the whole story. That's the sweet, deleted version."

Not understanding, Annie tried to smile as Vera went on. Leaning forward with her arms on the table, speaking quietly, Vera pronounced, "Charlie *Del* Vicario—get it?—is known as the Undertaker. He's the guy the mob took their bodies to, and Charlie got rid of them. In his junkyards, he had to shift bodies every time he sold an old car or a boiler for scrap. When he got into the construction business, he'd put 'em in the foundation of the buildings. Charlie's very smart; he never charged the hoods a fee for his services. So he got a lot of favors—contracts from City Hall, pussycat union deals, any building variance or code adjustment he needed. Now, nobody ever bothers him. He still gets a lot of respect because nobody knows better than Charlie where the bodies are buried, so to speak. They're all over town. Charlie could tell exactly where to start digging."

Annie was sitting straight in her chair. "Good Lord," she said. "Who's Teddy Lapps?"

"The word I heard is that once upon a time he used to work for Albert Anastasia at Murder, Inc. You're too young to know what that is, aren't you? Well, you don't want to know. Teddy got shot in the leg once, had a steel plate put in there. It couldn't be depended on; he couldn't run. So he got retired from the wars. Charlie Dell picked him up cheap when he was down; he looks after Charlie. Where Charlie's been, you can't be too careful. Probably more comfortable having a killer on his side."

"Does everyone know all this?" Annie asked, wincing slightly.

"No. Just a few of us. If the track knew his background, he'd never get a license to own horses. See, Charlie Dell and I had a wiggle for a while. He found me wrecking stock cars in New Jersey and put me on thoroughbreds. He's been nothing but good to me. I was about your age when he found me, almost twenty years ago. But if I had it to do over, I'd rather have known about him and his friends going in."

Annie stared at Vera, who smiled at her. "Couple of pieces falling into place? Like why this old broad gets to keep riding? Well, I'm a good rider, and Charlie pays his debts. Part of his 'honor,' and honor makes men feel good. Of course, men get to make up their own, don't they?"

"What about Phil?" Annie asked through a dry throat, pushing at the eggs and grits with her fork.

Vera laughed. "One day over at Jamaica Race Track, Phil came up, a total stranger, and asked Charlie for five bucks to bet on a lock in the next race. Charlie gave it to him, and he lost it. So much for locks." She saw the confusion on Annie's face. "A lock is a sure thing, a bet that can't lose. There aren't many. Phil should have been in school, and Charlie saw a kid headed into a lot of trouble. So he took him on, as a kind of junior partner. Charlie liked him, mainly because Phil was nuts about racing."

Vera leaned forward again and said quietly, "Last time I heard, he owed Charlie thirty-five grand. Phil can't stop gambling, on *anything*. Charlie covers his losses."

"Why?"

"To keep Phil from going to hell—which'd be fine with me —to have him do the dirty work . . . and who knows what in the future. Listen, eat your food. Then I'll show you around a little."

Annie tried to eat, but her nerves had killed her appetite. "I'm supposed to meet Phil at the backstretch gate for a driving lesson."

"I'll walk you over."

Outside, the cold clear air dissolved the thick odors of the kitchen. Annie breathed deeply. The sun was high and the sudden bright chill made her eyes water.

"You think they're dangerous?" Annie asked as she and Vera walked past the rows of barns to the gate.

"No. Charlie doesn't have a dangerous bone in his body. He's just real smart, does what he has to do to take care of himself. Teddy would kill for him if he had to, and Phil would like to be dangerous, but so far Charlie's kept him fairly harmless . . . Where'd you learn about horses?"

Annie smiled. "I started this morning."

"Oh, yes, I remember them calling 'green.' Well, if you want, I'll tell you whatever you need to know."

"That'd be fine, because I sure don't know much."

"You're doing all right. Just stay quiet and keep your eyes open. The track's a different world from any other, and it's got a strong pecking order. They say that there are only two places left in America where you have a real plantation social system, from slaves to masters—the army and the track. You and me, we're the peasants, though because I'm up on a horse, I rank you. A little. At the top are the trainers, who you obey like they were the Pope. Of course there are the owners, but you don't see them much. They're like God, usually a pain in the ass."

They passed by a barn with gold and purple featured on its stall webbing and boxes. "Here's an exception. The Wheatley Stable, owned by Mrs. Henry Carnegie Phipps. She's a smart old dame and knows about horses. Of course, she has Eddie Arcaro riding for her and Sunny Jim Fitzsimmons as a trainer. Now he's a genius, also trains for Belair Stud . . ."

"The Woodward Stable," Annie offered, pleased to know something. "They own Nashua."

"Right! Hey, it won't take you long. Oh, Annie, wait'll you see Nashua run. It makes living worthwhile. When you watch him go, you'll know why this business is more than a gambling game or a rich man's sport."

Annie looked over at her as they walked, surprised to hear such ardor from someone who seemed so mocking of everything.

"Keep your eye out for the best, the best horses, like Nashua, Swaps; the best stables, Wheatley, Belair, Caernarvon, Greentree; but most of all the best trainers, Fitzsimmons or the young ones coming up, like Woody Stephens and Frank Carney, and get connected somehow. Johnny Phillips is a good place to start; he's on his way. If you make it real easy for him to tell you things, he will."

As they rounded the corner of a barn, Sam Cumberland and another man were walking toward them. Vera nudged Annie in the ribs; she thought of turning away, but they were too close. Sam, wearing a dark suit and striped tie, was talking animatedly. The other man, about Sam's age, tall, with a face of hard angles, listened without reaction. He was as rawboned good-looking as Sam was stunningly handsome. His sandy-colored hair lay on his head like thatches of grain. In contrast to Sam's emphatic gestures, the other man walked with his hands stuck in the back pockets of his jeans. He glanced at Annie with cool blue-green eyes that held on her for a curious moment. She watched him because she was too scared to look at Sam as he came right by her. The other man courteously nodded in greeting. Glancing at her, Sam took a small step of courtesy behind the other man in order to allow the women the path. Then he walked by without any sign of recognition.

"*That* was the gentry!" Vera said excitedly. "Frank Carney just took over Caernarvon Farms. Everyone says he'll be one of the great trainers, if he can get on with young Sam, which is a big if, I hear— Hey, what's the matter, Annie?"

"I'm late; I gotta go," she said and started running down the road toward the gate. She could think up an excuse for the tears later.

FIVE

"WATCH THAT FILLY!" Johnny Phillips called to Annie from the door of the tack room. He did not yell, but he made himself heard easily enough. Nobody yelled on the backstretch. Annie turned in time to see her filly move sideways to kick out with her hind legs at another filly across the walking ring. When Annie jerked on the lead, the filly pulled back, almost yanking the leather out of her hand. She hung on and stayed still, watching as the filly pranced in place, trying to rear. The other hotwalkers quickly led their charges away from the fractious horse.

"Hey hey hey, come on now," Annie said, jerking the lead again. "No need to do that. Here, come on." Her voice stayed low and calm; she made eye contact with the filly and continued to reassure her.

"Listen, I'm just as scared as you are. Ain't no need to fight each other."

After a short struggle, the filly stopped prancing and stood, head drooped slightly for a better look at Annie. She smiled and said, "You about finished? We going to finish this dance together? All right, come on." She approached the filly, let her get a smell of her hand, and as she touched her neck, Annie thought she could feel the filly's body grow calm. Startled, she stood a moment, but then she became aware of attention. She turned and continued with the filly around the ring. In passing, she saw John Phillips, climbing into his western saddle on the stable pony. Without smiling, he nodded to her —appreciatively, Annie thought—then led a set of colts out toward the track for their works.

Annie had learned a lot in her first month, both on the backstretch and, in the afternoons, in the clubhouse box with Charlie Dell. From the grooms she befriended, she learned how to rub a horse with brushes and rags, how to clean a stall and lay in straw so that it would smell fresh and support a horse comfortably, how to wrap leg bandages to protect thoroughbreds' incredibly thin ankles both in the stall and on the track. "They got twenty-three little bones in those ankles," Burt, the black groom, told her, "all packaged in there as thin as your wrist. When you have a thousand pounds of thoroughbred crashing down on them every step of a race, you get lots of problems. No feet, no horse."

"What's 'thoroughbred' mean?" she asked, noticing the man's hands work the stall bandage over his colt's ankle with precision and care. Burt glanced up at her, his eyes lifting at yet another question. "It's the breed, the race horse breed. They been breeding the animal they call horse for a long time, getting different kinds to do different things. There's about two hundred of them now, cart horses, plow horses, carrying horses, stepping-out horses. But they bred this one for speed, nothing but speed." He finished wrapping the ankle and let it fall, at the same time running his hands up the leg. "Beautiful," he said. "God don't make anything this kind of beautiful, you know?" Then he looked at Annie and smiled. "Oh, you'll know. You will, Annie."

One day, she saw Nashua in action. The great colt's owner had been shot accidentally by his wife, and everyone on the backstretch was talking about the tragedy, conjecturing what the Woodward family would do with the Belair Stud and its champion. Word spread that Nashua was going to have a special work at exactly ten. When she arrived at the backstretch rail, Annie noticed that it was more crowded than usual, not only with familiar people, but with strangers carrying cameras, many important-looking men in silk ties, and even a television truck.

She saw the Cumberland Rolls-Royce parked ten yards from the gap. Recognizing the chauffeur, she felt her stomach tighten, and she leaned against the rail. She had not seen Sam since that first day, and had avoided going anywhere near the Caernarvon barn. Even glimpsing the new trainer, Frank Carney, or hearing someone speak of a Caernarvon runner made her feel jumpy.

Annie turned to see Nashua being led to the gap. She recognized Eddie Arcaro in the saddle. The greatest jockey in the world seldom took a horse out to work in the morning unless he was preparing for a major race. This was special. Walking along in the group that followed the colt was Sam Cumberland in a polo coat and tweed cap with a binocular case around his neck. Frank Carney, wearing old jeans and a leather jacket, kept his eyes ahead, oblivious of the crowd.

When Nashua started his work, Annie realized that, although she had seen many fine thoroughbreds in her month at Belmont, Nashua was identifiably different. Even to her inexperienced eye, he exuded nobility and purpose. Arcaro walked him the length of the backstretch past the crowd, which watched silently. Then at the far turn, the jockey started his mount galloping. Annie saw the huge, smooth gait and the restrained power in the glowing red animal, his black mane and tail trailing in the wind.

"At home in the going," someone said.

"They're doing a two-minute lick," someone else said, which Annie had learned was a one-mile gallop in that time. In the distance, the champion passed in front of the empty stands continuing his easy, even stride. The end of the mile brought him to where the morning crowd was waiting. Instead of easing the colt, Arcaro leaned down, crouched in his signature posture, and let Nashua see the riding crop out of the corner of his eye. The great colt needed no further urging. He leaped ahead with an explosion of speed that made Annie take in breath. In seconds, the champion's raw wild force shot past Annie, who was as overwhelmed by it as she was thrilled. People standing at the rail released their astonishment and respect with yells and gasps. As Annie watched Arcaro expertly ease the colt and bring him back, she, too, was awed by the exhilaration and inadequacy she felt in the presence of such perfection.

Something touched her back. "Excuse me, are you . . . ?"

It was Sam. She turned to him and tried to breathe.

"Annie? Are you Annie Long-Legs?"

She nodded, still unable to speak or even smile.

"I thought so. When I was following Nashua down the backstretch, I saw your hair through the binoculars. Couldn't ever forget that. What in the world are you doing here?" He smiled broadly, happily surprised.

She had been wearing Phil's cap that other morning; he had not seen her hair. "I work here," she said and finally smiled.

He stared at her a moment, amazed.

"What? How did . . . ?" Then his trainer came up, obviously wanting to leave.

"Oh, Annie, this is Frank Carney," Sam said, reacting habitually with the social courtesy of an introduction. "She's the young lady who rescued Certainty, and she's turned up here."

The trainer nodded to her; his blue-green eyes acknowledging recognition. Then he said, "If we're finished here, I better get on back." His quiet, firm voice seemed direct and honest, with the authority of a man who knew himself and disliked unnecessary words.

"We're not quite finished," Sam said; Annie thought he sounded tense. "Annie, good luck. I'm glad to see you." He started to walk away.

"How'd you like Nashua?" she said, not wanting him to leave so quickly.

He stopped and came back to her. "Can you keep a secret?" he asked, leaning close to her ear.

She bobbed her head, aware of his nearness.

"I'm going to buy him." He stood back and smiled with his finger to his lips. "Our secret," he said, then hurried to catch up with Frank Carney, who had not waited for him.

No one whom Annie knew had seen her talk to Sam. Her happiness at being recognized, spoken to, and allowed to share such an extraordinary secret was offset by the frustration of not knowing how to meet him again. Seeing him through Charlie's binoculars a week later in the Cumberland box did not help. Belinda was there. Wearing a bright green checked coat with a cloche hat to match, she looked beautiful. Annie put the binoculars down and did not use them for the rest of the day.

"Who do you like in the fifth race?" Charlie Dell asked as he studied his *Morning Telegraph*.

"The number four horse, Queen of Burma," Annie said with no hesitation.

"That's crazy," Phil said. "She's coming off a string of three losses at the same distance."

Annie shrugged. "We'll have to see, I guess."

Charlie watched her and his eyes squinted through his glasses as he smiled.

As Phil had predicted, Annie had quickly learned to drive, and as soon as she had her license, Charlie Dell asked her to move into the small apartment over his garage in Garden City. By then, Annie knew him well enough not to worry. Besides having a separate entrance, the apartment had a bedroom, living room, bathroom, and tiny kitchen. Charlie's house was one of several Tudor-style brick buildings built in a row of small lots. It had a lawn shaded by maple trees in front and back; it was quiet, modest though spacious, and twenty minutes from Belmont. Part of the arrangement was that Annie would stay to look after the house when Charlie and Teddy Lapps went to Florida and California for the winter racing season. Johnny Phillips kept his barn at Belmont throughout the winter, even though there was no racing at Belmont, Jamaica, or Aqueduct, the three New York City tracks. He went south with some of his horses, leaving his stable assistant in charge. Annie would still have plenty to do, and Phillips was glad to have her there.

. . .

She loved her garage apartment. In New York, the five-flight walk-up she had rented had one window with a view of a brick wall. From the windows above Charlie's garage, she had a view over Garden City trees all the way to the cathedral spire. In another direction, she could just glimpse the outline of the old Garden City Hotel and a golf course beyond it. The simple color coordination of light blue curtains, dark blue wall-to-wall carpeting, blue towels and china, made the place seem lavish to Annie. With her runner's money, she bought a bright red plastic 45 rpm record player and listened to Peggy Lee, Harry Belafonte, and Frank Sinatra. Around the backstretch she found used horse magazines, like *The Blood-Horse* and *The Thoroughbred Record;* she made neat stacks of them on the large pine table in her living room and read them from cover to cover. Occasionally she came across a picture of Sam in an article about Caernarvon Farms. Annie would clip it out and add it to the row of pictures she had thumbtacked to her bedroom wall. The separated picture of him and Belinda remained between the pages of *Great Expectations,* which she still had not read.

Each night before going to sleep, Annie spent several hours studying the *Telegraph*'s past performance charts for the next day's Belmont runners. When she drove Charlie to the track in the morning, they would compare notes. After hotwalking, she would visit the barns where horses were being readied to race that day. Keeping her eyes and ears open, she often picked up information that even Charlie could not know: whether a horse was ready, off his feed, or full of painkillers. Nothing gave Annie more pleasure than picking a different runner from the one Charlie did and having her choice come in a winner. When it happened, Charlie seemed to take pride in her win.

"You have to teach yourself, Annie. I taught myself English; you can teach yourself control of the facts. You never bet on every race. And you always bet to win. Some guy figured out once that there are more than ten thousand variables in any one race. You can't cover all of them, but you always try."

After the Belmont season ended, horses were shipped across Long Island by truck to the short race meetings at Jamaica, then Aqueduct. Annie's education continued on the backstretch. Vera became a combination of friend and mother hen, and the grooms in John Phillips' stable adopted Annie as a favorite. Burt said she had "the touch." She was soon assigned to walk the most difficult "rank" colts. Several times, she had some serious trouble when a colt suddenly reared or fought to get away from her. Although Annie was afraid, she also felt in control and never yelled. Holding on to her shank, she would jerk it hard, getting the horse's attention, reminding it of her control. Then she would talk quietly, finally reaching out to stroke the colt's cheek or neck, feeling the calm spread from her hand through the body of the animal.

A few of Phillips' horses allowed no one to touch them. If Annie tried, they would pin back their ears and reach for a bite of her hand. One colt got hold of her arm, and left some bruises and bleeding tooth marks. Even then, Annie did not yell or lose her temper, but made the colt get back into the walking ring, finish cooling out, and submit to her firm rule. Still, the bite hurt badly for a week.

"There's just a basic problem with race horses," John Phillips said grudgingly one morning. He was watching her help Burt put on stall bandages. Phillips was one of the few people on the backstretch who did not drawl. Even Yankees, after a few days around the barns, seemed to start flattening their words and dividing one syllable into two, such as "hay-und" or "say-ed." Phillips was from Brooklyn, and Annie figured that drawling was probably a physical impossibility for his mouth, particularly with a half-chewed cigar in it. "You gotta understand, Annie, they been breeding these animals for what, two hundred years, to do nothing but run. Here we are training them to race, and keeping them in a sixteen-foot stall for twenty-three out of the twenty-four hours of the day. No wonder so many of them are crazy. They're like humans get after a couple of days in a jail cell."

Annie kept her eyes on what she was doing as she carefully wrapped the bandages smoothly up and down over the bony bulges of the ankle.

"I always remind myself," Phillips mused, "that they only see shadow, no colors. They can hear anything from here to next Sunday; they can smell anything that's living or not; and they can remember better than elephants when they need to. But no 'touch' is gonna help their second-rate stomachs, which are more sensitive than your eardrum, or a third-rate breathing system, which'll break down easier than a flivver, or those ankles, which are twenty-three pieces of glass. See, the goddamn animal's impossible!''

In the final day of the Aqueduct meeting, Annie was watching the third race from the backstretch rail, having shipped over with Burt and two of Phillips' runners. The day's crowd was sparse but enthusiastic. A three-year-old colt in the feature race broke down not twenty yards from where she was standing. The crack of bone was clearly audible as his left front leg gave way, but the colt ran on. Still trying, unable to understand the pain and panicked by it, he lurched on the broken ankle until he slowed to a hobble on three legs and the jockey was able to stop him and dismount.

Annie ran out on the track with several others as the colt, by then confused and terrified by pain, tried to fight his way free from the torment. Screaming, he lurched around the jockey, who held his reins. Annie saw the box-shaped horse ambulance speeding down the track as the veterinarian's car approached from the other direction. Several men tried to stop the colt, but he was beyond control except for the reins. Suddenly he stood absolutely still. His eyes rolled to their whites, came back to focus; then he collapsed on his side.

Avoiding the danger of his thrashing legs, the men jumped to a safe position and held him down. Annie knelt beside him on the ground, talking softly, stroking his neck. The men talked in low voices as the vet examined the leg. A dark green tarpaulin screen was held up by the ambulance attendants to shield the scene from the spectators.

Annie noticed the crowd's silence. Across the infield, the thousands of racing fans had become chillingly quiet. Next to the horse's head, she saw a hypodermic needle and heard someone whisper, "Just keep stroking him, young lady."

Annie watched the colt's eyes; she went on talking, reassuring him as death fixed his stare. A long gasp came out of the colt's mouth, the gleaming muscles of his neck gave way, and his large head fell dead weight onto the track. Annie tried to lift his head, because it had fallen at an awkward angle, with one open eye against the dirt. But someone said, "Okay, let's move him." A wide leather cinch belt was strapped to his back legs and clipped to the ambulance's winch.

After the horse was dragged away from her, Annie walked off the track. She kept walking until she reached a barn. Around back she sank down and cried harder than she remembered ever crying before.

Aqueduct closed, ending the racing season in New York State. Those stables which headed south for the winter were soon gone, leaving a comparatively small contingent of horses and their handlers. The mood on the Belmont backstretch changed as quickly as the weather to a sullen gray.

Charlie Dell and Teddy Lapps prepared to travel to Miami for the Hialeah meeting, then on to Los Angeles and Santa Anita. They would return in May after attending the Kentucky Derby. The week before Christmas, Annie drove them into New York to catch their sleeper at Pennsylvania Station. A redcap ran up, unloaded the four leather suitcases from the Oldsmobile, and Teddy Lapps followed him into the terminal while Charlie stood on the curb with Annie. He took out a small gift-wrapped box from his overcoat pocket.

"We're on our way," he said.

"I'm really going to miss you," Annie said softly.

"That's nice to know. I got a Christmas present for you."

"Oh, Lord, Charlie, I don't have anything . . ."

"Don't think about it. Put this away until later. Your bonus is inside the package, along with a couple of phone numbers to call if you need me." He looked at her, as always, smiling. "I want you to call Phil if you have to. You have his number? You feel okay about doing that?"

Annie nodded gratefully, and Charlie adjusted his muffler and pretended to watch the traffic go by. "About your present. What I'm giving you is no big thing to me. They came my way a long time ago. I got 'em for nothing, thinking I'd have someone special to give them to someday, a wife, a daughter . . . I never had those, and I figure I'm not going to. Besides, it's a lot of fun watching you get hooked on the horses. I'm going to miss you, too."

"All set, Charlie," Teddy Lapps called from one of the station's granite portals.

Annie leaned over and kissed Charlie on the cheek.

"Hey," he said, taking her hand, "you can't do that out here on the street. People will talk." He squeezed her hand, shook it, then let go and joined Teddy.

"So long, Annie," Teddy Lapps called to her.

"Take care of him, Teddy," she said, hugging herself against the cold.

"I will. See you in the spring."

An icy wind whipped down Seventh Avenue. Annie turned to face it for a moment; then she got back into the Oldsmobile. Reaching to push the starter, she saw a festive group of people carry some large gift-wrapped packages into the station. She watched them until they were out of sight. Sitting back in the driver's seat, she thought of buying a Christmas tree for her apartment, then shook her head and slowly opened the paper around Charlie's present. Inside a long gray velvet jewelry box she found five hundred-dollar bills, a card with two phone numbers on it, one in Miami, one in Los Angeles, and a single strand of large, lustrous pearls. Tears welled in her eyes. She could not imagine where she would ever wear them, but she twisted the rearview mirror toward her and unbuttoned her coat. The clasp was a delicate embossed gold. She closed it and moved the pearls around her neck.

Looking in the mirror, she remembered a certain Christmas in the shack. After her mother had died, no one else paid much attention to the holiday. That year, Annie had cut down a tree, dragged it in through the woods, and decorated it with paper stars and strings of popcorn. In spite of what they had done to her, she made her father and two brothers presents. She knitted scarves and hand-carved wooden belt buckles. Her father surprised her with coloring books and a pencil box. After making pancakes for breakfast, he held her on his lap, laughing and telling her of places he had seen while working for the railroad. Afterward, he threw a new football to Jimmy Lee and Fungo. That was the good Christmas, the only one without her mother. She looked at her reflection once more, then readjusted the mirror and started the car.

She headed for the Midtown Tunnel to return to Long Island, but found herself turning north on Madison Avenue. The stores were closed, but the sidewalks were crowded with pedestrians, many carrying packages, most window-shopping in spite of the brisk wind. As she idly circled a block to glimpse the Rockefeller Center mall and its gigantic Christmas tree from Fifth Avenue, she suddenly thought of something she wanted to do. She sped back to Madison and headed north again.

Number 10 East Seventieth Street had thick holly wreaths with stiff red satin bows on each side of its double front door. A similar wreath, with a candle glowing through its center, hung in each window of all four floors. The draperies over the two center windows of the high-ceilinged second floor were left open, revealing a huge spruce supporting masses of blue lights and silver bulbs with spun glass layered over it so that it looked like a glowing blue cloud.

Annie sat in the Oldsmobile double-parked across the street, the motor running. She stared at the mansion's seasonal decorations, the double doors, the room on the second floor with the carved wooden ceiling and the green velvet walls, upon which she saw firelight flickering. She put her head down on the steering wheel, and wondered if the shack was still standing in the woods by the Ohio.

Headlights glared into the back window of the Oldsmobile and passed by. Then Annie heard a car stop. She looked up and immediately sank down in her seat. Through the windshield, she saw the back door of the Rolls-Royce open before the chauffeur could get to it. Sam's mother and father got out. She wore a long dress and a fur coat. Mr. Cumberland was in black tie, without an overcoat. They walked quickly to the front door, which was opened on their approach by a butler. The Rolls started forward again, but then stopped abruptly, and Sam got out. He turned, said something angrily back into the car, then gestured, ordering the car to go on, and slammed the door. Watching the car as it moved silently down the street, he seemed to lose his balance. In one hand, he carried a cut-glass bottle from the car's polished wooden rack, and he started walking unsteadily toward Madison Avenue.

Annie heard her heart beating. She reached up and took off the beret she had been wearing, letting her hair fall to her shoulders. Seeing him stop at the corner to wave down a cab, she put the Oldsmobile in gear and moved forward. After she jerked to a stop, she rolled down the window and called, "Need a ride, Sam?"

As soon as she said it, she gasped at what she was doing and at the shock of using his name.

Startled, he turned and, unsure of who it was, took several steps toward the Oldsmobile, then froze. "Good Christ, it's you! How did you hear?"

His bow tie was at the wrong angle, and with his overcoat unbuttoned he seemed oblivious of the wind, which blew it open. The look of perplexity on his face made him less formidable but no less overpowering to Annie.

"Hear what?" she said, then swallowed to loosen her voice. "I was just driving by and saw you looking for a ride."

He stared at her for a moment, then walked around the front of the car, struggled with the bottle and the door latch, and got in. A car behind them honked.

"Which way you going?" Annie asked.

"It doesn't matter. You can let me off somewhere."

Annie turned on Madison, going downtown. She took several slow deep breaths.

"It was our secret," he said, shaking his head in amazement. "You mean you were just here on this particular night?"

"I'm not sure what night this is, but I was in New York . . ."

"I lost him!" he blurted, then took the stopper out of the bottle and lifted it carefully to his lips.

Annie glanced over at him as she drove. His face was pulled into a tight grimace of anger and pain. "Who'd you lose?" she asked.

He turned. "Nashua," he said in a tone indicating that his answer was obvious. "Don't you remember? The lawyers for the Woodward estate opened the bids today." He slumped down in the seat and took another swallow from the bottle.

"I missed getting him by *twenty thousand piddling dollars!*" he said with disgust, staring through the windshield. "Mother and Father were just delighted. So was Frank Carney, the son of a bitch! They all fought me from the second I decided to go after him. As usual, Carney agreed with my father, just like he always has. Well, by God, it isn't Father's stable anymore! Ol' Frank better damn well learn that! Father said to me, 'You simply don't offer a million dollars for a horse. It's too gaudy. The most money ever paid for a single horse was seven hundred thousand by the Irish National Stud for the Aga Khan's Tulyar.'" The imitation of his father's pious superiority was exact in its satire. "'Try to remember that Caernarvon is *not* the Irish National Stud, and we do *not* need such a reputation.' Can't you hear him saying that? With that edge implying we aren't as common as a bunch of shanty Irish trying to get in with the Aga Khan? Can't you just hear him? . . . You met my father, didn't you?"

The question indicated his own foggy memory of a day she remembered in explicit detail. "Yes," she answered, which seemed to reassure him. He drank again.

"I bid a million two hundred and thirty thousand, and god-damned if ol' Cousin Leslie Combs didn't beat me by twenty thousand dollars. Mother spends that at the hairdressers. . . . Well, it's not the end of the world. We have a couple or three pretty good horses at Caernarvon." He lifted his bottle again in a toast to that comfort and drank it down. "I'd say we—" He was suddenly silent, and Annie looked over again to see what was wrong.

"Horseshit," he said. "I'm trying to convince myself that losing that colt doesn't matter. Well, it's killing me. I drank a lot of martinis tonight; I wanted to make them all furious. But none of them cares. Carney was probably relieved not to have the goddamn responsibility. Good Christ, you know Belinda laughed? Said, 'You win a few, you lose a few.' I'm supposed to rise above it, of course; be a good sport and a Cumberland! But goddammit, you can plan your whole stable, your whole life, around a colt like that." He looked at her, hoping for understanding.

"I'm real sorry, Sam."

"Annie," he said. "Annie Long-Legs, with the lovely amber hair." He started to reach over to touch it, but then pulled his arm back. "Listen, I'm very tired and very drunk, but before I pass out, I have to ask you what the hell you're doing here."

"Well, I saw you on the corner and just thought I'd say hello."

"But why were you . . ." He stopped, losing his concentration, then started fumbling to button his overcoat. "Listen, I don't think I can talk anymore. Just drop me at the next corner. I'll get a cab to the club. I'm damned if I'm going home!"

Annie slowed the car and stopped at a corner. "I'll be glad to drive you."

"No, no. Wouldn't trouble you," he said as he opened the door and stepped out. A freezing wind filled the car in an instant. Misjudging the curb, he lurched forward and fell. The cut-glass bottle shattered on the sidewalk.

Annie put on the emergency brake and slid across the front seat, but he was already standing by the time she reached him. A freezing gust hit them.

"Good Christ, it's cold. Here . . ." Instinctively he put an arm around her, then opened his overcoat and folded Annie into it. She turned slightly, her body against his. His arm tightened around her and she hesitantly she put her arms around his waist. She stood with her head against his shoulder, her breasts against the side of his chest, her stomach against his hip, her legs tight against the side of his leg. She did not dare to move. As she stared at the pieces of broken glass on the sidewalk, she felt his cheek on her hair. "I just don't want to go to the club right now," he said. "Could I come with you?"

Annie looked up at him, unable to speak. When he let her loose, she stepped toward the Oldsmobile. Sliding back behind the steering wheel, she tried to think of where to go. The door slammed shut.

"I live out on Long Island," she offered.

"Fine. I don't care." He leaned his head back and closed his eyes.

She watched him for a moment, then put the car in gear and drove to the Midtown Tunnel. He started to breathe deeply and hardly moved for the first half hour of the trip.

She did not know what she was going to do. He could sleep in Charlie Dell's house. She had the keys to everything but the study. No one came by except Phil just to check in, and Charlie's sister once a week to water the plants and collect his mail. The sister was not due; Phil always called first. Annie wanted Sam in her apartment. She thought of his pictures on the wall of her bedroom. She remembered him naked to the waist at the train wreck. Not sure of the order of seduction, she visualized him naked on her bed, watching as she undressed. Concentrated on the details of the scene, she barely saw the road.

"Annie." She felt his hand on the back of her neck, his fingers playing with the pearls. Looking over at him, she saw an expression on his face that stopped her heart and her breath. He moved across the seat, took off his overcoat, and threw it in the back seat. One hand went through her hair and held her head as he kissed her ear; the other hand pressed against her stomach, then moved up over her breast.

An aching jolt went through her body as she tried to drive, gave up, and turned onto the shoulder of the road. She wondered where they were; there was little traffic. After the car stopped, Annie let Sam pull her gently down on the seat. She saw him looking at her, his mouth open slightly, bending over her as if he would consume her. She pulled away, but he drew her to him as his mouth pressed down on hers and his tongue prodded through her lips.

Stretching her legs across the seat to the door, she felt him on top of her, his legs drawn up between hers. Her skirt was up to her waist and his hand moved easily into her underpants, touching her thighs, going under her and grasping her buttock, then coming back and moving through the hair between her legs. Still he kissed her, sucking at her tongue. With his other hand he unbuttoned her coat and pulled the sleeve of her blouse down her arm. Both his hands went under her back to undo her bra. She arched to help him, and the bra came loose. His mouth left hers as his head fell to her breasts, kissing one, then the other, his tongue playing on her nipples as his hands reached down and pulled at her underpants. She drew up her legs in order to help him get them off. As he pulled them down beneath her garter belt, somehow he managed to kiss her thighs, holding them up by lifting her buttocks.

Annie felt a sensation beginning in her which she had never felt before. She needed him to touch her. As he kissed her again, she began to twist against him. Suddenly she felt his hardness against her, then prodding into her, then, in one slow lunge, filling her. She felt as if her bones were melting around it, and could not control her need to move against it. He drove himself into her as his hand squeezed her breast and he sucked her tongue with his mouth. Rubbing against him, she began to feel her urgency growing to a point of bursting, tearing something open. Her fear restrained her, but only for a moment as she twisted against him again, wanting whatever was coming too much to stop. Annie was overwhelmed by sensation and fright and affection, so that, without a thought, she gasped, "Oh, Lord, I love you, Sam," and knew before she finished saying it what a fool she was.

She felt him drive up inside her and hold as his jaw locked and his tongue became hard in her mouth. Then his tension broke and, panting, he pulled back and looked at her, seriously at first, then with a little smile of sharing something forbidden, as if he had not heard what she said. He pulled away and sat up, checking to see if there was any traffic. Annie watched as he fumbled with himself and buttoned up his trousers. Then she too sat up and pulled her blouse on, reached back and hooked her bra. The skirt had torn, but she managed to cover her legs with it. She saw her underpants on the floor near Sam's foot.

"Where the hell are we?" he said, staring out the window so that Annie could not see his face. His tone was sober and distant. Annie suddenly felt desperately embarrassed, and was appalled that they were going to her garage apartment. Not knowing what else to do, she started the car and began to drive.

They rode in silence and after five minutes Annie looked at Sam. He was asleep again. She thought of turning around and taking him back so that there would be no time to talk. Driving carefully around turns in order not to wake him, however, she kept going, wanting to stay with him. She tried to think of

75

what she would say to him, rejecting every idea as soon as she thought of it.

She pulled into the driveway and stopped. Watching him, she reached to twist the rearview mirror and see how she looked. It was too dark. She finally reached over and put her hand on his arm. She shook him twice before he woke up.

"What?" He turned and saw her. "Oh," he said, and looked around. "Are we here?"

They got out and Sam tripped on something. She reached out her hand and they climbed the outside flight of stairs leading up to her apartment. As she unbolted the lock, she said, "This is where I live, but you can stay in the house over there if you want."

"Why would I want to do that?" he asked.

He chuckled as she went in and turned on a light. He took three steps to the center of the room and looked around. Then he smiled, but the look on his face was a judgment.

"You want to take your coat off?" she asked.

He hesitated, but then did. Annie had the impression that he was doing it to be polite. She took off her own coat and threw it on a chair.

"I can't offer you anything to drink, I'm afraid."

"Thank God. All I want is some sleep."

She watched him to see exactly what that meant, and chose to believe it meant that he really wanted to stay.

"Well, give me a second," she said. "I'm going to wash up and change, if you'll excuse me."

"Here." He pulled her underpants out of his overcoat pocket and handed them to her. Annie took them, feeling herself flush.

"I'll just make myself at home," he said, and even as he smiled, Annie saw the regret shoot across his eyes for using the phrase.

On her way to her bathroom, Annie tore the pictures of Sam off her bedroom wall and stuffed them in a drawer. The clasp on the pearls would not come undone at first. When it did, she put the strand in the same drawer. She undressed and washed herself as quietly as possible, not thinking beyond the excitement of sleeping and waking up with him. She wished she had bought some perfume, but the soap smelled nice and would have to do. Slipping into her nightgown, which hung on the door, she picked up her own clothes to carry out in case he wanted to use the bathroom before coming to bed. But when she went back into the living room, Sam was standing near the front door, again in his overcoat.

"I think I'd better go, Annie."

She felt as if something had cracked through the middle of her, and it must have shown on her face, for he looked alarmed.

"I'm really very sorry," he said. "I was selfish as hell, and you didn't deserve to run into me tonight."

"I'm glad I did. You don't have to feel bad because of me. I sure wish you'd stay."

He shook his head. "I really can't." He smiled sadly. "When I realized who you were tonight, I was so damn glad it was you and not some damn deb I'd known all my life. I felt I could tell you everything."

"I'm glad I was there."

They stood, looking at each other for a moment. Then Annie said, "I'll drive you."

"No, let me walk and sober up. Where are we?"

"Garden City."

"Where's the hotel from here?"

"You go down four blocks, then left for two. Turn right at the dead end."

There did not seem to be anything else to say. Sam glanced at the door, but then took two steps and gathered Annie into his arms. He kissed her again—longingly, she wanted to believe. Then he looked at her, curious and finally confused, at which point he let her go and went out the door, closing it behind him.

Annie stood, immobilized for a moment, then ran to the door, opened it, and called to him without knowing what she was going to say.

"Sam!"

He had reached the bottom of the stairs. "Yes, Annie?"

"I . . . um, you didn't tell me how Certainty is doing."

"He's coming together very well. We think he's going to be a champion."

"I hope so."

"Thanks. Good night, Annie."

"Good night, Sam."

She turned back into her apartment and closed the door.

SIX

ANNIE STOPPED to pick up Phil, who was waiting on a corner of Astoria Boulevard. He walked around to the driver's side and, expecting to drive, waited for her to slide across the seat. She did not object.

"I hate April," Phil grumbled as he drove the Oldsmobile through Queens. "Real New York prick-tease weather, you know? A couple of nice days, you think 'spring,' and then a week of this shit."

Annie stared ahead at the street as the windshield wipers smeared the sleet across the glass.

"I hope you like gnocchi, because this club has the best gnocchi west of Genoa."

"Where are we going?"

"College Point. You'll love this place. One family runs the whole thing. Mama's in the kitchen, sons and daughters are waiters, cousins at the bar or washing dishes . . . Hey, Annie, cheer up, will you? What's the matter, you hate gnocchi?"

Annie tried to smile and shook her head. "I don't know what it is."

"Oh, terrific. First I have to explain the track; now it's what to eat. I guess I should be grateful; at least you ain't asking about religion or something."

Annie made herself laugh, which he wanted. He looked at her quickly, checked the road, then looked at her again.

"You're very good-looking, Annie," he said objectively, "especially that smile. If you were a couple of years older, I might put some moves on you, but I'm not into child molesting, you know? You got that dimple. I mean, you turn that smile on, it lights the room. I knew a girl once, Francine Taliaferro, wanted a dimple so bad, she went to a plastic surgeon and had him carve one out. Didn't work so good, though. Came out looking like a bullet hole."

Annie laughed and said, "You made that up."

"Really! Scout's honor. We used to call her Holier-Than-Thou. Want to know what Francine's doing now?"

"No!"

"Works in a pool hall."

He waited for Annie to ask, "Doing what?"

Tapping his jaw, he said, "She puts chalk in the hole so guys can put their cues in her cheek to chalk up! And don't ask me what a cue is!"

She reached over and hit his shoulder, laughing enough to start coughing. With a wide grin and his toothpick dancing, Phil stopped the car in front of a torn sidewalk awning painted in a fading zebra pattern of pink and green. A sign over the door read CLUB TAHITI. Pressed between the glass and inside shutters of the two windows were green neon tubes, suspended by electrical cords, outlining a martini glass with a pink cherry. A man ran out of the front door wearing a frayed admiral's hat and a leather jacket. Seeing Phil, he greeted him effusively. "Hey, Angel, how ya doin'? I'll park this for you."

When they went into the club, the employees welcomed Phil with similar enthusiasm, everyone calling him Angel. Annie could hardly see at first, but as her eyes adjusted to the dark, she saw worn vinyl banquettes along the walls and about fifteen tables, half of them occupied, in the middle of the room. Fake palm leaves and fishnets hung from the ceiling. Island scenes were painted on the walls and lit dimly with green and pink bulbs. At the far end was a small stage. To one side were a set of drums, a piano, and three frayed cardboard music stands, stenciled with "Jack Straddler's Big Band." There were no musicians. The ashtrays on the tables were full of butts and the floor was littered with coasters, napkins, and cigarette packages. The air was warm and stale; it stank of cigarettes and liquor.

Phil greeted everyone by name without smiling and without acknowledging that anyone was with him. He and Annie were led to a table by an insistent headwaiter, whom Phil irritated by pointing to a booth. When they were seated, a waitress appeared and asked Phil, with a suggestive smile, what he would like. The club's costume was a long green slit skirt and a pink off-the-shoulder peasant blouse. As the waitress bent over to make her offer, Annie noticed that her large breasts were unconstrained by any undergarments.

Phil ordered a bottle of wine and two plates of gnocchi.

"You come here a lot?" Annie asked.

He shrugged. "I come by." He looked around. "This place is a toilet. When I take you to the Copacabana, or the Desert Inn in Vegas, and they welcome me like that, then you'll know who you're with. It don't mean anything in here. I come here for the gnocchi, which is the only thing worth the visit."

"What if I don't like it?"

"Don't worry about it. Just taste it."

The wine arrived, was opened, and poured with great display of cork screwing and breasts. Phil watched with brooding pleasure, sipped, and approved the wine. When they were left alone again, he looked hard at Annie. "So what's the matter with you? Until I told you about Francine, it was like driving around with a slab of concrete."

She looked down at her wineglass. "I just haven't been feeling too good."

"You keep saying that on the phone and I always have to call you. The deal was we'd check in with each other. You remember my number?" Annie nodded. "Well, listen, Charlie's worried about you. Johnny Phillips told him you'd quit, of course, which was all right. It's up to you, but Charlie—"

"I gave Johnny plenty of warning. He said he could get along—"

"Hey, wait. Nobody's blaming you for anything. Johnny thinks you're aces. It's just that Charlie wants to know if you're okay and he told me to find out. I haven't seen you for a while, so I thought we should have dinner."

"I'm fine."

"Everything all right at the house?"

"Yes."

"Nobody coming around, bothering you?"

"No. Charlie's sister comes by, but I never talk to her . . . Blimpie's called a couple of times."

"Blimpie? What the hell does he want?"

"Nothing. Just being friendly, or trying to be. I don't talk to him long."

"You just stay away from him . . . You got enough money?"

"Yes!" she said, irritated.

"Charlie asked," he explained with patronizing concern. "So what is it? Johnny said you pretty much stopped talking to people before you quit. Even Burt was worried. When I call, you sound like a robot. It's been bad since Christmas, Annie. What do you do all day?"

She tried to think of something, then told him the truth. "Listen to records, read Charlie's thoroughbred magazines, keep the house clean, eat, sleep."

"He has a cleaning lady."

"I *know*, Phil. It just keeps me busy. Look, I just didn't want to go out to the track anymore. I'll call Charlie and tell him I'm all right, hear?"

"Don't do that; it'll make me look bad." He grinned and raised his glass. "Tchin-tchin."

She did not ask what it meant. She lifted her glass and, taking the customary sip, was surprised by how good the wine tasted.

"I don't blame you," Phil said. "Winter on a backstretch is

the worst. They say the horses don't mind it, but five o'clock on a January morning ain't a swell time for humans."

"I really miss it," she said.

To her relief, Phil did not point out the contradiction. "Wait till spring; I mean the real spring. You know, those five New York days between winter and summer? About there, the races start again. Then you can go back."

Annie pretended to agree but did not believe she would feel any different. "Why do they call you Angel?" she asked, not wanting to talk about herself anymore.

"My last name's Angelo. Phil Angelo. You didn't know that?"

"I guess not. Do you live around here?"

"I grew up around here. I got a place over by Belmont, but I'm moving to an apartment in Manhattan. As soon as I find the right one. Hey, here it is! Wait'll you taste this stuff."

The two plates of gnocchi were placed in front of them and Phil started eating immediately. "Mmm! Mmm! Wherever we go, Annie, Miami, Beverly Hills, the Riviera, we'll look at each other across the table and say, 'The gnocchi was better at the Club Tahiti!'"

"You keep talking about all these places we're going," Annie said with a weak smile.

"I figure that we're going to know each other a long time, Annie. And you're growing up." He grinned suggestively. "You don't think we're going to be stuck coming to places like this, do you? Listen, if you don't dream big, how the hell do you know where you want to go? I mean someday I'm going to have a car like you've never seen. Right now, I can see my New York apartment in my head. All I got to do is go over the bridge and find it. As a matter of fact, I can see us sitting on some veranda looking out over the whole goddamn Mediterranean. See what I mean? Go ahead, eat your gnocchi and tell me your dreams."

She tried a piece of the potato dish and chewed it slowly. "This is really good."

"What'd I tell you?"

"You go on telling the dreams and I'll eat. Yours are better

83

than mine anyway, except I don't know why I got into yours, unless it's because I just happen to be the one sitting here."

Phil grinned. "You'll do fine, Annie. Of course in the dream you're just a little older, you know?"

She felt her face go hot, and concentrated on her food. "I got a postcard from Vera," she said. Phil did not respond; he went on eating. "She loves it in Miami, but says one out of every three horses is either infected or doped. What does that—?"

"Vera's mouth is bigger than her brain!" Phil said viciously, making Annie recoil. "Don't ever tell her anything you don't want the world to know. She puts that cute nose of hers into places it shouldn't go." He finished a glass of wine, then poured another, shooting a look at Annie. "It's hot and humid in Florida, easy for germs to grow around a barn. Horses get sick easy down there. A virus starts on the backstretch, it can knock out every horse there. Sometimes it kills them. It's almost as bad as a fire."

Across the room, there was a disturbance, a man talking too loudly to his wife. Phil glanced over and scowled. "Jesus Christ, this is my night off."

"But what does she mean about dope?"

"Goddammit, Annie, when the hell are you going to open your eyes and stop asking dumb questions? There's only one way for a horse to win a race and that's getting him to the track. Lot of times, they need some help. And if the horse ain't any good in the first place, dope makes him better. It's part of racing. I don't mean Nashua. I mean the ninety-five percent of the horses running that people don't care much about except that they win their race."

Across the room, the man who had been yelling at his wife smacked her across the face and she screamed, leaning down in the booth.

Phil breathed an angry sigh, stood up, and dropped the keys to the Oldsmobile next to Annie's plate. "You better go," he said, watching the couple. "I gotta work now."

"What do you mean?"

"I work for the guys that own this place. I keep the peace. It's going to get ugly, so you better go home."

The headwaiter came up ready to urge action, but Phil started over to the couple without any prompting. The man was trying to force the woman to sit up straight. Annie was on her way to the front door when she saw Phil grab the man's hand as he was about to hit the woman again. Holding the hand, Phil took hold of the man's hair and, with one jerk, yanked him out of his seat. The man fell on the floor, and before he could get up, Phil kicked him hard twice in his ribs, reached down for his hair, and, lifting his head up, smacked him back and forth across his face. The woman was screaming as Annie went out the door.

Phil called the next day. "You get home all right?" he asked.

"Yeah. What about you?"

"Yeah, sure. The happy couple was celebrating his birthday. Can you believe it? Moral, don't get married and don't get older. Call me. You got the number?"

"Mayflower 5-2760," Annie recited dutifully. "I went over to Belmont this morning, talked to Johnny's assistant about starting work again, maybe after the Derby, when Charlie comes home." Her excitement was obvious in her voice. "Will you tell Charlie?"

"Sounds good . . . 'Listen, when I take you to Vegas, I won't have to do any of that shit, you know." He hung up.

On the day of the Kentucky Derby, Annie bought a cheap radio to listen to the broadcast from Churchill Downs in Louisville. That morning, she had returned to Belmont Park to see Johnny Phillips, who was back from Florida. Burt was there and kidded her about her winter vacation. She knew she had missed the horses, but not how much until she went down the shedrow, greeting some of the colts and fillies. She and Burt made a bet on the Derby, and Annie went out with Johnny and watched at the rail as the horses worked. By then, her hands itched with wanting to wrap ankles and curry flanks.

Besides that anticipation, Annie was intensely eager for Charlie Dell's return two days after the Derby. As she tested to find the best place in her apartment for the radio to be clear of static, she imagined what Charlie and Teddy Lapps were doing. The race was a statewide Kentucky festival, yet she had never seen the Derby or thought much about it. But that day, she knew someone who was there, and from Charlie's thoroughbred magazines, she knew a great deal about every runner in the field.

The knock on her apartment door startled her; because the radio was turned up, she had not heard anyone coming up the stairs. Through the window in the door, she saw a vase filled with flowers on the landing. Carefully she opened the door. A bouquet of purple irises, pink tulips, and red carnations in a white plastic vase stood on the landing. She stepped out and, for a moment, hoped they were from Sam.

"Hi, Annie." At the foot of the steps stood Charlie's nephew, Blimpie. "Didn't want to scare you, so I came down here."

Annie felt the surface of her skin prickle. Remembering the freakish high-pitched singsong precision of his words, she just managed a pleasant nod. "What are they for?" She could see his mother's car parked at the curb.

"Well, I've wanted to apologize for ever so long, for how I behaved that day at the track. When you arrived that day, I was already furious at Phil Angelo, and I think I took it out on you. Please forgive me."

"That's okay," she said, glancing inside at the telephone, then smiling down at him. The radio was still playing. "Thanks for the flowers. They sure are beautiful." Hoping he would go, she tried to look confident.

"I've got a secret, Annie Grebauer."

She held her smile, but was alarmed by his use of her real name. "What's that?" she said.

"Well, I'd like us to be friends, because Uncle Charlie won't take me to the track anymore. Maybe you'd say something to him. In exchange, I'll show you the secret."

With a smile, he pulled out a metal key ring with three keys on it, and held it up for her to see.

"Do I get three guesses?" Annie asked, trying to keep the mood light without encouraging him to stay.

"They're to Uncle Charlie's house."

"I have those, too," Annie said. "Thanks anyway."

Rolling his eyes in that direction, he said, "Not to his office." Then he smiled wisely. "Want to see what it looks like?" Behind his thick glasses, his eyes stretched open with anticipation.

"Charlie gave you his keys?"

"No. He gives them to Mommie when he goes away. She's supposed to come down once a week to get his mail and water the plants. But she couldn't come today because of her sciatica. So I have to go over and water the plants. He's got two fica trees in his office."

"What's the secret?"

He swallowed, then smiled, quickly licking the saliva from the corners of his mouth. "See, Uncle Charlie has a file on you: 'Annie Grebauer.' I saw it on his desk once, 'Grebauer' was crossed out and 'Brown' written in. I didn't see what was in it. Want to come look for it?"

Annie stood rigidly on the landing. She could say no and lock the door. But there was a file with her name on it. Why did Charlie have a file? What was in it? "Blimpie, I'd like to, but I'm still kind of scared because of what happened at Belmont."

He stood up straight, swinging his bulk resolutely into place.

"Well, I didn't mean that. I was just angry. Really, Annie. Please forget that. Ridiculous."

She smiled at him with admiration, which seemed to have the effect she wanted. With an urgent nobility, he declared, "I won't *touch* you, I swear to *God!*"

"Then can I ask you a favor?"

"Sure! Yes! Anything you want."

"When we go over there, give me the keys after you open the door. Let me hold them till we leave, okay? Don't take it wrong, hear? I just got real scared, and that'd help me."

Blimpie watched her—a bit suspiciously, Annie thought. Then he put the keys down on the second step.

"You take them right now. You don't have to worry *one bit.*"

Annie looked around, smiled again at Blimpie, and said, "Let me turn off the radio. I'll meet you over there."

She carried the flowers into her apartment and thought of calling Phil, but she wanted to look at whatever file Charlie had with her name on it, and definitely did not want Phil to see it. Forgetting the radio, she went down the steps and across the lawn to Charlie's front door. Blimpie gestured gallantly for Annie to use the keys, which she did, allowing him, after the bolt was drawn, to open the door. As Annie stepped in, she felt a quick quiver in her legs.

With familiarity, Blimpie turned on light switches in the dark room. Annie put the keys in her jeans pocket as she followed him through the house. Heavily draped with thick maroon velvet and ball fringe, the rooms were lit by violet and green crystal wall sconces and small chandeliers. Oriental carpets, densely flowered wallpaper, and paintings of country views were in each room. There was a dark oak table set in the dining room, and old stuffed maroon sofas and chairs in the living room. Blimpie led Annie to the study door at the back of the house. Using the unfamiliar key on the ring, Annie opened it. The room had better light, and on all four walls were floor-to-ceiling shelves filled with books.

"You can start looking while I water the plants. He's got that *jungle* in the bedrooms upstairs. But be careful. Put everything back the way it was. If he found out we were in here, he'd kill us."

Annie waited. First she heard the water run in the kitchen, then Blimpie went past the door carrying a pitcher and wearing rubber dishwashing gloves. As she heard him climb the creaky stairs to the second floor, Annie went straight to the desk. There was nothing on top except two telephones and stacks of old copies of the *Morning Telegraph* and *The Blood-Horse.* All the drawers were locked. She felt around the edges of the desk and under the two phones for a key. Searching the room, she looked under pillows and on the bottoms of chairs. On one wall of bookshelves was a small vase placed in a space between the books. Annie picked it up and shook it. It was empty.

Putting the vase back carefully in its place, she decided she would not be able to find the key. Then she noticed the books themselves, leather-bound many of them, whole sets, sometimes twenty or thirty volumes in matched bindings. Perhaps a key was in one of them. She ran her hand along a set of volumes in old blue leather and was surprised to find the title *Great Expectations.*

She listened as Blimpie creaked around the floors upstairs, then took the book down from the shelf. It was heavier than her copy. When she leafed through it, she saw that many words had been underlined, and in the margins were notations in a foreign language.

A single piece of paper fell out of the pages and floated down to the floor. Annie stared at it a moment, stooped down, and picked it up. Written in the same tiny hand as the notes in the book, the paper had a numbered list of names, each followed by a date, an address, and a description, such as "second basement, northwest concrete pillar."

The stairs creaked. Without thinking, Annie slipped the book back in its place. Realizing that she still held the piece of paper, she jammed it down into her bra as she hurried out of the office. Suddenly she was covered with sweat and desperate to get out of the house.

"Hi," Blimpie said. Annie looked up and saw him standing in the hallway between her and the front door. His white socks hung around his ankles; the rubber gloves were still on his hands. He was naked.

"You said . . ." Annie could barely talk.

"I said *I* wouldn't touch you," he blurted excitedly. "I won't! See? I'm wearing rubber gloves! And I won't even do that if *you* touch *me.*" He started for her.

"What?" She leaped back into the office, slammed the door, and locked it. He was already yanking at the doorknob.

"I don't want to scare you," he called. "And you can scream all you want. There are bars on the windows. You can't open them, and the storm windows are unbreakable. Nobody will hear you. I know. This isn't the first time I've used Uncle Charlie's place." He pounded on the door, then giggled and went away.

Annie hurried to the phone and dialed Phil's number. While it rang four times, Annie started to dial the operator on the other phone to get the police.

"Hello."

"Phil, I'm locked in Charlie's office. Blimpie's trying to get at me."

"Jesus Christ!" He slammed down the phone.

Annie started shoving chairs and tables across the room to block the door. She piled up everything, then tried to push the desk against her barricade, but the desk was too heavy to move, as were the two tree tubs. Standing in the middle of the room, she heard the floor creak outside; then Blimpie giggled again. He started doing something to the door. She looked around the room for anything that could be used as a weapon.

"I know there are phones in there," Blimpie shouted. "If you call the police, I'll just say you came over while I was watering the plants, stole the keys, and locked yourself in Uncle Charlie's study." The scratching noise on the door continued. Then he laughed in a piercing falsetto. "Of course, I'd have my clothes on, and I'd tell them I was just trying to get in to stop you from searching or stealing, whatever you're doing in there." He laughed again.

"Blimpie, they'll never believe you. Even if they did, Charlie wouldn't."

He worked quietly without answering. "See, this is an old house. And did you notice these old metal strap hinges *out here?* They're on all the doors; makes the place look kind of antique. Each door has two hinges, and each hinge has, let's see, twelve screws, twenty-four in all. That's a lot of screwing, Annie! And *this* one is . . . number two!"

Annie went to a phone and dialed the operator. "How do I get the police?"

"I can connect you. What's your location?"

"Can you just give me the number?"

"Are you in Hempstead?"

"Garden City."

There was no pen or pencil. Annie repeated the number to herself. Blimpie said through the door, "Number three!"

There was nothing in the room that she could use to hit him. The vases were too small, the side tables and chairs too heavy to swing. She could hear him grunting on the other side of the door as he struggled with the screws, calling the number after each successful effort. She went to the windows and saw that they were painted shut. Taking a book, she used it to break out a pane, but she could not even crack the storm window, which seemed to be made of thick plastic. And beyond that were the bars. She listened to the screws coming out of the door, grateful that each took so much time.

"Too bad you're making such a mess in there, Annie. Uncle Charlie's going to be very angry. It certainly would be better if you just opened the door. It doesn't make any difference, you know, because . . . umph. Number seventeen is stuck. Well, I'm getting *tired* of this! I'm going to get the crowbar. Why should I care about what Uncle Charlie thinks?" He suddenly sounded enraged.

Annie listened as the floor creaked down the hall. When she began to tremble, she stepped to the desk and pounded her arms on it to make herself stop shaking. "Phil's coming," she said to reassure herself. "Phil's coming," and she pounded her arms on the desk again.

"My goodness, what's going on in there?" Blimpie said, and Annie heard the dull thud of a crowbar being jammed under a hinge. He grunted, and the hinge popped loose. The door shifted in its frame as there was another thud.

"Blimpie, you're crazy!" she shrieked. "You're crazy!" she shrieked again. She ran to the desk and started to dial one of the phones. He was laughing on the other side of the door; then he grunted with effort and the second hinge popped free. The door thumped down an inch in its frame, and immediately he charged against it. The furniture barrier held against the bottom of the door, but the top slanted in; then the door slid of its own weight into the hall. Blimpie yanked it out farther. Throwing the furniture aside and smiling widely, he stood looking at her, his lips pulled tightly away from his teeth, through which his tongue hung out. His white sagging chest had clumps of hair growing around his protuberant nipples. He was so fat that Annie could not see his crotch.

"I won't put a hand on you," he said brightly, "if you just touch me all over . . . *all over!*"

"I can't do that, Blimpie," Annie said quietly, hesitating even to move to dial the last number.

"Why not?" he demanded.

"Because if I touch you . . . I'LL KILL YOU!" She reached for a book on the shelf behind her and threw it as hard as she could. The phone fell to the floor. The book hit Blimpie in the face, knocking his glasses askew. He groaned and put his glasses right. His nose started to bleed, and she threw another book, then another, but Blimpie started coming for her, batting the books away, smiling, sweating, licking at the corners of his mouth.

Behind him Annie saw Phil with a gun. Just as Blimpie was reaching out to grab her shirt, he screamed and stood up very straight, his eyes popping.

"You move, Blimpie," Phil said, standing close behind him, "I'll give you a second asshole."

"Take it out of there!" Blimpie shrieked.

"It'll go off if you squeeze, Blimpie. Just stand there real still. Annie, get out of here."

Annie tried to slip past the trembling, bleeding Blimpie, but he leaped at her and fell on top of her on the floor. Annie smelled his breath and felt him writhe against her, even as Phil kicked him, bellowing obscenities. Grabbing him with both hands and hauling him off, Phil could not manage the weight as Blimpie attacked her. The two men fell down, beating at each other. Annie stood up and saw Phil's gun on the floor. She picked it up and stood above them, holding it with both hands. Phil rolled off Blimpie, who saw her pointing the gun at his head. When she lowered it to his crotch, his face twisted with fear.

"Annie," Phil shouted, "don't do it! It ain't worth the trouble!"

She did not move the gun. Her arms began to shake and she realized her finger was tightening on the trigger. She could not stop, and she jerked herself around as the gun went off. Then she dropped it. When she looked around, Phil was on his feet and Blimpie was cringing on the floor with blood from his nose all over his chest.

"Get back to your apartment," Phil said. "I'll take care of this. Where are the keys?"

After dropping them on the floor, Annie climbed over the

furniture in the doorway, made her way around the fallen door, and walked down the hall to the entrance. Crossing the lawn, she held her hand on her forehead against the sun. She felt as if it were a different day from the one she had left less than an hour before. Climbing the stairs, she heard music. It was the crowd at Churchill Downs over the radio. They were singing "My Old Kentucky Home," the traditional Derby post time anthem.

Annie walked to the radio and turned it off with such force that the plastic knob broke in her hand.

SEVEN

ANNIE SAT on the blue-striped couch in her apartment, staring at the names on the paper. She had to get Blimpie's keys from Phil so that she could put the list back. Panicked, she wondered if Charlie had put it at a certain page number in the book. If she could just put back the piece of paper, it would make no difference. He would not know she had been the one who moved it.

There were forty names. She did not recognize any of them. Several were repeated: Luciano, four times; Anastasia, six. Annie abruptly remembered that name from what Vera had said about Murder, Inc. Others were repeated but not as frequently. Genovese, Lansky, Zwillman, Costello, Siegel, Schultz, Moretti, Gambino, Colombo, Bonanno. The dates started in 1935 and continued through 1950. Fifteen years, three times five, Annie noted. Because of the repeated names, she reasoned that they were the people for whom Charlie Dell had done his undertaking favors. Most probably, the date and location recorded when and where the bodies were preserved in concrete.

She heard Phil coming up the outside stairs. She first stuffed the list under the couch cushion, but thought better of it and folded it back in her bra. When he knocked at the apartment door, she got up from the couch and let him in. He was carrying the gun, wrapped in paper towels.

"You all right?" he asked.

She was about to thank him when he shoved her and yelled, "What the *fuck* were you *doing* over there?"

"Blimpie invited me," she murmured.

He wiped off the barrel of the gun, balled up the paper towels, and threw them in the wastebasket next to the pine table.

"Blimpie invited you? Sweet Jesus! I told you about Blimpie. Are you *stupid* or *what?*"

Shaken by his yelling, she confessed, "I was."

"He's been arrested *three* times for molesting and exposing himself. He was at a private *funny* farm for two years. They had to sew him into bib overalls because he kept dropping his pants in the dining room." Then he snorted in anger.

Annie sat down on the couch. "I'm sorry," she offered. "I didn't know all that."

"You'd be a hell of a lot sorrier if my neighbor hadn't taken a hundred bucks to drive through ten red lights to get me here." He was still holding the gun and looking down at her.

"I'm sorry," she said again.

He was still angry. "Now listen real good. On the way to the doctor, I made it real clear to Blimpie that he don't tell no one about it, not even his goddamn bitch Mommie. It's gotta be just as clear to you. I have a friend coming in tomorrow to fix the window and the door. I got most of that fat pig's blood up and the rest don't show on the rug. Because"—he tugged loose his tie—"if Charlie ever finds out you were in his office, he'd have to punish you. I don't know how, but whatever he decided on, I'd have to do it. Get it?"

He stared down at her until she finally said, "I got it."

He reached over Annie's legs and dropped the gun on her lap.

"You know how to use that?" he asked.

"No."

"Take it and learn. Blimpie's crazy; you never know when he'll show up again, and I might not be home. Throwing books at him ain't gonna do the trick. Oh, yeah, the bullet. It went into a back corner of the leather couch. You can barely see it. I covered the hole with a pillow. Nobody'll ever move it, except the cleaning lady, and what'll she know?"

Trying to show sufficient gratitude, Annie said, "Phil, thank you. I'm really glad you got there . . . Do you still have the keys?"

He looked at her harshly. "Of course I got the keys." Then he grinned. "Do you realize how hard it is to find a fat man's asshole?"

So relieved that his anger had passed, she reached out a hand. He took it and, with a gentle tug, pulled her up. The gun fell from her lap to the floor. Then his arms went around her. He looked down at her, and she knew what was going to happen.

"So maybe you grew up faster than I thought," he said.

She had to get the keys so that she could put the list back, and dared not offend him. She suddenly thought of Sam Cumberland in the car with her. When Phil kissed her, she responded, trying to erase what had come into her mind. As his hand moved deftly into her bra, it stopped on the piece of paper.

"What the hell is this?" he asked, kissing her ear.

"Grocery list," she said, her eyes wide over his shoulder.

He hesitated a moment, then yanked the paper out and shoved her back down on the couch. He walked to the window with the list. "Bullshit, Annie. D'you find something over there?"

Annie saw the gun on the floor. Without thinking, she dove for it, picked it up, and pointed it at Phil.

"Put it down," he said viciously, "or I'll kick the shit out of you."

Annie shook her head. At the same time she felt she might

throw up. Phil held up the list. "Where the fuck did you get this?"

"Please just drop it and give me the keys." The gun was heavier than she remembered, and her hand was shaking. She grasped the gun with both hands, trying to steady it. Remembering the movies she had seen, she felt for the safety catch by the chamber, found it, and clicked it off—or on; she did not know which. Phil heard the click.

"Don't fool around, Annie; you'll get hurt. You don't know how to work it." He started toward her. Quickly, she pointed the gun to one side of him and pulled the trigger. The explosion again deafened her and threw her arms almost back into her face. But she immediately pointed the gun straight at Phil's head. He stopped moving. The bullet had gone past his ear into the wall near the window.

"Just drop the list and leave, Phil." Her hands began to shake again.

"What are you gonna do with it?" he asked as he let the piece of paper float down to the floor.

"If you hadn't seen it, it wouldn't matter. I could have just put it back. Now—"

"Annie, I *know* what to do with it. It's worth maybe *millions!* I'll split with you."

"Get out! Please!"

"Just take it easy, all right? We'll talk about it," Phil said as he moved to the door. "Before Charlie comes back. How about tomorrow? Sunday brunch. I can help you, Annie, and you know it. Just don't lose that list, and don't tell no one else about it." At the door, he looked back. "And don't think you're so smart, Annie. You do something wrong with that list, you're dead."

He left, closing the door behind him. Annie rushed over to turn the bolt, then fell with her back against the door and sank to the floor. She sat there listening to Phil going down the steps. One hand lay in her lap, holding the gun. She stared at her finger on the trigger, then looked at the bullet hole in the wall. Standing up, she put the gun on the pine table. She had to get away from Charlie Dell's so that she could think.

Picking up the list, Annie folded it back into her bra. When she had her coat on, she went to the medicine cabinet in the bathroom and grabbed the Band-Aid box where she kept her money. With the car keys in one hand, she switched the safety on the gun and held it in her pocket as she opened the door.

Outside on the landing, she saw Phil leaning against the Oldsmobile in the driveway. He made a mocking gesture of opening the door for her. She took the gun out of her pocket.

"Get away from the car, Phil."

"Hey, I left Blimpie's car at the doctor's, took a cab back here. I need a ride."

"No. Get away from the car."

He backed slowly across the lawn.

"Put the iron away, Annie. Just remember who saved your life today. I'm trusting you."

"The hell you are," she said angrily.

He shrugged and held his hands up as if surrendering. "Just stay cool, all right? Hear what I gotta say." He grinned ingratiatingly. "Don't forget, tomorrow brunch."

She came down the steps, watching him carefully. As she turned to get into the Oldsmobile, he said, "You know something, Annie? When you took that shot and missed Blimpie today, you were almost as crazy as he was. Be careful, okay?"

Annie did not respond. She started the car, backed out, and drove away. Phil watched from the lawn without moving. At the corner, she turned toward the Mineola station to catch the next express train into New York.

The railroad car was not crowded. She took the list out of her bra, unfolded it, and read the names again, beginning to realize what she had done to herself. The list contained the names of killers. They all knew Charlie Dell, and he had proven that they could trust him. They did not know Annie. If anyone on the list found out that she had it, he would probably kill her. Phil Angelo could tell any of them, and would. He had read it. Probably he recognized the names, but in that quick look he could not have memorized more than one or two addresses, if that. Still, whatever he knew he would use. Annie was sure of that. Somehow she had to figure out how to make the list useless to Phil. Looking out the window, she winced at how impossible it seemed.

When she arrived at Pennsylvania Station, she walked across the street to the Statler Hotel and checked into the cheapest room. The next morning, she went to the New York Public Library. She had no idea how to find information, so she stood in the Main Reading Room and watched. Finally she went to the librarian's desk and asked for help. A nice woman explained the card catalogue and, only by chance, mentioned newspapers. Soon Annie was using the *New York Times Index* and scouring back issues of the paper. She stayed in the reading room for the rest of the day. By the time she left and walked down the broad front steps to Fifth Avenue, she was terrified by what she had learned. The names on the list belonged to the most powerful men in organized crime. She had evidence that might convict every one of them of murder.

Annie walked aimlessly, trying to figure out what to do. She could not trust Phil. She also knew that she could not lie to Charlie. All at once she realized that if Charlie knew she had seen the list, he would have to kill her to protect himself. He would have to kill Phil as well. Phil was in just as much danger as she was. As she continued walking, an idea began to take shape. The first thing she had to do was hide the list, perhaps in a safe, a bank. She remembered passing a bank on Fifth Avenue and doubled back. After hurrying several blocks, she was standing in front of a new glass building with a huge silver safe brightly lit and visible from the sidewalk. Annie stared at the gleaming surface of the safe, its enormous hinges, its time locks, its massive bolts of solid steel.

The next morning she stood in the same place and watched as the safe was swung open. Inside, its bar doors slid back and bank employees began to walk in and out of it. She stood there for a long time until, stepping closer to the glass, she watched a customer enter the safe with a bank employee. They came out with a small metal box, which the customer took into a small room nearby. The bank employee, an older man with white hair and glasses hanging from a silk ribbon around his neck, saw Annie through the glass and smiled. She returned the smile, then took a deep breath and went into the bank.

Mr. Fogle was the man's name. He courteously explained to Annie how a safe deposit box worked. Enjoying his responsibility, he said, "I must tell you, miss, that it gives me great pleasure to see young people who want to save *anything*. No one seems to remember what the Depression was." When he filled out the signature card for Annie's pair of keys, Annie gave him the name Mary Lou McCasslin, and made up a New York address. He slid out a long flat box from the wall of the safe and led Annie to the small room she had seen just outside the safe's door. When she was alone, she took the list out of her bra and, without looking at it again, placed it in the box. She thought of putting the gun there, but did not. Returning the box to Mr. Fogle, she said, "Sir, can I ask you something else?"

"Surely," he said sliding the box back into its slot and using one of Annie's keys to lock the little door. "As much as you like."

As he handed her the key, she said, "Well, can I leave the keys with you somehow? I'm afraid I'll lose them, or someone else might find them."

"I'm afraid we can't do that, Miss McCasslin. Perhaps you could find a good hiding place."

"Well, let me ask you this. What if something happens to me and I want someone to get what's in the box?"

"Usually all those instructions are in a will, but you're too young for that, aren't you?"

"I'm getting older pretty fast," Annie said, making Mr. Fogle chuckle.

"Perhaps you should have your parents take you to a lawyer, who could record your instructions, even keep your key. You might sign what's called a power of attorney, allowing him or whoever you choose to gain access to the box in the event of your . . . unavailability. We open boxes under those circumstances all the time."

Annie said, "Where can I find a lawyer?"

Mr. Fogle laughed. "Everywhere." Then, seeing her consternation, he became serious again. "For instance, just off Fifth Avenue at Fifty-first Street is the Esso Building. There are any number of firms there. Look in the lobby directory for a firm with a great many names, and take your pick."

Carrying the small envelope with the two safe deposit box keys in her jeans pocket, Annie went to the Esso Building. She found a firm in the directory called Pickerell, Herskewitz, and Showalter. After taking the elevator to the fifteenth floor, she was confronted by a large waiting room, at the center of which was a receptionist sitting at an antique desk. She was dressed in a snappy silk suit with a colorful silk scarf arranged puffily around her neck.

"May I help you?" she asked through an already contemptuous smile.

"I need to talk to a lawyer," Annie said, conscious of the woman looking at her jeans, boots, and jacket.

"Do you have an appointment?"

"No."

The receptionist's eyebrow lifted. "Perhaps you'll have a seat. It may be some time."

Annie sat for two hours, smiling at the receptionist whenever their eyes met across the room. People came and went, none paying attention to Annie except to cast an occasional glance at her clothes. She was intensely embarrassed but was not going to be intimidated. One young man in rolled shirtsleeves and red suspenders hurried through several times. He noticed Annie the first two times, then smiled at her the third. Finally he came back, saw that Annie was still there, and said to the receptionist, "Toodie, is this lady waiting for someone?"

"She doesn't have an appointment," Toodie replied archly.

The man scowled and came over to Annie. "Hello, I'm Archibald Delansig. If you're looking for an attorney, come on with me."

He led Annie through a doorway, down a long hall, and into a small office with a desk littered with files and stacks of paper. "Forgive the mess. There's a clear surface on that chair there. Help yourself. Now what can I do for you?"

He collapsed in a leather high-backed swivel chair, took off his clear plastic-rimmed glasses, and rubbed his eyes. Annie saw pictures in frames on a shelf behind him of a woman holding two babies. There was a line of documents hanging on the wall as well as several paintings in vivid colors of what looked like smeared rainbows.

"Sir," Annie said, feeling very awkward, "I need someone to keep a secret. Can you do that?"

He put his glasses back on and said, "Well, there's the attorney-client privilege, and if I violate that or your confidence, you could have me disbarred." He smiled. "How's that?"

Annie had no idea what it meant, but she trusted him. She said slowly, "If I gave you my safe deposit keys to keep for me, and signed an attorney's power, or whatever it's called, so that you could use the keys, is there some way you could send what's in the box to the police if something happened to me?"

By the time she finished the question, Archy Delansig was watching her very carefully. He was about thirty, with brown hair and a high forehead over large brown eyes, which were penetrating even when they were half closed, as they were while he watched her. His face was quite handsome, but everything about it—his narrow cheeks, short pointed nose, and slightly tightened lips—seemed involved in his concentration. He wore a plain blue tie, which lay quietly between his fire engine–red suspenders.

"Yes," he said simply.

"How much would it cost?"

"I'll do the power of attorney and your letter of instruction for fifty dollars. It'll cost you fifty dollars a year to keep everything here in our safe."

"That'll be fine," Annie said.

"How often do I need to know you're all right? Every day, every week?"

"No, not that often. Maybe every month."

"Fine. Send me a postcard. If I don't get one, I'll open the box."

"Couldn't I just call you?"

"I don't trust phone calls. I wouldn't know if someone was forcing the call. If the postcard is forced, you'll sign it 'Cordially.' Otherwise, 'As ever.' All right?"

"Sounds fine," Annie said.

"I'll call my secretary in to dictate. Anything else?"

"Aren't you going to ask me what's in the safe deposit box?"

Delansig smiled. "Would you tell me?"

"Not if I could help it."

"When and if you want me to know, you'll tell me. I hope you don't have to. But if you do, you're welcome to call or come by at any time. My only advice is not to wait too long if the time comes. And don't let Toodie out there bother you."

Annie smiled and said, "Thank you, sir. I won't."

She took the train back to Mineola and drove to Garden City, hoping she could talk to Phil before Charlie returned that night. When she pulled into the driveway, Phil came striding out of the house and started ranting before she reached the steps to her apartment.

"Where the hell have you been? Don't you know Charlie's—"

"Phil, come on up. We've got a whole lot to talk about."

Enraged, Phil stared at her, then followed her up the steps. Inside the apartment, Annie began to talk before he could say anything.

"The list is in a safe deposit box. The keys are with a lawyer. It'll go to the district attorney right off if anyone bothers me."

Phil glared at her, eyes wide. *"You gotta be nuts!* Charlie's coming in tonight. We gotta get that piece of paper back to wherever you found it. Maybe Charlie won't check on it tonight. You get that list out of the safe deposit box tomorrow morning, and we'll . . ."

Phil stopped when he saw Annie shaking her head. "Phil, I'm not going to get it back."

"You stupid little bitch, do you know what you're doing?"

Annie ignored his anger. "Did you tell Blimpie about the list?" she asked.

"Shit, no. Does *he* know about it? Did he see you . . . ?"

"No. So that's one less person for us to worry about." As she sat down at the pine table, she took hold of it with her hands to keep from shaking. "From what you said about the list being worth millions of dollars, I figure you were already thinking about blackmailing some of those people on it. Phil, those men don't blackmail. It'd get you, me, *and* Charlie killed, because as soon as you mention to them where a body's buried, they'd know where the information came from." Her arms started to shake and she gripped the table harder as she continued. "This way, all I have to do is convince you and Charlie that I'm *never* going to use the list. It'll stay right where it is. So the best thing for all three of us to do is just forget about it."

Phil stared at her, then reached across the table to grab her. Annie leaned back to avoid him. *"Forget* about it? You're crazy! You're throwing away this chance of . . ." He stopped and sat tensely on the couch. "You think Charlie's going to 'forget' you went over there searching through his office; that you found something to get him killed thirty times over? You don't think Charlie can get Teddy Lapps to do to you the same fucking thing any guy on that list would do to you?" His lips curled, showing his teeth. Annie thought he would hit her if she hesitated.

"I know all that, Phil. But Charlie can't hurt me now or the list goes to the district attorney, and when the news of that gets out, Charlie'll be dead. The thing is, if Charlie finds out that you've seen the list, there's *nothing* to stop him from killing you." Phil's face went white.

"I'm going to tell him," Annie continued quickly, "that you never saw the list, didn't know I had it, that you came in there and saved me from Blimpie only because I called you, which is the truth."

Phil continued to stare at her, then ran his long fingers through his thick pompadour. "That's real nice, Annie, but you could tell Charlie I *did* see the list anytime you wanted, couldn't you?"

Annie watched him, then said quietly, "I don't have any reason to do that, do I?"

"You mean, as long as I'm a good boy, you won't tell him. Well, fuck that noise!"

"That's not it, Phil. I'm *scared* about this! I wish I'd never seen that list; I wish *you'd* never seen it. But we did, so I'm taking care of myself. I don't want to make any trouble, and I'm not sure I've covered everything. But no matter what, I really need you to be on my side." She wanted him to believe that her dependence on him was great so that he could accept the situation.

"Where's the .38?" he said, and started coughing.

"I got it here in my coat. I sure don't like carrying it around."

Phil went into the kitchen and filled a glass with water. He walked back in, drinking it. After clearing his throat several times, he looked at Annie again.

"Buy a purse. Keep the gun with you. Wipe your fingerprints off and start wearing gloves in case you need to use it. If you do, you drop it and run."

"All right," Annie said, taking orders.

"What the fuck do you plan to tell Charlie?"

He was trying to get control of the situation, but Annie recognized an edge of fear in him.

"Just exactly what happened to me over there," she answered, "even what you don't know about, which is where I found the list . . . and *nothing* about what happened over here." She looked away, embarrassed. "I mean about you finding the list. He'll check with you, try to find out if you know about it. You'll have to be a good liar."

"Thanks. I doubt if Charlie'll be too thrilled that you're holding on to all those names."

"I know. But Charlie likes me and knows I like him. I think he'll believe me, that I have to do it to protect myself even from him, and that I just want to forget about it. Tell me something, Phil. How much did you see?"

He sat silently a moment. "None of your fucking business! And I'll tell you something for sure. You're never going to forget about that list, Annie. Don't kid yourself." He stood up. "When you pick Charlie up, you better talk to him about it before he finds out it's gone." He looked perplexed for a moment, then went out the door, slamming it behind him.

Annie shivered. She was wet with nervous sweat. Exhausted, she put her head down on the table. Then, with an hour before she had to leave for the airport, she went into the bathroom and took a shower. As the hot needles of water ran over her face, she reviewed everything that she had told Phil and his reactions. She thought that he had been convinced.

• • •

When Charlie came out of the La Guardia Terminal, he looked better than Annie had ever seen him. He had a tan and had put on a little weight. He saw the car and, with Teddy Lapps and a porter following with the bags, he walked briskly over to greet Annie.

"How are they running, Annie?" Charlie asked, and gave her a hug.

"Not as good as they are in California," she replied.

"They ran pretty well for me," he said as he got in the Oldsmobile.

On the drive to Garden City, Annie let him tell her about the Derby, Santa Anita, and Hialeah, as well as the gossip and tips he had accumulated. When she parked in the driveway and Teddy got out to get the bags, Annie put her hand on Charlie's arm and said, "Charlie, I have to talk to you, right away."

He glanced at her and saw her intensity. "Didn't Johnny Phillips have work for you?"

"It's not about that, Charlie. It's about *Great Expectations.*"

Charlie's face lost so much color that his skin looked like gray rubber.

"What are you telling me?"

"I saw the list. I have to talk to you about it."

Charlie gasped twice to breathe. "Who else knows?" he asked, barely able to utter the words.

"No one. Only me."

He stared at her before saying, "Come over as soon as you want." Then he got out and walked across the lawn to the front door. Teddy Lapps was there waiting for him.

A few minutes later, Annie went over to the house and knocked on the front door. Teddy Lapps let her in and demanded quietly, "What the hell's happened?"

Annie shrugged and said, "He wanted to see me."

Looking confused but resigned, Teddy gestured toward the office and went into the living room.

"I'm down here, Annie," Charlie called from the office. When she walked in, he was sitting with the blue leather-bound book open on his desk. He looked up at her, still pale but deadly calm. "So what's the story?"

After closing the door, Annie told the story in careful detail, admitting her fault in accepting Blimpie's invitation, explaining but not excusing her reason as simple curiosity about the file Blimpie had mentioned. She described how she had discovered the list, then her regret and fear when she realized what she had found. Begging Charlie to believe that she had no intention of ever using the list to harm him, she nevertheless spelled out why she had to protect herself in the way that she had done.

Charlie listened attentively, and when she had finished, he looked down at the open book before him.

"I always tell people that Charles Dickens was the guy who taught me how to speak English . . . my private tutor. This is the first book I ever read in English. It's wonderful. After this, I read everything he wrote and then anything anybody wrote. Dickens got me through the first bad years, made me forget my stomach when I was hungry . . ." He looked up at Annie. "Have you read it?" he asked, turning some of the pages.

"Not yet," she replied regretfully.

"Ah, I envy you. You have all that to look forward to. How old are you, Annie, really?"

"Seventeen last month," she said.

He grimaced, saying, "Oh, God." Shaking his head, he looked away. Then he turned back, took a ring of keys from his pocket, and unlocked a drawer in the desk. From it he pulled a file and handed it across the desk to Annie. It had her name on it, but she did not look in it.

"Annie, I believe your story and I understand the trouble you took to protect yourself. You amaze me, how smart you are. About that file. You told Phil your name was Grebauer, from Catlettsburg, Kentucky. I have to check on anyone who works close to me. I spent a couple of hundred bucks on a private eye in Cincinnati to collect what's in there. Now, Annie, listen to me. I'm not worried about you, but you got to be sure that Blimpie or Phil didn't see you find anything."

"It's just like I said. I'm real sure." Annie stated it without the slightest waver.

"All right, then, I'll forget, and I'll trust you to forget. But I want to explain something about that list. I don't know how much you understand about it, but everyone on it wishes for one thing more than anything else: to die in his own bed. You know what I mean? Not in a gutter or in a cell. That's the biggest luxury they all know, and their millions can't guarantee it. I've set it up so that the list guarantees me that luxury, just like it does you, now. But if anyone ever finds out that somebody else besides me has seen what's on that list, I'll die shot up in a gutter. You understand?"

"Yes, Charlie."

"If that happens," Charlie continued dejectedly, "and don't misunderstand this, Annie . . . God, that I'd ever have to say this to a seventeen-year-old girl . . . but I got to protect myself just like you do. If that happens, I'll have prepared things so that Teddy Lapps will come after you."

Annie stared at Charlie, and he gazed back at her with deep regret.

"Oh, Lord, Charlie, I wish I'd never found that damn piece of paper," Annie said, closing her eyes, feeling an anguish that she had not felt when she said the same thing to Phil.

"So do I, but you did, so let's stay friends and make the best of it. You're just like I was. You had to grow up too fast just to stay alive. I wish I could give you a childhood, Annie."

Feeling tears coming into her eyes, she blinked them away. "I think it's probably too late," she said, and tried to laugh.

"Here, take the book, read it."

"I have my copy." Both smiled sadly.

"When you finish," Charlie said, "I'll give you another one." He stood up, and Annie turned to leave.

As they walked down the hall to the front door, Charlie said, "We'll talk about books on our way out to Aqueduct on Thursday."

She smiled at the prospect, as he did.

"Charlie, thank you for the pearls. I've never had anything so beautiful in my life."

"Nobody in my life deserves them more." As he opened the front door, he continued, "Annie, I'm going to have to punish my sister and Blimpie. You'll probably hear about it."

"I sure wish you wouldn't, Charlie," she said, turning back quickly. "He'll blame me for telling you and come after me."

"No, he'll blame Phil for telling me, because that's what I'll tell him, and I promise you Blimpie will understand that if he ever bothers you again, he'll die. Good night, Annie."

EIGHT

━━━━━━━━━━━━━━━━━━━━

━━━━━━━━━━━━━━━━━━━━

"SARATOGA" WAS SPOKEN so often on the backstretch that it seemed mythic. From the moment she returned to work at Belmont in May, Annie had heard it again and again. After the last Saturday of racing in July, Belmont Park closed down. That night and the next day, all its stables and employees, from the ushers in the stands to hotwalkers, moved a hundred and eighty miles north to the cool, clear air of the Adirondacks. The following Monday, Saratoga began its season. As she drove Charlie and Teddy Lapps up the Taconic Parkway, Annie was as relieved as anyone else to have a change of scene. She had become frustrated with hotwalking. She wanted to have something more to do with thoroughbreds than leading them around in circles.

Charlie owned a cabin on Saratoga Lake, a few miles out of town. He had gone to the old spa in August for the thorough-bred meeting every year for the past twenty, with the exception of three seasons during World War II, when the track was closed. To Charlie, Saratoga was the perfect race track, with good betting cards every day, occasional big crowds of innocents to jack up the odds, and a relaxed ease to the place that made attendance a joy. He paid little attention to the history of the nation's most tradition-encrusted race track, nor to the distractions of the social activities that swirled through the town for a single giddy month of the year. He was a gambler, and had no time for the "thin stew," as he called society.

"I can remember how the Whitney Stakes was run ten years ago," he said, looking out from the back seat of his Oldsmobile. "You think any of those high-class people can remember the conversation they had the night before at one of their parties? Well, that's okay. They're killing time, just like I am. But I'd rather be in my pajamas reading the *Telegraph* at night than in a tuxedo chatting with Mrs. Phipps, no offense to her intended."

Annie smiled. So far, the summer had been a financial success for her. By being Charlie's runner, and by putting down an occasional bet herself, she had saved nearly two thousand dollars. The amount might have been higher had she remained in the clubhouse when she saw that the Cumberland box was occupied. No one knew the reason for her sudden departures, or thought to ask why she abruptly chose to watch the races from the backstretch rail. Charlie would use Teddy to run his bets. Later, when she met them in the parking lot to drive them home, their minds were filled with the details of the day rather than with Annie's brief disappearance.

Phil had appeared infrequently at Belmont that summer. Annie overheard Charlie telling Teddy Lapps that the Angel had some big ideas that he was working on at some bush tracks somewhere, but Annie made a point never to ask about him.

Vera invited Annie to join her in Saratoga at the boarding house where the exercise rider had stayed for years. They would have the Oldsmobile to drive to the track in the morning. If Charlie wanted to breakfast on the track's terrace and watch the morning works, he and Teddy would use a local cab. If he did not come early, Annie would go out to Charlie's cabin when she was finished hotwalking, pick up the two men, then drive them to the track, parking in the owners' section near the front gate.

"Annie, you can have lunch with us, sit in the box anytime you want," Charlie said as they drove into town.

"Thanks, Charlie. I will once in a while. I just learn a lot on the backstretch."

"Oh, you'll learn a lot at Saratoga. Everyone has their stories, good stories, too. But most of them are lies."

Annie loved Saratoga from the first morning she and Vera drove from their boarding house across the sleeping town to the track's backstretch gate. Outlined by long rows of bright red geraniums, the old clapboard stands with their sloping roofs and high pointed cupolas were less awesome than Belmont; new paint gleamed white in the sun, which burned through the morning mist. The backstretch barns were clustered under trees at the main track and around a separate training track across Union Avenue. Vera loved riding at Saratoga because the stands' terrace was often filled with people each morning having breakfast. She was popular with the crowd, who recognized her platinum blond ponytail and usually gave her some applause as she rode by. There were few women working on the backstretch, and a pretty one received special attention. If she was going slow enough on her mount, she would acknowledge the response with a wave.

"They call this town the 'dowager queen of spas,' " Vera explained one evening, "and the track is the 'graveyard of favorites,' because so many great horses get beaten here. The big race of the meeting, the Travers Stakes, can be the Travers Swamp. The August weather up here is crazy; changes all of a sudden. Rain turns a fast track to soup in about two minutes. I've seen it happen."

"So why is there a track in Saratoga? Seems kind of out of the way," Annie said as they drove past some of the grand Victorian mansions of the town.

"Because of these godawful mineral waters. They were supposed to cure everything from hangovers to lumbago," Vera said. "Hotels got built here, along with 'cottages' of fifty rooms, casinos, and for something for the rich people to do in the daytime, a race track. For a while, this was the place to be, even if you didn't like horses that much. Then some scientists said the mineral waters were useless and people finally admitted the stuff tasted awful. I drank at the Geyser once; tasted like boiled owl. The one on Spring Street is sulphur. The casinos got raided from time to time, and the town closed down, except for the one month a year when New York racing took over the track. The racing's still the best, and it's everybody's holiday."

Annie felt at home working on Johnny Phillips' shedrow. The trainer was giving her more to do: mixing feed, checking the hay for quality when it was delivered, and being on hand to help the vet when he visited. Burt taught her what he knew about medication, and, one morning, showed her about poultices.

"A sore horse can't run, and sooner or later just about every horse gets sore," he said as he mixed ingredients with a pestle in a large mortar. "And there's only one cure for lameness. That's rest, to let the swelling and heat around the sore joint or muscle go down. But there ain't never no time for enough rest usually, so you mix up this stuff to draw off the heat. Everybody has his own recipe, everything from vitamins to buzzard's blood. I use this and that, boric acid and peppermint oil, a little creosote and kaolin. I spit in it once, mix it all up, slaver it on, and put a bandage over it to hold it in place. Works as good as what the vet gives, but don't tell him I said so. He'd rather charge for a shot of Bute."

"What's Bute?" Annie asked as she watched Burt mix his poultice.

"Butazolidin is one of these drugs supposed to do miracles. Pretty good one, too. Takes the heat in the joint right down, the swelling too. Problem is, it's a real good painkiller, which is fine for relieving the horse while it's healing, but people use it to get the horse to the starting gate. If a colt don't feel his pain, he'll go out to run and reinjure hisself, probably worse than before. You just can't do that to a horse, but people do. I'd rather use ol' Burt's poultice. Lot of horsemen choose their poultice over the drugs. Woody Stephens, he mixes up stuff like a witch boiling a brew. And Frank Carney makes a poultice so good he won't tell anybody what's in it. You know who I mean?"

"Yeah," Annie replied, then, to change the subject, asked why a blacksmith was called a farrier. As Burt explained that the term was one of many that had come with the thoroughbred from England, Annie thought of the tall, sandy-haired Caernarvon trainer whom everyone on the backstretch respected so much. She saw him often astride a stable pony watching the Caernarvon sets. Once, at Belmont, he had nodded to her as he went by, whether from courtesy or because he remembered Sam's introduction, she could not tell.

"I'd say Carney's one of the five best trainers around," Vera said that evening when Annie asked about him. "Real serious, very smart, a real horseman. Been at Caernarvon since he was a kid. Started as a hotwalker and worked his way up. Kind of adopted by old man Cumberland. I hear young Sam and him aren't exactly friendly. I also hear Carney drinks a little."

"Good Lord, so does everyone else around here."

"Ha! Ain't that the truth!" Vera was uncharacteristically quiet for a moment, then spoke quite seriously. "Don't ever start, Annie. It gets you to the grave real fast. My mother died a drunk at forty-six. It took her ten years of serious work with the bottle, but she made it. It gets to your face before it eats at your innards. If I hadn't watched it happen, I wouldn't have been able to recognize her, her face changed so much."

Annie and Vera passed a carton of ice cream back and forth between them, watching the sky darken, unwilling to go inside to escape the mosquitoes. They were sitting in old wicker chairs on the porch of their boarding house. Annie was holding a leather-bound copy of *Don Quixote* that Charlie had given her. Their rooms were on the second floor; by sharing a bath and kitchen privileges, they were able to live very inexpensively in the summer resort. Their landlady was an old friend of Vera's and enjoyed having them. She was a fanatic two-dollar player who asked them for, and received, a lot of good tips.

"My mother died when she was thirty-four," Annie said abruptly.

"That's really young," Vera answered. "What happened?"

"My father and brothers always said I caused it. I was a hard birth, and she never got well afterward. But it wasn't just me. They were so mean to her when she couldn't cook and clean. I think she died just to get away."

"How old were you?" Vera slapped at a mosquito and picked it off her wrist.

"Five. I don't remember her much. I miss her more than I remember her. She died in the summer. It was warm like this. I was sleeping on a rag rug beside her bed every night, holding on to her hand. I used to wake up and see her hand hanging out of the covers, waiting for me to take it. She always smiled at me, no matter how bad the pain was, and it was pretty bad at the end. One morning, I reached up for her hand and it was cold. When I looked at her, she wasn't smiling anymore."

They sat quietly for a while. Annie was surprised at herself; she had never spoken of her family to anyone.

"Did your father remarry?" Vera asked.

Annie shook her head. "He had three little kids. We lived in a railroad shack in the woods near Catlettsburg, Kentucky. No woman in her right mind would've come out there. Besides, he started drinking more. I wonder all the time how it would've been different if my momma had lived. I doubt if anyone could've controlled them. They got to be like, well, animals . . . Can I tell you this, Vera? Will you ever tell anyone?"

Reacting to the anxiety in Annie's voice, Vera turned to look straight at her.

"I've got a big mouth, but a deep heart, which is where I bury a lot of things. Tell me anything you want. I only blab about things that'll get me in trouble."

"My father started drinking this moonshine whiskey that they made up in the hills," Annie began, talking slowly, softly, as if telling a bedtime story. "It made him mean, and all three of us kids just stayed away from him when he was drunk. He worked mostly at night, so we were pretty much on our own. My brothers are three and four years older than I am, and they looked after me for a couple of years, but then they started getting mean, too. Not from moonshine; I guess just from growing up. When I was nine, they started taking my clothes off. About a year later, Jimmy Lee, he's the older one, made Fungo hold me up naked against the wall and he tried to get inside me, but I was too small. He got real mad and hit me, saying I was doing something to keep myself tight like that. Then he went over to the stove. I could see him in a mirror that hung over the kitchen sink. I can see it now. He took some bacon grease. When he started back, I begged him not to, but neither one of them listened. He hurt me pretty bad, but even so, after he was done and Fungo let me go, I ran out of the place to find my father. He was a switchman on the railroad and worked up the line about a mile away. I ran as fast as I could, but when I got there, he was drinking and got mad seeing me naked, screaming at him. He grabbed me by the arm and threw me so hard, my arm broke . . . I was ten. Two times five.''

Annie paused, feeling an excited flutter in her chest.

Vera cleared her throat twice. "What's that mean, two times five?'' Her voice was shaky and Annie turned to look at her. Vera stared into the near darkness, her eyes wider than usual.

"Nothing," Annie replied. "It's just a notion I have. I'm sorry I told you all that, Vera.''

For a moment, Vera did not respond. Then she asked, "What happened after that?''

Annie leaned back, making the wicker creak. Her eyes followed her friend's look into the dark. "It was bad for a while. They came after me a lot. But when I grew, I could fight and run. They did it once in front of my father when he was drunk. He *laughed.* He . . . laughed.'' She hesitated, then shook her head. "When I was fifteen I ran away from home.''

Crickets were filling the dark with their din. The two women sat listening on the porch.

"Are they still living there?'' Vera finally asked.

"No," Annie said, feeling suddenly exhausted. "They're all three in jail. I didn't even know, except that Charlie had me investigated when I started working for him. He showed me a file. My brothers got caught stealing. Grand theft, they called it; gave each of them seven years. My father caused a train wreck while he was drunk. Negligent homicide. He got twenty. They're all in the Kentucky state penitentiary at Eddyville."

"They're safer in there," Vera suggested.

"What do you mean?"

"Because if I ever happened to meet any one of them, I'd sure as hell kill him." She reached over, took Annie's hand, and held it for a time. Then she stood up and, without looking at Annie, went into the house and up to her room. Soon after, Annie followed. She managed to get up the stairs, but fell asleep without undressing.

The next afternoon in the third race, the best of Charlie Dell's colts, Jaybird, took the lead on the far turn. Annie was there on the rail and screamed encouragement as he sped by. She was sure he heard her. A long half minute later, he won, and Annie felt a sense of completeness that seemed to balloon her off the ground. She knew the colt well and had cooled him out from her first days at Belmont. He was a mean animal. Burt was his groom, and even he had to be careful walking around in the stall. Jaybird was known to kick with a devastating aim. When Annie walked him, however, he became relatively placid. She had gained his obedience with a time-tested method. Each morning after his work, she had slipped him a sugar cube.

As she waited by the gap in the far turn for Jaybird to be led from the winner's circle to the testing barn, Annie wondered if Charlie Dell had left his box to have his picture taken in the winner's circle. She doubted it. Then, remembering her own ten-dollar bet at twelve-to-one, she realized she would clear $120. "Free money," she called a gambling win. It made the bright, warm Saratoga day close to perfect.

Down the final stretch in front of the grandstand, Annie soon saw Charlie's colt among the other money winners. Stripped of the jockeys' saddles and the track's number cloths, they were being led to the gap by their grooms.

Surprisingly, Jaybird was being led not by Burt, but by another hotwalker, a Cuban boy who worked with Annie. When he saw her standing by the gap, the hotwalker led the winning colt to her and handed her the shank. "He's your horse. You take him." Jaybird recognized Annie and, in spite of his fatigue after the race, nickered and started to nuzzle around her, looking for his sugar cube.

A track official was eyeing them, so Annie led the colt through the gap to the testing barn, or spit barn, where blood and urine samples were drawn for analysis.

"Where's Burt?" Annie asked.

"He got sick. Bad. Big pain," the hotwalker said, gripping his right side. "They take him in the ambulance."

They entered the fenced-in compound of the spit barn, passing guards who checked badges of employment. Along with the other colts to be tested, Jaybird started walking around the barn, led by Annie, as the state vets watched, waiting for the runners to be ready to urinate.

When she came around a corner, Johnny Phillips was standing next to the hotwalker, sweating, having hurried over from the winner's circle.

"Congratulations, Johnny!" Annie said, still excited.

Phillips was all business. "Thanks. Let Humberto take him; I gotta talk to you."

Annie gave the shank to the other hotwalker and stepped out of the walking path.

"Burt got appendicitis," Phillips said around his wet cigar. "They're probably cutting him up right now. He'll be laid up a week, ten days. Think you can handle his horses?"

"Yes, sir," Annie replied while her eagerness overwhelmed any doubt. "I might need some help mixing feed."

Phillips nodded. "I'll help you with that. This is just until Burt gets back on his feet."

"That's good with me," Annie said, knowing that once she became a licensed groom, she could get other jobs at that level.

"All right, then, you're a groom. I'll go do the papers. Charlie sends congratulations, by the way. Thought it was a great idea."

"Did he get his picture taken?"

"Hell, no. Too busy sending Teddy Lapps to cash his tickets . . . Hey, Doc, my colt's ready," he yelled over to one of the vets, who showed Humberto which stall in the spit barn to use. Humberto left Jaybird inside, where an employee of the track held a two-foot bamboo stick with a plastic cup attached to its end. Known as a catcher, he closed the stall doors and started whistling. Annie and Johnny Phillips waited for the whistling to stimulate the colt's reflex to empty his bladder.

"Annie, Burt was my night watchman," Phillips said. "Slept in the tack room, fed the horses their evening meal, lit the gas fire to heat the morning bath water. I was wondering . . ."

"Yes, sir, I'll do it," she interrupted. "I'll still have to drive Charlie in the afternoon."

"That's all right with me. You'll get some more money for doing night watchman."

"I know," she said, and Johnny hurried back toward the stands.

The whistling in the stall stopped and Annie heard the resulting flow. Soon the stall door opened and the catcher came out with a full cup. One of the vets appeared and stuck a needle into the colt's neck to take a blood sample. Then Humberto took the shank and led the colt out of the spit barn compound back to Phillips' barn.

Annie walked along beside them, trying to control her delight that she had a chance to be a groom. They reached the barn, and as Humberto continued to walk the colt, Annie checked his stall, grabbed a four-prong pitchfork, and turned the straw, fluffing it up. Then she went out to fill buckets to give her colt a bath.

The new responsibility broadened her respect for her horses immediately. She spent increasing amounts of time handling her two colts and one filly, and began to observe the effect of human calm on a thoroughbred's fear.

"You gotta remember," Johnny Phillips told her one day, "instinctively they're wild animals. They're forced into captivity and all this training. But each one deals with it different. It's when you can understand these differences that you'll be a horsewoman."

When she watched her horses break from the gate and sprint for the wire, Annie urged them on with every stride. When they finished well, which they did often, she gave in to true joy. When they lost, she withdrew into gloom. If they were hurt in a race, as her filly was one day, clipping her front ankle with her back hoof, Annie felt a sympathetic pain cut through her. All of these feelings, however, were kept in control. She had learned that there was always too much emotion around horse racing to let any of it loose.

Her duties as night watchman required that Annie be a light sleeper. She had to feed all fifteen of Phillips' horses their evening meal, try to sleep on the cot in the tack room surrounded by saddles, bridles, and halters, then at four A.M. light the gas heaters under the water barrels in order to provide hot water for baths following the morning works. Her main responsibility was to make sure that no one bothered the horses. In spite of the track's contingent of Pinkerton guards on duty at night, Annie often woke up on her own and checked the shedrow.

Following his surgery, Burt became ill with pleurisy. Johnny Phillips asked Annie to remain as groom and night watchman at least until the end of the Saratoga meeting. She worked hard, proud of her growing skills. Her two colts and one filly ran well and always looked at their peak because of her endless brushing and currying. From an old Irishman in another barn, she learned several ways to braid the horses' manes for a race. Other grooms saw the handsomely twisted plaits and paid her fifty cents to do their charges.

One duty she did not perform. Claiming shyness, she always arranged for another groom to take her horses over to the paddock before a race. At Saratoga, the unfenced paddock was under the lush deciduous trees near the clubhouse entrance to the boxes. Owners wandered about, looking at the horses, and Annie had no wish to be in such likely proximity to any of the Cumberlands.

Almost every day, Annie had seen the crimson, gold, and royal blue silks on Caernarvon's beautiful horses, usually in the day's feature race. That was hard enough for her. One night at the store on Broadway where Annie and Vera bought their copies of the *Telegraph* and food for the next morning, Annie saw by chance a picture of Cornelia and Belinda Cumberland on the front page of the local newspaper, the *Saratogian*. They were wearing elegant print dresses, broadbrimmed summer hats, and white gloves. Both were smiling.

Annie did not pick up the paper, allowing herself to read only what was on the page. The two Cumberland ladies had attended a luncheon for the benefit of the local hospital, and together in the charity auction had been the highest bidder for a set of antique knife boxes.

Later, lying on her cot in the tack room, she read in the *Telegraph* that Caernarvon Farms' candidate for the Hopeful Stakes was shipping in, a colt named Certainty. Annie felt a jolt go through her. The Hopeful was one of the most important races of the year for two-year-old colts, indicating which horses were potential champions in their three-year-old season. Earlier in the summer, at Monmouth Park, Certainty had won his first race, or, in the masculine idiom of the track, "broke his maiden." Subsequently, he had won two more races in impressive times.

Annie put down her *Telegraph,* turned out the light, and tried to sleep. Several hours later, she heard a horse moving restlessly in its stall and whinnying in annoyance. Annie slept in her clothes, as much for efficiency as for modesty. She reached over a rack of saddles for a flashlight on the window-sill and leaned back to get a file-shaped steel hoof buffer from the tool board hanging on the opposite wall. Opening the door of the tack room, she crept outside. Several stalls down the shedrow, she saw an open door and moved silently toward it. Beside the door, she squatted down and held the flashlight at arm's length from her body. Then she crab-stepped in front of the door and flicked the switch. The first thing the flashlight beam hit was a hypodermic needle raised over the horse's flank. A man swore in Spanish, threw the hypo at the light, and charged for the door. Annie ducked and held the pointed edge of the hoof buffer above her. It hit him right between the legs. He stumbled over her and crashed to the ground. As he yelled in pain, Annie stood up, ready to protect herself. Shouting profanities in Spanish, he got to his feet and, still groaning, hobbled into the dark.

Annie did not get a good look at him. She waited until she stopped shaking before going into the stall and settling the colt. It was Jaybird. He was supposed to run again the next afternoon. Fortunately, he had not bolted out of the stall when the webbing was down. She used the flashlight to search out-side for the hypodermic needle. Finding it in the dirt, she took it back with her to the tack room. She stayed up until a Pinker-ton guard came by, and she told him what had happened. He agreed to stay nearby for the rest of the night. As she lay down on her cot, she considered getting the gun. It was at the board-ing house in the box she hid there which contained Charlie's pearls and the money she had saved. As sleep finally came, she decided against the gun.

That afternoon, Jaybird won again. Then three days later, the analysis of the hypodermic needle was returned. It had contained Phenobarbital, a strong sedative. Several investiga-tors came by the barn to question Annie. She felt she did not help them much.

The next morning, as the third set was getting washed and cooled out after their work, Phil Angelo drove up to Johnny Phillips' barn in a yellow Thunderbird convertible. The entire stable was on hand to watch his entrance, which he enjoyed. He was deeply tanned and was wearing aviator sunglasses. His pompadour and ducktail had been shorn and reshaped into a wavy nattiness. The light brown linen suit he wore fit him better than suits Annie had previously seen on him, and his shirt was open across his chest to reveal a heavy gold chain. That glittering effect was matched by a little gold buckle across the top of each shoe.

As he got out of the car, Phil saw Annie but did not ac-knowledge her. He went up to Johnny Phillips and exchanged a few fast remarks. Johnny walked Phil around the barn to where Annie was washing one of her colts, using a sponge and sweat scraper to dry him off.

"Hey, Annie, how ya doing?" Phil said, grinning inti-mately. Annie noticed he had no toothpick.

"Fine," she said, and went on with her work. As she led her colt into his stall, Phil came up behind her.

"I'll be back after the races to pick you up. We'll have a fancy dinner at a place I know."

"I can't leave. There are things I got to do around here."

"I've already arranged it with Johnny. He'll get someone to

cover for you until after dinner," he answered, grinning smugly.

"I don't want to go, Phil."

The grin disappeared into a vicious look. "No fucking excuses, Annie. You're coming! I got a message from Charlie for you. Get it?" Then he grinned again.

Beginning to shake, she grabbed a clean rubbing rag and started to work on the colt. Charlie had not come to the track for three days, not even to see Jaybird run. He had offered no explanations when she had gone to the cabin to pick him up, only a terse refusal.

"All right," she said to Phil. "I'll meet you outside the main entrance. I'm not too anxious to be seen driving off in your car."

He smirked, then sauntered back to the Thunderbird. Unable to resist digging up the dust, he drove away.

After the day's races, Annie approached Phil wearing clean boots, Levi's, and a work shirt. He was leaning against the Thunderbird, which was parked in front of the main entrance of the track. The crowd had gone, and only a few "stoopers" remained, obsessed men bending down to turn over the thousands of betting tickets discarded on the ground in the hope of finding a winner thrown away by mistake. When he saw Annie, Phil gave her a quick once-over and nodded appreciatively.

"Did ya know," he said philosophically, "that every thoroughbred in the world comes from three Arabian stallions that they brought to England in the seventeen hundreds? One of 'em, some guy found pulling an ice wagon, starving to death in Paris. See, it didn't make any difference what the horse was doing, or what it looked like right then. The guy could see class." He grinned and gave her the once-over again. "I'm like that."

Annie laughed at Phil's self-serving compliment. He opened the Thunderbird's door for her and she stepped in. As he drove her through Saratoga, Annie said, "Phil, I don't need fancy food just to get a message. Why don't you tell me what it is?"

He took off his sunglasses and she saw his eyes for the first time. She had forgotten how vicious they were.

"Put it this way, Annie. You eat or you don't get Charlie's message. And that'd be real dangerous for you." Then he looked at her. "Why the fuck can't you relax and enjoy yourself?"

She almost laughed, but made no response.

Scowling, he drove on. Then out of nowhere, he said, "I gotta tell you, you look beautiful." She felt her face go hot, but said nothing.

The restaurant was outside Saratoga on the main road to Lake George. Phil ordered steaks. As she ate, Annie noticed that the room was filled with familiar faces from the track. The voices were loud, the conversations often intense. A woman played popular songs on an organ. Phil ate quickly and said little.

Annie finally put down her fork. "Phil, what are we doing here? What did Charlie say?"

He grinned at her, then wiped his mouth with his hand. "Okay, here's what I gotta say to you. This isn't how Charlie would say it, but I know more about your relationship with him than he thinks I know, right? So I'll be straighter with you. You probably oughta be dead."

Annie watched Phil's eyes. "Why?"

"Hey, stop looking so grim. Show your dimple, look good for me."

"Just tell me why I ought to be dead," Annie said, her voice tightening.

"Don't worry about it. I'm looking after you. All right, Charlie's a gambler, dig? He ain't in horse racing to 'improve the breed.' He likes to win like everyone else. I've been traveling this summer, trying out some business for Charlie, and we've been doing real good at tracks all over the country. But we got screwed up the other day here at Saratoga, and that's because of you. This is the big leagues, and we didn't like getting screwed up."

Annie sensed the reason immediately but hoped she was wrong.

"Why because of me?"

He sat back, took a deep, bored breath, and said, "Charlie likes you, Annie, and not just because of what you got on him, okay? He's got horses running here. Jaybird got enough wins to be a favorite. That's a setup for a good thing, y'know what I mean? They only test the winners of races. They plan to change that soon, test favorites that lose, too. So we have to move fast. But you got in the way of our business, and Charlie wants you to stop it. That's the message. Get it?"

"You mean let his horses get doped?" Her disappointment was so great that she felt nauseated.

"Just go in the tack room and sleep through the night, Annie. Listen, if it weren't for Charlie, that spic would've beat the shit out of you."

Annie stared at him. "Is Johnny Phillips in on it?"

"No. It always works better with a stable everyone knows is straight. You stick a favorite so he runs out of the money. You pay off a couple of jockeys and bet the long shots."

"Is that how you've done so well this summer?"

His eyes hooded. "Don't get wise, Annie. That's none of your fucking business."

"Phil, I got to get back to the barn."

He reacted with disgust. "Fuck you, Annie." He pulled out some cash, put it on the table, and, taking her arm, left the restaurant.

They drove back to Saratoga without speaking, until he blurted, "Can't you figure out why I'm . . . ?" He did not finish.

"Figure what?" she asked.

He continued driving, then said, "There might be a reason I look after you, you know."

"I'm sure, so you can do a favor for Charlie." In spite of her fear, she was getting mad.

Phil looked over, surprised by her attitude, then stared forward again.

"Annie, just remember this, goddammit. I can either like someone or hurt someone. There's nothing in between for me. And I've *never* hurt you." He turned to her. "That oughta mean something to you, right?"

She nodded without looking over at him, afraid of what she

might read in the look on his face. Whether it was brutality or some strange expression of affection, she did not want to see it. They did not speak until they reached the gate to Saratoga's backstretch. Once through it, Annie said, "Phil, tell Charlie that I'm real sorry, but I can't go along with this. I suppose if he wants to dope his own horses, that's up to him—if he wants to take the chance of getting caught. But I'm not about to let *anyone* dope a horse I'm looking after. I'll tell Johnny tomorrow that I'm quitting."

He stopped the car in the middle of the road and pointed his finger at her. "Don't you even *think* about quitting!" Then he turned away, exasperated. "Jesus *Christ,* Annie, you can be a pain in the ass!"

"Listen, Phil, you know how hard I'm trying to keep out of Charlie's past! I didn't know you all were doing this kind of thing, and you come down here to hook me into it. Well, I'm not going to do it!"

He grabbed her arm and pulled her over to him.

"Just shut up and listen to me. You *owe* Charlie. You owe him for walking around, for your job as a groom, all the goddamn bread he's given you for running his bets. He takes a lot of trouble with you, and like I said, it ain't because of the list. He thinks you're tough and smart. He admires you. So why the fuck can't you—"

"Because I can't! And I won't take Charlie's payoff. Tell him." She started to open the door to get out, but Phil held on to her arm and gunned the car.

As he drove toward Phillips' barn, he said, "Goddammit, you don't quit, not till you see Charlie. Maybe he can talk to you." He let her go as they approached the barn. "He'll come over tomorrow."

When he stopped the car, Phil did not look at her. Someone was playing a portable radio several barns over. Night beetles swarmed around the light at the end of the shedrow. She got out of the car and started walking to the tack room.

Phil watched her for a moment, then said, "Smart is good, Annie, but too smart is dangerous." He shifted the gears of the Thunderbird. "You still got that list, don't you?"

Annie nodded; Phil nodded back. "Take care of it. Someday you might get smart and make me your partner." He grinned and drove away.

Annie did not sleep that night. Sitting in the tack room, she made her plans. She would leave a letter for Johnny Phillips, apologizing but not explaining why she was going. Vera would bring the Oldsmobile in the morning as usual. Annie knew where she parked it and knew that the keys would be under the floor rug. After driving to the boarding house, she would pack, leave a note for Vera, then drive to the owners' parking lot at the track and leave the Oldsmobile there. After that, beyond taking a cab to the bus station, Annie was not sure where she would go.

Before leaving the track, there was only one thing she could not resist doing. Early in the morning, after writing the letter to Phillips, she gave a Pinkerton guard five dollars to stay at the barn until the trainer arrived. It was still dark, and the backstretch workers had not yet begun to arrive. Annie made her way across Union Avenue to the barns near the training track. One of them, Number 71, was Caernarvon's. Not once during the Saratoga meeting had Annie gone near the barn. The previous day, however, Certainty had shipped in.

In comparison to most of the barns on the backstretch, the Caernarvon barn was immaculate. A carved wooden sign with the farm's crest, interweaving the C and F, hung from each end of the thirty-stall shedrow. Every stall had a wall box, webbing, and water bucket striped in the Caernarvon colors of crimson, gold, and royal blue. The straw pillow was packed and shaped into an exact crescent edge at each stall's entrance. The tack room at the center of the barn gleamed with polished leather saddles, bridles, and bits. On a wash line hung three-colored blankets and saddle towels with "Caernarvon" written in Old English script. White petunias in barrels painted with the farm's colors were placed every five paces along the barn. The flower boxes hanging from the tack room windows were similar to the ones at Number 10, Annie thought. She noticed that the dirt in front of the stalls and around the barn's walking ring had been carefully raked into a straight furrowed pattern.

Annie waited as the night watchman lit the gas jets under the tubs of water. No one else seemed to be there. Then

Annie greeted him, saying she was on her way to work but had just stopped by to take a look at Certainty. The night watchman saw her employment badge and, pointing to the colt's stall, told her to enjoy herself. Most of the other horses were looking out over their webbings, several nickering back and forth to one another. Certainty, however, stood heading in toward the back of his stall.

Annie waited at the webbing a moment before saying, "Hey, Certainty, remember your ol' swimming buddy?"

At the sound of Annie's voice, Certainty's head turned and his ears flicked toward her.

"Yeah, it's me again," she said, holding out her hand low so that he could see it. The colt came over and snuffled at it. Then he reached his head over the webbing to smell her face. Annie let him, not sure of recognition. She patted his neck. He had filled out in the year since she had seen him as a yearling. His front legs were strong and straight; his chest cavity had broadened considerably. Although she was no expert on what horsemen called conformation, Annie could see how well he had come together as a powerful running animal.

Out of her pocket, she took a sugar cube. No sooner had she extended her arm when someone grabbed it.

"Whatya got there?" Annie turned and saw Frank Carney holding her wrist. He let it go right away, but stepped between her and Certainty.

"Just a sugar cube," she said, aware of his authority and her trespass. "Didn't mean to bother you."

"I know you," he said, moving closer to her. "You're the girl who saved Certainty . . . according to our master." He smiled scornfully.

Annie nodded as she smelled the whiskey on his breath.

He looked at her, then blinked and turned toward the colt's stall. "Well, I want to thank you. That colt'll be our first champion . . . mine and Sam's." He laughed quietly.

"Hope he wins for you," she said, smiling but anxious to leave. "But would you do me a favor?"

"Seems I owe you one," tilting his head toward Certainty.

"Would you mind not telling anyone that I was around here?"

"'Anyone' meaning Sam?" When she nodded, he smiled and said, "Well, I don't tell Sam any more'n what I have to. There's a fine trainer out in California, says you treat owners like you grow mushrooms—keep them in the dark and feed them plenty of fertilizer."

Annie laughed and he joined her. Then he stopped. "It ain't too smart to talk about my owner like this." He reached out to shake her hand. "I won't say anything if you won't."

Embarrassed, she looked down. Taking his hand, she felt hard calluses and, in the light from the barn lamp, saw jagged scars that crisscrossed his knuckles.

"Thank you," she said and started to go.

"See you again," Carney said, and watched as Annie hurried into the dark.

NINE

FOR EIGHT MONTHS, Annie lived in a basement apartment on the West Side of Manhattan in the area known as Hell's Kitchen. At first she lived in fear of being found by Charlie and Phil, of being "punished" for having left Saratoga and for knowing too much. As the months passed and her money slowly ran out, her dread lessened and she began to look for a job. When she found one, it presented a number of problems. She decided she had to talk to the lawyer again.

"So." Archy Delansig leaned back in his swivel chair and clasped his hands on the top of his head. "Am I about to learn the mysteries of your safe deposit box?" His eyes closed halfway behind his plastic-rimmed glasses.

"I don't know," Annie replied and shifted in the straight chair across from his desk. She had forgotten how intelligent and distinguished the attorney looked, nor had she remembered his hair being so gray on the sides. But she did remember his colorful suspenders. This day, they were bright green and yellow. "You told me once that you couldn't tell anyone about anything I said to you. Does that include evidence about crimes?"

"Yes, it does."

"About murder?"

He nodded without revealing any surprise. "I'm your lawyer, Miss Grebauer. I'm not required to report to anyone anything you tell me. If the evidence is pertinent to the ongoing investigation of a crime, I might advise you not to withhold it, because that is against the law. But if you chose to ignore my advice, I am bound not to reveal anything."

Annie smoothed her gray flannel skirt over her lap. "And what if the evidence is dangerous for you to know? I mean, if certain people found out you knew about it, they might . . . You've got a family."

He thought for a while, rocking slightly in his chair, watching her.

"I think I'd probably arrange things as I gather you've arranged them, Miss Grebauer, so that any damage they caused me would cause them considerably more."

"Then I'd like to tell you about all this, if you don't mind taking it on, and then get some advice."

He did not respond for a moment, then stood up and paced to a corner of his office and back. "Before you tell me, what made it necessary for you to come here today?"

Annie took a deep breath and stared out the office window at the view of the sky. "I've been hiding for eight months. I'm running out of money, so I got a job. I'm supposed to start tonight, but I'm scared about it."

"Does the job jeopardize your secrecy?"

Annie shifted in her chair. She started to talk, but had to swallow first. "I'm going to be a showgirl at the Latin Quarter."

Archy Delansig stood bobbing slightly on the balls of his feet. Then he walked over to open the door and called to his secretary to hold his calls. Returning to his swivel chair, he sank into it and said, "Miss Grebauer, believe me, you have my undivided attention."

He listened for almost an hour as she told him about the list, the names on it, how she had found it, and her arrangement about it with Charlie and Phil. She also told him why she had left Saratoga the previous summer after Phil explained his race-fixing partnership with Charlie. When she finished, she realized the muscles of her back had become painfully rigid as she had kept from leaning back against the chair.

"Why did you come back to New York to hide?" Delansig asked.

"It's the only place I know. I thought if I went to someplace new, I'd stick out. No one sticks out in New York."

"And what have you been doing for eight months?"

"Not much. I spent most of my time at the public library reading."

"*Great Expectations,* I presume," Delansig said, smiling.

Annie nodded. "I read a lot of Dickens' books, all kinds of things. There's a woman who works at the library, kind of wanted to educate me."

"And how in the world did you ever get a job at the Latin Quarter?"

Annie smiled. "It's on the route I take between my basement and the library. I passed by there in the evening on my way home. The doorman got to recognize me after a while, said hello. When I started looking for work, I asked him about being a waitress or bar girl. He told me I should come to an audition. I thought it was to be a waitress." She saw that Delansig smiled. "So I went, and got the job. Seems there's so many nightclubs with shows that there's a shortage of tall girls. I've been rehearsing for a week. I don't do much except walk around"—she interrupted herself—"with no clothes on." That part of the job still bothered her.

"Miss Grebauer, how old are you?"

"I'll be eighteen in a couple of weeks, April twenty-eighth."

He nodded again. "I have to inform you that the evidence you have is indeed germane to, I would think, a great many cases now under investigation by state and federal authorities. To withhold it is a punishable offense, no matter what the circumstances. The government offers a witness protection program under which you would be protected and, after testifying, given a new identity. You would start a new life as another person."

"Is that your advice?" she asked, obviously disappointed.

"No," he said. "That's information I'm obliged to give you. My advice is to go to work tonight and leave things just as they are."

"What?" Annie exclaimed and laughed with relief, but, as suddenly, she stopped. "You're not giving up on me, are you?"

"On the contrary," Delansig said. "I'm assuming that, as a client, you will give my comparatively mundane practice a much needed jolt of glamour, not to mention excitement." He laughed, and then was quiet for a moment. "Let me explain my conclusion. The evidence on the list I doubt would convict anyone. It's largely hearsay; that is, it doesn't prove that the person named killed the corresponding body. Even if Charlie Dell testified, which he would never do, even if they exhumed the bodies from their concrete resting places, there's not much of a case. The list connects the bodies with the names of criminals, but all of them would have alibis and very strong defenses against cases that are now five to twenty years old. Therefore, you're not exactly withholding evidence that'd sweep America clean of these criminals. You are withholding evidence that would, in my judgment, simply create a good deal of heat for them. The authorities would be delighted to create such heat, and if they ever learned of the existence of such a list, they'd want it badly. Criminals don't like heat. The authorities' getting your list would lead almost certainly to the death of Mr. Dell, Mr. Angelo, and you, even if you took advantage of the witness protection program. It is run by a government bureaucracy, and since bureaucrats are notoriously inefficient with everything else, I would not trust them with your life for the sake of heat."

Annie watched him as she tried to assimilate all he said. Already she felt relieved, but then she asked, "What about Charlie and Phil? If I start walking around on the stage of the Latin Quarter, I'm pretty sure they'll hear about it. What if they show up?"

"I can't see that your knowing about their gambling fixes

makes you any more of a problem to either of them than your knowing about the list. You haven't told anyone about the fixing for, what, eight months. What's important is that the list can still get each of them killed, should any of those people on it learn of its existence. Your friends still know that, and that you've arranged for the list's disclosure should they cause you any harm. You've certainly done nothing to harm them; I doubt very much if either of them would dare to threaten the status quo. Also, from what you've told me, Mr. Dell seems to have a certain affection for you. If they show up, I think the question of seeing them is still yours to decide. I'd recommend against it, obviously, but I'm not certain of your affection for them."

"I'm not either." Annie stood up. "You sure have made me feel a lot better, Mr. Delansig. Thank you, sir."

"Thank *you*, Miss Grebauer. I think you should call me once a week for a time and keep me up on developments. I won't bill you for that, although I will for today."

"You'll get it out of my first paycheck."

That night, once again as Annie Brown, she arrived at the Latin Quarter to start work. At five-foot-nine, she was instantly christened "Shorty" by the other girls in the cramped dressing room backstage. Each of her colleagues approached or surpassed six feet in her mesh-stockinged feet. No one asked about Annie's age or anything else, which seemed to be an unspoken policy. Her youth and inexperience were obvious. One girl helped her learn to walk on the stiletto heels her costumes required, another to attach pasties so that they would not make her nipples sore, another to trim pubic hair, and all showed her the intricacies of applying body makeup to the best effect. Annie took their advice, seldom speaking, doing as she was told as if watching herself from a safe distance.

There were eight showgirls as well as seven female dancers in *The International Convention of Love*, the title of the Latin Quarter's production. They shared the jammed, noisy dressing room, which had costume racks down the center, and makeup tables with lights around the sides. There was little room for the women, particularly the eight big ones. Nevertheless, there was little friction; instead, Annie discovered a camaraderie of survival in a bizarre world of perfect bodies, naked glamour, and ridiculous fantasy.

Her first featured number was entitled "A Boudoir in Heaven." Making an entrance in a gondola as an angel wearing tiny wings on her back and a see-through shorty negligee, she carried a large globe. Once onstage, Annie stepped from the gondola and walked gracefully along the edge of the footlights to the beat of "I'll Build a Stairway to Paradise," played by the brassy Joe Lombardi Orchestra. Other duties included assuming various classically statuesque poses on cue while she stood on a pedestal as peripheral emphasis to the "Syncopated Waters" number. A miracle of onstage plumbing enhanced by multi-hued lighting, hundreds of spigots responded up, down, and sideways with geometrical water spurts to the incessant beat of the orchestra.

Grateful for an occasional backstage shove from a colleague, Annie went through her numbers without making any mistakes. What surprised her the most was her total lack of modesty. Before going onstage, she was as mortified as she had been throughout rehearsals by the thought of walking around nearly naked in front of a roomful of people. The moment she stepped out of the gondola, however, and she heard people gasp appreciatively or applaud, she felt that her nakedness was almost a costume.

During the first weeks on the job, Annie's effect on the audience began to give her a sense of authority. She learned that if she walked a certain way, smiled a certain way, or even turned on the runway with a certain excited anticipation, she could make the audience respond to her. Her salary was another surprise. Walking around naked paid three times what grooming horses did. She would have traded the jobs in an instant, but she needed the money and was happy to have such easy work.

One night before the show, another girl in the dressing room asked her if she wanted to "party."

"What's that mean?" Annie asked as the two of them applied their false eyelashes.

"Sometimes there's a party after the show," the girl said casually. "You know. They entertain us in a penthouse, we entertain them, well, wherever they want." She smiled at Annie in the mirror.

"I don't think so," Annie said.

"Listen, it beats noshing pastrami at the Stage Deli. These guys give presents. And it leads to other things—trips on yachts, weekends in the Hamptons. Georgine got a ruby bracelet last year, and Phyllis . . . you didn't know her, but she married this guy and lives in Palm Beach. You never can tell . . ."

Annie attached the lash and checked it by blinking several times. "You just don't know how much I like pastrami."

The other girl laughed and said, "Suit yourself, but let me know if you change your mind."

Breakfast at the Stage Deli became Annie's habit. When the show was over, she was usually too excited to go back to her basement room. She began living at night and sleeping through the day, but she was working, had made some friends, and when she thought of Charlie Dell finding her, she convinced herself that she was ready to face him.

But when she came out the stage door one morning and saw the Oldsmobile parked in the line of limousines waiting to pick up the party girls, Annie began to tremble. Teddy Lapps was standing beside the back door, ready to open it for her. Behind her, Annie heard a familiar mocking voice say, "How ya doin', Annie Brown?"

She forced herself to get into the back seat, and Teddy Lapps closed the door behind her. Phil got in behind the wheel and Teddy Lapps joined him in the front seat. Annie turned to Charlie Dell, who was in his regular place.

"Hello, Charlie," she said and sat back against the seat, trying not to shake. In spite of what Mr. Delansig had said, she thought she might not leave the car alive. The Oldsmobile pulled out into the light early morning traffic.

"Annie, tell me why you haven't called me," Charlie said, sounding as if he were offended. Annie looked at him, irritated at being mocked. She saw that the old man had changed; his clothes seemed too big for him, and he slouched into the back seat. In his lap, one hand quivered spasmodically.

"You know why, Charlie," she answered quietly. "I was scared to, just like I'm scared now."

"*Why?*" he asked with pained surprise.

"For Lord's sake, Charlie, I know an awful lot, don't I?"

Charlie was silent for a moment. "The Angel told you too much," he said angrily. Annie looked toward the front seat and caught Phil's eye in the rearview mirror. He shrugged and kept driving. Charlie leaned over close to her and whispered intently, "You know a whole lot, Annie, but you damn well should know by now that I *trust* you with it."

Annie also whispered but felt her voice shake and tears come. "I didn't trust *you* anymore, Charlie, not when I heard you were hopping your own horses."

With an effort, Charlie pulled himself back into the corner of the back seat. They drove silently for several blocks before he spoke again.

"It was my great mistake to think I could ask you to understand the kind of business I'm in . . . or even to want to understand it. I'm sorry, Annie. I was worried that if you got in the way too much at Saratoga, you'd get hurt."

He took a deep breath and suddenly began coughing, hard and deep. "We got out of it," he continued, "so you don't have to worry." He kept coughing until he hunched forward in the seat and took small, shallow breaths. Silently, Teddy Lapps looked back; he and Phil seemed used to Charlie's behavior. Annie reached over as he straightened his back.

"You all right, Charlie?"

He glanced at her with old affection. "We're driving out to Belmont; thought you might want to go. If not, Teddy'll get you a cab."

Annie watched his eyes and saw the trust there that she could not deny.

"Sure," she said. "Why not?"

Phil immediately turned the car. No one said anything more, and as the long row of tunnel lights rhythmically lit the car interior, Annie saw Phil watching her in the rearview mirror. When he caught her looking at him, he grinned, as if everything was just fine. She gave him a dirty look and turned to watch out her window. When they came out of the tunnel,

Charlie reached over, offering her a copy of the *Morning Telegraph*. Annie thanked him and took it. The favor made her feel uneasy again about Charlie and what he expected for all he had done for her. She also remembered the months before her job at the Latin Quarter, when she could not afford the fifty cents for the *Telegraph;* it was what her evening meal at the Automat cost. Glancing over the front page, she saw an article that made her forget such concerns. It named three new entries for the Belmont Stakes to be run in ten days. One of the entries was Caernarvon Farms' Certainty.

She read the article twice.

> . . . Certainty has been rested at Caernarvon's training center in South Carolina after recovering from the virus which swept through the Florida tracks this spring. The virus knocked out several contenders for the Triple Crown races, but Certainty has taken up daily training, "as if he's trying to make up for all the fun he's missed," according to the stable's trainer, Frank Carney, who is watching over the colt's recovery.

"How was the Derby, Charlie?" Annie asked as if they were taking just another drive out to Belmont.

"Crowded; a crazy race. Shoemaker thought he'd crossed the finish line at the sixteenth pole, and stood up in the irons. His horse broke stride and lost the race. Anything can happen at the Derby."

"Who do you think's going to win the Belmont Stakes? There's three new entries," Annie said, easing into their old banter.

"Who cares? You don't bet the Belmont. The Derby and Preakness horses come up here to run a longer distance. These new entries, nobody knows much about them, one of them's been sick. Not worth it."

"I wouldn't mind seeing it once," Annie said absently, trying not to show her excitement.

"You want to go, Annie?" Phil said from the front seat. "I'll get us some tickets." He volunteered as if inviting her to church.

Annie stared at him in the rearview mirror, knowing she had to make some kind of peace with Phil. "Let me think about it."

She saw Phil grin.

Charlie began to cough again, harder than before. Annie slid near him and put her arms around his chest; the cough seemed to tear through his body. When he sat back in his seat, Annie kept her arm around his shoulders. He acknowledged it with a quick smile, but then looked out the window.

"What's the matter with you, Charlie?"

He breathed carefully before replying. "They tell me I got a couple of asbestos-lined lungs, from when I was building things." He met her eyes. "When I built things, I used the best. Asbestos was the best."

Annie tried not to be affected by what he said. "Can't they do anything?"

He looked away again. " 'They'? I had to move into town so I could be closer to them. What they suggest is worse than dying. I'd rather talk about the horses."

Without thinking about it, Annie leaned up and kissed his cheek. Charlie continued looking out the window, but he reached for her hand.

They rode for a time, Annie wondering how sick he was. As they turned onto the Hempstead Turnpike, Annie considered the chances of Sam Cumberland's being at the Belmont Stakes. Certainty was his colt. Sam had bred him. Annie had saved him.

"Phil, if you're going to the Belmont, I'll go with you." She would rather have gone alone, but thought it would be a good way to find out what Phil was doing.

"Terrific," he said. "I'll see if I can fix the third race for us." He snickered at his own joke, which was met with silence. "Hey, just kidding." He checked his mirror again for a sign of shared levity. There was none.

Within a half hour of their parking near the rail of Belmont's backstretch, Annie saw Certainty come on the track for his morning work. She watched from the Oldsmobile, not willing to take the chance of being seen. Charlie had left his binoculars for her in the back seat. Frank Carney rode in tandem on his mount, ponying Certainty down the backstretch of the track before starting the colt on a gallop. When Carney let the colt go, Certainty leaped forward. He galloped for five furlongs in fifty-eight seconds, which Annie timed by counting, a technique she had developed at Saratoga; she had not wanted to spend money on a stopwatch.

Annie heard the *Morning Telegraph*'s clockers in the backstretch judges' stand next to the Oldsmobile talking excitedly, comparing their stopwatches. When Certainty and his rider returned to Frank Carney, he led the colt by the judges' stand. One of the clockers yelled down, "Pretty damn speedy work, Carney. What kind of time did you get?"

Without slowing his pony, Carney said, "I just got this real good feeling in my innards. What'd y'all get?"

The clockers laughed and one shouted, "Would you go with fifty-eight and two?"

"I'd go with anything you guys say." And the clockers hooted at his mock respect.

As Carney led Certainty off the track through the gap, he passed within a few yards of the parked Oldsmobile. Pressing herself back into the seat, Annie saw the scars on Carney's hand, resting on his chaps-covered thigh. She looked up at the intense concentration on his face. His blue-green eyes, for no apparent reason, began to slide toward the Oldsmobile. Abruptly, the trainer reined in, and along with his jockey, still seated on Certainty, looked back at the track as Eddie Arcaro rode by, driving his Belmont Stakes entry hard.

Annie also watched him. Sitting low in his saddle, back straight, head down with his chin almost in the horse's mane, Arcaro urged his colt with his hands, pushing as he held the reins. Annie knew what an advantage Arcaro gave to any horse he rode. Already Certainty's partisan, she watched him grimly.

Later, she saw Johnny Phillips and Burt leading a colt to the gap. Watching them from the Oldsmobile, Annie thought that if she talked to them, she would quit the Latin Quarter and go back to work. Maybe one day, but that morning was not the time. She watched for Vera, and on the drive back to Manhattan, asked Charlie about her.

"Vera took a fall in Florida, broke a leg. I convinced her to quit and run this manicuring shop I happened to buy in Queens."

Annie's only response was to kiss him again, which he shrugged off.

Over the next ten days, she returned to the Belmont backstretch with Charlie on three occasions. Half jokingly, Phil suggested she start driving again, because he hated the early hour. The idea was ignored. Annie knew the consequences her association would have if Charlie or Phil was ever discovered fixing a horse race. People with connections to gamblers, fixers, or the underworld were not allowed licenses on any track in the country. But Charlie had been good to her, and he was obviously ill. Annie could not turn her back on him. They fell into their old routine of comparing what they found in the *Telegraph* and what they saw in the works. Phil drove on the trip out; Annie took the train back to Manhattan after the works and went to bed. She never reacted when she saw Certainty, and was careful not to be seen, particularly on the morning when she spotted the Cumberlands' gray Rolls-Royce driving by the shedrows. Her anticipation of the Belmont Stakes grew with each visit. Arcaro's mount and the Derby and Preakness winners were getting all the attention. In spite of the published times of his works, the odds on Certainty were still long.

Annie had observed how the rich women dressed to stroll around the backstretch at Saratoga, looking at their horses, smiling like royalty at the help. Having noted their shoes, their jewelry, their hairdos, their makeup, she had understood the difference between showing off the goods a woman might have to offer and the elegant simplicity of someone so secure that showing off was never considered. As Annie had read in the gossip columns, with the rich it seldom was called showing off; instead, it was called style, and they were supposed to have been born with it, along with good breeding, good taste, good looks, and lots of money.

Annie spent a large part of the money she had saved on an outfit for the race. She bought a pale green crepe de chine silk dress with short sleeves, a deep scooped neckline, and a pleated skirt, sling-back dark green pumps, and a plain wide jade-green straw hat, the brim of which could be worn to cut straight across her eyes. And she bought her first pair of pure white cotton gloves. Early on the morning of the race, she paid to have her hair done for the first time, showing the hairdresser a picture, torn out of *Town and Country*, of exactly what she wanted: a waterfall of amber waves down her back, parted on top in the middle to frame her face, and held in place on each side by two simple tortoise-shell barrettes. The only jewelry Annie wore was the single strand of Charlie's pearls, which she had not worn since the night with Sam.

The day of the Belmont Stakes was cloudless and bright but became increasingly humid. Phil met Annie at Pennsylvania Station. He noticed how she looked, but made no comment about it. It was the first time they had been alone since their conversation at Saratoga, and neither was inclined to talk. On the train, both studied the *Morning Telegraph*, though Annie was not interested in any of the other races of the day besides the Belmont Stakes. That day's approximate betting odds, which included consideration of the weather, last-minute scratches, and the condition of the track, were known as "the morning line." Annie was happy to see that Certainty still was a fifteen-to-one long shot and had drawn a good post position, the third slot from the rail in the starting gate.

Idly, Phil said, "I caught your act at the Quarter a coupla times. I'd forgotten you had such a terrific bod." He grinned to emphasize his compliment.

"Gosh, thanks, Phil," Annie replied sarcastically.

Phil turned a page of the *Telegraph*. "You know Charlie's going to die."

"Yes," Annie said softly.

"When it happens, what are you gonna do with his list?" He pretended to keep reading.

So did Annie. "What list?"

Phil jammed the *Telegraph* closed and said, "Don't get smart with me, Annie. I mean the list that's worth maybe ten million bucks if it's handled right. It won't be able to hurt Charlie when he's dead, and *I* know how to handle it."

"You already digging his grave, Phil?"

He grabbed her wrist. "Listen, you—"

"Phil, let go of me."

He let go, but went on talking. "Nobody'll know who has the list. Every guy on it is a zillionaire, getting old, wants to live a quiet life, die in bed. They're all getting real dodgy about each other. Vito Genovese marked Frank Costello last month. You hear about that? The stupid jerk sent to do the job *missed.* Both those guys are on that list, right? Now listen, every time one of those guys gets killed or dies, the price of the list goes down. You don't think those guys'll pay five hundred G's *each* to keep evidence buried that'd yank them out of their fuckin' BarcaLoungers and put them in front of a grand jury? Just think about it, will ya? Just think about it."

"Sounds like you've been thinking about it a whole lot."

"Fuckin' A, Annie."

"Then why doesn't it get through to you that those people may be getting old and dodgy, but they aren't dumb? As soon as any one of them hears about an old body turning up, they'll think of Charlie and grab whoever was around Charlie before he died. That's you and that's me, Phil. I doubt if they'd blame it on Teddy Lapps. You might be able to talk your way out, but I'm a terrible liar. The list is staying right where it is."

"I saw some of the names, y'know, some of the addresses," he challenged.

"I figured that. If you use them and I get hurt, which I will because they'll *know* about us, Phil, the whole list goes in. Your couple of names'll be worthless, and we'll spend the rest of our lives, if we have any, running and hiding."

Exasperated, Phil sat rigidly and did not move. "You are the fuckin' dumbest white woman in this goddamn world!"

"You just keep thinking that, Phil. It'll make it a whole lot easier for you to *forget that list!*" Annie stood up and moved to a seat at the other end of the car. When they reached Belmont, she left the train alone and walked over to the grandstand entrance. As she paid her admission, Phil, who had followed, tried to stop her, indicating that he had Charlie's box seats. Annie bought her ticket and followed the crowd.

Just before the fourth race, Annie saw Phil watching her from the other side of the clubhouse divider. She ignored him, but soon after the race was over he came and sat in the seat next to hers.

"That seat's taken."

"Yeah, I paid the guy fifty bucks to go down and watch on the rail."

Annie stood up. "Sounds like a good idea."

"Look, sit down, will ya? Let's just forget about the goddamn list."

"As if you ever could."

"It's done. Forgotten."

Annie sat down again and absently watched the crowd. "Why do I know you're already figuring out another way to get it?"

He grinned. "Because you know what a smart-ass son of a bitch I am." He opened up his *Telegraph*. "Who do we like in the fifth?"

She reached over to take his binoculars off his shoulder. Her view of the Cumberland box was blocked by several columns and the clubhouse divider. Nevertheless, she focused the binoculars in that direction. She could see the usual knots of well-dressed people talking animatedly to one another. She thought she glimpsed Cornelia Cumberland, and put the binoculars down, suddenly realizing how nervous she was. Her stomach tightened and she felt sweat on her forehead. Worrying about sweating through her dress, she wished that she was on the backstretch, looking after Certainty. It seemed unnatural to be sitting in the stands when her horse was running.

For Annie, the next three races went by as irritating distractions. Phil won some money, but Annie did not join him at the betting windows. Instead, she waited and fretted until the seventh race was finished. Then she was on her feet, heading for the paddock. Phil could barely keep up with her.

The crowd was already packed five deep on the grandstand side of the paddock. Annie could barely see. As the horses were led in from the barns, however, she glimpsed Certainty.

Held firmly by his groom, he came prancing by, magnificent, ready, and nervous. His special Belmont Stakes saddlecloth bore his name as well as the numeral 3, his post position. Annie spotted Frank Carney watching his colt as he circled the paddock. The trainer looked uncomfortable in a coat and tie. Then she saw him greet two other men, one white-haired, the other with hair the color of newly poured tar.

Annie turned and pressed back through the crowd. She was not ready to see him. Returning to her seat, she waited alone, shaken by the longing she had felt when she saw Sam.

The bugler announced the post parade, and the horses, each led by a pony, came onto the track. Phil returned and sat down beside her.

"Arcaro's got a lock on this one. With those odds, there's no point in betting."

Annie hardly heard him. She wanted to look through the binoculars toward the Cumberland box again. Instead, she watched Certainty walk past the stands, still skittish, washing out with a light sweat over his flanks. Under control of his pony rider, the colt took off down the track on his warm-up. By the time he returned to the starting gate with the rest of the field, he was calmer. Some of his nervous energy had burned off and he entered his slot in the starting gate with no hesitance. There was trouble, however, with the colt that loaded after him, who balked and backed out. When he was shoved in by the starting gate crew, the colt grew increasingly fractious. One of the crew used a device similar to a large nutcracker, known as a crimper, to pinch the colt's ear in order to keep his head facing the track ahead of him and, presumably, his mind on the race.

Not a second after the last horse entered the gate, the starter triggered it. It opened with a bang, the gate bell ringing, and nine horses charged out. Number 3 broke well and was held by his jockey in fourth near the front of the pack. As the field of runners passed the stands and headed around the clubhouse turn, several bumped one another in a fight for the inside position. Phil took his binoculars back as Annie's eyes shot ahead and around the wide oval of Belmont's track. Once again, she was awed by its size and distance.

Down the backstretch, little changed, except for the plod-
ders, the long-shot field horses, who began to string out behind the five-horse pack in front. When they approached the
final turn, Certainty made his move, swinging wide without
worry. He drew up to the leader, and matched him stride for
stride.

"Come on come *on* come *on come* ON!" Annie bellowed,
startling Phil.

"Hey, Annie, shut up, will ya?" he muttered.

Certainty took the lead, breaking away from the field as he
headed around the stretch turn into the straight. Annie's
mouth suddenly dried. Coming up on the outside, Arcaro was
using his whip, demanding his mount to carry him to yet another win at the Belmont Stakes.

"You want the glasses?" Phil asked as the action came down
the stretch, where binoculars were unnecessary. Annie shook
her head, easily following the brilliant Caernarvon silks of
crimson, gold, and royal blue. The crowd noise boiled up as
the race came down to a contest between the will of the
world's greatest jockey versus a fifteen-to-one long shot. Certainty seemed oblivious of Arcaro's human purpose, and reacted only to the instinct that another horse was moving up
fast.

Annie found her voice but could shape no words. The noise
she made, a shouted holler, surprised her and further irritated
Phil. Annie's cry was lost in the massive wave of sound that
crashed down from the stands onto the fast June-baked track as
Certainty pounded with massive strides to hit the finish line
first by a nose.

In the resulting clamor, Annie stood absolutely silent; then
she moved quickly out of the row of seats.

"Hey, where ya going?" Phil called.

She did not answer, knowing he would shrug and go back
to his *Telegraph* to handicap the last race of the day. She de-
spised him.

"Where you headed, miss?" A Pinkerton security guard
stood at the entrance through the clubhouse barrier. Annie
had learned much about the understanding between those
who kept the law and those who broke it. She played on that

volatile intimacy with a smile that admitted everything and dared anyone to stop her.

"My horse just won!"

"Congratulations. The two-dollar windows are right up there."

"You didn't hear me. *My* horse won; I'm with the Cumberlands."

Annie knew the guard might not believe her, but her clothes were right, and so was her smile. Besides, he knew that the Cumberlands were Belmont royalty, and that there were a lot of other guards between her and the winner's circle. Passing the buck on to them, he let her go with a look indicating that he knew she was conning him.

By the time Annie had passed the fifth guard, her belief in what she said was so certain—"My horse won; I'm with the Cumberlands"—that doubt never formed in another guard's mind. As she edged her way toward the winner's circle, Annie saw in her mind the crooked smile Sam had given her so long ago in the back seat of the Rolls-Royce.

Above the heads of the crowd, she saw her horse. Certainty was being led from the track by Frank Carney. As Annie reached the low picket fence that held back the laughing, cheering people from the small area of dirt just off the track, she remembered Sam shaking her hand, thanking her for saving the colt. She remembered how embarrassed she was because she was only wearing a torn flannel shirt. Annie laughed at the memory just as she saw Sam take the bridle from Carney to lead Certainty into the winner's circle. The two men did not exchange any greetings. Several track employees maneuvered the traditional blanket of white carnations over the colt's withers.

Annie suddenly felt glutted with too much emotion. The three-year-old colt was still blowing from the race, his blood vessels pushed to the surface by the bunched, knotted muscles under his glistening chestnut coat. The noise and excitement from the thousands of onlookers made him prance, which caused the jockey to pass a laughing comment to Sam. He, in turn, radiated happiness; he made no attempt to contain it with dignity. Pure joy seemed to fill him so that he might have exploded with it. Annie loved him; she could barely stand. Of course Certainty was her horse! Of course she was with the Cumberlands! None of this would be happening if it were not for Annie Grebauer! A vision filled her mind of the Cumberland family embracing her as they thanked her and asked her to come with them, to share the glory of the win. As Sam came around once more with Certainty, Annie reached out a hand. The horse saw her and hesitated; Sam, however, was distracted by the arrival of his mother, father, and wife, who was carrying a baby. He led the colt on.

The crowd cheered as two elegantly dressed men appeared in the winner's circle. One had a gold crest on the pocket of his blue, gold-buttoned blazer. He was carrying in both hands the huge August Belmont Memorial Cup, which he placed on a cloth-covered table near the spot where Annie was standing. The other man was the tall, dignified governor of New York, Averell Harriman. He greeted the senior Cumberlands with pleased intimacy and joined Sam as the family quickly arranged themselves in front of Certainty for the bank of photographers who had assembled. Mr. Cumberland waved at Frank Carney to join them, but the trainer refused. As the cup was held up for the picture, the crowd gave a noisy cheer.

And then Sam saw her. He did not quite believe it at first, but then did. Immediately he started to walk over to her, but the press noisily demanded more pictures. He returned to his family as they glanced at Annie, then posed again with no indication of recognition. Sam looked back apprehensively, stared a moment; then his crooked smile slowly appeared. He whispered quickly to the others and gestured back at Certainty. Each of them glanced at Annie again, Belinda longer than the others, then exchanged tolerant glances of understanding among themselves. Belinda said something to Sam, but he did not respond. The Cumberlands smiled again at the cameras, the governor, the cup, and the colt.

Annie realized that, though she was standing fifteen feet away from the Cumberlands, they were on a separate planet. Abruptly, she felt she was wearing too much makeup. Until that understanding look was exchanged among the Cumberlands, Annie had felt attractive, even stylish. Now she began to sweat again; a trickle ran down under one arm. Sensing that someone was looking at her, she glanced across the winner's circle. Also standing outside it, Frank Carney was watching her. She tried to smile, wishing she could say something to him.

The jockey dismounted, and his valet gathered his tack. The blanket of carnations was removed and Certainty was quickly led away by a groom to begin cooling out. Frank Carney followed with no further reaction to the winner's ritual. The photographers begged for just one more shot of Governor Harriman with the Cumberland family. Sam again smiled unobtrusively at Annie and signaled for her to wait, then quickly turned back to the cameras.

Annie felt as if she had been thrown a bone. She looked at their shoes, the men's polished and buffed wing tips, inappropriate for the dust of the winner's circle, which indicated only that such a concern as dust never entered Cumberland minds. The women wore elegant patent leather pumps. Their dresses were cool, unwrinkled pastel silks. Their jewelry, though subtle, was rich and real, and from a few feet away, Annie could see Belinda's intricate gold bracelet, Cornelia's pearl pin, and her square emerald set in a heavy ring.

The two Cumberland men wore suits of linen that fit in a way none of Phil Angelo's clothes ever fit. Mr. Cumberland wore a boater, a bow tie of stripes, and in his breast pocket a silk handkerchief that, in a perfect pale way, coordinated but did not match the color of his tie, shirt, and hatband. Sam wore no hat. His deeply tanned skin and black hair were thrown into contrast by his light brown linen suit, blue shirt, and bright yellow silk tie.

Annie suddenly hated them all. They were there because, by running their colt into a freezing river and swimming him to safety, she had saved him from crashing through hedges onto a highway and being hit by a truck. No, she thought, they were there because they were born to be there, and the rest of the world was around to serve them, to applaud them, and to appreciate with respectful envy their pleasure. Annie had played her small part in their lives, been tipped for her services, had serviced Sam's drunken pleasure, and then been tossed a smile.

The baby started to cry. Annie watched the two women smile indulgently down on the heir. The photographers moved in a frenzy to capture the human touch of the moment. As they chatted with Governor Harriman, Cornelia Cumberland's tight blue-gray curls and Belinda's plain blond page boy stayed perfectly in place. Mr. Cumberland and Sam smiled congratulations at each other, their brows lifted, accepting their glory. Democratically, they both shook hands with the jockey and dismissed him. Then the two men offered their arms to their wives and, joking again with the governor, started back to the owners' boxes, leaving the gleaming cup they had won to be carried after them by the official who had brought it. The crowd cheered them; the photographers pleaded. The Cumberlands were heedless of all.

The official stepped to one side of the winner's circle, allowing the governor and the Cumberlands their courtly exit. Then he turned to lift the cup from the table. Without thinking, Annie reached out and gripped a silver handle of the August Belmont Memorial Cup. The startled official stared at her.

The resulting crowd reaction and photographers' excitement caused the Cumberlands to look back. Annie saw the family watching.

"You see, sir, I deserve this as much as they do," she explained quietly to the official, who turned beet-red. Annie held on for a moment, making the official tug for the cup and start barking for help.

Annie let it go as two security guards pushed through the crowd to her side. She recognized one who had let her through to get to the winner's circle. The official stopped yelping, tried to regain his dignity, and ordered the security guards to grab Annie. He began to brush dust from the crest of his blue blazer.

Before the guards could react, Sam was there, smiling, forcing calm, and easing the guards' grip from Annie's arms.

"She's with us, men," he said with easy command. "An old friend." Then he spoke to the official solicitously, which flattered the man so much that he burst out with a nervous cackle. Annie glanced at the other Cumberlands, who watched the scene with an air of distaste until Cornelia imperiously turned to Governor Harriman and went on, leading away her husband and Belinda with the baby. Sam urged the official to follow his family with the cup, which the man did with alacrity. Then Sam came back to Annie and smiled again at the guards.

"Thanks, men."

Thus dismissed, the two guards nodded and moved into the crowd.

Sam ran his eyes over Annie, appreciating how she looked as well as appraising what she wore. "I went back the next day and walked around Garden City for hours," he said. "I'd been too drunk to remember where you lived. I drove through for the next couple of weeks, hoping to run into you on the street. Then we left for Florida, and . . ."

Everything changed. He had looked for her. "Why?" she asked.

"To apologize. Because I wanted to see you." He smiled again. "You've grown up a lot, Annie."

"And you have another baby," she said coolly. "What's its name?"

"Named after me, but we call him Barky. As you can see, my wife enjoys presenting herself as a mother."

"What did she say just now when she saw me?"

"She wondered if your pearls were real." He chuckled.

"You like being a father?"

"On occasion." He laughed hollowly; she did not join him. When he looked at her, his eyes were serious. "What are you doing here, Annie?"

"I came out to see our horse win."

He acknowledged the shared possession with a long, easy smile. Moving closer, he said, "If I could give you the goddamn cup, I would. We only get to keep the thing a year; then we bring it back. It's an ugly old piece of junk, isn't it?" He reached out and took her white-gloved hand, not to shake it, but to hold it. "The important thing is, *our* horse sure did win, Annie!" As he held her hand, she looked at him directly and tried to judge her effect on him. "We're all still so grateful to you," he said.

Annie smiled. "I noticed how grateful your mother was, running over here to give me a big hug."

Sam laughed, then moved closer to explain intimately, "My mother's idea of gratitude is that the world enjoys doing her favors, and can figure out its own reward. Good Christ, I've got to go. Annie, please, tell me where you live. I want to see you again."

He was still holding her hand. She took it away. "If I told you that, I'd spend too much time thinking you'd come. It's better for me to think you wanted to come and didn't know where to find me . . . But I know where you live. Maybe we'll run into each other again."

They stood quietly a moment.

"Then I'll wait for you, Annie," he said as he took a step back and smiled. "But don't make me wait too long." He walked away. She watched him until he disappeared through a private door.

She leaned on the rail, the last person still standing at the winner's circle. Remembering her fantasy of the Cumberlands urging her to join them, Annie hated them again. Of course Belinda would wonder if the pearls were real, probably recognizing that the rest was just a little bit fake. Annie thought of what would have happened if Sam *had* found her on the streets of Garden City a year and a half earlier. She loved him for telling her he had looked for her, and hated him for thinking what he and his family surely must think of her.

"Dammit, I'm more than that," she muttered, then glanced around to see if anyone had heard her. Looking back at the winner's circle, she was glad she had grabbed that "piece of junk." She shook her head. Sam said that he had come looking for her, wanted to see her again. Could she believe that, or was he just making it up?

Depressed and shaken, she went back to find Phil.

TEN

THROUGH THE FIRST THREE NUMBERS of the Latin Quarter's late show, a ringside table for sixteen had remained empty. As the magic nozzles of the Syncopated Waters began to gurgle counterpoint to the Joe Lombardi Orchestra's plangent version of "La Mer," Annie and her colleagues arched, posing erotically on their pedestals, changing positions in unison every sixteen bars. Their flesh-colored pasties and G-strings gave the impression of nippleless, smooth-crotched nudity.

A raucous group was heard coming up the stairs. Annie glanced at one of the other showgirls, who rolled her eyes at the thought of another rowdy ringside party. The maître d' led the group of sixteen men, all in dinner jackets, to their table. None of them stopped talking, laughing, and, in one case, singing the lyrics of "La Mer" as the song stimulated the Syncopated Waters. Once at the table, the men yelled at one another about the seating. Unnoticed at first, a single member of the party climbed onto the stage. He announced in a loud slurred voice, which a nearby floor mike broadcast, "This is the goddamnest men's room I've ever seen," opened his fly, and contributed significantly to the Syncopated Waters. Several of his friends climbed up to grab him just before two stagehands and a bouncer arrived. Hauled back to the table, he struggled to zip up his fly over his protruding shirttail. The audience, swayed from their original irritation with the group's noisy entrance, gave him cheers and applause, which prompted him to climb onto the table, wave, and publicly struggle with his fly.

As the orchestra continued playing bravely, Annie and two other showgirls got the giggles when their eyes met. The audience quickly spotted the laughter, and it spread through the room. Still giggling, the performers nevertheless assumed their dramatic poses on every sixteen-bar cue.

Then Annie noticed the distinctive head of tar-black hair. She stopped laughing. Enjoying himself, Sam helped pull his friend down from the table and guided him into a chair. Over the music, Sam shouted an idea to both ends of the table as the rest of the audience continued to laugh. When the orchestra reached its appropriately sodden climax, all sixteen of the men at the ringside table stood up to applaud the girls, each with his shirttail hanging out of his fly.

At that moment, Sam saw Annie. She was staring at him. Glancing past her at the other hysterical showgirls, his eyes snapped back to her, riveted. The other men at his table turned to the audience and bowed to spontaneous howls and applause. Sam continued to gaze at Annie with his crooked smile as the music ended and a blackout covered the scene.

The band segued briskly into a loud introduction for the next act, and a deep voice announced profoundly in the darkness, "Lou Walter's Latin Quarter is proud to present, direct from . . ." At the same time, a contingent from the rowdy ringside party climbed onstage. Colliding with pipes, nozzles, and shouting stagehands, one black-tied swain chased a screaming showgirl. Flashlight beams spotted the upset as the man tripped on a nozzle and water sprayed into the audience. Shrieks and more pandemonium ensued.

Annie quickly climbed down from her pedestal and hurried around the back drape toward her dressing room. A hand took her arm.

"Annie," Sam said, pulling her against him and putting his arms around her. Looking up, she could not even see his face. His mouth came down to hers. She responded as his hands hurried over her. The backstage work lights came on suddenly and Annie pulled away to look at his face. He smiled, daring her to stay. On the other side of the back drape, they heard more screams, shouts, crashing pipes, the orchestra vamping endlessly, and the audience hooting and laughing. Apparently no one saw them. Sam kissed her again, deeply, as he put his hands on her breasts, covering the pasties.

"Oh, my Lord!" Annie gasped.

The master of ceremonies began again, "Ladies and gentlemen, Lou Walter's Latin Quarter is proud to present . . ." The audience was still restive, so he had to wait.

"Let's get out of here," Sam whispered.

The work lights went off as a dramatic drum roll began in the darkness. Relative order seemed to be returning to the stage.

"I can't. I have to finish the show. What are you doing here?"

"It's a bachelor party."

". . . direct from her record-breaking smash in Monte Carlo and Biarritz . . ."

"I'll be at the stage door." He kissed her and was gone.

". . . the wondrous Katinka!"

A juggler. She did twelve minutes, and a three-minute encore with flaming cossack boots. Annie had time to lean against the backstage wall to catch her breath. She did not dare to think, although she had thought of little else in the two weeks since the Belmont Stakes. She pushed off from the wall and moved slowly across the stage behind the back drape, in front of which Katinka was sending twenty daggers aloft.

Annie made two more appearances in the show, one as an orchid and one, in the finale, as Marie Antoinette. For the first time since appearing at the Latin Quarter, she felt deeply embarrassed. Refraining from even glancing at Sam or his table of friends, she made herself go on. She wondered if, surrounded by his friends, drinking champagne, and scrutinizing the bodies before them, he would brag to them about what had happened behind the back drape. In the finale she worked up enough courage to look at him. He was drinking coffee, watching her. When he saw her look at him, his mouth opened slightly. Annie smiled. His smile in return was enough to reassure her that he would be at the stage door.

As the applause dwindled after the final blackout, she maneuvered her open hoop skirt, shepherd's crook, and huge hat up to the dressing room. She hurried to be first in the shower, and as she lathered off her body makeup, she remembered what she had to wear—jeans, a shirt, and a sweater. Annie had planned to go out to Belmont. Charlie would be waiting outside.

It did not matter. When she walked out the stage door, the first thing she saw was the Oldsmobile. Half a dozen members of Sam's party were gathered, among them the one who had upstaged the show. He came over to her, stretching himself to stand up very straight, but still missed Annie's height by an inch. A blond, round-faced, amused young man with a narrow brush of a mustache, he had blue eyes that, in spite of a champagne glitter, seemed strangely shattered.

"Annie . . . 'Brown,' as it says in this vivid souvenir program?" he inquired, smiling lopsidedly, whether naturally or from champagne, Annie could not tell. She nodded.

"My name's Winton Sumner. I've been sent to escort you." And he grandly offered his arm.

"Just a sec," Annie said and hurried to Charlie's car. Teddy Lapps opened the door for her as usual, but she only leaned in the back seat.

"Charlie, I'm real sorry, I can't go this morning. Maybe next time." He let her see his disappointment before he nodded. Phil watched from the driver's seat, but turned away quickly.

Annie returned to Sam's friend and said, "Let's go."

The other black-tied members of the party shouted admiring remarks to their friend as Annie and Winton Sumner proceeded over to Broadway. He chatted aimlessly; Annie did not hear a word. They turned the corner of Forty-sixth Street. There, in a Checker cab, Sam was waiting.

He stepped out and held the door for Annie. "Thanks, Winnie." Sam smiled as he got in and slammed the door shut, calling an address to the driver.

For a moment, they looked at each other, considering what to say. He reached out and touched her neck, then pulled her slowly over to him. As the cab sped north through Central Park, they held each other, kissing and touching silently.

Finally, Sam said, "You sure you want to start something like this?"

Even in her most outrageous fantasies, Annie had never imagined such a suggestion. She felt herself flush.

"I haven't thought about it much."

"You'd better." It was a warning.

"Where are we going?"

"My old apartment. I had it after college, before I was married." He used the word purposefully and looked at her for a reaction.

Annie watched him. "What kind of thing are we starting?"

Sam took her head in his hands. "I"—he kissed her—"don't know. And I don't"—he kissed her again—"think we have to figure it out this morning." Although he smiled, he searched her face before saying, "I can't promise you anything, Annie."

She answered quickly, surprising herself. "Whatever this is going to be, it's not about promises."

He, too, seemed surprised. "I've been told I'm very selfish."

She watched him. "Why all these warnings?"

Seeing him struggle to answer, she said, "I want to have as much of you as I can. There's nothing that I expect. I just hope you want me the same way."

He moved toward her again and kissed her. She reached under his coat and pulled his shirt out so that she could touch his back. His hands went gently down her body. Then the cab pulled to a stop.

When Annie stepped out onto the sidewalk, she did not

know exactly where she was. Central Park was across the street; looking up, she saw two huge twin towers of the building they were about to enter. Sam took her arm and rang the bell at the front door. A sleepy porter let them in and took them up to the thirty-fourth floor. When the elevator doors opened, they stepped out circumspectly. Sam fumbled urgently for the end of his gold key chain, separated the keys, and jammed one into the apartment door lock. When the door flew open, they pulled off each other's clothes as they went through the foyer into the living room. Annie saw a couch; she was in her underwear. Sam was yanking apart his formal shirt, fighting studs and cuff links. He hesitated as Annie stripped herself bare and lay down on the couch. Sam was naked and on her in an instant. He slipped into her; she let one leg dangle over the side. As they made love, the same feeling Annie had felt with him before started through her, but faster, as if it had been waiting since they were at the Latin Quarter, ready to explode again. Sam felt it coming and held her hips down. She could not hear herself shout because Sam was shouting at the same time. They both collapsed, moving just enough to prolong the final aching tremor.

They lay on the couch a long time, utterly still. Annie finally reached out to stroke Sam's hair; he cupped a hand over one of her breasts. The door to the apartment was wide open, but that did not seem to matter. Annie could hear her heart beating. Sam coughed, which gave way to an exulting laugh, a deep, sharp report that led to another cough. Then he was quiet and Annie felt him looking at her. Before she turned to him, she smiled at his pleasure and pressed her breast farther into his hand.

"Annie, I'll have to go soon."

"My Lord," she said pretending amusement as she slipped out from under his hand and propped herself up on an elbow, "you thinking about that already?"

"You understand that I can't stay."

"I figured we weren't setting up housekeeping or anything."

Sam smiled gratefully but warily. "I wasn't planning on this."

"You think *I* was? When I saw you sitting out there tonight, I about fell off my pedestal."

Sam laughed, stood, pulled her to her feet, and kissed her. Then he watched her a moment, and went to close the front door. The key, as well as his gold chain and pocket watch were still hanging from the lock. He picked up his jacket and waistcoat, and when he came back, he snapped the key off the chain and handed it to Annie.

"You can stay," he said, "as long as you want."

Annie had to clear her throat. "I'm not staying here."

"I wish you would. I don't know where you're living now, but this place is empty; nobody uses it. Cleaning lady comes once a week."

She watched him carefully. "Kind of changes things real fast, doesn't it?" Annie crossed her arms over her breasts, feeling a chill.

"I don't want to lose you again, Annie." He put the key on a side table and came back to lie on the couch. "Remember, it's taken us more than two years to get this far." Annie put her head on his shoulder and looked around the living room. It was decorated in bright yellow-patterned upholstery, with a fireplace, pale green walls, and four tall windows. Through a haze behind the Fifth Avenue skyline across the park, Annie saw the sun rising huge and red.

"The bar's in the credenza, and the phonograph's there, in that cabinet," Sam pointed out, already assuming she would stay. "Terrific collection of jazz underneath . . . My gosh, I haven't listened to any of it for I don't know how long. Come on. Let me show you around."

He hurried her into a hall, pointing out rooms. "Dining room . . . kitchen has everything . . . the study over here . . . and, last but not least, the bedroom."

It was huge, with a ceiling as high as the one in the living room and corner windows overlooking Central Park to the south. Its walls were covered in dark suede; the sheets and comforter on the king-size bed were a cream color. At the foot of the bed was a large leather sofa with oversize fur pillows, facing a small fireplace.

"The bathroom's over there, best room in the whole place,

a tub you can dive into. And here's a robe." He opened a door; as the automatic light went on, Annie saw a large walk-in closet filled with men's clothes. From them, Sam selected a maroon bathrobe and held it open for her. Annie hesitated; smiling confidently, he urged her. She reached out an arm and turned as the luxurious silk covered her. Sam wrapped her in it and held her from behind.

"Stay," he said, and kissed her ear. "Please, Annie."

Annie already knew she would, in spite of all the reasons against her doing so. She had always considered any moment she had with Sam as the last one. Even now, she accepted that Sam would go back to Belinda, the children, Number 10, and the whole Cumberland legacy. He might reconsider his impulsive night with a showgirl. He might never return to the apartment, allowing her to reach the obvious conclusion that she should discreetly disappear. Nevertheless, Annie believed that, for once, she had some odds on her side.

"All those clothes?" she asked as a diversion.

"Mine," Sam said.

"Don't you need them?" Annie asked.

"I have others," he replied with the slight inadvertence of the rich when confronted with an example of their wealth. He took out a second robe for himself.

"If I stay, you have to agree to one thing," Annie said.

His crooked smile appeared. "Anything."

"If you ever want me to go, tell me right off."

"If it happens, I'll tell you," he said, then kissed her. "Come on, there ought to be some coffee in there."

Sitting at the kitchen table, they held hands and spoke of their previous meetings, until Sam brought up the present.

"Annie, I didn't know this would happen, but I know what I'm doing here," he said. "I really want this. I've thought about you so damn much since the Belmont." He offered the explanation seriously; then he laughed.

"I loved you for grabbing the cup from Sturdevant. He's such an ass! You know what happened? My father insisted that I write the son of a bitch an apology for any embarrassment caused 'by an uninvited acquaintance of ours.' Sturdevant and he are fellow stewards of the Jockey Club, and one steward does not embarrass another steward . . . all that horseshit."

Again Sam's imitation of his father's superior tone was exact. "So I wrote the damn fool, but I used a piece of my wife's pink stationery, which got everybody into a lather, because he dropped it publicly on my father's plate while he was having lunch at the Knickerbocker Club. Within *two hours,* my wife heard about it at the Colony Club, and my mother heard about it at Le Pavillon. Good Christ, can you imagine such a dumb thing being that important, taking that much time out of a day?"

Exasperated, he looked at Annie, wondering whether she understood anything of what he had said. She did, though not the social nuances. What she clearly perceived was his need for some area in his life free of the Cumberland legacy, and her being the one person Sam Cumberland happened to know who might provide it.

She smiled and said, "I know what I'm doing here, too. But you're taking a lot more chances than I am."

Sam nodded, then pulled her up from the table, and in a moment they were in the bedroom. Unlike their earlier urgency, their lovemaking was slow and languorous, with time for discovery. At one point, Annie noticed a deep, crescent-shaped scar on Sam's back, but like so many things that morning, it was something she refrained from asking about. Soon, her pleasure and exhaustion were so heavy and complete, she fell asleep.

When she heard the doorbell ringing, she did not remember where she was, what day it was, or where her clothes were. She jumped out of bed, noticing that she had been covered with a fur blanket.

Annie yelled, "Coming!" She picked up the robe, ran into the living room, and saw her clothes piled on the sofa. Gathering them up, she hurried to the front door.

"Who is it?"

"Um, Winton Sumner. We met briefly last night. I come bearing gifts and a communiqué of thrilling import."

"Will you give me a minute?"

"Centuries, dear Annie."

"I'll unlock the door, but let me get out of here before you come in, all right?"

"I'll count to one."

Annie laughed, turned the bolt, and hurried back to the bedroom to dress. When she returned, she found Winton Sumner in the kitchen, opening a case of champagne, one of four he had stacked in a corner. He was wearing a tailored seersucker suit, a bow tie, and wing-tip shoes. On the kitchen table between the used coffee cups was a vase filled with vivid poppies. The counter was crowded with brown bags of groceries yet to be unpacked.

"Hi," Annie said.

Winton Sumner held a bottle of Veuve Cliquot in his hands and gazed at her with his shattered blue eyes as if appraising a vision. "Ah yes, you're even more lovely than Sam said or I remember. You see, his opinion and my memory are notoriously untrustworthy."

"You're Winnie. You mind people calling you that?"

"It's an egregious nickname, but better than my grandfather's 'Win,' which his horses did always, or my father's sad 'When,' which alas, his never did. I'm the third of their name, and my mother, who nicknamed me, was a raging Anglophile who worshiped Churchill. 'Winnie' fit in very nicely with the horsy metaphor, but much to everyone's chagrin, I'm bored to oblivion by the beasts. May I have a glass of champagne? It's tea time."

"Help yourself. Where'd all this stuff come from?"

Winnie opened a kitchen cabinet and took out two champagne flutes, indicating his familiarity with the place. "Oh, well, that takes us quickly to the communiqué, doesn't it? Sam sends love and other greetings too complex to be entrusted to a mere messenger. Join me?"

"Can't. Haven't had any breakfast."

"Should I cook you some? I'm a Cordon Bleu with soft-boiled eggs."

"Whatever that is, I'm sure you are, but no thanks. Go on with the communiqué."

"One thing I need to know first. When do you have a night off, and could you play hooky for two?"

"The Quarter's dark on Sundays, but I'm not so good at fibbing about being sick."

Winnie nodded, further appraising her, but before a serious moment could descend, he raised his champagne glass. "Well, then, here's to you and Sam and me, which, as a matter of fact, is the beating heart of the matter."

He drank and, carrying the bottle with him, led Annie out of the kitchen into the living room. "Sam called me this morning—much too early by the way; only one o'clock in the afternoon—to tell me about you, quite endlessly. I won't bore you with the ecstatic details. I soon came to realize that he was deeply concerned about discovery, and rightfully so."

" 'Discovery' of what?"

He glittered a smile at her. "I mean the rotten world out there finding out about what seems to be happening to you two. Sam came up with the brilliant suggestion that I act as a diversion, so that we, rather than you and Sam, would attract the gimlet eyes of the social buzzards in their endless search for fresh meat on which to sup." Sipping his champagne, Winnie lifted his eyebrows over the glass in expectation of Annie's reaction.

"You'd want to do that?" she asked without indicating how she felt about the plan.

"Surely," he said, waving a hand idly in the air. "I'd love to see how long we could pull it off, maybe get myself thrown out of the Social Register, although that usually takes a questionable marriage, and I promise you, we won't go quite *that* far." Laughing in his snickering, nasal way, he refilled his champagne glass from the bottle he still held.

"You see, dear Annie, I've just survived unscathed one of the most convoluted plans to get me married that a rapacious mother could invent. Not *my* mother; she's dead. Kacky Mundlapp's mother. The Mundlapps already own Oklahoma, and they bought a big place next to ours in Locust Valley. They've spent enough time and money up here to want terribly to belong, and Mrs. Mundlapp came to believe that marrying Kacky to one of the Sumner boys—I have two brothers—

would envelop all Mundlapps in heritage, history, and New York's nonexistent social hospitality.''

He rose to pace the room, emphasizing his peroration with champagne bottle and glass in whimsical gesticulations. Annie listened, enthralled.

''Kacky was not without charm, but it was enormous charm. Everything about her was big—her hands, her mouth, her shoulders, which could easily drive Y. A. Tittle into the ground. When she walked across her lawn, I could feel the earth shake. When I danced with her, I feared the breath of life being crushed from my body. She proposed making love one night, managing to reveal her *enormous* self in one fast unveiling of what must have been a Gobelin tapestry that covered her. After one look—wide-eyed as you can imagine—I fled, howling, into the night.

''Worse luck, my father happened to start dying. Mrs. Mundlapp took full advantage of the situation and convinced him to make me swear that I'd marry Kacky, which he did, and which I so swore, both of us for no other reason than to let the poor old man die in peace, which he *finally* did. Kacky was at the funeral; black did not diminish her.''

As Annie laughed, he paused to finish drinking his champagne. ''Good Lord, what *happened?*'' she demanded.

''The American dream, my dear. Attending some bowl game on New Year's Day, in which the Oklahoma football team's Sooners were battling for the national title, Kacky's father, being a major Sooner alumnus and benefactor, introduced his vast daughter to the co-captain of the team, a pleasant colossus appropriately nicknamed 'Tractor.' Their love was so instantaneous, he barely could finish the game. After the team's triumph, which Tractor assured by plowing his way to three touchdowns, the two of them vanished for a week. This caused Mrs. Mundlapp to tear out a good portion of her already thinning hair, but her husband, a true Sooner, could hardly object. Tractor, after all, was proclaimed a State god. Soon after her return, Kacky revealed that she was indeed carrying what was perhaps a little pickup truck in her womb, and within moments, she and Tractor were wed, I believe in a dirigible hangar. I wasn't invited to the rite, but as a wedding present I sent them a lifetime subscription to *Trucking News*."

He paused long enough to finish another glass of champagne. "Let's just say, Annie, that as the rejected suitor of Kacky Mundlapp, I might be expected and forgiven a relationship with a Latin Quarter showgirl. In fact, it would do my image a world of good. Besides that, you seem to enjoy my anecdotes, which flatters me beyond comprehension."

"I sure do," Annie said. "But how would it work? For instance, what's planned for my day off?"

Winnie nodded. "Sam told me of your inclination to get to the point like a bat in the darkness. Well, you see, I have a plane, a war-surplus P-38 trainer, one of the few two-seater versions Lockheed ever made. I love it inordinately and must fly it every few days or I begin to molt. How would you like to fly down to Bermuda on Saturday night after your last show? Needless to say, Sam will meet us there on the tarmac, and I'll have you back for your Monday night curtain time."

Annie sat quietly for a moment, unable to adjust to such complex and lavish arrangements, in spite of knowing that Winnie and Sam regarded them as simple pleasures. "What happens between now and then?"

"You and I are seen. You'll be noticed as being as lovely as you are, and laughing at my jokes. I'll appear stricken by your charms and so earnestly attentive that anyone who knows us will regard me with envy, and you with compassion. We'll be seen at lunch at all the pack's watering holes, maybe even Pavillon to beard the Cumberland dragon in her lair, if you like." He snickered in anticipation.

"Winnie, I can't go to those places." Just the idea of being in the same room with Cornelia Cumberland made Annie uncomfortable. "I don't have anything right to wear."

Winnie watched her reaction, again with his brows lifted, the amused mask on his face concealing a perceptive concern. "Annie, I think it's time for us to discuss the true nature of money, don't you?"

Startled by his mention of a problem so complex that she had not yet dared to consider it, Annie replied, "I'd say your idea about money's a lot different than mine."

"Yes, definitely. That's the point. Well, let's just say right out loud that Sam and I are rich as hell and you aren't. Done! We have been for generations. What *you* have to understand is that from our point of view, it's like a family owning a desert, millions of acres of sand. Like most deserts, it keeps getting bigger without anyone's doing much of anything about it. Well, once you have a desert, sand doesn't mean anything. In principle, you don't want anyone to steal your sand, and you might trade off a mound of it to build a castle of rock. But giving a few cups away to someone creates no loss, and certainly has no effect at all on the whole big desert. Do you see what I mean?"

Annie smiled and shrugged. "I suppose, but—"

"Good," Winnie interrupted and poured the last of the champagne into his glass. "Now, dear Annie, when shall we go shopping?"

ELEVEN

IN ORDER TO ESTABLISH Annie's presumed affair with Winnie Sumner, they appeared together at nightclubs and restaurants, gallery openings and charity auctions, events from which they could escape if Annie began to feel uncomfortable. As soon as the gossip columnists discovered such a choice society-and-showgirl item, they besieged the Latin Quarter's stage door, offering Annie payoffs for interviews, bribing their way into the dressing room to take her picture, and following her and Winnie when he picked her up after the show.

The Latin Quarter, delighted with the free publicity, supplied the press with previously taken pictures of Annie in her most revealing costumes and most provocative poses. When the pictures appeared in the papers with the caption "The Showgirl and the Sumner Scion," Annie decided to quit.

By then, Annie had turned down Charlie Dell many times outside the stage door in order to go back to the apartment with Winnie and wait for Sam. Finally, one morning she slipped into the back seat of the Oldsmobile. As usual, Phil was driving, but Annie did not acknowledge him. Teddy Lapps got in, but when he heard the first part of the conversation, he stepped onto the curb again to let Annie out when she was ready.

"Charlie," she said, "I can't go to the track with you anymore. I'm quitting my job, and it's just not going to be so easy . . ."

Charlie was nodding. "Been reading about you in the papers."

Annie looked away, embarrassed. "Yeah."

He smiled affectionately at her. "Don't worry about it, Annie. In my kind of life, you get used to people coming and going. You do what's best for you. But be careful with these rich guys. They work different than most people . . . not that they have to work much at all." He smiled at his own joke, then looked at her as if he already missed her. "If you need any help, you got it. Here's a phone number; they'll always know where I am." He hesitated in order to breathe. "Be happy, Annie. Remember I trust you, and you can always trust me."

"I will, Charlie."

"If something works out, invite me to the wedding. I'll come as a duke."

Annie kissed him and got out without saying a word to Phil Angelo. Exchanging smiles with Teddy Lapps she shook hands with him silently, which suited him fine.

It was strange for Annie to leave the Latin Quarter. The anxiety she felt with Charlie Dell seemed easier than dealing with the world she entered. From her first shopping trip with Winnie, even buying clothes seemed both enticing and oppressive. They went to Bergdorf Goodman to find shoes. Annie tried on about twenty pairs in order to buy one that could be worn for both day and evening. The next day, a dozen pairs were delivered to Sam's apartment. Unknown to Annie, Winnie had instructed the salesman to send along anything for which she had indicated a liking. An entire wardrobe was quickly accumulated in the same fashion.

She admitted that there was nothing like the feel of putting on a dress or suit that had been made for her. At first, intimidated by their sure sense of what she should wear, she let Winnie and the designers decide on material and style. Gradually, she began to assert her own taste, until one day she came out of a dressing room and stood before Winnie in a silk suit she had chosen.

He gazed at her, his fractured blue eyes wide with pride. "Dear Annie, any number of women can buy the best clothes in the world. You can wear them."

"In something as beautiful as this, anyone would look good."

Winnie smiled patiently and said, "I cannot tell you how wrong you are!"

She was pleased by his praise, yet when the suit was delivered, she could barely find room to hang it in either closet, even though Sam had emptied his own. She stared at the long racks of her new opulent apparel, then quickly shut the doors.

"I can't do this anymore, Sam," she said late one morning after Winnie had arranged a delivery of not one, but two fur coats, a seal and a mink. She had sent them back.

Sam laughed. "That's just because it's summer. You'll need them this winter." He was lounging on the bed, wrapped in a towel.

Annie was toweling her hair, standing naked in front of the full-length mirror on her closet door. "That's not what I mean and you know it."

"Just think of it as a Broadway show," he said, watching her. "I'm the producer, Winnie's the director, and you're the star. The part you're playing takes a lot of costumes."

"I knew mistresses were expensive," she said, with no recrimination in her tone, "but you're really going overboard." When she took the towel away, she saw Sam in the mirror standing behind her.

"Is that what you think you are?"

Staring at his reflection, Annie said, "It's my part in the show. We want everyone to think I'm Winnie's mistress. You're just the guy offstage that I love."

It slipped out. Since the affair had begun, neither had made a statement of love. He put his arms around her waist and kissed her shoulder.

"What I feel about you seems a hell of a lot more than love to me. I'm not avoiding the word; I just don't know what it means with us. I've ducked saying so because . . ." He hesitated, unable to explain.

"I know," she said. "Well, it's easier for me to say. I think you're running in a whole lot of traffic. It's just that I've never had so much money thrown at me before, and I'm not sure I'm handling it right."

"Annie, the goddamn money doesn't matter," he said, slightly exasperated.

She turned around and looked up at him, putting her arms around his neck. "It does, Sam." She kissed him. "Money doesn't mean anything to you, but I've worried about it every day of my life. I can't forget about it all of a sudden. It's wonderful living here. All these clothes make me feel like a movie star. But it bothers me that you leave me those envelopes of cash, send all that food and wine, dress me.

"See, I don't *care* how much money you have. To tell you the honest truth, I wish you didn't have so much, because I think my chances would be a whole lot better. It's just that it costs you to keep me, Sam, and I wish to hell it didn't."

He stood on the other side of the bed.

"Annie, I have money that's put in special accounts to spend on whatever I choose. I want nothing more than you, so why not spend it on you? I'm finding myself being happy, which sure as hell justifies the expense. I wouldn't be spending it any differently if we were married."

Startled as she was, Annie saw that Sam was more surprised with what he had said than she was. Marriage was a dangerous subject. Sliding under the covers of the bed, she said, "Then tell me this, Sam. How much money *do* you have? Maybe if I know, I'll understand how unimportant a mink coat is, and I swear that's the only reason I'm asking."

He chuckled as he threw his towel across the room onto a chair and climbed into the bed beside her. On his back, he drew her over to lie on his chest. "No one's *ever* just come out and asked how much money I have, although they've skidded around the question a lot. The problem is, I'd say that there hasn't been a Cumberland for three generations who knew the answer to that."

Annie propped herself up. "You can't be serious."

"It's true. I can tell you the principal in the Cumberland Foundation, two hundred fifty-four million at the moment. I can show you my tax returns, but I have a private accountant who spends his life finding all the loopholes and shifting numbers. There are pass-over trusts that go way back, and just keep growing from generation to generation. Some people put it this way: I'm one of those who live on the interest from the interest on my money. So a mink coat doesn't really *cost* me anything. It's simply something that I can decide someone like you should have; that's all." He rolled over, obviously wishing to be finished with the subject. "If you rub my back, I'll rub yours."

Annie knew that the explanation made perfect sense to Sam. It did not to her, and never would.

"What's this scar here on your shoulder?" she asked as she straddled his back.

"Winnie and I used to play polo together while we were at Princeton. He took a bad fall; knocked him out and his helmet off in the middle of some heavy traffic. I jumped on top of him; got the shit kicked out of me."

"My Lord, that was pretty brave. Probably saved his life."

"I remind Winnie of that all the time."

"I thought he didn't like horses."

"Never did. Took up polo to please his father. After that fall, he never rode again. He started studying bloodlines, tried to get involved in breeding, but got bored."

"He never told me that."

"Ask him about Rosewood Stables sometime. Beautiful farms in Lexington and up in Millbrook, another over in France." He chuckled. "Wants me to buy them from him."

"Well, why don't you, and give them to me? If money doesn't really matter, I'd rather have horses than a mink coat."

He turned to look up at her, laughed when he saw her smile, and pulled her down in his arms. "Better be careful.

They say you can get what you hope for. I know people who own stables who go crazy."

"All I know is," Annie said as she ran her hands slowly down the hard cords of muscles next to his spine, "if I thought we could get away with it, I'd ask you for a groom's job at Caernarvon. I'd rather be doing that than anything."

Sam chuckled again. "You know, we're running Certainty in the Travers Stakes at Saratoga in August."

Annie's hands hesitated, and Sam felt it. "You'll be there, Annie. Winnie and I will work it out."

"Oh, I'm sure of that. He and I'll get up there and hide from all the Cumberlands, until you and I have a chance to sneak off together. What I was thinking about was that I wish I could look after Certainty for that race."

Sam kissed her and said, "Tell me something, Annie. 'Brown' . . . where'd you get that?"

She shook her head. "My real name's Grebauer," she said. "Somebody suggested that Brown sounded better, and I'm not too anxious for my real name to be known."

"Why not?" he asked.

She took a deep breath. "You probably can't understand this, Sam. You have all those generations, going on back to Adam and Eve, for all I know. I have one, and I'm not too proud of it. Except my mother, but she died when I was five. I hardly knew her."

Her throat started to tighten, but she went on. "My father was a drunk. He was the switchman who caused the train crash you all were in. My two brothers were the looters they caught. Remember? In the railroad car, stealing dead people's jewels? They're all in jail. Our shack was about a quarter mile from where the crash was. I left there with the money you gave me that same day. I haven't heard much about them since, which is just fine with me."

Sam stared at her. "You amaze me. You're quite incredible."

"No," she said, "I'm really what your family would call ol' Kentucky white trash."

"Well, if you're going to pigeonhole us, then I'm just a spoiled little rich boy who's nothing more than his trust account. That's horseshit, Annie. Besides, I already *know* you're unique. Winnie says it, too. And so will anyone who gets to know you. So please don't worry about all my generations and I won't worry about the one you have, all right?"

Annie smiled. She liked that word, "unique," and wondered if Sam had used it first, or if Winnie did.

The next day, Winnie took Annie to another cocktail party, this one in a Fifth Avenue apartment high in a building overlooking Central Park. By then, "the Showgirl and the Sumner Scion" was less of an item and more of an accepted social presence. Nevertheless, as they drove across the park, Annie felt the usual nervous knot in her stomach from dreading people's looks and her attempts at talk.

"May I say just once more," Winnie said, "how delightful it is to walk into a room with you?"

"Thank you, sir," she chirped, then laughed. "I feel like I'm diving into a cold pool full of fancy people."

"That's a perfect name for us," he replied, "and being one of the fanciest, I shall gladly guide you through those shark-infested waters."

He already had advised her not only about clothing designers, but about makeup specialists, jewelry ("Your pearls are very good ones, but you have to wear them frequently next to your skin to keep their luster"), hairdressers ("Keep your hair long and simple except for formal occasions; then wear it piled on top of your head. You'll devastate everyone!"), the complexities of manners ("The finger bowl and its doily are *never* used, but lifted up together over to eleven o'clock at your place *before* you take the spoon and fork off to the sides of the serving plate"), the intricacies of family relationships ("Because divorce is becoming so common, no inheritance is guaranteed. Even when a fellow is named for his father, if the father divorces the mother and remarries some luscious thing with six little darlings of her own, the poor namesake may be completely forgotten in his father's will"), and the affection for any kind of title, even ecclesiastical, in a society with no visible rank beyond the economic (" 'Venerable,' the honorific for an Episcopal archdeacon, guarantees a quite ordinary cleric

a place at the best tables; 'Very Reverend,' a dean, gets a cler-
gyman as far as the hostess's left; 'Right Reverend,' a bishop,
propels a man of the cloth to the level considered almost, but
never quite, equal. Such favor, however, doesn't apply to a
similar rank of Baptist, Mormon, or Roman Catholic, if any
are known. And 'Rabbi' is a term from an unknown foreign
language. Of course the whole ecclesiastical lot will eat in the
kitchen if a hostess comes up with some simpering British bar-
onet").

Later that evening, in the Cub Room at the Stork Club,
Winnie taught Annie about the status of seating and the sig-
nals (a tug of his tie, a fingering of his handkerchief), which
the owner, Sherman Billingsly, gave to an underling to indicate favored guests, who would receive gifts of champagne or
perfume. Then, in the early hours at El Morocco, before Sam
joined them, Winnie began to teach Annie how to dance, what
to tip the ladies' room attendant, and when to smile for the
occasional approaching photographer. "You never eagerly invite the picture. It's more as if you recognized the camera as
an old, but not quite a good, friend."

Over the next two weeks, they saw *My Fair Lady* three
times. It was the first play Annie had ever seen. Winnie
adopted the role of Higgins to Annie's Eliza Doolittle. They
learned all the songs and often sang them together. In his
assumed professorial role, Winnie addressed Annie's Kentucky accent, urging her never even to think of altering it. He
did, however, make occasional suggestions about her use of
the English language.

When the affair with Sam started, Annie had not understood
why Winnie went to such trouble to cover for his friend. But
as she learned about the ingrained habits of society, Annie
realized that Winnie's very visible relationship with her relieved him of a great many nuptial pressures.

"Being an extremely desirable social catch," he explained
one day in the Locust Valley lockjaw drawl he used to imitate
the fancy people, "I'm usually the object of innumerable mat-
rimonial strategies. Remember the siege of Kacky Mundlapp!"

They were sitting in the Oak Room Bar at the Plaza, as

usual waiting for Sam. "My avoidance of single women of my own social caste is to evade not only entrapment but boredom! I'm so damn familiar with their conversations that I break out in hives from hearing about one more season in Saint Moritz, or some Bailey's Beach romance at Newport. If you ever *smell* Bailey's Beach, you'll realize how idiotic a romance, much less even swimming there would be. It's absolutely foul! And yet every debutante for the last twenty years goes up to that stagnant tide pool and spreads her charms on that reeking sand hoping to snare some sad social snail!"

He was drinking gimlets as they watched from the cool darkness of the old paneled bar the pedestrians passing by the windows in the sweltering July heat. As Winnie talked, Annie sipped lemonade and watched women in short shorts, poodle cuts, and pop-it beads. Every other man was wearing a pink shirt, the fad of that year. "If the truth were known, dear Annie, this kind of rapacious debutante, after the first blush of her marriage to the social snail has faded, begins to have affairs. I have long been considered irresistible to this particular type of woman. She knows I'm safe and won't try to break up a financial arrangement she has worked so hard to secure. For the same reason, I know she's safe from exuding conjugal urgency. Your presence in my life makes my presence in hers hard to believe if her husband should ever conjecture about it."

He lifted his eyes to look at her for a reaction.

"Well," she said, "I'm glad to know I'm useful to you for something."

He was not sure whether she was irritated or not, and started to say something, but Annie smiled and said, "You've never told me about Rosewood Stables."

Relieved that he had not offended her, Winnie described his deep vexation. "Ah, you mean the cross of Rosewood I bear. Well, dear Annie, on the death of my father, I and my two brothers came into our inheritance, which included a great deal of land in Manhattan and Westchester County. As the eldest son, I grudgingly accepted the burden of the Sumner estate's management. My two brothers had little inclination toward sharing such duties. One is solely interested in fast cars and dropped out of Princeton to drive them. The other is devoted to fast women, and flunked out of the family's alma mater to pursue them. I resent my duty and curse the arbitrary order of our births, particularly because a major obligation of honor is the tradition of the family stable, and its hallowed chartreuse and blood-red silks. Can you imagine a worse combination of colors?''

He finished his gimlet and called for the waiter to replace it. ''My grandfather established the place before the First World War. 'Win' Sumner's Rosewood Stables developed into one of the spiffiest racing operations in the thoroughbred world, with the inevitable stud farm in Kentucky, another up in Millbrook, as well as a quite pleasant French *haras* in Normandy. Between the world wars, Rosewood's thoroughbreds won many of the major races on both sides of the Atlantic. But after my father, 'When' Sumner, took over in the late thirties and lost four Kentucky Derbies in a row, his heart was no longer in the thoroughbred game. The stable dwindled. My father kept it because of family tradition, not to mention the advantageous tax shelter it provided, which is the only reason I keep it.''

''You sounded pretty proud of it there for a minute,'' Annie said.

''For a minute, it was something to be proud of.''

''Could we go see one of the farms sometime?''

''I suppose so. Ah, here's Sam.''

The subject was forgotten as Sam slid into the booth. He had just arrived back from Newport that morning on his weekly business trip.

''I've been sailing around on my cousin's yacht, going crazy thinking of you.''

Annie smiled and squeezed his hand under the table, the one physical indulgence they allowed themselves in public.

''Please save the extravagant praise for later, old man,'' Winnie said, ''when you have her to yourself. What's the plan for the evening?''

''I have to go to dinner with friends of my parents who are in from Spain. I'll call after I get loose. Tell me everything. God, I've missed you . . . *both.*'' As they laughed, Annie was again amazed by how natural it seemed to sit in a bar joking with Sam and Winnie, knowing that it was really completely unnatural.

"Listen, I've had a fantastic idea!" Sam said. "I may have to go over to Deauville to the auctions in August. There's a pedigree line we've been looking for that's in the sale, maybe find some nicks for Certainty. Winnie, you want to bring Annie over?"

"You're absolutely prescient, old man. We were just talking about Rosewood. Would you like to go to Deauville, dear Annie?"

"Where's that?"

"It's on the Normandy coast in France," Winnie explained, "about thirty-five kilometers from Rosewood Stables' *haras*, known as Haras de la Brise, where we could all stay. I ought to look in on the stables, I suppose. God, it's been years. And I need to stock the wine cellar, anyway."

"What about it, Annie?" Sam asked keenly. "We'll go to Paris, too."

Annie tried not to appear flabbergasted and said, "Only if somebody'll tell me what 'nick' is, and somebody'll teach me how to ride a horse."

Sam looked startled. "Ride a . . . I thought you . . ."

Annie smiled. "Grooms don't get up on horses, Sam. And will we get back in time to watch Certainty in the Travers?"

"Yeah, the week before. Carney says he's never seen Certainty look better."

"I'll explain nicks, my one area of horsy expertise," Winnie said. "Sam can give you the riding lessons. Well! Let's have another and drink to France. What a splendid plan!"

That night at Sam's apartment, as they waited for him to call, Winnie drank champagne and talked about nicks. "In any thoroughbred, dear Annie, if there's a particularly advantageous combination of two good pedigree lines, that is known as a nick. It's valuable in the pedigree because doubling a specific quality may produce better than average results. So you try to mesh pedigrees when matching a stallion and broodmare."

"You mean you can control things that carefully?"

"No, not exactly. It's always a gamble, but in breeding you give yourself as many advantages as you can. You see, it's known that the horse, the *Equus caballus*"—he nodded pedantically to her—"is known for its genetic consistency, or prepotency. That means the power with which the parents' dominant genes will imprint hereditary characteristics on their offspring. In the trade, this is known as 'stamping the get.' The thoroughbred game, or business, depending on your bank account, is as much about prepotency as it is about racing."

As Winnie took a sip from his glass, Annie smiled outrageously and said, "Oh, Professor Higgins, why don't you tell me the whole story?"

Winnie snickered. "It's endless. God, the bloodlines I traced back to those three Arabians. Do you know about them?"

"Not enough to matter much."

"All right, Eliza. Well, first of all, since about three thousand B.C., when horses were first domesticated, humans have used the animal's incredible genetic consistency to breed them to various human needs, from war horse to children's ponies. There are about two hundred fixed breeds today, but in 1750, there was no thoroughbred. None. The thoroughbred breed came into being largely because of several English kings, Charles the Second, mainly—which makes every American owner feel thrillingly close to royalty. Of course they overlook what a dissolute reprobate he was, largely because of what he did for the breed, a rationale that bends the admissions policy of most of the world's jockey clubs. But Annie, the degenerate King knew the importance of bloodlines, and for that, I drink his health."

As Winnie toasted, Annie realized that she had never seen him so invigorated by a subject. "So what happened?" she asked.

He hesitated, then stood up and began to pace, his eyes glittering more than usual as he warmed to the subject.

"Well, the old rogue knew about Arabians. You see, there were a lot of horses in England at the time, including some good Arabian stock. This caught the King's attention; Arabians were known for quality, courage, stamina, and speed.

Even then, when Arabian blood was mixed with that of any other breed, it brought about an improvement in the quality of the resulting progeny. Incredible hereditary power, probably because of the Arabian's antiquity as a breed. For instance, a guy named El Kalbi, an eighth-century historian, traced Arabian pedigrees back to the great-great-great grandson of Noah. Then Mohammed came along and wrote that every grain of barley given to a horse would be entered in the register of good works. For centuries, Arabian pedigrees were controlled and handed down ceremoniously by word of mouth. The Arabian horse, therefore, was considered the most prepotent breed of a prepotent species." He stopped suddenly and turned to Annie. "Now, Eliza, what was the name of the eighth-century historian?"

"El Kalbi, Professor."

"Brilliant! Well, His Majesty sent his Master of Horse to the Levant to buy Arab stallions. He established a stud for what were called the Royal Mares, which gave rise to a great deal of badinage about the Royal Mistresses, of which there were almost as many. As a result, everyone was looking for good Arabian bloodstock. And it came to pass that three stallions arrived in Great Britain which established the thoroughbred breed. Now remember these, Eliza, and you can make endless conversation at any Turf Club about them: the Byerly Turk, taken as a spoil of war by a certain Captain Byerly in 1686, when he participated in one Turkish war or another; the Darley Arabian, traded for a rifle in Aleppo in 1703 by Thomas Darley, the English consul in Syria; and the Godolphin Arabian. No one knows where he came from. Supposedly he was discovered pulling a water cart in Paris, was imported, and eventually sold to Lord Godolphin's stud in 1730 as a teaser."

He glanced at Annie to see if she knew what he meant by the term. She shrugged that she did not.

"A teaser, dear Annie, is that unfortunate stallion with an inferior pedigree used in the breeding shed to arouse a mare so that she will be prepared for the primary stallion's advance. The Godolphin Arabian is said to have resented his role, fought off the established stallion for a mare, and covered her himself. For that, I drink his health."

Impressed, Annie said, "Winnie, you really know this stuff."

"Yes, I do—an attempt to please my father, or, since he'd lost interest by then, to irritate him. I've never known which."

"But if you know all of that, why don't you . . . ?" Seeing the irritated expression on his face, she did not finish the question.

"I suppose because the theory intrigues me," he replied, "or used to, but the actual practice is a big bore. I've been trying to get rid of Rosewood for years. I keep talking to Sam about buying it, feeling that my progenitors won't haunt me if a friend takes it over. But Caernarvon certainly doesn't need any more real estate. So I keep it and brood over it. I'm not quite able to put it up for public sale, God knows why." He drank some champagne.

Annie sat quietly, hoping he would go on. "Why brood?" she asked.

"Well, because of the *shame* I'm supposed to feel," he continued, "never to be expressed but definitely expected of me, of a family stable going bad. My father suffered a good deal of guilt because Rosewood meant so much to *his* father. I really don't care. But racing people look on it as a failure of blood, of will, a withering of family prestige similar to what happens when you commit treason or inbreed to idiocy. God, I hate it. What if I just give the whole damn thing to you, Annie?"

The phone rang as Winnie laughed. Annie turned to the table beside her to answer, but before she did, she said, "If you gave it to me, I'd make it something you'd be proud of for another minute." She smiled, then picked up the phone.

"Hello?"

"Hello, my darling," Sam said. "I'm here at El M. Come dance with me. Bring Winnie, and then we'll work out what we'll do later."

In the cab, she and Winnie talked about the plan for their trip to France, and whether or not to go to the theater the following Tuesday. Annie, however, was still reacting to his offhand proposal. Winnie had a stable he did not want, which

Annie knew she could not begin to run. And yet the idea distracted her enough so that she did not pay attention to what Winnie was saying, making him joke about what he thought was her eagerness to see Sam.

As the cab pulled up in front of El Morocco, Annie saw Sam in front of the entrance. The doorman opened the door; Sam hurried to meet them. She stood on the curb, smiling as he approached, when suddenly Winnie jumped from the cab between them and put his arm around Annie. He smiled broadly, looking pointedly behind Sam.

Belinda Cumberland was walking with two other couples to the club's entrance and, at that moment, saw them. Annie froze as the entire group melded together for cheek kisses. "What a surprise! What are you doing here?" Winnie guided Annie with a firm arm through some quick introductions. One man said, "Come join us, Winnie," to which he quickly replied, "Can't, old man; we're just on our way." As she shook hands with others, Annie heard Sam say, "How did you get down? I thought you were . . ." And Belinda said, "Phyllis called and Charlie Neal was flying down in his seaplane, so I decided to come along. Introduce me to Winnie's girlfriend." Annie tried not to turn, but Sam said, "Winnie . . ." and Winnie turned to Belinda. "Dear Belinda, what are you doing out on the streets with people like these? May I introduce Annie Brown? Belinda Cumberland."

Belinda did not offer a hand or a smile, only a curious perusal.

"Hello," she said. "You're much prettier than your pictures."

Annie said, "Hello, Belinda. Thank you."

Then Belinda noticed Annie's pearls. She cocked her head, a curious look of remembering on her face, which changed abruptly to brow-lifted suspicion. Then, eyes glittering with understanding, her gaze passed from Sam to Winnie, then back to Annie. "No, you don't look like your pictures at all. Shall we go in, darling?" Belinda said as she smiled at her husband.

"Taxi!" Winnie called to El Morocco's doorman, who hailed a cab from the waiting line. It drove up and Annie got in as Winnie called back witty goodbyes to the group going into the club. Sam was watching but turned without a sign and followed Belinda.

"She knows!" Annie said, her voice hollow with alarm.

"What are you talking about?" Winnie said, surprised. "I thought we got out of there as gracefully as a ballet exit."

"Belinda saw me at Belmont once. She recognized me tonight. I saw it in her face. Oh, Lord, I didn't want to meet her."

"Why does it matter? She's known about you staying at Sam's apartment, that I met you with Sam that night at the Latin Quarter."

"She hasn't known I'm the same girl who rescued Certainty and—"

"But dear Annie, that's easily explained. Sam simply says that he recognized you at the Latin Quarter and pointed you out to me. He can take care of himself, believe me."

"Women know things, Winnie. Explaining doesn't hide them." Annie grimaced, squeezing her eyes shut. "Besides that, we just stopped play acting and became liars."

"Stop it, dear Annie," Winnie said kindly. "There's no need at all for sackcloth and ashes. You're giving Belinda more credit than she deserves."

"Don't say anything bad about her, okay?"

They rode back to the apartment building in silence, and Winnie said good night at the front door. "Don't *worry,* dear," he said.

Sam said the same thing on the phone the next day. "She didn't bat an eye, Annie. Didn't ask about you, didn't say anything when the others talked about you and Winnie. You should have heard them, wondering if you two are going to get *married,* for Christ's sake. Darling, I'm so sorry it happened. It won't happen again, I promise you."

Annie did not respond for a moment. "She didn't even ask if I was the girl she'd seen at Belmont? Or if my pearls were real?"

Sam hesitated, then said, "No. She didn't."

Annie heard a brief pause and made her point. "She recognized me, Sam. If she hadn't figured out about us, she would have at least asked about my being the one at Belmont. She'll use it whenever she wants."

"Then let her. You don't know Belinda, Annie. She has what she wants and isn't about to do anything to hurt herself."

There was silence. "When will I see you?" Annie asked.

"Not today. I'm sorry. Charlie Neal is flying us back to Newport. Not going with them would be pretty obvious." He cleared his throat. "Look, Annie, I'll see you next week. And remember our trip. We'll make up for all this in France."

She closed her eyes, and relieved him by changing the subject. "Don't I need a passport?"

"Good Christ! You sure do. Ask Winnie to help you. I love you, Annie." Then he hung up—hurriedly, Annie thought. Sam was not used to turmoil. She wondered how he would handle it when it came.

TWELVE

IN SPITE OF WINNIE'S DISDAIN for the family stables, the Haras de la Brise, owned by Rosewood, provided the three conspirators with their happiest time together. The *haras'* fifteenth-century château was situated on a rise, surrounded by apple groves heavy with fruit. Ancient lilac bushes formed hedges leading down to the stone stables, beside which a deep stream cut through the rich Normandy soil. The Château de la Brise itself was modest, with twenty rooms, a mansard roof with dormer windows, two rounded turrets at each end, and four French windows arranged symmetrically on each side of the massively jambed and corniced front door. Inside were echoing stone hallways and a creaking wooden staircase with shaky balusters and steep risers. The rooms had huge fireplaces, enormous old armoires with intricately carved door panels, and in Sam and Annie's room, an ancient recamier and a large feather bed enclosed with tapestries.

Winnie supervised the cooking by an attractive, opinionated Frenchwoman from the local village whom he had known most of his life. With her expert advice, he went about restocking the château's wine cellar. In spite of his presumed purpose of checking on his bloodstock, he did not go down to the stables once, but spoke with his farm managers in the drawing room of the château.

From the moment she arrived, Annie was elated. Aside from finally learning to ride, she was able, as never before to spend time openly with Sam. Each morning, they went to the stables and saddled a pair of thoroughbreds chosen from the forty stalls. They rode on the several miles of soft sand tracks, called "gallops," that ran over the *haras'* five hundred hectares, then went out through the rich grass fields of the surrounding countryside.

"Go with your horse! Feel *her* move!" Sam yelled as he and Annie cantered in company down one of the gallops. *"Right!* Don't get rigid; you're a piece of her spine!" Sam rode a sixteen-hand horse and looked as if he had taken root there.

"That's terrific, Annie! You're *very good!* Okay, that's enough." Annie eased back on her reins, as filled with pride at his praise as a schoolgirl. As her mare slowed to a trot, Annie posted gracefully up and down in her saddle until they settled into a walk.

Sam had been watching. "Proud of yourself?"

"Damn right!" Annie replied.

"I think you're a natural."

"And I think you're a big flatterer, but I love it."

"I mean it. You look as if you've been on horses all your life."

"Don't I wish," she said as she patted the neck of her mare. "Then I wouldn't be this sore. Oh, Lord, I love this!" He laughed with her. "Do you, Sam? Did you always love horses, or did it just happen because of what you had to do with Caernarvon?"

He did not answer right away, thinking about her question. Then he shrugged. "Chicken-or-egg time; I don't know which came first. I knew I'd be running Caernarvon before I knew much about anything else, that's for sure. I also had a better chance than most to be around horses. Once you're close to them for any length of time, you can't help realizing how"— he searched for a description—"how really *grand* they are. You start to understand that they have something we've lost . . . that their 'heart,' or courage, whatever you want to call it, has none of the complications or shades that bravery and heroism always have in humans. With a good horse, what you call character is as simple and honest as anything God ever created. When you see it, you realize how pompous human beings get about most things." He laughed at himself. "I'll try to show you what I mean tomorrow at Deauville. I found a terrific colt in the sales catalogue."

They could see the château to the west on the horizon.

"Want to head back?" he asked.

Annie was moved by what he had said. "No! This is too damn perfect."

"Winnie's preparing a special lunch."

Annie laughed. "Don't worry; he and Madame Brunot won't mind if we don't show up all day. I just want to keep riding. Sam, this is the best place in the world."

She said it with such conclusiveness that he smiled and took her hand.

"You're just in love," he said.

"That, too."

He leaned over from his saddle and they kissed until the motion of the horses forced them apart.

"I agree with you," Sam said, looking westward over the endless fields that eventually led to the sea. "Great place to live, to love, to eat, to raise horses. What else is there?" He smiled wistfully. "We're two hours from Paris, Deauville is down the road, terrific racing in August, and one of the best horse auctions in the world. What could be better?"

"Then how come you don't buy Rosewood, sell off the farms back home, and hire me to run this place?" Surprising herself with the suggestion, she dared to mean it.

Sam laughed. "You could do it, too."

"Damn right I could; then you'd have to come over here once a week. That's all the time I could spare you. Really, if it's so great over here, how come you don't get Caernarvon to buy it?"

"We already own a stud at Newmarket in England and one in Ireland. We ship to stakes races all over Europe. Besides, who the hell wants to learn French?"

"I wouldn't mind, after I get English down."

Sam smiled, reached over, and touched her cheek. "Never change, Annie."

"I doubt if I could even if I tried. I just wouldn't mind talking right."

"Tell me you love me," he said.

"I love you, Sam."

"Sounds like you talk pretty good to me," he drawled, and leaned over to kiss her again.

The next morning, they drove their rented Peugeot to the auction ring at Deauville. Across the street from the race track, the Hippodrome de la Touques, the pavilion was filled with bidders by the time the trio arrived. Seated around a small sawdust-covered arena overseen by the auctioneer's pedestal, the buyers bid silently, their raises called up to the auctioneer by a number of bid spotters scattered around the ring. Above the auctioneer was a board of electrical lights, which changed to show the amount of the bid.

Sam was met by a French bloodstock agent who would do the bidding and, if successful, arrange the colt's transfer to Caernarvon's stud in Ireland. As they discussed details, Winnie, who had been studying the auction catalogue in the back seat on the way to Deauville, said, "The colt in the ring now is from the Nasrullah line. He'd match nicely with a couple of Rosewood's broodmares in Kentucky."

"That's a lot of nicks, right?"

"Might be," he said, pleased with the results of his teaching. "Buy him."

"No!"

"Go on, Winnie," she said, laughing, and then turned around and raised her hand. Her bid was immediately accepted by the auctioneer, who saw it without the aid of his spotter.

"Annie, no. The colt's conformation isn't right."

Another bid was accepted, and Winnie snickered at her impetuosity. "Nicks are a big gamble and are only part of the reason to buy a horse, dear Annie."

"What's conformation, Winnie? I've heard that word ever since I was a hotwalker and never did understand it."

"Simply put, it's the way a horse is put together. It's as important as pedigree when you make your choice, if not more so. There are a thousand rules as to how a horse should look, and just about every great horse breaks them one way or another. They say that the good-looking horse usually can't run. But you don't want to buy a horse with obvious problems just to see if you can get him over them. That colt's withers aren't well defined, which could mean he won't develop a good length of shoulder muscle, and the shoulder makes a strong runner. Why is he like that? Who knows? Somewhere along the pedigree line, the weakness was introduced, and weakness can be stamped on the get just the way a virtue is. That's why breeding is so . . . Good gracious, Annie." He laughed briefly and looked away. "I seem to be showing off for you."

"Well, go on and do it," she said. "If you don't, I'll start waving my hands around again."

He smiled at Annie; for the first time, he seemed rather shy, as if he had been asked to sing a solo. "Well, you remember the three foundation stallions of the breed I told you about?"

"Yeah, the Byerly Turk, the Darley and Godolphin Arabians," she said proudly.

"Yes," he said, pleased again. "Well, none of them ever raced. They proved themselves only generations later, when their progenies excelled on the track and were traced back to those three. By then, some people had started *The General Stud Book,* which ever since has kept records of the thoroughbred breed. The Darley Arabian was the progenitor of a colt born in 1764, the year of a solar eclipse, which gave him his name. Eclipse was never beaten in eighteen races, sired more than three hundred winners himself, and began the line from which ninety percent of today's top thoroughbreds descend."

Sam slipped into his chair beside them. "Well, we're ready for anything," he stated. "We just hope—"

"Wait, Sam, Winnie's explaining something."

"It's not important," Winnie said, opening the sales catalogue.

"Yes, it is. I want to know about this."

Winnie glanced uneasily at Sam, but Sam nodded encouragingly.

"Well, what a lot of people forget is that Eclipse was only fourteen and a half hands, and the kinds of races they ran in his day were between two and twelve *miles* long. Often, there were several heats in one day. Jockeys weren't thought of in terms of size or weight, so the horse might carry a hundred and seventy pounds. To do all that, a horse had to be fully grown, five or older. But keeping a horse in training for five years was a long time for a return of an investment. In the sport of kings, even the kings are interested in money. So races became shorter, and the runners younger. In a hundred-year blink of the evolutionary eye, the breeders developed the average thoroughbred from fourteen to sixteen hands high, and increased their speed over shorter race distances by twelve miles an hour. By 1850, the breed was fixed, and since then there's been relatively little increase in its size and speed. So what we're looking for here today is some kind of infinitesimal advantage, impossible even to hope for. But if you find it, you live with a miracle in your life."

Annie and Sam were held by Winnie's intensity until he glanced at them, snickered, and waved away the serious mood. "Please buy your horse, Sam, so that we can go to lunch."

Sam's agent bid for the colt soon after, and got him for forty thousand francs less than Sam thought he would have to pay. The trio walked from the auction ring through Deauville to Cyro's, a brasserie overlooking the beach and the English Channel. They ate Normandy crepes and drank Calvados. After a hazy, laughter-filled walk along the boardwalk known as the Planches, they went back to watch several races at the Hippodrome. It was a beautiful grass track with relatively small stands; geraniums grew around lawns filled with picnickers.

"Good Lord!" Annie exclaimed when a race started. "They're running the wrong way."

"Just about everything's different in Europe except the animal," Sam said with admiration. "They run clockwise; there's no backstretch, because the horses are shipped in from their farms on the day of the race; stalls are called boxes—oh, and this'll interest you, Annie. The grooms are called lads, and they do everything that hotwalkers and exercise riders do: ride them in the works and walk them out, as well as groom them."

"I'd love that," she said.

"And they race only on grass. Europeans look on us as barbarians for running on dirt. They say it's too hard on the horses' ankles, and compared to grass, they're right."

"I've never thought of it," Annie said. "Why do we have dirt instead?"

Sam pointed to a group of men walking along the grass track, each with a long tool used to replace turf kicked up in the previous race. "See those guys? They're the *reboucheurs des trous,* and they keep the turf in the best condition they can. In spite of them, a grass track won't hold up, especially if you have a week of rain. So European meets don't last very long. Deauville even has a second grass track to give the turf here a chance to recover. But on a dirt track, you can run every day of the year, if you have to."

"Is it really harder on the horse?" Annie asked.

Sam shrugged and smiled. "Depends on which horse you talk to."

After their day at Deauville, the rest of the visit was too hurried. They hurried back to Haras de la Brise, hurried to pack, hurried the next day to Paris, hurried to check into their hotel. It rained, and while Winnie visited a tailor, Sam quickly walked Annie around the city. She was appropriately overwhelmed by its beauty. The inclement weather kept people inside, giving her the feeling that she and Sam had the boulevards mostly to themselves.

He showed her favorite places he had known since he was a boy: a house on the edge of the Bois de Boulogne that the Cumberlands had owned for a time, Napoleon's tower monument in the center of Place Vendôme, which Sam had climbed with binoculars to spy into the windows of the Ritz Hotel, a restaurant off the Boulevard Saint Germain, where he had tasted his first bottle of Château Petrus.

"There's so damn much in the world I want to show you, Annie."

"I'd be happy seeing one tenth of what you've seen. It seems like you have to start traveling and getting culture and all that stuff when you're real young, about your kids' age."

"Hell, it starts earlier than that. My father took me riding when I was three months old, held me on his saddle when he rode in Central Park. When my mother was pregnant with me, she changed her seats at the Philharmonic from our box to the front row so that I could start appreciating music in the womb."

"Did it work?"

"Hell, no. I can't carry a tune. But that's how complicated upbringing can get."

"Do you and Belinda do things like that?"

As they walked along the Quai Voltaire, each with a hand holding the umbrella, Sam glanced at Annie, acknowledging the previously unspoken subject.

"Yes, I suppose we do, for continuity's sake. Barky was on a horse within his first three months, and of course started sneezing right away from his allergy. My God, I hope he grows out of that. Alycia, well, it's too early to tell, although she holds on pretty well when she rides with her mother."

They walked silently for a while. Sam was deciding whether or not to go on with the subject, which he did with an edge of irritation.

"Belinda's a good horsewoman, really knows what she's doing in a show ring. All that pretty running and jumping over those neat little white logs and plastic hedges doesn't much interest me, but I can't help admiring her. She's up every goddamn morning at six to drive out to some Austrian Nazi's riding academy in New Jersey . . ."

"What happens to the kids?" Annie asked as idly as she could.

"Oh, hell, she packs Alycia along with the nanny and leaves Barky with the maid. Except on weekends in town. Then she has a horse brought over from the stable across the park. If we're in the country, she barely gets up to the house, she's in the saddle or the barn so much."

"I'd probably do the same if I had the chance."

He shook his head cheerlessly. "She's trying to be a champion rider, something she probably can't be. She refuses to consider the possibility that she might not make it. It's a little crazy and it's getting worse. She'd take her goddamn horses into church if she had a chance."

Uncomfortable with the subject of Belinda, Annie said, "From what I've heard, the Cumberlands go to church a lot."

"That's different," Sam responded with an edge.

"How?"

"We go to church because it's part of who we are. My great-grandfather paid for the north transept of Saint Luke's. It's expected. They depend on us." He hesitated, unhappy with his reasons. "You do it for other people, for . . ." He did not go on.

"For continuity's sake?" she said, trying for the humor of the repeated phrase.

Sam glared at her. "That, too." When he saw Annie's vulnerable reaction, he frowned at himself and shook his head with regret. "Sorry."

They reached the Quai de Montebello across the Seine from Notre Dame. Automatically, they stopped and gazed at the view, but neither paid much attention.

"I guess you wonder where you fit in to all this continuity," Sam said.

"Not much anymore," Annie replied, "because I already know the answer. I don't."

They stared at the crowds of people in front of Notre Dame. Sam said nothing to counter what she said. He turned to Annie, suddenly smiling his crooked smile, laughing at himself. "How often has a married man fallen in love with another woman and brought her to Paris to walk along the banks of the Seine, for Christ's sake, to explain why his marriage doesn't work?" Then he scowled, disgusted with himself.

"Good a place as any," Annie said, "and better than most."

"Well, it *doesn't* work. We got married for a lot of wrong

reasons—parents, familiarity— God, I'd known Belinda since she was born. It was easy, and obvious, and it was time. The two families . . . *fit*. We *pleased* everyone." He watched the river, then shook his head. "So we're in it. We've both finally realized we're in a trap. We have two children; we both love them a lot. We perform the Cumberland duties, and we look so damn good together. I suppose that we respect each other somehow. But we sure as hell don't like each other much."

Sam put his arm around Annie, leaned down, and kissed her.

"I know how selfish this is," he said. "I've never loved anyone like this. I didn't know it was possible and I don't know how to deal with it. I want this, and I'm damned if I see any reason not to have it. I just wish we'd found each other earlier, before my life got so crowded with all this . . . this continuity."

Annie said, "That probably would've had to be before your momma and daddy stamped their get into you."

"Probably."

"Well, I'm not sure you have it right about Belinda. I don't know her. But whatever, you don't have to worry about me. I have no right to you. You're another woman's husband, the father of her kids, and your life was packed tighter than an egg before we ever saw each other. *I* was selfish enough to want in on it. I'm taking what I can get, which is more than I ever expected." She turned to look up at him under the umbrella, and several drops of rain fell on her face. "It's just that after having you all to myself this past week, it's hell giving you back."

She was not crying, but Sam thought she was.

"Don't cry."

"I'm not, but it's allowed, isn't it?"

"Yes, but once you start, it cracks your strength."

"Sounds like what Cumberland daddies tell their kids when they fall off a horse."

Sam smiled. "It is."

"Don't worry, I usually wait till I'm alone."

He smiled, but his frustration showed. Restlessly, they

started walking again, crossing the Pont au Double to the Île de la Cité.

"So if I feel this way," Sam continued, "why don't I break loose and do what I want? Believe me, Annie, I ask myself that every time I leave you. And the answer's always the same: it never works. I've known guys who said to hell with everything—wife, children, family, inheritance—and run off to do what was 'real.' Just about every damn one of them finds some pretty girl to marry, and uses her to shock his family and friends." He stopped walking and turned to face Annie. "That's not who I am, and that's not who you are." He kissed her gently before continuing to stroll.

"I've known several guys," he went on, "who got through it, but it usually took three or four marriages and a lot of trampled kids along the way. By the time the poor bastards worked it out, they were exhausted and more sick of themselves than happy."

The rain had stopped, and Sam folded the umbrella.

"I'm happy now," Annie said, smiling up at him.

"So am I," Sam agreed, taking her arm in his as they walked up the Quai des Orfèvres to the Pont Neuf.

That night, they dressed up. Just before they met Winnie, Sam presented Annie with a sapphire-and-diamond bracelet. He did not allow her time to thank him, only to put it on. Winnie joined them and, the rain having stopped, they strolled from the Ritz to Lucas-Carton, the red plush *belle époque* restaurant, which glowed across from the Madeleine. Annie was so self-conscious about the bracelet that she kept breaking into nervous laughter every time she spotted the glitter on her wrist. They ate, drank, and laughed enough to avoid thinking about the next day.

Later, when they were alone in their suite, Annie stood at the window, looking out on the Place Vendôme. Sam poured champagne into two flutes and handed her one. "What are we worrying about?" he asked.

She hesitated, then said, "How long we can get away with this, and what'll happen when it's over." Sam gazed at her, then nodded. "If we've pulled it off this long, it'll last as long as we can stand it. When it's over, you and I will find another way. I love you, Annie . . . Here's to Certainty." He held up his glass. "I'll see you Friday night at the Travers Ball."

What he said was close to what she wanted, as close as she could hope for. Annie raised her glass and they sipped champagne.

The next day at the Orly airport, Sam saw Annie and Winnie off on their plane back to New York. His plane left an hour later. Annie watched him standing at the gate. As the plane taxied away, he did not wave. When the aircraft turned and Annie could not see him anymore, she sat back and stared dully at the bulkhead at the front of the compartment.

"Oh, Lord, Winnie, how are we going to go back to play acting after this?"

He took her hand and held it. "They say the show must go on, but in this case, only as long as you want it to." Annie did not respond, so Winnie continued. "Not to extend the metaphor to oblivion, but if you say the word, I'll gladly pull the curtain, although, I must say, I'm troubled when I think what it will be like after the curtain falls."

Annie looked at him, surprised by his similar concern. He barely turned to her, his brows raised appraisingly over his blue shattered eyes. "I have a friend who's an actor," he went on as the plane trundled to the end of the runway. "A very good actor, as a matter of fact. He told me once that the danger of having a long run in a play was that the original creative joy of rehearsals and the early performances is deadened by repetition. Maybe we're experiencing something like that. What do you think?"

Annie only shook her head. "Keep talking, Winnie. I just don't want to think about seeing Sam with Belinda at the Travers Ball."

As the plane took off and gained altitude, Winnie continued to hold Annie's hand.

"Annie," he said and looked at her very seriously, "I *have* to tell you something." Then he sighed and seemed to change his mind. "About Belinda."

"I don't care about Belinda," Annie said. "I just hate her knowing that I'm sneaking around with her husband."

"I understand that," Winnie said. "But you should realize

that your involvement probably doesn't cause Belinda one iota of concern. A loose braid in the mane of one of her show horses would produce greater alarm. You see, dear Annie, Belinda is one of those Southern women raised on pasteurized magnolia sap and honeyed manners. One basic purpose is bred into the marrow of their bones—to give a man exactly what he wants in order to get exactly what she was raised to have. Southern mothers baste their daughters' brains with manipulation. Once their goal is accomplished, the man becomes a secondary consideration. Belinda is, at the moment, armed with the future that giving birth to two Cumberland children guarantees. She's now free to drive herself to a frenzy with her onerous ambition to become a champion show rider. From what I hear, she's not quite good enough, but her attempt, believe me, precludes any deep concern on her part about you and Sam."

"I'd sure like it to be as simple as that, Winnie," Annie said. "I just don't like the suspicion. Sam doesn't either. Don't you think the rest of the Cumberlands wonder why you haven't been around their place since you started seeing me?"

Winnie laughed and said, "The Cumberlands take it for granted that since I'm dallying with a showgirl, I would never be so gauche as to bring her with me to their social occasions or try to introduce her into society. My friends, on the other hand, are expected to look after me, and Sam is one. The fancy people regard this as a fling, and when it's over, as they are certain it will be, I'll be welcomed back again, as was once the Prodigal Son."

"Winnie—" she began, but a stewardess approached with a menu.

"What is it?" he said.

"I don't want to go to Saratoga and see all those people. There's no point. I'm never going to be like the fancy people. I don't want to be."

"Dear Annie, all that you lack is several hundred layers of the social varnish that makes us shine, but that, of course, often causes us to crack. But don't worry; the point of Saratoga is Sam and, if I'm not mistaken, Certainty. If he wins, he'll probably be the Horse of the Year. That's a good reason to be there. We'll avoid the fancy people as if they were spreading religion."

The next Friday, Winnie flew Annie to Saratoga in his P-38. They were to spend the weekend with Princeton friends of his who had a house there. By then, Annie was beyond caring that she was going to be in the same room with the rest of the Cumberlands for the first time. Standing in her guest room that evening, she snapped the clasp of the sapphire-and-diamond bracelet on her wrist. She thought of the only thing Sam had said to her when she tried to thank him in Paris.

"You don't ever have to thank me for anything, Annie," he said, and meant it. "I'll just sign a check for this. I'll never be able to give you anything close to what you've given me."

The "never" made Annie frown.

Walking across the room to the full-length mirror, she looked at herself and shook her head. The outfit was just as much a costume for a production number as what she used to wear at the Latin Quarter, except that the long black taffeta Mainbocher dress covered more skin.

There was a knock on her door. "The chariot awaiteth," Winnie called.

"Come on in," Annie said as she went to get her evening bag from the bed.

"Um, I think not. You come on out."

Annie scowled at herself, certain she would never get the rules right and sick of all of them. As houseguests, in spite of everyone knowing of, and long ago accepting their "relationship," she and Winnie were expected to observe certain proprieties, one of which was to appear to respect the privacy of their separate rooms.

Annie opened the door, and Winnie gazed at her, his usual look of amused assessment giving way to unexpected longing.

"Dear Annie, I could give up breathing, even talking, just to look at you." He stood in the hall in his black tie (". . . or dinner jacket, but *never* call it a tuxedo!").

She smiled back. "I'm ready if you are," she said, her voice giving away her concern.

Winnie recognized her anxiety immediately.

"If you really didn't want anyone to notice you, dear Annie, you shouldn't have made yourself look so ravishing. Come along; if any Cumberland eye isn't blinded by you, I'll spit in it." He offered Annie his arm, which she took as she leaned over to kiss him on the cheek. He pulled away as if she had shocked him. The look on his face was of pained despair.

"What's the matter?" Annie asked, surprised.

At that moment, their host and hostess came out at the opposite end of the hallway, calling greetings and compliments. Winnie reflexively answered in kind. They all went down the stairs and out the front door, where a butler helped them into a limousine (". . . preferably European, maybe a Lincoln or a Packard, but *never* a Cadillac; they're for rentals and undertakers"). Annie sat next to her hostess in the back seat, and Winnie had his Princeton classmate laughing on the jump seat. Sensing that something was amiss, Annie watched Winnie, until she began thinking of Sam and Belinda and Cornelia and J. Cardell Cumberland. At least the two children would not be at the ball.

While her hostess chatted amiably about the threatening weather, Annie thought of Paris again. The chauffeur turned on the windshield wipers, causing the hostess to announce that another Travers Stakes would surely be run in the soup. Winnie looked back at Annie and saw the apprehensive look on her face. He reached out to take her hand.

"I've always told you the truth, dear Annie, so I must finally tell you that I've fallen rather desperately in love with you," he said.

Their host and hostess regarded the statement as charming, but it had a devastating effect on Annie. Annie had given Winnie many indications of her own distress, but she had not noticed that Winnie was suffering as well. Remembering his reaction to the kiss she had tried to give him in the hall, she doubted that he had planned to tell her that particular night.

"I'm so sorry," Winnie said in such a profound and unfamiliar tone that their host and hostess were startled into nervous silence. For once, it was up to Annie to distract with words.

"You mean about the rain? Well, don't worry, Winnie. Some of us do a whole lot better running on a sloppy track."

The double entendre was lost on their host and hostess, but it succeeded in making Winnie smile in appreciation.

Held in a cavernous hall formerly used by patrons who took the mineral waters in the famous spa, the Travers Ball was packed to the bricks of the Georgian Revival building. Five hundred couples, including some of the thoroughbred world's most august personages as well as distinguished citizens of Saratoga, feasted and danced to Lester Lanin's Orchestra.

To Annie, it was a perilous place. She saw the Cumberlands' table across the dance floor the moment she sat down. She did not look at it again. Having seen how Belinda looked in a Dior strapless royal blue dress, which set off her emerald necklace, Annie tried not to wonder if Sam had written a check for those jewels as well. Of course he had; she was his wife. Comparing Belinda's jewelry and dress designers with her own made Annie wince.

Their party sat at a table of twelve. All friends of Winnie's, some of whom Annie had met previously, they were as usual courteous and carefully responsive to her. The decibel level in the room was high and reverberated against the thick walls, making it necessary to yell instead of talk. The colors of last year's Travers Stakes winner, black and purple, hung from every sconce and were woven into a crepe-paper tent over the dance floor. Lester Lanin's Orchestra was unremittingly danceable and drew octogenarians and teenagers alike onto the floor. Door prizes were awarded; an auction sold off donated antiques, local artists' horse pictures, and, capriciously, a racing scull.

Annie and Winnie sat together, grimly holding each other's hands under the table, as much in desperation as affection. Both kept smiles on their faces, and responded with increasing detachment to their dinner partners' conversation.

At the moment she turned to tell Winnie that she would not go on with the deception a moment longer, Sam came over to the table. He asked their hostess to dance, and exchanged some Princeton badinage with her husband. Automatically, Winnie joined in, allowing Sam to greet Annie with their long-practiced openness without a hint of intimacy. Annie responded as she always did when meeting Sam in public, with a pleasant but disinterested smile.

They watched Sam dance with their hostess, knowing from long practice that Winnie was expected to cut in on Sam so that Sam could then, with gallant social impunity, ask his friend's showgirl to dance. She started to tell Winnie again, but the man on her other side began a conversation. Winnie dutifully rose and excused his way onto the dance floor. Within moments, Sam returned.

"Care to dance, Annie?"

She stood up and, as usual, preceded him to a place close to the bandstand so that the music would lessen the chances of their being overheard.

As soon as she was in his arms, Sam said in her ear, "I've missed you. I love you."

Annie could not respond, except to hold him tighter.

He went on. "It's not going to work for us tonight; I'm really sorry. As soon as the Travers is over, things'll get back to normal. We've got houseguests coming out of the walls, and . . ."

"Sam, I can't do this anymore. I won't."

He kept dancing, looking off, not surprised, but obviously dejected. Finally he said, "Then we'll have to . . ."

At that moment, Annie saw Belinda, smiling, coming through the crowd on the dance floor, straight for them. When she arrived, she stood looking at Annie until Sam realized she was there. Annie knew immediately that Sam did not know a great deal about his wife. In spite of the permanent smile, her ready-for-battle eyes revealed the iron self-control of instinctual manipulation. Startled, Sam stepped back to make an introduction. Nearby, Winnie danced with their hostess. Seeing the situation, he suddenly looked alarmed.

"Bea, you remember . . . ?" Sam began.

"Oh, hush, Sam, I know exactly who she is. I just wanted to see her again right up close," Belinda said, her Kentucky drawl a hard purr. "What does Sam tell you about me?"

"That he admires you and respects you," Annie said. "But we don't talk about you that much."

Belinda's eyes squinted slightly, and her smile broadened.

"I'm sure you all have better things to talk about," she said, "probably in French. And let me just tell you that I don't care. But I'd as soon have you keep it to yourselves. People talk and I don't want my children ever to hear their daddy's running around with a . . . well, running around." She turned to Sam and said, "Neither does your mother."

Startled, Sam looked over toward the Cumberland table. "Does she know?"

"Course she does, honey. I just told her. She asked me who you were dancing with and I said your mistress . . . for lack of a better term." Still smiling, she turned back toward the table, but Sam grabbed her arm and swung her around. "You bitch," he said loud enough to be heard by several couples nearby.

"You bet, honey," Belinda said, and jerked her arm away from him. Still smiling, she again turned away and made her way through the crowd back to her seat.

Leaving his hostess at their table, Winnie hurried over; the music played on, although several orchestra members and dancers were watching, wide-eyed.

Sam looked dismayed. He turned back to Annie. "You were right. She knew."

"You better go look after your family, Sam," Annie said. "We're finished here."

Sam edged his way through the standing crowd, grown thicker as news of the scene spread across the dance floor.

"I'll take you home, Annie," Winnie offered, taking her arm.

"Dance with me, Winnie."

"What?"

"Come on, dance with me. We'll stay."

As word of the altercation spread, the Cumberlands' guests remained discreetly engrossed in their own conversations as Belinda offered further explanation to Mr. and Mrs. Cumberland, and Sam countered it angrily. Cornelia made one loud remark, which silenced everyone. Then, with a saber-thrust smile, she started a conversation with the man on her right.

Winnie danced with Annie to the other side of the floor, occasionally looking at her with concerned admiration.

"Does Belinda ever stop smiling?" Annie asked.

Winnie snickered and said, "Not even when she falls off her horse."

"It's all over, Winnie."

"I know."

They smiled sadly at each other, and they twirled around the emptying floor, clearly aware that they were the center of the room's attention. Annie glimpsed Cornelia as she carried on her conversation with her dinner companion. She watched Annie with a look of malice that changed to contempt when she met her eyes.

The orchestra segued into a fast-stepping medley from *My Fair Lady*, which Winnie and Annie appreciated and used to full advantage. She leaned on him as he twirled her around.

"You are, dear Annie, a magnificent woman," Winnie said. As they danced, they saw Cornelia Cumberland rise and, acknowledging no one, lead the other three Cumberlands on a circuitous route around the dance floor to the exit. Mr. Cumberland followed her, his eyes raised above everyone's head as usual, implying a consideration of more important matters. Still smiling, Belinda stared straight ahead. Sam followed, visibly furious, but at whom, no one could be sure.

As Annie watched, Winnie said something that she did not hear, because Sam walked out of the hall without looking back at her. She knew he did it purposely, perhaps with difficulty, to avoid giving grist for further speculation. For Annie, the dread of ending was so strong that she wanted to go after him. But she kept dancing.

"What'd you say, Winnie?"

"I said, will you marry me?"

Annie stopped. She gaped at Winnie. He was not smiling, and seemed to be in as much pain as she was. She closed her eyes and hugged him. For a moment, the two of them stood and embraced on the dance floor, eliciting even more comment.

The orchestra started a familiar tune, one of their favorites. They looked hopelessly at each other and began to laugh. Winnie started to sing, and Annie joined him as they danced around the floor again.

THIRTEEN

Dear Sam,

I've never written a letter before, except thank you notes that Winnie taught me to write. I don't believe I can write everything I want to say to you, but I doubt if I would say it any better.

You said in Paris that when this happened, we'd find another way. I believed it then, probably because I needed to so much. But I don't anymore. We'd never be able to have what we want, which is everything. Anything less would be just as painful as last night was, and it would only get worse. Please don't think I love you any less. I probably love you more. We just found each other too late.

Winnie asked me to marry him. I'm going to do it because I can't see any good reason not to. He knows better than anyone about us, so he and I aren't fooling ourselves. We'll leave right after the Travers. I won't be able to congratulate you for Certainty's win.

I'm so sorry, Sam. I love you. Goodbye.

Annie

Winnie hired a car and driver to take Annie and him to the track. They excused themselves from sitting in their host's box for the Travers. Their absence was understood because of the previous night's difficulty. They had their bags loaded into the car, then waited to go until it was time for the sixth race. At the clubhouse entrance, Winnie got out and gave twenty dollars to an usher who said he knew the Cumberlands. His instructions were to deliver Annie's note to Sam by calling him away from the Cumberland box after the Travers Stakes. Then they drove around to the backstretch gate.

Dressed in crisp twill trousers, a sheer white blouse, and a summer jacket, Annie felt exhausted and knew it showed on her face. They stood on a tree-shaded path along the rail among a large group of track employees and their families. Certainty came by on his way to the paddock, led by a groom and accompanied by Frank Carney. Those around Annie took pictures and shouted encouragement to both horse and trainer. Carney, looking shy and uncomfortable in his coat and tie, muttered "Thank you . . . appreciate it" to the ground five feet in front of him. His lanky body moved gracefully with his colt as he reached up nervously to run a hand through his hair.

Then Certainty stopped in the path and looked at the group of people, pulling his groom back and causing Carney to stop. Several of the onlookers laughed, one saying, "That colt's getting so famous, he's looking for the cameras *before* the race." Annie saw that Certainty was looking at her and tossing his head up and down. Carney saw her and nodded. Annie walked over to the colt and let Certainty nuzzle her hand. Carney watched his horse but said, "You sure do turn up in surprising places."

Annie stroked Certainty's cheek, then backed away. "I love this colt. He'll win today. He just told me."

Annie smiled, but Carney looked away. "That's good to know," he said. The colt nickered, then started again toward the paddock. Carney stepped out to keep up with him. He looked back at Annie as if he wanted to say something, then went on.

As she joined Winnie beside the path, Annie said, "He's going to win."

"Cornelia will be so pleased," he replied sarcastically. Annie smiled and took his arm.

They walked over to the rail and waited across from the half-mile pole. The trumpet call to the post was an echo bouncing off the crowded stands. The horses warmed up, then were loaded into the starting gate, and suddenly they were off, the resulting cheer reaching the back rail several seconds later. As Annie and Winnie watched, Certainty came by six lengths back in seventh place. With little anxiety, she saw the jockey ask Certainty by urging him with his hands and showing the whip. The colt moved through the pack and took the lead going around the far turn. From where she stood, Annie's view of the final stretch and finish line was partly blocked by shrubbery and the tote board. A few seconds later, when the booming roar from the stands flowed across the track's infield, Annie glimpsed the Caernarvon silks between the bushes and the tote board. Certainty was in the lead by a length. Annie turned to Winnie and said, "Let's go."

They were driven to the airport, where the driver transferred their bags into the small compartment of the P-38. Winnie helped her into the seat behind his and made sure she was buckled in properly; then he climbed in.

Through the propeller blades, Annie saw a convertible come speeding through the open gate and skid to a stop on the tarmac directly in front of the P-38. Sam jumped out and ran toward the plane. His navy blue tie hung loosely and his linen suit was rumpled.

Winnie turned grimly back to Annie and said, "Let's get it over with." He opened the old fighter's canopy to help her climb down to the ground.

"Well, old man, this is very dramatic," Winnie said, his eyebrows raised in his usual amused expression. Both Sam and Annie knew he was feigning. His face was moist with sweat.

"If you're marrying her for some noble purpose," Sam said, "it won't work, y'know." Annie felt he had practiced the line.

He continued, "We *knew* that sooner or later people would find out about us. So what the hell is this all about?"

Sam's eyes bore into hers. "Annie, come back with me. Right now. We haven't even had a chance. We can find another way. This"—he gestured toward Winnie and the plane without looking at them—"is absurd if not downright farcical."

"It's probably 'absurd' to everybody," Annie said quietly, "except to Winnie and me." She looked at Winnie, whose forlorn smile held on his face.

"Annie!" Sam commanded. "Aren't you even willing to try? You never struck me as the kind who ran away from anything." He stood squarely on both feet, as if ready to fight.

"Don't turn this back on me, Sam," Annie said. "Try what? Another apartment closer to yours so that you could sneak over faster? Waiting for you more and more? Seeing you less because everyone would be watching? Wondering what Belinda suspects or knows?" She heard her own sarcastic drawl as she said Belinda's name. Seeing Sam standing so aggressively, his angular chin jutting out, she felt furious with him.

"Belinda doesn't care!" Sam spat out in exasperation.

"She does!" Annie shot back. "That's only what you'd like to think. I don't know her, but I've seen enough to know that she cares, or she wouldn't be fighting you and enjoying it so much . . ." She hesitated, then said sadly, "Sam, don't you see? There was nowhere for us to go."

His head arched back and he looked at her, pained and suspicious. "Are you asking me to get a divorce?" he asked rigidly.

Annie stared at him. She felt her throat tighten with rage. "I'd *never* ask you that. Don't you dare put those words in my mouth."

His arm snapped out and his hand gripped her wrist. She froze, then said with slow deliberation, "Come on, Winnie. It's time to go."

Winnie stepped forward and said, "Let go of her, Sam."

"You can't do this," Sam said, ignoring him. "I love you, and you still love me. Don't you understand that?"

At that point Winnie grabbed Sam's hand and awkwardly

pried it off Annie's wrist as he said, "We *do* understand, old man. You see, I love her too, *knowing* that she loves you. And as you know, I'm rather fond of you myself." He gave an imitation of his own laugh.

Sam yanked his hand away. "Don't give me any of your glib horseshit, Winnie. You think she'd be running off with you if you were broke? Don't kid yourself."

For a second, the three former conspirators looked helplessly at one another. Abruptly Sam turned and walked toward his car. Annie almost started to follow, but Winnie took her arm firmly and led her back to the plane. As she was climbing back into the cockpit, Sam yelled from his car, "It'll never work! I'll be there. Every day. Every night. You'll come back! You'll—"

The door of the convertible slammed shut. Sam started the motor and Annie heard his tires squeal as he drove away.

"Oh, Lord, Winnie, please hurry up," Annie urged, pressing her forehead against the canopy, trying not to look at the car but then watching. As Winnie turned over the two engines, she saw that Sam had stopped the car on the grass. He was slumped in the front seat, staring at the plane. When the P-38 started to move, Sam started pounding on the steering wheel, his mouth open, yelling. Then the plane taxied to the end of the runway and Annie lost sight of the car until Winnie turned the aircraft to gather speed for takeoff. Annie could see Sam again, now standing beside his car. As the plane became airborne, he raised his arm in a wave. Winnie banked the plane, she lost sight of Sam, and she closed her eyes.

After landing at the Brookhaven airport on Long Island, they went into New York and checked into separate rooms at the Plaza Hotel. The next day, they met movers at Sam's apartment and supervised packing Annie's clothes and belongings, which were sent to Winnie's apartment on Park Avenue. Annie had never seen it, but their awkwardness with each other precluded their staying there. They spoke little, and then only with a grim determination. Winnie offered suggestions, Annie agreed to them, and arrangements were made. Early the next

morning, they returned to Brookhaven and flew to Nassau to
be married after lunch.

The Nassau civil ceremony only added to their sense of
dejection. At the appropriate moment, Winnie produced an
antique ring of rose-cut sapphires surrounded by diamonds set
in a serpentine pattern. He placed it on her finger apologetically, and said, "It belonged to my grandmother. It's French."
Later, when the Honeymoon Suite was enthusiastically suggested by the desk clerk at their waterfront hotel, they instead
took a penthouse with separate bedrooms.

"Now, dear Annie, we are not children," Winnie said, trying to be humorously pontifical as soon as the bellboy left.
"We both know that sex is always a comedown after an airplane ride, and I hate obligatory gestures like wedding night
rites. Besides, I haven't been to a drugstore, have you?"

"I've had a diaphragm for a long time."

"Ah, I see. Well, I guess Sam will be hovering around more
than just the frayed edges of our consciousness."

He smiled, trying hard to ease the situation. They stood at
opposite ends of the suite's strange, overdecorated sitting
room. A pool table was at one end and a baby grand piano at
the other, both painted white with gold leaf. The rest of the
furniture was fake French antique. The August heat was wilt-
ingly humid, and the air conditioning threw an uneven chill
through their clothes, which still stuck to their skin. Winnie's
brows raised resolutely above his grim, shattered eyes.

"This place is about as surreal as the world gets. I'm so
sorry, dear Annie."

"You know, I *do* love you, Winnie," Annie said with all the
conviction she could muster. It was true, but they both knew
the limitations of that truth.

"Of course you do. I know that." He strolled over to her
and took her hand, as he had done so often when she needed
his support. Annie reached out and hugged him but felt a
resistant tightness even as he courteously put his arms half
around her. His body felt thinner than she had remembered.
Then he laughed gently in her ear.

"What?" she asked, still holding him.

"I looked out the window at that corrosive sun out there,

and at all this ludicrous *faux* Louis Sixteenth furniture, and for just a moment I forgot where in the world we are. Decorators are the true devils!" He turned away and continued, "God, this could be a set. That musical about the French Foreign Legion in the Sahara, what was it? The goddamn *Desert Song!*"

"This ain't no musical," Annie said with an embellished twang as she lowered herself into a hard, upholstered chair. She slipped off her shoes and crossed her legs on a fat ottoman, trimmed in gold braid.

"No, most surely not. It's so odd, Annie. Here we are, just married, and I don't have the faintest idea of where we're going to go. How long are we going to stay in Nassau? What to do next? The very thought of—"

"Winnie, I'm too tired to think about it. I want to take a bath and try to get some sleep. Let's just stay here in this strange penthouse until we're ready to go. No itinerary. No grand plan."

Winnie agreed. She went over to him for a good night kiss, but as their eyes met she saw how self-conscious he looked.

Annie tried to tease him. "Winnie, we've *always* kissed each other good night. Just 'cause we're married, we don't have to start shaking hands."

Winnie smacked his hand on his face. "I can't believe myself. Suddenly I'm shy! I've never been shy in my life. Annie, this marriage thing is very tricky."

"I've heard that," she joked, but he remained awkward, unable to play a light scene with her. Finally, they kissed.

"Good night, dear Annie. And let's agree that if either of us can't sleep, we'll meet out here for a game of pool!"

"That's a deal," she said.

Once in the tub, Annie recalled the scene at the airport in Saratoga. What Sam had said made her stomach clench: "You think she'd be running off with you if you were broke?" It was a dirty thing to say. Annie did not think that Sam believed it. He had said it to hurt her and had succeeded.

Willing herself to think of something else, she quietly recited the names of the mares and stallions at the two Rosewood farms. As she slipped on her nightgown, she remembered that Winnie had told her he lost three hundred and fifty thousand dollars a year on the stables. She had been astonished, and told him he had to do something.

As she sat on the side of her bed in the dark, she asked herself if Sam had been right, if she was marrying Winnie for a chance to do something about Rosewood. She realized what a mess the marriage could turn out to be. A nervous sweat began. She thought about Sam's suggesting his own divorce, and how he had tried to make it her idea. But what if he did it on his own? What if he walked away from everything and came looking for her?

Holding her head between her hands, she tried to figure out the real reason she was in a Nassau hotel married to a dear friend instead of the man she loved. She was eighteen years old. She felt as if she had given away the rest of her life.

She and Winnie barely left the penthouse for several days. Meals were ordered in, naps were a daily ritual, and long baths took up as much time as possible. When they did go out, they walked along the waterfront or took a cab to a beach and walked some more. Then they returned to sleep again, in their separate rooms.

As the week passed, they went to several movies and did some sightseeing. At last they were ready to celebrate a little. They found a waterfront dive with a tacky trio playing dated songs. The seafood, however, was good, and they toasted each other with Veuve Cliquot. As they began dancing, the same memory hit them. They looked at each other and knew it.

" 'Seems like old times . . .' " Winnie sang, in spite of what the trio was playing.

"Well, let's not let it seem like that," Annie said, feeling the confidence of champagne. "Lord knows this isn't El Morocco or the Travers Ball, and Sam Cumberland isn't about to walk in here. It's you and me, Winnie, in this raunchy hole in Nassau. And I love you. So *now* what are we going to do?"

Winnie was silent for a moment. Then, with a dry mouth, he said, "I think we should finish this dance and go back to the hotel." He went on, his brows rising to the speculation, "And we could tear our clothes off and see what, if anything, will happen."

Annie laughed. "I'll tear yours off if you'll tear mine."

"All right. Just be careful with your fingernails."

"Let's go now."

"What a good idea."

The champagne mood continued as they walked back to the hotel. "I should warn you," Winnie said, "I have scars and moles, I'm ticklish, and I . . ."

"Is that right? You better warn me about everything."

"Everything? Well, I have a tendency to sneeze . . ."

They crossed the hotel lobby and took the elevator up to the penthouse. Once the door of the suite was closed, Winnie leaned back against it and said, "My God, I feel as if it's the first time!"

"Well, it is, for us."

"Where should we start?" he asked.

"Where do you usually start?"

"How does champagne and a diaphragm sound? I can't believe I said that . . ."

"It sounds fine." Annie laughed.

Winnie went to the bar next to the pool table; Annie went into the bedroom. She slipped out of her shoes and unzipped the back of her dress, then caught her own eyes in the huge framed mirror. Once again, the situation seemed impossible to her. She returned wearing a silky sapphire-colored kimono as the champagne bottle popped and Winnie poured two flutes.

"You know, dear Annie," he said still with his back to her, "when I lost my virginity, I was a very ignorant thirteen. Our gardener's daughter was a very curious sixteen. I'm really too old to go through losing it again, so you must convince me somehow that I really have nothing to lose. I—" Holding the glasses, he turned to find Annie standing completely naked, several steps away. He gasped and comically sank to his knees without spilling a drop.

"Champagne?" he asked.

"Sure," Annie said and sat down beside him to take a glass. She noticed that his hands were shaking.

"You are, simply, amazing. I'm . . . overwhelmed."

"You've seen most of me pretty much like this before, remember? It's your turn, you know."

"To what?"

"To take your clothes off."

He took a long swallow of champagne. "Show business has one wise rule: never try to follow an act like that."

"All right, we can just sit around and drink champagne if you want."

He looked at her, then formally handed her his glass. "Would you be kind enough to hold this a moment?"

Without getting up from the floor, he started to hurry out of his clothes, throwing shoes, shirt, tie, coat, socks, and underwear in all directions. Once naked, he reached casually for his glass. "You see, every act needs comic relief, and I'll drink to that."

He clinked his glass against hers and drank. Annie joined him, then reached up and put her glass on a nearby table. Winnie watched her as he drank, his eyes widening as she slid over next to him and embraced him. He rolled his empty glass away across the rug and put his arms around Annie. Silently they held each other, kissing each other's neck, avoiding each other's eyes. He made several hesitant attempts to touch her breasts, but self-consciously withdrew his hands. Annie tried to position herself to best advantage for him and finally he entered her. They held tight to each other, tensely, silently, both responding hopefully. Winnie gave no indication of his climax, but slowly stopped moving. He lay on her for a while, saying nothing; then he rolled off and sat up. He reached for the empty champagne glass and turned it around in his hands.

Annie did not move, but stared at the ceiling. Slowly she propped herself up on her elbow and then turned to look at Winnie.

He said, "Well, he's certainly right here with us, isn't he?"

"No, he's not."

He smiled sadly. "Let's not ever lie to each other, dear Annie, even about what we think. If we don't want the truth, let's not ask."

"I'm not lying, Winnie. He's not here. I love you."

Leaving the name unsaid, he stood up and started for his bedroom door. "I think it's time to leave Nassau. Why don't we pack and take off tomorrow?"

"Winnie, stop it!" Annie said as she stood up. "We know each other too well for something like this to bother us. We don't have to prove anything tonight."

The look on Winnie's face gave Annie the first glimpse of what a disaster their marriage might be. "Yes, we certainly have time on our side, don't we? Would you mind putting something on?" He picked up her kimono and held it out for her. "I know you're used to running around like that; still . . ."

"Winnie! Don't do this! We both were so nervous about it, we—"

"Don't patronize me, Annie. Ever! Take your robe!"

She did, her mouth open with surprise at his harsh tone.

"I'm so sorry," he said pressing his hand on his forehead. "I'm going to go pack." He went into his room and closed the door. Annie heard a click. He had locked it.

Annie hardly waited a second before trying the door.

"Winnie!"

"Not now, Annie!"

"Then you tell me when!" She went to her own room.

Before dawn, Annie heard Winnie moving around in the sitting room. Quickly, she put on her kimono and went out.

"Dear Annie, can you forgive me?" He came rushing to her and kissed her quickly on the cheek. "I acted imbecilic last night. Did I wake you up?"

"No. And you didn't do anything you need to be sorry about."

"Well, *I* thought so, and I'm truly sorry. Did you pack? I thought we'd have coffee and go on out to the airport. What do you say? I've had a perfectly brilliant idea and I want to try it out on you. It's about Rosewood. Remember how we used to talk and talk *and talk* about it, and you used to say how easy it would be to bring it back, to bring in new bloodlines . . ."

"I never said it would be 'easy.' "

"But it's something you'd like to do, isn't it?"

"If *you* would, sure," she said, trying not to sound too eager.

"Well, I'd like it *done,*" he said.

"Aren't you going to help me?" Annie smiled, feeling their friendship.

"Yes, of course. You've rather stimulated my interest again. Besides, I'll pay for everything. I've heard that's the best help you can get."

"Where will we live?" she asked, beginning to sense the excitement of it.

"That's up to you. We have a choice of Lexington, Millbrook, or Normandy. Of course, I'll have to be in New York a good deal because of family matters."

He watched her. Realizing instantly the separation he was suggesting, Annie wanted to cry out against the idea. But she saw Winnie's fear of what they had done by marrying, and this was his instant remedy. If she hesitated to accept it, they might not have any chance at all.

"Let's go on out to the airport, Winnie," she said brightly. "I don't need coffee."

FOURTEEN

ROSEWOOD FARM in Millbrook, New York, was two hours north of New York City. The distance between the two places became a barrier that Annie never broke. As the months passed, it became only one of the barriers between her and Winnie, who spent more and more time in the city, slipping away with a charming excuse that seldom disguised his deepening despair. Their few moments of genuine happiness occurred when he assumed his role of professor and taught her more about breeding and bloodlines.

The farm, nearly two hundred acres, was situated around two hills; four large streams traversed it, two of them running into a five-acre lake. Paddock fences ran over the level ground, which had been cleared by numerous generations of farmers before the Sumner family bought the land. There were about two dozen broodmares in the barns when Annie arrived, and from her first morning there, she had ridden one or another of them, investigating every acre of Rosewood's property.

The main house, its symmetrical Colonial structure and center chimney built two hundred years earlier, had had two architecturally similar wings added during the Sumner years. It stood on one of the hills, with a view to the west that stretched for miles. Too large even for a couple, when Annie was there alone she felt burdened by its size, even though she had a full staff to look after it. The rooms had wide-board oak floors and were filled with early American antique furniture and Georgian silver, which had been lovingly collected by Winnie's grandmother. He quipped once that everything in the house was original except the people.

During the first year, Annie was alone much of the time. She filled it by gradually taking on the responsibility of overseeing the farm, working in the stables on the horses, and studying bloodlines. The winter was a long one. Winnie used bad weather as an excuse to stay longer in New York. A number of invitations to dinner at neighboring farms arrived at Rosewood, mainly from friends of Winnie's family. Never sure when Winnie would be there, Annie turned them down with the excuse that she and Winnie would be at the other Rosewood Farm, in Lexington. They did fly down to Lexington in the P-38 on several occasions, but it was more for the flying than for the visit, and they always returned quickly.

Tentatively, Annie began to make suggestions about what should be done to improve Rosewood. Winnie gave her a free hand, dropping discussions of the subject as quickly as possible. During the early winter, she arranged to have nearly a dozen of the best Millbrook broodmares bred to a number of stallions standing in New York. Dealing by telephone with Kentucky breeders was more difficult, but the Rosewood broodmares there were of such high quality that she was able to secure for them the services of several first-class stallions.

By the date of their first wedding anniversary in August, Annie had prepared a surprise for Winnie. As he had done for Christmas and her birthday, he would, she knew, give her jewelry, which she never wore. Annie's surprise was Rosewood, what it could be and mean to both of them.

As expected, Winnie arrived in time for dinner and presented her with an antique sapphire bracelet that went nicely with her wedding ring. After telling her about the bracelet's history, and receiving her happy gratitude, he changed the subject. "When do you think you'll want to go down to Lexington again?" he asked idly as he began to cut into his salmon, a dish Annie had prepared, knowing it was a favorite. Not having become used to servants as a constant presence, Annie had given them the night off.

"I don't want to go down to Lexington." She regretted saying so, but she had been uncomfortable in Rosewood House, the old brick-and-pillared plantation, from the first day she walked into it. "But if we're going to finally start doing something about the stable," she suggested, casually, hoping to lead into her surprise, "I figure we ought to go down there for the Keeneland broodmare sales in November."

Winnie chewed for a moment. "You sound . . . confident."

His slightly bitter tone alerted Annie. "What do you mean?"

"I mean, dear Annie, that you seem poised to bring Rosewood Farms back to the forefront of the goddamn thoroughbred world . . . Perfect salmon by the way."

"Wait, Winnie. *I'm* not so ready; *we* are. It's what we decided together; all you've taught me . . ."

"Dear Annie, we mustn't kid ourselves to death. The bank account is open. Do with Rosewood what you will. The truth of the matter is that I really don't care, as long as I don't have to be involved in any way."

"I don't believe that, Winnie," she said. "I remember how excited you were when you taught me about finding bloodlines, and how we—"

"I was happy," he cried out, "because I was having at least one effect on you!" Then, controlling his outburst, he took a long swallow of white wine. "Did it never occur to you, dear Annie, that delving into all those endless pedigrees and plotting out little nicks as if we were planting diamonds also served to drag me back through several sad generations of misplaced family glory? Good God, I learned all that garbage in the hope of getting my father to come alive again. He was so overwhelmed by the failure of his obligation to these goddamn stables, he gave up on everything else, most certainly his sons." He looked apologetically across the table at her. "That's the kind of rationale I've developed in order to understand myself, not that such burning truths make life much easier."

"Winnie, I'm sorry you're hurting so much."

"I know," he said quietly. "And I'm sorry you just happen to be so handy to beat on. One reason it's so difficult to stay out here is that I end up loathing myself for doing that. I often wonder how long you'll stand it."

She got up and went over to hug him. His body remained rigid in the chair. "Longer than it'll take for us to work it out," she said. "I want to show you what I've been up to out here, and it has nothing to do with your father or any other Sumner. It has to do with you and me."

He reached up and hesitantly stroked her hair as he said, "Dear Annie, why do you put up with me?"

"Oh, Winnie, nobody's ever loved me as much as you do. We've just got to keep trusting each other."

She kissed him and looked for his reply. He smiled doubtfully.

"Come on," she said, taking his hand. "I want to show you something."

She led him out of the dining room and down the broad hall to the parlor, a room paneled in chestnut with a fireplace and crowded bookshelves. Used as a study, the room was one of the few in which Annie spent time. On a Duncan Phyfe dropleaf table were Rosewood's pedigree books and numerous volumes of thoroughbred history. She lifted them aside, using them to pin down the corners of several sheets of blueprints as she unrolled them.

Winnie stared down at them and said noncommittally, "Gracious, you've been busy."

"You said that if we were going to really do it right, we'd need a new stallion barn and twenty more stalls for broodmares," she said, pointing to the blueprints, her excitement uncontained. "The north paddock is perfect for the stallions.

There, and over to the west, behind this stand of oak trees, is a place for the broodmare stalls, with room for paddocks for them and their foals. The brook goes right through there. I had a new survey done, the first, by the way, in sixty-five years, and do you know you own two hundred and four acres instead of a hundred and ninety-seven? Some of it's wetlands, but they're beautiful. A lot of dogwood and deer."

For a moment, there was a spark of interest as Winnie went over the plans. "Room for how many stallions?"

"Three, but it's designed to be expanded when we need more. We have twenty-three broodmares here, a hundred and forty-two in Lexington. It'll depend on what we want to do down there."

"It looks quite splendid, Annie. Really."

"I'd like to put it out for bids so that we could break ground in the spring. Then at the summer sales, we'll buy some first-class yearling colts and get this place going. If it works out here, we'll go down and make it work at the Lexington farm."

Looking up from the blueprints, he smiled at her, acknowledging her enthusiasm. "Do it, Annie. It sounds wonderful."

She did not mention the Haras de la Brise. The memory was too vivid. She was grateful that Winnie did not either. "Tomorrow, I'll walk you around and show you exactly where everything will be. Oh, and about three quarters of all the paddock fences have to be replaced, but we can save a lot if we have three-board fences instead of four."

Winnie assumed his Professor Higgins demeanor and stated, "There are three-board farms and there are four-board farms, Eliza. Three-board means sleazy, tacky, probably a seedy riding school run by some little dictator, attended by eager young girls and deeply frustrated women. Four-board is for a horseman or horsewoman. If you see a three-board farm, pass it by." He started for the bar at one end of the room. "Join me?"

"Sure," she said, willing to drink if that would make him stay. "Make it a small one. I have to be up early."

"Of course you do," he said as he put two glasses on the bar and poured Scotch. "And after mucking out the stalls, you'll come back here and study your *books.*" Again there was a bitter tone, but he snickered to counter it. "I can't imagine why I spent all that time plotting the course of a gene through the myriad canals of equine reproduction. That only leads to winners and losers. On the other hand, the breeding of *human* families leads to the occasional sublime, or the more typical ridiculous, often within a single generation. Human genes get mixed up with money, love, lust, illegitimacy, ambition—certainly a much more amusing subject for study." He returned, handed her a glass, and drank deeply from his own.

"Not if you want to run a horse farm," she said.

He glared at her a moment, then took another swallow.

"No, of course not. The purpose is all for the breed, isn't it?" He began to pace angrily as Annie stood by the table. "Well, I have to get up early, too. Because I have *my* purpose —getting to the office by eleven, glancing over the family real estate holdings, then calling, in order, my broker, lawyer, banker, accountant, and, most important, my tailor. Then lunch, at one of my clubs. The Brook has the best silver, the Knickerbocker the best food, the Racquet the best friends, the Union the biggest snobs. Each provides me with companionship of sorts for a long afternoon of drinks with pool, bridge, or backgammon. Even after such an exhausting day, my evenings are again filled with dinner invitations, my standing as an extra man having been somewhat reestablished this season with the knowing few."

He stopped pacing and glared ruefully at Annie as he drained his glass, then started toward the bar.

"Winnie, do you want to get rid of Rosewood, just forget it, and have me come live in New York? I'll do it tomorrow if you want. I can't stand seeing you hating everything so much."

He did not answer until he had filled his glass and let a drop fall from the lip of the bottle. "We agreed that you'd never have to put up with the fancy people, or take the chance of running into . . ." He turned quickly and put the bottle back on the shelf behind the bar. "I'd never ask you to do that. And be assured, dear Annie, that I hate nothing so much as I hate myself, and I'll drink to that." As he swallowed, his brow lifted over his glass, once again appraising her reaction. Seeing only her discouragement, he said, "I think I'll go to bed now. I'll sleep in the guest room."

"You sleep where you want," she said intently. "But *you* 'be assured' that whichever of those nine antique beds you choose, I'm sleeping with you. Because I love you, Winnie. I really do."

They stared at each other. Winnie put his glass down, came over to Annie, and they embraced, holding each other silently for a long time. Then he took her arm and led her out of the parlor.

"I think of you so much," he said. "Are you all right out here, dear Annie? Do you go out, see people?"

"No. People are friendly, or maybe they're curious. I think they're still suspicious about a showgirl marrying the Sumner scion." She frowned, trying to explain carefully. "Don't worry; I'm not afraid of them. It's just not important to me to know a lot of people. What we're doing here is, and I don't really have too much time for anything else." They reached the stairs, and she turned to Winnie. "Does that make any sense to you?"

He smiled, his eyes glazed with whiskey and admiration. "It makes perfect sense, dear Annie, just as being a vegetarian does. Unfortunately, the fancy people are addicted to raw meat as well as to glitter and chat."

Annie laughed, took his hand, and led him upstairs to their room. "I never will understand why the fancy people got involved with horses. I suppose it's one way to show off money, but horse sweat and manure just don't seem to fit in with glitter and chat."

"Well, we have to have something to chat *about*," Winnie said as Annie began to undress. Winnie did not watch, but kept talking rapidly as he slowly took his clothes off. "What's called society in this country isn't much more than various circles of money—new, old, Wasp, Jewish, legal, or illegal—swirling around each other like another inferno. When one circle does something, the others either try to join or they do something bigger on their own."

He kept talking as he put on a pair of pajamas hanging inside the closet. "August Belmont, one of the great social climbers of all time, started it up here. Racing was wrecked in the South after the Civil War and it moved north. He and Leonard Jerome started a track on Long Island called Jerome Park. They were both rich and they made racing respectable. High society returned to the clubhouse, along with gambling and corruption, which, for the rich, gave the enterprise the thrill of wickedness. Leonard Jerome did nothing of greater importance with his life except that—through no fault of his own—he became Winston Churchill's grandfather. Belmont's son founded and ran the Jockey Club with an iron bigoted hand, built Belmont Park to keep himself on one social forefront, and then did something for which his many sins will always be forgiven. He bred Man o' War! But he sold him for five thousand dollars, and had to watch the greatest colt of his time win twenty of his twenty-one races while setting five world records. I'd drink to that kind of sublime justice, but I left my glass downstairs."

Winnie slipped under the covers and lay there without touching Annie. She moved over and rested her head on his shoulder with her arm over his chest.

"I saw Man o' War once," she said.

"You did? When?"

"When I was five. I barely remember. I think it was a year or two before he died, so he must have been almost thirty. My mother took me on a trip to Lexington, she said to celebrate the end of the war, but I think it was because she knew she was going to die and wanted to take me somewhere to talk to me. We sat up on a milk train from Ashland to Lexington. That's what I remember, the train. It was my first trip and I stayed up all night. When we got there, we walked through the stores and had lunch. I can remember the apple brown Betty. Then we got on a tour bus and I fell asleep. We went out to the place where Man o' War was standing . . ."

"Faraway Farm," Winnie said.

"I guess so. I didn't want to get off the bus to see some old horse. My momma pulled me off and we looked, together with what must have been a thousand other people, got back on the bus, and I went back to sleep. On the train that night, she told me she was sick inside and wanted me to help her. She died later that year. I don't remember Man o' War at all."

He put his arms around her and they lay quietly together.

"And what did the professor tell you about Man o' War?" he said pedantically with Higgins' rain-in-Spain tolerance.

"That he's one of the best examples of the fact that mares are more prepotent than stallions." Unlike Winnie and his excellent imitations, Annie did not dare attempt any accent but her own.

"And how, Eliza, is that example manifested in Man o' War?"

The familiarity of their old roles relieved the mood. Annie chuckled. "Because his sire was a runty runner named Fair Play, who sulked his way out of winning any races. And *his* sire was Hastings, who bit any horse that tried to pass him on the track."

"Correct, my child. I've taught you so *well!*"

"But Man o' War's momma, Mahubah, was an amazon. From her he got a thirty-foot stride, a shinbone—no, what's it called—a *cannon* bone an inch longer than the average, a chest five inches broader, and a sweet disposition that made the whole world love him. All he got from his ornery daddy was the habit of chewing on his hoofs, like people chew on their fingernails."

Winnie laughed, and soon they began to drift. Winnie said, "Somebody wrote once that he was as close to a living flame as a horse could get. God! Think of finding something like that . . ." It was the last thought Annie remembered.

The next morning when she woke to go down to the barns, Winnie was gone. He called later that morning—"after my banker, but before the accountant"—to explain that he had suddenly remembered, in the middle of the night, his early morning appointment with his tailor. "I loved seeing you, and your ideas about Rosewood are first rate. Full speed ahead, dear Annie."

The winter began, and Winnie's weekly visits became briefer. They flew to Lexington together in the P-38 for the Keeneland broodmare sales. As planned, Winnie attended the open-

ing evening session alone with Annie's well-annotated catalogue. Their understanding was unspoken; both realized that
Caernarvon would be buying at the sales. She waited for him
at Rosewood House, her own excitement dissipating as the
hours passed with no phone call. She wandered aimlessly
around the mansion, looking at portraits of scowling family
members and the Rosewood champion horses of the twenties
and thirties. In the trophy room were gold and silver plates,
trophies and cups blazingly polished in glass cabinets, with
albums on shelves of photographs and press clippings covering
the careers of each of the winners. Clustered on the grand
piano and numerous tables in the living room were thickets of
silver-framed photographs of Sumner family members and
family friends, some of whom Annie had met, others whom
she recognized only from the pictures she had put away in
Millbrook.

On a table in the hall was a thick guest book stamped with
the Sumner crest, which included a rampant horse and a Latin
phrase. Winnie had explained that the crest had been created
for the family by a Broadway designer in sycophantic admiration, only to have the design filed by an Anglophilic great-
uncle at some British college of heraldry as the family escutch-
eon. There were only a half-dozen entries in the book for the
preceding eight years. Annie leafed back through the thick
pages, and saw that in previous eras there had been great gath-
erings of famous friends and relatives in the spring and fall,
culminating in Derby Week and Thanksgiving. When she
closed the book and looked around the hall, Annie shuddered
at the emptiness of Rosewood House. She hurried to the only
room in the mansion where she was comfortable, the old
kitchen, and sat down on a stool to wait.

When Winnie arrived, it was very late and he was very
drunk. Before he fell asleep on one of the living room
couches, he told Annie that he had overbid on three broodmares they had picked out, mainly because he was bidding
against Caernarvon. "No, dear Annie, Sam wasn't there," he
blurted, suddenly angry. "His trainer, Frank Carney, did his
bidding, as we all do for Sam. I bid like a fool to prove something, I hate to think what."

Annie let him sleep on the couch, and the next day he flew back alone to New York without making any effort at an excuse. Annie stayed at Rosewood House only long enough to supervise the arrival of the three new broodmares. The more than two thousand acres of the Lexington farm oppressed Annie with the amount of work that they, the paddocks, and outbuildings needed. She tried not to think about it, or the staff, or Rosewood House. Until Millbrook was established, Rosewood in Lexington would have to coast. She flew back to New York, where a car from the farm picked her up at the airport.

From then on, Winnie's visits seldom lasted for more than a day, and even those became tense with obligation. Annie continued to do whatever she could to relieve him, but nothing seemed to help. She filled her time with hard work and plans to break ground for the new barns. When the bids came in, Winnie would not even discuss them, saying only that she should go ahead with whatever she wanted to do. He came for Christmas Eve, presented her with a diamond necklace, and spent Christmas morning passing out bonus envelopes to the farm staff. He then returned to New York for a round of parties he said he could not miss. Annie offered no objection and, after he left, admitted her relief. She did not bother to wonder if he was once more bedding any of the eager ex-debutantes who regarded him as safe game. When she realized she did not care, she began to fear that time was not going to help them.

When foaling season began in February and March, Annie began to shuttle between the two farms. It was the busiest time of year for the attending veterinarians, and several in Kentucky were perplexed or outright irritated by Annie's insistent questions, for which she apologized but which she never held back. As spring approached, she felt a growing sense of being part of the farm. Each foal's birth solidified that feeling, as if each was a part of the new beginning at Rosewood.

As the ground thawed and the spring rains came, Annie remained at Millbrook to start building the new barns. She continued to hope that, with the commencement of construction, Winnie somehow would be drawn back to the farm.

One day while she and the contractor were showing the fencing men the outline of a new paddock, she saw a limousine drive up to the cottage that was used as the farm office. At first, Annie thought Winnie had hired a car to bring him out from the city because he had consumed too many drinks to drive. The limousine was a Cadillac. The driver stepped into the cottage for directions, then drove the car down to where Annie was working.

The back door opened, and Phil Angelo stepped out. He grinned at her obvious surprise, and put a toothpick in his mouth.

"Hiya, Annie, how ya doin'?"

Her stomach tightened as she walked over so that they could not be heard.

"Are you here for blackmail or as a messenger boy?"

His grin faded to a dirty glare. "Charlie wants to see you. It's been a long time, y'know. And he's got maybe twenty-four hours," he said as a casual rebuke.

Annie felt no shock or guilt. She had hoped that Charlie had died peacefully. She wanted to remember him as the first person since her mother who had genuinely cared about her, and not think of all the rest, particularly Phil Angelo.

"Where is he?" she asked.

"Back in the city. Hey, don't worry about it," he reasoned. "He paid for the limo, for Christ's sake. You coming or not?"

"Only if you sit up in the front seat."

His face tightened into a brutal mask. "Listen, bitch, you can use your cunt to get what you want from the bluebloods, but it never meant shit to me."

She hit him, as hard as she could. The toothpick flew out of his mouth and fell to the ground. The fencing crew started to move, ready to help her.

Phil smirked. "You ever do that again, you'll be picking your teeth out of the back of your throat." He prodded at his cheek from the inside with his tongue and said, "You coming?"

"Go wait up in front of the house." She walked back to the crew to give them final instructions about the fence. As she heard the limousine drive away behind her, she felt a cold sweat on her forehead.

She rode her stable pony back to the barn and walked to the main house. While she changed out of her work clothes and quickly showered, Annie wondered if Charlie was scared. She doubted it. He had been close to death all his life, and had his own ideas of what to expect. Once, he had said to her, "Gods and heavens were made up by the first guy who got scared about dying. Take it from me, Annie; death created God in six seconds."

Annie smiled. She was glad she was going to see him, even if it meant being in the same car with Phil Angelo.

FIFTEEN

"HELLO, CHARLIE."

Annie spoke loudly. He was asleep, propped up on pillows in an oxygen tent. The thick plastic that enclosed him from the waist up distorted his face. His skin was sallow, and one side of his mouth hung open at an odd angle. When he blinked and saw her, a weak smile raised the other corner of his mouth, and his eyes locked on hers in recognition. She had worn her navy blue blazer over a white blouse and slacks to please Charlie. In the antiseptic room, she realized that nothing mattered.

"Everybody else please get out," he rasped, loud enough to be heard. The nurse looked to Teddy Lapps, who nodded agreement, and Phil followed them out the bedroom door. Standing alone next to the huge old oak bed, which barely fit in the low-ceilinged room of the new East Side high-rise building, Annie glanced at the double cylinders of oxygen. The apartment was filled with Charlie's heavy oak and stuffed maroon furniture. The small rooms seemed overwhelmed with it.

"You lied to me, Annie." His mouth held the same half smile, and his voice sounded as if he had already forgiven her.

Realizing instantly that he was talking about the list, and that Phil Angelo had betrayed her, Annie said, "I'm sorry."

Charlie feebly waved her concern away. "I know why you did it," he said. Pausing between each phrase to gasp in oxygen, he continued. "So I wouldn't have to kill the Angel. For him knowing too much. You did him a favor. Poor jerk. Doesn't know when he's well off . . . When I started getting real sick, he tried to blackmail me. Wanted me to tell him the whole list. Said he'd seen Vito Genovese's name. He had it right, knew where the body was. Said he'd tell Don Vitone that I was daffy, talking about old times." Charlie laughed, a short windy groan.

Twisting a small brass button below her lapel, Annie could not speak. She knew who Vito Genovese was: Lucky Luciano's partner in brothels and narcotics since the thirties. When Luciano had been deported, Genovese had taken over their interests. He had called a meeting of a hundred of the top Mafia heads from all over the country in order to be proclaimed the boss of bosses. By a fluke, it was raided by local police from Apalachin, Pennsylvania, the tiny hamlet where the meeting was held. The resulting attention spurred the federal government to quickly establish a solid narcotics case against Genovese. Only several months before, Annie had read that his sentence was fifteen years in the federal penitentiary in Atlanta.

"Charlie, it's my fault," Annie said, furious at what Phil had tried to do. "I'll do anything you say."

"I didn't ask you to come here to apologize," he replied. "You just should have told me. I could have killed the Angel then. Now I can't."

"Why not?" Annie said. *I'll* do it!" She meant it as she had never meant anything in her life. Nervously, she twisted the brass disc tighter on its threads.

Charlie smiled again. "I can't, and you can't. He doesn't make any difference to me now, but he does to you. He's set it up that if anything happens to him, Don Vitone will hear about you and my list. So what you and your lawyer figured out won't work anymore. Genovese is already in jail, and he's really insane. He orders people killed from prison. If he ever hears your name, you're dead."

He had spoken too much. Grimacing with pain, he lay back, trying to breath. The rasping noise he made grew deeper. Annie turned to call the nurse, but Charlie moaned and said, "No! Wait!" She stood, watching as he breathed in the oxygen and gradually relaxed.

"Aren't you going to ask me what to do?" he said, trying to smile.

"Yes, but don't talk if it hurts you."

"Listen . . . Phil will try to scare you into giving him the list. *Never* do it. He thinks he can get rich off it. It'll only get you both killed. Arrange it so that if the Angel touches you, everyone on the list will know he's seen it. That way you'll equalize him."

She nodded, then her lips tightened with rage. "How can I keep him away from me?"

"You're stuck with him, Annie. You were from the moment he saw that list. Life does that, sticks you with dirt you think you can wash off. You can't. You have to live with it. But here's what you do. You remember the name Carlo Gambino?"

Annie nodded.

"When Vito Genovese ordered the death of Albert Anastasia, Carlo Gambino was one of the guys who shot him up in the barber chair. You remember the pictures?"

"Yes," she said, her mouth going dry.

"You tell Phil, and I'll back you up, that I've made a little arrangement with Gambino, his favor to a dying friend, that if anything happens to you, Phil's done for. So that's that. But you have to promise me you'll never give him the list."

She remembered holding the gun on Phil as he let the piece of paper fall to the floor. "I promise," she said, wishing she had shot him.

"All right. Now, tell me how you are. And if you have any more secrets, you might as well tell them. They're pretty safe with me." He struggled to stick his hand out from under the oxygen tent. Annie drew a chair close to the bed so that she could hold his hand, and began talking. Without hesitation, she told him about Sam, Winnie, and her hopes for Rosewood Stables. She had not intended to talk so much, but Charlie obviously enjoyed it. While describing the stables she noticed a bluish pallor spreading over the loose skin of his face. He squeezed her hand.

"I'm leaving you my horses, Annie, and my books."

Annie held his hand and leaned down to put her cheek against it. It was startlingly cold.

"Thanks for coming," he mumbled. "You're the one person I wanted to see." His eyes opened briefly. "You look so lovely, that amber hair." Then his eyes closed. "Tell them I'm going to sleep. Maybe they'll just leave me alone." He squeezed her hand again and said, "Watch out for those rich guys, Annie." Then she felt nothing but the cold in his fingers.

She kissed the back of his hand. Lifting the edge of the oxygen tent, she put his arm underneath and laid it over his chest.

"Goodbye, Charlie," she said, not sure that he heard her. "I'll always love you."

When she came out into the hallway, she saw Teddy Lapps and the nurse sitting in the living room. They stood up expectantly. Phil remained seated in a large stuffed armchair, his arms and feet so symmetrically planted that he looked enthroned. He gave Annie a small sneer, which she ignored.

"He said he wanted to sleep," she said as she buttoned her jacket.

The nurse nodded and picked up a cup to take into the kitchen.

Annie turned to Teddy Lapps. The big man still wore clothes that were too tight for him. He stood awkwardly, as if lost. "Goodbye, Teddy. I'm going to go. I hope you'll be okay."

"I'll make out all right, Annie. Thanks."

They shook hands and Teddy walked her to the door. Annie heard Phil rise and quickly follow. Presumptuously, he took her arm and guided her toward the elevator. Annie lifted her arm away. "You don't have to come down. I'll get home on my own." She pushed the elevator button.

Obviously he had been waiting for this moment, expecting her to be scared or shocked by what Charlie should have told her. Doubt hooded his eyes.

"We got something to talk about."

"Not me. I having nothing to say to you."

"You dumb bitch, didn't Charlie—?"

"He told me how smart you thought you were, trying to blackmail him, and he laughed."

She saw his hands clenching at his sides. She pushed the elevator button again.

"I want the fucking list."

"You're never going to get it, Phil, so the only thing you can do is blackmail Vito Genovese. I'd sure like to watch you try that, except it'd get me killed along with you. So I'll tell you once more. Don't even think about what you know. Your name's in with the list at my lawyer's. You say a word, and the dons will be all over you." The elevator seemed to be taking forever.

Phil stared at her, his lips tightening over his teeth. "Now that you're married to all that money, you don't know what it means anymore. We could make millions, Annie." He saw her give an impatient blink. He looked both ways down the hall, then back at her. "I'll find a way to get you for this, Annie. Somehow, someday, when you don't know it's coming—"

"Phil, don't try to scare me anymore. We're just stuck with each other. So don't get greedy and stupid."

His fist drew back just as the elevator door opened. Stepping in, she turned and met his eyes with a hard stare. The elevator operator waited, looking apprehensively at Phil.

"And don't forget to ask Charlie about Carlo Gambino," Annie said.

"What about him?" Phil said, made wary by the name. His foot jerked out to keep the door from closing.

"Charlie really didn't like what you tried to pull on him. So he asked Gambino to look after me, as a favor to a dying friend. If I'm bothered, you're dead."

The elevator operator was staring at Annie. Phil stepped

back, his eyes and mouth open wide, and the doors closed in front of him.

When she reached the street, she began to sob and could not stop. Hurrying past the waiting limousine, away from Charlie's building, she covered her face with a handkerchief. As she blindly crossed the street, she lurched in front of the traffic. A horn blared, and a cab screeched to a stop near her knees. She hurried on, around another corner, down another street. The tears continued as she walked, staring at traffic lights, aimlessly following their direction. She took no notice of anything for many blocks until, stepping off a curb, she twisted her ankle. She limped over to the nearest building and leaned against the wall. The sun glared, reflecting off a window across the street. She held a hand up to block the harsh light as people passed in front of her. She stared at their faces; several stared back. Then someone stopped and spoke to her.

"Annie." It was Sam. Her heart stopped. Without looking, she ran into the street. She heard brakes screech and a crash as one car hit the bumper of another. A man yelled at her. She tried to turn. Sam's hand was on her arm, leading her away from the traffic. He said, "Just keep walking. You're okay." No longer crying, she did as she was told while gulping in air. The angry driver yelled again. They walked quickly as Sam led her around the next corner, stopped, and turned toward her. His blue eyes glittered and his mouth broke slowly into his crooked smile. She leaned against him. The familiarity of his body sent a shock through hers.

"This is Seventy-eighth Street, Annie. For us, it's cannibal country," he said, gently moving his hand through her hair. "Not a good place for us."

"Where else can we go?" she asked.

"If you can manage two blocks without getting run over, Bemelmans Bar. I'll meet you there."

Annie looked up at him. She nodded.

"I'll be watching you from across the street," Sam said. "If you change your mind and run for it, I'll come after you."

He kissed her quickly, as if nothing had happened in a year and a half, then walked toward Madison Avenue.

Wiping her face, Annie did the best she could with her soggy handkerchief. At Madison, she saw Sam standing across the street. She walked quickly and reached the revolving door of the Carlyle Hotel's famous bar. Not seeing him when she looked back, she went in.

Because of its proximity to Cumberland Country, as they called it, Annie and Winnie had waited at Bemelmans Bar for Sam many times. On this occasion, she chose a table across the room from the one they had usually occupied. When the bartender approached to take her order, she suddenly realized how she must look. After ordering a lemonade, she hurried out of the bar across a small lobby to the ladies' room. She bathed her red, swollen eyes in cold water. The attendant handed her a towel, and as Annie fished a fifty-cent piece from her purse, she felt her hands shake. She hurried back to the bar, expecting Sam to be there.

Instead, a bellhop was calling out, "Miss Grebauer, message for a Miss Grebauer." Annie's stomach sank; Sam had changed his mind. It was probably better, but it hurt badly. Finding another fifty cents in her purse, she exchanged it for the envelope the bellhop was carrying. Without going to her table, she tore it open. There was no message, only a room key.

Annie was relieved and elated as she turned back to the lobby, hurried down the steps to the elevator, and gave the operator the key's floor number. In a moment, she was there, knocking on the door, trying not to laugh or to cry again.

"The door's open," he called, and Annie went in. He was standing in the center of a lovely sitting room, in a gray shepherd's plaid suit, dark brown shoes, and a red-and-gray-striped tie. His black hair was slightly mussed and fell on his forehead, and his hand rested on the back of a tapestried wing chair.

"We're lucky," he said. "It's the only suite they had left."

He started toward her, but stopped. Annie reached back to push the door shut, then ran across the room into his arms. She kissed him deeply and clung to him. Sam picked her up and carried her into the bedroom. Laying her down on the bed, he began to undress her. The brass button she had twisted popped off her jacket. Sitting on the bed, she quickly undressed herself. Looking up, she met his eyes as he undressed. His look of desire frightened her.

"I don't know how we got here," he said, "and I don't know when we'll see each other again, so I want you all."

He put his head between her legs, his hands reaching up to her breasts. When she began to writhe, he kissed his familiar way over her stomach, her breasts, her neck. As she wrapped her legs around his waist, he slipped into her, barely, tantalizing her as he covered her mouth with his and drove himself in deeper, then deeper.

She cried out with longing. Suddenly, he lifted her up and pressed her back against the padded headboard of the bed. He held her buttocks and she reached down for his, grabbing at him, giving in to the explosion of senses that was coming, then came, then, achingly to a point of pain, came again. And still he went on, holding her up, supporting her with his thighs. Kissing her neck and breasts, he pinioned her arms against the headboard, thrusting harder, faster, from one side, then the other, until his body clenched and he bellowed, grabbing her shoulders and falling back on the bed, pulling her down on top of him.

They lay, not moving, a sliver of afternoon sunlight edging through the drawn curtains and crossing their bodies.

"I have . . ." he started, then paused. "I have so damn much to say to you, I can't think how to start. How much time do I have?"

"I don't know," she said.

"All right, listen. Last week—you won't believe this—I went over to my old apartment and just sat there, remembering us." He waited, as if she were supposed to answer a question.

"And . . ." she offered.

He put his hands on her hips and pressed them tight against him. "I reached for the telephone over and over again, even dialed your number, but I hung up, not knowing who would answer." He shifted under her; then he went on, his voice edgier. "What's happening to you two? There are a lot of rumors whipping around town."

Irritated, Annie pushed herself up with her arms so that she could look at his face. "Why? What could they say? My Lord, I've lived at the farm like a nun."

Sam watched her for a moment. "Winnie hasn't been much of a monk. He's arrived drunk at a lot of dinner parties, and then gets drunker."

Annie sank down on his chest again. She tried not to think of Winnie, but a sadness had begun to spread.

"Sam, tell me the truth. Doesn't he sleep with a married woman or two here and there?"

"I honestly don't know, but I doubt it. He makes these drunken propositions loud enough for everyone, including husbands, to hear. The former debutantes don't like it. I've tried to talk to him, but he gets very nervous with me. Won't get into anything private, calls me 'old man,' and tells me some dirty joke he's heard over drinks at the Brook."

She slipped out of his arms, stood up, and walked quickly to the center of the room. Picking up the button, she put it in her jacket pocket and gathered up the rest of her clothes. Sam came up behind her and held her by the shoulders.

"Tell me," he said, "what's wrong."

"I don't know what to do. I'm ashamed, but I've tried everything I can think of. Oh, Lord, Sam, I'm sorry I still love you so much."

As she started to tremble, he reached around to put one arm over her breasts and the other across her stomach. "Annie," he said softly in her ear, "get a divorce."

The word hit hard. She took a quick breath, then edged out of his arms and began to get dressed.

"I can't do that. It'd hurt him too—"

"What do you think it's doing to him now?" Sam said as he watched her step into her underpants. "Neither one of you is going to get out of this without some pain, for Christ's sake. Look how you went into it."

Hooking her bra, Annie recognized the edge of anger in Sam's voice. "I went into it to be a good wife to someone I loved a lot. I still love Winnie," she added, hating how righteous and defensive she sounded.

Sam sat down on the bed. He picked up her slacks and

handed them to her. "That may be true, Annie, but he's hurting now, and you aren't."

She grabbed her slacks and turned away. "What the hell do you know about it?"

"Not much, but enough. He talks endlessly about how happy you are, how hard you're working for Rosewood. Says you'll take it over any day now. Get a divorce, Annie. He'll *give* you Rosewood, gladly."

"My Lord, Sam, you sure do give advice easy." She stepped into her spectator pumps. As he stood, still naked, and reached his arms out for her, she thought of Charlie's hand poking out of the plastic tent, of Phil's raised fist at the elevator. Sam's hands held her shoulders. "I don't know what goes on between you two," he said, "but it's killing him. Did you know they'd grounded him for flying while he was drunk?"

Embarrassed that she had not known, she shook her head and backed away from him. Lifting the shade, she stood at the window. The sunlight was slanting from behind the cold gray concrete building across the street. She had to get back to the farm. The night watchman was new; she had to supervise mixing feed for the horses' evening meal. Biting at her lip, she wondered how she could think of such things.

She turned back and watched Sam slip into his pants and reach for his shirt. His body still had the sweat of their lovemaking on it. She stared at him, trying to memorize details.

"Annie, I'm only half alive without you. I will *not* stop loving you." She smiled gratefully and wanted to believe him.

As Sam dressed, he spoke of when they might see each other, but nothing could be resolved, so unexpected had been their meeting. Sam called for a limousine to pick up Annie at the entrance of Bemelmans Bar and take her back to Millbrook. She noticed the odd tone in his voice when he gave her name, "Yes, the party's name is Mrs. Winton Sumner."

They kissed each other longingly before leaving the room. Holding her hand, Sam walked her to the elevator. "You're missing a button," he tried to joke, fingering the thread wisping off her jacket. Then he pulled her to him, but the elevator door opened. She stepped in and watched helplessly as the doors closed.

As she walked through the bar, her eyes had difficulty adjusting. It was dark and she hesitated for a moment. She saw that the limousine was waiting outside the revolving door. Then she heard a familiar voice. Instinctively, she turned toward Winnie. He was at their regular table with the lacquer-haired wife of a man they both knew. The wife saw Annie and gasped. Winnie turned, looked at Annie, then closed his eyes as his face drew into a pained grimace. He bowed his head.

Annie moved through the revolving door and got into the limousine so quickly that the driver did not have time to assist her.

"Mrs. Sumner?"

"Yes. Can we go quickly, please?"

The traffic out of Manhattan was a long agitation. Annie wept silently in the back seat, avoiding the driver's rearview mirror. Her greatest concern was for Winnie when he got over his own embarrassment and began to wonder why Annie had been in New York, hurrying through Bemelmans Bar. The question would surely occur to him, and Annie began to prepare a lie, which she knew would never work. She thought of the effect that her being Sam's lover again would have on Winnie, and was terrified.

It was nearly eight-thirty by the time the car pulled through the gates of the farm. When she went into the main house, the telephone was ringing. She hoped it was not Winnie. She had given up on telling the lie, but was not yet ready to tell him the truth. "Hello."

"What the *hell* did you tell Winnie?" It was Sam and he was angry.

"Nothing. I just—"

"Don't lie to me, Annie. He said you told him all about this afternoon."

"No, I didn't. And I don't lie to you, Sam! He saw me leaving the hotel. He must have made a good guess, and it sounds as if you've just proved it." Sam was silent. "When did you see him?" she asked.

"I didn't. He called me from the Racquet Club."

"Was he drunk?"

"I haven't heard him so sober in years. He said he'd run

into you at the hotel, and you told him you'd been with me. He wanted me to know it was all right; that he'd known from the beginning that all you really cared about was me, and then Rosewood—''

"Oh, Lord, Sam, where is he?"

"I don't know. I'm at the club now. I came right down here, but he'd gone. The bartender said he was here about an hour, drinking coffee, full of jokes and 'old mans' to other members coming through. Then he asked for some stationery."

"Stationery?"

"Yes, he wrote a letter or something and left." His tone was still accusatory.

"Could you ever believe that I told him anything?" She felt her throat tighten. "I only saw him. He was with . . . a woman. I didn't say—"

"Who?"

"I'm not getting her into this."

"All I know is, I want to find him," Sam said. "If you hear from him, tell him to call and leave a message at my home."

"Are you going out to Brookhaven?"

He paused a moment. "We think alike, Annie, always have. I've already called out there, but nobody was around. I'll talk to you later." He hung up.

Annie went upstairs to her room and changed into a work shirt, faded sweater, and old jeans. Switching the private line to the barn phone, she hurried down to help mix the feed for the horses' evening meal. The new night watchman, checking the feed chart, pointed out three mistakes she made. Annie let him do the rest and tried to concentrate on getting the right bucket to the right stall.

When the feeding was done, she busied herself with various chores: currying a colt, fluffing up straw with the pitchfork, resetting bandages on the horses' legs. Finally left with nothing else to do, she stood in the stall of an old broodmare and stroked her withers.

After saying good night, the watchman bedded down in the tack room. The broodmare finally tired and sank to her knees, rolled over on her side, and went to sleep. There was a dampness in the chilly night air; Annie sat down in the straw and leaned against the broodmare's back for warmth. She remembered the cold of Charlie's hand, then the weight of the room key she found in the envelope at the hotel. Staring into the darkness of the stall, she saw Winnie's look of agonized self-reproach. She wished she had been smarter, strong enough to walk over to the table, take his hand, lead him out to the limousine, and bring him back with her. She might have done it, had she not been hurrying away from her own affair. Eventually, Winnie must have realized that.

She wrapped her arms around her knees and put her forehead on them, hoping that Winnie would be all right. She understood why he had told Sam the lies. Winnie was hurt enough to say anything.

She began to bite at a fingernail. One brittle hangnail tore down into the flesh. By the time the phone rang, three of Annie's fingers were sore and bleeding. The clock above the wall phone outside the tack room said it was two-twenty.

"Hello."

"Is this Mrs. Winton Sumner?"

"Yes."

"This is the Federal Aviation Administration office at Idlewild Airport. There's been a crash of a private P-38 on Block Island. We're trying to locate . . ."

The plane had flown over the Block Island lighthouse once, then circled back and headed straight for it until, at the last moment, it side-slipped and crashed into the cliff two hundred yards away. There was an explosion; the wreckage had fallen to the beach below. The body of the pilot had not been recovered.

Annie walked back to the main house. She switched the phone line back and sat beside the extension in the kitchen, waiting for Sam to call.

When dawn came, she knew he never would.

SIXTEEN

ANNIE FOLLOWED the unctuous St. Luke's vestryman in his black swallowtail coat through a side door to the front pew in the nave. Winnie's two brothers were already there, the racing-car driver with a beautiful blond girlfriend, and the younger brother with his third wife in as many years, a thin-lipped, acquisitive-eyed former stewardess.

A tightly woven black veil concealed Annie's face, and in spite of her intention not to look, she saw in a glance that the church was packed. The vestryman retreated, and instantly, from the back of the church, the rector's voice rang out compassionately: "I am the resurrection and the life, saith the Lord. He that believeth in me, though he were dead, yet shall he live, and whosoever liveth and believeth in me shall never die . . ."

Behind Annie, the congregation stood up; she, too, rose as the minister continued to intone. He processed up the center aisle preceded only by a single acolyte carrying a plain brass cross. Both wore black cassocks without the usual white surplices.

As far as Annie knew, Winnie had never attended a service at St. Luke's other than weddings. He had made an annual contribution, however, as his father had done. Annie had been informed of this custom by the bravely smiling, magnificently attired rector, who had been the first to arrive at Millbrook the morning after the plane crash. He came in a car with a driver. By then, the phone had been ringing incessantly. The farm manager answered it and took messages. Occasionally, Annie glanced through the slips to see if Sam had called. She was perplexed to find that most of the calls were from newspapers and magazines.

The rector of St. Luke's was, despite his stateliness, a worldly man who was familiar with death, its rituals and knotted social complexities. He recognized that a former showgirl who had become Mrs. Winton Sumner III might not know exactly what was expected of her. Apparently familiar with the undertones of her marriage as well as with the stresses it had caused in the Sumner family, he asked first if she would like to pray with him, and then suggested she call her lawyer. Annie turned down the prayers but took his advice.

Archibald Delansig arrived from New York two hours later. Shaking her hand, looking down at her with his half-closed eyes, he offered his condolences as he seemed to perceive that the situation was more complex than he had thought. By the afternoon, he had taken on the responsibilities of dealing with the police and FAA investigations, the funeral, and the press, the last of which had become increasingly insistent as the day wore on. Hiring off-duty local constables from Millbrook to patrol the farm and control access through the front gate, he secured Rosewood so that Annie felt safe from the photographers who hovered at the gate, as well as from any last-minute gestures by Phil Angelo.

But even with the serene cooperation of the rector and St. Luke's unruffled staff, controlling the memorial service was more difficult. On the morning of the service, the press staked out the church's stone portals on Fifth Avenue, and the back entrance to its offices around the corner. A contingent of New York policemen guarded both, contributing to the tense conditions. Delansig directed one of Millbrook's constables to the front entrance of the church, where he turned on his car's siren just long enough to get the photographers running toward it. Double-parking the farm's station wagon at the office entrance, the attorney quickly slipped Annie through the police guards inside to the rector's vesting room, where they waited for the service to begin.

Sitting in the pew, Annie listened to the rector as he read a psalm, and to someone crying in a pew behind her. She had not cried since the night of Winnie's death. Crying did not seem an appropriate way for her to mourn. She knew that Charlie Dell was also dead, but she had not been told and dared not ask. One day, she had answered the phone and heard a man say, "You slut chorus girl, you drove him to do it, bitch, to get his . . ." Shaken, she hung up. The same day, Winnie's brother with the many wives talked his way through the farm manager and Delansig to say to Annie, "Well, sis, how much do I get and how soon?" He was seated next to her in the pew.

Many of Winnie's Princeton classmates, as well as uncles, aunts, and cousins, had called or written, each one careful to say the right thing, but with the cool distance of fulfilling a social obligation. They were sitting behind her as part of the congregation at St. Luke's. And somewhere, Sam was there, probably with Belinda and Mr. and Mrs. Cumberland. Annie glanced up at the stained glass windows on one side of the nave, remembering that a Cumberland had donated some section of the church.

In her black alligator purse was Winnie's letter. She had brought it in case she saw Sam. Only an hour before she left for the service, Annie had read the letter again, smoothing out the two pieces of heavy rag paper, which bore the embossed crest of the Racquet Club just above its name.

April 17, 1959

Dearest Annie,

Please don't think I'm writing alcoholic maunderings. The amount of caffeine in my brain has me in a state of alertness similar to that of an assassin.

The realization of my utter uselessness on this planet began many years before I had the good fortune of meeting you. Having charmed my way through life, I'm nevertheless aware of most of my problems. Their remedies don't make much sense to me anymore.

The moment Sam asked me to be involved with him and you, I thought the whole idea was a stroke of brilliance, a chance to send up the whole social pack by infiltrating it with someone genuine. You were delightful from the first. Sam was my best friend. For a moment I felt, yes, useful.

Alas, as fate would have it, I fell in love with you. I began to create the most elaborate fantasies, but they made sense only to me. As events around our little ménage à trois took their inevitable sad course, I waited patiently for the chance to marry you. You seemed the perfect addition to the Sumner line, representing the new blood of reality, or some such nonsense. I truly believed that with time, and love, we might very well have been a happy couple. And I confess, I imagined our children. But like all such utopian visions, this too had an inherent fatal flaw, and its name, of course, was Sam.

Dear Annie, I just spoke to him on the phone, for no other reason than to be certain of what I'd already concluded from seeing you this afternoon. What I didn't realize was the slipperiness of my own emotions at the moment. I said many terrible things to him just now, all lies, because, for reasons I can't explain, I wanted him to hate you as much as I hate myself, or some such neat psychological equation. Just show him this letter if he was fool enough to believe me.

He's coming down here, so I must hurry. It occurs to me that your birthday is soon, and I'm bound to spoil it. But dear Annie, be assured that what I'm doing is a gift, to you and, even more, to me. Believe that—and believe that I love you, hopelessly and stupidly perhaps, but as completely and honestly as I have ever been capable of loving.

W

The letter had arrived two days after the plane crash. Annie wanted to call Sam, but calling him was impossible, and sending Winnie's letter through the mail was no guarantee that he alone would see it. The way that Delansig had organized the memorial service did not present any opportunity for her to see anyone, least of all Sam. She would have preferred not to have any funeral at all, but Delansig had insisted. "Mrs. Sumner, there's a real purpose to having a ceremony," he had reasoned. "Let everyone have his day in church and think whatever he wants. It's a conclusion. After that, it's over." Annie had accepted that argument. At least there was no coffin. Winnie's remains had been cremated, and would be buried privately in the Sumner plot near Locust Valley.

Suddenly the processional cross was passing by her. Annie stood, feeling a weakness in her legs as the rector approached from the chancel, intoning, "Man, that is born of a woman, hath but a short time to live, and is full of misery. In the midst of life we are in death. Of whom may we seek for succor, but of Thee, O Lord . . ." He paused by her pew, reached out in a gesture both of compassion and of official church forgiveness, Annie thought, and clasped her hand for a moment, bringing her attention she did not want. The rector smiled consolingly, then went down the aisle, delivering his final words with mellifluous grandeur.

Annie ached to leave. When finally the usher swept across the front of the church, Annie left the pew and strode out through the side chapel before him. Two more ushers, similarly swallowtailed, waited at the door to guard the vesting room. When Annie walked into it, she thought Delansig might have to catch her, her legs were so shaky. Delansig, however, was not alone. Sam was standing next to him.

"Mr. Cumberland came in during the service, Mrs. Sumner," Delansig explained hurriedly. "I thought you might want to see him?" His voice lifted to imply a question.

"Yes," Annie replied, lifting the veil back over her small velvet hat.

"Don't take long," Delansig advised. "It's crazy out there already." He went out and closed the ornately carved wooden door behind him.

Wearing a dark suit and tie, Sam stood next to a black wooden cabinet that held various eucharistic vestments in thin, flat drawers. The room was shadowy, and Annie felt the air was stale. She could not see his face clearly. Fumbling with her purse, she opened it and put her hand on Winnie's letter.

"I don't know what you plan to say to the papers, Annie, but I don't want it to include me." His disdainful voice stopped her hand. "You told me that you didn't talk to Winnie. But he said you did, and it's hard not to believe him now, isn't it?"

"Sam!" She gasped, trying to see through the room's shadow. She stepped toward him, but his lowered head and forbidding stance stopped her.

"I'm pretty sure I'm the only one who heard about what you said to him," he continued coldly. "I haven't heard about any woman who you say was with him that afternoon. I haven't said anything, and won't, as long as you say nothing about why you were at the Carlyle or anything else about me."

She held Winnie's letter in her purse. "Anything to protect the Cumberland name," she said bitterly. "Even calling me a liar. The woman was married, Sam. Did you expect her to announce—"

"Why would Winnie say . . . ?" he said angrily, then stopped, controlling his temper.

Annie took her hand out of her purse and snapped it shut. "I doubt if you'll ever know why, Sam. And I'll never know how you could think . . . ." She was not able to finish.

She turned and opened the vesting room door. Delansig was waiting for her and they could hear the crowd outside. As she reached up to lower her veil, he said, "Here we go," and took her arm.

Annie let herself be half guided, half shoved by Delansig and the policemen into the station wagon. A New York City police car was in front and the constable's car behind; both turned on their sirens. Even with her eyes averted, Annie was blinded by the popping flashbulbs aimed at her window and through the windshield. She covered her face with her hands. Several people were pulled off the car as it began to move away from the church. The sirens continued for two blocks; at last there was quiet. Only then did Annie look out. They were speeding into Central Park. Annie took off her hat.

"Are you all right, Mrs. Sumner?" Delansig asked.

She reassured him as she wrapped the veil around the hat and put it in the back seat.

"I never told you anything about Sam Cumberland," she said. "How come you let him in there?"

Delansig paused a moment. "I heard that you left instructions with your farm manager to come get you if Sam Cumberland called. I assumed he was important."

"He was."

Responding to the cold finality in her tone, Delansig glanced at her but said nothing more. In spite of the many details they still had to deal with, they drove back to Millbrook in silence. She remembered the rector intoning, "In the midst of life we are in death . . ." She was not yet twenty, and already she was numb with death. Charlie was dead, Winnie was dead, Sam was dead. As the station wagon drove through the countryside covered by a bursting spring, Annie saw nothing.

Through the following weeks, she worked whenever she was able in the Rosewood barns. The new construction was canceled until the estate was settled and Annie decided what she was going to do. At night she battled sleeplessness and despair. She had told no one of her birthday; she hardly remembered it herself.

Annie responded to Delansig's many questions about Winnie's estate as best she could. She trusted him. He traveled to Millbrook almost daily, went through files and legal documents in the farm office, then hurried back to Scarsdale each night to be with his family. Whenever he spent the day at his office in New York, or conferred with the Sumner family's attorneys, he called Annie with new details of the estate as he discovered them.

The reading of Winnie's will took place three weeks after the funeral in the ancient offices of the Sumner family's law firm. Again Delansig delivered Annie, but he waited outside the sooty Wall Street building to take her home. She wished he could have come in with her, but all parties had agreed that their lawyers would not be present.

Sitting in a straight-back chair at a long, inlaid table in the law firm's conference room, Annie waited as others took their seats. Neither of Winnie's brothers spoke to her when he came in; each found a place at the table where he would not have to face her. A large number of other people were present; Annie nodded to a small group of farm employees, several from Lexington. There were representatives from various charities, some of whom courteously came up to her chair and introduced themselves. Annie did her best to respond, but her tension made it difficult for her to talk.

The firm's leonine attorney, an older man with flowing white hair and imperial visage, took his place at the head of the table, proceeded immediately with various legal explanations, and began to read the will. As Annie listened, an extraneous thought suddenly slipped into her mind. Her period was late. More than a week. Almost two. She sat absolutely still as Delansig had instructed, but under the table she began to tear at a hangnail with her thumb.

". . . I name my wife, Ann Grebauer Sumner, as executrix of this will, with all power and . . ."

If she was pregnant, it was Sam's child. In the last several months, she and Winnie had not even tried to make love. When she had seen Sam that day at the hotel, she did not have her diaphragm with her, even if she would have thought of using it. If she was pregnant, Annie knew that the pack and the press, when they found out, would get their enticing little thrills by counting on their fingers back to the date of Winnie's death. But they could not connect Sam. If a child was born, it would be named Sumner.

". . . and to my wife, Ann Grebauer Sumner, I leave all assets currently held in the Sumner Trust IV, these assets as of January 1, 1959, totaling at least twenty-six million dollars . . ."

The two brothers looked quickly at each other, then turned and glared at Annie. She looked down at her hands. The finger was bleeding. Winnie's letter was in her purse, useless now, except to prove what the pack had speculated, that the plane crash was not the accident which the investigations had concluded, with apparent official compassion. She kept the letter because she missed him so much.

". . . also to my wife, Ann Grebauer Sumner, I leave in its entirety the corporation known as Rosewood Stables, including all stock and contents on the two properties so named in Millbrook, New York, and Lexington, Kentucky, as well as at the Haras de la Brise in the Département de Calvados, Normandy, France. The box at the New York Racing Association tracks is included . . ."

Without Winnie between her and the fancy people, what chance would a child have? And Sam would figure out the timing. When the baby was born, he too would be able to count back nine months. However, being unaware that Annie had not slept with Winnie, Sam could argue away any speculation of his paternity. If he did admit to himself what the truth might be, his denial of it, if he was ever confronted, would be total. As she sat listening to the droning details of her inheritance, she found herself suddenly hoping that she was actually pregnant. Under the table she counted on her fingers. A baby would be born in January. That would be 1960. She would be twenty, four times five.

". . . and in the apartment at 600 Park Avenue, those items listed in the fine arts and silver inventory in Policy Number 667883HJ4 from the Summerville Insurance Company are also bequeathed to my wife, Ann Grebauer Sumner. All other contents of the apartment are to be divided between my brothers as they see fit, as is the family estate in Locust Valley, Long Island, New—"

"Holy Christ, she's getting everything!" the brother with the wives interjected. There was a heavy pause, broken by the other brother.

"Most of that silver belonged to my mother," he said in a tone implying a desecration.

As Delansig had advised her, Annie said nothing and did not react. The attorney reading the will cleared his throat commandingly as a warning and continued.

"And to my brothers, James Delany Sumner and George Lawton Sumner, I bequeath all the real estate currently held by the family-owned Glendenning Realty. The value of these properties, as of January 1, 1959, is conservatively estimated at 51.7 million. These are not liquid assets, and they will have to be managed. The Glendenning Box at the Metropolitan Opera is included. Combined with the trusts set up for my brothers by my father, these holdings make an equitable division of the main assets of the estate which my father entrusted to me—"

"What does that mean, 'have to be managed'?" the racing-car driver shouted.

"We'll break it, goddammit, we'll break it!" the other brother blurted.

"I doubt it, Mr. Sumner!" the attorney shouted back at both. "I wrote that will, and my wills don't get broken!" He stared down one brother and turned to look at the other. "The need for management means that you will have a choice of liquidating or going to work for the first time in your lives to make sure your assets are not squandered. I should also remind you both, and you can remind your lawyers, that your parents were enamored of the British tradition of primogeniture; hence your eldest brother, now deceased, inherited *everything* from your parents, which you did *not* contest. Quite legally, he had every right to leave *everything* to his wife, but he chose to be equitable. I would assure you any judge in this land would see that, even if you cannot. Now may I continue reading this will?"

Effectively silenced, the two brothers listened as bequests to some two dozen servants and thirty charities were announced. Annie noted only one, $25,000 to St. Luke's Church. The rector would be pleased, Annie thought, and understood why the fancy people remembered churches, hospitals, clubs, and boxes at Belmont and the Metropolitan Opera in their wills. It was for continuity, which death must enhance and not deter.

When the reading of the will was done, the attorney stood up to hand out copies and to shake the hand of anyone who approached him. The brothers avoided him and were the first to leave the conference room. Annie waited for them to go, then rose and thanked the attorney. Notwithstanding his spirited words on her behalf, the attorney barely touched her hand. She sensed a familiar contempt. Annie realized he had not been defending her at all; he was upholding his own creation. As a long-time attorney for the Sumner family, he looked at Annie as if she were nothing more than a successful fortune hunter of alarmingly young years. Annie turned and left the room.

As she and Delansig drove up the West Side Highway, Annie reported to him the details of the will from her copy. Quite unexpectedly, in the middle of telling, she knew exactly what she was going to do.

"I'm going to sell the two Rosewood Farms and go live in France."

"Excuse me?" Delansig said, trying to look at her as he drove. "You were telling me about the fine arts in the apartment."

"We'll sell what we can, give the damn silver back to the brothers, and put the rest in storage. I don't want to stay here," she said quietly. "Everything I planned here was for my husband. He hated Rosewood and I wasn't able to change that in time. It'll be better to let it go and start over in France."

"I'm not sure that's such a good idea, Mrs. Sumner," Delansig said with genuine concern. "Do you know anybody over there?"

"No. No one. And nobody knows me. I spent some time at the *haras* with Mr. Sumner, so I know what's there . . . You might as well hear this now. I think I'm going to have a baby."

Delansig tried to exercise a lawyer's rigid control over his surprise, but he failed. "My God, I'm so sorry."

"Why?" Annie asked.

"Because it's certain to complicate your life . . . and it's sad that, well, the child won't ever know his father."

Annie did not respond.

"Mrs. Sumner, I suppose I should advise you that if you're going to France soon, my firm has contact with several excellent doctors in Paris. Certain procedures are illegal in France, so they would fly down to meet you in a private clinic in Casablanca if you should wish to exercise any options regarding termination of . . ." Again he stopped.

A clinic in Casablanca. The rich had everything worked out

so neatly, Annie thought, realizing for the first time that she was one of them. When she had married Winnie, she was given access to as much money as she had ever wanted or needed; however, she had no sense of being rich herself. She was merely playing a sumptuous role, and was never in control of what was to happen. Now, the authority was hers. She ignored Delansig's offer and startled him with a question.

"How many months does it take for a woman to show?"

"Well, as I remember, three or four."

"I want the two farms on the market tomorrow. We'll set up a dispersal of all the Rosewood bloodstock as close to the Summer Select Sales at Keeneland as we can get. I'll ship the stock at Millbrook down to Lexington. I'd like you down there to manage the dispersal. Anyone who's worked for Rosewood longer than two years, and doesn't want to take a chance on new owners, gets six months' pay . . . You think we can do all that in three months?"

"I doubt if Rosewood will sell that fast," he opined, "and six months' pay is an awful lot."

"Can I afford it?"

"Oh, yes, Mrs. Sumner," he replied, "you can certainly afford it."

Annie looked at him inquisitively. Something had changed about the way he said "Mrs. Sumner." It had always sounded a little unnatural after his use of "Miss Grebauer." They had spent almost every day together for weeks, and he was at least a dozen years older than she was. She had been planning to suggest they call each other by their first names. The way he had just said "Mrs. Sumner," however, sounded right for the first time—not careful, or respectful, or formal, but authentic. Annie wondered if money had changed her in his eyes, or if somehow she herself so quickly had been transformed.

A month later, her pregnancy was without doubt. Not only had she missed her second period, but the Manhattan doctor with whom she had consulted called to inform her that his tests were positive and to give her advice about diet. The inevitability startled, frightened, and exhilarated Annie. She continued to work at the barns, hoping that preparation for the dispersal sale would distract her. Feeds were being changed to fatten up the horses. She taught her grooms how to take particular care with currying and grooming, and told them to keep their horses out of the bright sun, which burned their coats. With Delansig, Annie shuttled between Millbrook and Lexington, arranging for the dispersal sale and for the sale of real estate. One day, with no more warning than a grumbling phone call from an unknown trainer at Belmont Park, a twelve-horse van pulled into the farm at Millbrook. The first horse led off was Jaybird, one of Charlie Dell's runners, which Annie had walked out and groomed at Saratoga. Fortunately, there were enough empty stalls at Rosewood for his string of horses, as well as room in one corner of a barn for the sixteen crates of books that arrived by truck later the same day.

According to the papers that came in the van with Charlie's consignment, Jaybird and the others had been shipping out to claiming races, which they lost. They arrived at Rosewood in poor condition, in need of care from the vet and the farrier. Over the following few months, Charlie's horses responded well to the special care Annie lavished on them. She took Jaybird on long, easy rides in the morning, which benefited them both. Riding over the Rosewood acres one day, Annie remembered how Mrs. Cumberland had sat in the front row of the Philharmonic so that Sam would learn to appreciate music. She laughed out loud, startling Jaybird, who shied sideways.

By July, both farms were being looked at daily by prospective buyers. Delansig began to hear about the resentment in the thoroughbred world at the Sumner widow's hasty sale of Rosewood and its noble tradition. Offers were made, though none met Annie's price. Her wardrobe was requiring more loose, presumably casual clothes. In drawstring pants and long work shirts that covered her expanding abdomen, Annie supervised the shipping of the Millbrook horses south. The Rosewood Stables dispersal of a hundred and thirty head of thoroughbred bloodstock was set to take place two days before the Keeneland Select Summer Sales, an event that drew buyers of the finest bloodstock to Lexington from all over the world. With a series of advertisements in *The Blood-Horse* and *Thoroughbred Record,* in the *Morning Telegraph* and the Lexington and Louisville papers, Annie and Delansig hoped to convince the Keeneland buyers to start their purchases a few days early.

The dispersal was set to begin on schedule at ten in the morning of what turned out to be the hottest, muggiest day that summer. Annie wore a cotton shirt with a wide-cut jacket and a long scarf centered down her torso. The ensemble was a smart and effective disguise.

Outside the Rosewood barns, the auction company had set up two hundred folding chairs and an auction ring. Annie welcomed people as they arrived, but she received more curious or resentful looks than courtesy. Thirty minutes before the hour, the seats were nearly full. Watching and talking quietly among themselves, a few men stood in back.

Annie recognized one of the men. It was Frank Carney. He was talking to a stocky, bald man who watched Annie as he listened. Then, with an angelic smile, he came over, easing along as if running into her on a country road. Behind him, Carney watched Annie and nodded. The strength of his look and the blue-green eyes had an unexpected effect on Annie.

"Miz Sumner, I'm Albert Beasley. How're you doin' this morning?" He reached out his hand, which she took.

"Not too bad, Mr. Beasley. This is Archy Delansig; helps me out on just about everything."

"Must be a lawyer," he said, chuckling. "Well, ma'am, I was noticing what you're doin' here, and I have to tell you, I feel it's a terrible shame. I'm wondering if you'd consider an alternative?"

She looked down at the ring where the auction workers were raking the circle of sawdust. Then she looked back at Frank Carney. He was still watching her.

"Mr. Beasley, if you can tell me a way I can keep a hundred and thirty head without worrying about them, I'd be interested in hearing what you have in mind."

Delighted, he laughed with more stomach shaking than sound. "Ma'am, just about everybody around here calls me Chigger. Please feel free. I own Blue Bell Farm out on the Versailles Road. Sent a boy over here to get your catalogue the other day, and I've been studying it pretty good. Talking with a couple of friends of mine over there, we think you got a couple of lines of broodmare families here that it's a real advantage to own. Since you're selling the Rosewood Farms, I'm wondering if you and I couldn't figure out a way for me to look after your horses at my place, selling off some of them here today, of course, but seeing what we could do with all that quality."

Annie and Delansig exchanged a quick glance. They both knew of Blue Bell Farm. It was not one of the famous Bluegrass stables, but was highly respected for boarding, breeding, breaking, and foaling thoroughbreds.

"I tell you, ma'am," Chigger Beasley continued, "you've got some bloodstock here that don't come along too often. You may just want to be done with it, and I'd understand that. It happens to people. On the other side of the fence, someday, when things are different for you, you might regret it a whole lot. Unless you're just dead set on giving these horses away this morning, I'm pretty sure we could work something out. Now you just can't cancel the auction, but if you bought some back, you'd only be losing the auction people's commission."

Annie looked at him quizzically for a moment, then turned to the ring. "Will you stand here with me and tell me which ones to let go if I'm willing to buy the rest back?"

"Yes, ma'am. Sure will."

"Mr. Delansig, you'd better tell the auction people to keep their eye on us."

Delansig hurried down to the auctioneer as Annie looked past Chigger Beasley to the group of men with whom he had been standing.

"What's Caernarvon Farms doing here?" she asked.

"Ma'am, Caernarvon Farms isn't really here today. They're down for Keeneland, of course, but Frank Carney says he got curious about your bloodstock, and Frank goes his own way. Knows more about horses than anyone I've ever known. Matter of fact, it was Frank who called me and put the idea into my head that we ought to talk."

Frank Carney saw Annie looking in his direction. She smiled her thanks as Beasley continued to talk to her. Frank's face softened, but he looked away before it could break into an expression that meant anything.

"There's one thing you don't have, Miz Sumner, if you don't mind my saying it."

"What's that?"

"The Rosewood stallions are about tuckered out, seems to me. I'm wondering, if you're going to be around a few days, whether you'd be going to the Keeneland sales. There's a couple of colts that might be real nice possibilities for you."

"I suppose everyone goes to Keeneland, Mr. Beasley," she said.

"Yes, ma'am, everybody does, and Blue Bell Farm has a bunch of seats right down front. Won't you please call me Chigger."

"Why do they call you that?"

" 'Cause I get in under people's skin real fast, and if they scratch at me too hard, I drive 'em crazy. Now listen, you're from Kentucky, ain't you? You sure do sound like you're from around here somewheres."

Annie had to laugh. He used his accent the way she did, to ingratiate, disarm, and make people think he was not as smart as he most surely was.

Over the next two hours, Annie, Delansig, and Chigger Beasley bought back sixty-four horses, then worked out their deal. For their benefit, and with taxes in mind, Delansig drew up corporation papers for Fair Lady Stable with Annie as president, Chigger Beasley as vice president, and himself as secretary-treasurer. They studied the Keeneland sales catalogue and found a colt to be auctioned the first day, hip number 38, with bloodlines that would be a strong complement to the broodmares Annie owned.

"Buying yearlings is a crapshoot, ma'am," Chigger told her, "and you might have to pay nearly a hundred thousand for the privilege of wondering if he can run frontward and worrying if he's sterile."

Annie was staggered by the amount, but she had her own purpose in mind.

"Can I afford it, Mr. Delansig?"

"After my instant thoroughbred education, I'd say you can afford it, Mrs. Sumner."

The day before the sale, she closed on offers for both Rosewood Farms. The prices were not as high as she had asked, but she wanted them sold before she left the country. Then she packed, starting with her accumulation of maternity clothes. The stretch-stomach trousers, ballooning dresses, and blouses with nursing flaps were still folded in tissue paper with their price tags attached. A train was leaving Lexington's Union Station the evening after the sale, and she had reserved a compartment. She laid the new garments in the drawer of the steamer trunk, suddenly abashed by what was happening in her body, for as she leaned over, she felt the baby move. She stood up, waited for it to happen again, then cried out happily when it did. In that moment, whatever else she had to do seemed insignificant.

When she and Archy Delansig arrived at the Keeneland Sales Pavilion, she was wearing a dark raincoat over a plain black high-necked jersey dress, black stockings, and black shoes. The outfit announced her mourning and, without the coat, clearly revealed her pregnancy. Chigger Beasley was waiting for her in the crowded lobby, and he and Delansig escorted her to the glassed-in amphitheater. As they opened the door leading to the center aisle, Annie saw that the auction was in progress and that every seat was taken. The bid board said that number 36 was being sold. The horse was being led around the sawdust-covered ring in front of the high rostrum on which the tuxedoed auctioneers called out their expostulating, incessant repetition of the bids and raises.

Chigger Beasley started to lead the way.

"Just a second, Chigger," Annie said as she took off her coat. "I'd appreciate it if you'd both let me go down there and sit alone. I'll buy the horse."

Seeing her without her coat, the men were hesitant to let her go alone. "Well, ma'am, my momma always told me to escort a lady to her seat," Chigger said, smiling.

"Well, that's all right," she said, handing him her coat and using her deepest accent. "I'm not too sure I'm whatever a

257

lady is, and if your momma knew I was pregnant, she'd have told you to let me have my way."

Chigger laughed with his stomach and agreed. Delansig said, "We won't be far."

Annie walked down the steps of the center aisle. Whispered reactions of recognition from both sides of the semicircular audience section filtered into the rhythmic chant of the auctioneer. She stepped slowly until she reached the third row, where the four seats on the aisle had taped to them pieces of paper reading BLUE BELL FARM. Instead of quickly sitting, she turned to one side, then the other, on the pretense of looking for her seat, but with the purpose of demonstrating her pregnant profile as obviously as possible.

A number of horsemen were there who had no idea who she was, and looked at her as a pretty mother-to-be in a black dress. There were, however, many familiar faces from the past staring at her, Winnie's friends, people from Saratoga and Lexington, and, two rows above her, seated across the aisle, was Sam Cumberland seated next to Frank Carney. Before she sat down, Annie saw the look of shock on Sam's face.

Hip number 36 was sold, and number 37, a chestnut filly, was led in.

Annie picked up a sales catalogue from the seat next to hers and pretended to read it. The auction hall was never quiet, but her appearance had caused an audible reaction, which continued through the short period of bidding for the filly. She was sold and led out. Then number 38 was led in, the colt's identifying number on a small square of paper stuck to his hip. He gave an immediate bleating whinny and tried to rear from his handler.

The bidding began quickly at $25,000, and Annie was delighted to hear Frank Carney come in at $50,000 and drive the bidding in five-thousand-dollar increments to $75,000, when two other parties dropped out. The hall had become attentive, and as the auctioneer called for further bidding, the room was silent out of respect for so much money being spent and made.

As the auctioneer raised his gavel, however, Annie held her hand up and was noticed by one of the dozen bid spotters around the amphitheater. He recognized the bid with an instant shout. The auctioneer recorded it, as well as the very rapid following bids from Frank Carney, which drove the price to Annie's bid of $90,000.

"Ma'am," the auctioneer said from his podium, "we're unfamiliar with the bidder. Are you bidding for Blue Bell Farm?"

"No, I'm bidding for myself. My name's Mrs. Annie Sumner." She said it clearly, and there was an intense reaction throughout the hall.

Then Sam's voice called to the same spotter, with a false casualness that Annie knew so well. "A hundred."

From the podium, the auctioneer picked up the bid and proclaimed, "A hundred thousand dollars is bid," and went on chanting.

The effect of a sudden doubled raise to the psychological boundary of $100,000 was supposed to freeze opponents.

"A hundred twenty-five," Annie said to the spotter, who turned to bellow the bid up to the auctioneer. The auctioneer's mouth automatically ran with it, but got nowhere. From behind Annie across the aisle, there was silence, and the auctioneer finally dropped his hammer, as a floor man rushed to Annie to get her signature on the sales slip. She stood to sign it in order to allow the crowd another look. Walking up the steps, she smiled graciously at Sam for all to see. He glared at her, then looked away. Frank Carney, however, smiled slightly, offering his congratulations.

Someone started clapping, and Annie thought that, having won the bidding, she might be getting a little appreciation. The clap, however, was not spontaneous; it was a steady, contemptuous parody of applause. Quickly taken up by many others in the hall, it made the air crack in rhythm around Annie as she reached the top of the stairs. Nevertheless, her smile remained, and at the door, she turned back as if acknowledging the room. She stayed there long enough to let them know she would not run, and she would not be mocked.

Chigger Beasley and Delansig were waiting for her. Full of congratulations and admiration, they drove her straight to the train station and helped her board. After their good wishes and reassurances, she sat alone at last in her compartment. For several hours, she stared out into the moonlit night until the train passed by the bank of the Ohio where she had grown up. She stood, her hands and face pressed against the window. In the bright moonlight, she barely saw Cowell's Bluff, then the service road, and the dirt road leading up to the shack. In a moment, the view was gone. As the train trundled across the bridge over the Big Sandy River and sped into West Virginia, she sat again and put both hands over her stomach. Remembering her mother's flower garden, she smiled. Later, when the porter came to make up her bed, she had already fallen asleep.

Once in New York, she transferred directly from Pennsylvania Station to Pier 43 and found her cabin on the S.S. *Independence,* sailing to Southampton and then Cherbourg.

PART TWO

Glorious Girl

1965–1975

SEVENTEEN

▬▬▬▬▬▬▬▬▬▬▬▬▬▬▬▬▬▬▬
▬▬▬▬▬▬▬▬▬▬▬▬▬▬▬▬▬▬▬

"BONJOUR, MAMAN."

Annie sat up in bed, startled from a dream that she immediately forgot but that left her feeling troubled. Eager for an invitation, the little boy stood in his pajamas, his hand gripping her big toe under the quilt. Smiling, she held out her arms to him. He leaped onto the bed and crawled up into her embrace.

"Good morning, Henry," she said purposefully in English, her attempt to equalize the French he was learning. "How'd you sleep?"

The boy was still a towhead, with just a hint of his mother's reddish gold blending in. His eyes were as deep-set and blue as his father's, but the resemblance ended there. His smile was his own, wide, with a small wrinkling of his nose. Already he was quite handsome, quick to laugh, as quick to go silent when

263

disturbed. But even his pensive quiet held the enthusiasm of a five-year-old discovering the world.

"*Maman, allons-y!* I'm hungry," he yelped, jumping to the floor and tugging at Annie's hand.

"Go get dressed; I think Yvette is making brioches. And wear the sweater I laid out on your chair. It's supposed to be cold today."

As the boy ran across the hall to his room, Annie opened the draperies on the windows in her bedroom and looked out. The three stable lads were already busy around the boxes of the barns. Beyond the bare black branches of the apple orchards was the rolling countryside of the Calvados region leading to La Côte Fleurie, the flowered coast.

Abruptly, she remembered her dream. She was back in Saratoga, but working for Caernarvon Farms, grooming Certainty with a curry comb. As she brushed, hair from his coat pulled out in thick bunches, leaving large patches of raw skin. She tried to hold the hair on, but more and more pulled out from his hide until the colt was a skeleton, who turned his skull to face her, his hollow eyes staring, blaming her.

Hurrying to put on her dressing gown, Annie shuddered from the dream and the chill room. In spite of new central heating, and a three-year struggle to eradicate the dry rot in the timbers and walls of the old château, fall and winter mornings were still bone chilling. Even when the oil burners kicked on, heating the stone floors took much of the day. Still, it was a great improvement over the first winter Annie had spent there, when the baby was born and she had held him against her body every night under three quilts.

Annie was proud of what she had accomplished at the Château de la Brise. Not only had it been modernized, with new plumbing and wiring, but the rooms had been refurbished, redecorated, and, in some cases, redesigned. A crumbling larder had been made over into a pristine laundry, and what had been a basement scullery now glowed with botanical lights so that it was a year-round hothouse filled with flowers, herbs, and plants. An unused storage space became Annie's dressing room and bath, both done in pale green marble, luxuriously warm because of newly installed radiant heat.

And another winter, the fifth for her. Henry was born in the middle of the first one, in January. He had been a colicky baby, and Annie had had to carry him in her arms for months, sleeping when she could. During his first three years, he'd been subject to sundry fevers and illnesses, but in these past two years he'd gained strength and vigor, and she had a funny, energetic little man on her hands.

As she sat down on an ottoman to put on her slippers, Annie remembered what an older woman had said to her the previous night.

"My dear, you obviously have a passion you do not allow to breathe." The woman had smiled, but her eyes indicated an accusation.

Madame Marie Pichon was a houseguest at the *haras* of the Comte and Comtesse de Deaubry, one of the few couples in the area who had broken through Annie's protective reticence. The comtesse was an American from Burlingame, California. The couple had two small daughters and bred horses. In the local village on market day, when she heard Annie struggling with a six-month-old baby and French, she had offered to help. Annie was still reserved with the Comtesse de Deaubry but continued the relationship, based on sharing the problems of young children and being Americans living in Normandy.

Madame Pichon had been seated to the comte's right at the opposite end of the dinner table from Annie. During the course of the meal, Annie learned that the woman was the most famous horsewoman in France, and had been decorated with the Croix de Combattante for heroism during the Nazi occupation. Before his death, her husband and she sent horses to all the great races of Europe, and won many of them. Annie saw Madame Pichon watching her. When the party moved into the Deaubrys' drawing room for coffee and Calvados, she took Annie's arm and said, "Come sit and talk with me. I hear you have horses."

They had an instant rapport. They talked for an hour, comparing ideas and learning of each other's lives. After the other guests said good night, they talked for another hour, until the comte and comtesse went to bed, leaving the two women by the fire. Annie sat watching the white-haired woman as her restless though penetrating gray eyes reflected the firelight. Physically, she was a woman of hard angles, flat cheeks, straight mouth, sharp elbows under her maroon velvet dress, a solid uncurving back, and a prominent chin, which emphasized everything she said in her clear, level voice.

"You know, Ann*ie*," Madame Pichon said, accenting the second syllable, "I have a program at my Haras de la Poire for young people who wish to learn my way with horses. I call them my *stagiaires*, pupils who work very hard. They live in the château as my guests and help me do everything. It's not far, about an hour, in the heart of the Pays d'Auge near Potigny. We raise great thoroughbreds there. Perhaps you and your son would like to come for a time. We would find him a pony, and we're about to have a litter of springer puppies, so we would keep him busy . . . and you, too."

Annie had an impulse to accept, but at the same time felt a familiar alarm. "Madame, thank you, I'd love to do that, but the . . ."

"Ah, yes, of course, the eternal 'but,'" she said, smiling pleasantly, except that her eyes revealed her disregard for the unspoken excuse. "Let's have one more swallow of this beautiful Calvados and hope it will dissolve all the 'buts' in our lives."

The evening had ended there, and Annie had returned to her château. As she brushed her hair, she realized how automatic her rejection had been and admitted to herself that for five years she had stayed in the Haras de la Brise as if it were a fortress, carefully avoiding any possibility of intrusion, emotional or otherwise. At the very occasional neighborhood dinner party, she was inevitably seated next to an eligible man. Charming, handsome, amusing, or intelligent, but always hound-eager, he would invite Annie to the Casino in Deauville, to his yacht, to watch him play polo, or go for a walk in the moonlight. Annie always refused, graciously but rigidly enough to dampen ardor and, on a number of occasions, wound vanity. A number of Frenchmen simply could not accept her rejection. One angrily accused her of frigidity, and was surprised when she agreed to the possibility. Annie had not made love since the afternoon in the Carlyle Hotel when her son was conceived.

A few months earlier, she had gone to Paris for the first time since her return to France. She wanted to take Henry to the Louvre. Although he liked the train ride, he was quickly bored with the art. Annie discovered that she was grieved by memories of the hurried day she had spent with Sam and Winnie. She and Henry returned to La Brise early. Such memories did not affect her there, for the *haras* was filled with the experience of her son.

From the moment she had arrived at La Brise, Annie began to revive the farm and the stock, which had been neglected for so many years. Throughout her pregnancy, she supervised the barns' renovations. She sold off stock that had no use, and by the time Henry was born, she was down to ten horses and a small staff of local lads to keep the barns immaculate. Within weeks of the birth, she began riding again, and since then had never missed a day.

She bred her best mares to good stallions standing at one or another of the two hundred *haras* in the province. The resulting foals were usually sold as yearlings at Deauville in the summer, although she kept a few. Annie never went to the sales, nor did she accompany her mares to her neighbors' breeding sheds. Occasionally she had been asked to board horses for other owners, but she always turned down such offers. The Haras de la Brise had been safe for five years, and Annie was unwilling to jeopardize that security with outside commitments.

Hurrying to her bedroom to finish dressing, she picked up the *International Herald Tribune* from the floor, where she had dropped it the previous night. She held the paper a moment, remembering that nearly two years before, she had read in the *Trib* of the death from natural causes of J. Cardell Cumberland and, a week later, of the death of his wife, Cornelia Talasker Cumberland, presumably from a combination of grief and self-will. According to the obituary writer, she had stated commandingly at her husband's grave side, "I do not wish to continue living without him," as if informing God what she expected of Him.

After considering the idea for several days, Annie wrote a short note of sympathy to Sam, a simple statement with no undertones of the past. Three weeks later she received an engraved card which informed her that "the Cumberland family deeply appreciates your expression of sympathy." Annie imagined Sam reading her letter and ordering the impersonal response, or Belinda handling all the condolence mail and never showing it to Sam, or of no one seeing it but a social secretary.

A second incursion of memory, less painful but more frightening, usually followed any thought of the death of the Cumberlands. As she dressed in her breeches, riding boots, sweater, and jacket, she remembered the unannounced visit. It had happened just after her twenty-second birthday. From her office window she watched a car approaching the château. The vehicle moved slowly up the long drive between the rows of apple trees, which were covered in pink blossoms at the time. Annie noticed that it was an American car, a black Chevrolet, and as it got closer, she saw that it had a French diplomatic license plate. The two men who came in were dressed in dark suits and one carried an attaché case. In the entrance hall, the man with the case said, "I'm Ben Stewart of the United States Department of Justice. This is Lyle McCracken of the FBI." Each produced an identity badge.

Smiling hospitably to cover her agitation, Annie escorted them into the small parlor she had made into an office and closed the door, which she seldom did. When they were seated and the attaché case was opened, she asked, "Should I have my lawyer here?"

"Gee, I think you have to be the judge of that, Mrs. Sumner," the Justice Department man said earnestly. "We certainly wouldn't mind. We're only looking for some information."

Annie smiled back, but she was disturbed. "Well, let me see if I can help you. I'd as soon not bother my lawyer." She hoped the response would give the impression of her having nothing to fear. For the first time in probably a year, she thought of the gun she had brought with her from America and kept in the glove compartment of her Renault Ondine.

"Do you know, or have you ever had contact with someone

named Vito Genovese, known as Don Vitone?" Ben Stewart asked. He used an ingenuous tone, as if trying for a manner of mild curiosity.

"No, sir." Annie wanted to reach for the telephone instantly, but it was too early to try to reach Delansig in New York, even if she could manage to get through the French telephone system.

"Do you know, or have you ever had contact with a Joseph Valachi?"

"No, sir." She had never even heard the name. Perhaps she was all right.

"Did you know, or did you ever have contact with a Charles Del Vicario, known as Charlie Dell?"

"Yes, sir. I worked for him once." She noticed that the FBI man had said nothing, but only watched her.

"Were you friends, Mrs. Sumner?" Stewart asked.

"I drove him to the track a lot. He helped me get a job on the backstretch."

"I see," he said, looking down at his papers. "Gosh, he left you a dozen thoroughbreds and sixteen crates of books." Smiling at Annie as if confused, he obviously was aware of what he had revealed.

"Yes. By then I was running a stable and could look after them. The books, well, he got me started reading . . . Is something wrong? Because if there is, I really think I ought to call my lawyer, and I'd have to ask you to come back another time when he was here."

The two men glanced at each other, and the FBI man took over. "Mrs. Sumner, there's nothing wrong and we're not here to intimidate you in any way. We're here because we have a witness, Joe Valachi. He's a very important witness, a member of the Mafia or, as he puts it, La Cosa Nostra. He's been exposing to us the entire structure of organized crime in America. But in order to use his evidence, we have to be sure he isn't lying, or exaggerating for purposes of revenge, or trying to please us in the hope of gaining leniency. The reason he's talking to us is that he was in the Atlanta penitentiary with Vito Genovese, who ordered him killed. Valachi doesn't know exactly why. Apparently a body had been buried for Genovese some years ago by Charlie Dell, who, Valachi tells us, was known as the Undertaker. Somehow Genovese became convinced that Valachi knew about the body and was trying to blackmail him. Genovese gave Valachi the kiss of death, so Valachi came to us for protection. For us, knowing Genovese's motives and Valachi's motives is vital. That's why we've come all the way over here to talk to you."

Terrified, Annie watched McCracken, realizing he could know much more than what he had told her. She tried hard to hold her voice steady. "I'm not sure I can help, but I'll do what I can. When I knew Charlie, he was an old man. He was pretty sick, and seemed to love only one thing, the races. He paid me to drive him out to the tracks, but we didn't talk about his past."

"Did you know about it?" Stewart asked. "That is, that he buried the mob's bodies in buildings all over New York?"

"I heard about that," Annie replied, feeling that every word she spoke was like a razor blade between her lips, "after I'd known him awhile. I couldn't believe it. He was very kind to me . . . I was sixteen when I first met him. He was kind of like my grandfather. He'd never had children, so . . . ."

"Who told you about him?" McCracken asked pointedly.

Annie suddenly realized that she would not have been the first person they contacted. "Some other people who worked for him."

The two men glanced at each other.

"Mrs. Sumner," Stewart said, "do you know, or have you had contact with, a Philip Angelo, known as the Angel?"

"Yes." Already realizing that the Angel had gone ahead like the fool he was and tried somehow to blackmail Genovese, Annie wondered how much Phil had told them.

"Could you tell us about him?"

Annie smiled grimly. "Now I am getting worried. I have the feeling you're after something that I doubt if I can give you, but I sure don't want to get into trouble trying. I'll tell you about Phil, but if we're going any further, I really do want to call my lawyer."

McCracken watched her for a moment. "Tell us about Phil."

"He bet the horses with Charlie. He knew about Charlie's past and told me about some of it, I think to impress or scare me. I didn't like Phil Angelo very much, and he didn't like me."

"Was Phil Angelo involved in any way in Charlie Dell's undertaking business?" McCracken watched her intently.

"I don't know," Annie said. "I don't think so. From what I heard, Charlie retired from that before they met. They just played the horses. I think Phil owed Charlie some money."

The FBI man nodded, then stood up. "We're done, Mrs. Sumner. No need to call your lawyer. If we need to talk to you again, we'll give you plenty of warning." He hesitated; then, as the Justice Department man closed his case and stood beside him, he asked, "You don't happen to know where we could reach Mr. Angelo, do you? It seems he's disappeared."

Deeply relieved, Annie replied, "Sir, I never even knew where he lived."

"Thank you for your time, Mrs. Sumner," Stewart said. "Oh, and by the way, Vera Kovalchik sends her love."

McCracken glared at him for revealing the information, at which Stewart only shrugged. Annie laughed. "I didn't know her last name, either."

After they left, Annie placed a call to Delansig at his home in Scarsdale. Two hours later, the call went through. That evening, a professional bodyguard arrived from Paris and took up residence at the château's small gatehouse. Fitting in easily with the rest of the staff and enjoying his life in the country, the former paratrooper was always in sight when any stranger appeared at the *haras.* His presence reassured Annie but did not end her fear. As long as Phil Angelo was alive, "disappeared" or not, she expected him to come after her.

"*Maman! Maman!* Yvette did *not* make brioches. She's making omelettes. I hate eggs! *Les oeufs sont écoeurants!*"

Henry stood with his legs astride in the middle of the downstairs hall, hands on his hips and eyes blazing. He was already such a man, Annie thought, making his French objections. Still amazed after five years even to have a son, much less one who spoke French, Annie resisted picking him up to hug him and instead answered his stern tone in kind.

"Eggs are *very* good for you; of course, that doesn't matter much to you, does it? What kind of omelette is it?"

"Je n'sais pas." He shrugged. "She hasn't cooked them yet."

"Well, what if it was an omelette with the strawberry jam we made inside it?"

"Jam, in an omelette?"

"It's really good."

He considered it a moment. "I'll try a little bit." Then he smiled and reached for her hand, grabbing at her wedding ring as he had done since he was a baby. He tugged her along through the dining room and into the kitchen, where they both greeted the cook.

Annie had struggled to learn enough French to communicate with her staff. They stood stoically before her as she pointed, gesticulated, and pantomimed her wishes. Preferring an incoherent woman to an absentee landlord, they waited until they understood what she was trying to say. Then, in the Normandy fashion, they raised their eyebrows, said, "Ah," and went on their way. Fortunately she had found a head lad to run the barns who had apprenticed at Newmarket in England. He had as much "struggling English" as Annie had "struggling French." In the last year, however, Annie had used Henry on a number of occasions as her translator.

As Yvette poured a large cup of café au lait from two long-handled copper pots, Annie watched her son carefully cut into his omelette, put a tiny piece into his mouth, and acknowledge his satisfaction.

"Chew it fifty-seven times," Annie said, an old joke of theirs.

With his mouth still full, he said, "Maman, did my father die here or in America?"

There were times when Annie was grateful that English was not understood by her employees. "In America, remember?"

"In an airplane?"

"Yes." She watched his reaction, which was, as usual, a look of anger that Annie did not understand but did not yet question. He took another bite and spoke as he chewed. "When are we going there?"

"Don't talk with your mouth full, Henry. I don't know. You want to go?"

"Mais certainement. For school. I'm an American, Maman."

Yes, he certainly was an American, which he announced whenever he was introduced. "I'm Henry Sumner. I'm an American." The question of school had been pushing itself into Annie's mind. The next fall, he should start kindergarten, the following year, first grade, unless he went to school in France, which did not appeal to either son or mother. Yet for Annie, the idea of going back was like returning to a nightmare.

"Henry, you and I have been invited to stay at one of the greatest stables in France. Would you like to go?"

He looked at her warily as he ate the omelette. From his earliest days, Annie noticed his caution about any variation, anything new. There always had been deep caution in him. Annie often wondered if he had inherited the trait from her or had assumed her attitude.

"We have *un grand haras* right here," he said, using his French as a shield, which he often did.

"Yes, it's a very nice stable. But the woman who invited us has a pony she'd like you to try, and she wants you to help take care of the puppies that—"

"Puppies? What kind?"

Henry had his own pony, which he was learning to ride at La Brise, but there were no dogs on the place and he often had asked to have one. Annie suspected that puppies would decide the issue for him. Later that morning after her ride, as she sat down to write to Madame Pichon, she still was not sure what had decided the issue for her.

Chère Madame,

   The Calvados worked; the "buts" are dissolved. My son is eager to be present for the puppies' birth. When may we come?

By return mail came Madame Pichon's reply:

Ma chère Annie,
  I am delighted. Come as soon as you can. The puppies are due in two weeks, but anything can happen.

Three days later, Annie and Henry drove between knotted brooding branches of the plane trees that bordered the road on each side. The long avenue led straight to a pair of huge wrought-iron gates, then curved to the cobblestoned courtyard of a château. Larger than that of La Brise, the building was an amalgam of architectural periods. Turrets and irregular trusses supported the roof; from it protruded four different kinds of chimneys. On one end was a small Italianate balcony, on the other was a second-floor terrace bordered by a balustrade. Surrounded by carefully pruned pear trees, perverse in Calvados country, the ancient building looked over a small lake. Beyond it were plowed fields, then the immense main barns, with dense forests of oak darkening the landscape behind them.

Madame Pichon, dressed for work in boots and riding breeches, met Annie and Henry at the front door, and showed them to their room, which overlooked the lake. After unpacking and changing, Henry was introduced immediately to Vouvray, the white wine–colored springer bitch who rested comfortably in a warm kitchen corner, waiting to give birth. Then he was taken off to a stable in the woods to meet "his" pony, a chestnut Landais with a fine coat and a friendly personality. Thus occupied, the boy was content to stay as his mother and Madame Pichon continued to survey the *haras*.

"I have many rules here," Annie's hostess said, "for the horses and for myself. I assure you I've broken every one of them, but it is necessary to have them. For instance, we dress respectably for dinner, and we are always on time. We grow our own food because the food in the stores is filled with chemicals. I insist on the same purity for the animals, from the most prized stallion to the chickens. *No chemicals!* The best cure for any disease is to keep everyone healthy in the first place. If disease comes, isolate it and give good care, which of course includes medicine. That's the time for a few carefully selected chemicals. After all, my horses are not Christian Scientists, nor am I."

She gave a low, rolling laugh. Stopping to rest at a field gate, she turned to Annie. "But the most important rule we have here at the Haras de la Poire is to wake up with a purpose, and work toward it every second of the day. Whether it is a large purpose or a small one makes no difference; whether you accomplish it that day doesn't matter. You will the next. But you must know what it is the moment your eyes open, or the day will be lost to busy-ness, which is how most people waste their lives. There! That is the *first* sermon!"

Annie laughed with Madame. As they walked along a rutted path leading through the woods to another stable, however, Madame began again.

"That's what we must find for you, Ann*ie*—a clear purpose to wake with. And I must be honest with you. I hope it will turn out to be the same as mine."

Annie smiled. "I doubt if I could do it as well as you, but you might as well tell me what it is."

Madame Pichon hesitated, glanced at Annie, then said, "But of course. To raise classic thoroughbreds, nothing less. And of course there *is* nothing else."

Annie looked away and did not answer. The two women continued walking through the forest. They heard cowbells, then glimpsed a herd of dish-faced spotted Normandy cattle in a nearby field.

"You're so sure, Madame," Annie said finally. "I'm afraid I'm *not*. I thought I'd better tell you that right at the beginning. I used to think that horses were the only thing that mattered, but now sometimes I think it's the dumbest thing in the world for people to spend their time on."

"Ann*ie,* of course there are more important things to do in this life, and perhaps some of them will come your way. But without a purpose of your own, one that comes from your own passion, you cannot confront anything well. I have sixty families who work on the *haras,* from generation to generation. When the Nazis were here, we naturally fought against them for our country, for our souls. But without my purpose to wake with, how could I have dared be responsible for sixty families? How could I have dared stand up to the Gestapo when they discovered I was caring for horses belonging to Jews? Annie, my purpose, *c'est moi!''* She laughed exultantly.

For the next several months, Madame Pichon consistently wore out her half-dozen young *stagiaires*, who struggled to keep up with her as she supervised her nearly two hundred horses. Henry thrived at the *haras*. His pony took much of his time; he made many friends his own age from the farm families; and after Vouvray gave birth to eleven puppies, the boy was constantly distracted.

Annie worked harder than she had ever worked before in her life, and soon realized that she had never been so stimulated, so excited, or so happy. She did not have time to consider what she was going to do about her reaction. Blaming it on Madame Pichon, she gave in to the woman's method and, in private, jokingly called her a sorcerer. Madame arched an eyebrow at the designation but seemed to enjoy it.

"To raise classic thoroughbreds," Madame Pichon said after dinner one night to the assembled *stagiaires* at the table, "simply means to breed colts and fillies that can win the classic races, distances of a mile or longer. Pedigrees, of course. Know them all by heart. But the whole business of pedigrees is vastly overrated.

"I will tell you about an acquaintance I have in England, a book collector. He discovered that in the second volume of their sacred *General Stud Book*, published in 1827, a preface admitted that the original volume on which *everything* is based was compiled too hurriedly for the editor to validate many of the early pedigrees! That means all this business of Byerly Turk and Godolphin Arabian is a myth!"

She sipped her Calvados and hoped for an argument.

"But surely, Madame, the stud books are necessary," another *stagiaire*, a young Englishman, suggested, "as a record of the purity of the breed."

"I say let into a race anything that can be called a horse," Madame Pichon said, enjoying the challenge. "If performance rather than blood proves itself, then let the animal in the books, whether it's a Clydesdale or a Shetland pony! There is such a thing as too much purity of breed for nothing more than its own sake. Look at England!''

The young *stagiaire* smiled and rolled his eyes, familiar with her Anglophobia.

"The British Jockey Club," she continued, "upheld a rule until 1949, barring American thoroughbreds from their stud book for being half-breeds! Typical nonsense! They had to change their minds because the American half-breeds kept coming over and winning all their best races.''

After dinner, Madame Pichon took Annie aside with their coffee to sit in the drawing room's bow window seat, a place where it was understood Madame wished to speak to someone alone without interruption.

"Annie, tell me what is happening to the horses you left in Kentucky. I've been looking at the pedigrees you told me about, and you should be getting some results by now.''

"We have some yearlings—well, after New Year's they'll be two-year-olds—that Mr. Beasley seems pretty pleased about.''

"I have a very good idea," Madame said, already pleased with it. "Why don't you bring two yearlings over here to La Poire, and together we will break them and teach them to run. Then you'll really see what we do here, how we feed them, treat them, introduce them to themselves as race horses. The first eighteen months are when bone and character are formed. It is a vital time to spend with them. After that, it's up to the trainer and the lad to find whatever greatness there is, and to keep it *au point*. But before that, we can have our fun.''

Since coming to La Poire, Annie usually fell into bed after dinner and barely remembered lying still before going to sleep. Madame Pichon's idea excited her so much that she could not sleep that night. After she had left Kentucky, she received monthly reports from Blue Bell Farm along with the boarding bills. Every three months she was sent individual reports on each of the horses Beasley kept for Annie. She and Chigger spoke on the telephone about breeding and which weanlings and yearlings to sell off. Chigger did a very good job, and Annie did not take an active part in her string's management. She read the reports, finding them a painful reminder. The thought, however, of bringing two yearlings over to La Poire, and actually breaking and working them with Madame Pichon, kept her wide awake with anticipation.

She looked down at Henry on the small bed that was at the foot of hers. He breathed heavily, lying on his back under two blankets and a quilt, his face comically distorted against his pillow. Not once had he complained about being away from his own room. Granted, he very much enjoyed sharing the spacious room in the La Poire château with his mother, watching her light the fire before the sun came up, then jumping into bed with her until the room was warm. She remembered asking him if he missed his home. His answer was brief. "You mean La Brise? That's not home. My home is in America, and we'll find a father there."

She heard the telephone ring downstairs in the château and looked at her alarm clock. It was two-fifteen. A call at that hour was unusual, but Annie thought no more about it until she heard people moving about in the halls. Then, outside, several cars drove up. Henry ran to the window. He folded open the wooden shutters and looked down into the courtyard.

"Maman, something's happening."

"Get some clothes on. We'll go."

They dressed quickly, and he grabbed her hand, pulling her out of their room and down the long stone stairs. Many of the household servants passed them, but said nothing, looking so grim that Annie did not ask any questions. The front door had been left open; Annie and Henry slipped outside into the cold damp night and stood to one side of the courtyard under the stark branches of a pear tree.

Headlights from several farm trucks lit the steps in front of the château. Wearing a black cloak, Madame Pichon stood in the center of two dozen farm workers and servants, all of them talking at once, their breath visible in the air. For a while she listened to her workers without response; then she spoke with grave intensity.

"What did she say, Henry?" Annie whispered.

"Something like 'They've brought men before. We must be sure, and not say yes because we want it so much.' "

At the curve in the drive, headlights appeared, flashing between the gnarled and knotted trunks of the plane trees. Three black Citroëns sped into the courtyard and pulled up just in front of the group surrounding Madame Pichon. All the cars' doors opened at once, and, with orderly efficiency, a man and a woman in soiled and torn civilian clothes were pulled out of the middle car by uniformed soldiers. Shoved into the glare of the headlights, the man and woman were held by their arms by soldiers on each side. The other soldiers held automatic rifles at the ready.

"Bonsoir, Madame Pichon," an official in a black hat and heavy civilian overcoat said as he walked up to her. Then he escorted her to face the prisoners. *"Voici nôtre homme."*

The woman in the headlights fell to her knees on the cobblestones. The soldiers guarding her let her stay there. She remained still and silent. The man stood staring into the darkness with an arrogant disregard of what was happening.

From those watching, there was silence, until one woman cried out incoherently. Whispers began which quickly died out when Madame Pichon walked into the light and stood in front of the man, staring at him with spectral gravity.

"Bonsoir, Capitaine Hultz."

A woman who worked in the kitchen began to cry. Several men shouted. The man in the headlights disregarded them all and said something in French.

Annie looked at Henry, hoping for more translation.

"Madame Pichon called him Captain Something," the boy said, "but he says he forgot everything."

Another woman from the farm walked into the light and stood next to Madame Pichon. Before anyone could stop her, she tore open her coat and shirt, exposing the scarred and mangled remains of her left breast. *"Un petit souvenir, Capitaine!"* she shouted, and spat in his face before Madame Pichon grabbed her and hugged her in her arms, where the woman wept.

"Allez," said the official, and the former captain was shoved by the soldiers into the back seat of the middle car. The woman who was with him struggled to her feet and attempted to follow, but was held back. Annie saw that she was pregnant.

"Vous-êtes sûr, Madame?" the official asked.

"Demandez-les," Madame Pichon said.

"He asked if Madame is sure," Henry said. "She told him to ask—"

Without waiting to be asked, the farm workers rang out a chorus of *oui's*, along with curses and sobs.

"Merci bien," the official said to them all, then gravely saluted them. Then he turned back to Madame Pichon. *"La femme n'est pas importante. Est-ce-qu'il y a un hôtel par ici?"*

"À Potigny."

Henry whispered, "He says the woman isn't important, so they'll take her to the hotel in Potigny."

The official then saluted Madame Pichon and said, *"Au 'voir, Madame,"* and returned to the first car. The woman was shoved into the back seat. The three Citroëns turned in the courtyard and sped down the drive through the plane trees. Those watching stood silently, then, with few words, walked to their trucks or returned to the château. Madame Pichon held the woman who had spat at the captain until several people came and led her away. She was no longer crying, but walked as if lost.

When the trucks and people had gone, Madame Pichon started up the steps of the château. When she saw Annie and Henry standing under the pear tree, she reached her arms out to them and held tightly to both. She said, "That man made our memory a wound. You cannot know what it was like, and you should not. We do not dare to remember for fear of pain. Even knowing that they finally caught the slaughterer gives us as much agony as satisfaction." She leaned on them as they silently climbed the steps and entered the front door.

Annie asked, "What are they going to do with the woman?"

"Do not ask me that," Madame Pichon snapped, then shot a look of warning toward Annie. "She deserves anything that happens."

"I think she's pregnant," Annie said.

As they went through the hall and into the drawing room, Madame Pichon's face showed a momentary concern. Then she shook her head.

"Twenty years," Madame Pichon said. "Twenty years, and

the man still stinks of arrogance and torture." Annie had never seen the older woman in such a state of agitation, and watched her pace the drawing room, enraged. She took Henry's hand and they sat beside each other in the bow window seat.

"Hultz commanded the garrison at Caen, which he hated. His ambition was Paris. So was *hers*. She was of the Austrian *nobility* and insisted on her 'von' from the shopkeepers. Ah, she was incorrigible! After the Third Reich made peace with the Vichy government, Hultz came here looking for horses that belonged to Jews. My husband and I had kept horses for Joseph Widener for years. Jean Stern had horses here, as did Lord Dolby, an Englishman, an enemy of the Germans. We changed all their papers, their stalls, destroyed their name halters. But the Reich was very interested in all kinds of breeding."

Annie watched as Madame Pichon drew in a deep breath and then continued. "Pure blood appealed to Hitler like nothing else. He sent officials to 'buy' French bloodstock. And they took it. Oh, we hid a few of our best in the forest, but they took so many, so many . . ."

She stopped a moment, looking desolate. "Of course the Nazis suspected they had been fooled," Madame Pichon continued, pacing again, "and blamed Captain Hultz. He stayed in Caen throughout the war, frustrated, bitter, giving the Haras de la Poire his special attention, threatening us, sending my husband and me to the Gestapo in Paris, confiscating our grain. But he could *not* defeat us! We harvested grain at night and hid it in the forest. We fed our horses what little there was, all of us, the farm families, feeding horses and often going hungry ourselves. Madness!" She turned suddenly and looked at Annie, her eyes burning. "You see, Ann*ie*, about purpose!" Annie nodded and felt Henry's hand squeeze hers.

Madame Pichon continued to pace. "As the end neared, he tried to impress his superiors by claiming he had discovered a pocket of the Resistance. They sent the S.S. torturers, and of course Hultz used them on anyone he wished, taking part whenever it appealed to him. He was a monster! You saw what he did to Émilie."

As if noticing Henry's presence for the first time, Madame quickly went to the boy and knelt on the floor before him.

"Ah, *mon petit chèr*, you should not be hearing of this. Not yet."

"What happened, Madame?" the boy asked, wide-eyed.

She sat beside him on the window seat, held his hand, and said, "We survived. The Germans never could prove we did anything for the Resistance, although we took messages every day, once hid an American pilot who crashed. They watched us day and night. Hultz would have killed us. The day after the Normandy invasion, he drove up here in his staff car. We saw him in the courtyard from our bedroom window. He got out with his men and drew his pistol. But just as he started up the front steps, he heard the American tanks coming through the fields. We could see them! His Austrian woman screamed at him, and they jumped back in their car and drove away . . . I have not seen him for twenty years."

"What's the Resistance?" Henry asked quickly.

"I'll tell you all the stories tomorrow, but now you must go back to bed. *Embrasse moi.*"

Henry gave Madame Pichon a kiss on the cheek, and the three of them walked to the hall.

"Go on up, Henry. I'll be right there," Annie said. As the boy ran up the stairs, she asked, "What about the woman?"

Madame Pichon responded with scorn. " 'Madame Von,' we called her. One of those silly stupid women who has one talent—to fit herself into whatever man's underpants can do her the most good."

"But what'll happen to her now?"

"Who knows? They'll pay for her hotel for a week. They brought Hultz here in the middle of the night for us to identify him before the newspapers make it a circus. He's a criminal, so he'll go to prison. She is garbage, so she'll be . . . thrown away."

Annie watched her a moment, then said, "Good night, Madame," and hurried up the stairs after Henry. As she climbed the stairs, Annie remembered the hotel in Potigny. It was only eight kilometers away, an old establishment next to the railroad station. Annie had seen it numerous times when picking up supplies for the *haras*. She also remembered being pregnant and alone, and what fear could do.

After only a few questions about the "horses kept secretly in the woods," Henry fell back to sleep. Annie had made up her mind. She put on her riding breeches and gabardine shirt. Grabbing her sheepskin coat, she hurried downstairs. As she crossed the hall, she glanced into the drawing room. Madame Pichon sat in her chair, watching her. Annie took a step toward her, trying to find words to explain what she was doing.

Madame Pichon, however, said, "Go. You can; I cannot."

In the Renault, Annie sped over the icy road to Potigny. It was slick from a dusting of snow. The main street led to the square, on one side of which was the ancient stone station and timbered two-story hotel. As Annie drove toward it, she saw what she had anticipated. Farm trucks were parked haphazardly in front of the hotel, some with the doors left open and headlights still on. The snow had stopped, but the wind blew harshly. As Annie drove her car around the square, the front door of the hotel opened, throwing a shaft of light onto the street. A knot of men and women pushed out, dragging the Austrian woman by her arms. Her hair had been cut off, revealing patches of her scalp.

Annie stopped her car and watched as one of the farm women brandished a gleaming pair of scissors and lunged at the shorn head. There was little hair left to cut. Fearing that the scissors would soon be stabbing at the victim's face, Annie started to get out of the car. The Austrian woman was thrown on the ground, and men and women started to kick her. Hurriedly, Annie unlocked the glove compartment. She grabbed the gun and, stepping out of the car, fired it toward the sky. The shot was deafening.

There was silence from the mob. Barely an eye moved. Then murmurs began, broken by angry shouts. One of the women began kicking the Austrian woman again. Clutching her stomach, she cried out in pain.

Annie raised the gun, shot it again just above the crowd's heads, then lowered it, aiming directly at them. She tried to think of the right French and yelled, *"L'enfant est innocent! L'enfant est innocent!"*

She could not tell whether they had realized the woman was pregnant. Some of the men obviously had not, and looked down at the Austrian woman. One of the women whom Annie recognized from the farm at the Haras de la Poire leaned over and spat on the fallen figure. Most of the others did the same; some looked at Annie with anger, but they walked away. The Austrian woman lay in the street, moaning, as the last farm truck drove off into the darkness.

Annie ran to the woman and tried to help her up. *"Venez! Venez avec moi!"* Annie shouted as she pushed the gun into her sheepskin pocket. The Austrian woman looked up at her, fearful and suspicious.

"My Lord, how can I talk to you?" Annie said as she indicated her car and signaled for the woman to come. *"Venez! Vitement!"* Annie thought about the police coming and her possession of a gun.

The Austrian woman looked around the square. With Annie's help, she struggled to her feet and limped to the Renault, where she fell into the passenger seat, gripping her side. Annie watched her as the ignition key turned and the motor raced. The woman's large blue eyes were hollowed by exhaustion and sunk below her prominent brow, but her aquiline nose and her lips, drawn in like a tight bud, still held a reserve of dignity. The car sped out of the town square.

They drove in silence. When they came to the main intersection in the town, Annie turned at a sign indicating the direction to Paris. The Austrian woman said in a gruff, throaty voice, "Where do you take me?"

"You speak English?" Annie asked.

"Of course," her passenger said, with an attitude of superiority that seemed to have survived the past twenty years and two hours.

Annie glanced at the woman's arched eyebrows and the imperious tilt of the chin. "Paris is two hours from here," Annie said, controlling her anger. "Can you make it that far?"

The woman put her hand on her stomach reflexively. "Yes."

"I'm taking you to the American Hospital in Paris," Annie said. Out of the corner of her eye, she saw the Austrian woman's surprise; then she turned away.

For a long time, neither spoke. Eventually, the Austrian woman asked, somewhat commandingly, "Who are you? Why are you doing this?"

Annie did not answer for a moment; she felt wary. "I was at the Haras de la Poire tonight. I saw that you were pregnant."

"But you are American."

"Yes," Annie said.

"Did *la grande* Madame Pichon send you?"

"No. I thought you might need help."

The Austrian woman stared ahead, then said, "I do. Thank you." Annie heard that she meant it, in spite of her patronizing edge.

After miles of silence, a pink dawn outlined the rolling horizon. Annie thought her passenger had gone to sleep, and was grateful. The woman seemed to flaunt disdain as a virtue.

"My family's name was Von Herschfeldt," she said suddenly and glanced over at Annie, but then shook her head. "No, Americans understand nothing about this. It is a name that commands respect. Our home in Vienna, one of the largest, gone now. Everything, everyone is gone. We had a mirrored ballroom where I take my dancing lessons . . ." She leaned back to let her head fall on the back of the seat and closed her eyes.

Then she looked at Annie and said with disgust, "I tell you something will make you laugh. My grandmother, my mother's mother, is a Jewess. The Von Herschfeldts are powerful enough in Vienna for such a thing to be overlooked, not even spoken of. But not by the Germans. Hultz is a captain, a rank high enough to find out about the part-Jew Von Herschfeldts of Vienna and to protect me when others find out. But he blames me for being sent to Caen, and threatens me all through the war to keep me with him. Do you understand me?"

Annie nodded. The Austrian woman watched her, then, out of habit, reached up to pat her hair. When she felt the shorn patches that were left, she turned the rearview mirror toward her. Gasping, she stared at herself. Annie heard her sob. Annie drove on, but as the sobs continued, she reached over and put her arm around the woman's heaving shoulders. She went on crying for a considerable time. Then, without any warning, she opened the car door and tried to leap out. Her lurch caused the car to swerve, but Annie braked hard, grabbed the woman's arm, and held her.

"No, let me die!" the Austrian woman yelled.

"Stop being a damn fool!" Annie shouted back as the car skidded on the icy road, heading sideways for the shoulder. The car hit a dry spot, which jerked them to a 180-degree stop.

Annie's heart was pumping erratically. The motor was still running; the passenger door hung open. Annie coughed, feeling a deep soreness spreading through her shoulder.

"Don't do that again!" Annie suddenly shouted. "You don't have any right to get me or that baby killed!"

The woman reached out and slammed the door closed.

"Who are you?" she asked. For the first time, there was no hint in her voice of superiority.

Annie turned the car around and started driving again. "Look, I'll help you. That's all you have to know. When your baby grows up, you'll be glad about tonight." She reached one hand over the other on the steering wheel, adding, "Here, take this."

Annie struggled to pull her wedding ring over the knuckle, then put it in the Austrian woman's hand. "Wear it. People look for rings when you're having a baby."

"It is your wedding ring?" the woman asked, amazed at the gift.

Annie did not answer. Neither spoke again until Annie asked directions for the hospital in Neuilly, right outside Paris.

As soon as the woman was under a doctor's care in the emergency clinic, Annie went to the admissions office, arranged for a private room, and called Delansig at his home in Scarsdale. Astonishingly, the call went through immediately.

"I'm sorry to wake you, but this won't wait, I'm afraid. Please apologize to Mrs. Delansig."

"It's all right. I'm due in court early tomorrow, so I'm up late tonight. Is there a problem?"

"Not with me, you'll be happy to hear. You told me once

you knew some fancy doctors over here who'd fly off to Casablanca for enough money?''

There was a pause. ''Are you in need of such a doctor, Mrs. Sumner?''

In spite of her fatigue, Annie laughed. ''No! As everyone always says, 'It's for a friend of mine.' She's at the American Hospital in Neuilly, and needs what they call 'discreet' care. When you arrange it, tell the doctor that his job is to make sure she has this baby; she's very scared and depressed. And tell him not to concern himself with her appearance. Her hair's been cut off.''

''That's intriguing,'' Delansig said. ''May *I* ask?''

''No,'' Annie said. ''And one more thing. Find out if there's some kind of relief agency still operating for people displaced by World War Two. This woman has no papers, no identity, and has been wandering around Europe for the last twenty years.''

''What's her name?''

''Make one up.''

''Now?''

''Yep. I'll tell her what it is.''

''Is she Jewish? There are several good agencies still working on relocation.''

''One-fourth.''

''That was enough to get her into Auschwitz, so it's enough for the agencies. I'll see what I can find.''

''What name are you going to give them?''

''I'm not very good at this. What is she? Polish? German?''

''That's close.''

''I don't know. The name of the best criminal lawyer in our firm is Herskewitz.''

''What's his wife's name?''

''Georgia.''

''No. How about Vera?''

''Vera Herskewitz, the bald lady. No, the bald pregnant lady.''

''Go back to work.''

Annie hung up, then called the Haras de la Poire and left a message that she would return by dinnertime. She gave the hospital administrator the name and phone number of her Paris banker, whom she would instruct to arrange, without revealing from whom the money came, all medical payments, as well as a lump sum to "Vera Herskewitz" to cover expenses until the baby was born.

An hour later, Annie was standing in a private room of the hospital as a distinguished, silver-haired, immaculately tailored French gynecologist, who had trained at Columbia Presbyterian in New York, examined Vera Herskewitz. The patient barely responded, either to her new name or to the examination.

"The lacerations on her legs and back are severe but don't require stitches. She may have some broken ribs, but I don't wish to use X-rays to check . . . Perhaps we could talk outside a moment?"

"Might as well say it all here, Doctor. She has to hear it."

"May I suggest a wig as soon as possible? The staff is naturally curious."

"I'll tend to that. You won't be seeing me again, Doctor. Please take care of her. When she's released, she'll have money to find a place to live until the baby comes. By then, I hope a relief agency'll be involved, because Mrs. Herskewitz hasn't any papers and doesn't remember very much about what's happened to her," Annie said pointedly to the patient as well as the doctor.

"I understand. I'll come around again this evening." He said goodbye to both women and left.

Annie turned to the Austrian woman, who stared at the ceiling. The ring was on her middle finger. Without looking at Annie, she blurted, "I *hate* you for making me live!"

"I know," Annie said quietly. "The past does that. It comes after you. But maybe the baby'll get you away from it."

The woman did not respond. Annie left the room. She made arrangements for a wig maker and an apartment rental agency to call at the hospital. Then she filled the car with gas, ate a quick lunch, and started back to Potigny. She stopped along the way, so exhausted that she could not hold her eyes open, and slept in the car for two hours.

Arriving late for dinner at the Haras de la Poire, Annie

hurried through the downstairs hall, hoping not to interrupt the meal. As she let the weight of her sheepskin coat slide down her arms, she heard laughter, a new voice, and Henry, who sounded like the center of attention. Just as she stepped on the stairs, Madame Pichon called, "Ann*ie* . . ."

She turned and saw the older woman's arms reach out for her. She dropped her coat and they embraced. Madame Pichon asked, "You are all right?" When Annie nodded, she went on to say, "Let us never speak of it." Then she led Annie into the dining room.

"Maman!" Henry yelled as he jumped up from his seat at the table and ran to her. Annie's fellow *stagiaires* rose to greet her, and as Henry grabbed her hand, Madame took her around the table to introduce her to someone.

"And we have a guest visiting us for a few days. Lord Dolby, may I introduce Ann*ie* Sumner. Lord Dolby owns one of England's most ancient stud farms, and he allows us to care for several of his best . . ."

Annie was not listening. The man who stood up with a smile of casual interest shook her hand. He was about thirty, enormously tall, perhaps six-foot-seven, with wild, wavy chestnut hair falling down his back, glinting blue suggestive eyes, and a meticulously cut beard. He seemed to be dressed in a costume made up of a florid striped shirt, a bright ascot, and a coat cut to his knees in the Edwardian style.

Annie pushed back a wisp of her hair. Looking up at him gave her the unfamiliar feeling of being small.

"Maman, where's your wedding ring?"

Before she could respond, Lord Dolby offered in a ringing voice, "Well, obviously, Henry, she lost it so that she could marry me!"

Everyone laughed at the preposterous suggestion except Henry, who ran out of the dining room.

EIGHTEEN

WHILE THE OTHERS remained at dinner, Annie hurried upstairs after Henry. When she entered their room, she found him standing in the middle of the room, crying with rage.

"That was my father's ring!"

Annie went over to hold him, but he backed away.

"What happened to it?" he demanded.

"I gave it to the woman we saw here last night."

"She's a Nazi!" he yelled.

"The farm workers cut off her hair and broke her ribs, kicking her. She's going to have a baby. She had no family, no friends, no one to help her."

Henry looked away, trying to stop crying. "Sometimes, when we were taking a nap in the fields, I'd stare at the ring so that when I closed my eyes I could see an eight, the way the diamonds were." Without warning, he ran to her, and she hugged him tight. "It was the only thing of his that we had," he said.

"Oh, Henry," Annie said softly, "everything we have came from him."

He stayed quiet in her arms, his sobs subsiding. "Maman, am I ever going to have a father? I mean one that's alive?"

"I don't know, Henry. We'll keep looking, and if we find someone we like—"

"We'll kidnap him!"

"We sure will!"

She put her son to bed and sat with him while he drifted off to sleep. Then she washed and changed into a clinging soft jersey dress, which, when Annie returned to the dining room, Madame Pichon noted with a wry smile. A seat was waiting for her next to Lord Dolby, who occupied her the rest of the evening until everyone else in the château had gone to bed.

"You're really outrageous," Annie said, standing with her back to the fire in the drawing room. A gale blowing in from the English Channel made the old chimney moan. He sat in a stuffed armchair, smoking a cigar and drinking Calvados, with his long legs stretched into the center of the room. Annie noticed that he was wearing slippers made of green tapestry.

"Absolutely," he replied. "Outrage runs in the family, actually. My grandmother's great-uncle, for instance, was a Ukrainian count who was hauled up before the Tsar for deflowering seventy-two local virgins in a single all-night session. And please don't attack me with the new feminism. I have it on the best authority that the virgins attended willingly and thoroughly enjoyed themselves."

"What'd the Tsar do to him?"

"I believe he gave him some sort of medal. So you see, Annie, we inevitably must do something about this mad attraction we have for each other."

Annie laughed. "Let's just enjoy it from a safe distance," she said.

"That's already barely possible, so when you feel yourself giving in, warn me so that I may prepare myself to amaze you."

"Oh, you want a medal of your own. What kind of thing do

you do?" she asked, then turned to the fire so that he would not see her surprise at her own flirtation.

"Words fail the experience, so there's only one way for you to find that out." She heard him puff on his cigar. "But in the meantime, I've been invited to a gala at the Rothschilds'. It's in two weeks. Want to come?"

"Sure," she said, turning back. "Why not?"

"Splendid. It's a fancy dress ball. Would you be my Dulcinea? I'm going as Don Quixote." Cigar smoke clouded over his head as he flicked an ash into a silver ashtray and showed Annie another provocative smile. Watching her, he stroked his beard.

Annie remembered when Charlie Dell handed her the large leather volume with CERVANTES embossed on it. She had taken it to Saratoga with her and finished reading it in the New York Public Library soon after her return. Now, smiling down into Bernard Dolby's eyes, she wanted him to know she had read the book. At dinner, he had told her of his Eton and Oxford education. Annie was more than a little awed; she wanted to impress him. "I guess Dulcinea's better than Rocinante," she offered with a self-conscious laugh.

He made no response to her literary reference, but instead rose purposefully to loft the last of his cigar into the fireplace. Then he leaned his elbow on the mantel, standing next to her.

"I have a proposition for you," he said, impishly smiling down at her. "A business proposition rather than a personal one. I have a two-year-old colt that's the result of a breeding program I started for our stud nearly ten years ago. Since my father had to sell off everything to pay taxes after the war, it's taken this long to turn the Dolby Stud around. I believe this colt may be the one to put us back on the thoroughbred map. His name is Dionysus, by Stamblit out of Pollygraph. He's in training at Newmarket. I'm pointing him toward the Prix Morny at Deauville in August. I was wondering whether you might be interested in being in on it."

The Prix Morny was one of the most prestigious races for two-year-olds in Europe. "In on it how?" she asked. "I don't know if I'll even be here by then." Annie felt the familiar surge of excitement for the track.

"Madame Pichon told me you *could* be here if you wished," he said, studying the Calvados in his glass, then swirling it. "She thinks very highly of you, says you have 'the passion.' " He raised an eyebrow suggestively. "I also understand you're a superb rider and may bring some yearlings over here to work. So it would all fit together rather nicely." He drained the snifter and said, "You also have some rather extraordinary broodmares in Kentucky. Say you bought half of Dionysus at a price we agreed on if he wins the Prix Morny. We could share the progeny in future years."

Annie was flattered by the offer and by what Madame Pichon had said, but she was thinking about something else. "Isn't Stamblit a full brother of Nearctic?"

He glanced at her, his brow lifted at her knowledge of the pedigree.

"Yes, he is," Lord Dolby said, "but he's been rather overlooked as a stallion, all glory in hindsight now going to the incredible Northern Dancer. God, what an animal that Dancer is! Still, I rather like the unfashionable, unproven fellow, don't you?" He looked down at her, amused.

"Madame Pichon would be proud of you," Annie said, feeling a bit flustered, and realizing again how tall he was. She was also acutely aware of having a man so close to her, of how long it had been. "I tell you what, Bernard—I mean," she corrected herself, putting the emphasis in the British manner on the first syllable, "*Ber*nard. I'll agree to stay here and take a look at Dionysus. If I like what I see, we'll agree on a price if he wins and if he *doesn't* win the Prix Morny, both."

The idea of owning part of the colt, win or no win, intrigued her. Nearctic, the sire of Northern Dancer, was the son of Nearco, the great Italian champion, who was proving himself to be one of the greatest sires of the century. Northern Dancer, one of his grandsons, had been the Horse of the Year in America, breaking the record of the Kentucky Derby the previous spring. To have access to the Nearco line was an opportunity that Annie wanted, particularly if Lord Dolby's colt was a winner.

He held out his hand to shake on the deal.

"To seal the agreement, don't you really think it's time we

went to bed?" he asked, not releasing her hand, and offering the dare with an impish smile.

"You really are outrageous, aren't you?"

"What I'd find truly outrageous is sleeping alone when I could be making love to you."

Slowly he raised her hand to his lips, then, when she did not object, drew her to him and kissed her. His size made her feel as if his body could envelop hers. His beard brushed over her nose and chin. There was an appealing masculine scent about him, and his mouth tasted of sweet Calvados and rich Cuban tobacco. Although he made no further move, holding only her hand, his tongue began to play in her mouth with a subtle delicacy. Feeling her heart pound, Annie drew back and looked up at him.

Without the slightest suggestion of insistence, he smiled at her casually; then his head tilted quizzically to one side.

"You're used to this, aren't you?" Annie asked. "Are you always so good at it?"

He chuckled. "I work very hard to be proficient at what I enjoy." He kissed her lips again. "In order to succeed, I take every opportunity to practice. Occasionally, this leads to a triumph. Not always, though." He drew her closer to him and kissed her eyes. "But, Annie, I assure you, the pleasure of this particular attempt is triumph enough."

"I think you practice the words, too," Annie offered gently. "Don't women mind being practiced on?"

He straightened up slightly and shrugged, "Apparently not. Women have their own agendas." His voice kept an amused confidence. "And I'm always delighted to serve them."

She watched him a moment. "I never heard it called an agenda before," she said.

"Shall we go?" he asked.

Annie stood, watching him. The wind blew, rattling the room's wooden shutters. She opened her mouth to say no, but nodded before the word came.

He led her out of the drawing room and up the stairs. The gale evoked a strange harmony from the château's chimneys and whistled through the cracks in its walls. The two candles that Bernard Dolby lit wavered in his drafty bedroom. Standing at the foot of the ancient canopied bed, Annie faced the man as he began to undress her. But then she stopped him and let him watch as she slowly removed her clothes in the candlelight. His face seemed to soften. He quickly undressed and they moved against each other. He lifted her onto the bed.

At first, she was doubtful of her capacity, but he took care, and slowly his tongue and fingers made her ready. When he held his broad muscled body over her, the thick hair of his chest brushed over her breasts and she began to relax and grow more eager. He was very careful with his size, very gentle while easing into her, nimble with his hands and mouth, and always aware of keeping the full extent of his weight from falling on her.

She saw him watching her, breathing hard, a mixture of surprise and admiration spreading his smile. Annie reached for his head and pulled it toward her, kissed him deeply, and forced him to slide backward from the edge of the bed to the floor. Still mounted on him, she rose up on her knees and squeezed her hips as she repeatedly lifted and plummeted down on him. His mouth opened, wider and wider, until at last he gave out a whispered bellow as he bucked her repeatedly into the air.

Annie was delighted. She gave a quiet laugh when the massive Bernard Dolby finally collapsed on his back in exhausted satisfaction. Annie leaned over, kissed him again, then stood up and slipped into her dress.

"Wait, Annie." He groaned. "I haven't finished with you. I *always* return the pleasure."

"Always? You mean it's guaranteed? Well, I'm sure you'll get a medal for that." She laughed again, kissed him as he started to stand, and, carrying her underclothes and shoes, moved quickly into the hall. Hurrying quietly down the hall to her own room, she controlled her laughter but skipped several steps. She was not scared; she did not ache with love. She had been gloriously laid and had enjoyed every second of it. She could not ask for more, and as she pulled the covers around Henry's shoulders, she realized she wanted nothing more. After undressing and washing, she climbed under the quilts of her own bed. The events and names of the day made an enlivening traffic through her mind: Bernard Dolby, Dionysus, Vera Herskewitz, Rothschild. She was smiling when she fell asleep.

For the gala, Annie drove to Paris to buy a suitable dress for Dulcinea from Christian Dior. When she and Bernard arrived at the Rothschilds' country château, there was a major domo in powdered wig and full Louis XIV livery to announce the guests. At the top of a flight of stairs leading to the ballroom, Bernard whispered to the major domo, who promptly bellowed, "The Right Honorable the Lord Dolby, and the Countess of Catlettsburg!"

As they descended, Annie and Bernard laughed all the way to the bottom of the stairs. Many pictures were taken. He introduced her to a great many "*very* fancy people," as she called them. In spite of their titles and long bloodlines from all over Europe, Annie experienced none of the nervous awkwardness she had felt when confronting the pack in New York. Annie was exhilarated, and they in turn regarded her as a delightful surprise. Bernard Dolby watched her shine and was suitably smitten. The next morning, before leaving the inn where they had spent the night, he asked her to another party in Paris two weeks later.

"Sure," she said happily, "why not?"

Three days later, her two yearlings arrived at the Haras de la Poire, exhausted after an eleven-hour flight from Kentucky and a three-hour truck ride from the Orly airport. Within days, however, Annie had them kicking up their legs in the paddock, mingling contentedly with other yearlings, and gobbling down their special diet of oats.

Immediately, Madame Pichon and Annie began hand-walking the two yearlings each morning from their boxes out through the barn's cobblestoned stable yard. The damp winter cold held over the fields and pastures of the *haras*. As soon as they were released, the yearlings, a colt and a filly, whinnied to each other and cantered around their paddock.

"As yearlings, they're like teenagers," Madame Pichon said, ever instructing, "with too much energy, more size than they can handle, and therefore quite likely to get into trouble and hurt themselves. But we will treat them as adults. We'll feed them like adults from the beginning, insisting that they grow up. Soon their bones join, or 'come together,' as you say in America. They must have room; it's absurd the way some people keep them in their boxes. If they misbehave, they must be controlled, but never with punishment to make them fearful or keep them from going on. A yearling must always go on, now, forward, always toward *l'arrivée*, the finish!"

Through the winter months, Madame Pichon showed Annie how to feel a joint for joining, as well as for the heat of injury. Probing with her fingers at the knees, pasterns, and hocks of her yearlings, Annie felt the space between the bones, a natural condition of their immaturity.

"I will give you diagrams of these bones. You must learn each one, and how it fits in with all the others. This is the cause of most horses going lame; they are run too hard and too far before these bones have grown together and are ready for their weight. Once those legs are misused and injured, it is an endless problem to bring them back. That is often when drugs are used, to rid them of any painful symptoms of their injuries, to keep them running at all costs. It is a *crime!*"

Even when it rained or snowed, the women watched the two yearlings. While they shared a thermos of coffee one day, Madame Pichon watched them silently for a long time; Annie tried to see what her teacher was seeing.

"They are growing so fast now that each day they are different," Madame Pichon said. "You must recognize the difference, see it, understand how the yearling is changed by it."

She smiled at a memory. "One of the great breeders of this century, Federico Tesio, used to sit on a shooting stick in his paddock for hours and do nothing but watch his horses. If anyone dared to speak to him, he would cut him dead. He had little money; his stud in the north of Italy had none of the modern conveniences. Even at the sales in England, he would watch the horses in their boxes for hours. He couldn't buy the expensive ones, but he found what he wanted. By the time he made a match, he could predict the horse that would be foaled, practically see it. I think he was a bit mad. But his success was astonishing, and he produced the great Ribot and, of course, Nearco. Only by knowing how to watch do you know your animal, whether to fatten it up and shine its coat for the summer yearling sales, or to break it and prepare to put it into training. You must decide, though. Being vague can make you bankrupt."

"That's the hard part," Annie said. "I can't imagine selling either one of these two."

"Never fall in love with your horses. They are not your children; they are part of your business." Madame Pichon made an atypical pause, then sighed and said, "That rule I break the most. My heart is so scarred, it looks like an old walnut."

"When do I have to decide?"

"Well, Deauville is the best yearling sale, in August. It's on a level with Keeneland and Saratoga. You should allow several months to prepare the yearling for the sale. If you decide to put a horse in training to race, we break them here in June, so you must decide for that."

"Could I sell at Deauville?" Annie asked.

"Their pedigrees alone would get either one in the select sales for the better horses. What we do will assure it, and if they're consigned from the Haras de la Poire, that will guarantee it," she said proudly. "Cheegar Beasley has done very well for you . . . Annie, tell me, what is this 'cheegar'?"

"It's a bug that lives all over the South, bores in under your skin. If it gets in, sometimes you have to use a knife or a match to get rid of it. Mr. Beasley's like that. Proud of it, too."

"I think Cheegar Beasley is a good horseman. These are beautiful yearlings."

"Henry wants to call the colt Moonshot," Annie said. "He's pretty amazed by the astronauts, cuts out their pictures from all the magazines. He says he'll let me name the filly."

"He must realize that you may sell them."

Annie nodded. "He knows, but he doesn't like it."

A few days later, Henry was cutting pictures from magazines on the floor of the drawing room. As he thumbed through a stack of them in search of illustrations of the flights of the American astronauts, he was startled to see a picture of his mother with Lord Dolby at a party. Running into the kitchen, he proudly showed it to the staff and Madame Pichon, all of whom started to laugh. When he wanted to know why, Madame asked Henry to help her with a joke.

That night at dinner Madame Pichon stood at her place, her wineglass raised, and said, "I propose a toast to our distinguished friend and colleague, who has concealed all this time from us her true heritage. We have thought her to be a child from the hills of Kentucky who made her way through the travails of the hard world she found. Instead, we find she is titled, and who knows what stories she has to tell. Ladies and gentlemen, the Countess of Catlettsburg!"

The *stagiaires,* already in on the joke, rose as Henry lay the magazine on the table in front of his mother. When she saw it, Annie put her face in her hands and laughed. From that night on, "the Countess" became her sobriquet around the *haras.*

Each day Henry brought the two yearlings a bunch of carrots from the kitchen. The colt and filly quickly learned the routine and responded to it by racing each other across the paddock when they saw the six-year-old boy approaching.

"Look at them, Maman!" he exclaimed one day. "They're both so fast. They'll win everything!" Then he looked up at his mother to see if she was convinced.

"They're coming along very well," Annie said.

Aware that his salesmanship was only partially successful, Henry fed the carrots, holding one in each hand. "Where are their mothers and fathers? Back in Kentucky?"

"Yes," Annie replied, "except that Moonshot's daddy is at a farm in Maryland."

"Don't you think he misses them?"

Annie glanced over at him, standing on the first board of the paddock fence holding the carrots. She said, "Animals are different from us. They go their own way when they're very young. I wouldn't be surprised if these two have forgotten about their dams."

"I don't believe it," he said firmly. "How could that be?"

"Well, for instance, most foals never even see their fathers . . ."

As soon as she said it, she winced, then turned to Henry. He stood down from the fence and faced her, legs astride. Gripping a stump of carrot in each hand, he said through gritted teeth, "Then they're lucky, aren't they, to forget so easily."

"Sometimes it seems that way," she answered, "but there's so much else to remember, we're the lucky ones."

She started to reach out to hold him, but he stepped back. "Why did my father have to die?" he shouted angrily. "I want him back! I want him back!"

"I miss him, too, Henry," she began.

"But you can remember him. I can't do that. I have a picture of him, but that's not anything. Who am I supposed to remember?"

His deep eyes welled with tears he did not want to fall. Annie knelt on the ground and took him in her arms. He did not resist, nor did he respond.

"There's a lot of life that isn't fair, Henry," Annie said quietly. "Sometimes there are reasons, and sometimes there aren't. It isn't fair that you don't have a father. We both know that. But what should we do, spend a lot of time looking for the reasons that we don't have something, or do the best we can with what we do have? We're a whole lot luckier than most, Henry, even without a father. There's so much for us to do."

As she held him, she knew the day would come when she would have to tell him all the reasons. Although she had not lied, and would try not to, she accepted that one day she would probably have to.

"Maman," the boy said over her shoulder, "do you think Moonshot is going to forget me if we sell him?"

"You can't tell. Horses have incredible memories sometimes. I helped a horse in trouble once who remembered me a couple of years later."

She leaned back to see if the idea gave him any relief. He was watching Moonshot, who remained at the paddock fence, hoping for more carrots.

"I hope he does forget," he said. "It isn't fair to sell him and have him remember us." He walked back to the fence and gave Moonshot the last of his carrots.

Ironically, it was during those quick sprints for Henry's carrots that, day by day, Annie saw minute changes in the yearlings, having to do with acceleration and concentration. The colt would break into a gallop first, but would inevitably frisk about and look around for his paddock mate. The filly, whom Annie called Moonglow after a song she liked, started late, but ran straight for her carrot, never deviating. As the two of them grew, their conformations became clearer. There, too, Annie recognized the filly's superiority. Her length of leg seemed better proportioned to her body; her stride was easier and less choppy than the colt's.

In late April, the *haras'* training ring was surrounded by blooming pear trees. The sweet gusty winds kept promising warm weather, but more often delivered rain. Working the yearlings around in a circle, first one way, then the other, Madame Pichon taught Annie how to use a twenty-five-foot lunge line and long training whip.

"This develops their running muscles without need for the weight of a rider. You see, the horse's body is bent slightly as it goes around the circle, which supples it, first one side's muscles, then the other. The exercise tenses their spine, causing the back to round. And watch how it brings the hind legs under the body for better balance. See that?" Annie was about to respond, but Madame began again.

"Just as important as the physical work is the discipline. We've been handling them every day for weeks. Now they trust us. Very soon they'll take the bit. We put them on the bit earlier here than other places, again, because we treat them like adults."

Annie's assurance with the lunge line and whip grew. Moonglow began to develop a supple, fluid movement, with her hind feet neatly covering the tracks of her forefeet in a trot, and her stride lengthening in her canter. By June, the idea of matching the filly to the grandson of Nearco was clear to Annie. On the other hand, she knew that she was going to sell the colt.

Surprisingly, Henry knew it, too. A week before the breaking of the *haras'* yearlings began, the boy walked back to the château with his mother, unusually silent. Annie asked him several questions about his day. She knew he had gone swimming in the lake with some of the farm children and was surprised by his reluctance to talk. Suddenly he stopped in the middle of the lawn. His mouth trembled.

"You'll have to sell Moonshot, Maman. There's something wrong with his way of going. I don't think he likes to run."

Annie was amazed. "I think you're right, Henry."

He came into her arms and whispered, "Maybe it's better not to love anything at all."

"You can't do that, Henry, just because sometimes you get hurt. What if you and I stopped loving each other just to protect ourselves? I couldn't do that. Could you?"

"No. But why do we have to lose the things we really love?"

"I guess so that we can lose the awful things, too."

He drew back. "Like what?"

"Mistakes," she said, "bad people you run into."

He nodded wisely. "Yeah, I know what you mean. But losing them is easy. You feel happy. What do you do when you lose your horse or your best friend or something like that?"

"You get through it, and you find something else. It won't be Moonshot, or exactly the same friend, but there are a lot of possibilities out there."

The boy's face closed into its familiar anger. "I'll never find another father, will I?"

"You won't find Winnie Sumner. I won't, either. Maybe that's something we've lost that we'll never find anyone to replace. But we have to do whatever we can to go on and try."

"You think that's one reason why you gave your wedding ring away?"

Surprised, Annie chuckled. "Maybe it is, though I haven't thought about it that way till now. You're not supposed to know things about me that I don't know."

The anger on his face gave way to a grateful smile. "I love you, Maman."

"I'm so glad, and I love you too, darlin'."

"I'm not going to love anything else," he declared.

"Well, I wouldn't plan on that. We'll just take things one at a time," Annie suggested.

He took her hand, pulling her toward the château. Then he looked up at her slyly and added, "Like Lord Dolby."

"Yep, like Lord Dolby."

"I like him," the boy said. "He's very funny, and *so big.*"

"That's . . . true."

"But will you marry him, as he says?"

"When did he say that?"

"The first night, when he met you."

"He was just kidding, Henry. Getting married is a very complicated thing to do. The whole idea is a joke to Lord Dolby."

"The last time he was here, he invited me over to England to visit his castle," Henry said with impudent pride. "Was that a joke, too?" He watched her.

Annie shrugged. "I don't know. I'll have to ask him next time he shows up. Now come on. I want you to have a bath before dinner."

Annie learned from Madame Pichon, as well as from the English racing magazines and papers, that Lord Dolby's stud had been revived by him with considerable cunning, care, and intelligence. Having made several killings as a merchant banker in the City of London, he not only could afford to begin renovations of Tavellay Hall, the family castle in Warwickshire, but also to rejuvenate the family stud. He himself explained to Annie that he had begun with five years of serious study of bloodlines and another five years of careful selection of broodmares at auctions. Finally, he purchased a number of expensive stallion nominations and matched them to his broodmares. The results were coming onto the tracks that year, running as two- and three-year-olds, carrying the purple, pink, and white Dolby silks for the first time since World War II.

The connection between the Dolby family and the Haras de la Poire began with Bernard's father between the wars. The senior Lord Dolby had sent many high-priced yearlings to Madame Pichon for early care and breaking. During the war, the Dolby stock at La Poire was taken away by the Nazis. After D-Day, however, Madame Pichon went to Germany and located three of the best. She brought them back to France, where they recovered under her personal care. Therefore, when Bernard began to reestablish the Dolby Stud, one of the first people he came to was Madame Pichon.

"He is just like his father, although thinner and more ostentatious," Madame Pichon told Annie. "His father was so enormous, across as well as top to bottom, he could not fit in our bathtubs when he stayed here. His servant had to pour the water over him as he stood. And the *moment* I was a widow, he became amorous. He would creep down the hall late at night, making as much noise as a rhinoceros in the bush, and rap on my door, suggesting that he tell me of his dreams. I never dared let him in, but he was a dear man."

With Madame Pichon's guidance, Annie had put a saddle on Moonglow, worked her in deep sand on a lunge line to let her get used to the cinch, then "backed" her, lying across the saddle to give the filly an idea of a rider's weight. At last Annie mounted her and, from then on, rode her over the gallops through the forests every day. At the same time, Moonshot was put on a fattening diet to prepare him for the sale. Henry continued to go to his box every day with carrots.

The arrival of the Dolby Stud's ten-horse contingent for the race meeting at Deauville was led by the two-year-old, Dionysus. Bernard Dolby had rented a villa on the beach in Deauville for the season. He and his trainer commuted the half hour to the Haras de la Poire each day to supervise the works of Dionysus and the other Dolby horses on the sand gallops through the forests.

Annie watched every morning. Dionysus was a beauty, a big solid roan whose joints Annie could feel had already knitted together like steel mesh. When he was let loose, he was a smooth study of speed. Annie began to believe he might win the Prix Morny, and negotiated his price.

At the same time, Annie was supervising the final stages of Moonglow's training before she was sent off to a trainer, and was also preparing Moonshot for sale at Deauville.

"I'd rather not see you again until after the Morny," Annie suggested one morning between her duties with the two year-lings. She and Bernard had spent an occasional night at his beach villa, but both were tense with the pressures of sale and race. "When I stay over with you," she explained, "I have to get back here by five in the morning. And I don't like to leave Henry overnight."

"Well, you could bring Henry along," Bernard Dolby said as they walked through the forest for lunch at the château. "You met Mrs. Forbes. She's a wonderful housekeeper and there's a beach outside the front door. Besides, you don't really want to miss Deauville in August, darling. It's one of the most elegant, enchanting places in the world. We've been invited to a number of rather splendid parties, and every night at the Casino there's a big fête. Everyone is there."

"I'm not too interested in 'everyone.' And I haven't minded missing Deauville in August before now. I'd like to go with you, but I just can't go to parties or dancing at the Casino all night and then run back here to work."

He sighed. "I'll try to muddle through the season without you."

"You'll do just fine. I can already see those gorgeous long-legged title searchers lining up."

"It's not the title they're after, darling; it's my stellar character. Now listen to me. We do need something to look forward to. If Dionysus wins the Prix Morny, you must celebrate his victory with me. Your duties will be done. Your filly will be placed with the best trainer in France. Your colt will have sold at auction for thousands of francs, and Henry will join us until he falls asleep. You'll have absolutely no reason to avoid enjoying yourself . . . with me."

"You've got yourself another deal." She shook his hand as she had before, and he drew her to him to kiss her as he had before. Then she pulled back. He taunted, "I'm sure Madame Pichon wouldn't mind if we ran upstairs for an hour or two."

"Get out of here," Annie replied. "I'll see you in the winner's circle."

The Prix Morny was run on the second Sunday of the Deauville meet. On the same morning, the select sales of the yearling auction commenced. Moonshot was scheduled to go through the ring in the first session. He was one of eleven yearlings from the Haras de la Poire selected for the prestigious first days of the sale. During the two days before the sale, Madame Pichon drove Henry and Annie to the boxes near the auction pavilion where the yearlings for the sale were shown to prospective buyers. The boy stood next to Moonshot's box, scowling at each potential buyer who had his colt led out and walked around for inspection. Annie saw that several buyers had expressed real interest; all she needed was two of them ready to bid against each other.

On the morning of the race and the sale, Madame Pichon and Henry left the château early to be with the yearlings for one final currying and brushing before they went into the auction ring. Annie stayed to watch as Dionysus was prepared to be shipped the short ride to the Hippodrome de la Touques. Lord Dolby and his trainer arrived, and Annie watched with them as several lads loaded the colt into a van. Annie rode with Bernard and the trainer, who followed the van in their car as the convoy made its way to the track's receiving barn. Once the two-year-old was settled in his box, Annie kissed Bernard and hurried across the street to the sales pavilion.

The three hundred seats were filled and the bidding was active. Annie grabbed a sales catalogue while checking the sales board for the hip number currently being sold. She found Henry and Madame Pichon at Moonshot's box. The boy was behaving bravely, but both women understood the despair he felt as his colt's sale approached.

"If I had a million francs, I'd buy him myself," Henry said. Then, looking for a last chance, he offered, "If you'll lend me the money, Maman, I'll take good care of him, and pay you back as soon as he wins a race."

Annie would almost have given in, he wanted it so much, but Madame Pichon was more practical. "Henry, we must always do what is best for the horse. In this case, you and your mother made a choice. You concluded that the colt was not right for you. It was a hard choice, a brave one, and it is better that the colt go to someone who wants him and will try to prove you wrong."

The boy looked thoughtfully at Madame Pichon. "I hope they do."

Moonshot's hip number was called, and the three followed

the yearling to the holding corral behind the auction platform. Henry reached up to rub the colt's nose and said a quavering goodbye. Then they went into the pavilion and stood at the back. By the time the yearling was led into the small sawdust ring over which the auctioneers chanted, Henry was watching the proceedings with a sullen detachment. Annie thought he had suddenly grown up a little, but was not sure she was glad.

Madame Pichon nudged Annie with her elbow. The bidding was fast and strong, climbing quickly to and beyond a hundred thousand francs. Unable to tell who was bidding, Annie could only stare as if instantly hypnotized by the rapid French trill of the auctioneer. Francs were quickly converted into dollars on the sales board. She saw "$18,000" appear, and the figures grew steadily until 200,000 francs had been reached. There was a pause. The auctioneer scolded and cajoled, and the bid suddenly was raised by 25,000 francs, which seemed to satisfy the auctioneer, who dropped his hammer quickly. Delighted, Madame Pichon hugged Annie, who watched over her mentor's shoulder as the amount was again quickly shown on the sales board as "$40,909.00." The price was better than Annie had ever expected.

Then she saw Henry start to walk away.

"Where you going, Henry?"

"I want to tell the new owner his name."

"Darlin', whoever buys a yearling gets to name him."

The boy shrugged. "I'll just suggest it."

Annie let him go. She watched him idly as she anticipated telling Chigger Beasley of their success, and of enjoying Bernard Dolby's reaction. The boy followed the floor man as he approached the buyer for his signature. Annie thought how she might splurge a little on some surprises for Henry, Madame Pichon, and . . .

The new owner turned to sign the sales slip. Henry began talking in his most serious grown-up manner, and the man listened, smiled, then squatted down to reach out and shake Henry's hand. Annie saw her son's lips move as he said proudly, "My name's Henry Sumner. I'm an American."

The buyer was Sam Cumberland. His shock was obvious. He rose quickly and began searching the crowd.

"Look after Henry for me, will you please?" Annie said to Madame Pichon, and walked out of the pavilion.

It was the longest afternoon of her life. Staying near Dionysus' box, leaving it only when she saw a silhouette at the end of the receiving barn that might be Sam's, Annie waited for the Prix Morny to be run. Henry and Madame Pichon hurried in, eager to return to the pavilion for the rest of La Poire's yearling sales. Looking somewhat mollified, Henry said that the colt's new owner had promised to consider the name Moonshot. Madame Pichon told Annie that Caernarvon Farms was the buyer and that Sam Cumberland had come over with the boy to introduce himself to her. "He said he liked the colt's pedigree better than his conformation." She watched Annie carefully for a reaction, but getting none, hurried away with Henry. Bernard breezed through, set off from the crowd in a white Edwardian suit and broad-brimmed panama hat.

Attentive to their own excitement, no one noticed Annie's dead calm. She knew Sam would look for her; the expression on his face when he had met Henry told her that. Finding her would not be difficult; Deauville, even in August, was an intimate town, particularly in the world of thoroughbreds.

A festive crowd filled the stands of the Hippodrome de la Touques, and the first races were run. Annie remained in the shadows of the receiving barn. To keep busy she braided Dionysus' mane, thinking of Sam without remorse or longing.

"Le Prix Morny. Préparez pour le rond de présentation," a voice said over the loudspeaker at the end of the barn. Annie followed Dionysus and his lad out of the box and through the track gates toward the paddock, which was already surrounded by crowds. A sudden covering of clouds moved in from the Channel, darkening the ancient Normandy timber-and-plaster buildings around the saddling enclosure. The thousands of geraniums, begonias, and pansies bordering the ring and the nearby stands began to bend in the menacing breeze.

The beauty of the Hippodrome added to Annie's sense of anticipation. Trying to control her nerves, she followed Dionysus into the walking ring.

Bernard Dolby was there, holding his hat against the wind.

As his trainer and the jockey's valet cinched on Dionysus' saddle, Bernard and Annie exchanged quick smiles. She watched as the jockeys appeared and spread out around the paddock. Madame Pichon and Henry joined her, letting the excitement of the sale be overtaken by that of the race. By then the crowd was packed against the rail to watch the ritual. As the track official called for the jockeys to mount, Annie heard the familiar voice say, "Hello, Annie."

In the barest glance, during which she replied, "Hello, Sam," with prepared ease, she saw his questioning though protective smile, and knew that he was as wary as she was.

She automatically followed the horses out of the paddock with the other owners. She did not join Lord Dolby's party in his box, but watched from the back of the stands. From the moment the starting gate opened, the result of the race was never in doubt. Dionysus led from wire to wire and won by a decisive three lengths, running the twelve hundred meters, or six furlongs, near to record time for a two-year-old. Annie's emotions had gone elsewhere. As the jockey brought the colt back, she went down to the winner's circle, where the jubilant Bernard Dolby rushed forward to greet his winner. Annie watched with an indifference she regretted deeply but could not help.

At that moment, a flash of lightning and crack of thunder announced a sudden Normandy downpour. Umbrellas sprouted throughout the stands and around the winner's circle, but in his joy, Bernard disregarded them. He saw Annie and waved for her to join him in celebration. As he moved along with the colt, turning him, obeying the photographers' shouted requests, Annie slipped away.

Already soaked, she went to the parking lot and hired a taxi. Madame Pichon would bring Henry to the Dolby villa. A celebration was planned there in the event of a win, an open house for well-wishers, followed by dinner at the Casino's Les Ambassadeurs, and then dancing at the nightclub. When she arrived, Annie hurried into the villa. She was shown to her room, where her clothes and Henry's had already been sent.

Still in her dripping dress, Annie looked at herself in the mirror over the dressing table. She saw the open closet where

Lord Dolby's butler had hung her dress for the evening. She looked at herself again, then quickly turned away, not willing to acknowledge what her eyes admitted, that she could fall in love with Sam again in a minute.

At dinner, Annie was seated on Bernard Dolby's right. She wore a new dress of jade silk with a long full skirt and a plunging neckline. She greeted and talked with Bernard's guests, the British bankers, a marquis, a Greek shipping tycoon, several French thoroughbred owners, as well as an endless line of people who came to congratulate the winner's owner. Madame Pichon, who sat across the table, noticed Annie's attempts to cover her anxiety, but said nothing. Several times, Bernard commented on Annie's seeming distraction, but it did not interfere with his triumph.

As the party walked from the restaurant along the plush carpets under the Casino's huge chandeliers, past roulette tables and the *salles privées* where no-limit baccarat was played, Annie consciously stopped herself from looking around for Sam. She took her place at the table in the Casino's nightclub, unable and unwilling to concentrate on what was happening or what people were saying around her. Champagne was poured; toasts were proposed. A magician entertained; Georges Guetary sang, and then there was dancing. Annie performed such a concentrated, if perfunctory routine, that she hardly noticed when Sam was there, standing behind her chair.

"I was wondering if the Countess of Catlettsburg would give me a dance?" he said as a joke between friends.

She had not seen him coming. Nevertheless, she responded easily, "I'd love to, Sam. Do you know Lord Dolby? And you met Madame Marie Pichon. Sam Cumberland . . ." She introduced him gracefully. Most of them knew of Sam, and he of them. He greeted them, congratulated Bernard Dolby, complimented Madame Pichon, and then followed Annie to the dance floor.

"So you saw a picture of the Countess?" Annie said over her shoulder.

"In *Town and Country.* Made a big impression in Lexington. They loved it," he said as they walked onto the floor.

"Lord, I'll bet they did." She laughed as she turned around and held up her arms to start dancing. He stopped a moment to look at her, hesitance and decision both playing hard in his eyes. Then he took her in his arms, and they danced. Neither spoke. Annie closed her eyes and tried not to think, or feel, or wonder. She almost succeeded, except for remembering the little catch step on the half-beat they used to do, and the still familiar blend of their bodies when they danced.

The music stopped abruptly, and they let go of each other slowly to join the applause.

"Is that boy my son?" Sam asked steadily, as if he had rehearsed the question many times.

Annie thought she had prepared herself for anything, but not to lie. "No, he's not."

He knew her too well and smiled knowingly. "Thanks for trying. I wish I'd known. I'm such an *idiot,* it didn't occur to me until today when he . . . I'd have tried . . ." He hesitated, then shook his head and took her arm to lead her back to her table. "It's a little late to make noble statements of intent, isn't it? Thanks for the dance, Annie. It's good to see you looking so . . . happy."

"Thanks, Sam. I am," Annie said, moving with him. "How about you?"

He laughed hollowly and let her go ahead of him between tables, but held on to her hand. Before they reached the Dolby table, he drew her back to him and said, "The last time I was happy was the afternoon I ran into you on Madison Avenue."

Annie watched him, taking a long breath before saying, "What about right now?"

His crooked smile spread across his face, as full of appreciation as of despair. He glanced at the Dolby table and back at her. "I'm supposed to be in Paris; my plane leaves at dawn. I stayed to find out about the boy. If you ever need anything for him . . ." He looked away, frustrated, and shook his head. "Annie, there are too many questions and too little time. A lot of people are waiting for us. I'd rather be standing here with you than anywhere else in the world, but you know, and I know, that we have to be very careful."

He watched her for understanding. She gave it to him. He smiled, bent forward, and kissed her on the cheek, then turned and walked away through the tables toward the main entrance.

Annie watched him a little too long before returning to her table. In spite of being in the middle of an uproarious discussion, Bernard gave her a quick look of curious concern. Annie smiled to reassure him, but her smiles had no effect on Madame Pichon, who said to Annie when she excused herself to go home, "Come talk with me tomorrow."

She did not want to think about what had happened with Sam. She made herself enter into the spirit of the evening, talking animatedly, dancing with the other guests, and making Bernard laugh. The party continued, moving from the Casino to the Greek shipping tycoon's villa for ouzo, the smashing of glasses in the fireplace in honor of Dionysus, and some drunken, passionate, and frequently hilarious Greek dancing. Annie continued in apparent high spirits until she was alone with Bernard, being driven home in the back seat of the Greek's Rolls-Royce.

"My darling," Bernard said, "I believe that tonight we've suddenly become the best of friends."

Annie looked over at him to see if he was hurt or angry, but he picked up her hand and kissed it fondly. "And now that I'm your best friend, you can tell me all about him. I've seldom seen Cupid bludgeon someone quite so severely as he did you tonight. The Cumberlands come from Wales, as I remember reading somewhere."

Annie told him as much as she could, not everything, not that Sam was Henry's father, but about the conspiracy, her marriage, and Winnie's death, and more than she had thought about in years. Their conversation continued with Calvados on the villa's terrace overlooking the sea. The breeze from the Channel was warm and pleasant.

"I didn't know Sam would be here," Annie said, "and I'm really sorry he showed up during your party."

"Darling," Bernard said, waving away the problem, "he had no effect on the party, except on your enjoyment of it. Selfishly, I wish he'd appeared tomorrow. But this way, we can be friends for life as well as partners in a great colt. So that's that. The major question is, what are you going to do about Sam?"

"I don't know," Annie answered, although fantasies had been popping into her mind throughout the evening, only to be dissolved in her determined talk and laughter. "There are too many things I don't know."

"None of any importance, if I may say so. From what you told me he said, the poor sod seems to have been unhappy for quite a long time . . . if you can believe him. Or was he just plucking an old familiar tune on your heartstrings?"

"No, I believe him," Annie said.

"Then, my darling, your course is clear," Bernard said. "Go get him. He and whoever else is currently in his life have had a good deal of time together, and if they haven't worked things out, then he has the right—as I remember all patriotic Americans have—to pursue his happiness."

Annie smiled doubtfully. "Go get him? Don't you think that'd be kind of obvious?"

"My darling, it's outrageous. And so what? And speaking of outrageous, I'm going to bed alone." He smiled, sadly. "Come, we must learn to kiss each other as chastely as children."

Affectionately, they kissed each other's cheeks, then hugged. "Annie," he said, "you are the kind of woman who convinces a man like me that he's a fool to let you get away. Does this Cumberland know how lucky he is?" He bade her good night and left her on the terrace.

Slowly Annie finished her Calvados, watching the waves overlap as they spread their foam over the beach. Dawn began in the cloudless sky; the air of the flowered coast, washed clean by the previous day's rain, seemed even to taste sweet. The soft pounding of the waves and the soft hiss of the surf seeped through Annie's mind and washed away her objections.

She felt as if the whole of what she was going to do was already formed, and that all she needed was to discover and act on the details. No longer a nightmare, the idea of going back to America and making a home excited Annie so much that she stepped out of her shoes and peeled off her stockings to run down to the beach. The full skirt of her gown billowed around her. The water was frigid, and as she gathered up her skirt and walked through the shallow tide, she was glad for the Calvados, happy that she was a bit drunk.

She laughed, then saw something out of the corner of her eye, and stopped. Looking up, she watched the white contrails from a plane dividing the sky as it headed toward the still dark western horizon. Annie laughed again, not believing for a moment in the coincidence that Sam might be on that particular plane, but enjoying the possibility.

Behind her, suddenly, there was a pounding. She turned to see an early morning set of ten thoroughbreds lope easily through the shallow water of the surf, the icy temperature tightening and soothing the animals' ankles. As they went by on either side of Annie, the lads waved and called to her. She waved back and watched the horses pass, automatically appraising them, noting a flaw of conformation in one, the fluid stride of another, moved by their beauty as if they had happened by at that moment as approval of what she was about to do.

NINETEEN

THE COUNTESS
BUYS LIMETEEN

October 21.—One of the oldest
stud farms in the Bluegrass
changed owners last week. Mrs.
Winton Sumner III, widow of the
former owner of fabled Rosewood
Stables, bought Limeteen Farm for
a reported $1.75 million. The 450-
acre Fayette County stud farm is
one of only three in central Kentucky with a training track.
Limeteen had fallen on hard times
since the death of its longtime
owner, Colonel Matthew Scanlon,

and was placed on the market two years ago by his estate.

Mrs. Sumner, a native Kentuckian, has been living in France. According to an associate, Mr. A. R. Beasley of Blue Bell Farm, Mrs. Sumner's intention to expand her thoroughbred interests is due to her recent stay at the famous Haras de la Poire, where a number of Europe's greatest trainers and horsemen have been trained by the distinguished breeder Madame Marie Pichon. "As far as I can tell," Mr. Beasley said, "she [Mrs. Sumner] just wants to dig down into this business deeper, so she's bringing her shovel to the Bluegrass."

A former resident of Catlettsburg, Mrs. Sumner was known as "the Countess" of that community while residing abroad. After inspecting Limeteen over several days, she has returned to France to prepare for her change of residence.

THE ARTICLE appeared on a back page of the *Lexington Herald-Leader* in the business section, where it shared the page with news concerning the Bluegrass industries—barley, tobacco, bourbon whiskey, and breeding thoroughbreds. Belinda Cumberland read the article early on the morning of its publication. She was being driven from Caernarvon Farm to take her honored place behind the master of foxhounds of Lexington's ancient Iroquois Hunt. The news further exasperated her. She had not been able to button the waistband of her buff-colored riding breeches, and her three-button black shadbelly hunting coat was uncomfortably tight. The diet pills were not working, but instead were causing sleepless nights and a short temper.

Belinda displayed her temper to her fellow hunt members,

chastising several of their guests for riding too close to the hounds. Increasingly angry as they rode on, she drove her six-year-old hunter with her whip, finally lining him up to take a jump they had never tried. The hunter pulled up at the last moment; Belinda went over the jump by herself. She landed on her shoulder and cracked her collarbone. The first hunt member who came to her aid heard her spouting words he never believed could fall from a Southern lady's lips.

At the hospital, the left part of her torso was put in a cast; nevertheless, later that day Belinda was able to throw the newspaper at her husband when he came into her private room.

"Go on, honey, read it!" she yelled at Sam. "Business page, lower left. I know you'll be pleased as punch!" Then she turned away from him as best she could.

After he left the room, Sam read the article. A smile spread over his face as he stood in the corridor. He read the article through again before striding happily to the elevator.

Two days later, the paper arrived by mail forty-seven miles south of Lexington on Highway 25, at the Slate Lick Truck Surplus. A used-farm-truck dealership, its owner subscribed to the city paper so that he could compare truck prices. The young salesman read the newspaper, looking for his next opportunity. Not many customers came to the Slate Lick lot, but when they did, his curly blond good looks, coupled with his easy convincing lies, made a sale almost a sure thing. The owner of the lot recognized the young man's talent, and even gave his hulking brother a job spinning wheels backward to adjust the odometers and cleaning the vehicles before they went on the lot. On Thursday mornings, both brothers were let off work to meet with their parole officer in Berea.

The young man did not plan to sell trucks much longer. When he finished reading the article, he ran his hand through his blond curls, checked to be sure he was alone, and grabbed the showroom phone to dial.

"Can I help you?" the operator drawled.

"I want to call New York, person-to-person collect. To the Angel. The number's 212-555-2837."

"And your name?"

"Just say Jimmy Lee."

After he hung up, Phil Angelo sat staring at the phone. It was on a bedside table crammed into the dingy Broadway hotel room where he had resided since Charlie Dell's death. "Twenty-six million dollars" floated through his thoughts, as it always did when Annie came to mind. He had first read the amount in the papers when her Sumner inheritance was an item in the gossip columns. It had enraged him. To his way of thinking, he deserved a lot of that money. After all, she had kept him from making use of Charlie Dell's list. When Phil had tried to use the little information he had, sending an anonymous blackmail note to Vito Genovese himself, he had almost had himself burned for his trouble. During a scary six-month period, after Joe Valachi started singing, Phil was grilled by the FBI, then yanked off the street and kept in a cellar for a month by members of Vito Genovese's Mafia family.

They had not suspected him as the blackmailer, but they did not want him available to the FBI. He had talked his way out, but it was close both times. He would have gladly implicated Annie, but such information would have made it clear to everyone that it was he, not Joe Valachi, who had tried to blackmail Vito Genovese. So Annie owed him for staying quiet; he had probably saved her rich little life. Now that she was coming back, he would collect somehow. He did not have a scheme, but he would work on one, maybe with her stupid brothers, he thought, maybe not.

He twisted the cord of the phone, knitting it around his long fingers. After the mortician had taken away Charlie Dell's wasted body, Phil had been left alone in Charlie's apartment for two hours. He had rifled the place, breaking into Charlie's desk, going through his papers, taking a last shot at finding the list. He did not find that, but he ran across a copy of Charlie's will, as well as a payment record to a Cincinnati detective agency, marked ANNIE GREBAUER, CATLETTSBURG, KENTUCKY.

From the copy of the will, Phil learned among other things

that Teddy Lapps had been left $150,000 in cash, that Vera Kovalchik was to receive ownership of her two fingernail-and-hairdressing salons in Queens, that Charlie's sister would get a half-million-dollar trust that she would lose if her son ever left the institution where he resided, and that Phil Angelo was forgiven all debts owed. In other words, Phil did not receive a penny from Charlie Dell—although by then his debt had risen to $168,000. Phil spent the afternoon of Charlie's funeral in a bar, shooting pool.

For a price, the Cincinnati detective agency gave Phil the same information about Annie that it had previously provided to Charlie Dell. Without revealing his identity, Phil contacted both of her brothers in the Kentucky state penitentiary and sent them cash in return for any information about their sister. Even Phil Angelo found the brothers' claims about what they had done to Annie to be disgusting, but he kept communication with them open, figuring that one day they might be useful. Phil also realized that Jimmy Lee was by far the smarter, so eager to get into "the big time," as he kept calling it, that he would do just about anything.

The radiators in Phil's room started banging as he stared out through the grime of his window. He hated living poor. Annie had screwed up his big chance. His teeth clenched hard together. He would get his share soon and live the way he was supposed to live.

He grabbed his overcoat and hurried out. On the street, he walked fast, a persistent cough catching in his throat. His office was in "Needle Park" on the West Side. He was selling heroin to junkies. The Genovese family had requested that he join them in the lower echelons of their drug enterprises, an invitation no one ever turned down. Now he took orders from punks, and forced some of his female customers to screw him to get their next fix. Phil was a good salesman; he made enough to pay for his suits and his gambling. But he wanted off the streets, to convince his bosses to let him get back to fixing races. Soon things would change. He was going to get his share from Annie.

• • •

During the year-end racing lull, when the New York season was over and Caernarvon's runners were shipped to South Carolina and Florida for the winter, Frank Carney usually spent time at Caernarvon's stud farm in Kentucky. He did not read the article in the *Herald-Leader.* Someone told him about it. Frank had been noting Limeteen's deterioration. The caretaker there, Hugger Elway, had been a friend of Frank's since they were both boys, hotwalking for Caernarvon.

Frank Carney had a deep respect for the permanence such a farm represented. After three generations of wise buying and smart breeding, the farm had turned out a number of stakes-winning thoroughbreds for the young Colonel Scanlon, a real Kentucky colonel in the First World War. He built Limeteen Hall as a wedding gift for his bride.

It was a gracious house of classic Colonial lines, built of brick and fronted by a wide stone porch with an impressive portico supported by six wooden Doric columns. Beyond it, down a small hill, was the farm. But the training track needed resurfacing. The breeding, foaling, and stallion barns needed major renovation and modernization. The paddocks needed mowing and new fences.

Standing at the front door of Limeteen Hall one morning, he saw torn and faded velvet draperies, peeling wallpaper, and water damage on the ceiling and the broad curving stairs leading to the upstairs gallery.

"That Countess better get on over here," he said to Hugger Elway as they shut the door. "Pretty soon she'll be moving into a pile of rubble."

Frank Carney never showed emotion, having nurtured the belief that any such display was unmanly and interfered with the business at hand. He had intense feelings, however, and none went deeper than those for horses and long-owned land. Growing up with neither, he had moved through the South with an ever expanding family, his father sharecropping, going bust, moving on, finding another stake, and working it for three years at the longest. As soon as Frank and his eight siblings were old enough, each was set to work, and left behind if the employment offered a future. Frank had been lucky enough to be dropped off at Caernarvon Farm when he was ten. At the age of thirty-three, he still did not own horses or land, and it was a need he felt deeply.

Walking back to his pickup after his tour of Limiteen Farm, Frank thought about the new owner. He remembered catching her that time at Saratoga, years earlier, when she tried to give Certainty a sugar cube. She was as pretty a girl as he had ever seen on the backstretch. Because he always was made uncomfortable by female beauty, he had dealt with her by using his authority.

The next time he saw her, at the winner's circle of Certainty's Belmont Stakes, she had grown up. Then, later that summer, Certainty stopped in his tracks on his way to the Travers to greet her. She looked so beautiful that Frank hardly watched her for fear of breaking his concentration on the race. A year later, after telling Chigger Beasley he ought to do business with her, he managed to nod to her at the Rosewood dispersal sale.

The last time Frank saw her was when she stood up to the crowd at the Keeneland Select Summer Sales in that black dress. He thought that she bid too high for the yearling she bought, but he recalled that it certainly did irritate Sam Cumberland. Frank had smiled his congratulations, but never knew if she noticed. Then, when some of the audience tried to embarrass her, she had handled herself admirably, standing at the top of the stairs, looking down on all those people clapping as if they were monkeys. He had heard the rumors about her driving her husband to suicide. Having glimpsed Annie Sumner over a number of years, Frank Carney figured that anyone married to her would have had to be near crazy to end his life.

He drove down the five hundred yards of cracked and potholed asphalt of Limiteen's front drive. On each side was a line of oak trees and broken paddock fences. The muscles in Frank's left arm cramped, a familiar occurrence from years of posthole digging and fence building. He worked out the cramp and looked at his hands on the steering wheel. They had barbed wire scars, calluses, and a long rope-burn scar on the right one from his wrist to his knuckles. A stallion had dragged him across a Caernarvon paddock.

He scowled, remembering his argument the previous

month with Sam Cumberland. As he turned onto Ironworks Pike, Frank opened the glove compartment. In it was a pint of Maker's Mark bourbon, the only daily luxury he allowed himself. Although it was early in the day, he took the bottle to his mouth and unscrewed the top with his teeth.

In January, a week after they celebrated Henry's seventh birthday and said goodbye to their friends at the Haras de la Poire, Annie and Henry flew into Bluegrass Airport. As they drove up the long drive to Limeteen Hall, Henry exulted, "We're home!"

Stepping out of the cab, he grabbed his mother's hand as he always did. Annie let him pull her up the steps, across the front porch to the immense front door. Together they opened the antique lock with a large iron key. They walked in and stood in the wide breezeway, just as they had done months before when they came over from France to buy the farm.

"You still like it?" Annie asked.

"I love it!" Henry shouted, grabbing a curl of faded wallpaper and peeling it up to the seam of the ceiling. Without hesitation, he tore at another piece.

"Now don't make a mess, Henry."

"I'm going up to see *my* room!" he shouted and ran up the stairs, two at a time.

Annie saw the parcels that she had shipped from France stacked against a wall. She had decided to come two days before anyone expected them; she wanted to be alone with Henry before the workers arrived. As the cabdriver lined up their luggage inside the door, Annie noticed that the heat was on in the house, for which she was grateful.

She paid the driver, then wandered through the empty rooms, the library with its warping oak paneling, the dining room with stained and spotted mirrors, one in shards on the floor. Then she entered the enormous drawing room. Paint and plaster had fallen from the ceiling, littering the floor. The room's six French doors hinted at elegance despite some broken panes and missing hardware. The doors opened onto a stone terrace that overlooked a frozen creek-fed pond, fifty acres of paddocks, and a gently rising hill with a dense stand of oak at its crest. A light rain was washing away the last of a thin snow.

She ran a finger along the dust of a windowpane, then started at what she saw. Outside on the porch were Hugger Elway, the caretaker, and his wife. Annie smiled a greeting; she and Hugger struggled to open one of the French doors. A rawboned, down-to-earth, middle-aged couple, they were deeply chagrined that they had not cleaned up the house before Annie came. She reassured them that it had been her intention to arrive without warning. Without further discussion, they went to work.

Hugger Elway distributed the luggage and boxes between the two upstairs rooms with beds in them; Mrs. Elway began to clean up the kitchen. The rest of that day was spent unpacking, testing which lights and toilets worked, and discovering new parts and new problems of the house that they had not noticed on their previous trip. Annie did not go down to the barns. She was saving the business part of Limeteen Farm for her second day.

That night, after the Elways had returned to the caretaker's cottage, Annie and Henry sat in front of the fire that Mr. Elway had laid in the library. They sprawled on a thick pile of quilts that Annie had sent from France, eating a dinner of burgoo and pecan pie, both of which had been brought up to Limeteen Hall from Mrs. Elway's freezer.

"Maman," Henry said, staring at a bowl of the strange-smelling concoction. "What *is* burgoo?"

Having grown up on it, Annie knew that any honest definition would not enhance the urge to eat it. "Well, it's kind of like a Kentucky bouillabaisse, but without fish. Everybody makes it a different way, but I'll bet Mrs. Elway makes it better than most." She quickly tasted it and hummed her praise. "Umm-mm. You're going to love it."

Henry liked bouillabaisse and Mrs. Elway. After spooning a bite into his mouth, he quickly finished his first bowl. Only then did Annie tell him the bromidic recipe of "okra, beans, and anything the farm truck runs over that ain't still wigglin'." He cocked his head and said, "Maman, that's really disgusting . . . but can I have some more?"

323

As he ate, Henry said, "Sometimes I can't understand what Mr. and Mrs. Elway say, they talk so funny. And Maman, since we arrived, you've begun to sound just like them."

Annie laughed. She was aware that she was slipping back into the familiar drawl of her childhood. "You'll get used to it, Henry. You'll probably start to sound like this yourself sooner or later."

"If I do, it'll be my third language!"

She put him to bed, letting him keep a light on in answer to his need of "getting to know my room." She had no worry that he would not sleep; the day had been a long one and they were both exhausted. Annie, however, was still too excited by being at Limeteen. She changed into a warm velvet dressing gown and went back down the buckling, creaking stairs.

Outside, the rain had become a driven snow, and she heard the wind rattling over Limeteen Hall's windows. The place seemed similar to the Château de la Brise the first winter, when Henry was born. She sat down on the bottom stair. Noticing that dust had already streaked the skirt of her gown, she felt foolish sitting on the stairs. She knew she should go to bed, but she sat there, looking around at the decay and wondering where to start.

Headlights suddenly raked across the front porch and glared through the glass panels that bordered the door. When the light darkened, Annie instinctively thought of the gun. It was upstairs in one of her bags. As she stood to get it, she heard a loud knock.

"Annie!"

It was Sam. He knocked again and she hurried to the door so that he would not wake Henry. Unlocking and opening it, she reminded herself how quickly her feelings for him could trouble everything else she wanted to do. He lurched in; snow blew in behind him. Annie closed the door and leaned against it to look at him.

"What in the world are you doing here tonight?" she said as he took off a wide-brimmed leather hat. He was wearing a heavy leather jacket, corduroy pants, and boots. After hitting the hat against his leg to get the snow off, he stood in the center of the hall, watching her.

"Did you think I wouldn't hear that you were coming?" he asked. "Did you think I wouldn't arrange to be here? I've been driving by here for the last four nights. I saw the lights."

Annie heard the familiar logistical concerns and decided to confront them right away. "How *did* you arrange it, Sam?"

He brushed snow off his shoulders; then he looked at her and said, "You do get right to it, don't you? All right, here's the happy picture. We were in Palm Beach for the Christmas holidays with the children. Belinda hit thirty-five last year, and she performed badly at the horse shows in Europe. She blamed it on her weight, which she blames on her unhappiness, which she blames on guess who. She ran into a very smooth society doctor at a ball, and he's hooked her on some kind of diet drug. It isn't working and she's getting heavier and unhappier." Perplexed, he looked around at the empty hall, then took a deep breath and continued. "I heard from people in Lexington when you were expected. When it was time to get the kids back to New York for school, I told Belinda I was going to stop off here. We don't offer excuses or explanations to each other anymore. I've had to be here a lot since Father died . . . Did you know that Mother and Father . . . ?"

Annie nodded. "I wrote you."

He stared at her. "I never got it. I suppose the secretaries . . ." Then he started to pace uneasily around the hall, pushing a large strip of wallpaper aside with his foot. "I'll be honest with you. It probably wouldn't have made much difference if I'd seen your letter. I wouldn't have answered it. I was still shaky about Winnie's death, and I blamed you."

"What about now?" Annie asked. "Do you blame me now?"

He stopped pacing, and leaned an elbow against the banister.

"The blame stayed right where it was until I saw you at Deauville. Then I thought, even if it was true, it didn't matter. But after I left the Casino that night, I went over all of it again. It suddenly seemed damn strange that I believed what Winnie said on the phone about you, especially since telling him about us that way was so unlike anything you'd ever do. It was so unlike you."

He pushed off from the banister and stood up, running the brim of his hat through his fingers, watching her as he talked. "At the time, I think I had to believe the worst about you, because I'd just admitted to my best friend that I'd made love to his wife. After he killed himself, I needed to believe it even more."

The wind blew through the outline of the front door. Annie moved toward the drawing room, uncomfortable in the criss-cross of drafts in the hall. But then she stopped.

"Winnie wrote me a letter that night," she told him, "about why he'd said such awful things to you about me."

Sam took a step toward her. "Why didn't you show it to me?"

"I never had the chance, Sam," she said, controlling the anger in her voice. "Besides, the fact that you believed him so completely seemed like a betrayal to me."

He looked down at his hat. "It was."

"In the crunch," she said, raising her voice and fixing on his eyes, "you slid right back into your upper-class superiority, because it was safer and more comfortable."

"Horseshit! That has nothing to do—"

"Don't kid yourself, Sam," she said. "I was forbidden plea-sure, outside the rules. You had a lot of fun breaking them, playing our secret little game. But the betrayal was more than that. You loved me." She started to walk across the hall. "But even that wasn't enough when the excitement turned into a tragedy. You tried to make a deal with me. Remember? At *church?* So that nothing dirty and low would touch your glori-ous name and perfect family!"

They stared at each other. The wind blew a piece of loose wallpaper. It lifted slowly, then fell.

"If you still feel that way," Sam said, his voice low and menacing, "what the hell am I doing here?"

"I *don't* still feel—"

"Maman . . ."

The boy was standing at the top of the stairs, looking sleepy but curious.

"Henry, you're supposed to be asleep. Come on down and say hello. Careful of the stairs."

Henry hurried down, seeing who it was. "I know you! You're the man who bought Moonshot! How is he? Is he here? I didn't know you lived here."

"This is Mr. Cumberland, Henry. Shake hands and look him straight in the eye." Her instructions were rote, but suddenly seemed too pointed.

"Moonshot's fine, Henry," Sam said, shaking the boy's proffered hand. "He's down in South Carolina with our trainer, learning how to run. But I wouldn't be surprised if he'll be up here this spring."

"Really? That's super! Can I come see him?"

"Anytime. And the Jockey Club let us keep the name Moonshot, so if I'm not there, you can just ask for him."

"Now, Henry, up to bed," Annie said.

"We should have never sold Moonshot, Maman," the boy said as he kissed his mother on the cheek. "Mr. Cumberland is going to win a *lot* of races with him."

They both watched Henry take the creaking stairs two at a time and disappear down the upstairs hall to his room.

"Do people back here suspect anything about who Henry's father really is?" Annie asked quietly.

Sam turned to look at her. "There were the basic nasty reactions when you proclaimed your pregnancy at Keeneland. None involved me. Winnie's the father as far as anyone knows. The Sumner family was pretty horrified, but that's passed. Hell, even I didn't suspect anything until I met him."

"What made you so sure?"

Sam looked off into the dark, shook his head, and started pacing again. *"I don't know.* As soon as he told me his name, the idea became so obvious."

He shrugged, stopping to look at her. She met his eyes steadily.

"You think it'll be obvious to people if they see us together?"

"I think enough time's gone by." He answered the question quickly, but hesitated before he addressed the implication. *"Will* they see us together?"

327

"Well, I don't sneak around anymore."

"I'd never ask you to do that again."

"Then I'd say the fact that you and I managed somehow to get to this drafty hallway, talking to each other, makes the chances that we might be seen together pretty good."

"You sounded damn angry."

She turned and drifted away from him.

"I'll always be angry, hurt, whatever, about what happened to us when Winnie died. But that's not all I am . . . or all I remember. That night in Deauville, you said we had to be careful. I agree with you. The problem is, I don't think we have a choice. I know I don't. We didn't see each other for five years! It sounds as if we even stopped thinking about each other. And then, a couple of glimpses and a dance at Deauville . . . and here we are, walking around each other, being *real* careful, because everybody will be watching what happens if they've a mind to." Hearing herself, she put a hand to her head. " 'If they've a mind to'? I haven't said that in years."

Sam said slowly, "I don't care, Annie." The tone made Annie want to go to him, but she held back and let him speak. "So let them watch. I love you. I don't believe I ever stopped. For five years, I guess I just suspended it. Being together may still be our problem, but as for love, you have all of mine."

Sam did not move. He waited for her to come to him.

"Sam," she said, "I've become somebody I like, and what worries me most about you is that somehow I'll lose hold of myself."

He dropped his hat on the floor and took a step toward her. She hesitated for a moment, then ran across the hall into his arms. Clinging to each other, they kissed longingly, then stood silently holding each other, hearing the wind blow and staring at fallen plaster and shadows.

They both started talking at once, and chuckled.

"Were you going to say something about Henry?" Annie asked, speaking close to his ear.

"Yes, about how heavy a sleeper I hope he is."

"It's his first night in a strange house, and I wouldn't bet that he won't come wandering down here again."

"I don't want to leave you."

"Then stay. I suppose we can neck a little."

He kissed her, and slowly his hands moved down her back, then around to the front, over her breasts.

"Oh, Lord, Sam, don't do too much to me."

"Can't we at least sit down, or . . ."

"No chairs. No nothing. Come on, there's a fire." She took his hand and led him into the library.

Looking around, Sam saw more decay. "I don't know how you're going to do it, Annie. The place is falling apart. Everyone says that Colonel Scanlon started keeping his money when he turned sixty and let everything go, with the idea it'd all collapse the day he died. Looks as if he didn't miss by far. It's going to take millions to get this place—"

He stopped abruptly. He was regarding Annie as if he had made a small gaffe.

"Well, well," she said. "One thing I learned about the fancy people, they're only comfortable talking about money with equals. I must be making progress, at least with you."

Sam laughed. "Obviously you are." He went over to throw more wood on the fire.

"So tell me how you are, Sam. What's been happening to you?"

"Well, they made me a steward of the Jockey Club, to occupy the family seat, I expect. They have a real fight on their hands. All of a sudden, people want to legalize using drugs on the day of the race. I'm getting into it, although the Jockey Club has no clout except for its prestige. Politicians regard us as being just as important as used-car salesmen."

"If they legalize drugs on the day of the race, the trainers who don't want to use drugs will have to, just to keep up."

"I know," he said, shaking his head. "It's all changing, Annie. You'll see. Too many drugs and too much money." Then he smiled. "So tell me your plans. What *are* you going to do here?"

"Whatever it takes to have the best. No compromises. Quality from the first day to breed, train, and run classic thoroughbreds." She sat on the pile of quilts and hugged her knees as the fire rekindled itself.

Sam stood, looking down at her. "You may not have enough money for all that, Annie. I'm not sure anyone does."

"Maybe not. Maybe I'll lose it all trying, and end up just the way I was when you found me."

"It isn't so easy. You get used to money," he said.

"I know that, and I've already taken care of Henry's future. But the money isn't mine. It came to me because of a lot of sadness. I want to turn it over and make it mean something better."

He took off his jacket and spread it out on the quilts. "Horses don't often cooperate with such noble sentiments."

"I know that too, but that's what I'm going to do."

"Tell me about it." He sprawled down on the quilts at her feet, leaning on an elbow and facing her.

"I aim to have a hundred broodmares, eight stallions of my own, and twenty first-class nominations to others, including Certainty, if you'll sell me one. Say we have a seventy percent live-foal rate. With seventy yearlings each year, we'll send half to the sales and put half in training."

"I'll give you a nomination to Certainty. A 'farm-warming' present."

"No you won't. You and I are going to keep business and pleasure in separate counties."

Sam chuckled. "Who's going to be your trainer?"

"Don't know yet. Whoever's the best. I'd like to find a private trainer just for Limeteen, but if not, I'll try to get the best of the public trainers to take us on." She was rocking back and forth, enjoying the excitement of telling about her plans.

"Finding the right trainer's really hard," Sam said, staring into the fire. "You never know where he'll come from. Frank Carney was a hotwalker for us when he was a kid. The most natural horseman I've ever seen. Father was as proud of finding him as of any yearling who won a Derby. I'm not sure Frank knows that Father died. And he drinks." Then he turned to her. "If you do all that, in three years you'll have a hundred horses in training. How can Limeteen handle all that?"

"It will. I'm putting in four hundred acres of new paddock fencing, building two more twenty-stall broodmare barns, which'll make five, redoing the two foaling barns, and building a brand-new stallion barn and breeding shed with more scientific gewgaws than they'd find in a hospital. The yearling and training barns may have to get torn down and rebuilt; I haven't decided that yet. The track needs a new surface and a new starting gate. Other than that, we're ready right now."

Sam chuckled again and shook his head. "You've been doing a lot of thinking."

"About a lot of things," she said and leaned back on her elbows. The motion was an old familiar invitation, which Sam recognized immediately. Annie regretted it. She rolled away and stood up. "I'm sorry, Sam. Old habits. I'm not quite ready yet."

Sam watched her as she stood looking down at him, both wary and loving. Then he too stood, picked up his jacket, and put it on.

"Okay," he said, "but don't worry about us; it's different now. We aren't going to be as crazy as we were. Annie, we're brand-new."

Annie smiled and took his arm. Together they walked to the front door. He picked up his hat and zipped up his leather jacket. Then he leaned over and kissed her gently on the lips.

"I'll never get in the way of what you want to do," he said, "or whoever you want to be. Just let me love you and help out with Limeteen if you need anything. Oh, and one thing. When you put in your paddock fences, just use pressure-treated wood. All those pretty white fences are for people who want their pictures in the magazines."

He kissed her again, said, "God I'm glad you're here," then opened the front door and pushed out into the wind.

TWENTY

HOLDING THE PEDIGREE CHARTS of two stallions that she was considering, Annie walked across the hall to grab a hat before going out to the construction site. The front doorbell rang. Although her new housekeeper appeared at the top of the stairs, Annie motioned her back.

"I'll get it, Josie," she called and opened the large door.

She saw the blond curls first, so much lighter than the burned amber of her own hair. Jimmy Lee and Fungo were standing there, awkward and surly. Annie took three steps back and began to tremble visibly. Her first thought was of the gun, now in a locked drawer of the library desk.

"You all right, Annie?" Jimmy Lee said slyly, with false concern. "It's just us, Jimmy Lee and Fungo." Annie heard his voice hiss, saying "jist" for "just."

"Hi, Annie," Fungo said, his voice still a hollow rumble.

She reached out for something to lean on, but nothing was

there. The sun was bright behind them; she had backed up far enough so that she could see little more than their outlines. Fungo's arm rose to swat at a fly crawling on his crew-cut head.

"What do you want?" she said, her throat so tight that the question sounded as if she were clearing her throat. She suddenly remembered that Henry would be home from school in two hours.

"Well, we got some good news and bad news," Jimmy Lee offered. In spite of not being able to see his face clearly because of the glaring light behind it, Annie saw the white teeth of his mocking smile. "Can we come in?" he asked.

Annie's back stiffened, but she nodded. Josie was working upstairs, the cook was in the kitchen, and four carpenters were putting up molding in the dining room. Nevertheless, Annie's hands still shook. Trying to control them, she folded the pedigree papers and put them in the pockets of her jeans.

The brothers stepped into the newly painted and papered hall and looked around. Fungo was wide-eyed, but Jimmy Lee acted amused. They were both wearing old work shirts, overalls, and work boots. Each carried a duffel bag.

"Real nice, Annie," Jimmy Lee said and smiled as if suggesting an intimate secret of corruption. Then, without being asked, he dropped his duffel bag and said, "The good news is that we've served our time and finished with our parole officer. We wanted to come welcome you sooner, but only when we had that behind us. Like they say, we paid our debt to society, and we're clean as newborn."

Annie could smell Fungo, a once familiar odor of sweat that terrified her. He said, "You want me to close the door, Annie?"

She stared at them. "How can you dare . . . ?" She stopped because she knew the answer. Jimmy Lee could do anything, and Fungo would do anything Jimmy Lee told him to do.

"Yes," she said. "Close the door, Fungo." She stared at Jimmy Lee. "What's the bad news?"

Jimmy Lee's expression changed to a mournful look that appeared as false to Annie as if he were mugging. "It's Pa," he said. "He's still in the castle, and he's got a tumor in his brain

333

. . . We call the penitentiary the castle," he explained earnestly. "See, they won't let him out on parole because, about three years back, he killed this dumb guard who'd been hassling him. Used an ice pick." Then Jimmy Lee smiled as sweetly as Annie remembered his doing just before he pulled a knife.

She started walking toward the library. Inexplicably, the news of her father had caused tears to come to her eyes, and she did not want her brothers to see them. "Come in here," she called back to them, trying to keep her voice firm.

The oak paneling in the library had been stripped from the walls and sent to a restorer. Aside from a partner's desk covered with a protective drop cloth, there was no furniture; drop cloths and fallen plaster covered the floor. Annie started to close the door, then left it open. Standing near the threshold, she took a deep breath and stated, "You better tell me what you want, because you aren't about to stay on this place!"

Fungo blinked his small eyes and peered dumbly at Jimmy Lee for a signal about how to react. Getting none, he lowered the fleshy overlay of his brow in a frown.

Jimmy Lee never took his eyes off Annie, and again smiled. "The past is over, Annie. We're just looking for a way to get our shit together, y'know? It looks like you've done real good for yourself. That's fine. We're your brothers, and we sure don't want to cause you any problems, do we, Fungo? But maybe you could think about what we need, Annie. We want to make a living. If you don't want us around here, well, maybe some of your rich friends . . ."

"Wait here," she said, understanding his threat as she slipped through the open door and closed it behind her. She ran up the stairs and told Josie to watch the library door and call her if it opened. Then she went to the phone by her bed and called Archibald Delansig in New York.

When she returned to the library twenty minutes later, Fungo was sitting on the floor, his back against the wall. Jimmy Lee was looking out the window; in the distance, a crew was building paddock fences. He turned to Annie, grinning expectantly.

"There's a car out front," Annie said. "Two of my security

people are driving you to a motel. They'll give you some money when you get there. Stay there until you hear from me. We're trying to arrange a visit to Daddy in the next couple of days if you want to go. If you don't, that's fine. You'll hear from me before I go."

"Oh, we want to go," Jimmy Lee remonstrated. "Don't we, Fungo?"

His brother, unsure, let his cruelly curved mouth hang open under his flattened, broken nose. He stared at Annie with the same kind of dumb malice she remembered from when he would come for her in the shack. She turned quickly and left the library.

The brothers followed her. One of the security guards was waiting in the hall. He led the two brothers out to the farm station wagon and loaded their duffel bags in the back. The brothers said nothing as they left. Neither did Annie. She watched the station wagon drive down through the two rows of oaks past a tree surgeon's truck. As soon as it was out of sight, she looked at a clock, again thinking of Henry returning from school. Then she went to get the gun.

She kept it with her through the night. Even with one of the security men stationed in his car in front of the house, Annie could not sleep. Wandering through the house, sitting in different rooms, some nearly finished, some still crowded with scaffolding, Annie listened for any sound of break-in. She checked and rechecked the locks on the doors. When dawn came, she sat exhausted in a chair in Henry's room.

Delansig arrived later that morning. He contacted the governor's office about a possible pardon for her father, and the warden at the penitentiary about a visit. Then he and Annie worked out a plan for her brothers.

After another nearly sleepless night, she drove with Delansig to Bluegrass Airport, where a small chartered plane waited. A Limeteen security guard had already delivered the brothers from their motel. They stood by the plane on the tarmac and waited as Annie climbed up the small ladder. Fungo still wore work clothes, sweat-stained at the armpits, his dirty jeans cinched by a wide belt under his protruding belly. In contrast, Jimmy Lee had dressed for the occasion in slacks and a clean shirt. Delansig introduced himself to the brothers and shook their hands. Fungo was embarrassed by the gesture and barely gripped the proffered hand; Jimmy Lee squeezed it firmly, smiled brightly, and said, "Real glad to meet you, Counselor."

The two brothers sat behind Annie and Delansig in the plane's cramped cabin. No one spoke during the flight or in the car riding from the Paducah airport to the Kentucky state penitentiary.

"Gee, it's great to be back, ain't it, Fungo?" Jimmy Lee said as they drove into the dirt parking lot. "But dammit, I thought they'd have a brass band out here to welcome us." He looked at Delansig and Annie in the front seat, waiting for some acknowledgment. When none was forthcoming, he leaned close behind them and said, "I know we're here to see poor old Pa, but don't we have something to talk about first? I mean, like Fungo and I can only stay in a motel for so long."

"Jimmy Lee," Delansig answered quickly as he parked the car, "Mrs. Sumner has a proposal for you, but she'd like to get through this visit first. We thought we could talk on the way back to Lexington."

"Oh, well, listen, anything that Mrs. Sumner wants is okay with us," Jimmy Lee replied.

In the century-old fortresslike limestone facility, they were escorted and passed on through sliding barred doors by a series of guards. Walking down one corridor, holding Delansig's arm, Annie began to tremble. Delansig felt it and glanced over at her, indicating to her that she could change her mind. She kept going.

A guard led them to the hospital ward where a doctor and a nurse were waiting. Introductions were brief, and the doctor quickly let them know he was a busy man.

"The tumor was far advanced when they brought him in here," he explained perfunctorily. "His speech and memory are affected, one side of his body is increasingly paralyzed, and he's incontinent."

"Does he recognize people?" Annie asked.

Ignoring the question for the moment, the doctor signaled to a guard through a set of barred doors. "This is a high-security ward. Please stay together," the doctor said in a routine way as he led the party into a twenty-bed ward. It was a cavernous room, reeking of disinfectant. The thick mesh windows high in the walls let in small filtered strips of the bright spring sunlight.

"He may recognize you. He has his days." The doctor answered Annie's question as an afterthought, walking on in the flickering glare of the fluorescent tubes overhead.

"Hey, looka here!" an inmate called as they passed his bed. "It's the pig turd. What you doin' back here?" Annie saw Fungo hesitate and turn menacingly toward the inmate before Jimmy Lee pushed him on. Intravenous bottles hung dripping from old metal stands. A bedpan had been left on the floor; the nurse stepped over it. A hamper of soiled sheets was rolled past them.

The three siblings stopped at a bed that the doctor indicated with a nod. The nurse busily straightened the covers. The brothers remained at the foot of the bed. Annie moved up one side and looked down at her father.

The edges of his milky eyes showed under half-closed lids. Deep breathing rasped through one side of his mouth, which hung open. His left arm was drawn up in a contorted angle on his chest like a bird's broken wing.

Annie looked across the bed at Delansig. "Can't we get him out of here in this condition?" she asked.

"We'll make the appeal to the governor if you want, but it'll take his office some time."

"They ain't going to let him out, Annie," Jimmy Lee whispered impudently. "He killed this guard in here."

Annie ignored her brother. "Doctor, what about surgery?"

"Oh, you can find somebody who'll operate, cut out as much of the tumor as he can without touching any brain tissue. But he can't get it all. It just grows back."

"How long does he have?" she asked, looking down at her father again.

"Depends. Could be weeks; could be months."

Annie stood silently a moment, then reached out to touch the crooked arm. "Daddy . . . Daddy."

"Oh, hell, Annie, let him be," Jimmy Lee said, his body tensing as he leaned on the rail of the bed.

"Daddy," she said again, and shook her father's arm gently. "Daddy . . ."

"Let's get out of this goddamn place," Fungo growled.

"Come on, Annie," Jimmy Lee wheedled. "This ain't such a happy place for us to be."

"I came down here to see him. I want to stay for a while," Annie answered icily. "You two can wait out by the car if you want."

Jimmy Lee looked at Delansig, smiled shamelessly, said, "Goodbye, Daddy," and started out. Fungo followed, scowling.

"So long, pig turd. You'll be back," the inmate called.

Fungo started for him, but with both arms Jimmy Lee grabbed his brother around his ample waist and said to the man in the bed, "Not before you die lying there in your own shit, ol' buddy. Maybe we'll come back for the funeral, right, Fungo?"

The guard at the door approached and they hurried out of the ward, the guard close behind them.

"Daddy, Daddy," Annie repeated as she gradually straightened his crooked arm, then held her father's hand in both of hers. Her face contorted with the struggle of finally saying, "It's Annie."

The reaction was immediate. His eyes blinked, trying to focus.

"Annie? Is that m' little gal? Merry Christmas, darlin'!" He spoke as if his tongue were wooden, slurring the words. As soon as he began to talk, saliva gathered in the slack corner of his mouth. A folded towel was already in place to absorb the flow. Annie stood rigid. She had forgotten how brutal he looked. His forehead folded under above his eyes, his cheeks caved inward, and his almost lipless sharklike mouth had crooked, protruding, broken teeth, made more prominent by his paralysis.

"Merry Christmas, Daddy," Annie said. She forced a smile in case he could see her. "I made you a surprise."

"Ain't you a sweetheart. You always do that, don't you?

Well, I have one for you, and your momma. Where is she? You tell her to get on in here. That woman shouldn't be out in the garden too long in this hot—"

"Daddy," Annie interrupted, still holding his hand. "She'll be here in a minute. I just want to tell you that I love you. And she does, too. Momma loves you too."

The patient stared at his visitor, his eyes moving back and forth, searching for a better angle. "I never seen you before," he said suspiciously.

"I'm Annie, Daddy. I'm grown up." She smiled urgently again, hoping to hold his memory.

"Your momma don't love me. She's dead. She started dying the *day you were born!*" He began to chuckle low in his phlegm-clogged throat. "Where're my boys?" he said, sending a gush of spittle onto the towel.

Annie tried to pull her hand away, but he grabbed her wrist with his good hand and held on, starting to laugh loudly. "Let's have one of them little shows, hear?" Annie pulled away harder.

"Come on, Annie. You know how long it's been in here?"

Annie jerked her hand back so hard, he was pulled halfway out of the bed onto the floor. The catheter was loosened and his diaper torn open, soiling the bed. Delansig grabbed her as the doctor and nurse struggled with their thrashing, shouting patient. The patient in the next bed began to laugh; others yelled encouragement, enjoying the excitement. Delansig guided Annie away from the bed and out of the ward as two guards hurried in through the door. She did not look back as her father continued to bellow.

Once in the corridor, Annie broke down and started to cry. Delansig offered to let her lean on him, but she shook her head and went to the wall, reaching out one hand for support, using the other to cover her eyes. The doors of the ward opened briefly, allowing a guard out. Her father's shouts echoed down the corridor until the door closed again. Delansig signaled the guard to wait.

Finally, Annie pushed back from the wall. Delansig offered her his arm, and they walked down the corridor, followed by the guard. Annie stared straight ahead, seeing nothing until they reached the front gates of the penitentiary. Her brothers were waiting at the rented car. Jimmy Lee was throwing rocks at a bird on a telephone wire, and Fungo watched, sitting on the hood of the car.

Annie said, "I can't get in the car with them. Settle it here. Give them extra money to get back to Lexington and go wherever they're going."

Delansig and Annie approached the car. Jimmy Lee mockingly bowed and opened the front door for her, but she did not get in. Delansig took his briefcase from the trunk. While the brothers watched, wary and curious, he spread a document on the front fender. Two thousand-dollar bills were paper-clipped to the document, which the attorney made sure the brothers saw before he began to speak. Neither Jimmy Lee nor Fungo, who still sat on the hood, missed a move Delansig made.

"What's this about, Counselor?" Jimmy Lee asked, grinning with camaraderie.

"This is an agreement between both of you and Mrs. Sumner. She'll pay each of you a thousand dollars a month if her instructions are followed."

The two brothers looked at each other. Then Jimmy Lee turned to Annie with an elated smile. "Hey, Annie, that's . . . I was about to say 'too much,' but, hell, it's just about right. Hot damn! Real good!"

"There are some conditions," Delansig continued.

"Yeah." Fungo grunted. "I bet there are."

"The first is that Mrs. Sumner will never see you again. You will leave the state of Kentucky and never return. The second is that you do nothing to publicize in any way your relationship to her. That means you tell no one from this moment on, and if you're asked, you don't answer."

Fungo's mouth started to open and he slid off the front of the car. Jimmy Lee silenced him with a look, then smiled at Delansig. Neither looked at Annie.

"The third is that, wherever you do go, if Mrs. Sumner sees you, even by mistake, the payments end. It's up to you to avoid her. And last, the agreement takes effect immediately. You find your own way back to Lexington to pick up your clothes and then get out of the state. I'll give you another hundred dollars." He took his wallet out of his pocket.

"Each?" Jimmy Lee asked brightly.

"Each," Annie snapped.

"That ain't what we're supposed to do," Fungo said anxiously to Jimmy Lee. "He said to . . ."

"Shut up, Fungo," Jimmy Lee ordered. "Ain't nobody else about to pay us regular like this, is there?"

"Who said what you were supposed to do, Fungo?" Delansig asked.

"Hey, Counselor, this ain't a courtroom," Jimmy Lee said, still smiling. "Stop showing off, hear?"

Both brothers then looked at Annie, Fungo eager about the money, Jimmy Lee impudently grateful. "Okay, Annie. Let's sign these papers."

The two brothers signed. Delansig handed them each a copy and the cash. Annie got into the front seat and waited as Delansig closed his briefcase, got in, and started the car. Jimmy Lee knocked on her window. She rolled it down but looked straight ahead.

"Thanks a lot, sister. And *fuck you!*"

Delansig accelerated, glimpsing in the rearview mirror the two brothers standing in the parking lot. Fungo was staring at his thousand-dollar bill; Jimmy Lee picked up a rock and threw it after the car.

Annie was silent, riding with her eyes closed. Delansig did not try to start a conversation. They returned to the Paducah airport, where their chartered plane waited. Only after takeoff did Annie speak.

"What you saw today must have made you feel sick. I was." She let her head fall back on the seat. "If he'd just stopped after he heard me say I loved him."

Delansig watched her, expecting her to cry again. She stared intently ahead and said, "I won't let any of this touch Henry."

Trying to ease her concern, Delansig said, "Your brothers seemed pleased with the money."

"Yes," she said slowly, "but what happens when they want

more? Henry and I are only half a family. We're wide open on one side. Those two could get to us." She winced.

"You're not as vulnerable as you're feeling now, Mrs. Sumner," Delansig said. "And they're too greedy to dare threaten their income."

"You're thinking like a lawyer, Mr. Delansig, that a good contract makes a good deal. This is family, *my* family. Nothing about it works the way it's supposed to."

Annie did not rebound from her visit to the penitentiary for some time. In the weeks following, she spent many sleepless nights wandering the scaffolded shell of Limeteen Hall, making sure the doors were locked. She hired more security men to guard the property around the clock. One was responsible for driving Henry to and from school. A security company installed an elaborate alarm system throughout the house, including panic buttons connecting directly to the Fayette County Sheriff's Office. During her nocturnal wanderings, she impulsively moved the gun from one hiding place to another. Each day, when more than a hundred construction and farm workers came on the property, Annie scanned the crews, fearing she would see the familiar blond curls or the thick slouching body sneaking in among the other men.

Annie told Sam nothing of her brothers or the trip to the penitentiary. Once it began again, their affair was discreet but not secret. They saw each other whenever they could, and made love wherever they could. The logistics were always difficult. Sam's life was heavily scheduled, and even getting to Lexington was a struggle for him. Once he was there, Annie was not inclined to talk about her family.

"You know," he said one day in early summer, "if you'd told me we'd be making love at high noon in a room at the Campbell House Hotel, I'd have never believed you."

"It's strange," Annie agreed, spooning her body next to his back as they lay in bed. "But it sure is better than nothing."

"I don't see anything wrong with your staying overnight at Caernarvon. Nobody's there except me."

"And the butler, cooks, and maids." She kissed his back and

reached around to put her arms on his chest. "I can't do that yet, Sam."

"Why not? Who the hell do you think they're going to tell?" He sounded angry suddenly. "And even if they do, so what?"

"It's just a bad time right now," she said softly.

"Well, I hope you don't think it gets much better," he said as he rolled out of her arms and lay on his back. "You're just starting a stable. Wait till it gets going. It never stops, Annie. You're already working too hard. You walk in the door, but it's about fifteen minutes before you get here."

"And it's about fifteen minutes after we make love that you always get mad at something." She sat up and put her feet on the floor, but his hands were on her shoulders and she let him pull her back in his arms.

"I'm sorry," he said. "I'm having some problems of my own, and I obviously let it out here."

"What's the matter?"

He let out a long breath of irritation. "Frank Carney. He's a real drunk."

"He is?" Annie was surprised. "I heard he drank a little, but whiskey isn't exactly unknown in this business. He sure does well by Caernarvon."

Sam shook his head. "It's worse than that. He can't get through the day without his pint of bourbon. It's really sad. I grew up with him. He told me once that his father made moonshine. Used to test it by giving some to his kids to see how fast it would put 'em to sleep or make them sick. Alcohol's in Carney's bones."

"I've heard about him since the first day I was at a track. What'd he do?"

"He's a great horseman, has an eye for horseflesh that never misses. But the bourbon's getting to him. And ever since Father died, he acts as if *I* were working for *him*."

"I'd say that's the problem more than liquor is."

"Horseshit, Annie! It's one hell of a lot more complicated than that. He ran a colt last week at Belmont that broke down. Didn't even call me. Said he tried to call, but he had to put the horse down. Horseshit! I found out later that he'd worked the

343

colt hard that morning and everyone at the barn had smelled the whiskey on his breath. He never behaved this way when my father was running things. Since the day Father died, Carney's been acting as if he'd inherited the place!"

Annie did not argue. "What are you going to do, Sam?"

"I don't know," he said with irritated concern. "Finding the right private trainer to look after a single owner's stable is hard as hell. It's a lifetime commitment. Father was a gent; he wanted a nice steady routine with no new faces and certainly no arguments from an employee. Winning wasn't so important as living well and behaving properly. That's the way it was then. Today, if you don't win, you're nothing but a rich joke . . . I'll tell you one thing. I just wish to hell that Frank Carney wasn't . . ." He did not finish, and Annie did not ask him to.

A week later, Chigger Beasley called Annie. "Caernarvon Farm's trainer, Frank Carney, got fired," he told her. "It'll be in the sports section tomorrow."

"That's a big loss for Caernarvon," Annie responded noncommittally.

"Well, it sure is," Chigger said. "But it might be real good for Limeteen. Frank's a good old friend of mine. He's coming down to visit next week, and, Annie, you might talk with him. Limeteen Farm has everything but a trainer, and this man's the very best."

"Why did Caernarvon fire him?" she asked, already considering Sam's reaction if she were to hire Frank Carney.

"Well, that depends on who's dealing the reasons," Chigger replied. "Caernarvon *says* that it just came time for a change, but it's going around that it's because he drank. Frank tells me it was a difference in thinking between a trainer and his owner. Now that kind of difference is the oldest argument in horse racing. Whatever the real reason, you don't stay around when there are feelings like that."

"Does he drink?"

Chigger sighed. "Well, ma'am, I've known Frank Carney twenty years and he's been drinking a little bourbon for a long time. But you know, I've never noticed a problem with him running a stable, and neither do his horses. They just win."

The next week, she drove out to Blue Bell Farm. Turning off the Versailles Road, she recalled the first time she had pronounced the name of Louis XIV's palace. With her Kentucky pronunciation, she had said, "Ver-sales." *"Non, non,"* her French friends had corrected with that particular Gallic scorn they reserved for the misuse of their language. "Ver-*sigh!* Ver-*sigh!*" they said with the *r* she had never learned to pronounce.

As she drove beyond the airport, Annie saw the open fields of grass catching the morning sunlight. The lush color was glorious; however, "bluegrass" was a Lexington exaggeration. "The longer you look at the grass and think blue, the bluer it gets," she had said once to Sam, making him laugh. Frowning, she thought how seldom they laughed now.

When she reached Blue Bell Farm, Chigger Beasley was sitting on a paddock fence with Frank Carney. Both were watching a mare and her new foal getting used to the outside world. The two men started to climb down to greet Annie, but she waved them back and climbed onto the fence herself. Chigger introduced Frank Carney, who reached across Chigger to take her hand, briefly looking straight into her eyes. "Nice to see you again, ma'am."

Annie felt the calloused palm of his hand and noticed the uncomplicated decency in the brief glance he gave her.

"Thank you," she replied warmly. "The last time I saw you was at the Rosewood dispersal."

"No, a couple of days later at Keeneland."

"That's right, I remember."

He nodded slightly and looked back at the mare and her foal. He had strong good looks—not the stunning handsomeness of Sam Cumberland, but a powerful rawboned face of strong, hard angles. His eyes were the color of the paddock grass. Bluegrass eyes, she thought, and smiled to herself.

"What do you think?" Chigger asked, his attention back on the foal.

"Dunno yet," Frank replied. "Lemme watch a minute."

"Take your time. I'm going on up to the office, if you two'll excuse me."

Chigger winked at Annie as he climbed down from the

fence. She and Frank Carney sat staring at the mare and her foal.

"Well, that was pretty obvious, wasn't it?" Annie said.

"Chigger's as stealthy as a hungry mule sometimes," he said, never taking his gaze off the horses.

"Sorry to hear you left Caernarvon after so long."

"Well, life goes on." He squinted against the sun and tilted his head slightly to watch the foal trot away from its mother. His hair was a sandy brown and cut, Annie thought, in an old-fashioned way, short on the sides and unevenly on top. It lay flat on his head in many different directions, like rain-flattened grain.

"Why don't you tell me what Chigger said about Limeteen so that I don't repeat anything," she suggested.

"Well," he said, stepping down from the fence, "from what he told me, it seems you have almost as much money as you do ambition, but probably not quite." With that, he started walking across the paddock toward the broodmare.

She was stung as much by his forthrightness as by his walking away. She started to go after him, but called to him instead, "That's exactly right. You have any good ideas for me?"

"I might," he called as he continued over to the mare. The foal, made anxious by a stranger's approach, ran to its mother and peered at Frank through her legs. The broodmare watched Frank, ears and nostrils actively searching for clues. Annie could not hear if he was saying anything, but he continued walking with a slow, unbroken stride until he reached the broodmare. She smelled his hand, and he was accepted by her, though the foal shied away. Scampering back with a comically bobbing head, it moved slowly closer to smell the strange man. Soon Frank was stroking its neck as he carefully observed its legs. Then he walked back slowly to Annie. The broodmare grazed, but the curious foal tried to sneak up on Frank; when discovered, it frisked away, bleating its excitement.

At the paddock fence, Frank hooked his arm over the top board near Annie. "What do you think of that foal?"

Annie had watched the foal and hoped she was right. "A little bit of funny action on his front off leg, but that'll probably get grown out. Otherwise, a nice little foal."

"One of yours," he said, "sired by Little Slam."

Little Slam was the name given by Chigger Beasley to the yearling for which Annie had outbid Sam Cumberland eight years earlier at the Keeneland sales. Racing under Blue Bell Farm's colors, Little Slam had won four stakes races and been successful at stud, his first progeny just now reaching the race track. Chigger had used the stallion to breed many of Annie's broodmares, so far with excellent results at the yearling sales.

"I'm lucky I got Little Slam away from you that night," Annie said.

Frank glanced up at her, then away. "Well, I'm not sure luck had much to do with it. I'd told Chigger that yearling was a good one. But I stopped at eighty thousand. Sam Cumberland liked the horse and he usually gets what he wants, but both of you bid a lot more than the yearling was worth . . . for your own reasons, I guess." He paused to watch the foal.

"I figured I could afford it," Annie said, "and *I* liked the horse, too."

Frank Carney observed, "Spending too much money on a horse just 'cause you can afford it is the best way I know to go broke."

Annie sat perched on the fence, feeling irritated and trapped. She looked down at Frank Carney's head with its cross-thatched hair. "You sure do say just what's on your mind, don't you?"

"Yes, ma'am. Always have."

"I suppose I can depend on that."

"Oh, yes. For instance, about why you and I are out here talking to each other. You're looking for a trainer; I'm looking for a job. Since I left Caernarvon, a couple of owners have come to me saying I should start a public stable and take care of their horses for them. Good horses, to run in New York and Florida. Belmont Park and Hialeah have both promised me as many stalls as I ask for. So why do you think I should tie myself to the problems and restrictions of being a private trainer for one unknown stable?"

"I'll answer that," Annie said as she climbed down from the fence and stood next to him until he looked at her. "But first

347

you have to answer something I have on *my* mind. What about your drinking?"

Nothing registered on his face. Then he started walking away along the paddock fence.

"Well, Frank, don't you think people are going to ask about that?"

He stopped. "Sure they'll ask, but damned if I have to answer." He turned. "Let me ask you the same kind of question. What goes on between you and Sam Cumberland? People talk about that, too. It's none of my business, is it? Except he's sold you some stallion seasons, and I used to work for him. Both reasons could make things real tricky if . . ."

He paused and watched her.

"About being a private trainer," Annie said. "Well, here's what I think. With a public stable, you spend all your time hustling after the best horses you can get, making yourself attractive to the owners who have them. With good horses like that, you have to make a lot of money real fast or you'll lose them. Owners may let you have a say about what they're going to buy or how they're going to breed, but most of the time, you wait for other people's results to show promise, and hope they come into your barn. Besides all that, in a public stable you're holding the hands of five or twenty different owners, each one knowing everything about how you *ought* to be doing *your* business. Working with a private stable, you only have one owner who tells you that."

She smiled at him; he squinted at her, but then looked off at another paddock. Annie continued. "At Limeteen, the trainer's going to be coming into a new stable to shape every part of it into one of the best in the world. I have enough money to get it started, and I'm not in a big hurry to get into a winner's circle. I plan to do it right from the very beginning, but it's going to depend on my trainer to make it last."

Frank did not answer. Annie said nothing until he responded. He put his hands in his back pockets and kicked at the grass. "Let's agree on something. If it works out, any questions about my drinking or Sam Cumberland don't get asked, unless either one gets in the way of the work."

Annie thought about what liquor had done to her father.

She did not believe this man was a drunk. Sam was wrong about that. "Fine with me," she said.

Frank nodded. "Then I guess you ought to invite me over to see what's going on at Limeteen."

Frank sat silently beside her in her new car, a Jaguar. The leather and the plush carpeting seemed to make him uncomfortable, although he said nothing about it. As they drove through Lexington, Annie asked, "How's Certainty doing?"

"Good. Fourth leading sire of stakes winners last year. A really fine stallion."

"The best you've trained?" Annie asked.

"Hard to say. Close to it. Caernarvon has a lot of good horses. But he has something few have. He's the most honest horse I know. Never showed off, no ornery habits. Just the finest kind of horse . . ."

He looked uneasy. When he started talking again, Annie thought it was to change the subject.

"I might as well tell you this. I don't run horses that aren't ready, and I won't use any kind of drug to make them ready. If a colt is sore or hurt, I'm not going to fool him by killing the pain. I'll rest him or retire him. That has to be my decision."

"A hay-oats-and-water man?"

"No, not at all. I just want a horse fit when he runs, not full of drugs."

"That's fine," Annie replied, "but I'd want to know about your decision, and I may decide to scratch a horse myself at any time for any reason. That right I keep."

"You're the owner," he said factually. "They're your horses."

Annie replied, "I never did believe that. When I was a groom, the owner was nothing. Every horse I took care of was *mine!*" She glanced over and caught him smiling.

As construction workers, bulldozers, and back hoes continued their work around the new buildings, Frank Carney inspected Limeteen Farm. He liked what he saw, or at least he seemed not to dislike it. He suggested that one of the new broodmare barns, which had not been started, be located separately from the others, in case isolation was needed in an epidemic. Walking the training track, which was being dug out, he urged a thicker cushion of loam than was planned over the base of sand in order to protect young ankles. While discussing European training and the use of gallops, they decided that Limeteen should have them if a relatively flat length of land could be found on its rolling acres.

Back from school, Henry appeared with his new friend, Speed Oliver, a black boy who was the same age as he. He and his parents had taken up residence in one of Limeteen Farm's houses. Both of the Olivers had worked on Lexington stud farms and traveled to race tracks for nearly fifteen years. Their son, George Junior was known as Speed, because of his tendency never to walk but to run everywhere. He was their only child, and Limeteen was the Oliver family's first permanent home since he was born.

Annie called the boys over and introduced them to the trainer. "This is my son. Henry, this is Mr. Carney."

On cue, the boy stuck out his hand and said, "Hello, I'm Henry Sumner." He had given up stating his nationality.

As he shook the boy's hand, Frank said, "Hello, Hank."

The new name surprised Henry, but he immediately responded with a shy smile.

"And this is Speed Oliver," Annie said. "His parents are living on the place."

"I know your daddy," Frank said, shaking Speed's hand. "Used to work over at Calumet, didn't he?"

"Yes, sir," Speed answered proudly. "Sure did."

"We're going over to see the new starting gate," Henry said. "Come on, Speed," and the two boys raced each other toward the training track.

Frank watched them go and noticed that Annie was looking at him. "Nice boys," he said quickly and started walking up the farm road to where the Jaguar was parked. Annie let him go, realizing that he was not being rude. He had walked away three or four times during their conversation. It seemed to be a technique, surprising the person he was talking to, putting her more off balance than he was, and effectively breaking any conversation that might become difficult. When he reached the car, he put his hands in his back pockets and waited, watching his boot tracing a square in the dirt. Annie followed slowly.

When she arrived, he glanced at her.

"George Oliver is one of the best grooms around," he said. "How'd you get him?"

"I offered him and Mrs. Oliver a home. They were tired of traveling. Wanted to settle. He's going to run the stallion barn."

Frank nodded. "I'll tell you a secret. Bruna Oliver's the best cook in Kentucky."

"We've already found that out."

Then he asked, "You have your racing colors yet?"

The Jockey Club had notified Annie of their acceptance of her choice the previous week. "Yellow and white stripes," she said.

Watching a crane lift a steel beam above the foaling barn, Frank crossed his arms and leaned back against the car. "What happened to that filly Chigger sent you over in France last year?"

Annie was almost certain he already knew the answer. "I called her Moonglow. We had some bad luck. I broke her myself, really thought she was a good one. But when I put her in training at Chantilly, she hurt herself in her stall somehow, fractured her cannon bone. Carpitis set in and there's new bone growth. I'm afraid she'll never race, but she's still a beautiful filly."

"You might think about bringing her back here and sending her to Certainty."

Annie stared at him. Certainty's pedigree flashed through her mind, then Moonglow's. She did not know the pedigrees of all the horses in the world, but those two were special to her. The match might be a good one. She had bought a nomination to Certainty from Sam; the filly could be flown over from France within a week.

Frank was tracing with his boot in the dirt again.

"Frank, I'd like you to be the trainer for Limeteen Farm." She watched to see what he would do. Between Annie and the car, he had no clear route to walk away. "I'll give you the standard ten percent of any purses we win and a salary the first

351

year of five thousand more than Caernarvon paid you, whatever it was."

"I'll think on it," he said, opening the car door behind him and sliding easily inside. The door slammed shut.

Annie smiled to herself and drove Frank Carney back to Blue Bell Farm. During the trip, Annie outlasted his silence and said nothing more. After he got out of the car in front of Chigger Beasley's office, he leaned through the open door and said, "Let's not have any contracts. If one of us gets unhappy, I go. That's enough. And if it's all right with you, I have no great need of any announcement. People will hear."

Annie agreed. He reached in and they quickly shook hands. Once again, he walked away.

Oh, yes, Annie thought, people will hear.

Two weeks later, Annie was notified by the state that her father had died. She hired a Paducah mortician to claim the body, which was cremated. The small box of ashes was buried in a local cemetery with just the identity marker required by law to mark the plot. Annie's only mourning was several months of nightmares. They were so vivid that for hours each night she believed she was in the shack with Fungo holding her against the wall for Jimmy Lee, and her mother dying in the bed by the stove. When she was lucky, she woke up. Even after the exhausting days of building Limeteen Farm, she was afraid to go to sleep.

Delansig was instructed to inform her brothers of their father's death. He did so when he sent their next monthly payment. According to their address, they had found their way to Brooklyn.

TWENTY-ONE

THE SIMPLE INTENT of winning a horse race, even with its ten thousand variables, defies the convoluted machinations of governmental function. In the late sixties, however, rapacity drew the two together and bound them irredeemably. A temptation nearly impossible to resist moved slowly but obstinately through the state legislatures of every racing state. Many called it a blessing; others called it a disaster.

"D'you find me ten million more dollars for this goddamn annual budget?" a leading state senator in one such legislature demanded one morning at the beginning of the session. He tasted, then glowered at the thin coffee his secretary had placed on his cluttered desk.

"Yes, sir, Senator," his alert young legislative aide answered, having learned in his first four months on the job that his boss, known statewide as "the politician's politician," liked to hear the title often. He also learned in the first hour that his boss lusted after national office and was determined to balance his state's budget in order to enhance his chances of getting to Washington.

The senator squinted at his aide through eyes creased by years of suspicion and compromise. "Where?" he asked threateningly, eyeing the embroidered patterns of the aide's psychedelic tie and the tiny initials stitched on his shirt pocket. The thick wavy cut of the aide's hair was irritating. He obviously was trying to look like Bobby Kennedy, and worse for the old-school, old-style, old state senator, the kid did.

"At the race track," the aide answered brightly, making the mistake again of thinking that his youthful gall would please the old elephant.

"If that's all you came up with," the senator said, his voice rising, "you can take your third-rate law school degree and shove it! What do you mean? We already take out seven percent of this state's handle. Two of the tracks are screaming at us to take less because they're going broke!"

Unintimidated, the aide shot back, "And we license only a hundred and forty days of racing at all three tracks. At the moment, there are three hundred and sixty-five days in a year, Senator," he reasoned, "and twelve thousand voters who are directly involved with the state's horse-racing industry. You scratch their ass, they'll vote for yours." He laughed presumptuously.

The senator took a swallow of coffee without tasting it and glared at the young man, whom he was beginning to detest. The idea, however, was very interesting. "Who've you been talking to?"

"All *sorts* of wonderful people," the aide replied, opting for sudden charm and enjoying the senator's irritation. "The chairman of the state Racing Commission, who by the way was appointed by your friend the governor, the national office of the Horsemen's Benevolent and Protective Association, which is the most powerful group of thoroughbred owners and trainers in the country . . . and my dog's vet."

"Your *dog's* vet?" the senator rumbled. The coffee and the kid were both bad tastes. Jutting out his jaw, he smoothed back his jowls with his thick fingers and stared ahead dismissively. The aide hardly paused.

"Yes, he just moved here from out of state, where he was the head vet at two race tracks until he started shooting his mouth off. Says he gave it up because he loved horses and hated people too much. He's sensational with Frankfurter, though." He grinned at the senator. "My dachshund, named for Felix."

"Stop playing with me, boy," the senator said fixing his eyes on the upstart's chipmunk teeth. "What'd they have to say about extending the racing season?"

"Everyone can go for it except my vet," the aide replied.

"I don't give two turds for your vet. How soon can the Racing Commission have hearings? I want that added take-out in my budget *this year.*"

"Well, Senator, there's a slight complication."

"Shit! What the hell is it?"

"The horses."

"The horses?" he shouted. "Listen to me, boy! In thirty years of working this goddamn capital building, I've never seen a horse vote. So what's the goddamn problem?"

"It seems that if we expand the meetings at the three tracks, say, to two and a half times what they are now"—the aide paused to allow the mathematics of the added revenue to pass through the senator's brain—"you know, that's three hundred and fifty racing days a year. There are going to be a lot more races to fill, but with pretty much the same number of horses. I mean horses that are good enough to race. That means the horses are going to have to run more, and, what's even a greater difficulty, run longer through the year. I mean, like, year round . . . in *winter,* when the *track surface freezes.*" The last phrase he said slowly and precisely for emphasis.

The senator was further irritated by the condescension, but he sensed that some important new information was forthcoming. "So what? The horse was bred to run, just like beef cattle were bred for steak."

"That's a brilliant point, Senator. The difference is that when we eat a steak, we don't have to see it being slaughtered, do we? If horses run too much, they can get sore, or they can break down; that means they hurt badly and run badly, or they die during a race. Their legs break right off. Or their hearts burst. They collapse on the track, maybe killing a jockey, taking other horses down with them, you know? People pay to go to a car race hoping to see some guy smeared all over the pavement. But nobody likes to see an animal hurt or die, particularly something as big and beautiful as a thoroughbred. If that happens too often, people might find somewhere else to bet their money."

"So are you telling me we can't go year round?" the senator demanded.

"Oh, no, Senator, we can," the aide replied. "We just have to let the trainers and vets help the horses a little, which it seems they're eager to do."

"How?"

"Certain drugs that—"

"Shit!" The senator stood, knowing that finally the kid had delivered and wanting to punch him in his schoolboy face. "We have hippies stoned on marijuana, and heroin addicts mugging anything that moves. And you want me to legalize doping horses!"

"At the moment," the aide continued, disregarding the senator, "we have very strict regulations in this state about medication on the day of a race. But the Horsemen's Benevolent and Protective Association is lobbying for what they call 'a controlled medication program.' "

"Well, fine! If the owners want it that way, then what's the problem?" The senator glanced at his watch.

The aide knew that the senator had a Finance Committee meeting and time was running short; he savored adding to the tension. "The owners want winners. Very few are willing to give or can afford what a sore horse really needs—rest and time. I mean, it costs ten thousand dollars a year to keep a horse in training to race, and not that many runners make that much. So if a shot of something called Bute will save a couple of months by letting a horse run the way it should and win a purse, fine. The problem is—and here's where my vet comes in—a lot of these drugs don't cure anything. They only mask pain, ease inflammation. So if the horse, say, pulls a tendon and you give it a shot of Bute, it'll run pain free and maybe shred the tendon, turning itself into a cripple. If there's a chronic problem in a knee joint, and cortisone or steroids are injected for any length of time, the drug will eat away at the joint like termites gnawing a wooden leg."

The senator winced. "The racing people want to do that?"

"It's a starry-eyed business, Senator. Like they never believe it'll happen that way to *their* horse. But it might if they run all year. If and when it does, they want to be able to use whatever it takes to get their horses back on the track. And we need these horses to run, to fill the racing cards, to bring in those bettors, to give us our take-out . . . and to give you your balanced budget."

The two men stared at each other. "Write me up a bill about the drugs," the state senator said, "but make damn sure it sounds like it's for the good of the horse. And get a press release out that reads like the goddamn Old Testament. I don't want any gray hairs from the Humane Society screaming at me. Doping their own animals . . . It's hard to believe."

"They say that the rest of the world is only a metaphor for the race track," the aide expounded, then chuckled knowingly. "Not the other way around. You know?"

The news of yet another racing state extending its racing season or legalizing a varied list of drugs for use on race day was always a front-page story in the *Lexington Herald-Leader*. Colorado and California were the first; Florida, Pennsylvania, Maryland, and fourteen other state legislatures studied their examples and began to consider the relief to be provided by expanded race track revenues in annual state budgets. Concurrently, each state studied a permissive medication program; Kentucky quickly legalized the use of some forty drugs on race day. Only New York, of the major racing states, held out against any race-day use of drugs, although the season was extended year round, with racing scheduled six days a week through the winter at Aqueduct, frozen track or not.

After Sam Cumberland became a steward of the Jockey Club, he jumped into the middle of the controversy. Joining the Jockey Club's efforts, he lobbied to convince other state

legislators and the public of the threat to racing that legalized
race-day drugs represented. By necessity, his trips to Kentucky
were more and more subject to rescheduling.

A week after Annie hired Frank Carney, Sam called her.
"Annie, I can't get down on Thursday as I planned, but maybe
I have a better idea."

She listened while she was seated on a sawhorse, holding
the phone on her leg as the carpenters worked in the room
next door; it was to be her farm office. Having expected Sam
to be angry about Frank, Annie remained wary, wondering if
Sam had heard. "I've always liked your ideas, Sam."

"I have to testify that day before a bunch of state legislators
in Harrisburg, Pennsylvania. What if you came with me? I just
bought a plane and I can pick you up on the way out."

"Oh, you do know how to turn a girl's head, Mr. Cumberland. For Lord's sake, what kind of plane?"

"It's a little jet. I named it the Gwydian, after the old railroad car, remember? And what would you say if I asked you to
testify, too, as another thoroughbred owner?"

She stood up. "I'd say that I wouldn't know what to say."

"Oh, yes, you would. Just tell them what you've said to me.
We've talked about this. And listen, there aren't many of us
who think this way. I need as much help as I can get. I could
pick you up at ten that morning, we'd fly over and pound on
them for a couple of hours in the afternoon, and I'll get you
back by Henry's bedtime, I promise. I have a foundation
meeting the next morning, so I'd have to get back. Oh, yes,
lunch and dinner on the plane thrown in."

"That's showing off."

"That's right. Coming?"

"Yes, but I don't promise to testify."

He paused, then said, "You will, Annie. I know you. So you
may as well prepare something. I'll see you Thursday morning
at Bluegrass Airport. I love you."

"Sam . . ."

"Yes?"

"Have you heard that I hired Frank Carney?"

"Yes."

"Well, aren't you going to say something about it?"

"That's your business, Annie. You didn't talk to me about it, so I don't have anything to say."

"I did talk to you about it, at the Campbell House, remember?"

"No, I talked to *you*. You just listened. I told you he was a drunk. If you'd asked, I'd have told you he's also a lowlife. Real white trash, pure and simple."

Having anticipated his anger, Annie abruptly felt her own. "Those were *your* problems with him, Sam. As I'm sure you remember, I'm more experienced with both of them."

There was a pause before he said impatiently, "I'd very much appreciate it if you don't send any broodmares he picks over to Caernarvon." The threat was obvious.

"Well, Sam, I'll be sending a mare called Moonglow over to Certainty. Your stallion manager accepted her. Frank Carney suggested the match, and the mare's pedigree is good enough for your stallion. I paid for that service. If you stop it, you'll be breaking a contract, not to mention your word."

"Goddammit, Annie, what's the matter with you?" he shouted back. "*Of course* Carney suggested Certainty. He's getting back at me, taking a part of my best stallion away with him . . . though I'm damn sure he thinks of Certainty as *his* horse!"

Annie was swayed for a moment, until she remembered the two horses involved. "The pedigrees mesh too well for this to be his little revenge, Sam. He made a good choice, and I'm going along with it."

There was another pause. "Annie, let me tell you something you *ought* to know already about this business. Everyone in it thinks he's smarter than the other guy. Winning's even nicer when you take someone's loser, turn him around, and show the other guy how dumb he was. Well, don't think you're going to show me anything about Frank Carney. Try all you want, but one day you'll call to say I was right."

"I doubt it. Frank Carney was no loser for you, but thanks for the advice." In spite of her anger, she did not want the conversation to get nasty. "I know this was a business call. What time did you say on Thursday?"

Again he paused, said, "Ten," and hung up.

Annie put the phone on the floor and leaned on the saw-horse. Their relationship was public knowledge; the need for discretion had passed. Again there was gossip and speculation, yet there was also acceptance. The sixties was not a time of narrow-minded judgment, and Lexington had long been inured to the entangled matings of the thoroughbred people.

She walked over to the large plate glass window that overlooked the construction of the new buildings and the training track beyond them. She wondered what would happen with Sam. What could happen with Sam? Since her return from France, she had heard ever more rumors about Belinda Cumberland. She had given up riding and become increasingly erratic, then reclusive. It was open knowledge that she went from one fashionable doctor, spa, diet, and prescription to another in a frantic effort to stay thin. At New York charity parties and Cumberland Foundation functions, she appeared bejeweled by Harry Winston, coiffed by Kenneth, and dressed by Blass, but photographers inevitably revealed a grim look and a pudgy body. The joke being told was that Belinda and Sam arrived together, sat apart, went home together, and slept apart. Between social engagements, they saw as little of each other as possible.

Annie left the shell of offices and went up the farm road to Limiteen Hall. Henry was due home from school. Wondering if she and Sam could ever be married, she turned around to look back at what was taking place at the farm. Walking on, she had no answers to her questions about Sam, and decided not to hope for any in the near future.

Not only was she a good witness before the Pennsylvania legislators, Annie was so effective that Sam pressed her into service whenever there was an opportunity. Throughout the rest of the year, Annie went before the microphones in hearing rooms with her prepared statement and then answered the legislators' questions. She did her homework so that no question would surprise her. The surprise was her growing passion about the subject.

During their campaign, much of the construction of the new Limiteen Farm was completed. As soon as possible, Annie's broodmares and the stallion Little Slam were shipped over from Chigger Beasley's Blue Bell Farm. Throughout the summer and into the fall, Limeteen became a major buyer of more first-class broodmares, as well as yearlings and future stallion seasons, the choices of which Frank Carney supervised. He trained the farm workers to his own exacting standards of thoroughness and care. As the stable grew, Limeteen Farm acquired a reputation for class even before there was any record on the race track.

Frank lived in a small bungalow three miles away from the farm and was at Limeteen from five in the morning until nine or ten at night. He made a point of never entering Limeteen Hall, even though Annie's hospitality was frequently offered to him. He covered any business he had with her quickly in the barns or at the new farm office, then, with a typically abrupt exit, went back to work. Not once did Annie see any indication of his supposed alcoholic habit.

What she did notice was Henry's growing rapport with the trainer. Each afternoon, when the security man dropped him from school, Henry met Speed, home from his own school, and the two boys ran to the barns to find Frank. One day, the boy introduced himself to a visitor by saying, "Hello, I'm Hank Sumner." He never asked his mother to call him Hank, but he obviously preferred it. Annie noticed that his school friends also used the nickname.

The boy and man became a familiar pair. When Annie saw Frank in the afternoon without Henry dogging along behind, she wondered where her son was. He was learning about horses from Frank, and often showed off his new knowledge to his mother. A slow imitative drawl also developed in Henry's pronunciation, negating fully his first seven years in France. Only "Maman" was not superseded, though it, too seemed slightly prolonged.

One night, as Bruna Oliver served them supper in the pantry, Henry asked, "Maman, did you know that Mr. Carney chose the mares that Mr. Beasley mated with Little Slam to get Moonshot and Moonglow?"

"I didn't. Did Frank tell you that?"

"No, not exactly," Henry answered. "But that's what happened. Mr. Beasley told me. You always breed the best to the best and hope for the best," he said, quoting the tired axiom with all the earnest importance of newly discovered truth. "That's why Moonglow's foal is so special to Mr. Carney. It'll be the third generation that he's been watching."

"I'm glad you like Mr. Carney so much," Annie said. "I do, too."

"I wish he was my father," Henry said cursorily through a mouthful of Bruna's apple brown Betty. "He's going to let me and Speed raise Moonglow's foal."

Annie did her best not to overreact to these two pieces of surprising information.

"You know, the grooms call me and Speed the Scotch boys," he continued, "after Black and White whiskey. They call Mr. Carney and me Hank 'n' Frank, and they call you the Countess."

"Oh, they do." Annie had tried to discourage the epithet by ignoring it, but its occasional repetition in the press helped make it stick.

"Yep, everyone says it except Mr. Carney."

"What does he say?"

"Mrs. Sumner. Why is that, Maman? He sure knows you well enough to call you Annie, doesn't he?"

"I suppose," she said. "But he and I work together, and I suppose he calls me that to be respectful."

"But you call him Frank. Is that because you're the boss?"

Annie laughed. "I guess it is."

Henry remained serious. "That's too bad. I guess you can't be just friends, can you? He's the best friend I have, besides Speed. I think he'd be a better friend for you than Mr. Cumberland."

Annie kept eating. Henry saw Sam Cumberland only when he came by Limeteen Hall to escort her to a dinner party. "Why do you say that, Henry?" she ventured. "I thought you liked Mr. Cumberland."

"Oh, he's all right. He's kind of nervous when he comes over, but he sure does love you! When he sees you coming down the stairs, his eyes get all mushy! Really sickening."

Annie laughed again, more for disguise than humor.

"Maman, is he married?"

"Yes," she said simply.

"Is he going to get a divorce?"

"No, not that I know of."

"Good. That means you won't be marrying him. Oh, I was supposed to tell you the bug fogger in the training barn is busted."

Foaling season was a busy time at Limeteen Farm, as it was throughout the Bluegrass. The original Rosewood broodmares, along with their offspring and the acquisitions Annie had made, brought the number of expected births to thirty-five.

Moonglow's foal received particular attention. Both Henry and Speed mastered brushing, rubbing, and currying the broodmare, and they assisted her groom with mucking out her stall. So devoted were they that both were in the broodmare barn by five-thirty, working on Moonglow before school. Each afternoon they took turns riding, then walking her—outside if the day was good, in the training barn if it was cold. In February, when Moonglow was finally moved to a larger stall in the foaling barn, both boys insisted that they be allowed to watch the birth, and would not stop nagging until Annie and Bruna agreed to let them.

"Just remember one thing," Annie explained to Henry over breakfast one morning. "And tell Speed. It usually happens in the middle of the night, and it only takes about thirty minutes if everything goes right. It could be that none of us will see it."

"Frank'll be there," the boy said, showing off his use of the first name. "He'll know when it's happening and he'll call us. See, Maman, Moonglow waxed this morning. That means the col—, the col—, the colostrum appeared on the teat," he said as casually as possible while spreading jam on his biscuit. "I'd say tonight, or tomorrow at the latest."

When the phone rang next to Annie's bed the second night after waxing had appeared, Henry was instantly at her door. Annie heard Frank say, "Moonglow's in labor but there's a problem. I've called the vet, but he's on an emergency over at Spendthrift. I'm calling some others . . ."

Annie saw Henry and said, "We'll be right down."

At the foaling barn, they found Frank with Al Hawkins, the broodmare manager, watching at Moonglow's stall. Standing quietly across the barn was Speed with his mother and father.

Frank Carney talked barely above a whisper. "She's stood up and gone back down twice. It's getting on to an hour now. She's getting real tired, and the foal can't take too much more."

Moonglow was lying on her side and steam was rising from her body; her legs were stretched, straining with each contraction.

"What's wrong?" Annie asked.

"I think the foal's locked in the wrong position. Moonglow keeps getting up, trying to move it around . . . Uh-oh."

The broodmare had stopped straining. Her eyes were rolling, and her mouth opened to gasp air.

"Hank! Speed!" Frank called the two boys. "Talk to her. She knows you best. Get her up. *Make her stand.*" As the two boys went into the stall, Frank tore off his heavy shirt and went to a washtub.

"George, Al, lift her up if you have to, but get her on her feet," he commanded George Oliver and the broodmare manager. Putting each of his arms under the stream of hot water, he grabbed a bar of soap and scrubbed himself. "Annie, when she stands, grab her tail and keep it out of the way."

As Annie followed the two men into the stall, she realized it was the first time Frank had ever used her name. The two boys urged the mare to her feet. At first they pleaded; then Henry yelled at her. "You have to get up, girl! Your baby's going to die if you don't!"

Moonglow lifted her head and tried to struggle. "Come on, you girl!" Speed Oliver shouted. "You got to get up!"

Annie heard Frank give a harsh groan and turned to see him rinsing his arms again under the scalding water. Then, bare-chested and dripping wet, he came into the stall and joined the others urging Moonglow to her feet. Gallantly, the mare struggled, rolled onto her knees, then rose. Immediately the two men and boys moved around to help support her. Annie grabbed her tail and held it wide to one side as Frank carefully put his hand into the vagina and slowly pushed his arm almost to his shoulder into the uterus.

He and Annie faced each other, only inches apart. He looked at her with a combination of tenderness and intensity she had not seen before, as if the circumstance allowed it. "I've got a leg here . . . all right, fine, good pulse . . . Can't find the other foot, and it feels like the head's over in Jessamine County."

He continued to work inside the mare, locked in concentration on Annie's eyes. "All right, keep her real steady. Hank, go up where she can see you, and keep smiling, let her know everything'll be fine." He withdrew one arm, turned his back to Annie, and put his other arm deep into Moonglow. Annie watched the muscles of his neck and back strain as he tried to reposition the foal. Occasionally he murmured, "Come on now, little one." Suddenly there was a lurch and Moonglow shifted and tossed.

"Hold her!" Frank commanded quietly, as he withdrew his arm and turned back to insert the other arm again. His upper body was covered with placental fluids, and as he faced Annie again, he smiled briefly and said to her, "It just slipped around. All we need is that one leg . . . and *there it is.*"

Annie stared at him and her mouth went dry. His tenderness and sure control made her shudder. "I'm going to pull the foal into the birth canal," he said calmly, just loud enough for the others to hear. "It should start her contractions again, so watch out. She'll go down pretty fast then, and this foal is going to move on out. Here we go."

Annie saw his shoulder tense as, very gently, he pulled. He was sweating now, and his jaw tightened with the pressure of his effort. Still, he watched Annie, and she found herself unwilling to look away.

Moonglow shuddered, fell to her knees, and rolled to her side. Frank pulled his arm out as everyone jumped out of the way and left the stall.

"Al, get me the iodine bottle and the bulb," Frank said as he hurried to the tub and began washing himself again. Annie turned back as Moonglow began to work and struggle. Within minutes, the front hoofs and nose of the foal were visible. "There it is!" Henry called, trying to keep his voice calm and quiet.

"You boys get your towels ready, and remember, not too hard," Frank instructed.

After another few minutes of intense struggle, the foal was nearly out, still covered with the white-blue amniotic sac. As its hocks appeared, it seemed to quiver. Frank, still wet from washing, grabbed a suction bulb to clear the sac from the foal's nostrils and suck away any excess fluids. Immediately, the foal gagged in air. Frank nodded to the two boys, who began to rub the foal vigorously with their towels to stimulate circulation.

"Watch out for the umbilical cord," Frank said quietly as he nodded toward the two-foot length that still connected the foal to its mother. As the two boys worked, Frank carried the remains of the amniotic sac to the exhausted mother's head and gently held it for her to smell and then nibble. Soon after, Moonglow rolled up and turned to see her foal. She extended her neck to caress her offspring with her nose. Frank picked up the umbilical cord as he held the foal close against its mother's body. "Here, Speed, hold this."

The boy took the cord, automatically following orders, but was startled by holding it, particularly as gobs of blood the size of bird eggs pulsed through it. His eyes opened wide with wonder, and Henry gave a laugh as he continued rubbing.

Suddenly the foal lifted its head and blinked at Henry. Reluctantly, the two boys knew it was time to leave the stall. They checked with Frank, who nodded, just as the foal thrashed out with its front legs, naturally severing the umbilical cord. The boys hurried out to watch over the stall partition. Only Frank remained. He stroked Moonglow until, with surprising agility, she rose and stood near the foal. It moved its neck back and forth and then rolled up on its sternum. After a short rest, it struggled, fell, and finally wobbled to its front feet. It seemed hung in that position.

"Well, we have a little filly. Usually you let them work at this, but I'm going to tail her. She's had a hard trip and needs some food." Frank took a firm grip on the foal's tail and quickly lifted. In response, she put her back legs under her and suddenly was standing. Frank gently encircled the foal's girth and supported her as she staggered over to her mother to nurse. At first struggling to find the almost inaccessible udder, the foal fastened on to her mother's leg and started to suck. Moonglow pulled away, and Frank guided the foal's snout to where it needed to go. When the foal was standing in place, eagerly consuming her first meal, Frank took a shallow cup of iodine and held it over the stump of the umbilical cord. Then he left the stall. Spontaneously everyone gathered around him and they all hugged happily but silently in deference to the new mother and foal.

"We did it!" Henry whispered, and everyone agreed. Annie found her arm around her son on one side and around Frank's waist on the other. Suddenly conscious of his body, she avoided looking at him until she realized his hand was clasped over her ribs. He turned to her at the same moment she glanced up. The meeting of their eyes lasted only a moment.

"Oh," Bruna Oliver said as she approached the stall, having watched the birth from across the barn. "She's such a glorious girl!"

The group turned to look into the stall. Frank went to put on his shirt, and Annie held Henry's hand as the boy pulled her over to his vantage point. "That'd be a great name, Maman! Glorious Girl!"

Enthusiastically, everyone looked at Annie, and she quickly nodded. "We'll try it on the Jockey Club tomorrow. Is it less than eighteen letters?"

"Twelve and a space," Speed Oliver said.

They stayed a few minutes more. The vet finally arrived and the two boys were ordered home to bed. As she left, Annie passed Frank.

"Thank you, Frank. That was a beautiful thing you did."

"Glad it worked out."

They parted without any further gesture.

TWENTY-TWO

OVER THE NEXT TWO YEARS, Limeteen Farm reached its full population of horses. Through buying at the sales and claiming at various tracks, as well as by keeping the best foals her broodmares produced, Annie could look out of any window in Limeteen Hall on a summer day and see thoroughbreds grazing or galloping in every paddock.

The white and yellow stripes of the Limeteen silks were seen winning on tracks from Florida to New York. The first stakes race win for the stable came during the 1970 spring meeting at Churchill Downs. It happened a week after the Kentucky Derby. When the winner was shipped back to Limeteen from Louisville, Annie gave a victory party for the entire staff at the barns.

In a brief speech, she toasted the four-year-old gelding that Frank Carney had claimed for six thousand dollars at Keeneland the previous year. She gave Frank the credit he was due for turning the twelve-times losing horse into a winner, and then said with passion, "Remember this day. This is only the first stakes win for Limeteen Farm. There are going to be a lot more!"

Annie was a popular boss, mainly because she was not an absentee or social owner, insulating herself with the trappings of wealth or playing gentry during occasional visitations to the morning works. She began her daily routine in one of the barns, mucking out a stall chosen at random, then exercising horses on the training track or gallops according to Frank's instructions. Only then did she go to the office to decide how to spend her money. And spend it she did.

From the time she bought Limeteen Farm to the day of that first winning stakes race, Annie went through $12.5 million. Everyone working at the farm knew that Limeteen needed a big winner to validate the place and change the cash flow from gushing out to at least trickling in. From the moment that Glorious Girl was born, the hope grew that the daughter of Moonglow and Certainty might be that winner.

Under Frank Carney's tutelage, Henry and Speed Oliver were involved in every step of the filly's life. They grew as she did, and each boy was given his duties in tending to her. She became a graceful long-legged chestnut speedster who loved to run. Both boys begged to exercise her in the morning, but Frank would not allow it. Although the size of jockeys, the two boys, only ten years old, needed more strength and considerably more experience before they could control a thoroughbred in training. Both boys tried to gain those qualities, racing each other on stable ponies over the farm's two miles of gallops. Their rivalry in the races became intense but never interfered with their care of Glorious Girl.

One evening, as Annie and Sam drove to a neighboring farm for dinner, Annie said, "I think we're going to run Glorious Girl at Churchill Downs this fall." She was excited and it showed. "Frank doesn't like racing two-year-olds, but he thinks she's . . ." She noticed Sam's scowl, and shook her head. "I'm sorry. I just wanted to tell you about—"

"Oh, that's all right," he interrupted sarcastically. "I can't think of anything I'd rather talk about than what Frank Carney thinks about a horse."

They drove in silence. She was wearing a new white-and-black-print summer dress, bare-shouldered except for thin straps. Her hair was pinned high on her head, an elegant and cool style in the sticky heat. She had been pleased when she put on the dress. She had anticipated the evening.

"What *can* we talk about, Sam?"

"Oh, for Christ's sake, Annie, anything you want."

"Really? Well then tell me about Barky and Alycia. Tell me about Caernarvon. Tell me about Belinda. My Lord, there's so much we can't talk about, our conversations are like creeping around in a mine field."

"Telling you about Belinda isn't going to create a happy mood here."

"It might help," Annie said quietly.

"I don't come down here to cry on your shoulder about my family troubles. I come down here to forget them."

"That's the trouble, Sam. We get together and have to forget everything else. It's awful. I want to know everything. Don't you want to hear about what's going on at Limeteen?"

"I tell you what. I'll read about it in the *Morning Telegraph,* all right?"

"All right." They drove on silently, went to dinner, departed early, and made love at Sam's house. When he was asleep, Annie left as usual to be home in the morning for Henry and work. The routine with Sam had become more habit than joy to Annie. As their silences increased, the habit became tinged with obligation. When he called to cancel a date, Annie realized she often felt as much relief as disappointment.

Her attention was on Glorious Girl. Training continued, and Annie made sure she was at the track for the filly's works. On weekends, Henry and Speed were there, too.

"We've been working on her changing leads," Frank Carney said from his stable pony, looking out over the training track. Annie and the two boys were nearby, leaning on the outside rail. "Watch her when she comes into the turn."

They saw the filly at the far end of the track approaching the straightaway.

"What's changing leads, Maman?" Henry asked low enough so that Frank would not hear his ignorance.

"It's probably the most important thing a race horse has to learn," Annie replied. "In each stride, a horse leads with one leg and the others follow. That lead leg takes a lot of strain just on a straightaway, but going into a turn, there's even more. In this country, the turns are all to the left, so to relieve the strain and to help the horse lean into the turn, it has to be taught to lead with its right or off-side front leg on the straightaway, then change its lead to the left or near-side front leg, going into the turns. Watch her now. Watch her stride."

With a fluid motion, Glorious Girl came toward them into the turn. Without an awkward move, the near-side leg shot out, taking the lead in midair and hitting the ground, to be followed by the familiar pounding rhythm of the gallop.

Both Henry and Speed let out a whoop of recognition.

"Oh, Frank," Annie called, "she's so easy with it."

"She's at home in the going," Henry said, showing off another phrase he had learned.

"That filly sure does like to run," Speed said seriously, watching Glorious Girl as her exercise rider eased her. Then, with his shank over his shoulder, he hurried over to the gap to lead Glorious Girl back to her stall. It was his day, but Henry ran after him anyway.

"I'm thinking the Pocahantas Stakes," Frank said. "At the Downs, first week in November. Let her run her maiden three weeks before."

"What's the distance?"

"A mile."

"Pretty long run for a two-year-old filly."

"Same distance for the other fillies in the race. It'd be nice for Limeteen to have a two-year-old stakes winner in the barn for the winter. I don't often run two-year-olds. But she'll be ready, Annie."

At his use of her name, she looked up. He acknowledged nothing, still watching the filly from the back of his pony. They had worked together every day for more than two years since the birth of Glorious Girl, and he had never used her first name again.

"You haven't called me that since the night she was born."

"I'm sorry," he said without looking at her.

"I don't mind," she said. "I guess it's kind of strange that you haven't after so long. I wish you would."

He squinted down the track, but at that moment there were no horses working. Annie saw the muscles of his jaw tighten.

"All right," he said abruptly.

She sensed that a barrier was breaking down. "I know that Henry's asked you up for dinner a hundred times. You want to come tonight?" She tried to make the invitation humorous, but it sounded too intense, and he did not smile. "Bruna's off, but there's leftover rhubarb pie, and Henry and I do a pretty mean chicken diablo."

Holding the reins, he leaned down on the pommel and looked at her. She saw his blue-green eyes fall from her face to her body, then quickly back to her eyes. "Let's get this filly to her race," he said in the intimate way he had spoken to her the night of Glorious Girl's birth. "Then we'll see about dinner."

He booted his pony, which carried him to the gap and back to the barn. Annie stood at the rail for a long time, trying to figure out what was happening between her and Frank. Coming to no conclusions, she went up to the office to send in the entry forms for Glorious Girl to run in the Pocahantas Stakes.

The filly continued to train well. As the weeks passed, her body seemed to come together and she stayed surprisingly fit. In October, she broke her maiden in an allowance race at Keeneland, winning by two lengths with a strong stretch run. Three weeks later, when she was shipped to Churchill Downs for the Pocahantas, she took the three-hour drive so effortlessly that Henry and Speed, who rode in the van with her, swore she had taken a nap.

The day of the race was a different matter. Throughout the morning, Glorious Girl was skittish about visitors. The two boys took turns walking her out, but she remained restless. In the paddock, she reared several times and had to be held firmly for Frank to get her saddled. Once the jockey was legged up, however, she seemed a filly with a purpose.

From the toss of a coin, Speed Oliver had won the honor of leading Glorious Girl around the paddock. He did so, his smile showing his pride. When he gave the filly over to be led to the track by a pony rider, Speed followed the other grooms through the tunnel under the stands.

Annie and Henry hurried to an owner's box; she did not expect to see Frank Carney during the race. His habit was to find a place to watch unnoticed. Then he would appear on the track with the groom to accompany the runner back to the barn. If the horse was a winner, Frank avoided the winner's circle, despite anyone's urging. "Only two people win a race and deserve their pictures taken—the jockey and the horse," he had explained. "And most of the time, the jockey ought to bow out."

Glorious Girl broke well from the starting gate. Coming out of the one-mile chute at the back of the track, she found a position on the rail. Her jockey held her in back of the leaders until an opening appeared coming out of the final turn. As Annie and Henry bellowed with the crowd, Glorious Girl saw the hole and shot through it, driving past the leaders down the stretch to win by half a length.

While Henry pulled Annie along down the stairs, people she had never seen before called their congratulations. Several called her Countess. She greeted them all, pride and exhilaration making her feel as if she were a balloon that Henry held on a string. Once she was in the winner's circle, Henry rushed out to join Speed. The two boys pounded each other on the back, laughing and yelling happy congratulations at each other.

Annie suddenly felt Frank standing behind her.

"Well, she did it for us," he said.

Impulsively, Annie turned and hugged him. She felt him hold her briefly. Awkwardly, he touched her hair. She pulled back to look at him, and he looked down into her eyes with the most raw yearning she had ever seen. When Glorious Girl arrived and the crowd's appreciation swelled, Annie turned away to watch, startled by Frank's attention.

Frank left the winner's circle, allowing his place be happily filled by Henry and Speed. After the pictures were taken, they all accompanied the filly to the spit barn.

During the celebration with the Limeteen crew, Frank and Annie avoided looking at each other. Then Annie drove the two boys back to Lexington, delivering a sleepy Speed to his parents' house and barely managing to get Henry up the stairs of Limeteen Hall before he fell asleep. She bathed and went to bed, then lay there, watching the race in her mind over and over again. She saw the look that Frank had given her, and let herself admit some of what it meant.

The emergency phone from the barn rang. It startled Annie. Her clock read three-fifteen. When she answered, Frank said, "I'm real drunk, so we better talk. I'll meet you on your front porch."

Annie put on her robe and walked down the stairs. She heard his truck stop on the gravel driveway and the door slam shut. When she opened the front door, he was leaning against one of the pillars. He stood up, legs astride for balance, his hands slowly coming out of his jacket pockets. Annie closed the door behind her. It was cold, and she felt the chill through her robe. A nearly full moon cast angled shadows of the pillars across the porch, producing spaces of darkness and moonlight. She was in a shadow; he was in the light. His hair slanted down over his forehead, and the intensity of his face caused Annie to stop breathing.

"I can't stay working here," he said, watching her without wavering. "You know what's happened. I can't work this way anymore. So I'm going to go, like we agreed."

Annie said quietly, "Tell me what's happened, Frank."

"You know damn well," he said with either pain or irritation, Annie could not tell which.

"I suppose I do, but aren't you drunk enough to say something outright to me? Or are you just going to walk away again?" She took a step forward into the moonlight.

He stared at her and put up one hand, as if trying to stop a vision from getting too close. Then he let his hand fall back to his side. "I came to this place, fooling myself that all the work would be enough so I wouldn't be bothered by you. As soon as I found out I was wrong, good old sour mash bourbon helped me deal with it. But that doesn't work anymore. I've had to drink too much at night to forget being around you in the daytime." He took a step toward her into a shadow, but stopped, even though Annie made no motion to avoid him. "Anytime now, the night's going to run over into the day and cause problems with the work we're doing. I don't want anything to bother that, so I'm leaving."

He brushed his scarred hand back through his hair and waited for her response.

"How is leaving going to help you? And what about the farm?" Annie asked, unsure of her intention.

He shook his head. "Don't do that to me. Hoping won't keep me here. You can find another trainer now, easy."

Annie hesitated a moment, then walked over to him, lifted her face to his, and said, "Frank, I'm not talking about trainers or owners, and neither are you."

She stood on her tiptoes and kissed him. Her body leaned against his, her breasts against his chest. Slowly he circled her back with his long arms, pressing her against him. They kissed longingly, resistance gone. When the kiss ended, they still held each other, not daring to let go.

He said, "This shouldn't be happening."

"I'm not so sure," said Annie.

"I didn't think you had any idea . . ."

"I knew something the night you delivered Glorious Girl."

She kissed him again. He responded eagerly, but still was restrained.

"It's not real easy to believe this," he said.

"Why not?"

"Well, two reasons come to mind. I seldom get anywhere near to what I really want, and then there's Sam Cumberland."

Annie rested her head on his shoulder. "I just don't know. Give me some time for that. I didn't expect this to happen either."

He took a deep breath and let it out. "I suppose it's best you know the whole story. I've thought about looking after you and Hank, maybe having others. That's how bad it is."

Annie pulled back, amazed. He gazed at her with simple,

honest intent. She smiled her gratitude, then felt her throat start to harden, and hugged him. "How drunk are you?"

"I've had more to drink tonight than any night that I can remember, so I ought to be *real* drunk. But I haven't felt so sober at three in the morning for a long time."

"You think you could ever stop drinking?" she asked.

She felt his body tense, but then one of his hands ran through her hair several times before he answered. "I could try, but you might have a crazy man around here for a while."

"That's all right," Annie said. "We'll just keep you busy. I'd say we have a few other things to sort out. But if you'll do that, I'm willing to see what happens."

They looked at each other, and Frank nodded. "That's good with me." He kissed her gently. "I can't believe you even want to try."

"I do. I really do . . . We'd better go now," she said and smiled. "We have to be up in about an hour."

They kissed each other again and she watched him walk down the steps. The gravel crunched under his boots as he approached his pickup truck. When he opened the door, he looked back at her. Annie could see his eyes move in the moonlight to the facade of Limeteen Hall.

"It's just a house," she called.

"Kinda big, ain't it?" he drawled as he lifted himself into the front seat and drove off down the front drive.

Nearly a thousand miles away, Annie's two brothers were at their jobs on the backstretch of Suffolk Downs outside Boston. Fungo heard Jimmy Lee running toward him in the dark. The moonlight was too bright, and the brothers had worried about it. Fungo bent down and, with brute strength, bent up the bottom of the chain-link fence just as Jimmy Lee hit the dirt and rolled. Then Fungo bent the fence back as quickly as he could and tried to catch up with Jimmy Lee, who was running down the road toward a rusted station wagon.

Inside the car, Phil Angelo was reading the *Morning Telegraph* with a flashlight. He saw the brothers coming and started the motor. As soon as they piled into the back seat, he drove away.

"You got all the needles?" Phil asked.

"Yeah, sure," Jimmy Lee answered.

"Let's see them," Phil demanded.

Offended, Jimmy Lee retorted, "I said I got them."

Phil jammed on the brakes and turned around. "I want to see them, asshole! You dropped one that night at Timonium, and the Pinkertons were looking all over for me the next afternoon. I've got a reputation to protect, dig?"

Jimmy Lee grudgingly reached inside his shirt to the cloth halter strapped around his chest and tore at the Velcro strips. Four hypodermic needles were firmly in place, and he showed them to Phil. "All right?"

Phil started the car again. "All right, tell me who you hit again."

Jimmy Lee's patience was running out, but he had something important to talk to the Angel about, so he stayed cool. "Cable Jumper, Bluebuster, Charlene G, and Maxomachine."

"What barn was Bluebuster in?"

"Shit, Angel! Barn Eighteen, fifth stall in, white socks on the back legs, crooked blaze on her nose."

Phil Angelo nodded. "Hind legs," he corrected. "Good. You're getting to be a pretty good sticker, Jimmy Lee. You and the Monster make a good pair. Where'll we go for breakfast?"

Fungo hated Phil Angelo and wanted to reach for him, but Jimmy Lee's eyes stopped him. "We got an idea we want to talk to you about."

"Oh, yeah?" Phil Angelo said. "Is this one of Fungo's or one of yours?" He chuckled.

"It's about Annie," Jimmy Lee said and watched in the rearview mirror as the grin on Phil Angelo's face faded.

"What about her?" Phil said.

"We want you in on it. You have the connections we might need, to hide out, things like that. It'll take some time and money to set it up, but we got it all figured out."

"So what the fuck are you talking about?"

"She's got millions of dollars . . . and one little son," Jimmy Lee said dramatically, and watched Phil's face with anticipation.

Phil did not respond for a moment, but when he did, he surprised Jimmy Lee. "You stupid fuck!" Phil shouted. "You think because you can keep track of a couple of horses in your head, you could pull off something like that? Let me tell you something. Kidnaping is a federal crime. You ain't fooling with the dumb Pinkertons at a track. If you get caught, some local judge won't be there to listen to green reason. You kidnap somebody, you got the goddamn FBI coming up your ass. And if something goes wrong, you're talking Murder One! No connections of mine like that kind of attention. So just sit back there and say 'stupid' a hundred times to each other."

The brothers had worked hard on their plan over many weeks, and Phil's succinct reasoning deflated their dreams.

"Of course if you had any brains, you'd see the obvious way to go," Phil said and tossed the *Morning Telegraph* into the back seat. "Limeteen Farm had a winner yesterday, a two-year-old filly in the Pocahantas. That's a pretty big stakes race. She got some nice attention. If she keeps winning, she'll get very valuable." He reached up and twisted the rearview mirror so that he could see the brothers' faces. "And who's going to come after you if you kidnap a horse? Or even if you have to kill it? The makers of Meaty-Treat dog food, that's who!"

Phil laughed enthusiastically, a series of high nasal bursts. The brothers had never heard him do that. They looked at each other. Jimmy Lee raised his eyebrows. Fungo took it as permission to smile. Finally they had the Angel's interest.

An hour later, the Gwydian landed at Bluegrass Airport. Sam Cumberland was met by a Caernarvon car and driven to his farm. By then it was after five in the morning, late enough to call Annie.

She was mucking out a stall when a groom came to get her. Hurrying to the tack room to take the call, she began to feel how tired she was.

"Hello?"

"Congratulations," Sam said.

"Thank you, Sam. Where are you?"

"Here. I flew in about an hour ago."

"On your way to a hearing?"

"No, on my way back to New York. I heard about Glorious Girl in Kansas, and I'm very happy for you, Annie."

He was; Annie could hear it. "Sam, she ran such a beautiful race! I wish you'd been there." She put her hand over her eyes, recognizing her habit of wanting him to see anything she did, but knowing that if he had been there, Frank would have never touched her.

"Tell me all about it tonight," Sam said. "Come over for dinner. The staff's off, just us, wear something easy. About seven."

"Oh, Lord, we're having a celebration for Glorious Girl this afternoon."

There was a silence. Then he said, "Can you come over afterward? I really want to see you."

Something was wrong. Annie heard it in his voice. "I'll get there as soon as I can."

She managed a short nap in the middle of the day. When she woke up, Bruna Oliver presented her with the Lexington and Louisville papers, each of which had a lead article on the sports page about Glorious Girl. The *Times-Herald* had a picture of the filly approaching the winner's circle. In the background, Annie was hugging Frank. Immediately she thought of Sam seeing the picture.

Frank Carney appeared at the celebration and gave no indication to Annie that what had happened the previous night was anything more than a dream. But when he had to give a short toast to the filly, he made sure Annie saw that he filled his glass with ginger ale.

She arrived at the great Colonial mansion at Caernarvon Farm just after nine. At the front door Sam looked haggard. He smiled and gave her an affectionate kiss, explaining away his fatigue as the result of flying all over the country in recent weeks. Then he led her into the library, where the fire burning in the fireplace lit up the potted chrysanthemums. A small table had been set for two, with a single candle and a bottle of wine. Lying on an ottoman in front of a wing chair was a copy of the *Times-Herald*.

"I hope you like lamb chops," he said. "It's the only thing I know how to cook."

Sam wore brown corduroy pants, a dark green plaid shirt, a camel-hair cardigan sweater, and a yellow knit tie. Annie listened as he talked about his lobbying efforts with various state legislatures and the depressing results. Without warning, the image of the scars on the back of Frank Carney's hands came into her mind. Shifting uneasily in her chair, she said to Sam, "Maybe it's time to forget about the politicians and go directly to the public."

"No, that's not the point," he said, his contradiction angrier than it needed to be. "The public doesn't care. They just don't want to know. If their favorite quarterback has a cortisone shoulder, who the hell really cares as long as he can throw the bomb? You think they'll give a damn about a horse?" He glanced at her and tried to shift his angry tone to one of a more reflective calm. "The public comes to the track to bet, not to watch horses run. Hell, a lot of them don't even watch the race. They just wait for the results."

"I don't think they're all as bad as that. I've known some betting people who really loved—"

"Oh, I'm *sure* you have," he said, "The same kind of people who'd bet on cockfights and bearbaiting if they had the chance."

The implication was clear, but she wanted him to admit it. "What's that supposed to mean?"

"Nothing," he said as he stood up and walked over to the wing chair. Slumping into it, he said, "Did you know they're going to stop publishing the *Morning Telegraph,* and spread the *Daily Racing Form* all over the East?" The non sequitur embarrassed even him, and he offered a weak smile before looking away. "Sometime next year."

Annie waited for him to look at her again, then spoke quietly. "I've never thought you were a snob, Sam. That takes insecurity; Winnie taught me that. But, my Lord, you sure do get intolerant about people who aren't as lucky as you."

Quite suddenly he looked exhausted; his chin rested on the thumb of one hand and his forefinger pressed his temple. "Are you seeing Frank Carney?"

"I see him every day," she said easily.

"All right. If you insist, let's be literal. Have you been to bed with Frank Carney?"

"No," she said resentfully. Then, "Not yet."

" 'Not yet,' " he repeated. "And what do you hope for in a relationship, whatever it is, with a drunk?"

"Is there more hope in a relationship with a married man?"

"Oh, I see." Sam shook his head with disgust.

"What?"

"A divorce, I presume. I'm really sorry you asked, Annie."

"I didn't! Sam, I've known you for fifteen years. You've *always* been married. Nothing I can do is ever going to change that, or it would have by now. And I'll tell you something else. Even if you get a divorce, I know damn well you'd never marry me."

He stared at her for the first time, she thought, with hatred. "And I'm sure Frank will. Oh, yes," he said as he stood, "I can see him reeling around, the master of Limeteen Hall with a silver julep cup permanently stuck to his hand. You'll make a lovely couple."

Annie stood up. "I'm leaving now, Sam."

"Yes," he said, not turning to look at her. "I'm sure you two will be blissfully happy."

She left the library, but he followed her to the front door. "I'm sure that the romance of two noble rustics making it together in the pureblooded world of thoroughbreds looks good to you. Don't kid yourself, Annie. He's not in your class. He may hover around for a while—"

"Shut up, Sam," she said, stepping out the door. "Your ideas about bloodstock have always depended too much on pedigree." Before she could go, he grabbed her, lifted her up the step in his arms, and kissed her. She was too angry to respond in any way but to push him back and hurry to her car. As she sped around the circular driveway, she saw him standing in the door.

Passing under the immense Caernarvon iron arch held high over the gravel drive by two old brick pilasters, Annie felt absolutely calm. Previously when she and Sam had left each other, it had been shattering to her. She wondered what was so different. Was it because of Frank? Was it Sam's last kiss and the possibility of a return that it implied? Or was it simply the person she had become?

She hoped it was the last.

TWENTY-THREE

IN DECEMBER, Annie and Henry flew down to Florida for the Christmas vacation to watch Glorious Girl's training at Hialeah for her first race as a three-year-old. New Year's Day is every thoroughbred's birthday no matter when it was born. Although Glorious Girl was born in February, she became an official three-year-old on January 1, along with every other colt or filly born at any time in the same year. Frank wanted to start her early in the season and was pointing her toward an allowance race in mid-January.

From Turf Club gossip, Annie heard that Sam recently had taken his wife to Topeka, to the famous Menninger Clinic for psychiatric disorders. There were rumors of a divorce. When she pinned down the dates, Annie realized that Sam must have flown in from Kansas for their last dinner together.

The information disturbed her deeply. Each time she considered calling Sam, she decided against it. The break between them seemed final; an attempt at compassion would be gratu-itous, if not cruel. Recalling the copy of the *Times-Herald* she had seen in his library that night, she wondered what he might have said to her if the picture of her and Frank had not been printed.

Limeteen had eight other horses in training at Hialeah. While they were there, Annie and Henry met Frank every morning on the backstretch to watch the works, banter with the press, gossip with other owners and trainers, and finally decide about Glorious Girl's campaign. When Henry went exploring around the barns, leaving Annie and Frank alone on the rail, they found themselves edgy with anticipation. It was a state of mind that neither was used to, and both tried to con-trol it.

"Thirty-eight flat," Annie said as one of Limeteen's colts finished a three-furlong breeze.

"And some," Frank said, also without a stopwatch. "You're getting a pretty good clock in your head."

The early morning air was cool but heavy with humidity. The track's famous flamingoes preened and strutted for one another in the infield. Glorious Girl came through the gap, ready for her work, and the exercise rider trotted her over to the rail.

"Take her around once easy," Frank said, "then let her out for four furlongs in about fifty seconds. You'll have to hold her. She likes to run."

"Yoho!" the boy said, and started around the track.

"Fifty-two," Frank said.

Annie did not know what he meant. "What?"

"Days without sour mash."

She smiled and decided to chance taking hold of his arm. "Is it getting any easier?" she asked as she pulled away, conscious that they might be seen.

"Not a damn bit," Frank replied. "But at least my brain doesn't have that red-hot horseshoe nailed into it every morn-ing."

"When it's sixty days, we'll celebrate . . . with ginger ale."

"Let's make it ninety-six days."

"What do you mean?"

"If Glorious Girl wins down here, I mean Oaklawn Park in Hot Springs. There's a good prep race up there, then the Fantasy Stakes. That'll be ninety-six days for me, and she'll be eligible to go on up to Churchill Downs for the Kentucky Oaks. If she wins that, you'll really have yourself a filly."

The Kentucky Oaks, run the day before the Derby, was the most important race for fillies at that point in the season. Annie felt a nervous rush. "Frank, my Lord! You think she can do it?"

"If we can keep her fit. I'll be glad to get her to Arkansas. There's so many drugs around here, they say the damn flamingoes are hop-heads."

Instinctively, they both turned to watch Glorious Girl start her work. Frank continued, "I'm still fighting this drinking thing. Let me go on up to Arkansas. You come down for Glorious Girl's two races. Then let's see where we are." Without taking his eyes off the filly as she passed the second-furlong pole, he reached over and put his hand over Annie's on the rail. "I'd never have even thought to stop drinking if you hadn't asked."

It was an offering. Annie wanted to return it. "Sam Cumberland and I aren't seeing each other anymore."

His hand pressed hers.

"Forty-nine and two," she said as Glorious Girl passed the finish line and her boy rose in the stirrups.

"I'd say forty-nine flat," Frank said. "A little too fast, but that's all right. She'd run a hole in the wind dragging an anvil, just like her daddy used to do. Got to be careful not to fall in love with a filly like that." He gave Annie a look.

"Very careful," she acknowledged.

Glorious Girl won the allowance race at Hialeah by a commanding seven lengths. The filly drew increased attention from the press. After Annie returned to Limeteen, she and Frank spoke on the phone every day, always about business. Only at the end of their conversation would there be any reference to their personal life.

"Sixty-eight," he would say just before hanging up.

One night, instead of goodbye, Annie said, "Twelve."

"What's that?"

"The number of days until I get to Hot Springs."

He did not respond for a moment, then she heard a low chuckle. "You can really sidetrack a man, saying a thing like that," he said and hung up.

Annie arrived in Hot Springs on a bright April day. It was afternoon. The fever of spring was high and filled the atmosphere with dogwood and magnolia blooming in every yard. The breezes were warm and the clothes were light; seersucker and linen were the fabrics of choice. In a rented car, Annie drove straight to Oaklawn Park's backstretch and found her way to Limeteen's barn. Most of the stable help was watching the races. She found Frank alone in Glorious Girl's stall, working over her with a curry brush.

"This is just where I'd want to find you," Annie said before he realized she was there.

He did not look up, but finished working the filly's flank. "I've been waiting for you so long, I've just about curried the hair right off this filly." Then he turned and unsnapped the stall's webbing. She hurried to him and they stood, holding each other silently in the stall's clean straw and dark shadow. After a time, they pulled away to look at each other, then kissed, remaining in their embrace until Glorious Girl shifted restlessly. When they moved out of the stall's privacy, they stopped touching. Standing together outside the webbing, they watched the filly nibble at her hanging bag of hay as they talked.

"I don't know a thing about this, Annie," he said. "But if you think about it at all, seems there's only one thing for it. I want to marry you. If you feel the same, maybe we should, no matter about the rest."

Annie thought it was exactly the way Frank Carney would propose, no overtones, no hesitance, reaching his conclusion with simple honesty.

"What do you mean, 'the rest'?" she asked, trying to keep an even tone.

"How it looks to everybody for a trainer to be marrying up. You know, out of the shedrow into the main house."

Two grooms passed behind them, and Annie did not reach

for his hand. She said, "I haven't much cared about what people thought for a long time."

Frank was silent a moment.

"Then I guess it's up to you," he said.

"I guess so."

"A couple of things you ought to know. If you turn me down, I'll still be your trainer if you want me to. And whichever way you decide to go, I intend to stay sober."

Focusing on the filly, Annie touched Frank's hand. "There's just an awful lot we don't know about each other," she said gently.

He held her hand. "We come from the same kind of life, Annie. And we've come to the same kind of place. The only difference we have to worry about is that you've got some money. We know most of what's important. The rest we can learn."

"We haven't even made love to each other," she said, turning to him.

He kept his eyes on the horse, whether embarrassed or not, Annie could not tell. "From what I've heard," he said, "that used to be the custom."

Annie started to laugh, and he turned to her, smiling. Then he reached out, snapped open the webbing, and pulled her back into the stall.

"Excuse me, girl," Frank said to the filly as he closed the webbing and pulled Annie into his arms, kissing her again. He became increasingly ardent, but then moved back and held her shoulders. "I'm not superstitious or anything, but I have things pretty clear in my mind how all this ought to happen."

Annie hugged him. "Then you'd better tell me about it."

He watched Glorious Girl. "If she runs well tomorrow, we enter her in the Fantasy Stakes. That'll give you a couple of weeks to think about all this. Then you, with Hank and Speed if you want, come back down here for the race. I'd appreciate it if I didn't see you before it's run, because I'll have a lot on my mind. You can give me my answer in the winner's circle."

"You usually don't come to the winner's circle," Annie said. "And what if she doesn't win?"

Frank reached out and patted Glorious Girl's neck. The filly nickered back at him. "She'll win, and I'll be there for that one, that's for sure . . . By the way, did you know in Arkansas you can get married around the clock in one hour?"

Annie stared at him. "My Lord, you do have this worked out! You didn't choose Arkansas for Glorious Girl just because they have fast marriage licenses here, did you?"

"No," he said. "The timing just happened to be right for the Fantasy. Of course, if it does work out that way, it means I can ask Hank to be my best man."

In her prep race, a six-furlong sprint, Glorious Girl was bumped by another filly coming out of the starting gate. She stumbled, and at the quarter was dead last. But coming around the turn she ran the others down, and missed catching the leader at the finish by only half a length. Although second, she ran much the best race, and neither Frank nor Annie doubted her ability to win the next time.

Once back at Limeteen, Annie had a hard time keeping herself from calling Frank on the phone four times a day. The farm staff noted her exuberance and shared it. Everyone anticipated Glorious Girl's run in the Fantasy Stakes. Henry was almost as excited as Annie was. Five days before their trip, he and Speed Oliver were packed. This time they would miss doing any of the groom's work; they had relinquished those responsibilities when Glorious Girl left Kentucky. Nevertheless, "their" horse was suddenly a major contender, and they could barely contain themselves.

One night after dinner, Annie took Henry into the library and lit a fire. The fine old paneling glowed as they settled into the large leather chairs. Henry waited expectantly, for usually after dinner he was sent off to his room to do his homework. For a moment, Annie's eyes wandered restlessly over the shelves of Charlie Dell's leather-bound books.

"What are we doing in here?" Henry asked.

"I have something I need to ask your advice about."

"What?" Henry asked, eyeing the closed door.

"Frank Carney," she said. Despite her attempt at control, too much happiness showed in her smile.

"You're going to marry him!" the boy shouted with no surprise and total delight.

"Shush, Henry! I'm supposed to be telling you, not you me. How did you know?"

"I didn't. But I've thought about it for a *long time!* I really hoped it would happen." Then, with eleven-year-old self-consciousness, he looked down at the floor and said, "Ever since we came from France, I believed I'd get a father here. I'm so glad it's him and not Mr. Cumberland. It took so long, Maman, but it's worth it."

They hugged each other. Annie felt her eyes fill with tears and blinked them away. "I'm real glad you're happy about it," she whispered.

"When's it going to happen?" Henry asked.

"Well, I think right after the Fantasy Stakes, but you can't tell anyone about it. It has to be a secret until it's over."

"Maman, that's soon . . . but I have to tell Speed."

"Why?"

"He's my best friend. We've sworn we'd never have a secret from each other. Besides, he'd really want to know. He thinks as much of Frank as I do."

"He does?"

"Speed says that Frank doesn't see black. He told me that it's a lot easier at Limeteen for the niggers—Speed used that word, not me—that if the head man was black-blind, it seemed to spread. Besides, Frank treats Speed just like me . . . like a kind of, well, son." He smiled brightly. "I mean, I could really use a father around here."

Annie laughed. "Can Speed keep a secret?"

"Yes, Maman, he really can! Can I go tell him now?"

"Tomorrow morning."

Speed Oliver kept the secret, even from his parents, and only when the three confederates were on the plane to Arkansas on the morning of the race did they dare to discuss it out loud. With grave shyness, Speed said to Annie, "I'm just real happy for you, ma'am. I don't think you could ever marry a finer man."

Their excitement and happiness lasted until Annie saw the outline of Oaklawn Park and drove into the owners' parking area. Her body tensed and her mouth went dry. The two boys suddenly became quiet with a similar anxiety. Because no one under sixteen usually was admitted to the track, Annie had written for the special permission granted to young members of owners' families. They found their way to Limeteen's box seats without saying a word.

As they arrived, the third race was being run. Annie was startled to see her white-and-yellow-striped silks cross under the wire on a horse running second. She remembered Frank had mentioned that a Limeteen colt would be running. Ordinarily she would have known not only her own horse, but most of the others in the race. She felt strangely off balance.

When the boys became restless, Annie let them go exploring on their own, with strict instructions not to go to the backstretch and to return for the featured race without visiting the paddock. Races were run that Annie barely noticed. She was going to get married. Could Glorious Girl lose? Not this race. Another time, maybe, but not now. Then Annie remembered the prep race, the bump and stumble, and she tortured herself all over again.

The boys were back in their seats for the Fantasy Stakes post parade. All three watched Glorious Girl through binoculars as she pranced in front of the grandstand, then ran to the back of the track for her warm-up. There were eight other fillies in the field; three of them were stakes winners. Annie's stomach turned nervously as she glimpsed the tote board. Glorious Girl was the third favorite at seven-to-one. The filly moved into the starting gate easily, and waited patiently as the other runners followed.

The start caught Annie off guard, as it always did. She expected an instant of calm before the gates sprang open, but no official starter ever waited for such an improbable moment. Glorious Girl broke well and took the lead on the rail, just as she liked to do. Her jockey held her pace back, saving as much of his horse as he could. No one challenged her on the backstretch, but Annie winced when she saw the first two quarter-mile split times as they flashed on the tote board. The race was a mile and an eighth, a furlong longer than Glorious Girl had ever run, and she was setting too fast a pace.

Approaching the far turn, two other fillies made their moves, and for a few moments all three were head to head. Then Glorious Girl faltered and the other two pulled ahead as they came around the final turn into the stretch. Annie heard Henry and Speed groan in unison. The two lead horses closed in front of Glorious Girl too quickly and caused her to stumble. She almost went down, but her jockey pulled her neck up and kept her going. By then, two other fillies had passed her.

Without hesitation, Glorious Girl went to the outside and started to run, catching first the two fillies that had passed her when she stumbled, then, with a courageous effort, leaping ahead to run with the two leaders. One of them began to fade and suddenly cut out, bumping Glorious Girl hard. She seemed to ignore it, not losing her stride but stretching it out, gathering distance beneath her with long, flashing four-legged grabs at the track. The other filly surged forward, but Glorious Girl had gained a momentum that carried her across the finish line ahead by half a length.

Only then was Annie aware of the shrieking, bellowing noise around her. The two boys were pounding on each other, jumping up and down. First they hugged Annie; then they all hurried into the aisle and to the steps leading down to the winner's circle. The inquiry sign was flashing on the tote board, but Annie knew it was for the horse that had bumped Glorious Girl and come in second. It would not affect her win.

They all saw Frank at the same time. He was not smiling as he waited in the center of the track with the grooms for Glorious Girl to return. His obvious concern abruptly quieted their elation. Frank watched carefully as the filly cantered easily back, then trotted to him. While the Limeteen groom attached his shank, Frank shouted a question to the jockey, then quickly leaned down to feel the filly's back off-side hock and cannon. The jockey answered, apparently happy. Frank stood up smiling with relief, more of a smile than Annie had ever seen. Then, as the groom led the winner toward her, Annie watched Frank. He saw her. His look of momentary doubt passed as soon as he saw the smile on her face.

The two boys ran out to greet him, each grabbing a hand and pulling him along into the winner's circle. The governor's wife arrived with the chairman of Oaklawn to present the Fantasy Stakes trophy. The track photographer and several others were shouting for positions. Frank reacted stiffly to the cameras, but managed to stand next to Annie and say, "Well?"

"You already know. Of course."

They looked at each other as flashbulbs popped. "Well, let's not do anything to help them sell their newspapers, but I managed to get a justice of the peace to wait for us back at the barn, just in case."

Astonished as she was, Annie could only laugh. "That's fine with me. Glorious Girl can be my maid of honor. Is she all right?"

"Fine. That bump worried me. But, my God, what a race she ran! I've never seen such heart. Come on, let's get out of here and go get married. We've got to get that filly up to Churchill Downs."

The brief ceremony took place in front of Glorious Girl's stall. The filly whinnied and nickered as Henry handed Frank a narrow gold wedding band, which he placed on Annie's finger. The honeymoon began that night in a nearby Holiday Inn.

Henry and Speed were unnaturally silent after their first champagne dinner in the motel's restaurant. Annie and Frank walked the boys down the motel's corridor to their room. The foursome had already elicited a number of shocked and deploring stares from the other occupants. The idea of a black boy sleeping on the motel's sheets could have been cause for random violence by some.

"You all put the chain across the door," Frank said, "and don't open it for anyone but us, hear?"

The two boys had long since accepted the complexities of their friendship and agreed without apparent concern.

"Where's your room?" Henry asked.

"Just down at the end of the hall."

The boys exchanged quick looks, and then, with beaming smiles, chorused suggestively, "Good n-i-i-i-ght!"

Frank and Annie, caught off guard, chuckled and left the room, closing the door behind them. Over the boys' unrestrained laughter, they heard the chain slide in place. Frank took Annie's hand and they walked down the hall. She shrugged at Frank, and he shook his head at the boys' presumed sophistication. He reached into his jacket pocket for the room key, opened their door, and slid the chain across it. Annie stood in the space between the bottom of the two double beds and the TV table. She noticed a picture of a sailboat on the turquoise wall. Then, on the table by the window, she saw a vase holding a huge bunch of black-eyed Susans.

Frank came up behind her and put his hands around her waist.

"There are ninety-six of them," he said, and kissed her softly on the neck.

She leaned back and placed her hands on top of his. "I've never known anyone strong enough to do what you've done. We can stop counting now."

She lifted one of his hands and slipped it into her dress inside her bra. Already hardened by anticipation, her breast was so sensitive that when his rough palm covered it, her entire body trembled.

He held her gently, tenderly rocking her against him as he stroked her breast, kissing her softly on her neck, her ear, her hair. With his other hand he unbuttoned her dress from the hem to the neckline. Then he stepped back and slid her dress off. Annie turned to face him, feeling strangely shy. He let the dress fall, came to her, and kissed her lightly as his arms went around her back and he unsnapped her bra. His hands moved slowly down her back.

Annie felt as if the world were stilled and that nothing moved except his hands over her body. She allowed the waves of urgency to pass through her with quiet ease. He pulled down her underwear and hose, and she moved out of them as if she were floating. When he picked her up, she felt herself to be very light but very vulnerable; she was naked and he was dressed. Their eyes met, and Annie gave in to trusting him. He laid her on the bed and, still without undressing, caressed her with his hands as he kissed her everywhere.

By the time he took off his clothes, Annie was so lost in her own rapture that she was barely conscious. He moved lightly and glided into her, seeming to hover over her, touching her only where her flesh seemed ready to melt around him. She heard herself groaning and had no idea how to stop. He moved in her with deep consistency, allowing her to be engulfed by a flood of sensation that saturated her body and flooded her with emotion. He kept on without pause, and without resistance a deluge swept through her again and left her submerged, barely able to breathe. She did not realize when he left her, and remembered only turning on her side and feeling his hard body spooning her into its curve, and his scarred hands holding her breasts.

Annie woke once in the night, turned in Frank's arms, and saw that he too was awake. "My Lord, Frank. My Lord," she said, and fell back asleep.

Such nights were not uncommon as their honeymoon continued. It was a time of unbelievable intensity, which lasted throughout the training period for the Kentucky Oaks. In spite of Frank's concentration on the filly, and Annie's need to commute between Churchill Downs and Limeteen Farm to look after Henry, the couple spent the three weeks together as if separate from the rest of the world, lost in the usual preoccupation of a major race.

Glorious Girl took the lead from wire to wire and won the Oaks by two lengths. Together with the marriage, the victory brought Limeteen Farm, its owner and trainer, considerable recognition. The first, uneven edge of fame was not easy, particularly for Frank, who resented its instant intrusions. The day after the race, Annie drove Frank away from Derby Day in Louisville. Their drive back to Lexington was a great relief, but as Annie's Jaguar approached Limeteen Hall, Frank said, "Well, this may be the hardest part of it."

"Remember, it's just a house," Annie said.

His eyes slid over to her, but she did not see a smile. As they drove up, Henry ran out to greet them. A big party was planned for the farm that evening, by which time Glorious Girl would have shipped in from Churchill Downs.

"It's going to take me some time to be comfortable in there, Annie," Frank said before he stepped out of the car. "Don't take it personally."

"How do you know? You've never even seen it."

"I saw it once, before you came. It's just not my kind of place."

"Well, it's your place now, and I can't wait to show you around."

Henry and Annie guided Frank through Limeteen Hall, and in spite of an initial resistance, he seemed to accept what he saw. The phone kept ringing. Half a dozen women were in the kitchen with Bruna Oliver and Mrs. Elway, cooking for the party. Ostensibly for the filly, the celebration was turning into something of a wedding reception. In preparation, employees came into the house, offering congratulations, asking for instructions about parking, chairs, and bartenders. More guests wanted to come; the *Herald-Leader* wanted to send photographers.

Frank tried to avoid the confusion by searching the house with Annie for a small room—"someplace where I can keep a lot of my junk that you won't want around anywhere else, believe me."

"A room of your own, already?" Annie smiled.

"There won't be a bed in it," he assured her, then said seriously, "I'm not too good at handling all this public attention, Annie. I hope you're willing to do that. I can talk pretty good to horses, but these newspaper people make me real nervous. God Almighty, all that junk they said about us getting married."

"The day after newspapers come out, they're used to line garbage cans," Annie said as she showed him an old storage room on the third floor. As Frank considered it, they heard someone come pounding up the stairs. It was the farm manager.

"The state police are on the phone," he yelled, breathing hard from the stairs. "Glorious Girl's been kidnaped!"

TWENTY-FOUR

THE INVESTIGATOR from the Kentucky State Police, Lieutenant Ben Reed, had twenty-one years of experience, but none involving a kidnaped horse. A heavy, dolorous man with thinning gray hair and a weathered, jowly face, he knew only one thing about kidnaping, as he explained soon after his arrival at Limeteen Hall.

"It's over fast if you're lucky. If something goes wrong, it's real slow. The best thing to do is find out what they want, give it to them, and get your horse back. I don't believe much in tricks, although the FBI is awful good at setting things up for catching them later on."

Shifting his weight in a leather chair, he watched Frank Carney standing with his hands in his back pockets, leaning sideways against the library's shelves of books.

"Is the FBI involved?" Annie asked, more wary than pleased. Sitting at her desk, she had noted the policeman's

396

tendency to address his conversation to Frank, even though Frank hardly seemed to listen.

Outside, they heard another truck pull up on the gravel drive. People kept arriving for the victory party for Glorious Girl, which had been canceled. When they heard news of the kidnaping, they stayed. Newspaper people soon followed, then the first of several television trucks. Frank suggested locking the main gate, but it was too late. His recent experience had taught him that it was often harder to manage one member of the press than a group. It galled him to know that a crowd of people was on the front steps with nothing else on their minds than using the pain and excitement of this horror to fill their papers.

"Well, ma'am, as for the FBI," the lieutenant replied, "we always ask for their cooperation when a kidnaping is involved, so we called 'em. Frankly, we can use them. There's no particular law on the books about stealing or killing a horse, not even in Kentucky. All the kidnapers have done is steal something that's worth something. They *might* take it across a state line. That's enough to get the FBI into it, though we've already thrown up checkpoints all over the state, and every airport within five hundred miles has been alerted. I tell you, everyone's going to be looking for that horse. I mean to say, that's a Kentucky Oaks winner!"

"There are maybe three or four hundred thousand horses in the Bluegrass," Frank said flatly. "Most people don't know the difference between a chestnut and a bay. I wouldn't be surprised if tomorrow everyone'll think they've found her. What'd the kidnapers look like?"

"From what your driver and groom said, a couple of hippies, stringy black hair, dirty beards, dark glasses, those little gold rings in their ears, wearing tie-dyed T-shirts, jeans, and those running shoes all of them wear, if not smelly sandals. Only one of them talked, and from what your driver says, the accent sounded like it was from somewhere around here. But whoever they were, they knew what they were doing. This was a well-planned operation."

Annie again went through the details of the kidnaping: the Limeteen van pulling up at the first stop sign off the interstate, two stolen cars boxing in the van, the two male hippies, the two shotguns, the groom and driver tied up and thrown in the van with Glorious Girl, then being driven for twenty minutes, pushed out on a dirt road near Elizabeth Station, and struggling for an hour before getting loose and finding a telephone. The Limeteen van had been found abandoned a mile away.

Lieutenant Reed did not tell the Carneys about the blood that had been found in the empty van. It was being analyzed to see whether it was horse or human. "I need to ask you a couple of things, if that's all right," he said. "Can you tell me about the horse? Well behaved? Or will it be a problem for them?"

Annie and Frank glanced at each other, admitting their dread. "She's fine if she's handled right," Frank said. "Just like any high-strung race horse, if something bothers her, she'll balk. I just hope those two know something about horses." With his hands still in his back pockets, he walked restlessly over to a window.

"What's the horse worth? I mean to say, what are these people after?" Lieutenant Reed asked.

"After the Oaks, I reinsured her for a quarter of a million," Annie said. "But that isn't her real value. If she keeps winning, it's double, and then her foals, depending on who we breed her to, say a dozen foals in her lifetime, takes it into millions. And if any of them are stakes winners . . ."

She stopped, unable to continue for a moment, thinking of the plans she and Frank had of running Glorious Girl in the Filly Triple Crown at Belmont, then the Alabama Stakes at Saratoga, and, with that record, taking her to Dionysus, who had become a European champion for Lord Dolby, or even to Northern Dancer some year if they could buy a season.

"But, Lieutenant," Annie said, continuing resolutely, "I have to tell you one thing right now. We won't pay one dollar of ransom. I don't care how much they ask for, there's no deal."

The police officer's face furrowed. "Why not?"

"If those two men make any money at all on this, there won't be a horse in the Bluegrass or anywhere else in the world that's safe. Kidnaping a horse is too easy to do. You can't guard them that well. My Lord, the security that the insurance companies require now is overwhelmingly expensive. If we pay the ransom, even if we get Glorious Girl back, you'll have more experience with kidnaped horses than you want or the FBI will care about."

"D'you mention not paying ransom to your insurance company?" Reed asked.

"They know what I think," Annie replied. "They're considering it. But that doesn't make any difference. The decision is mine."

"I see your point, Mrs. Carney," Lieutenant Reed said as he hauled himself up out of the chair's low seat. "But if you take that position, and we can't find her first, I'm afraid you'll lose your horse."

Annie looked down at her desk. The lieutenant ambled over to the door to let himself out. "I have a man setting up to trace and record the phone. If they call, keep them talking. Make them prove that the horse is well. I'll leave some officers to keep people back from the house." At the door, he hesitated. "You know, I can't help but wonder why they came after your filly. Even I know there are a heck of a lot more valuable horses. Why not the Derby winner? Or Nashua? Whatever, is there anyone you know who might want to pick on you in particular?"

Annie did not respond, not wanting to admit her suspicion. Frank, however, came back from the window and said bitterly, "It's all these damn newspapers and TV, saying all this business about 'the Countess' getting married, and how much money she has. And then on top of it, she has a champion filly. My God, everybody knows everything about this place, and they're crawling all over it right now."

Annie was surprised at his hostility, and alarmed by it.

"If you can," Lieutenant Reed said sympathetically, "try to cooperate with them, Mr. Carney. You want them on your side, because the more information they get out there, the harder it'll be for the kidnapers. Just keep giving them pictures of the filly. Pictures seem to satisfy them for a while." He nodded. "Be seeing you."

When they were alone, neither Frank nor Annie moved toward each other. Annie, having called Delansig and told him to locate her brothers, had not mentioned them to anyone else. There was no specific reason to suspect them; since they had signed their agreement with her, she had heard nothing from them. They had received their monthly fee and, as promised, stayed away. Annie found it hard to believe that they were smart enough to plan such a kidnaping, though she knew it was a mistake ever to underestimate Jimmy Lee.

Frank started toward the door.

"Where are you going?"

"I can't stand this. I'm going out to look for her."

"We're supposed to stay by the phone."

"Only takes one to talk on the phone."

"Please don't walk away from me now, Frank." She made the request with as much irritation as pleading.

Before he had a chance to respond, there was a knock at the library door.

"Who the hell is it?" Frank asked angrily.

"Just old Chigger" came the reply, and Frank opened the door. Chigger Beasley entered and started talking right away. "I been entertaining those press people with every hardboot story I could think of, but if you have a mind to, you might talk to them."

"Not me," Frank said.

Chigger glanced at him, and said, "Well, Frank, they don't want you anyway. They want 'the Countess.'"

"That's just fine," Frank replied disgustedly. "She can get their attention, and I can get out of here."

He reached for the door.

"Frank," Annie said, suddenly alarmed. With Chigger there, she could not say what she wanted to say. "Don't be too long. Whatever happens, I really do need you here." She said it as lovingly as she could, but she knew he might take it as an order. In front of Chigger Beasley, he expressed nothing, only nodding as he left the room. For a moment, Annie and Chigger stood looking at each other.

Then Annie said, "All right, let's go talk to them, Chigger."

The phone rang. Annie froze. Beasley hurried to the door, but a state policeman was already there.

"Go ahead and answer it, ma'am. We're set up," he said and hurried back to his equipment.

Annie reached for the phone.

"Hello?"

"Annie, this is Sam. I just heard the news about Glorious Girl. Anything I can do?"

Her throat tightened hard. She knew his pride and what it had taken for him to call. Clearing her throat, she tried to control her voice. "You want to go out and talk to the press for me?"

"Don't worry about them; they'll love you," he said, a familiar reassuring humor in his voice. "Annie . . ."

There was a pause, which made Annie nervous about what he might say. "They're recording this," she said as Henry came in hesitantly through the open door.

"Okay," Sam said. "I'm here in Lexington. Call me if I can do anything."

"Thank you, Sam."

She hung up and quickly went over to Henry.

Having heard whom she was speaking to, he took a step back.

"Where's Frank going?" he asked.

"To look for Glorious Girl."

His eyes widened anxiously; then he ran for the door. "I'm going with him," he called back. But outside, he saw Frank's pickup already moving down the farm road to the back gate. Annie watched as Henry cut across a paddock, hoping to catch the pickup, but it was too late. He stood in the paddock, waved and yelled a few times as the truck disappeared over the county road.

In a boarded-up garage on the outskirts of Frankfort, about twenty miles from Limeteen Farm, a small fire of hair burned in an oil drum. Jimmy Lee and Fungo had shaved in water heated on a hot plate. As a result, both had numerous razor nicks on their throats and chins. Previously, they had given each other haircuts with the electric trimmer the Angel had brought for the purpose.

They soaked their tie-dyed T-shirts and dirty jeans in gasoline and threw them on top of the burning hair. Dressed in clean work shirts, cotton wash pants, and work boots, Jimmy Lee reached down to straighten the knife he kept in one boot, and looked over at his brother, who stared at the flames.

"Shit, Fungo, I'd forgot how much you look like Cary Grant."

"Hey, shut up. You ain't no pretty face yourself, you know." He rubbed his earlobe. "That goddamn thing infected my ear."

Jimmy Lee nodded. "You'll live." He ran his hand over his head again, glad to be free of the growth begun the previous fall. The inch-long hair on his head was still dyed black, but it would grow back, and by then, they would be rich.

They heard the horse stir, and looked over at the makeshift stall they had built on one side of the garage. The pickup truck and two-horse trailer they had used after abandoning the Limeteen van were on the other side.

"That goddamn horse," Fungo snarled.

"Hey, just take it easy, brother," Jimmy Lee said calmly. "That animal's worth a million bucks."

"It kicked the shit out of me," Fungo replied, reaching gingerly to touch his ribs.

Jimmy Lee laughed. "Ain't seen nothing knock you down like she did, Fungo. She just lifted you up, sent you flying ten feet down the road." He shook his head with feigned amazement at the memory, then grew serious. "Just don't hit her again. She's gotta stand up and look pretty for the camera. A four-by-four causes damage."

Glorious Girl lay on her side, front and back legs hobbled, with a rope around her neck. There were two deep gashes on one hip where flies had attached themselves to the dried blood. The filly's eyes were open, but she was not conscious, breathing in short spasms.

"You just keep your needle ready," Fungo muttered. "That horse kicks me again, I'll kill it."

"No you won't," Jimmy Lee warned. "That horse is going back to Sister, and we'll be leaving Kentucky with a load of her money."

This was another sore subject with Fungo. "Not near

enough. We took all the chances. How come that son of a bitch Angel gets half the money, and we have to split the other half? And don't tell me no more that we couldn't have done it without him. We did it, goddammit, with him sitting in his motel room waiting to hear from us so's he can run over here and take his fucking picture and then drive off to Cincinnati! We could've done all that!"

Jimmy Lee smiled impishly at his brother. "Maybe he's not going to get half."

Fungo's mouth dropped open in thought. "What's that supposed to mean?" he asked.

"I'll keep the needle ready, and you keep the four-by-four ready, all right?"

Fungo stared, then said, "No shit," and the two brothers laughed, their money instantly doubled in their minds.

Over the next two days, Limeteen Farm and the state police received four hundred and ten definite sightings of Glorious Girl, as well as two crank phone calls demanding ransom. The head of the FBI field office in Louisville came on the case. He suggested that Annie tell the press that Glorious Girl had an illness that needed a special medicine each week in order to survive, the idea being that any vet in Kentucky who received a request for such medicine would alert the authorities. Annie worried that the kidnapers would try to inoculate the filly and hurt her, so she refused the plan.

On the second day, an envelope arrived, postmarked Cincinnati. It contained a Polaroid picture of Glorious Girl with a copy of the *Herald-Leader* and its headline about the kidnaping taped to the filly's flank, thus proving that the photograph was taken after the event. A message made up of words cut out from magazines was glued to the back of the picture: LOVE FROM DARK HORSE.

Later that day, Annie picked up the phone and heard a strangely altered voice say, "Hello, Countess. This is Dark Horse. I know this is being traced, so I'll have to talk fast. Listen carefully. I know the value of your filly, so don't try negotiation. She's safe; if you want her back, go to the bank and get one million in hundred-dollar bills. If they're marked,

I'll be unhappy. Put the money in something that's easy to carry. I'll tell you what to do with it tomorrow at around four."

"Tomorrow?" Annie said, trying to keep whoever it was on the line. "I can't get a million dollars that fast. And how do I know she's still safe? It's real easy to hurt a horse."

"Nice try, Annie," the voice said. "One million, one-hundred-dollar bills. Tomorrow at four." There was the click of a disconnected line.

Annie was alone in the library, where she had been told to wait. Lieutenant Reed and the trooper who had been recording all the phone calls both hurried in, looking at her questioningly.

She shook her head despairingly. "I couldn't tell if it was a man or a woman."

"I think it was a man," the trooper said. "He used a phone filter of some kind."

"He called you Annie," Lieutenant Reed said, hoping it meant something.

"He called me the Countess, too," she said. "Everybody knows my first name. What am I going to say to him tomorrow?"

The two men stared at her. Reed finally said, "You'll ask for more time. You'll argue that a million is too much. You'll keep him talking as long as you can, and if you have to, that's when you tell him you're not going to pay."

All of them knew what that meant. Annie stood up and walked to the window. "Could you please ask your people to keep an eye out for my husband's pickup, and ask him to come home?"

"Yes, ma'am," Reed said, "and we'll take the phone calls from now on, until tomorrow at four."

They left the library, and Annie looked at the clock on the mantel. It was two-fifteen. Less than twenty-six hours to find her. Frank had been gone all day and night. The press was still waiting on the front porch. If he had come back and seen them there, he would have driven off again.

Annie took another look at the clock. Henry would be home from school in an hour and a half. She started toward the door with a vague idea of preparing something for him, but stopped. Should she tell Lieutenant Reed about her brothers? If they were the kidnapers, would the information help catch them? She did not see how. And whether it did or not, if she revealed who her brothers were, eventually their story would get to the press, and then Henry would have to confront that part of his heritage. She would have to tell him sooner or later, but he was only eleven. Not now, she concluded yet again, and looked at the clock. Two-twenty. They had to find Glorious Girl. Jimmy Lee and Fungo must not be mentioned. She hurried out of the library to do something.

The FBI field office in Louisville sent reports about the case to headquarters in Washington, D.C., where they were disseminated to a varied list of cross-referenced offices and agents for whom the case, in some way, might hold interest. Special Agent Lyle McCracken was on the list. Working in the Bureau's New York office that day, he picked up the report about Glorious Girl's kidnaping.

He skimmed it and put it aside at first, having a number of more pressing matters to consider. A longtime expert on the inner workings of the New York Mafia families, McCracken had benefited from the recent interest that J. Edgar Hoover and the FBI finally had taken in the existence of organized crime. In spite of the Bureau's desire to bring in the big names at the heads of the crime families, the Joe Valachi case had taught McCracken an important lesson. The head of a family who had the power to kill witnesses, to corrupt judges and juries, and to buy the slickest lawyers was not easily frightened. One could often learn more by cornering a low-level soldier and using fear to crack him open for information.

Applying this strategy, Special Agent McCracken had been tracking, among many others, Phil Angelo, who, after the Valachi case, became a small-time member of the Genovese family. After selling heroin for a while, he had successfully fixed races over the previous year or two by using drugs. More recently, from what McCracken's informants told him, the Angel had been bribing jockeys to hold back their runners. McCracken was about to make a move on Phil Angelo when, abruptly, the race fixer dropped out of sight.

The special agent, therefore, went on to other cases. As he worked at his desk, however, a phrase from the Kentucky field office report slipped back into his mind. "The owner, Mrs. Ann Carney, formerly (three weeks) Mrs. Winton Sumner III . . ." The connection to Phil Angelo clicked. McCracken remembered his trip to France, the lovely young woman with —what was it? Blond hair? Somebody had said amber. He smiled to himself, knowing he was no good at description, although he never forgot the details of a face. Hers had been a pleasure.

When he called the field office in Louisville, he learned of the million-dollar ransom demand, and Mrs. Carney's intention not to pay it. He immediately suggested that he get involved. His secretary made a plane reservation and called up the Bureau's file on Mrs. Sumner. Phil Angelo's file he knew by heart.

An admirer of Machiavelli's philosophy more than that of J. Edgar Hoover, McCracken practiced the techniques of the great Italian master when dealing with the baroque politics of the FBI. A million-dollar ransom for a winning horse owned by a beautiful woman with something of a past would be big news, especially if the horse was killed. Mr. Hoover's only lust seemed to be for glamorizing press reports about his Bureau. Besides, the director loved horse racing. McCracken sensed that in this case he might be able to please Hoover and gain a bit more favor for himself.

That evening, on the plane to Lexington, he read Annie's file again. Remembering most of it, he noted that she had registered a .38 caliber pistol and been licensed to carry it "for farm work." McCracken had forgotten that her two brothers and her father had been convicted felons. He planned to call up their records as soon as he landed.

Through the night, the troopers of the Kentucky State Police did their best to check out the myriad tips received about Glorious Girl. One trooper or another had inspected every abandoned barn in the five counties and thirty square miles of the Bluegrass. Hundreds of horse vans and trailers parked at rental lots, movies, and shopping centers were searched. Consideration of the town of Frankfort was far down on the list. It was by pure chance that at three in the morning a trooper on his way back to his barracks decided to drive by a garage whose owner had called in to complain about the man who had rented it a couple of months before. The renter had refused to let the owner even approach the garage. In any public investigation, a great many private arguments were phoned in to cause trouble or embarrassment, so the trooper planned only to eyeball the place as he drove past. It was just a mile from the interstate, so the visit would not delay him.

The garage was on a deserted stretch of Old Duckers Station Road, across the street from the Louisville and Nashville Railroad line. As the trooper's car approached the garage, he saw light leaking out from around the edges of boarded windows. Immediately he turned off his lights and motor and let the car coast, looking for something behind which to stop. There was nothing, so he let the car roll down the road as close as it could to the garage, and cleared his service revolver from its holster.

Inside the garage, Glorious Girl had struggled to her feet. Although she was hobbled, she tried to rear, causing Fungo to yank hard at the rope around her neck in order to hold her down. As the bare hundred-watt bulb swung above them, Jimmy Lee gave the filly another shot. Fungo's anger had increased and focused. "That fucking Angel! Why ain't he here for *this!*"

Jimmy Lee did not reply while he waited for the injection to take effect. The filly whinnied once; then her front legs folded, and she crashed to the ground.

"Goddamn, how long will that stuff . . . ?"

"Shut up!" Jimmy Lee said.

Outside, they heard a car start. Jimmy Lee ran across the garage, grabbed one of the shotguns, unbolted the door, and dashed outside. He reached the corner of the building just in time to see the outline of the police car moving away fast with no lights. A cop never comes in alone; he was calling for a backup. Jimmy Lee knew it was all over.

"D'you see anything?" Fungo said as he came up behind his brother.

"Some asshole in a lowered Chevy, probably out here trying to get laid." Fungo grunted a laugh and followed Jimmy Lee back into the garage.

"Damn, I'm tired," Fungo said.

"You know, Fungo, you're right," Jimmy Lee responded as he casually replaced the shotgun, then put on his denim jacket and duck-brimmed B & G Feed hat.

"About what?" Fungo replied.

"About the Angel. I'm going to walk up to the pay phone and call the son of a bitch, tell him to get his ass down here, give us a chance to sleep in the goddamn motel for a while. I'm tired, too."

"Goddamn *right!*" Fungo agreed. "Wake him up, and tell his ass to *hurry!*"

"I'll be right back," Jimmy Lee said. "Don't kill that horse, all right?" He grinned affectionately at his brother, sharing the joke.

Fungo laughed as Jimmy Lee went out. After unscrewing the bare bulb, Fungo went back to the mattress beside the horse trailer and lay down; he was soon asleep again. He was hungry. The Angel never brought enough food. He dreamed of ham with red-eye gravy, eggs, and grits.

When the bullhorn woke him up, he could not remember where he was at first.

"This is the Kentucky State Police. The garage is surrounded. Come out the back door with both hands flat on top of your head." Fungo ran toward the door, tripping in the dark over the mattress and fell hard on the concrete floor. He saw headlights and red flashers shining through the boards over the windows. Then he heard the bullhorn. "You have thirty seconds to come out of that door! You are surrounded! Thirty . . . twenty-nine . . . twenty-eight . . ."

Fungo looked around and realized he was trapped. He had been trapped many times before and his reaction was always the same—rage at whatever had surrounded him yet again. This time, however, he had a focus for his rage. He picked up the shotgun, then lurched over to the horse trailer. Inside was the bloodied four-by-four he had already used on the horse. Putting the shotgun down, he grasped the wood. The grip of it felt good to him; it made his arms seem longer and full of power.

"Sixteen . . . fifteen . . . fourteen . . ."

Fungo stepped into the stall and stared down at the unconscious horse lying on its side. He raised the four-by-four above his head. Annie's horse. He bashed the wooden board down across the filly's front legs. She lurched in spite of the drug and shrieked a high-pitched whinny that startled Fungo, but caused only a moment's hesitation before he raised the piece of lumber and chopped down again.

"Seven . . . six . . ." Outside, they heard the horse bleat, and stopped counting. With tear gas guns and shotguns, the troopers rushed the garage, crashed through the door, and, in the blinding beams of their floodlights, saw the four-by-four raised high in the air.

"Hit her again, you're dead!" a trooper yelled, and fired a shot of warning. The wooden club stayed in the air, held there as two officers rushed at Fungo and knocked him to the ground. The piercing screams of the filly continued as a trooper turned his floodlight on her.

"Oh, Jesus God," he said.

Annie was awakened by the roar of a helicopter landing in the paddock next to the front drive. It had landed there the previous day to report on its aerial search. She saw that it was still dark outside, and dressed quickly in jeans, boots, and a sweater. Grabbing her shoulder bag, she felt for the gun, which she had kept there since the filly disappeared. Henry met her in the hall, already dressed. By the time they reached the bottom of the stairs, a trooper was letting Lieutenant Reed and another man in the front door.

"We've found her," Reed said without any tone of triumph.

"Is she alive?" Annie asked.

Lieutenant Reed only nodded, then said, "This is Special Agent McCracken of the FBI. We have to hurry. I think the boy better stay here. No room in the chopper."

Annie instantly recognized the FBI man, but there was no time to consider what his presence meant.

"Maman, I want to go." Henry clung to her hand.

Annie knelt down on one knee. "When it's time to get up, go tell Speed we've found her. Then you can both drive over in the van." She turned to the police officer who stayed in the house; he indicated his understanding. "Where should the van come?" she asked Reed.

"I don't know the exact address," he answered impatiently. "We'll call it in. We have to go."

Annie kissed Henry and hurried out the front door with the two men. Not until they were in the air did she begin to fear why the lieutenant had not wanted Henry to come. She looked over at McCracken, who was listening and talking on a headset, as was Lieutenant Reed. They were reassigning units, urging careful secrecy.

With its landing lights blazing, the helicopter descended on the asphalt of Old Duckers Station Road beside the garage. Annie ran with Reed and McCracken under the rotors, and followed two troopers, who led them inside. Even over the helicopter's motor, Annie heard the filly scream. In the garage, portable floodlights lit the interior and the makeshift stall. Annie ran to it and instantly saw the filly's eyes rolling white in pain, the white foam and blood on her muzzle, and the white bones of her front legs sticking out of bloodied, torn skin.

"We didn't know what you'd want," Lieutenant Reed said. "If you needed a vet for your insurance, or . . ."

Without hesitating a second, Annie reached in her bag for the gun and approached the filly. A state trooper sat on the ground next to the horse's head. He held his own revolver, and when he looked up at Annie, she saw tracks of tears on his cheeks reflected by the light.

"Be glad to do it for you, ma'am," he offered.

"No, I have to do it," Annie said as she quickly traced an X running from Glorious Girl's left ear to her right eye and right ear to her left eye. At the cross, she placed the barrel of the gun. The filly focused on her a moment, at first terrified; then seeing Annie, she tried to lift her head. Annie pulled the trigger and watched the head fall. Deaf from the shot, she reached out and stroked the filly's cheek, as yet unbloodied by the wound. Then Annie turned and said to anyone who could hear, "Where are they?"

No one said anything. Annie stood up and put the gun back in her bag. She saw Lieutenant Reed and the FBI agent. "Have you found them? Where are they?"

McCracken stepped forward and took her arm. "Come with me," he said. He guided her through the door and outside. They were led to one of the ten state police cars parked near the garage. A trooper opened the back door; McCracken reached in and pulled Fungo into view by his handcuffs.

His face was bleeding from when he had been knocked to the ground, and he was sucking on his lower lip, as he always did when he was scared and powerless. He did not respond when he saw Annie. Her hand started toward her bag, but then she stopped. She did not want the gun taken away.

"Where's Jimmy Lee?" she yelled at Fungo.

"This is your brother?" McCracken asked, not with surprise but for the record.

When Annie nodded, Lieutenant Reed said angrily, "You should have told us about them, Mrs. Carney." Then he turned and walked away.

"Yes, probably. I have trouble admitting it to myself," Annie said.

McCracken shoved Fungo back into the car and shut the door. Without any tone in his voice that might imply he was judging her, the special agent said to Annie, "He says that the other two men involved in this are at the Best Western Motel in Frankfort. We're going after them now. I'll have a trooper drive you home. It'll take about a half hour, forty-five minutes from here."

"Wait! Other *two* men?" Annie asked.

"Yes. Your brother, Jimmy Lee, and the Angel, Phil Angelo." Noting Annie's appalled reaction, he said, "After we get those two, we'll have to talk, Mrs. Sumner . . . excuse me, Mrs. Carney. This time, you'll definitely want to have your lawyer there."

Annie did not respond to the obvious warning. She watched as McCracken stepped into one of the state police cars with Lieutenant Reed and, with half a dozen other cars following silently, sped off down the road. When a trooper approached her, Annie automatically started to walk back toward the garage to be with Glorious Girl. Then she stopped. Henry had to be told. Closing her eyes, Annie saw herself pull the trigger and the filly's head fall.

"Mrs. Carney, I have orders to take you back to Limeteen Hall," the young trooper said.

Annie looked back at the garage for a moment, then hurried to the police car.

On Route 60, between Winchester and Lexington, a state trooper turned on his red flashers and pulled over Frank Carney's pickup truck.

"Mr. Carney?" the trooper asked.

"Yep."

"We've been asked to find you and tell you that Mrs. Carney would like you to return home."

Frank scowled at the public nature of the request. "I was just on my way."

"You been looking for the filly?" the trooper asked. "I doubt if we'll find her over here in Clark County."

"Another pair of eyes," Frank replied. "Thanks for the message," he said and drove off. He had barely slept for three days. Too tired to do any good now, he wanted to see how Annie was. He had returned to Limeteen once, but halfway up the front drive he saw the TV trucks and the crowd on the front steps, and had turned the pickup around and driven away.

Never in all the time since he had stopped drinking did he want bourbon as much as when he was looking for the filly. He had passed more bars and roadhouses than he had ever noticed, but he stopped only at barns, sheds, warehouses, any building where a horse might be hidden. He drove back toward Lexington with a terrible feeling that he had lost the filly, and tried not to think about it.

Annie managed to thank the trooper who had driven her to the front steps of Limeteen Hall. It was a bright morning, the early sun outlining the oak-crested hill behind the farm. At the barns, the stable workers were arriving and beginning their morning routines. When she stepped inside the hall, she heard breakfast noises from the kitchen, and went into the dining room. Through the windows, she saw that two horses with their exercise riders were already circling the training track.

Bruna Oliver was in the kitchen, making coffee. She looked up when Annie came in. The question was on Bruna's face. Annie shook her head.

"I had to put her down," she said, and swallowed hard to control her voice.

"Oh, Mrs. Carney, I'm so sorry."

Annie thanked her. "Can I have some coffee, please? What happened to the trooper at the front door? And all the press?"

"He's down at the farm gate. A lot of the troopers left after you did in the helicopter. The ones who stayed moved the press away."

Annie collapsed into one of the kitchen chairs and started to take her bag off her shoulder. "Where's Henry?"

"Not down yet. I was about to get him up for school."

"No school today," Annie said, taking the mug of coffee from Bruna and standing again. "I'll go get him. If you want to go and tell Speed . . ."

"Thank you, ma'am, I'd like to. It's going to break those boys' hearts," she said, tears welling in her eyes.

Annie quickly headed for the stairs. As she climbed them, she steeled herself for Henry's reaction to the news. Opening his door, she was determined not to give in to her own sadness, but to—

Her coffee cup fell to the floor, breaking and splashing the hot liquid on her boots.

"Heard you coming, sister," Jimmy Lee said in a whisper. "Real glad it was you. Close the door." Standing in the middle of the room, he smiled, his face just beside Henry's.

Jimmy Lee was holding the boy with one arm around his waist, a knife in his other hand at the boy's throat. Annie barely heard her brother; a sound like a high violin note pierced her mind. She closed the door, the terrified look on Henry's face quelling her own hysteria.

"D'you get your horse back?" Jimmy Lee asked. "I hot-wired a car and got over here just in time to see you go off in that helicopter. Real big time, Annie."

"Please, let him go," she said as calmly as she could.

"Who? My *nephew* here? Oh, hell, he's all right. We been having a real nice talk." He chuckled, then glared venomously at Annie. "This is what I wanted to do in the first place, but your buddy Phil Angelo wanted to take a fucking *horse!*"

"Please . . ." she pleaded, and at the same moment realized that her bag was still over her shoulder.

"Keep begging, sister. I like that. Did you collect the million dollars?"

Somehow her mind started working. "Not yet. We had until four o'clock. The bank's delivering it this morning."

"What time?" Jimmy Lee demanded.

"Right after they open at ten."

"Ten? Well, we can wait for that, can't we?" His eyes were wide with anticipation. "And that's when you and my nephew drive me out of here, far enough to be real sure no one's following us in helicopters or any other goddamn thing. And if that happens, you two might get out of this without getting carved up too bad. Right, Henry?"

The boy stared at his mother and said bravely, "That'll be fine with me."

"Jimmy Lee, you can't hold that knife there until ten o'clock. I'll do whatever you want, but please put the knife down."

"I'll tell you exactly what you're doing, Annie," he said, suddenly vicious. "You stay right here until the first person comes up looking for you. Then you tell them what's going on in here, and to get things ready for us to leave when the money comes." He dragged the boy over to a chair and sat him in it, still with the knife under his chin. "So, Annie, how's Uncle Fungo? Go back to that wall and tell us."

As she spoke, Annie backed up slowly until she reached the wall. "They found him at the garage. He told the police where Phil Angelo was. They thought you were there, too."

"Ha! Goddamn, I wish I could see the look on the Angel's face when they walk in! Did Fungo kill that fucking horse?"

"No," Annie said, and let herself start to cry.

"Well, ain't you lucky, sister," he said exultantly as he stood up behind the chair, gesturing above Henry's head with the knife. "What the hell you crying for? You probably won't lose a thing, except a million dollars."

She reached slowly into her bag, pulled out a handkerchief, and, holding the bag open, sobbed harder.

Jimmy Lee stepped to the side of Henry's chair, still pointing the knife at the boy. "You're breaking my heart, Annie, so stop it, hear? We don't need . . ."

She grabbed the gun out of her purse, pointed it at his head, and fired. He ducked, but the bullet grazed his ear. Stooped over a foot away from Henry, he froze in shock, the knife still in his hand.

"Henry, *run!* Get help. Don't move an inch, Jimmy Lee. Don't move anything an inch."

Henry stared, then jumped out of the chair and ran from the room.

"Jesus, Annie, you about shot my ear off," Jimmy Lee said without moving. "Listen, help me. I'm your brother."

"Drop the knife," Annie ordered.

"Lemme just get out of here." He put his other hand up to his ear. It was quickly covered with blood.

"Don't move anymore, Jimmy Lee. Drop the . . ."

He was staring at his bloodied hand, slowly standing up straight. Then he turned the hand to her, and smiled incredulously. "How could you do that?" He leaped at her. She fired twice rapidly. The force of the bullets hitting his chest countered the thrust of his leap, and for a second he stood upright, still smiling but with utter surprise. Then, as the blood flowed through the white teeth of his smile, he fell forward, his head landing on Annie's boot.

TWENTY-FIVE

AS THE NEW YORK Racing and Wagering Board's commissioners conferred at their table, the noise from the crowd in the hall grew louder. Archibald Delansig sat with Annie behind a small table near a grimy window. They watched the commissioners, some of whom glanced nervously toward the door, where two bored police officers stood on guard.

For three years, the newspapers had referred to Annie as "tough." From the investigations of Glorious Girl's kidnaping and Jimmy Lee's death, through Fungo's trial and Phil Angelo's devastating testimony about her past, to the steady disintegration of her relationships with Henry and Frank, Annie never felt tough. She thought she was lucky if she felt numb. After the first wave of sympathy for the killing of Glorious Girl and the near catastrophe of Jimmy Lee's attempt to abduct Henry, the public was calmed by the fascinating stories, carefully released by the FBI for its own purpose, of Annie's former connections to organized crime figures. Then a storm of contempt and anger followed, not only from the public, but from the racing establishment. As a result, she had been forced to fight for the right to race her horses, and in four other racing states she had lost her license. New York did not offer her much hope.

The temperature outside in Manhattan was ninety-six degrees. In the state office building the air conditioning only rattled with a malfunctioning effort. Pounding and an occasional distant yell came from the air ducts, but no hint of cool air reached the humid room.

Annie's wooden chair rubbed into her spine. She stared out at a treetop through two broken slats in the venetian blind. "What are they waiting for?" she whispered rhetorically. "We all know what they're going to say."

Delansig leaned over quickly. "It's how they say it that'll be important if we have to go to court," he explained, sotto voce.

Annie turned and gave him a quick, hopeless smile. "I've been in hearings for three years," she said. "You think I have another lifetime to spend in court?"

He looked at her sympathetically. She smiled, again asking forgiveness for her frustration. He shrugged as he had a hundred times. Looking again through the venetian blind's opening, she saw the hot haze and wilted leaves of a summer day in New York City. Having sat through hearings in four states, she knew the results here could only be the same.

Shifting in her chair to relieve her back, she saw Special Agent McCracken sitting in the spectators' section of the hearing room. He was waiting, as he had waited for three years, ready to testify on her behalf. That was the deal he had offered her. He would testify against his own damning FBI report on her "consorting with criminal elements," based on the information he had collected from Phil Angelo, if she would give him Charlie Dell's list. McCracken felt Annie's look and turned to meet it. She stared at him for a moment, then shifted again in the chair.

Every state racing commission had iron rules about any relationship with the underworld, implied or overt. Because the reputation of racing was always subliminally suspect in the mind of the public, a commission could not allow even a hint of taint. The racing establishment's usual reaction to any mention of impropriety was to deny it, then attend to it as quietly and privately as possible. Should the matter be large enough to reach the public, however, committees were formed and studies were made, or investigations took enough time for the public's notoriously short attention span to lapse and the curiosity to subside. Conclusions then became an exercise in evaporation.

Annie's past, her marriages, and, most important of all, her photogenic image in newspapers and on television had made the killing of Glorious Girl, the coroner's inquest into the death of Jimmy Lee, and the subsequent trial of Fungo a highly visible scandal. Journalists, in print and on the air, had waxed hyperbolic in describing her. "Mrs. Sumner-Carney's luscious, dimpled smile" was only a florid beginning. "Legs long enough to ride and tame any stallion alive" and "hair the color of blazing dew-covered autumn leaves" were some of the descriptions Annie endured. The racing establishment was unable to suppress the negative implications of her story. It had to appear righteous; thus, her punishment had to be severe.

The commotion outside the hearing room meant that the press was waiting faithfully for her once again. She knew the commissioners were nervous. The pressure on them obviously meant that they would strip her of her owner's license, as had been done in the other states, Florida, California, Kentucky, and Maryland.

"It is the ruling of the board," the chairman droned as the other members scraped their chairs into place, "that there is clear evidence establishing a relationship between Mrs. Ann Carney and certain elements deemed improper and injurious to the best interests of racing. In spite of her current standing, and her explanations regarding her past activities, the report from the Federal Bureau of Investigation concerning her relationship with one Charles Del Vicario, alias Charlie Dell, and one Philip Angelo cannot be overlooked . . ."

"I want to make a statement," Annie whispered to Delansig.

"Just remember that one day you'll be coming back here for your license," the attorney advised.

The chairman continued, and Annie watched the court stenographer pressing her keys. Annie thought how every word was recorded here not so much for the record as for the press, to show the public how the state had exerted itself against evil, which here took the form of "the Countess" Carney.

"It is therefore the ruling of this board that Mrs. Ann Carney's license as an owner be rescinded, and that any horse owned by Limeteen Farm be barred from participation on all tracks in New York State." He lifted a gavel, but before he had a chance to bang it down, Delansig was on his feet.

"My client has a statement," he said and sat down.

Several board members had started to stand in anticipation of their exit. They settled back with bored impatience. Sweat stood out on their upper lips and stained the arms of their summer suits. They were probably just as hungry as she was, Annie thought.

"Gentlemen, I've done nothing wrong," she said, her Kentucky drawl sounding more pronounced than usual, a change that frequently happened in public. "I've explained my relationship with the two individuals who bother you, and I did nothing wrong with either one of them. Since the purpose of my punishment is to preserve your public image, the public and you should know that this board is being used by the FBI in its effort to intimidate me." She saw one of the commissioners glance nervously at Lyle McCracken.

Annie followed his look. McCracken gazed back at her with the same irritatingly impassive manner he had used when he requested Charlie Dell's list. Even when he explained to her and Delansig the pressure the FBI would exert if she did not cooperate, he had done so with the same passionless attitude.

"Well, I have nothing to admit to the FBI," Annie continued. "I have nothing to admit to you. You have *nothing* that you can say I've done wrong. New York was my last hope. I have fifty-eight horses in training. They deserve a chance to run. If they can't run in my country, I'll take them to Europe. I regret that you've been used like this. I regret most of all the seventy or eighty people I'll have to put out of work. But I *will* be back. You can expect me. Thank you."

As she sat down, she heard the nervous noises of throats being cleared, chairs scraped, and papers shuffled. Then, behind her, the door opened, and the waiting press outside crowded toward it. Annie turned in time to see McCracken go out. An unknown face, he was ignored by the journalists.

The crack of the gavel snapped her head around. The commissioners who had started to move away from the table stopped. Much to the annoyance of the reporters, the door was closed again. The chairman glared at Annie and lowered his voice. "I want to tell you one thing, Mrs. Carney"—he waved his hand at the court stenographer—"and it's off the record, Ethel; we're adjourned. We haven't been used by anybody, Mrs. Carney, and you and all of racing are damn lucky that they're trying to impeach the President, or you'd be getting a lot more attention than you already are. You should be grateful."

Annie started to answer, but Delansig put his hand on her arm and kept it there. The commissioners filed silently by them. The hearing room door was again opened by the two guards. The shouted questions rose in volume.

Delansig stood as he put files in his briefcase. Annie said, "I should have just given him the list."

"Once more, may I assure you that you should *not* have done that," Delansig responded patiently.

"I'd still be able to race my stable."

"And you'd be in a federal penitentiary for withholding evidence."

It was an old argument; she knew he was right. After Phil Angelo had been given immunity from prosecution in the kidnaping of Glorious Girl, he had not only testified against Fungo, but had told the FBI about the list. Delansig and Annie had denied its existence, insisting that it was a creation of an FBI informer, and that he had concocted the idea of a list to ingratiate himself while making his deal with them. Delansig had been able to convince the courts; subpoenas for the list and lie detector tests were quashed. McCracken, however, believed Phil Angelo and never gave up, even after Angelo disappeared. The FBI's strategy was to provide sufficient information to the state racing commissioners and the press to allow them to judge Mrs. Carney guilty of being associated with the underworld.

Almost every murderer on the list was dead: Vito Genovese, Frank Costello, Lucky Luciano. But Meyer Lansky and Carlo Gambino were facing jail for tax problems. A murder charge, even one for a crime thirty years old, might help them get there. McCracken had conjectured correctly that if there was such a list, Lansky and Gambino would be on it.

"Ready to exit?" Delansig asked.

Annie stood up. "We have this routine down so cold, I feel like we're a nightclub act."

Delansig smiled. "You're sure your car's down there?"

"It'll be there," Annie said and fixed her mouth into the public smile she had perfected. As Delansig nodded his recognition of it, Annie said, "Thanks again. I'd have never made it through without you."

"I'm sorry we couldn't do better than this."

"There was no better. The past has been coming at me for a long time. I'm just glad it's over." As soon as she said it, she thought of Henry and Frank, and knew she was wrong. It was not over. It was still coming.

The two guards at the door prepared for them. Delansig took out a twenty-dollar bill and asked one of them to lead the way to the elevator.

Through the mass of microphones, floodlights, flashbulbs, and television cameras, they moved slowly ahead. Annie smiled and Delansig replied to questions. The press knew the results of the hearing and wanted remorse, which Annie refused to give them. The jostling, both physical and verbal, grew more frenzied. Annie's eyes were caught by one flashbulb only inches from her face; she was blinded for an instant. Down the hall another policeman waited at the elevator. Annie kept moving, focusing on the elevator, her smile fixed rigidly.

The policemen and Delansig held back the press. The attorney shouted, "I have a statement from Mrs. Carney . . ." as the doors closed.

In the elevator, Annie watched as people came in from the lower floors. Only two seemed to recognize her and only one of those glanced back. He smiled, presuming familiarity. Annie smiled in return, not needing to alienate anyone. She had never minded being recognized around the track, but such general fame as discovery in elevators was unnerving.

The elevator reached the main floor and Annie hurried across the lobby to the revolving door. She knew the car would be there. Still, the sight of it was so reassuring, she smiled her relief. The chauffeur opened the back door. Annie stepped in and sat back in the deep, soft upholstery of the old Rolls-Royce.

"Did they do it?" Sam asked, taking her hand.

She nodded, remembering the first time she had sat in that car with Sam Cumberland, after rescuing Certainty. She winced.

"Are you all right?" he questioned solicitously as the Rolls pulled into the traffic.

"I was just remembering when I threw up in here."

At first he did not understand; then he smiled and leaned over with a kiss. "That was one of the great days." Putting his arm around her, he eased her head onto his shoulder. "And the day you win your next stakes at Belmont will be another great day. Those bastards . . ."

Annie did not respond. She had harbored anger for a long time and was exhausted by it. She needed desperately to relax, about everything. The public fight was over. Now the private ones had to begin.

"Sam, let me tell you this. Right now. I'm pregnant again."

He did not move. Still with her head on his shoulder, Annie felt completely enervated.

"Does Frank know?" Sam asked calmly.

A knot of bitterness tightened in her stomach. "If it's after one o'clock, my husband has started drinking his way across Lexington. I doubt if he'd be interested."

Drunk or sober, Frank would be devastated, and Annie knew it. However, her anger with him could no longer be contained. It overflowed into cruel fantasies of punishing him for his abandoning her and Henry for the bottle. She believed that any cruelty she inflicted on Frank was justified by his silent, torturous, steady desertion since Glorious Girl was killed.

"Will you marry me?" Sam asked.

Annie was so startled by the question that she pushed back and gaped at him. "No, of course not. We can't."

The Rolls-Royce moved into the Midtown Tunnel. The darkness was a relief. She could not believe that Sam had proposed to her. They held each other's hand.

Annie found herself thinking of Sam's wife. More of the past, she thought, always coming after her.

After her initial stay, Belinda had been an outpatient at the Menninger Clinic for more than a year. When she returned to New York, she lived at Number 10, where Sam had moved in her absence. Belinda gave up society altogether to stay at home, intending to dedicate herself to her children, though neither Barky nor Alycia had much inclination to respond to such dedication; the girl was at Sweet Briar and the boy at St. Paul's. Spending day after day in a studio she had had built on the third floor, she sculpted in clay. Pictures of her work had appeared in several glossy magazines, but she would not allow any photographs of herself. The private curator who selected art for the Cumberland Foundation assisted in selling some of Belinda's pieces. They closely resembled the elongated figures of Giacometti, a similarity so obvious that it was always noticed though rarely mentioned. Sam had spoken of her only once in the year that he and Annie had been seeing each other. Belinda had asked him if he was Henry Sumner's father. Sam admitted it. Belinda had laughed and said she'd always thought so, and never mentioned it again.

When the car sped out of the tunnel, the daylight seemed as blinding as the photographer's flashbulb had been.

"I meant what I said," Sam said.

"I know you did, and I love you for it."

"We could both get divorces."

"Not now. Good Lord, not now. Everything's so shaky, I feel that if I change anything else, it'll all come crashing down. Besides," she said, speaking very quietly, "I'm not sure you and I were ever intended to be married."

She sensed his surprise; the grip of his hand tightened. " 'Intended'? What the hell's that supposed to mean?"

She shook her head; she had no answer for him.

"Well, let me ask you this," Sam said, disengaging his hand and leaning away to look at her. "What do you plan to call the baby? Carney?"

Annie bowed her head and closed her eyes. "Yes, I suppose so."

"It's our child, Annie, just as Henry is. I hate having a son of mine being a stranger. I don't care what anyone thinks anymore. I can't tell you how many times I've wanted to tell him that I'm his father. You know he won't even look at me?"

Not at me either, she thought, but said nothing. She recalled the look on Henry's face when he had rushed back into his room after she shot Jimmy Lee. He had stared at her, horrified, and she dropped the gun to hold him as other people ran into the room. But Henry had stepped back from her. "I'm all right," he said, then looked down at the body of an uncle about whom he had never heard a word until that morning. "Where's Frank?" he asked, and when he saw Annie had no answer, he let her take him into her room and had listened while she told him about her family. He did not respond, except to ask if he could sleep at Speed's house for a while.

An hour later, Henry had looked at her again in the same devastated way when Sam arrived at Limeteen Farm to help. As she and Sam went into the library with the coroner and the state police, Annie saw her son watching from the stairs. "Where's Frank?" he demanded. She hurried across the hall and took his hand. "They're trying to find him, Henry," she said. He pulled his hand away. "What's *he* doing here?" Sam did not hear him. "Mr. Cumberland's trying to help . . ." Henry ran past her out the front door.

When Frank finally came back to Limeteen Hall, the boy could not be found. Sam was still there, as Frank saw the moment he came in. Sam left immediately, but the damage was done. Time took care of the rest. The last time Henry looked at her with such pain was when he walked into her room early one evening and said, "Why isn't Frank living here anymore, Maman?"

"He chooses not to, Henry."

"Is it because he gets drunk?"

"Where'd you hear that?"

"At school."

"I don't know all the reasons, Henry. No one at your school knows them either. I just hope he comes back."

"Please, Maman, you have to get him to come back." That was the closest he ever came to tears. After that, he watched what happened without really looking at her again. Frank began drinking earlier in the day and was not at the stable when the boy came home from school. Then Henry began to avoid him. When Annie told Henry that she and Sam Cumberland were going to see each other again, Henry said nothing.

Annie stared out the window of the Rolls-Royce. Henry was going to boarding school in the fall. When she had suggested the idea, he agreed so quickly that she was saddened, sensing his relief to be leaving his home.

Sam continued with his questions. "And how the hell can you conclude that we're not supposed to be married?" The edge in Sam's voice gave way to anger. "Haven't we done everything to stay away from each other? And nothing works. We come back together, time and again. I want to share this child, Annie. After all, it's our second, and here you are, going to Europe again in time to give birth . . ."

In the silence that followed, Annie admitted to herself that she had been careless about taking her pill each day. The idea occurred that she had become pregnant because of the unformed notion of punishing Frank for abandoning her, as well as the idea that she might have lost Henry and wanted someone to take his place. She hated both ideas, and herself because they might be true.

The limousine's air conditioning had chilled the air. "Sam, I don't know if there ever was a time for us, but it's too late now. I shot one brother, sent the other back to jail, I've been thrown out of racing, people think I'm connected to the Mafia, and my husband's drinking himself to death. I just can't run off with my lover, taking him away from his wife and having his baby."

He reached over and ran his fingers through her hair. "But you *are* going to have the baby, aren't you?"

"I thought about an abortion, but I don't want that. I want to have a baby."

"Then can't you understand my wanting to be the father? Everyone'll know it's me anyway. We haven't been particularly discreet this last year."

"Sam, would you have asked me to marry you if I weren't pregnant?"

He hesitated. "Perhaps not at this moment. But I think it's fair to say that it's been in my mind off and on for what? Sixteen years?"

She smiled. "I wish I'd known."

"Annie, you've known. You've known what's important about us better than I have." He folded his hands and smiled agreement with his own truth.

"You're my best friend and my deepest love," she said, taking one of his hands. "But I won't marry you—and I can't believe I'm saying it."

He let her hold his hand as he shifted close to her, but Annie watched his face harden into disappointment. Patches of gray hair mixed with the black on his temples, and his eyebrows were thicker, even bushy, compared with how sleek and exact they had been. His blue eyes were still alive with suggestion and possibility, although the creases of his laughter had become permanent in the corners.

"So do we pretend again," Sam asked, "the way we have with Henry? How long do you think it'll work? My God, he should know!"

"I have to tell him that I'm pregnant, Sam, and that you're the father. That's enough for the moment, don't you think? I plan to tell him about you when he's a little older, a little more mature. I can't do it now . . ."

They sat stiffly, each unwilling to let go of each other's hand for fear that the movement would be misunderstood. The Rolls-Royce sped through the heat waves and water mirages on the surface of the Long Island Expressway. Annie suddenly thought of their plans. Knowing they were all wrong, she closed her eyes and tried to think of how to change them.

During that summer season, sixteen Limeteen horses were running in the Belmont meeting. Annie had been on the backstretch every morning to watch their works and talk with their trainers. Frank Carney was not there; by mutual though unspoken agreement, he remained in Lexington "to run the farm." That responsibility, however, had steadily shifted to the farm manager and his assistants. When Frank started drinking again, Annie gradually had shipped her runners to a number of public trainers at various tracks. As far as she knew, Frank never reacted to the empty stalls when he arrived at the Limeteen barns. Sullenly, he went about his business until he left at lunchtime.

While working at Belmont and preparing for the Racing Board hearings, Annie again lived at Sam's old apartment on Central Park West, where they had begun their affair. He spent most nights with her, and in the morning often drove Annie out to the track, where Caernarvon had its own full contingent at Belmont. When the hearings started, however, Annie spent as much time in Delansig's office and the hearing room as she did at the track. Everyone on the backstretch knew what the Racing Board would do; the only question was how many races Limeteen could contest before Annie's license was rescinded. Sam suggested that when the board finally acted, they go out to Caernarvon Farm on Long Island to think of the future. Now her suitcases were in the trunk of the Rolls-Royce. The idea had sounded so right when they planned it.

"Sam, I can't go with you today. Tell Simon to turn off and drive me to La Guardia, will you please?"

"What?" he said, irritated.

"I just can't go there. I've got to get back to Limeteen, start shipping the stock, getting things planned for going to Europe . . ." They were bad excuses; both Sam and Annie knew it, and she admitted, "I have to tell Frank about the baby."

"You could call him," Sam said, barely controlling his anger.

"I'd never tell him something like that on the phone."

Sam pulled his hand from hers and pressed the button to lower the glass between them and the front seat.

"Simon," he said, in an even tone with scrupulous courtesy, "a change of plan. La Guardia Airport, please."

"Yes, sir," the chauffeur said.

Sam closed the window again. "You know, you still haven't admitted the whole reason for this sudden change of plan, but I'm damned if I'm going to sit here questioning you about it. Maybe you don't even know what it is. I suppose one thing I've learned through the years of this . . . turbulent relationship is that for you instinct is stronger than reason when it comes to a decision, and there's never any point in my trying to change your mind. As you damn well know, I'm not particularly fond of inconsistency. I don't say that's a virtue on my part; it's just that sudden change is difficult for me. Even though I'm surrounded by several piles of life's painful debris, I try to walk among them as an orderly man." Then he made fun of his high parlance. "God, that sounds like something Winnie would have said." He smiled at her quickly and went on. "I hope you've noticed a new degree of tolerance in me, but goddammit, Annie, there are limits. I really looked forward to this time together. I suppose I'm just learning the outer edges of my own adaptability, but damned if I can generate endless tolerance. Knowing myself as I do, I suspect there'll be a last straw."

"I hear the warning," Annie said.

"I hope you hear a hell of a lot more than that," he retorted. "I'll fly down in a few days, as soon as I can change every damn plan I've made for the next two weeks. Will Henry be there? Maybe that'll be the time to tell him about me."

"He's at camp. Not yet, Sam. Please."

He lifted his hand in acceptance and let it fall in his lap. They spoke about the logistics of a European move until they reached La Guardia. Sam walked her to her gate, and when her flight began to board, he kissed her longingly and said, "I'll be as good a father as you'll allow me to be."

"I know," she said, and went to the plane. She tried to read on the flight, holding a magazine in front of her but not registering a word. When she got off to change planes in Pittsburgh, she placed a call to Sam, but canceled it before it was connected. Instead, she called the farm to arrange for someone to meet her at Bluegrass Airport.

On reaching Limeteen Hall, Annie changed into her work clothes and walked down to the barns. She went into the stallion barn first and found George Oliver working with Speed on riding technique. They had put a saddle on a hay bale and hung a racing bridle on a support post. They greeted Annie with surprised enthusiasm.

Speed barely reached her shoulders; just as Henry shot up into sudden height, Speed had stopped growing. He remained five-foot-three while Henry, still growing, was an awkward, skinny five-ten. Speed never let his size bother him; it had in fact given him new purpose. He was passionately committed to becoming a jockey.

Annie told Speed and his father what the New York Racing Board had done. Limeteen would continue its breeding operation, but training would stop. The farm's runners would be either dispersed or shipped to Europe, where she planned to campaign them until her American owner's licenses were reinstated.

"We're going to miss you real bad, Mrs. Carney," Speed said sadly.

"You and your momma and daddy have to keep this place going, Speed. I'll be back, I promise you that. By then, you'll be riding in the Derby."

"I'll wait for a Limeteen horse to do that," he responded emphatically, then returned to his hay bale mount and continued to work on his form.

Left alone with the boy's father, Annie said quietly, "George, I want to tell Frank about all this before he reads it in the papers tomorrow. You have any idea where I could find him tonight?"

The black man's head bowed for an instant as he considered how to provide such information about an alcoholic white husband to a wealthy white wife. "From what I heard, he don't start off any one place, but usually he ends up at the Campbell House Bar." Again he hesitated, and Annie could see the sadness that the subject caused him. "They put him to bed there if he can't drive."

"Thanks, George."

"Yes'm."

Two hours later, Annie sat in a booth of the Campbell House Bar watching the ice cubes melt in her ginger ale. A four-piece rock band had started playing about a half hour before, and Annie thought she might go deaf. The room was the requisite dark, and the small dance floor allowed space enough for only the few businessmen and local women to gyrate around the floor, looking too old for the music and too alone despite one another.

Frank strode in and put a bill on the bar. Without saying a word, the bartender put out a jigger and a bottle of Jack Daniel's. Frank took them and started over to a corner booth. When he saw Annie, he stopped. Even in the dark, Annie could see the red rims of his eyes. He stood silently for a moment, figuring the situation.

"D'you lose your license?" he asked loudly over the music. His words were without malice or slur, but spoken more slowly than usual.

Annie nodded. He scowled, then looked at the empty booths to the left and right. After considering a moment, he sat down opposite Annie in her booth. Tearing off the bottle's plastic sealer with his fingernails, he unscrewed the top, filled the shot glass, and drank. Not cruelly, but as a joke, he held the bottle out to Annie, willing to share. She looked at the dancers.

He filled the shot glass again. "You didn't have to come in here to tell me. I'd have read about it tomorrow." He drank another jigger and poured again. "If I knew you were coming, I'd have started earlier."

"How much does it take, Frank?"

"What?" The music was too loud, even though they sat in a booth.

"How much does it take?" she repeated, louder.

"Well, I try to get the bottle down. And don't lecture me, Annie. This is my territory. I work on yours, but this is mine. Besides, I like the band."

Self-consciously, he turned to watch them as he sipped, a little more slowly, from the shot glass.

"Well, while you can still understand, I want to tell you something else. I'm going to have a baby."

His scarred hand shot out and he grabbed her shoulder. The jigger fell to the floor and bounced without breaking. He stared at her, his eyes hauntingly wide, exposing the white around his pupils. His mouth started moving, but no sound came out. As the grip on her shoulder began to hurt her, he let go, pushed himself out of the booth, grabbed the bottle, and walked straight out of the bar.

Annie started to go after him, but then, wondering what more she could say, sat down, allowing him his escape. Walking away was his choice; it had been ever since she had known him. Since Glorious Girl's death, he had deserted her, first moving out of her bed, then her house, then her life. What did he expect would happen? Then she remembered their honeymoon, between the Fantasy and the Oaks, when he told her how much he wanted to have children and she had promised him that they could start on one as soon as they took Glorious Girl back to Limeteen.

Annie slid out of the booth. Maybe if she had tried . . . what? She had tried. Frank had left her, long before she had started to see Sam again. Even so, as she walked out of the bar, accompanied by the deafening noise, she felt a deep remorse and a horrendous guilt.

Sitting in his pickup an hour later, Frank finished the bottle of Jack Daniel's. He smashed it on the dashboard and held the jagged neck up in front of his eyes. Then he threw the remains of the bottle out the window.

He got out of the truck, forgetting to close the door, and began walking. Knowing the dirt road well, he turned off where the four-board fence of Caernarvon Farm's back pasture came closest to it. As he climbed the fence, he slipped and fell, hurting his shin. He kept going, knowing the farm's routine well enough that he was sure not to bother anyone or be bothered. Walking beside the dark brown fencing, he headed toward the stallion barn.

The large sliding doors were closed, but Frank knew the

side door was always open. He also knew that a groom usually lived in a room above the barn. What he did not know was exactly what he was going to do.

From above came the sound of a radio evangelist's exhortations about hell and eternal damnation. Frank thought that the groom had probably fallen asleep with the radio playing. There were four stallions in that barn. It was one of three architectural marvels the Cumberlands had built just before Frank had been fired. He still knew by heart the pedigrees of the four stallions. He greeted each of them as he passed their stalls, and just before he reached Certainty's stall he saw, encased in glass above a row of fire extinguishers, a brightly painted red fire ax, one edge sharp for cutting, the other pointed like a pick. He stared at it as he recalled Annie standing outside the winner's circle when Certainty won the Belmont. As a jolt of hate went through him hard enough to knock him down, he heard the stallion nicker.

Frank saw a neatly coiled leather lead hanging beside the sliding stall door, as he had taught his grooms to place it. He took the lead and slid the door open. Certainty was standing in the center of his stall, his head held high for better smell and sight. Frank stepped through the hay bedding and attached the lead to the stallion's halter, then knotted the lead to one of the bars running along the top half of the stall wall. As he walked back out of the stall, Frank recalled the story of Annie's rescuing the stallion on the day she met Sam Cumberland. Studying the glass case for a simple way of opening it, he finally smashed it with his hand and lifted the ax from its holders. His hand was cut, but he felt nothing. His blood was hardly noticeable on the red ax handle.

When Frank reentered the stall, Certainty was already objecting to the restraint of the lead, snorting and tossing his head, trying to pull it loose. He saw Frank with the ax, and his instincts panicked him. He reared up on his hind legs and sent a whinny tearing through the night. Frank heard footsteps above, and the radio crashed to silence. He moved closer to the stallion, raising the ax high, moving with the animal, knowing surely how he would rear, where his front hoofs would flail, and when his head would have to lower to regain

432

momentum and balance. It was like a killing dance, Frank thought, like his with Annie, though not on a dance floor. For an instant, he remembered the stallion stopping on his way to the Travers to greet Annie. A hoof swept by Frank's ear, then Certainty's front hoofs fell to the ground just as someone yelled from the other side of the barn. Frank swung the ax, hitting the stallion's skull and splitting it wide open.

TWENTY-SIX

DURING HIS FIRST THREE YEARS in Virginia at the Colonial brick-and-pillared Seminary High School, Henry Sumner realized that the institution's true purpose was to instill tradition. The sponsors of this particular educational method were the fathers, alumni who funded the school's endowment. They wanted not only to educate their sons but, more important, to have them continue the never-to-be forgotten image of Southern radiance. To Henry, the main point of the place was to keep this glorified past alive, with its insistent masculine ideal of courtly but rigid feudalism. Therefore, each son was indoctrinated first in the nonacademic paternal model of manners, custom, dress, ambition, manhood, prejudice, and vision. S.H.S. was a place not for discovery, but for being molded to the fathers' form.

Unlike most of the other future embodiments of this legacy at the school, Henry did not have any memory of a father.

Nor did he consider himself much of a Southerner. Never truly identifying with his high school or its subliminal purpose, Henry regarded his presence there as an escape. Over the years, what had happened at Limeteen Farm became an area of memory that Henry did not enter.

He had discovered that one gained good grades at S.H.S. by memorizing facts. The columns of French or Latin verbs, algebraic equations, chemistry tables, historical dates, were valued only for themselves, separate from any meaning or application they might have. Moving from the facts to their interpretation, Henry learned, was to take an unnecessary chance. Such free thinking suggested to the venerable masters of S.H.S. a certain mental individuality and potential rebelliousness.

On the other hand, an entire year could be glorified by a completed pass, a perfect tackle, a successful run down the sidelines of Blackford Field. At S.H.S., as at any other American high school, a few brilliant seconds on the football field could exempt a person from almost all further effort, at least until the next game. At S.H.S., football, aside from being an athletic requirement, was analogous to God, the Confederacy, and, most assuredly, Father. There was a team for every student group, beginning with the Cookie Team for the youngest, who were traditionally given milk and cookies after they played. Next came the One-thirties, so named for their weight, then the JV's, the B Team, and, ultimately, the Varsity.

Members of the Varsity were an elite—the recipients of privileges and awe. During the fall, they had their own training table in the dining room, which was, according to rumor, the only table where saltpeter was not put in the food. In the gym, they had their own locker room and showers, as if their physicality deserved its own sanctuary. Henry always watched when members of the Varsity were excused early from eighth period, the afternoon study hall, for they moved away from the rest of the students with an air of security and self-assurance that he could only envy. Even if they were dumb enough to fail Sacred Studies, even if they picked their noses or emitted a personal smell, a great many of their less-than-godlike qualities were redeemed in the S.H.S. tradition of honoring the Varsity.

Henry never made a football team. He was on one squad or another because all students were on one squad or another, except for some boys who went out for cross-country and therefore were considered to be fairies. Tall and gangly, Henry was not fast or good at holding on to a ball. In a full football uniform, he saw himself as the Walt Disney armadillo in *The Three Caballeros*. Throwing himself at some runner, without fear but with bad aim, he was inevitably left sprawling in the dirt. When catching a pass, he would guide the ball into his body, only to have it bounce loudly off some part of his padding. Blocking an opposing player and driving with all his strength, he usually slipped off and was ground into the increasingly familiar dirt. With each fall, he would suffer bruises, pulled muscles, and jammed joints. Henry took such pain as he was expected to, jumping up immediately and never acknowledging discomfort with so much as a limp or grimace.

When he was little, he had developed a secret theory. He realized that he could distract himself from pain if he concentrated on its details. In his mind, he would describe and report things, trying to observe each affected component. For instance, when a hypodermic needle neared his shaking arm, he would examine its slanted point as it slid into his skin, picturing its passage in slow motion through the various levels of tissue until it punctured through the walls of the blood vessel. When the needle slipped out, he pictured each layer of skin closing so quickly that there was barely any blood. By mentally examining the elements of a particular pain and dispersing its concentration over its many parts, he made the total pain seem less.

Henry used the technique with his football injuries. Closing his eyes and concentrating, he saw the blood pulsing through the damaged cartilage of a throbbing knee. He pictured the torn capillaries, muscular ganglia, and the intricate process of healing. Because he excelled in biology, much of what he learned in class aided his visualization.

During his years at S.H.S., Henry began to regard physical pain as something of a secret partner. At football practice, having such discomfort under control meant that he could continue, not as a star, not even playing on the first two strings of that football purgatory for untalented juniors, the B Team. Nevertheless, he was a player. He could take his knocks, get up, and go on, thereby exemplifying the S.H.S. ethic of manhood.

For reasons Henry did not understand but did not question, Jim Rathbone, the star quarterback of the Varsity, had befriended him. Both juniors, they were total opposites, which was the only reason anyone could see for the friendship. One Friday afternoon, Jim was taken out of the practice scrimmage to avoid overtaxing him the day before the St. Mary's game. He trotted back toward the line of B team players, who, with arms crossed and hands in armpits, disconsolately watched the Varsity scrimmage. Jim saw Henry and jogged over to stand beside him. They watched the second-string quarterback fumble, and heard Mr. Leeny, the backfield coach, say, "Jenkins, don't stand there like an obelisk when you fumble. Fall on it!"

Jim Rathbone turned to Henry and said quietly, "The Leeny Peeny of Pizza!" Startled by the image, Henry laughed, drawing to him the attention of the subject of their joke. Henry felt a sudden constriction of his lungs as well as a nervous sweat running down his ribs.

"We don't laugh at fellow players' mistakes, Mr. Sumner," Mr. Leeny announced.

Henry would have stayed quiet, but Jim kept the joke going.

"He wasn't laughing at him, Mr. Leeny." Rathbone smiled with a combination of gall and pride. "Ol' Hank here was laughing at me."

No one had used Henry's nickname before at the school. The sound of it rang oddly through his brain.

"I see," Mr. Leeny responded. "Well, perhaps Ol' Hank will excuse you to run fifty-one-pass for us."

In the way of such boarding school transactions, the story of Jim Rathbone's put-down of Mr. Leeny spread quickly through the entire student body. By dinner, not only was the anecdote ubiquitous; even some of the masters had replaced "Henry" with "Hank."

Henry realized that the nickname was permanent, as if somehow he had been rechristened. The name itself did not matter, but hearing it recalled memories he had carefully walled up, as well as something weird that he called "the silence." It was a feeling of everything falling away around him, like being in a sound vacuum except that the air felt solid. He would begin to be drawn down toward some strange barrier, which, if he went through it, he could not survive.

The sensation had begun at home some years before he came to S.H.S. He did not remember the first time he experienced it. When he felt "the silence" start, Henry forced himself by sheer will to do an imitation of himself, not only to cover his fear in front of others, but to try in some way to stop whatever was happening. It reached a point of terror where he believed he inevitably would be drawn through the unknown barrier and never be able to get back.

Since his arrival at school, however, "the silence" had not visited him, except when he went home on vacations. Even then, it was never so bad that he was unable to fight it. The night he became "Hank" at S.H.S., however, he lay on the bunk in his dorm room after lights-out and saw himself helping Frank Carney and Speed Oliver dig Glorious Girl's grave. It was in the west pasture under the oak trees that lined the front drive. Then he remembered Certainty, and pictured the ax still in his head. He remembered saying goodbye to Frank Carney during a visit to the county jail before he was sent to the penitentiary.

"I don't care what happened, you're still my father."

"I'm not your father, Henry. You don't deserve that."

The devastated look on his face would not leave Henry's mind. Trying to erase it, he thought of the time he first saw his little sister, whom they called Helena Carney. It was in London, when he flew over from school for Christmas. Sam Cumberland was there, and Henry remembered not liking the way he held the baby. Then he thought of his uncle Fungo, who was killed the previous year in a fight at the same penitentiary where Frank was.

Henry could not relate the images one to another, or control them. The confusion was terrifying enough to thicken the air against his eardrums. He remembered his mother explaining that it was her brother lying there at her feet with blood pouring out of him. Henry felt the bunk and floor under him give way. He was falling. He jumped off his bunk and lurched down the hall to the head. There was a light on, and he stayed, pacing back and forth between the shower stalls and sinks, finally falling asleep while sitting on a toilet.

Hearing the rising bell as it began to toll over the main building, Henry forced himself back to his room and slowly dressed in his khaki pants, the disintegrating loafers, the blue button-down shirt with the meal tie already through the collar, then the daily coat, worn for all required occasions.

The two meal bells rang, and he found himself drinking his juice, unaware of how he had got to the dining room. He felt as if the air were too thick to breathe. Not knowing how he could get up from the table, he no longer felt capable of going back to his dorm to brush his teeth or make it back across the campus.

In chapel, Henry thought about his sister, whom people called "illegitimate," and then thought of Frank bellowing after he had killed Certainty. That was how they said they had found him. Bellowing. No words; just noise. Henry went to his classes, mute and unresponsive. The air thickened; he neither saw nor heard his teachers and only followed the motion of the other students as he moved from one class to another. In study hall, he desperately tried to concentrate on what was happening to him, but it was not like pain. He could not identify *feeling* anything, much less breaking it down and examining its parts. Somewhere he knew there was a torn edge that was slowly tearing further, but he could not focus on exactly where it was. He was submerging, and could neither see direction nor sense balance.

At lunch, new half-semester table assignments took effect for dining room seating. Henry found himself across a table from Jim Rathbone.

"Hey, Hank, look who's here!"

The headmaster pinged a small bell, silence descended, and grace was said. Henry closed his eyes. "Bless, O Lord, this food to our use and us to Thy service . . ."

439

The headmaster said the prayer in a monotone. Henry blinked his eyes open and saw Jim Rathbone looking at him with his finger far up his nostril, as if picking at something on the inside of his skull.

". . . through Jesus Christ our Lord. Amen."

Three hundred chairs scraped, and Henry let out a snort of laughter as Jim quickly drew his hand away and assumed innocence.

"Gentlemen," began Mr. Wilder, the master at the head of the table, "it is a pleasure having you all at my table. I demand only two things: promptness and neatness. Remember when coming to a meal that Mrs. Wilder and I have to look at you, an experience you should make as pleasant as possible. In return for these considerations, I will see to it that you get as much food as the kitchen can provide. If you fail in these gracious obligations, you'll be walking demerits until the nether regions experience a glacier. Do we understand each other, gentlemen?"

The boys liked "Eagle" Wilder's high-toned admonishments. He was the school's most popular master. Highly respected for being the track coach as well as the best teacher at S.H.S., he taught physics and biology classes that were regarded as the school's most reliable tests of intelligence. He was adored for his Southern cotton mouth, his rapier glance at stupidity or rudeness, and an undefined air of manhood.

"Mr. Sumner, would you pass the mashed potatoes, please."

Henry felt the attention of the entire table on him. As he passed the white porcelain dish with the plop of potatoes in it, he started to drift down again. "Yes, sir," he said, hoping the Eagle would move on to some subject not involving him. He knew Mr. Wilder liked him; Henry had received the highest biology grade given in the last decade, and at present was getting straight A's in physics.

"You know, Mr. Sumner," the Eagle said loud enough to include the entire table in his confession, "before I met Mrs. Wilder, I used to handicap the horses on a regular basis. Have any tips for me from Limeteen Farm?"

A pit opened. Henry felt a panic of loneliness. He had to say something.

"Ah, well, sir, I never bet. I'm more into breeding."

The use of such a word had an electric effect on the table. The Eagle looked at Henry with a warning to contain the conversation. "Perhaps I can use your expertise in biology class."

"Yes, sir."

The Eagle turned to serve his wife a portion of ham and pineapple ring, and the business of the meal began. Henry was sweating. The smell of the main dish almost made him gag.

He looked over and saw Jim Rathbone watching him with a quizzical look on his face. It broke into a smile of appreciation. Henry looked down at the pineapple ring and tried to figure out some way not to eat it. He felt trapped. He turned away only to confront the effete stare of Allen Sneed, a senior from New York, who, although a Yankee in a Southern school, was given a modicum of respect because his family was old Baltimore. He also was snidely amusing with snobbish put-downs. Henry disliked him but could do nothing at that moment, as Allen Sneed and Jim and the Eagle were gliding past him. He slid down through the thickening air, which seemed to harden around him like the transparent glue on model airplanes.

He did not remember the next few hours. He did not reconnect with what was happening around him until he felt an excruciating pain in his shoulder, and found himself lying on the practice field, holding on to Bubba Dawson's knees.

"Good tackle, Hank," Bubba said as he got up, and smacked Henry cheerfully on the same shoulder that was causing the pain.

"Mr. Sumner, are you hurt?" Mr. Leeny was standing above him. Jim Rathbone was there, too.

Henry nodded. He did not dare talk because he might laugh. He was no longer falling. He could feel the calcium pumping, flushing over the shoulder, the tiny particles clinging to bone. The faces looking at him were still, no longer gliding away. He became aware of the ground under him, solid, and the smell of the dirt and torn grass. He breathed in deeply, which caused the pain to grate against itself. He smiled again, feeling an edge of bone move over torn nerve endings, like the pictures he had seen in *Scientific American* of underwater telephone cables with myriad individual wires that miraculously search for their match across a break.

"Hey, Hank, what are you smiling at?" a player asked. "You hurt or what?"

"It's *Henry,* goddammit!" he yelled, but he was still smiling.

Overlooking his peculiar behavior, they helped him to stand up. The pain hammered at him as Mr. Leeny and the Varsity manager walked him across the field to the infirmary. By the time the school nurse had cut off his jersey and pads with surgical scissors, he could see incredible colors, which the pain pumped behind his eyes with each heartbeat. His vision seemed to filter through alternating spectrums that changed with each pulse, like a shaken kaleidoscope. By the time the school doctor arrived, Henry was completely unaware of pain. And somehow his falling through "the silence" had stopped.

What turned out to be a dislocated shoulder kept Henry out of football the rest of the season. He continued to go to practice, to help the manager, and, as his shoulder improved, to warm up Jim Rathbone's passing arm. Henry became adept at catching the ball with one arm and flipping it back to the star quarterback. As expected, Jim led the Varsity to triumph at homecoming over the school's arch rival, Seabury Prep, and Henry shared vicariously in his friend's glory.

Jim never called him Hank again, and several others also avoided using the nickname. Nevertheless, he was always aware of the images of Limeteen Farm hovering in his memory. He fought them off, spending many nights pacing in the head while studying for exams.

Henry and Jim often worked off their demerits together, either by walking four times around the quarter-mile road that circled the main buildings of the school or by doing some small jobs around a master's house for fifteen minutes a demerit. Neither Jim nor Henry collected a great many demerits, but it was fairly easy to pick up five over a week by talking in study hall or by neglecting to wear a necktie "up" at the Eagle's table. When he "stuck" them, the Eagle had Henry and Jim cut firewood and kindling at his house. This was a highly prized method of working off demerits, as Mrs. Wilder generally provided hot chocolate and pecan rolls when the work was done.

A large tree had been cut down near the Wilder house several years before, leaving a perfect knee-high stump to use as a chopping block. There was a two-man saw, an ax, and a hatchet. Henry and Jim started as a team on the saw; then each would break down the cut logs. At first, Henry worked on kindling with the hatchet until his arm improved. After that he started with the ax. He liked the feel of swinging the ax, felt how completely it concentrated all his kinetic energy into one narrow edge of steel. With each cut, the blade sank through the wood and made chips of it. He and Jim often had a contest to cut through a log with the fewest strokes. Henry usually won, not because of superior strength, but because his aim and control were more exact. Doing anything physical better than Jim Rathbone was something to be proud of, and Henry took pride in the accomplishment.

During the last two weeks of the quarter through the exam period, winter athletics began on a "voluntary" basis. In the past, Henry had gone out for winter track, for no other reason than that he could at least run, although he had not won races. Worried about French, English history, dates, masculine and feminine nouns, names, irregular verbs, he did not even think of starting track practice until after exams and Christmas vacation. But a week before exams started, the Eagle, who coached winter track, walked up to him in the hall of the main building.

"Well, Mr. Sumner, may I presume that you're coming out for winter track?"

"Yes, sir, I thought I would."

"Fine." He gave the boy a challenging look. "I realized for the first time the other day that you're a miler. I should have seen it before, but obviously I was blinded by your talents in physics class. I want to see you out there this afternoon. Rasmussen's graduating this year. Perhaps there's a future for you at the distance—Speedball." He gave a smile of daring, then moved quickly across the hall to the faculty lounge.

Speedball!

Henry stared after Mr. Wilder, the shared joke of the name

filling him with anticipation. He was amazed that anyone actually wanted him to do something athletic. The Eagle was famous for naming S.H.S. track stars. Everyone at the school had heard of "Swifty" Logan, the holder of the school record in the hundred-yard dash, who had gone on to run in the Olympics. But the mile?

Running the mile at S.H.S. was looked on as something to be done by a stoic weirdo. Jordan Rasmussen, the current miler on the track team, was perfectly cast. A notorious "conch," he did nothing but study and was accused of being strange about dogs. Henry doubted that there would be much competition for the miler's place on the team, and thought that just by running a lot he could get in shape enough to justify the Eagle's apparent confidence.

As he went through his classes that morning, Henry became more excited. He saw himself running around the winter track, the old wooden banked oval set up on one of the practice fields during the time the new indoor field house was under construction. He could feel his muscles leaning into turns, his legs reaching out and easing over the distance.

And "Speedball." What would it mean? It certainly seemed to be something special between him and the Eagle. Wondering if Mr. Wilder had heard about the Hank-Henry story, he knew that if the Eagle used "Speedball" in front of other students, they would never use "Hank" again! Speedball Sumner! He wanted it. It was his name.

At lunch he listened to grace, smiling at what he thought Jim Rathbone, across the table, would say when he heard "Speedball" for the first time. He ate the Spanish rice and hot dogs, containing as best he could his growing excitement. Jim caught his eye and let him know he thought he was acting a little weird. Henry smiled and looked idly away.

"You know, *Hank,*" Allen Sneed said with a contemptuous emphasis on the name, "I learned something interesting about you when I was home last weekend." His tone was menacing, although his voice was loud enough only for the end of the table to hear.

"And you just couldn't wait to tell it, could you, Sneed?" Henry replied, knowing that there was no defense against Allen Sneed's cruel observations, except to show that they had no effect.

"Oh, I *could* wait, but why should I? See, my family knows all the Sumners. They grew up together. As a matter of fact, your father and my father played backgammon at the Racquet Club for years."

"Long game," Henry said. The other students at the table laughed, particularly Jim Rathbone.

The laughter stung Allen Sneed, whose eyes narrowed as he continued. "Except that from what a lot of the Sumner family says, your father wasn't really your father. They seem to suspect that it's Samuel Cumberland of *the* Cumberlands." He looked around the end of the table to see the other boys' reactions.

"Shut up, Sneed!" Jim Rathbone said.

Allen Sneed ignored him. "Winton Sumner, your 'father,' thought the same, apparently. They say that's why he killed himself."

Lurching across the table, Henry grabbed Allen Sneed by his necktie and started slugging him. Sneed pulled back hard, and the two of them fell to the floor, along with plates, glasses, and utensils, which crashed around them.

Henry was still slugging when he felt himself pulled off, stood up, and held firmly by Jim Rathbone. The Eagle was picking up Allen Sneed, who seemed more concerned with the stains on his shirt than with anything else. The entire dining room was silent.

"You have twenty demerits each, gentlemen," The Eagle said, in a deadly calm voice. "You're both excused to go to your dorm and clean up."

Henry realized he could barely breathe and went immediately to the nearest door, which led outside. When he heard someone following him, he looked back and saw that Jim Rathbone had walked out with him.

"He's a shit, Henry," Jim said.

They walked quickly toward Henry's dorm, saying nothing more until they reached the door. Henry stopped and stared at it.

"You okay?" Jim asked.

445

Henry nodded, and with sudden urgency wanted to tell him about "Speedball." He hesitated, because it would be better if Jim and everyone else just heard about it. The Eagle would use it at practice, the other track team guys would hear it, and it would spread all over the school.

"Listen," Jim said, "I'm going to play B-ball this afternoon." He pantomimed dribbling and then a hook shot. "Fsh-shew! Two big ones. Why don't you come out with me? Jesus, you're studying too hard. Your eyes look kind of weird."

Henry tried to respond casually. "The Eagle asked me to come out to track practice. For the mile. I might go on out there."

"He asked you? Hey, that's great. But shit, the mile?" He smiled. Henry shrugged acceptance of how crazy it was, and forced a return of the smile.

Jim watched him a moment. "Don't worry about what Sneed said," he offered. "He's prime asshole and everyone knows it." Henry stretched his smile wider, turned, and went into the dorm.

There was an hour to kill before practice. Henry stood in his room, desperately concentrating on "Speedball." Abruptly, he decided to write a letter to London, telling Maman that he was cramming hard for exams, trying to hold down the demerits, looking forward to Christmas vacation and seeing her in two weeks. At the very end, he could not resist writing, "By the way, they've begun calling me Speedball around here. I'm going to run the mile. All my love, Henry." As he sealed the letter, tears fell on the envelope, blotting the address. Holding the letter in front of him, he said angrily, "How many fathers . . . how many lies . . . ?" Then slowly he tore the letter in two and threw it away.

As he hurried down to the gym, large flakes of snow began to fall and melt on the ground. He changed and jogged from the locker room out to the field. The other members of the team were gathered at one side of the black wooden track. When their eyes met his, Henry saw that they all knew of Sneed's accusation. Their gray sweat clothes matched the cold color of the sky. As they did their warm-up calisthenics, the snow thickened on the playing field around them. Mr. Wilder wore his ancient dark brown overcoat, a rumpled tweed hat, and galoshes. He walked among his team and watched them stretch muscles. As he passed Henry, he nodded. Henry made no show of noticing, but anticipation clutched at him as he wondered when the Eagle would give him his name.

He had to keep moving. As other workouts were run, Henry jogged on the outer edges of the board track, getting used to the banked turns, keeping a sweat going, feeling the soles of his smooth black track shoes meet the damp wood firmly like a handshake.

Then he heard the Eagle call out, "All right now, I want the distance runners over here."

Henry jogged over and joined a group of four other runners. All were seniors, except Henry and a gangly freshman who looked like Ichabod Crane.

"All right, Mr. Rasmussen," the Eagle said to his current miler, "take them around for a half, and take it easy. This is shin-splint weather and the boards are wet."

A half mile on the small wooden track took five laps. Without a start of any kind, Jordan Rasmussen turned and began running in long, easy strides. Henry started after him with the others, the suddenness causing his heart to pound. He hit the first banked turn and felt the now familiar smack against his shoes. Picking up his pace, he moved closer to Rasmussen on the straightaway. The other runners were bunched around him, each trying to find a position. It was not a race, but all of them were racing.

At the end of the first lap, Henry felt fine. As he passed by Mr. Wilder, he thought he saw him smile again. Henry sprinted ahead and passed a runner just going into the turn, the freshman who looked like Ichabod Crane. Henry kept his eyes ahead. There was only one runner between him and Jordan Rasmussen. The wood under him seemed to spring him forward each time his foot hit.

As he sailed by Mr. Wilder and moved into the third lap, Henry figured he would overtake the runner ahead on the next straightaway. Coming out of the turn, however, something grabbed in his stomach. In that instant, he knew he would throw up. It surprised him and made him angry. Two more laps; that was all. He heard breathing behind, then beside him, and saw the skinny freshman begin to pass him on the straightaway. Henry felt an unfamiliar sweat break out on his scalp and under his arms. Then he heard Mr. Wilder across the track.

"Come on, Speedball, stretch it out!"

Henry gagged, but held it down, and forced his feet to move faster against the track, which suddenly felt like soft sand. He could hear his heart beating in his ears, as well as some of the students laughing and yelling, "Speedball! Hey, Speedball! Come on, Speedball!"

He tried to make his legs go on, but they hardened. He dry-gagged again and knew it was going to come up the next time. He did not want the mess on the track, so he ran off the top of the banked turn and fell down into the snow.

He tried to throw up quietly, and heard the others on the track team yelling, "Speedball! Hey, come on, Speedball!" When he was done, Henry jumped back up on the track to finish the race, but the other runners were just coming into the turn of their final lap. He had to stay out of their way. As they went by, he heard someone yell, "You got him, Speedball!" The freshman who looked like Ichabod Crane was catching up to Jordan Rasmussen.

Henry watched the snow fall. He began to fall down through the white covering. The clear airplane glue flowed around him and hardened more quickly than usual, because of the cold, he figured.

"You all right, son?" The Eagle was standing on the track next to him. Henry looked through the snow and saw Jordan Rasmussen slapping the freshman on the back. "You'd better go on in and take a shower," Mr. Wilder said and smiled regretfully, acknowledging what had happened to the name. Henry turned and jogged back through the snow to the gym. In the basement locker room, he could hear the pounding of basketball squads above him, running from one end of the gym floor to the other, Jim Rathbone probably laughing as he sank another for a big two. Henry realized the breadth of his mother's lie, which was his whole life, and felt everything under him begin to collapse. Gasping for breath, he felt as if he would panic and start screaming, as Frank had done.

With a will he did not know he had, he dressed himself and walked over to the Eagle's house. He went around to the back and pulled the ax out of the chopping stump. Knowing he was about to scream, he pushed the log off the chopping stump, stretched his leg in its place, and raised the ax high above his head. He felt his strength move up to the sharp edge, and sank it just where he had aimed on his shinbone two inches above the ankle. Before he felt anything, he heard the crack of the bone. Certainty's skull had probably sounded the same. Then the pain hit him and he fell backward onto the ground. Feeling the wet on his leg, he turned his head to see blood spreading out through the snow.

The door slammed. "Willie, go next door and get help!"

"What's the matter with *him?*"

"Shut your mouth, Willie, and *get help!*" There was terrible pain as Henry felt something being tied around his leg. He saw Mrs. Wilder and smiled.

At the very edges of the cut, Henry knew that the torn capillaries were already searching for each other. The coagulation of the blood had begun. The break was a simple one; he knew it would heal well. He hadn't hit as hard as Frank did, but she had done more damage to Frank. The blood that flowed over the raw bone and torn skin—probably an artery was cut as well—was confronting the incoming germs, and white cells were battling them off. The bone had split cleanly, and the flow of blood was depositing a soft mush of calcium so that when it was set, the join would begin immediately. Until then, the battle between blood and infection would rage, and pain would occupy every synapse of the brain as it sent complex patterns of urgency throughout the nervous system. Concentrating, Henry followed an impulse from the shinbone up to the brain, through it, then down the system to the nerves, which seemed to be responding with a musical rhythm this time rather than with colors. He closed his eyes as the door slammed again, and he heard people start yelling.

Then he could not hear them or see them. Along with the pain, he felt something new and strange passing through his

449

body. It was hate, and it cleared his mind. He knew that he would not take his exams, that he would leave S.H.S., that he would not go to London for Christmas. He would go to see Frank Carney in the penitentiary. Frank would understand what he had done, and would tell him the truth.

PART THREE

Base Blood

1980–1990

TWENTY-SEVEN

LATE IN 1980, California appeared to be the first state willing to consider the return of Annie's owner's license. When Delansig called her in London to tell her of the possibility, she was delighted and held no grudge. The process might take a year or two, but it was becoming increasingly important to bring Limeteen's runners back to the United States as soon as possible. Besides, being in California would help with other, more personal plans.

The detectives Annie had hired when Henry disappeared from S.H.S. eventually located him. He was living in a trailer on a small ranch south of San Francisco, where he groomed horses. Once discovered, he informed the detectives that he had nothing to say to his mother and requested that she leave him alone. Annie's subsequent letters to her son went unanswered. On the occasion of her surprise visit to the ranch, Henry saw her get out of her car and he vanished.

Annie had no delusions that her eventual presence in California or Limeteen's return to America would draw Henry back into a close relationship with her. She believed, however, that she might be able at least to talk with him. The straw she held to was their mutual affection for Speed Oliver.

During Annie's European stay, the young black man remained at Limeteen. There, he had gained a reputation for exercising horses; it spread throughout the Bluegrass as many owners, breeders, and trainers brought their horses over to use Limeteen's training track. Speed had matured into a hundred and twelve pounds of nimble strength with lightning coordination on his five-foot-three-inch frame. When Annie returned to Limeteen on one of her many visits, Speed asked her to sponsor him as an apprentice jockey when Limeteen returned to the American tracks. She agreed immediately. It was in their subsequent conversations that Speed revealed he had received several letters from Henry. Perhaps the bonds of their friendship would at least get mother and son to the same race track. It was a long shot, but Annie had played plenty of those.

Limeteen's good showing in Europe had been expensive and difficult. Buying an Irish stud farm in County Limerick, running the Haras de la Brise in France, and purchasing yearlings and broodmares with worthy pedigrees had cost Annie much of her remaining inheritance. Nevertheless, she bred her best to Europe's best, and her hopes were often rewarded. With the guidance of a happily married and successful Bernard Dolby in England and a still vibrant Madame Pichon in France, Annie campaigned Limeteen's yellow and white silks at all the preeminent meetings of Europe. She took her place in the winner's circle at Goodwood, Ascot, Doncaster, the Curragh, Chantilly, Deauville, and Longchamp as she waited impatiently to return to race tracks in the United States.

Yet despite winning her purses and selling her stallion seasons, or nominations, as they were called in England, the costs of running Limeteen's three farms in Lexington, County Limerick, and Normandy rose precipitously, even faster than the rising worth of her bloodstock. A value was creeping into the thoroughbred business, a value based less on racing horses and more on speculation, taxes, and investment strategy. There was a new kind of ego involved. Instead of "My horse can beat your horse," the contest was becoming "I have more money than you have." After paying an enormous sum to buy and thus establish a horse's worth, an owner would only have to let it run enough to establish promise, not greatness.

At the end of the seventies, Annie had an experience with "the new money men" that she never forgot. Quite suddenly, the price of yearlings at the Newmarket and Dublin yearling sales became astonishingly inflated. At a Goff's sale one fall, Annie bid on a filly whose pedigree included Nearco and Hyperion. Annie intended to race her and, if she went well, to breed her to Northern Dancer, thus taking advantage of the similar progenitors. Limeteen had won a number of Irish races at the Curragh, so Annie was regarded as an interesting foreigner who had bought wisely for her Irish stud farm. Because Irish auctions were less pretentious and friendlier than their British or American counterparts, talk around the auction pit seldom let business inhibit humor or opinion.

Annie's opening bid for the filly was a strong one, and she stayed in as the amount climbed beyond 100,000 Irish guineas. She thought she had won the filly at 115,000, but just as the hammer was about to fall, two sets of new bidders began bidding against each other. In seconds, Annie was facing a price of 225,000 Irish guineas for the filly.

"Who'm I bidding against?" she whispered to a trainer sitting next to her.

The man peered around the hall, his eyes barely showing beneath the visor of his cap.

"The Gangsters and the Arabs. You might want to say good-bye to that filly."

As he spoke the words, the bidding passed 300,000. Annie said goodbye in a stunned silence.

"Sangster's Gangsters" was a journalistic sobriquet for a group of experts in conformation, pedigree, and money. Robert Sangster, the heir to an immense British soccer pool fortune, gathered them around him in an effort to corner the Northern Dancer line. The Gangsters included Vincent O'Brien, a Sangster in-law and the trainer of six previous Epsom Derby winners, as well as Stavros Niarchos, the Greek shipping magnate and Sangster's former rival at such auctions.

Across the Goff's pavilion Annie saw a row of Arab men dressed in casual Western clothes. They barely reacted to the numbers, but ended winning the bid. Annie had never met them and was not sure which family it was. There were several oil-rich British-educated sheikhs who came into the auction market at the same time. The most visible were the four sons of Sheikh Rashid al-Maktoum of Dubai, one of the Persian Gulf city-states that had joined with its neighbors to form the United Arab Emirates. Each of the brothers from Dubai was rumored to have a personal income of one million tax-free dollars per week. With the guidance of their British advisers, the brothers also became intrigued with the Northern Dancer line and joined the accompanying money contest with Robert Sangster. As a result, in the 1981 summer sales at Lexington and Saratoga, the Arabs spent $10.7 million on twenty-seven yearlings. One of them, a Northern Dancer colt that Sheikh Mohammed bought as a gift for his elder brother, Sheikh Maktoum, was hammered down for $3.3 million. At the same sales, Sangster bought two Northern Dancer colts, one for $2.9 million, the other for $3.5 million.

Each year of her European exile, Annie flew back with her daughter, Helena, to meet Sam for the summer sales in the United States. She became convinced that the Northern Dancer fixation was a fad. She knew several American breeders with mares worthy of Northern Dancer in his declining years at stud who jittered with anticipation of the Sangster-Arab bidding duel. No one knew how long it would last, but the breeders were frantic to get in on it. Everyone seemed to overlook the fact that Northern Dancer's offspring excelled only in Europe on grass. The whole thoroughbred world was affected as a few rich men inflated prices beyond exorbitance. To them, the race track became a useful advertising tool for selling their breeding rights. The only real issue at stake was how few races a horse had to run to justify his pedigree, his price, and his standing as a sire.

When Annie attended the select sales again in the summer of 1982, the formalities of her California owner's license were being completed. The previous month, two Northern Dancer grandsons owned by Mr. Sangster had won between them the Irish, English, and French Derbies, thus proving his Northern Dancer theories and setting in motion a frenzy of high bidding, first at the Keeneland and Fasig-Tipton auctions in Lexington, then a month later at Saratoga. Mr. Sangster paid, among his other purchases, $4.25 million for another Northern Dancer grandson. The brothers from Dubai arrived at each auction in a private Boeing-747 with their advisers and an occasional secondary British aristocrat who came along for the free ride. The brothers spent almost $30 million for sixty-one yearlings.

In the auction pavilion at Saratoga, a reporter sat down behind Annie one day. He commented with a feigned interest on the return of her license and continued with a question about Sam and her. Annie cut him off, saying, "You know, this summer there are twenty untried colts and fillies at one year of age selling for more than a million dollars each. That's really frightening. So why don't you settle for a horse story?"

The reporter, undaunted, whispered back over her chair. "Tell me what's so frightening about that? The breeders love it."

"Sure they do, but what's it doing for the two-dollar handicapper? Because without them, all these high prices are nothing but an orgy for eunuchs."

The reporter guffawed. "Can I quote you, Countess?"

"Sure," Annie said. "It'll probably help my reputation. But think about what I'm saying. Two dollars buys a small dream at the track. That's why people come. But we're losing them, to Atlantic City, to state lotteries."

The reporter countered, "Yearly attendance figures say that horse racing still draws the highest number of paid admissions of any professional sport."

Annie replied fast. "Track numbers are a well-known lie. Those totals describe the same people who come over and over again. The king of this sport of kings is the two-dollar bettor, and he wants to see good horses run. But when the prices get this high, no owner will keep such expensive horses on the track any longer than he has to. When the good horses stop coming, why should the public show up? And that, my friend, is frightening."

The next day, the interview appeared in the *New York Post*, pointedly on the same page as an interview with Sam Cumberland. Elsewhere in the paper, a gossip column synopsized their "friendship." Sam had been as businesslike in his column as Annie, obviously dodging the personal, as she had done. A famous owner and breeder with long-standing prominence in the Jockey Club, he blamed the attendance problem on the tracks themselves. In the seventies, track owners had fought against television broadcasts of racing cards. "At the time," Sam was quoted, "they believed that if people could watch the races in their living rooms, they'd simply telephone their bookies, and the tracks would lose attendance and their essential on-track bets. The logic was badly skewed; the public watched television and became addicted to football, tennis, baseball, basketball, even bowling! As a result, they bought out tickets to most spectator sports and almost forgot about horse racing."

Sam described how he had traveled throughout the United States to any group that would give him a hearing on the subject of getting television back to the tracks. He explained that in order to get networks interested, racing had to be made important, and the fastest way to do that was with money. Beyond the three Triple Crown Races in the spring, there had to be more newsworthy events. The first million-dollar race, the Arlington Million at Arlington Park in Chicago, in 1981, had been a great success. Therefore, Sam joined with the breeders who thrashed out the concept for a ten-million-dollar race day, titled the Breeders' Cup. Meant to be the Super Bowl and World Series of racing, Sam promoted it outrageously for the remainder of his interview, admitting candidly that such a day of racing, scheduled for 1984, was aimed at securing four hours of prime-time television.

Annie had spent eight years racing in Europe. Returning to America much poorer, she undertook racing again at American tracks with anticipation, though it was primarily a financial necessity. The Internal Revenue Service had a strict rule: a stable had to make a profit for two out of every seven years. If it did not, the farm operation would be taxed as a personal capital gains hobby rather than at corporate business levels. Limeteen needed a profitable season; if Annie did not win on the track, she would have to sell some of her prized blood-stock to make a profit.

Attending the Lexington and Saratoga yearling sales, she tried to pick up some of what Sangster and the sheikhs over-looked. For the first time, however, she and Delansig had to go to the banks for cash, using Limeteen as collateral. It was unfamiliar and worrisome. Several days before her license was officially restored, she flew to California with her daughter, any gratification about returning tinged with the hard neces-sity of success.

As she stood at the rail of Del Mar's backstretch, Annie felt the warm sea breeze from the Pacific and the heavy moisture of the early morning mist.

"Mummy, I'm tired," Helena said, leaning against her at the rail.

"You said you wanted to come, Helena. You can go back and sleep in the car if you want."

The girl shook her head, causing her black curls to spring comically around her face as her dark blue eyes scanned others who stood at the rail watching the early morning works. Annie smiled, knowing her daughter had come to look for movie stars. Somewhere Helena had heard that the old track at-tracted many of Hollywood's most famous faces to its Spanish mission–style clubhouse, and that many were owners who came to watch their horses train, just as it had been when Bing Crosby was one of the owners and promoted it. For her daugh-ter's sake, Annie hoped for a recognizable presence. Helena Carney had stood at the rail of most European tracks in her seven years and seemed to have grown bored by it, or so Annie surmised.

"Mummy, how long are we going to stay?"

"We'll leave as soon as all our horses have worked," Annie said, noticing again her daughter's occasional British accent, gained from many weekends spent at the Dolby castle in War-wickshire.

Helena sighed, shifted her weight from one leg to the

other, crossed her arms, and rolled her eyes with exasperation. When she saw her mother watching her display and smiling at her performance, she laughed and put her arms around Annie's waist. "I love you, Mummy," she said, smiling up at her mother, "and I don't really *need* a daddy."

Helena had said the same thing several years before when Annie had explained as best she could that Carney was the girl's name, but Sam Cumberland was really her father. Oddly, the line had become a running joke, an automatic refrain in a moment of affection.

The girl had seen Sam regularly over the years in England when he visited Annie. Helena asked him any question that occurred to her in her attempt to understand their unique circumstance and to charm him into explaining their bond. At one point she asked brightly, "Mummy, am I a bastard?" with wide-eyed hope. With Sam, Helena was even more precocious, asking him, "Then why, if you love Mummy and have me, are you married to someone else?"

Sam worked hard at avoiding too deep an emotional connection, but failed; he adored Helena. He tried to describe to her his obligations to his wife and other children, to which Helena responded with what was to her an obvious solution: "Why don't you kill them?" Such questions brought out some tortuous explanations that ended in either distraction or hilarity. Helena knew she had a brother but did not speak of him, because she noticed how sad it made her mother. As to Carney, it was simply the name of a man her mother had divorced.

"Look, Mummy, here comes Speed!" Helena said with enthusiasm as the young rider breezed by on a three-year-old colt that leaned into the turn and changed leads nicely. Speed crouched in the saddle, keeping the colt firmly under control. Speed had traveled with the Limeteen horses when they were shipped to California. He was exercising them every morning, and that afternoon he was riding in his first race as an apprentice jockey, one of fifteen races Annie hoped to enter in the few weeks before Del Mar's season ended and the Limeteen horses were shipped to Santa Anita. Speed's maiden was an allowance race for fillies with a five-thousand-dollar added purse. Annie needed every penny of it.

After galloping at a two-minute lick, Speed walked his colt down and came toward Annie and Helena.

"Morning, Mrs. Carney. Hi, Helena," he called, pulling the horse up in front of them.

Helena lurched awkwardly against Annie and demurely said, "Hello"; then she hurried away to the car.

"I think she's a little shy, Speed," Annie said, again amazed that the girl was so at ease with grown-ups and so ill at ease with anyone around twenty or younger.

"That's all right, ma'am. We'll be friends." He smiled and patted his colt.

"How is he?"

"At home in the going, ready as I am," he said with confidence.

"I know you are. And Speed, I have to admit something to you. I'm using you as bait."

For a moment, the rider was puzzled, but then he understood. "You mean for Hank?"

"I haven't seen him in a long time. I'm hoping he'll show up to watch you win. Maybe not today, but sometime while we're out here."

"If he does," Speed said, smiling even more at her assumption of his winning, "I'll drag him right over to you. Every boy ought to talk to his momma."

As Speed guided his colt away toward the gap, Annie felt a jolt of anxiety. What if Henry did come? Then she thought about the possibility of his not coming at all, and went to look for Helena.

They drove back to their beachfront apartment at the La Jolla Beach and Tennis Club. Helena took a tennis lesson while Annie had a massage. She tried to nap, but was unable to sleep. That afternoon, she was relieved that Helena chose to stay on the beach with Bridey, the young Irishwoman who traveled with them. Annie changed into a silk print dress and comfortable pumps. The winner's circle was not as much on her mind as the possible attention of the press to her past. She arrived at Del Mar too early and drove twenty miles past the track on the freeway to kill time. She was in her box in the stucco grandstand an hour before the first race, went to the Turf Club, ordered a huge lunch, then could not eat it. She stared at old photographs on the walls of Crosby, Durante, Cantor, Jolson, Bob Hope, Betty Grable, Paulette Goddard, and the clock. She wished Sam were there, then remembered that Caernarvon had three runners that afternoon at Saratoga.

Through the plate glass windows, she watched the Del Mar Special express train arrive from Los Angeles. The passengers hurried through the swaying palm trees as Crosby's recorded voice warbled the track's theme song over the loudspeaker: ". . . where the surf meets the turf at Del Mar." Annie returned to her box. She absently studied her *Form,* reading over the past performance charts of the race in which a Limeteen runner would start on an American track for the first time in more than eight years.

"Hello, Ann."

Not recognizing the female voice, Annie expected a stranger, since no one who knew her called her Ann. The woman standing at the entrance to her box wore a bright red-flowered muu-muu over her bulk. Her wispy blond hair was unstyled, cut short, and her face seemed to swim on a surface of flesh. The features were familiar, although Annie could not place them. Nevertheless, she stood up and smiled a greeting.

"Belinda Cumberland," the woman said, then watched Annie's attempt to cover her shock. "Yes, I know, there's enough in here for two of me." She held out her dress and gave a quick bitter smile, as if sick of saying the line. In spite of her obvious tension, her soft drawl had not changed.

"Come sit down, Belinda," Annie offered, and together they took chairs. Staring out on the empty track, they watched the tractors go by in staggered formation, furrowing the surface.

"I drove down to see Sam," Belinda said without any pretense of excuse. "I read about your big day, and I thought he'd be here with you."

"Caernarvon's pretty busy at Saratoga," Annie replied as a way of eluding the subject of Sam.

"As always," Belinda answered with an edge that Annie chose to overlook.

"What are you doing in California?" Annie asked.

Belinda looked at Annie, but Annie kept her eyes on the lead tractor as she sensed Belinda's eyes going over her.

"Originally," Belinda said, "I came out here to go to the Golden Door, but after four weeks, I flunked out." A sudden cackle of laughter made Annie turn to look at Belinda as the manic grin on her bloated face faded away. "I've been up at Esalen for the past six months."

"Is Esalen another spa?" Annie asked.

Belinda threw back her head and laughed again, so piercingly that people in neighboring boxes turned to look. "Exactly! Another spa! But this one they say gets rid of the fat in your brain. The problem is, it leaves my head and goes elsewhere; as a matter of fact, just about anywhere." She shifted in her chair but did not seem to find a comfortable position.

"How's the sculpture going?" Annie asked, eager to change the subject.

"Don't patronize me, Ann!" Belinda shot back.

Annie met her look. "Belinda, I wouldn't dare."

The two women studied each other briefly. When the trumpeter blew the call to the post, they turned with relief to watch the horses come onto the track.

"All that sculpture was so much horseshit; that's what Sam always says: horseshit." Belinda leaned forward and propped her arms on the rail of the box for support. "Well, it was. All that goddamn *clay* was just some very expensive insulation between me and the rest of my life." She snorted a laugh. "Those figures got skinnier and skinnier as I got fatter and fatter. Oh, they *love* that at Esalen! Where's your daughter?"

The question came with no transition and no apparent anger. "She's on the beach," Annie said. "She's not too interested in the track."

"Ha! Just like my little darlin's! Neither one of them can *stand* horses. Barky still breaks out in hives and sneezing when he gets near one, and I suppose Alycia hates them because I made her ride so much when she was . . ." She looked at Annie again and smiled conspiratorially. "Well, here we are,

Sam Cumberland's two broodmares, talking about the foals we threw. Isn't that sweet?''

At that moment, Annie saw Henry coming down the aisle toward the box. She recognized his walk more than his face. He was wearing boots, jeans, an open shirt, and an old linen jacket. His sandy hair was cut short and parted near the middle, so that wings of it fell evenly on his forehead. As he approached, Annie saw that he was wearing circular wire-rimmed glasses, which she had never seen on him. The glasses could not hide the startling light blue eyes of his father.

"Hello, Mother," he said, a blank smile on his face.

Belinda gasped. "What?"

"Hello, Henry," Annie said, trying to stay calm, more aware of the strange word he had called her than anything else. "This is Belinda Cumberland."

Henry took a quick breath, turned to look at the other woman, and smiled wryly. "No kidding," he said and held out his hand.

Belinda looked down at it but did not take it. "I don't think I'll deal with this today." She said it precisely and coolly.

"Belinda . . ." Annie started.

"You could've warned me he was coming, Ann!"

"I didn't know."

"I'll bet!"

"She's right, Mrs. Cumberland," Henry interjected softly. "She hasn't heard from me for five or six years."

"Dear God, we're all crazy!" Belinda said pushing past Henry and hurrying down the aisle of boxes.

"Henry, please don't leave," Annie said, moving into the aisle. "I'll be back."

"Oh, I'll be here," he said, almost mocking.

As Annie followed Belinda through the crowd, which was pressing forward to view the first race, she tried not to think about the word "Mother." She caught up with Belinda outside by the paddock, now deserted before post time.

"Belinda, wait a minute." Reaching out, Annie took hold of her arm.

"Let go of me, you goddamm whore!" Belinda blurted as she stopped and turned. As soon as she said it, her eyes and mouth opened in shock, spreading her face wide. "I didn't mean that. Dear God, I didn't mean that."

"I know you didn't," Annie said quickly. "Belinda, can't you stay?"

"No, no, no, honey, I couldn't possibly do that," she said in a little-girl singsong. "You've got your big *race* and your *son* . . . and my *husband.*" She turned and stared up into the bright sun. She seemed to have forgotten her anger. "Tell him I said hello, or goodbye, or whatever . . . and don't you dare try to do anything for me, hear?"

Annie heard the familiar Southern plantation tone of master to white trash, and realized she could do nothing more. Belinda started walking toward the main gate, patting what was left of her hair, hauling her weight with each step. Annie turned back to the stands as the crowd noises began to build in reaction to the race.

As she started into the clubhouse, she had to fight her way through the crowd hurrying out to the paddock, to the betting windows, or to the food stands. She thought of Henry learning to ride at the Haras de la Poire and could not connect the memory with the person waiting in her box.

He stood up when he saw her coming, and moved to one side as she went by to her chair. When they were both seated, he said, "Mrs. Cumberland is different from the pictures I remember."

"Yes," Annie responded, not willing to talk about her.

"You haven't changed a bit," Henry stated, not as a compliment.

"You have," she replied.

"Yes, a lot."

"Why don't you tell me all about it," she suggested, smiling.

He said caustically, "Well, why not?" The flat, cold smile Annie had noticed previously settled on his face as he began. "Let's see, where should we start? I suppose at the point when I heard I was a bastard after all those really neat lies you told me."

His words were emotionless, but Annie closed her eyes. "Please," she said.

"It's just a fact, Mother. I got used to it pretty easily. It's just a point in time . . . kind of 'before' and 'after.' Anyway I wasn't too hot to stay at the Seminary High School with that particular status, so as soon as I could, before you could fly back from London, I hobbled out of there and . . . well, the first thing I did was go up to New York to murder Sam Cumberland." He chuckled and shook his head. "After that dramatic exercise, I ended up out here, found a job, and settled down." He gave a brief, mocking laugh. "You know where I live from your detectives," he said in accusation.

Annie nodded silently, wanting him to go on, yet not wanting to see his smile.

"I also went to college. Stanford, as a matter of fact, and graduated summa cum laude. Not that anyone at Stanford knew about it. See, I started going over to the campus and dropping in on classes. Then I realized nobody really kept track of who was sitting in a classroom. So I began to buy the books. The labs were the hard part; they're pretty strict about who gets in where, so I hustled a janitor's job working nights, got clearance to the buildings, and I'd just stay all night and drive back to the ranch in time to feed the ponies. You with me so far?" he asked as if he were dictating.

Annie said, "I'd have paid your tuition. I wouldn't have bothered you."

"It would have bothered me . . . then. But times have changed," he said suggestively, though of what, Annie did not know. "See, a professor found out what I was doing, discovered me one night. Turned out to be the resident Nobel genius, working in genetics, which is what I was into. Instead of turning me in, he took me on as an assistant, graded my exams, all that shit, and got me published."

"I'd like to read whatever it was," Annie said.

"Fine. I'll include copies along with everything else I'm going to send you. I want you to know what a good boy I've been."

Annie tried to ignore the sarcasm. "What else are you going to send me?"

"A prospectus," he replied. "See, the professor at Stanford and I came up with some stuff that we want to patent and then license; has to do with genetic engineering. We need some capital to start a company. I mean, we've had more offers than we can beat off with a stick, but if we take somebody else's money, we'd have to share with them, and we're greedy." He laughed at himself and looked at his mother.

"Henry, I'm afraid this isn't a good time for me to be lending money."

"I don't want your money. Of course, it wasn't really yours, was it? But let's forget about that. I want the trust you set up for me. The principal. It should be about a million and a half by now." He put a foot up on the rail and tilted his chair back. "My lawyers were going to write you about it, but when I read you were coming out to Del Mar, and then that Speed was riding for you, I thought I'd come down to ask you myself, and put ten bucks down on Speed. You think he'll win?"

"The purpose of that trust," Annie began, feeling an increasing irritation with his mocking style, "was to make sure you'd never be broke. You've chosen not to use the income, and it's been accumulating. I'll gladly send that to you, but the principal . . . that's something else."

"Mother," he said rocking slowly back and forth, "I appreciate your deep concern for my well being. But I haven't needed it for some time. I'm twenty-two, and—"

"I know how old you are," Annie said angrily enough to cause him to glance at her.

"Oh, dear," he said and let his feet and chair fall back to the ground. "Well, I suppose we are pretty pissed off at each other, so let me just say this . . ." Annie felt her stomach tighten as if preparing to be hit. He continued, still smiling, speaking easily, as if passing the time. "My lawyers are really good at this kind of thing. I'll sue to break that trust. Maybe I'll lose. But I'll keep it going in court for five or six years, getting depositions, going to trial, making appeals, and all through it reminding everyone about your Mafia friends, and telling the press about my choice of fathers, and what a wonderful mother you were." He chortled. "Isn't the American justice system terrific?"

Annie stood up, which surprised Henry, but he did not move. "In my experience," she said, "you can find a lawyer who'll do anything you want as long as you can pay. But who's going to pay these lawyers of yours after five or six years when you lose?"

He gazed up at her, still smiling, but his eyes went cold with disdain. "You'll give in before that."

Annie hesitated. "You're probably right. I'll go off and think about it." She started out of the box, then said, "I don't know who you are now, so if I treat you like a stranger, don't be surprised. It's just that I've missed my son so much."

"Oh. You mean the one you lied about so long, the nice legitimate one you made up for seventeen years and let fall on his face? He got lost. You're stuck with me . . . Mother."

Annie started out of the box.

"We'll meet in the winner's circle," Henry said. "You gave Speed a good horse for his first race, didn't you?"

She hurried up the aisle, realizing he had come only to get money and to see Speed.

Not until she was hugging the rail in front of the grandstand and saw Speed ride by in Limeteen's white and yellow stripes was she startled out of her bleak thoughts. She had missed conferring with her California trainer and Speed in the paddock before the race. The crowd was yelling as her filly rushed to the wire, winning by three lengths.

Annie made her way to a gate between the grandstand and clubhouse, showed her owner's pass, and went toward the winner's circle. She arrived as Speed returned with the filly, proudly saluted the stewards with his crop, and dismounted. Then he saw Henry, and the two young men ran toward each other into a hug, laughing and both talking at the same time.

For a moment, Annie saw her son again. Love for him swelled painfully as she gave in to the memory of the two boys hugging her and Frank the night they all delivered Glorious Girl. In the winner's circle, she smiled her congratulations to Speed, and the three of them lined up in front of the horse as the track photographer took the pictures. Then Henry and Speed headed back toward the jockey's dressing room, leaving Annie alone.

When she arrived back at the beach club, there were five dozen yellow and white roses already in her room with a card from Sam: "Caernarvon welcomes Limeteen back." She ate dinner with Helena in the Marine Room and found her daughter's lack of interest in the day's events a great relief. After the girl went to sleep, she called Sam at the Cumberland camp at Saranac Lake, eager to speak with him. The butler said he had not returned from Saratoga. Annie left a message for him to call the next day.

At four in the morning, the phone rang. It was Belinda.

"You've sure caused me a few sleepless nights, so I'm not going to apologize for the hour. I want you to give Sam a message. I'm suing him for divorce. I'm going to live in Venice, if it doesn't sink under me. I've bought a palazzo . . ."

Annie thought she sounded suspiciously calm.

"Belinda, are you . . . ?"

"Drunk? No. Crazy? They've told me up here that this is the sanest thing I could ever do. Seeing you and that boy today made me believe them. Sam's all yours, honey. Hope you enjoy him just as much as I have."

The line went dead.

TWENTY-EIGHT

BARKY CUMBERLAND'S FRIENDS could hardly believe the news. After flunking out of Princeton, he had gained the reputation of trying to lay every deb on the Wasp horizon. He succeeded often, for he was an unusually eligible bachelor, rich and not bad-looking, if one overlooked some thickness of body as well as of mind. He did not have his father's still stunning handsomeness, but Barky's Cumberland blue eyes sparkled attractively enough over a thin-lipped, usually sardonic smile. No one imagined him succumbing to matrimony. A June wedding was announced, a main aisle wedding at St. Luke's, with a reception at the Museum of Modern Art, where his father served on the board of trustees.

Around the Wall Street brokerage firm where Barky worked, earning his bonuses by churning the account of his main client, the Cumberland Foundation, he was dubbed "the Swordsman" to his face, and behind his back "the Hacksaw."

The idea of his marrying seemed all the more bizarre because the bride was Jewish and the daughter of a cook. No one would acknowledge the slightest prejudice or snobbery, but their tone revealed what a vivid piece of gossip they felt the marriage to be. Raising an eyebrow over an interfaith marriage was a bit old-fashioned, but to Barky's friends, the economic polarity of the match seemed to invite their comments. Eventually, as RSVP's were sent and wedding presents purchased, subtlety gave way to waggish responses. "At least she's white" was one of the favorite laugh lines.

And she was strikingly beautiful. Envy and jealousy inspired at least part of their disposition. A brunette with high cheekbones, sensuous mouth, flaring nose, and thickly lashed eyes, Greta Herskewitz, after doing some modeling in Albany to earn tuition, had come to New York City to study at Columbia. She let it be known that her widowed mother had died recently of cancer. And she earned the rest of her college expenses by modeling for much higher pay than at home. There was time for enough photo sessions to pay for good clothes and a modest apartment.

Greta had met Barky at a party on his family's yacht, one of the last privately owned oceangoing square-rigged schooners. The *Merlin,* the hundred-and-twenty-foot vessel, had been berthed at the Seventy-ninth Street Yacht Basin for Barky's twenty-seventh birthday party. Their meeting started typically. Barky saw a beautiful new face, explained away the luxury of his yacht and life, told her the difference between a stay sail and a gaff sail, then asked her, in his inimitable style, "to fuck." Greta's response was original: she pushed him overboard. From that plunge on, Barky was immersed. He pursued Greta with uncharacteristic ardor and lavish gifts. When she finally rewarded his diligence by joining him in bed, she had a six-carat square-cut diamond engagement ring on her finger, and an appointment for lunch at Number 10 to meet Barky's father.

By then, Greta had observed that New York, the modeling world, and the Cumberlands were all active in the frenetic exchange of money for beauty. The models with whom she worked spoke endlessly of the huge houses and distant vacations provided by their men as a preview of married life and an enticement for sex. With Barky Cumberland, Greta met many of the astonishingly good-looking women married to the unthinkably gross men who lived in carefully restricted bliss amid their heretofore unimagined luxury.

To Greta, marrying Barky was a trade-off. His worth and her pulchritude made the transaction socially acceptable. Barky was something of a bore, not very bright, with little ambition but nó need for it. Greta had enough ambition for both of them. Just as she had learned modeling, she wore whatever ensemble was required and assumed whatever attitude best served her purpose of joining the distinguished generations of Cumberlands, even if it meant being Barky's wife.

In preparation for her lunch at Number 10, she did her homework. The extent of the Cumberland financial interests amazed her, everything from airlines, to resort hotels, to shipping, to computer hardware companies. The Cumberland Foundation supported hospitals, universities, charities, and the arts with annual grants amounting to millions of dollars. The Cumberland Gulfstream jet was named the Gwydian, after the private railroad car it had replaced. The five Cumberland residences, in New York, Long Island, Palm Beach, Lexington, and Saranac Lake, were all staffed and ready to be occupied at any time. Each had its priceless collection of art and antiques, along with the precious memories and anecdotes of generations. Although Caernarvon Farms was regarded as one of the last of the great privately owned stables in America, Greta read that the only thing Barky's father did not have and really wanted in his lifetime was a Derby winner. A Caernarvon two-year-old had won the previous year's first running of the Breeders' Cup Juvenile, and was one of three colts being pointed by the stable toward that spring's Kentucky Derby.

She also learned everything she could about the family scandals, the "other woman" who apparently had given birth to two children fathered by Samuel Cumberland III, and the vicious divorce and flamboyant Venetian exile of Barky's mother, which everyone blamed on this "Countess" Annie Carney. On their way to lunch at Number 10, Greta asked Barky about the woman, which resulted in the only vehement opinion she had ever heard from him. However, it withered as they approached his father's house.

The butler opened the door and led them to the drawing room. Barky joked with him, and Greta noted that the butler responded with cool dignity, obviously a trained tolerance. The drawing room was filled with spring flowers, which accented the pale salmon walls of the room. A young woman sat knitting in a tapestried armchair.

"Alycia!" Barky exclaimed. "What the hell are you doing up here? Oh, this is Greta Herskewitz. My sister, Alycia Stewart."

The woman stood up and greeted her brother with a kiss on the cheek, then took Greta's hand. "I'm sure this is why I'm here—to meet you." She smiled warmly, and Greta did so in return.

"A command from the Old Man?" Barky asked with a breezy lack of concern.

"Yes; he sent the plane down for me. Said something's up."

"Well, I told him I wanted to marry her."

"I thought so," Alycia said, again smiling. "That's why I came. Well, Greta. Welcome to the family. Barky, bring her duck shooting next time you come down."

"Good God!" he said. "What's that?" He was staring at an oil painting over the mantel that featured the Doges' Palace in Venice.

"The new Canaletto," Alycia said. "Papa's very proud of it, but don't remind him Mummah lives nearby."

"Where is he?"

"Coming soon, I think. He's upstairs in the study with a brace of lawyers. Greta, would you like a sherry?"

"No, thank you," Greta said, already liking this big-boned plain woman dressed in a tweed suit and wearing no jewelry except a double strand of pearls. What she lacked in good looks, she made up for with a high-spirited personality. Greta envied her sense of assurance, recognizing a birthright that came with old money. Alycia handed her brother a sherry and began a monologue about her dogs, Welsh corgis she bred on the farm in Maryland where she lived with her husband.

By the time Sam came in, the three young people were

laughing. Greta was relieved by her own sense of ease in the Cumberland drawing room. But the moment she met her future father-in-law, she knew he was wary of her. His charm was immediate and considerable, and Greta was surprised at how astonishingly good-looking he was, even though she had seen his picture many times. He made fun of Barky, harmlessly perhaps, which the son seemed to accept. Still, Greta sensed his power.

"Well, Greta, it seems that you've turned my son into a rhapsodic goof," he jested as he led her into a small dining room. The butler seated the ladies. "But I think his sister and I should acquaint you with the awful truth about him . . ."

As lunch progressed, Greta watched, noting that one maid brought the soup bowls and plates, the butler poured the wine and served the food, another maid removed the china. Greta ate little, on her guard to enter their badinage and to attend to her own apprehension. Although his occasional questions to her about Columbia and modeling were delightfully ingenuous, Mr. Cumberland did not look at her, even when he talked to her. He kidded his daughter about her infernal dogs, Barky about a certain terrible stock he had bought for the foundation's portfolio. He told several stories about how the Arabs were tiring of their shopping trips for thoroughbreds, surmising that they might buy the state of Kentucky and proclaim it an independent emirate called Kentuckistan.

Not until after a chocolate soufflé was passed by the butler did the questioning turn.

"Greta," Sam Cumberland said, "Barky's mentioned that you have a rather extraordinary history. Tell us about your family." He was casually concentrating on his soufflé.

Greta smiled at Barky, who gave her a warning look, patronizing in its transparency. "Not extraordinary at all, Mr. Cumberland. There's not much of it, as a matter of fact. The only family I know about is my mother." She knew Sam Cumberland had probably done his homework as well as she had done hers. "Something happened to her during the Second World War. She lost her memory and for two decades, it seems, wandered around Europe. The first thing she remembered was being in a hospital in Paris, pregnant with me. She probably survived hell. I think she was a very great woman."

"And then she came to the United States?" Sam asked before taking another bite of soufflé.

"Yes, after I was born in Paris," Greta said, sharply aware of the cross-examination. "The Displaced Persons Fund of the Hebrew Immigrant Aid Society relocated us to Albany. My mother worked there as cook until she died of cancer just a few years ago."

Barky furrowed his brow but said nothing.

His father gazed across the table at him, and said, "Yes, Barky mentioned the fund. They did extraordinary work with Jewish refugees after the war. As a matter of fact, the Cumberland Foundation was a contributor." Finally, he looked at her, still smiling. "Incidently, if your mother had lost her memory, how did she know she was Jewish?"

"While she was in Paris," Greta began, "waiting for me to be born, she wandered into a synagogue one day and instantly realized it was a familiar place, that she'd been in synagogues before. She went back every day . . . Are you getting at something, Mr. Cumberland?" Then she tried to eat her soufflé as casually as he had. Out of the corner of her eye she saw alarmed looks pass between Barky and Alycia.

"Amnesia is such a fascinating phenomenon," Sam responded. "And often so convenient. You were born in the American Hospital. The doctor, now dead, who attended your mother was one of the most distinguished, and expensive, gynecologists in Europe. Refugees, particularly those who've been wandering for years, seldom have access to such care. How'd she do it?" he asked guilefully.

Greta put her heavy silver fork across her plate. It was the third fork she had used during lunch. She wished Barky were on his feet, objecting to his father's probe, but there was only silence. "I don't know, Mr. Cumberland," she said, smiling at him directly. "I'm sorry my mother isn't alive so that she could explain . . . if she even knew. But I see that you've done some serious checking. Is it appropriate for a major donor to get confidential information from a charity? I wonder if you

475

inquired about Alycia's husband as carefully as you've obviously been investigating me."

Sam's only reaction was to wipe his hands carefully with his napkin and drop it on the table beside his place.

"Horace was investigated, Greta," Alycia said, "down to his toenails." She allowed no bitterness in her voice.

"A fine fellow, Horace," Mr. Cumberland said. "He had absolutely nothing to hide. And as a matter of fact, he was perfectly happy to sign a prenuptial agreement. Alycia will explain it, Greta."

Barky finally reacted, snapping a look at his sister. "Did Horace do that?" he asked, amazed.

Alycia nodded, realizing the true reason she had been summoned. Looking down at her fingers busily entwining themselves in her lap, she said absently, "Where's my knitting?"

Sam stood and said, "Coffee in the drawing room. By the way, did you notice the Canaletto?" He smiled warmly at Greta, who instantly returned his smile and held up her hands. On one was Barky's engagement ring, on the other was a sapphire ring with diamonds in a serpentine pattern, which her mother had given her. She took the engagement ring off and placed it on the lace tablecloth.

"The Canaletto's stunning," she said. "You should be proud that you spent the family money so well. But no coffee, thank you. I'm leaving now."

She stood and walked to the door leading to the hall.

"Greta!" Barky said, and hurried to stand beside her.

She smiled sadly and said, "You didn't tell me your father was quite such an anti-Semite, Barky." Glancing over at his father, she saw the profound effect the charge had on him. "He lets his foundation give money to all those Jewish charities, but he doesn't want to think of his son marrying one." Then she let herself grow angry. "And I don't want a person with his own well-known reputation using the influence of all his money to try to defame my mother. She had a hard life; she deserves to be respected."

She walked out of the room and down the hall to the front door. The butler was on his way to the drawing room, carrying a silver tray with demitasses and a silver coffee urn.

Adroitly, he placed the tray on a hall chair and opened the front door for her. Greta heard some raised voices but did not hesitate. She walked out the door, through the massive iron gates, then down the sidewalk past concrete tubs already overflowing with spring flowers.

"Greta!" Barky yelped as he ran out of the house to her side. He was holding the ring between his finger and his thumb. "There'll be no more investigations! There'll be no prenuptial agreement! I'll marry you no matter what!"

"We'll see," Greta said doubtfully as she let Barky slip the engagement ring back on her finger.

In the weeks that followed, Greta was selectively discreet about the altercation. A photographer who worked for a slick Manhattan gossip magazine took a stunning picture of her, and a paragraph hinting at the anti-Semitic situation appeared the next week. The text ran beside some awkward stolen shots of Barky and Sam Cumberland.

Barky portrayed to Greta his father's rage over the story. The arguments between father and son seemed to stimulate Barky's love for her, and he narrated his standing up to his father in minute detail. Greta was a responsive audience, but carefully avoided saying anything against the father. So certain was she of the outcome, she found herself considering which designer she would ask to make her wedding dress.

Her bookings for modeling tripled, and she dropped out of Columbia for the rest of the spring term to take advantage of them. The modeling world became feverishly aware of her connection to the Cumberlands, and her picture began to appear in national magazines for the first time. Finally, she received a handwritten note on the heavily engraved stationery of Samuel Barkeley Cumberland III.

Dear Greta,

I deplore the vicious rumors that are drifting around. I am not an anti-Semite in any way, shape, or form, and regret any misunderstanding which may have given you that impression.

Will you join Barky and me for dinner at Le Cirque on

Thursday at 8? I've become convinced that you and my son love each other, and the three of us have much to discuss.

> *Cordially,*
> *Sam Cumberland*

"He wanted to include his 'friend,' Mrs. Carney, in the occasion," Barky said when Greta showed him the letter. "A kind of double date! But I absolutely forbade it." Greta almost smiled at the adamant tone Barky had perfected.

"Le Cirque isn't very private," she said.

"Pa's no fool. He wants everyone to know about it. It's either that or a million dollars to the United Jewish Appeal or something."

"Fine," she said, thinking of which friends she would want there.

On Thursday night, more than twenty photographers waited outside the restaurant on Sixty-fifth Street. The next day, pictures of the smiling trio appeared in all the papers except the *New York Times*. The gossip columnists' conjectures were rewarded a few weeks later when the engagement was announced officially in the *Times*. A June wedding was planned for the week following completion of the Triple Crown.

During the preparations for the event, Greta received another letter. It was addressed to her modeling agency, without her name but with a small picture of her from a magazine layout stuck on it with cellophane tape. Folded inside was a message attached to a larger picture of Greta from the same layout, advertising executive jet aircraft. The double-page promotion had appeared in various aircraft trade magazines. The picture sent in the envelope was a half-page close-up of Greta with her hand casually supporting the side of her head as she stared through the plane's porthole at a beautiful sunset. A felt-tip pen had been used to circle her mother's ring on her finger, and scrawled across the bottom of the picture was the line "Where did you get the ring?"

Greta usually took the ring off for her sessions, but the photographer had liked it. Clipped to the picture was a piece of graph paper on which was scrawled:

The magazine gave me your agency, who then wouldn't give me your name. The ring looks like a wedding ring my mother had once. Don't worry; I don't want it back. I'm only curious.

Henry Sumner
415-555-3128

Greta was more than curious. She was astonished and frightened. The name on the graph paper meant nothing to her. She quickly found out that the area code was for the San Francisco peninsula. The letter could be from the usual crank trying to meet a model. On the other hand, the writer might be the son of the woman who probably had saved her mother's life and her own in Paris. At the same time, he represented the risk that her mother's background might be revealed.

Two months before she died, Greta's mother had described for the first time her supposedly forgotten life to her daughter, with the primary intent of instilling in her a sense of her noble heritage. "Never forget," her mother concluded, "you are a Von Herschfeldt. You can go to Vienna *today* and discover for yourself the greatness of your family. I want you to have everything that I lost."

She gave Greta the ring and a bank book listing weekly deposits totaling a few thousand dollars. Greta realized that she was expected to fly to Vienna after her mother died, as if the young woman would automatically be welcomed by the Von Herschfeldt family and taken into their presumably gracious lives. Her mother said more than once, as she drifted on painkillers, "I can see you, my lovely Greta, dancing in the mirrored ballroom, with handsome officers and members of the nobility all hoping to take you away for a moment alone . . ."

Instead, Greta had stood through the Kaddish prayer, buried her mother in Albany, and come to New York. The young woman had no faith in her mother's fantasy of Viennese hospitality and mirrored ballrooms. Her mother's story made no difference in her life until Sam Cumberland began to investigate her background. If the truth was revealed, her heritage would appear more Nazi than Jewish.

Whoever Henry Sumner was, his mother perhaps knew of

479

"Madame Von," and Captain Hultz, the war criminal. If Mr. Cumberland ever discovered that part of the story, Greta doubted that Barky would be able to withstand the pressure to break the engagement.

For a week, Greta debated whether or not to ignore the letter. Yet her own curiosity about the unknown woman who had saved her mother from the French mob and given her the ring, coupled with the fear of leaving so much information uncontrolled, wore Greta down. She stood in the kitchen of her West Side brownstone apartment and dialed the number.

"Mr. Sumner's line," a businesslike female voice answered.

Unprepared, Greta stammered, "I . . . Is Mr. Sumner there?"

"Who's calling, please?"

"My . . . Tell him, tell him I'm calling in response to his inquiry about a ring."

"Mr. Sumner's in a meeting. May I have him call you?"

Greta paused, irritated by secretarial ploys. "This is a personal matter. If I were you, I'd tell him right now."

There was a moment of silence; then "Just a moment, please."

As she waited, Greta suddenly realized that whoever this man and his hypothetical mother were, they might be setting her up to be blackmailed. She started to hang up but heard a voice begin to talk rapidly. She put the receiver back to her ear.

". . . and so you *are* curious. Well, we might as well start in France. I don't remember much because I was only around five years old. The ring was something I hadn't thought about for years until I saw it in your picture. I suppose it was one of those glittery things that embedded itself somewhere in my mind and set off all those recessive vibrations from lost childhood or something. Anyway, my mother gave the ring to a woman in Paris, sometime around 1965, 1966 . . . Does that mean anything to you?"

Staring at the ring on her finger, Greta saw that her hand was shaking. When she tried to speak, she found herself fighting panic. Hoping to find out what he knew, she said, "Who was this woman in Paris?"

The pause at the other end of the line was too long to be about memory. "I have a feeling you know that part of the story, and I'm at a disadvantage. You know who I am and where to get me. I only know what you look like."

Greta knew that, with the slightest effort, he could find out her name. She asked, "What do you want?"

"Nothing," he said, surprised by the question. "Oh . . . wait a minute. I get it. You're worried that I know something that might be harmful. Well, I don't think I do. All I remember is that this woman showed up in the middle of the night at a stud farm in Normandy where my mother was working. It had something to do with the war and the Resistance; I don't know. But the woman was in trouble and my mother went off to help her. When Mother came back, the ring was gone. That's all I really remember.

"I wrote to you about it because, well, the ring was given to my mother by the guy who was supposed to be my father. It turned out that he wasn't, but, what the hell, bastards are always curious." He chuckled, and Greta was amazed by his manner.

"Is your mother still alive?" she asked, trying to sound casual.

"Very much so. Look, I'm not into scaring people or causing anybody problems. All of a sudden I see that my letter might seem pretty weird, so let's leave it at this. I'm going to be in New York next—wait a minute, where's my book—next . . . a week from Wednesday for two days. If you want to talk, I'll be at the Ritz-Carlton on Central Park South. If I don't hear from you, I'll forget about the ring. It's no big deal.

"Let's see, what else? Oh, my mother. If it'll help, she was called Annie Sumner when I was born, but she remarried and is Annie Carney now. Runs Limeteen Farm. If you're into horse racing at all, you may have . . ."

Greta slammed the phone down and backed away from it. She knew very well who Annie Carney was, and now who Henry Sumner was, and that sooner or later he would know everything. There were too many pictures of her with Barky for her to hope this bastard child of her future father-in-law would not see one. She stood staring at the phone as she wrote on a used envelope, "Wednesday, Ritz-Carlton."

For the next few days, Greta was short-tempered and jumpy. Barky objected, and gave in to his own pique; but in his mind, he excused Greta's behavior as premarital nerves. When he offered to give her more privacy by sleeping back at Number 10, Greta further irritated him by accepting his offer with alacrity and relief. The days passed slowly; the Kentucky Derby came and went without a Caernarvon victory. The wedding, therefore, became the center of Cumberland attention. Greta believed that the June wedding would be easy compared with her meeting with Henry Sumner. She tried to prepare for it, thinking of what she would say, what she would offer him to keep quiet. If it was money, she would get it, probably from Barky. If going to bed with him would make him somehow assailable, she would do it. Nevertheless, she doubted each strategy, and spent most of her sleepless nights fighting down her anxiety.

Wednesday night finally arrived. That evening, the wedding party was being given a black-tie dinner by some Cumberland family friends. Greta planned to go to the Ritz-Carlton Hotel as soon as the party was over. What she did not anticipate was meeting Annie Carney.

"Goddamn son of a bitch!" Barky whispered indignantly as he handed his coat to the maid in the marble-floored foyer of the Park Avenue apartment. "Pa brought his lay with him."

The spring night seemed too warm to Greta, and her off-the-shoulder black water-taffeta dress with its floor-length skirt already felt confining. She saw Mrs. Carney instantly, slipped off her mother's ring, and put it in her evening bag. Surprised by Annie's beauty and apparent youth, Greta admired the shimmering burn of her amber hair and the perfectly placed dimple in her smile. Her body was firm and thin, which her strapless, full-skirted dress of pale green crepe de chine revealed. There was enough of a crowd to allow Greta time to recover and prepare, as well as for Barky to control his indignation.

The introduction between the two women finally was made by Sam Cumberland. It was followed by a rigidly courteous greeting from Barky. Mrs. Carney reached out and took Greta's hand, saying, "Hello, Greta." Then she held the hand and cocked her head to one side, responding to Greta's look of curiosity.

Greta smiled to cover it.

"Barky's a very lucky boy," Mrs. Carney said without even a glance at Greta's future husband. Then their hostess interrupted and took the guests of honor off to greet others. By then, Greta was trembling but was able to hide it by holding on to Barky's arm.

Throughout the evening, Greta avoided looking in Mrs. Carney's direction. Fortunately, they were seated at tables in different rooms. At the end of the party, as Mrs. Carney left with Mr. Cumberland, she again spoke to Greta but said only, "Good night, Greta."

Barky dropped Greta at the door of her West Side brownstone, and, still complaining about Mrs. Carney's presence and Greta's preoccupation, passionately kissed her good night. As soon as his car disappeared around the corner, she hurried over to Columbus Avenue and waved down a cab. She arrived at the hotel fifteen minutes later. It was one-thirty in the morning. She went to the house phone and asked for Henry Sumner's room.

"Hello?"

She hesitated, as if about to pull a trigger. "I'm . . . the ring. I'm in the lobby."

There was a pause. "Great. I'll be right down."

She saw several chairs but paced the lobby. Before she was able to calm herself, she saw a man wearing boots, jeans, an open shirt, and a leather jacket step out of the elevator. When he saw her, he smiled and started over. Greta had an urge to run.

"It seems I'm underdressed," he said.

She did not return his smile. Staring at his face, she saw Sam Cumberland's blue eyes looking at her. Probably no one would recognize the similarity if they did not know the relationship, because little else was duplicated. He wore glasses. His hair was sandy; his mouth was straighter, even when he smiled. Taller than Sam by a few inches, he was thinner and moved with a more sinewy stride.

"Henry Sumner," he said as an introduction and held out his hand, jokingly suggesting a return of a name.

"Greta von Herschfeldt," she heard herself say, as if she were listening from a distance. Then she gasped suddenly and started to throw up. As she put both hands to her mouth, she dropped her evening bag. Henry picked it up, grabbed her by the waist, and lifted her across the lobby and out the front door.

He held her head as she leaned over the curb and gagged. Having eaten little at the dinner party and drunk even less, there was nothing in her stomach but bile. She spat out some and stood up, unable to look at him.

"I'm sorry," she said.

He shrugged. "It saved us a lot of time. There's a kind of real intimacy when you hold someone's head while she's barfing. You feel any better?"

She shook her head.

"You want to walk around?"

"I'm cold."

"You can wear this." He slipped off his jacket and put it around her shoulders.

"What about you?" she asked, still not able to look at him.

"It's a spring night. If you start feeling faint or anything, let me know."

They began walking across the street from Central Park. He asked no questions and made no idle conversation, for which Greta was grateful.

"What do you know about me?" she said, controlling herself rigidly and feeling vast relief at the same time.

"That the photographer didn't do you justice"—he took a few steps before continuing—"and that whatever that ring means to you, it's scaring the hell out of you. Why, I don't know, and I don't need to know. I meant what I said. I'll forget it."

"You will know, sooner or later," Greta said as she opened her evening bag and handed him the ring.

"I will?"

Greta stopped and looked at him. "I met your mother tonight at dinner. I'm marrying Barky Cumberland in three and a half weeks."

She watched his face carefully for a reaction. He blinked once.

"Congratulations," he said evenly, and handed the ring back to her without having looked at it.

Greta could not control her curiosity any longer. "Does your mother know about me?" She slipped the ring back on her finger.

"I don't know," he answered guardedly. "I've never heard the name Von Herschfeldt before. But my mother and I don't talk to each other." Then his eyes softened and he said, "Greta, what the hell are you so scared of?"

"I've never said that name out loud before."

Her sob burst out before she could suppress it. Greta put both hands over her mouth. Standing in the eerie purple-white brilliance of the streetlights, she knew she was going to tell him everything. She knew no way to stop herself from doing so, in spite of not having the faintest idea of what would happen.

When they started to walk again, she was breathing in gulps. An hour later, she was digressing to explain what her mother had told her about Vienna and the Von Herschfeldts, laughing with disturbed wonder and then going on to describe what she knew about her natural father, the Nazi captain, the murderer, the war criminal. Henry asked an occasional question, but never made an observation. She talked about growing up in Albany, about the lie of her secret life, about modeling, and then about Barky.

Henry chuckled often at the Barky story, and Greta began to laugh loudly. She had never laughed quite so freely before, and gave in to it. It felt wonderful.

Then a question occurred to her, and without considering the consequences, she asked it. "Is Sam Cumberland really your father?"

He kept walking; Greta watched as his face went blank again.

"I've told you everything," she said, "so I can ask you anything."

For a few steps, there was no response. Then he stopped and looked at her. A flat smile spread across his face. "You want to hear about it?"

"Yes!" she said and, with the exuberance of the moment, leaned up and kissed him.

Slowly his arms came around her and he kissed her as gently as if it were the first kiss in his life.

When Greta pulled back and looked up into his eyes, she said, "I think I'm going a little bit crazy here tonight."

"That, or a little bit sane. So you want to hear the story of my life? It isn't as good as yours, but at least I'm a bastard, too."

They walked on. After another hour they went into an all-night coffee shop on Broadway and had a huge breakfast. Greta could not remember being so hungry. Afterward, they walked to Lincoln Center and sat on the rim of the fountain. Dawn began to light the sky as Henry was saying, "I haven't seen my little sister since she was a baby. She barely knows who Frank Carney is. She was told about Sam Cumberland's being her father from the very beginning. My mother didn't want to make the same mistake twice . . . I've heard Helena's a real wild one. She's ten now. Goes to school here in New York. My mother bought a town house; splits her time between here and Limeteen."

"Why don't she and Mr. Cumberland get married?" Greta asked. She sat close to Henry, her head on his shoulder and her arm around his waist.

"Beats me. They sure do deserve each other."

They were silent for a moment, watching long shadows appear on the plaza.

"I've got to go," Greta said, standing up.

"Where?"

"Back. A friend of Barky's mother is hosting a ladies' lunch at the Colony Club today."

Henry shuddered humorously. "You can't."

She smiled doubtfully. "Why not?"

"The truth's out."

486

"What do you mean?" she asked, afraid of the answer.

"Before tonight, the lie was the real thing for you. Now it's only a big lie, and it'll get bigger every day if you go on with it." He stood up smiling and put his hands on her shoulders. "I know how you feel. It's pretty scary. When I found out my own little true story, I'd have done anything in the world to keep things the way they should have been." Slowly he shook his head. "But it was too late. Once you know it's a lie, there is no going back to it." He leaned over, put his forehead against hers, and recited her names slowly. "Greta von Herschfeldt Hultz, can you imagine what Barky Cumberland will do if you tell him, which you'll do now, because that's who you are?" Then he started to laugh.

Greta backed away. "But I have to go . . . to *lunch* today," she blurted between bursts of laughter, "at the Colony Club!"

The line broke Henry up and he shouted to the surrounding facades of Lincoln Center, "Of *course* you do! That's how the really big lies keep going!"

"What can I do?" she asked.

He thought a moment, then reached out to take her arm and whisper into her ear. "I've heard about people, who wanted to end one life and start another, going down to a beach, taking off all their clothes, jewelry, and identification, and swimming away to something new."

"I can't swim," she said, and felt his smile spread against her cheek.

"You can walk," he replied. "Hell, you've been walking away from lunch at the Colony Club all night. Better keep going, Greta."

She leaned back to see his face. "What are you saying? Where can I go?"

"Anywhere you want. But since you're asking me, I'll take advantage and say, disappear and come with me. Back to my hotel. You can send messages; then we'll be out of here tonight."

Greta stood transfixed, unable to speak.

Henry chuckled again. "Don't worry about clothes or toothbrushes or your apartment. If you want it to happen, it can happen."

Greta heard the dare, but her habit of careful appraisal was not so easily discarded. "You said you're some kind of mad scientist tinkering in a barn. You live in a trailer."

He took her hand and they started walking toward the street.

"Careful," he said. "You said that just the way a Cumberland would. All right, here's the story. I bought a ranch a couple of years ago. The so-called barn's a state-of-the-art lab. My partner and I have a company that owns some patents. I'm in New York to work out final details with the investment banking house that's taking us public. The offering's for a hundred and ten million; my partner and I are keeping fifty percent of the shares between us. In two weeks I should be worth twenty-five million on paper, small change compared with the Cumberlands, but enough to buy coffee beans. The banking people flew me here in their plane. I was planning to stay an extra day, but we can leave whenever you want. And the trailer's pretty nice. I just haven't taken the time to move into the main house."

Greta walked silently to the hotel, holding Henry's hand. In his suite, she stood in the middle of the living room, still wearing his leather jacket over her evening gown.

"I've disappeared," she said.

"Not yet," he said as he came over to her and began to undress her. The black water-taffeta fell away quickly. In one easy stroke, he peeled her panty hose and panties down her legs. Her bra snapped open behind her back, and he gently pulled off her diamond clip earrings, then her bracelet. She took off Barky's diamond engagement ring and let it fall to the floor.

Henry stepped back to look at her as she stood naked except for their mothers' ring. She did not move to cover herself, wanting him to see her, feeling no embarrassment or apprehension.

"Now you're invisible," he said, which made her smile. She watched him undress. On the bed, they pressed into each other. As they made love, Greta did not feel the usual obligation to please. Her own pleasure was enough for both of them. She could barely stand him to leave her when, after making love three times, the telephone rang announcing that a car was at the door waiting for him.

Henry arranged for a sales lady from Bendel to visit the hotel. Greta wrote two letters on some of Henry's graph paper: a short one to her hostess at the Colony Club, and a long one to Barky that was placed in a box with the jewelry she had been wearing that he had given her, including the engagement ring. In neither of the letters did she say why the wedding would not take place, only that it would not. A messenger service picked the letters up for delivery. The details of Henry's public offering were worked out by early afternoon, and by the time the sun was setting, he and Greta were taking off in a Learjet, heading for California.

They heard none of the repercussions. Greta experienced her disappearance with exultant relief. On the ramshackle horse ranch with several corrals (not paddocks, as Henry explained), some twenty broodmares, and a trailer set in the middle of a grove of eucalyptus trees, she felt that her life was a reality for the first time. Several of the barns were high-tech laboratories for a corporation called Dynagen. Nearly a hundred people arrived and left daily, including the security guards who patrolled the discreet wire-mesh fences around the fifty-acre property. The cars were parked in a lot densely lined with eucalyptus and shrubs. Sometimes Greta could not believe so many people were around, because she saw so few.

Henry enjoyed explaining about both the laboratories and the horses, but Greta found the theories and details somewhat daunting. She met his colleagues and became comfortable at the ranch. The clapboard two-story main house, although unlived in for several years, was solid, spacious, and filled with possibility. Behind it, enclosed by ancient, gnarled California oak trees, was an empty swimming pool and a neglected tennis court. On several weekends, they drove to San Francisco, where Greta completed her wardrobe. They ate well and walked for hours, catching up on more of what they did not know about each other.

"I have to go to Kentucky this week," Henry said one night over steamed dumplings at his favorite Szechuan restaurant. "I'm going to buy a very good horse for a project we're doing at the ranch. You might enjoy coming. It's the Keeneland Select Summer Sales. A guy named Sangster and some Arab brothers from Dubai—everyone calls them the Doobey Brothers—all bid against each other and buy yearlings for millions."

"Sure," Greta said. "I'm not too eager to be away from you yet."

Henry smiled, then took her hand. "One thing you ought to know. Sam Cumberland will probably be there. He's tied in with a group of investors who are going to try to stop Sangster and the Arabs from running off with all the best bloodstock. My mother will probably be along. But I'm pretty sure we can avoid them."

Greta stared out the restaurant's plate glass window. "Barky?"

"I doubt it. I always heard he was allergic to horses. Breaks out or something."

"And sneezes," Greta said. "It sounds as if they'll be pretty busy. If you can go, so can I. I don't want any fear of them making me stay behind. Besides, I'm still invisible."

Henry and Greta arrived in Lexington on Tuesday and went directly from Bluegrass Airport across the highway to Keeneland Racetrack's auction pavilion. The parking area was filled, and the valet boys were kept running at the entrance of the impressive limestone building. The auction was in progress as Henry led Greta to the seats reserved in his company's name. Even before they sat down, the intense atmosphere inside the pavilion was apparent.

A yearling was standing in the sawdust of the pit. On his hip was the number 215. The auctioneer was chanting with barely controlled zeal, but before they heard the figures, Henry and Greta saw the bid board. As they looked, the bid changed from $6.5 million to $7 million to $7.5 million to $8 million. The black-tied bid spotters were bellowing and waving with a frantic intensity. The auctioneer continued his rapid singsong. ". . . Okay, I've got nine million in back on Dale. Nine million would you bid ten? Nine million five, would you bid ten? Nine million seven would you bid, would you bid ten million, would you do it, sir? The Lord loves a cheerful giver.

Nine million eight, ten million. At nine nine, would you bid
ten? Ten, in back . . .''

The catalogue explained the incredible price. The yearling's
sire was Nijinsky, a son of Northern Dancer who was already
the sire of eighty stakes winners. The yearling's dam was My
Charmer, who had given birth nine years earlier to Seattle
Slew.

At the same moment that Greta saw Mrs. Carney and Sam
Cumberland, she heard somewhere behind her a familiar
sneeze, then another. She was too terrified to move. Mr. Cumberland was seated the next aisle over, about ten rows down
from where Greta and Henry were sitting. He was leaning
over with several other men conferring with a handsome man
with perfect teeth, carefully blow-dried graying hair, and
tinted glasses.

"That's Wayne Lukas," Henry whispered. "Red-hot trainer
with a lot of money behind him. Sangster always bids from out
back. Don't see the Arabs.''

Lukas gave a nod to the bid spotter, and the figures continued to rise. Again, Greta heard a sneeze and turned to see
Barky standing at the top of the aisle, staring at his father's
group. She grabbed for Henry's arm just as Barky started
down the steep steps of the pavilion. No one was watching
him, so intent was the crowd on the colt and the bid board,
which read "$11,700,000."

"Do you want him for twelve. Twelve, do I hear it. Be
bold, sir! This one's surely bred to win, but then aren't we all!
All right now you're talking my language. Twelve million dollars is what the bid is!''

Barky was halfway down the aisle when he pulled a small
pistol out of his coat pocket and sneezed again. Greta and
Henry saw the gun, but before Greta could shout, Henry was
on his feet, jumping nimbly across the rows of startled spectators, stepping on the arms of their chairs until he reached the
next aisle. As Barky said something and shoved the gun toward the back of Mrs. Carney's head, Henry leaped from ten
steps above him. Mrs. Carney turned to see the gun in her face
as Henry's shoulder hit Barky in the back. The two men tumbled to the bottom of the aisle and came to rest at the feet of

the bid spotter, who did not take his eyes away from his work for one second, but shouted Wayne Lukas' latest offer up to the auctioneer.

"Thank you, sir! Dale, out in back, I have twelve million four here. How about thirteen million dollars and let's just stop this? Thirteen . . . ?"

Henry and Barky were struggling while security guards were surrounding them. Henry's glasses were smashed, and one cheek was bleeding. Grabbing the gun out of Barky's hand, the guards dragged the half brothers through a back door leading behind the auctioneer's pulpit. The yearling stood serenely on the sawdust and took no notice.

Greta looked around the pavilion. The men with Wayne Lukas were conferring, except for Sam Cumberland, who was speaking urgently to Annie Carney. She sat rigidly in her chair. Then as the couple stood and hurried up the aisle, Wayne Lukas said, "Yeah!"

"Thank you! Thirteen million! At thirteen million, Dale! Do you go to thirteen million five, back there, Dale? Did that plum choke you down? Okay, I'll wait for you. Thirteen million dollars . . ."

Greta stood and made her way out of the pavilion to find where Henry and Barky had been taken.

Robert Sangster won the bidding out back with a bid of $13.1 million, the highest price ever paid for an unraced, untried yearling. Two years later, as a three-year-old racing under the colors of Sangster's associate Stavros Niarchos, the colt, auspiciously named Seattle Dancer, struggled through five races in Ireland and France, won little, and was retired to stud.

TWENTY-NINE

SITTING in a Madison Avenue coffee shop, Phil Angelo wiped away the moisture on the window next to him so that he could see down the sidewalk. The March wind was blowing street debris against pedestrians and buildings. Even so, there was a perverse hint of spring warmth in the air. He looked at his wristwatch. He had taken the Rolex off an overdosed customer of his. At the time, Phil had not been sure the man was definitely dead, but later he learned that when the police arrived, he was.

Phil's toothpick broke in his mouth and he spat the two pieces onto the floor. As he turned, he caught sight of himself in the coffee shop's mirrored pillar nearby. He scowled. No matter what he did with the hair that was left, he was still going bald, right on the front of his head. He recalled the luxuriant pompadour he had had when he was young. Once, he tried to get away with wearing a pair of dark glasses casually pushed up to cover the blighted area, an accepted affectation of the time. But his supplier had laughed and said, "What the fuck are those for? You protecting your head from sunstroke, or are you going to be some fucking Hollywood faggot director?"

Phil checked through the hole in the steamy window again. Late. But she would come. They always came. That was the one thing in his life that Phil could trust.

The waitress came by and, without asking, refilled his cup. She was young, pretty, with dyed blond hair and a nice ass. Probably an out-of-work actress. Phil gave her his special smile of gratitude and suggestion. She saw it, looked through it, and went on to the customers in the next booth. As Phil followed her ass, he again confronted himself in the mirrored pillar.

Cheap. His shoes, the suit, the tie, the knock-off Burberry trench coat with that stupid ugly brown plaid. Cheap. Everything he wore looked cheap. He hated to get dressed in the morning, hated having anyone he knew see him, hated seeing himself. He stared at his reflection and felt genuinely sorry for himself.

Nothing had gone right since "the stupid brothers" had fucked up kidnaping that horse. Phil had stayed out of jail, but had received too much attention, first juggling for the FBI, then tap dancing for the mob.

The dark suits were easy; all they wanted was for him to send Fungo away and to talk about the Cosa Nostra. He told them about Annie's list, which distracted them from asking what else he knew, and they gave him immunity.

His immunity had no meaning to the Genovese crime family. When they heard about the list, they grabbed him off the street and put him in a meat locker. When he was blue, they took him out and asked about the list. Phil told them he had made it up so that he would not have to sing to the FBI. Explaining that he had known Charlie Dell and that he remembered the Joe Valachi blackmail try, he described how he came up with the idea of the list and made the FBI believe him. If the Genovese family needed proof of that, let them watch what the FBI was doing to Annie Carney in order to force the list out of her.

The mob boys beat him up, then threw him back in the meat locker. Phil took it all, knowing it was the only chance he had of staying alive. He turned blue again and passed out. They carried him out and kept him in a room for two weeks, eating tuna fish and granola. Then, without any explanation, they let him go. Apparently they believed him. He went into hiding and stayed out of sight for a couple of years, doing occasional errands for the Gambino family in order to support himself.

After that, Phil could never get near a track. The Pinkertons spotted him coming through the turnstiles and ran him right out of the parking lots. In the hangouts near the backstretch, jockeys treated him as if he had AIDS, and trainers with whom he had worked told him point-blank to get lost. Even grooms and exercise girls got the word and moved away from him. He realized that no one would even join him for a drink when he was buying a round. After a while, he stopped trying.

The bookies talked to him; Phil put thousands down and could not stop. Once he went to Gamblers Anonymous in Las Vegas, told everyone what a terrible addiction he had, and got a big kick out of shocking them with the sordid details. After receiving lots of earnest support, he celebrated by walking right over to the horse room at Caesar's Palace and laying a thousand dollars on a thirty-to-one long shot running at the Meadowlands. The odds were right; the winner distanced Phil's horse by thirty lengths.

At one time, Phil owed the bookies over a hundred grand. That was when the moneylenders showed up. The first time he missed his bimonthly twenty-five percent interest payment, their goon collectors appeared as a warning. The second time, they beat him up and tore his last tailored suit right off him. The third time, which they said was the usual "last warning," they broke his wrist with a tire iron.

As a result, Phil returned to the streets, selling drugs. Over the years, his debt shrank, but he was living in one room again and wearing cheap clothes. Besides that, the word was out about him, and no bookie would take his money until he paid off his debt. It was killing him. As he stared at himself, Phil thought that with a life like his, it was hardly worth going to the toilet.

"Who're you looking at, John Travolta-Ravolta?"

He grinned into the mirror, saw too many of his own wrinkles, and turned to the girl as she slipped into the booth across from him, a cocky little smirk on her milk-white face. Framed by the black curls that tumbled over her head, the face was already gorgeous, Phil admitted. She had long legs and breasts that pushed firmly against her school blouse and jumper. And the dimple.

"How ya doin', Helena."

"Sorry I'm late," she said breathlessly. "Had to ditch the witch who guards me."

"She'll have a Coke," Phil said to the blond waitress.

"I don't want that kind of a Coke," Helena said with a try at sophisticated flirting. "You know what I want."

Oh, yes, Phil thought, she's ripe for picking. *How* old are you?" he asked her once again.

She rolled her eyes, acting as if terribly bored by the question, but smiling at the flattery of his interest. "Old enough to know not to touch a dirty old man with a ten-inch pole." She laughed, having never used the line with anyone else but her girlfriends.

The waitress put the Coke down with the check.

"No, really," Phil insisted as if it were in jest. "How old?"

The smile disappeared, and she looked at him apprehensively. "Who cares?" she said with irritation. "I'll be fourteen in December, all right? Did you bring me my stuff?"

"No."

Her back went rigid. "What?"

Phil grinned. "Just remember what that felt like the next time we meet, the feeling that I don't have any stuff for you. Because next time I won't, if you don't bring me twice as much money."

Her mouth dropped open. "You prick! I can't . . ."

"Shut up. This isn't a public discussion, you know."

"I'm taking all the money I can get away with out of my mother's purse. I can't get . . ."

"Take more. Take things out of your apartment. Sell them. I don't give a shit how you get it. But you better get it."

"I'll kick, cold turkey," she said with intense resolve.

"Fine," he said and started to slide out of the booth.

"Wait a minute!" she whispered urgently, and as he sat back in the booth, she looked around desperately as if for help. "Do you have any with you?"

"I'm used to seeing money first, remember?"

"You're a real pusher, aren't you? Is your name really Mr. Pope?"

"No. I'm Nancy Reagan in disguise."

As she rummaged in her schoolbag, the girl said, "Yeah, 'just say no,' as if it were so goddamn easy . . . You used to be so nice."

"I am nice," Phil said, idly checking around the coffee shop before the money changed hands. "Think of the chances I take getting this stuff to you. There are people who think I should die for doing this."

She handed him bills. He did not look at them and put them in his pocket. Then he slid out of the booth and stood up. "It's under the napkin thing. Don't go after it until I get out of here. Drink your Coke; I'll pay the check. And don't smoke too much of it at once. It'll blow your pretty head off." He grinned a warning. "Don't forget. Double next time. Remember when and where?"

"Thursday at the skating rink."

As he stood at the cashier's stand, Phil watched the girl. She reached for the napkin dispenser, then turned to see if he had gone, saw him, frowned, and sat back tensely.

Oh, yes, Phil thought, ripe and hooked. He pictured how high her breasts were. When he got his change, he selected a new toothpick and walked out of the coffee shop, feeling proud of himself.

He had stayed away from Annie. The people he worked for let him know they would not be pleased if he got any more attention. But when he heard Annie was living in town with a daughter, it was too good to resist. It had not been easy getting to the girl. Her fancy school was a fortress, and Annie's housekeeper met Helena at the end of classes and drove her back to their town house. Every Saturday, however, Helena walked with three friends up Madison to the movies on Eighty-sixth Street. After the movies they ran over to Ninetieth Street and Central Park to smoke cigarettes. It took four weeks for Phil to figure out an unsuspicious introduction, but his strategy worked. He carried a bag of oranges, which split open as he walked past the girls in the park. Giggling, the girls retrieved them and he tried to stuff them in his pockets. The next week, he lent them cigarettes and was charming. Soon after, he suggested better stuff. First, it was good marijuana, and then it was crack.

Helena was their leader in daring, a smart-mouthed snooty-sounding girl who was ready to try anything in front of her friends. Phil provided for her showing off, and when the others finally lost courage, he made it easy for Helena to come back alone. Often, he righteously refused to supply anything, expressing concern that she was getting in too deep, but she begged him. She did not like it when he started charging her money, but when he explained his expenses, she accepted the price.

Phil put the new toothpick in his mouth and danced it across his teeth with his tongue. It was just the right time to double her price. She was going to need a stronger dose soon, which was fine with him. As he stepped off the curb to cross the street, he wondered when Annie would discover what was happening. Savoring what he fantasized would be her reaction, he thought about how to make sure that Annie knew he had done it.

Still, he would have to be careful. Walking downtown, he headed for his favorite Off-Track Betting parlor. He was pretty sure he could not only hook Helena deep, but that sooner or later he would get into her young, tight-fitting pants. Annie would go nuts with rage. Phil smiled. Thirteen? Hell, going on thirty. He felt so terrific, he just had to put a bet down—not a big one, but that morning in the *Form* he had spotted a long-shot lock in the ninth at Aqueduct, and if he hurried, he still had time.

What Phil had no reason to suspect was that Bridey, the Irish housekeeper who looked after Helena when Annie was in Lexington, was watching him at that moment. Having been suspicious for some time about the girl's erratic behavior and sudden disappearances, Bridey had allowed her charge to escape that day, then followed Helena to her meeting with what Bridey regarded as bog slime with a toothpick in its face.

When the girl came out of the coffee shop, Bridey kept watch at a careful distance. Helena hurried over to Fifth Avenue and into Central Park. Then she started to run, too fast for Bridey to keep up, heading north toward the Metropolitan Museum. The housekeeper watched her go, then went back to the town house on Seventy-third where she had lived with the girl and Mrs. Carney since the latter's return to New York racing. Bridey decided to call her employer to report what she had seen. She once had caught Helena smoking in her room but had given in to the girl's tearful begging that she not tell. The current incident, however, seemed much more troublesome; the man whom Bridey had seen sitting in the coffee shop with Helena alarmed every instinct of responsibility.

As soon as she heard from Bridey, Annie flew back to New York from Limeteen Farm. She had no idea who the man was or what he was doing, but Annie had already noticed that Helena was growing distant and experiencing unfamiliar, alarming mood swings. The night she arrived, Annie, Bridey, and Helena had a pleasant dinner together. Mother and daughter caught up with each other's news and made plans for a trip to St. Bart's during Helena's spring break.

"But no horses!" Helena kiddingly insisted. "And if I see you reading the *Racing Form,* I'll set it on fire!"

"I promise," Annie said, laughing happily with her daughter, wondering if, after all, she and Bridey were being alarmists.

Helena stood up abruptly and said, suddenly angry, "I can't speak French! Why do we have to go to some stupid island? I don't want to go to *Saint Bart's!*" She pronounced the name with intense sarcasm and marched out of the dining room.

Annie, after exchanging quick looks with Bridey, followed her daughter up to her bedroom.

At the door, Annie knocked.

"I *knew* you'd come up here!" Helena blurted from inside the room. "I just knew it!"

"Well, here I am. Can I come in?"

"I'm sure you *can* come in, but *may* you?" she said in a

sarcastic singsong. "That's the kind of crap they teach us at my *wonderful* school." She swung the door open. "Sure, *Mom,* come on in." Striding to the opposite wall, she turned around and crossed her arms, staring insolently at her mother.

"Are we having a fight?" Annie asked.

"No!" Helena replied with exaggerated petulance.

"Then why are you acting like this?"

Helena's eyes shifted to points all over the room. "I'm sorry, Mummy," she said genuinely, talking her way out of a trap. "Really. Let's forget it. You should *see* the homework I have tonight. Algebra. Do you understand what happens when you move the x to the other side of the equal sign? It gets divided or something." She dashed over to the table she used as a desk and opened her schoolbag.

"Something's happening to you, Helena," Annie said, trying to sound more concerned than threatening. "I want to know what it is."

Helena let her head bow down and leaned on the table. "Well," she said, "I think it's two things. Having these periods gets me really nervous. Ever since they started, sometimes I feel like my skin has been peeled off." Then she turned to her mother and looked at her angrily. "And you know, Mummy, being illegitimate just isn't what it used to be. People talk about it a lot now, about me *and* Henry, wherever *he* might be. I mean, like bastards run in the family or something . . . Family! What *family?* My brother's on the moon, my father lives somewhere else, and my mother, even if she's here, goes off to the track at dawn. There are a lot of parties I don't get invited to, you know. You're not around that much, so you don't hear about them. And at dances I know damn well that by intermission everybody there knows that I'm the bastard in the crowd. So, Mummy, why the hell don't I have a father?"

"You do. Sam Cumberland is your father," Annie said, shocked by the outburst, but somehow disbelieving its indignation.

"Oh, sure," Helena challenged. "Well, why isn't he here? Why does he live three blocks away? Why doesn't he come see my school on Fathers' Night? Why does he sneak in here to sleep with you, and why the hell don't you two get married?"

"There are answers to that last question that I don't know, but he doesn't sneak in here. You know that; he comes to see both of us. That's the main reason we live here. Helena, I'll try to answer all your questions if you'll answer one question for me."

"What?"

"Who was the man you met at Jenny's coffee shop yesterday?"

Helena's pale face mottled in an instant and her eyes opened wide. "How . . . ?" Then she glared at her mother and yelled, "That's none of your business!"

"It hasn't been because I haven't known about it," Annie said, "but I can promise you it is now. Who is he?"

Helena stood, lifted herself on her toes as if about to fly. "His name is Mr. Pope, but he's really Nancy Reagan in disguise." Then she started laughing, too hard and too loud.

"Helena, if you won't tell me, I can only promise you that you won't have another chance to meet him alone."

"Mummy, please don't do that," the girl begged earnestly.

"I have to. You're my daughter, whom I love very, very much, which may not be an important reason to you, but it's the most important reason to me. Something's happening to you that I don't like. I don't know if this man has anything to do with it, and if you won't tell me about him, I'll have to stop your seeing him. Do you understand?"

Helena looked down at the floor and mumbled yes.

Aware of the pressure she had exerted, Annie walked back to the door in an attempt to relieve it. "So why don't you try to figure out some way to talk to me about this, and I'll try to figure out just why Sam Cumberland and I don't get married. Deal?"

"Deal," the girl said, but did not look up.

Annie did not press any further. She worked late at her desk, reviewing Limeteen's financial statements, tax returns, and debts to the banks. She kept hoping Helena would appear before she went to bed, even if it was just to say good night. But she did not come down from her room and when Annie went up to give her a kiss, Helena was balled up in her usual position, apparently asleep.

Fatigued by her trip from Lexington and depressed by the figures, which showed Limeteen's worsening fiscal condition, Annie slept heavily. When she woke up the next morning at five, as she always did out of habit, she did not feel at all rested. Fretfully, she lay in bed, falling asleep and waking again. Finally, she went down to the kitchen for coffee, which Bridey was already making. Surprised at seeing her employer and not her young charge, Bridey went upstairs to see why Helena had not come down yet, ready for school. Annie heard the housekeeper open several doors, and was on her feet before Bridey called. Helena was not in the house; some of her clothes were gone. In a matter of minutes, Annie discovered that her purse was missing.

She called the police and once again hired her own private detectives. By noon, the detectives had discovered that Annie's Platinum American Express card had been used at three twenty-four that morning at a twenty-four-hour automatic teller machine to withdraw eight thousand dollars in traveler's checks. Annie went to a file in her desk and found that the American Express slip with her access number on it was missing. Later that day, the traveler's checks, immediately flagged by the company, were reported already cashed at a bank on the West Side. It was particularly bad news; the checks would not leave a trail for the police to follow, and with eight thousand in cash, Helena could hide or go anywhere.

While searching the girl's room, a private detective found a small plastic vial crammed into the inside of one of her thirty-five stuffed toy pigs. The vial was sent instantly for analysis. As soon as traces of crack were discovered in it, Bridey was taken to a police station to try to identify mug shots.

Annie called Sam, could not find him, and left messages marked "urgent" at his offices and at Number 10. Usually able to reach him on one or another of his private lines, she seldom left messages. Although their relationship was well known, they preserved certain habits of discretion. Annie had not had a chance to tell Sam of her sudden return to New York or the reason. Helena's disappearance had shaken Annie, more than when Henry had run away, more than when Barky had made his attempt to shoot her. Helena's involvement with drugs meant that her disappearance might not be entirely her choice.

Annie stared at the phone as she sat in the small den. For her, the last five years had been a commute. Trying to save Limeteen, she had had to fly from Manhattan to Lexington sometimes twice a week. She knew her absence was hard on Helena, but Annie had not realized her daughter's anger about that or about Sam. She should have known. Restless, she decided to take a walk and told Bridey to write down any messages. If Mr. Cumberland called, she was to say that Annie would be back in half an hour and that it was absolutely imperative that she see him.

As she walked up Madison, she found herself searching every face that passed, even checking people on the opposite side of the street. Knowing that Helena would not be walking on Madison Avenue, she tried to think about other things. A March wind was blowing. In the window of an expensive optical shop, she saw a pair of wire-rimmed glasses. The image of Henry's shattered glasses on his bleeding face at the Keeneland pavilion came into her mind again. Annie kept walking and tried to distract herself, but she felt there was not a safe subject in her head.

She had not seen Henry for almost three years, since those horrifying moments when he and Barky tumbled down the steps at Keeneland and were dragged away by the guards. Annie was immobilized by what Barky had said: "You and your bastards are destroying my family!" She saw the gun in her face and the murderous look in Barky's eyes the second before he was hit from behind by her son. Sam had led her up the pavilion steps, then to the office of Keeneland's director, who found out exactly what the security people had done with Barky and Henry. By the time Annie and Sam went down with the director to the security office, Henry had been allowed to leave. He had given the security guards a false name, saying he did not know Barky, had reacted only to seeing the gun, and did not want any thanks or attention.

Using his considerable influence, Sam managed to arrange Barky's transfer to a hospital instead of to the county jail.

Barky was out of control, boisterous and incoherent, with Greta Herskewitz's name constantly recurring in his tirade. Never having seen Henry before, Barky did not know his half brother; even so, it was difficult to take his insistence that he had spotted Greta as anything more than further proof of his derangement.

The incident was largely overlooked by both the audience and the press in the excitement of the astonishing record-shattering sales figures. Henry, however, called his mother at Limeteen two days later.

"I hear that Barky is saying he saw Greta and that nobody believes him," he said with no greeting. "I don't know if he's crazy for wanting to shoot you, but he did see Greta. She was with me."

"Thank you for—" but Annie heard the click of the disconnected line before she could finish.

She told Sam what Henry had said. After trying to figure it out themselves, Sam passed the information on to Barky's doctor at the clinic in Michigan where he had been sent to "convalesce" from what was referred to as a nervous breakdown. The doctor said the information about Greta was no longer germane, that Barky was spending his days reading the Bible and seldom mentioned his former fiancée in his therapy sessions.

As Annie continued her walk along Madison, she wondered if Barky might be the man whom Helena met in the coffee shop. Shaking her head, Annie rejected the idea almost as quickly as she had it. Since leaving the clinic, Barky had been working for the Liberty in Christ Ministry somewhere in North Carolina. She doubted that he knew much about drugs. Remembering what Sam had gone through to cut off Barky's access to the funds he wanted to donate to the ministry, Annie sighed and shook her head again with tired regret.

Suddenly she saw Sam across the street. She checked the traffic and crossed in the middle of the block. Halfway there, she saw him laugh and lift the hand of a woman walking with him. He kissed her hand with loving affection; she reached up to touch his cheek. Annie stopped and turned back, but the traffic came and horns blew. When she looked again, Sam and the woman had seen her. They looked caught, but with no regret. Then Sam glanced at the woman, left her, and came toward Annie. The woman was lovely, dressed beautifully in a Chanel suit, gold necklaces, and a mink coat, her brown hair coiffed classically. And she was young, quite young. She understood Sam's look, and walked away without a word in the opposite direction.

When Annie reached the sidewalk, Sam said, "I thought you were in Lexington," as he came up to her.

"Obviously," Annie said, hoping he would explain it away but knowing he would not.

"I had every intention of telling you about this—"

"Oh, Lord."

"—the moment there was something to tell."

"And that moment's here." She tried to get angry so that she would not fall apart.

"Yes," he said without apology, but not unkindly. "Annie, we have to talk. Alone. Can we take a cab back to your place? Or will Helena be there?"

"Let's just walk," Annie said and started again down Madison Avenue. After a few steps together, she said, trying not to sound bitter, "Do me a favor, Sam. Tell me all about her. I don't want to have to wonder, or hear it from anyone else."

"I didn't go around looking for this," he said. "It just happened. She's divorced from Charlie Pendergrast's nephew. Charlie was a classmate of mine at Princeton. We've known all the Pendergrasts forever. I met her at her wedding, as a matter of fact, years ago. She's a Buchanan. I hadn't seen her for years, ran into her at a dinner party in Palm Beach, and, well . . ."

They stopped at a light, then crossed. Annie could not understand where her anger was. He had said so much that under other circumstances would have infuriated her. She needed rage and began asking questions that she hoped would stimulate it.

"When was that?"

"The first of the year, some time after the holidays."

Annie tried to remember the times that she and Sam had

been together since then. "Three months . . . How old is she?"

Sam walked silently, then answered with irritated coldness, "Thirty-two, almost thirty-three."

More than twenty-five years younger than Sam; worse, more than fifteen years younger than Annie. "Just Alycia's age . . . Does she have children?" The question was an obvious one, but it smothered the anger she had begun to feel by reminding her of her engulfing concern for Helena.

"No, she doesn't, fortunately," Sam said. "I don't say that because of us; just that when there's a divorce, it's so much better . . ." He stopped, knowing he would only go deeper into that subject's bottomless hole.

"What's her name, Sam?"

"Glynn."

"Glynn," Annie repeated, then walked quickly, aware of Sam's restless obligation to stay with her. Even under the circumstances, she wanted him there. "Well, do you think it's just a passing thing, or something . . . more permanent?"

"I don't think it's 'just' a passing thing, but we haven't discussed permanence. The point is, Annie, I've become involved enough to believe that you and I . . . can't . . ." He did not finish.

"No, we can't," Annie agreed. "Will you just walk me back to the house?"

"Of course," he said, relieved to have a defined conclusion to the conversation. "There's one other thing I want to say. I've said it before and you've chosen not to take me up on it. We've known each other a long time, Annie. I don't want to forget it, or lose it to bitterness. I hope I can still see Helena and help with her expenses. I also know about the pressures you're facing with Limeteen. As I've said, you can depend on me for as much as you need at any time. Just let me know."

They walked without speaking for a block before Annie said, "If we were married, we'd get our lawyers and use money to punish each other, get revenge . . . and then turn all the memories, guilt, and failure into contempt by signing checks. Payment in full, so to speak. I'm never going to put a price on us, Sam. No payoffs."

"That's not what I meant."

"If I asked you for ten million dollars right now, you'd be able to go home, write the check, and close a lot of doors. You could go breezing into this thing with . . . Glynn, worrying a lot less about walking away from whatever it was that we've shared for almost twenty-three years. Other than that, she sounds perfect for you. After all, a Buchanan . . . Good Lord, Sam! Is this the rich man's right, to trade in for young flesh? Why didn't I see it coming?"

"Listen to me, Annie. Every relationship either grows or dies. I asked you to marry me, more than once. It was the most obvious step for us. I wanted it and needed it. You turned me down. More than once. *You* wanted to live separately, and even after what happened with Henry, *you* were content that Helena had no live-in father—"

"I wasn't content! There were so many reasons, Sam. Don't make it sound so simple now."

"I know it wasn't. God knows that nothing about us has ever been simple. But we could have fought to get closer. Instead, we leveled off at a comfortable distance from each other. Obviously, it left a good deal of empty space to fill."

"With someone young and fresh who has none of the problems we have from . . . what do we call it? Our history?"

"Annie, the problems weren't . . . the problem. We'd reached an impasse; we were treading water. Good Christ, you know what I mean. You tell me why we didn't get married."

Annie looked up at the sky, hoping to see the stars. There were none. "Helena asked me the same thing last night."

"I'm not surprised. And let me tell you this. No matter what's happened, we've come as close as we ever could. You'd never let anything or anyone interfere with what you've worked for. You're first and foremost a horsewoman, Annie. Running Limeteen, making it work, finding the goddamn horses; that excludes me and Henry and even Helena, as a matter of fact. I'm sure they'd agree with me. That's who you are. There's nothing wrong about that—though maybe they wouldn't agree on that point."

Annie closed her eyes for a moment, refusing to cry.

"You're hitting me where it really hurts. You don't know about Helena, so I know it's not on purpose. But this is horrible."

"What's the matter?" he said, concerned.

"I made some bad mistakes. Other things have happened that I had no control over. I blame myself for a lot, but not for everything. I'm not going to give up or fall apart now that you've found someone to fill your 'empty space.' I *just won't* do it. And there's more important things, anyway." She looked at him imploringly.

"I know that. What's happened to Helena?"

Annie told him the details; he offered to help, with influence, with money, with whatever it took. Annie realized that he could offer help but that he was not compelled—as a parent is. His love came from choice; hers from instinct. Perhaps that was the greatest difference, and Annie could not keep from resenting it.

He made her promise to call him if she needed anything. When they reached the door of her house, Annie put the key in the lock and, as she opened the door, said, "I know women who put up with little flings and wait for their men to return. I don't know if this is a little fling for you, but whatever, don't come back. I'd never take another chance."

Sam said nothing, but nodded his acceptance. Quickly, Annie closed the door behind her. She felt herself ready to fall, and hurried to the stairs to get to her bedroom. She heard noises in the living room just as Bridey appeared in the hallway, looking shaken, saying nothing, but motioning apprehensively in the direction of the living room.

When she followed Bridey into the brightly lit room, Annie's stomach knotted. A uniformed policeman stood awkwardly by the fireplace, and two men sitting in the twin chintz chairs rose to greet her. One of them was Lyle McCracken.

Annie was almost grateful. "You're not welcome in my home, Mr. McCracken." Fury held her together as if she were riding herself, a phantom jockey whipping herself to stay in control.

"Mrs. Carney," the FBI agent said blandly, "this is Lieutenant Donner of the New York Police Department, and Patrolman O'Fallon. We have something to show you."

By way of introducing himself, the lieutenant held out a police record with mug shots on it. It showed full-face and profile pictures of Phil Angelo. Stunned and confused, Annie looked at the lieutenant; then, understanding, she turned to Bridey. The housekeeper, still uncomfortable in the presence of the police, said, "That's the man. I saw him."

Annie stared at Phil's pictures again. "If I see him before you do," she said with calm rage, "I'll kill him, and I won't care that you know it was me."

The two men glanced quickly at each other; then the lieutenant spoke. "Mrs. Carney, you ought to know a couple of things. Today in New York, we got around three hundred calls about missing children. Our resources aren't that big and our authority pretty much ends at the city limits. Mr. McCracken has assured me that he and the Bureau have no interest in you, only in the Angel. For your daughter's sake, you and I could sure use the FBI's help, you know what I mean?"

Annie glanced at Lyle McCracken. "I do, Lieutenant," she said. "But I've had some experience with the Bureau and Mr. McCracken. I don't trust anything they say, and you shouldn't either. He was happy to ruin me, and came pretty close." Then she turned back to the police lieutenant. "But if you think he'll help find my daughter, I'll do whatever you say. I want some ground rules. I work with you, Lieutenant, and Mr. McCracken doesn't come into my house, ever."

The FBI agent said, "I'll wait outside," and left the room. Annie noted how he had aged—the slump in his shoulders and the added weight around his waist. His eyes were the same: cold, emotionless gray.

As soon as she heard the front door close, Annie said, "Lieutenant, either he's lying or you are. Phil Angelo worked *with* the FBI. He was their witness against me, and they let him go free. Do you know about that?"

The lieutenant smiled. "It's like throwing a fish back after you catch it. The bigger fish usually eat it right away, but if they don't, your fish grows and learns a lot about what goes on down in the pond, you know? So when you catch him again and really get a good hook into him, like selling drugs to a kid, then you can let him hang on it until he talks a lot, or you can make a really good deal to throw him back again, or both."

"I'm damned if I want my daughter to be used like that!"

The police officer squeezed another smile on his face and shook his head. "No, don't worry about that. From what I understand, and I don't mean this to hurt you, your daughter made her own choices, you know? All she'll have to do is testify that he sold her drugs. For that, you *might* get her back." He watched Annie's reaction. She went very pale and quickly sat down on a nearby couch. The lieutenant shrugged fatalistically. "McCracken has a lot of juice at the FBI. He wants this Angel guy a lot. I have to tell you that if that guy's file hadn't had a Bureau referral on it and McCracken hadn't come roaring downtown, the odds against your daughter's case even getting to someone's desk before Christmas would've been off the board."

Annie caught the handicapper's phrase. "Interested in horse racing, Lieutenant?"

"Oh, yeah, and Limeteen's been good to me. There was a thirty-to-one long shot a couple of years ago at Belmont . . ."

"Sweet Steven."

"You got it. I owe you."

"You don't owe me anything. Just find my daughter. What do you want me to do?"

He pressed his lips together and shook his head. "You're stuck with waiting. Just, if she calls, make it easy for her to come home. I mean, don't be angry or anything. If she contacts you, let us know right away. While you're waiting, I'll tell you about everything that comes in. I'll do everything I can to find your daughter. It ain't that much; she could be in South America by now. But it's the best I can offer."

"She didn't take her passport. I checked."

Lieutenant Donner said, "That's helpful. Maybe she wasn't thinking about going too far. Let me ask you some questions about her friends, hangouts . . ."

The lieutenant was as good as his word. He called Annie once a day to tell her everything that had developed, which, day after day, was nothing. Her ground rules were obeyed scrupulously; she never heard from or saw McCracken, although from what she heard from Lieutenant Donner, the FBI was mounting a nationwide effort to find Helena Carney and Phil Angelo.

Annie stayed in the town house, barely sleeping, barely eating, staring at the street from the front windows, grabbing the phone when it rang. Each time it did, she expected to hear Helena say, "Mummy, please come get me." Instead, she had to speak to the trainers who were readying the Limteen runners for the coming season, or the stallion and foaling managers at the farm. Early spring was the busiest time for a breeder-owner, and that year, every decision was crucial to Annie. Now that Sam was absent, she realized how often she had used him as a sounding board for problems and how much she had valued his advice as a horseman. She admitted to herself that the main reason she would not go out was the devastating chance of running into him and Glynn on the street again.

A week passed. Helena was twenty blocks south and five avenues west, in the fourth-floor railroad flat in Hell's Kitchen that Phil Angelo called home. He had taken all of the girl's clothes away so that she could not leave. He also had taken the eight thousand dollars that she gave him, believing he would help her hide. In return, he provided her with take-out Chinese or Mexican food, almost as much crack as she could smoke, and his bed.

Helena quickly lost track of time and much of reality. When she was alone, she occasionally tried to open the door of the apartment, but it had dead bolts, and she had no key. Not ever sure of when Phil would return, she always waited with desperate agitation. What he usually did to her before relinquishing the drug was painful and brutal, but she barely remembered from one time to the next.

Then someone banged on the door, and yelled. Phil recognized the voice, put on his pants, and unbolted the locks. Three men came in, staring at Helena on the bed as one of them talked. She pulled a sheet over her body and looked at the ceiling. Phil argued and yelled. The man who spoke said something that caused Helena to remember.

". . . But we don't want the FBI, Phil. They're looking for you all over the fuckin' country. So zip up your fly. You're takin' a vacation." The man looked at Helena on the bed. "Jesus, Phil, you're real class, y'know?"

Phil did not respond, but dressed quickly, then came over to the bed. He smacked Helena across the face, jerked her up to a sitting position, and said urgently, "Remember this. Tell your mother that the Angel sent his regards. Say it!" When he raised his hand to hit her again, she said quickly, "The Angel sends his regards."

He let go and she slumped back on the bed. When she looked again, the men were gone and the door was open. She rushed to close it. It was still dark, and she searched the apartment for something to wear. Finding only Phil's clothes, she dressed in a shiny dark suit of his, rolling up the sleeves and putting on enough socks to hold the shoes on. She opened the door and for a long time stood there, too terrified to go through it. Finally, she walked down the seemingly endless steps and reached the street. Not remembering where she was, she went to the corner and stared at the street signs. A police car cruised by, then jammed to a stop. Two officers jumped out and came toward her. Helena started to run, and lost both shoes before they caught her.

Annie stayed with Helena in her hospital room for a week. Other than delivering Phil's message, the girl remained silent, she was sedated. When the doctors recommended a private clinic in Connecticut that specialized in drug detoxification, Annie arranged for the transfer and rode out with her daughter in an ambulance. Only then did Helena offer the slightest communication. She reached for her mother's hand and gripped it hard for the rest of the trip. Annie learned from the staff of the clinic that her support would be vital at a certain stage in the treatment, but for the first few weeks, she should not plan on visiting or calling. She hugged and kissed Helena goodbye. Annie left the clinic feeling as if a part of her had been torn out.

Depending on Limeteen to help her get through the weeks

of waiting for Helena and the pain of losing Sam, she flew to Lexington. On her arrival, she was informed by her farm manager that a meeting was scheduled in two days with the three banks from which Annie had secured loans based on Limeteen as collateral. Annie went to the meeting with Delansig and Chigger Beasley. The banks were blunt. They were going to consider forcing the farm into Chapter 11 if Limeteen's debts could not be restructured to their satisfaction. Delansig managed to convince the banks that such an action would jeopardize the possibility of their ever realizing repayment. Like the hardboot snake charmer that he was, Chigger made it clear that such an action would scare the whole thoroughbred industry into never trusting banks again. The banks gave Annie a six-month extension of her loans to the end of the current racing season.

The same afternoon, as she went through the stacks of mail that had piled up in her absence, she opened a padded envelope, and Winnie's wedding ring fell out. A letter accompanied it:

Dear Mrs. Carney,

Henry knows that I'm writing this, although he doesn't agree about it. I've wanted you to know about me for a long time, but I couldn't tell you for many reasons. You may remember that we met when I was about to marry Barky Cumberland. I enclose the ring. You gave it to my mother just before I was born. So first, I must thank you for my life, and all you did for her. And now, my incredible happiness.

Henry and I were married last week. I wanted very much for you to be here, but Henry said no. I promise you I'll do everything I can to bring you two back together. It will not be easy, as I'm sure you understand.

In the meantime, know my deep gratitude.

Greta

Annie shut the door and sat alone for several hours in her study. For the first time, she could not make herself go down to the barns for distraction. She did not cry; instead she felt a deathlike numbness begin to spread. Believing that she had to leave instantly or Limeteen would die with her, she hurried to her room, stuffed some clothes in a bag, and ran out of Limeteen Hall. She drove away knowing that she was not escaping from anything, only freeing the place of her presence.

THIRTY

ANNIE PICKED at a piece of cuticle on one finger. She put the brittle irritation between her teeth and tore the flesh, slowly, painfully, unwilling to stop pulling until the hangnail was off at the root. When she sucked at the finger, she tasted blood. She thought of other bad times when her fingers stayed sore and scabbed for weeks.

She felt as if her nervous system were lying on the surface of her skin, a razor was scraping over it and shaving it raw. Annie's despair was not about being alone. She had accepted that as a condition of her life a long time ago. Whether she was driving around all day going nowhere, or, as at that moment, sweating on a sagging bed in the Dixie Motel, her anguish led to no answers. There was only the futile question: If this is how it's going to end, why had they come into her life at all?

No one was left who saw her as she was and who still wanted to be with her. She mistrusted any need for others.

Her tendency was to define herself by what she had survived rather than by whom she knew and loved, or what she had accomplished. She had not seen her son for years, she could not see her daughter, her molested, drug-addicted daughter, for weeks. Damnably, most destructively, so much of everything involved Sam. Losing him was the worst, for he knew her the best. And how, after all this time, could he . . . ?

Fury only deepened her depression, and Annie tried to control the thought of him. She knew Sam better than he knew himself, and therefore knew all the answers to "how could he?" She lay on her bed in the roadside cabin with the acid of anger and poison from pain moving through her as steadily as her blood. Wishing the feeling would jolt her enough to make her move, she knew it would not. She felt paralyzed, smothered, and she choked for a breath of humid, spring air.

Another spring. Hope and expectation. She had met Sam in early April. She realized it was almost exactly thirty-three years ago. In spite of the heat, she began to shiver, and gasped for another breath. Covering her face with her aching fingers, she said aloud, "That's so *long,* Sam," and thought again, as she had over the past ten days, of her life as a terrible waste, and of ending it.

Again she became aware of the bugs crashing into the screens of her cabin. Covered only with a light sweat, Annie lay naked on her back. She wondered how many other people were lying alone, ready to die in a motel on some decaying highway. For no other reason than fellowship, Annie gave a low throaty laugh. The humidity of a Southern spring morning was getting thicker. She picked up the lumpy pillow to wipe the sweat off her face; the pillow case was cleaner than the crusty towel hanging on a nail by the sink. Then she thought of why she had arrived at the Dixie Motel, which gave her reason enough to sit up and swing her feet to the floor.

She walked over to the sink, willing to trust the water but not the towel. Turning on the twenty-five-watt bulb above the cracked mirror, she looked at her body and wished Sam were standing behind her, reaching for her, touching her where he knew she liked to be touched. Without any warning, too many memories hit her at once. Her throat closed and she had to struggle again for breath.

She braced herself on the sink with her arms and let her head hang down. The pain went into her stomach, then weakened her legs. She could hear her heart beating; twice, it skipped, built up pressure, and then pounded hard. She muttered quietly, "Well, what else do you think about alone in a cruddy motel except suicide and sex?"

She turned on the spigot and threw cold water over her face and body, oblivious of the growing puddle on the floor. Her finger stung but she did not think about it. The rest of her body was all right; riding kept her back straight, upper arms and shoulders tight, breasts firm, stomach flat, butt small, and thighs hard. Her skin was not as soft as it had been, despite her wearing straw hats against the sun. Her hair was a mess at the moment, but was still thick and amber blond, though there was the occasional gray filament. She saw one, but let it be, brushing it back with her hand.

Still wet, she quickly turned away from the mirror and walked over to the chair where she had put her clothes. Without looking at any clock, Annie knew it was five. It made no difference where she was or what she had done the night before. In New York, in California, at the stud in Ireland, or the *haras* in France, when it was five A.M. in Kentucky, Annie would wake up. A twenty-year habit is not broken by time zones, obligations, or, in this case, despair, which prevented much sleep anyway.

Since Annie had driven away from Limeteen Farm ten days before, five o'clock had been the hardest time of every day for her. At that hour, everything that she was trying to face came in hard, particularly blaming herself about Helena. So far, none of the defenses had developed that perspective and distance were supposed to provide.

She had found her way to the Dixie Motel because it was about a half mile from a race track running the last card of its spring meeting that day. The track was not a first-class one; in fact, it was seedy and rumored to be closing down. Annie wanted only to get close to some horses in order to help her through the five o'clock horror. After that, at least the sun came up.

She pulled on her pants and boots, and tucked in her shirt. Taking her bag, she unhooked the screen door and stepped outside. The spring on the door stretched noisily, and she turned quickly to keep it from slamming, not wanting to wake someone who was fortunate enough to be able to sleep. The farm's station wagon was parked beside her cabin; Annie got in, backed it out, and drove onto Highway 207. She opened the windows, and the wind cooled her as it dried her clothes.

She supposed that people at the farm would think she was having some kind of breakdown. No one had called the police; though she was driving around through several states, the station wagon would have been pretty easy to find. She glanced over at the glove compartment, then back at the highway. The .38 was in there. Four images that the gun summoned up flipped through her mind: Blimpie on the floor of Charlie Dell's study, the shots fired above the heads of the French mob, the surprise on Jimmy Lee's face just before the blood gushed out of his mouth, and the barrel placed against Glorious Girl's head. Only the last caused her tears, as it always did, and the new image of the gun came again—holding it to her own temple. Annie figured that the idea of putting the gun to her head had as much to do with blowing away memory as it did with ending her life.

"Radical surgery," she said out loud.

The first light of dawn was beginning. In the distance, Annie saw the outline of the grandstand. Unfamiliar with the track's layout, she slowed down, looking for an access road. Several other pairs of headlights turned in the darkness, and Annie followed them. None of the vehicles hesitated for the guard, who was leaning with his hands in his pockets against his cubicle beside the chain-link gate.

She had owner's stickers from Saratoga, Churchill Downs, Keeneland, and Belmont on her front bumper. The guard, an old man wearing the track's security shirt, pulled at his cap with the Confederate flag above the visor. He had no intention of holding her up, so she kept moving. Then she saw the track on her right.

Outlined in the dawn light, one by one, three thoroughbreds came out of a ground fog that covered the mile oval. Their exercise riders were straight-legged in the irons. The horses galloped easily by, made the stretch turn, and disappeared into the mist again. Annie heard more coming and smelled the sweet odor of manure in the fresh morning air. She pulled up to the nearest barn and parked. Not wanting to be recognized, she took an old tweed hat from the door pocket and hid her hair under it. Then she got out and walked over to the track, putting on her dark glasses.

She reached the rail and gratefully put her hands on it. Several colts went by, one breezing in company, another roaring a rhythmic natural groan as it pounded along in a slow gallop.

Then, for a moment, everything became incredibly still. Annie looked around, and it seemed to her that time had stopped, leaving her for an instant in a place of pure calm. The thousands of empty seats in the grandstand were witnesses. The sun burned orange above the mist, which rose with its new heat. A single dying oak tree in the infield stood like a sentry. The moment was broken by the pounding approach of a thoroughbred and a yell from the man on his back.

"Whoa, whoa, WHOA, goddammit!"

The colt appeared, swirling the mist around him. He rose up, leaped sideways, and neatly threw the rider out of the saddle.

"She-e-e-*it!*" the rider yelled as he fell and hit the ground. Without hesitation, the colt shot forward in a flat-out run, picking up speed as he passed Annie. Automatically she began timing him in her mind as he passed the four-furlong pole, irons flying. She had seen his one white sock on the front off side, the crooked lightning bolt of a blaze dividing his face, the slight foamy wash over his reddish bay coat. She also noticed his way of favoring his near back leg, and the enlargement in his back joints. But the speed! He passed the track's finish line, going on around the clubhouse turn until he passed the second-furlong pole.

Annie said a number to herself and could not believe it.

"My Lord!" she said aloud. Even for a riderless horse, the time was unbelievable. Across the infield, the colt began to pull himself up. The siren from the track's ambulance parked by the officials' stand finally sounded the warning for a loose horse.

"Goddamn horse can't wait for the goddamn card!" The exercise rider was up, holding his ribs and limping off the track. Seeing Annie, he smiled and shook his head.

"Looks kinda ouchy on his back legs," Annie offered, trying not to show she wanted to know more.

"Oh, yeah, toes out like hell, but it don't stop him running none. Trouble is, he don't get too far." They looked down the backstretch; an outrider was closing in on the colt, who offered no resistance. Even at the distance, Annie and the exercise rider could hear him roaring, different from the normal rhythmic noise of a gallop. It was deeper, harder, down in his lungs.

"Well, he had a good work, I guess," Annie said.

"Yeah, 'cept he's in a claimer this afternoon. I was supposed to hold him in for a little jog. Shit, my trainer's going to have my ass." He spat as the outrider led the colt, roaring badly, over to him.

Annie stood near the rail, watching every move the colt made. The outrider was laughing. "You want to try again, Benny, or you want me to lead him in?"

"I tell you, this sucker's got three balls and it's springtime, that's all."

Taking the colt's reins, the exercise boy jumped easily back in his saddle. The colt remained placid, standing with his head down, still trying to get breath. Then he saw Annie looking at him. He lifted his head high, distracted from his need for air. His ears pricked up hard and straight to forty-five degrees; his nostrils flared. He stared at her and she met it.

"Come on, you goddamn plater," the exercise rider said. "If somebody claims you today, I won't have to begin another day of my life on *your* back and *my* ass."

"Could you walk him over here a second?" Annie asked.

"Oh, sure, hon."

Without breaking his gaze, the colt moved slowly forward,

watching Annie. When he reached the rail, he shuddered. He looked down, put his teeth on the wood, then starting gnawing at it, convulsively arching his neck, and sucking air.

"A cribber, too?" Annie asked.

"As advertised. His stall looks like the termites had an orgy."

"Who's your trainer?"

"Willie Sorby, or he was until I lost this damn horse. Come on, back off that wood, you crazy—"

"What kind of race today?" Annie asked, too urgently, she knew.

"Five furlongs, maiden two-year-olds, five-thousand-dollar claimer," the exercise rider said, misinterpreting her excitement and smiling his presumption. "But hon, don't bet on him. He only runs three or four furlongs like that before he can't breathe. Hey, listen, aren't you new around here?"

Annie smiled to keep him talking. "Sure am. What's his name?"

"Base Blood. But he's a quitter. I got a filly in the fifth, a real lock . . . Maybe I'll tell you about her over at the backstretch kitchen. We call it the Armpit, but the coffee's not bad."

"Don't you think you'd better walk that colt out?"

Looking surprised, he said, "Oh, well, thanks a whole lot for the advice, hon. I sure do need advice this morning. Come on, you goddamn piss bag." Irritated, he pulled the colt back and turned him down the backstretch. Defiant, Base Blood resisted a moment, glanced at Annie, then followed the exercise rider's command.

Annie quickly moved down the rail so that she had a straight-on view of the colt walking away. The drop of his hips meant he had some serious soreness in the hocks. The toeing-out was pronounced. But the rest of Base Blood's conformation, his unique structural relationship between the limbs and body, made Annie's heart stop and punch through the second time that morning. Knowing that nobody had taken the trouble to look beyond the cribbing and the toeing-out, she wanted to follow him to his stall, go down his bones, feel for heat in the joints. Unconsciously rubbing her fingers together, she guessed he was sixteen and a half hands, with a back the perfect length for his legs. Contrary to what the roaring implied, he had an enormous chest, plenty of room for the lungs to expand if he could just use them.

Annie ran to the station wagon, grabbed her binoculars from under the front seat, and hurried back to the rail. She watched Base Blood walk through the gap in the rail until he was lost from view behind the barns. By then Annie was smiling. She took no time thinking of consequences; she wanted only to find a phone and wake up her farm manager. He would crank up the computer and plug in to the Jockey Club's twenty-four-hour on-line service to find out Base Blood's breeding, not that the information would do anything to change Annie's mind. She would also order the farm's small van to start driving down to pick up the colt.

She walked quickly toward the station wagon. At the barn, she noticed the hotwalkers leading horses around their ring, grooms mucking out stalls and rubbing down horses, exercise riders waiting for the next set, talking with their trainers. In midstep she saw Frank Carney staring at her as if he were facing a firing squad. Annie stopped as another man took the shank of the colt Frank had been leading. He let the colt go, never taking his eyes off Annie. She had not seen him in twelve years. His hair still lay at all angles on his head like grain after a rain, but it had turned gray, almost white.

"Hello, Frank," she called, unwilling to pretend she had not seen him.

Her voice caused him to grimace. Then he shook his head and walked over to her.

"I didn't really need this today." His voice was worn rough, like a cough.

Annie tried not to react to what she saw. Lines cut deep into his leather face. They ran through his cheeks and the skin around his eyes. His mouth and jaw were still set hard, his body was straight, and his blue-green eyes still gleamed with hatred.

"Well?"

"I didn't know you were here, Frank. I came for my own reasons."

Surprise lifted his creased face. Then it fell again, closed by suspicion and malice.

"Don't fool with me, Annie."

"I won't bother you."

Over the years, an occasional rumor had reached her that, after he was released from the penitentiary, he began working tracks at fairs. Annie always stopped people when they mentioned him. She did not wish him any more ill, but she had never wanted to have anything to do with him again. Until that moment.

"Except I could really use a favor."

Frank Carney looked at her with growing anger. "What?"

"I need someone to claim a horse for me."

He looked away and ran his hand through his hair. "There are twenty trainers on this backstretch who'd go through hoops to claim a horse for the Countess of Limeteen Farm."

"I can't trust them, Frank."

The implication surprised Annie as much as Frank. His reaction was to walk away from her. She did not hesitate to follow, and quickly caught up with him. They both walked in a hard silence.

"D'you ever marry Sam Cumberland?" he finally asked. "I haven't been reading the society pages for a while."

"No, I never did. You still drinking enough Jack Daniel's to fall in a ditch twice a week?"

"I can't afford Jack Daniel's," he said.

A horse being led past them shied and whinnied, but neither of them turned. They walked tensely.

He coughed, then said, "Where's this claimer?"

"I don't know. Willie Sorby's his trainer."

"Oh, fine. The milkshake man."

"What's that mean?"

"You got a problem horse, you take him to Willie's drugstore and he makes a shake that'll get the poor damn horse around the track."

"That's probably why he was washy on his work this morning."

"What's his name?"

"Base Blood."

Frank stopped walking. "A bay, toes out pretty good?"

"You know him?"

"I've seen him. Annie, he's a cribber."

"I know. He ran four furlongs in forty-six seconds! That's incredible even without his rider—"

" 'Without his rider'? Annie . . ."

"He *wanted* to run; the boy wouldn't let him, so he threw him. I've never seen a horse who wanted to run so much. He's not a beautiful horse, but he's strong-made around the shoulders, ran right on the rail with no one telling him how to go. He's sore because of running on that bad foot, but his legs—" She stopped abruptly, and stood staring at Frank Carney. "My Lord, here I am again, trying to convince you about a horse."

"You're an owner, Annie," he said with forthright contempt. "That's what owners do."

Grooms and exercise riders, shouting greetings and insults at one another, led colts and fillies by. Annie and Frank angrily looked off in separate directions. She had not been to a bush track like this one for a long time and was depressed by the condition and quality of most of the horses she saw. Misformed or old, sore, sick, swaybacked, they represented the sad remainder of the tens of thousands of thoroughbreds foaled every year who failed to make it. Sent to tracks like this one, they were run into the ground for any money they could pick up before they broke down. When they finally did, the truck from a dog food company was always nearby.

"We might as well get coffee," Frank said. They walked silently to the backstretch kitchen. It was a purely functional, unpainted, screened-in cabin on a concrete slab with a basic coffee shop chow line. Frank held the screen door open out of habit. Annie accepted the courtesy without comment. In the food line, she took two doughnuts along with her coffee, suddenly hungrier than she had been for a couple of weeks. They sat down on folding metal chairs facing each other across a small plastic table. Annie watched Frank pour a steady stream of sugar into his coffee, an unfamiliar custom.

"What's the deal, Annie?"

"I'd like you to claim that horse for me this afternoon. I'm not licensed at this track and I don't want anyone to know I'm the claimer."

He stared at her, took a swallow of the burning coffee, and let out a deep breath. "My groom quit a week ago. I'm mucking out my own stalls with a green boy says he wants to learn something. I told one of my owners I wouldn't run his filly today because she was so sore she could barely stand up. The owner has a girlfriend coming all the way from Atlanta, wanted to show off his silks out on the track. So he called up this morning early and ordered the filly out of my stall. I just walked her over to a fella who'll pump enough cortisone into her ankles to grow a beard on them if she lives long enough . . ."

"Still a hay-oats-and-water man?" she asked with an edge of respect in her voice.

"Pretty much. It isn't easy on this backstretch. There's so much elephant juice back here, a horse can get hopped just taking a deep breath. But what I'm telling you, Annie, is that I'm down to two horses. One's six years old, and you don't want to hear about the half-blind, all-lame gelding. The racing office knows I sleep in the tack room. They wouldn't accept my credit to claim the trash."

"I'll have cash here by post time to cover the claim and your fee."

He glared at her, any easing of his animosity forgotten.

"I want to tell you something. In the penitentiary, they 'suggested' that I go see this lady shrink they had there. I refused until a fella told me it'd look good to the parole board. So I went. Big waste of time and tax money, this smiling crazy lady and me talking for fifty minutes a week. But she did say one thing, that killing Certainty wasn't only about hooch or you having a baby with Sam Cumberland. I did it to kill the part of me that ever loved you. I believe that, and I'll *never* take any kind of fee from you!"

"Then Limeteen Farm will owe you a favor."

"I don't ask for favors."

"What the hell can I do, Frank?"

"You can tell me why you had to turn up on this particular backstretch on this particular day."

"That's too long a story, Frank. All that matters here is that I want that colt. What do *you* want?"

He watched her, then finished his coffee in a gulp. Hers was still too hot, and she no longer was hungry for the doughnuts.

Putting his mug back on the table, he said, bitterly, "Nothing." Then he stood up. "Get your money. I'll meet you in front of the racing secretary's office at noon to put in the bid. And keep your hair under that hat."

He gazed at her a moment, then walked out the screen door and let it slam shut. Annie watched him stride away along the dirt path back toward his barn. She wondered what he would have asked for if he were not so stubborn, proud, and strong. Probably he would want nothing more than a decent horse to train. There was no doubt in her mind that he still knew more about horses than anyone in the world, and that it probably was killing him not to be able to work with good quality. Her mind jumped to a conclusion before she knew the reasons for it. If Base Blood was the horse she thought he was, Frank Carney would . . .

She shook her head and drank her coffee. After what he had done to Certainty, she could never give Frank another horse. She thought of the time it must have taken for an ex-convict horse killer to get a trainer's license in any state, then to convince any owner in the world to trust him. She wondered how many years he had been nursing cripples on bush tracks, waiting for something to come along that he could help win. He could have asked her, but Frank never took a shortcut in his life and never would.

What the prison psychiatrist had told him was true, Annie thought. She recalled what Frank had said to her at the time. "If I hadn't killed Certainty, I'd have killed you."

She was sorry she remembered that, and got up to look for a pay phone.

THIRTY-ONE

AT THE END of four furlongs, Base Blood had six lengths of daylight between him and the horse running second. Then he hit the wall. Coming around the final turn into the stretch, he faltered. Annie could hear him roaring over the yells of the sparse crowd. Base Blood had started at twenty-to-one with relatively few supporters in the stands. Even those who had put their money on him did not advertise their wisdom with the usual shouts of encouragement. The jockey thrashed with his whip as Base Blood's neck sank lower with every stride. The rest of the field was closing fast; then Base Blood stumbled.

Annie flinched and muttered, "Dammit." Frank Carney kept watching the colt. In a glance, Annie recognized his familiar anger at the mistreatment of a horse. Base Blood pulled himself up and lurched forward, oblivious of the jockey's whip. The pack of horses rushed up beside him. Gasping for more air, he lunged. One of the other runners caught him at the finish line. Annie took a quick breath. The track had its excuse to flash the pulsing PHOTO sign, a feeble attempt to instill a little excitement into the long afternoon.

"See what I mean?" Annie said as the field went by. She and Frank Carney stood with the grooms in their area near the finish line. Annie still wore her hat and sunglasses. Her adrenaline was flowing and her eyes narrowed. Watching the colt return, she hoped he would not collapse. The roaring of his lungs continued as he shuddered again to a walk. Then he stopped and stood still, much to the jockey's irritation, who whipped him toward the finish line. Annie started toward the track, but Frank held her, his calloused hand gripping her left elbow.

"You'll have your time with him," he said. "Don't worry. That horse can take whatever that dumb boy gives him." Then he turned and looked at her. "You're right. That's a lot of colt"—he turned back to watch— "with a lot of problems."

Annie did not speak for a moment, grateful for Frank Carney's approval of her judgment. She felt his fingers drop away from her arm. His opinion about a horse still meant more to her than anyone's. She knew that he would never offer a positive assessment without believing it.

They watched the field of horses trotting back to the finish line. Base Blood came last, so noticeably sore in his back legs that Annie grimaced sympathetically and Frank indicated his agreement with her expression. The jockey lofted his crop over his valet's head. The crop fell in the dirt near Annie's feet. Picking it up, she walked along with the track official, who would inform the jockey and groom that the horse had been claimed.

Exhausted, whistling from his throat, Base Blood looked up and saw Annie. He lifted his head in recognition.

The numbers flashed up on the totalizer board across the track from the stands, proclaiming another horse the winner. As the jockey slid off Base Blood, he saw Frank Carney standing nearby and understood he had made the claim.

"D'you buy this shit maker, Carney?"

Frank nodded once.

"Well, congratulations! You got a great buy. Five thousand bucks for a thousand pounds of dog food." He laughed until he felt something flick his ear.

"This yours?" Annie said. When the jockey turned around to face her, she held the crop to his nose.

"That's right," he said, his hands on his hips. Annie dropped the crop in a pile of dung, then stepped on it with her boot.

"Hey," the jockey bleated, "what the hell d'you do that for?"

"To let you know what I thought of that ride," Annie said tersely. "I ought to whip you the way you whipped that colt!" She turned and followed Base Blood. Several grooms and jockeys who had heard the exchange hooted.

Annie ignored them; she was watching Base Blood as he was led around the track by his groom. Walking beside the colt, she tried to sense how badly he was hurting. He was watching her as well, even though his neck drooped almost horizontal to the ground and the whistling from his throat continued. Then without warning, he hacked out a cough hard enough to stop his walking.

Frank quietly came up beside Annie. "Real sore," he said quietly.

"Yeah," Annie said, wanting to ask more but holding back.

"He might have some hemorrhaging in the lungs. If he does, let it heal natural. Don't give him—" Abruptly, he stopped talking.

Annie knew why and did not look over at him. Their past had broken into his present again. Annie regretted it. She wanted him to help her, and somehow had to make him overlook their history.

When they passed the guards at the spit box's chain-link enclosure, Annie approached Base Blood's groom. "Mind if I wash him down?"

A young kid of about seventeen with bad teeth and lank hair, he looked around to make sure the guards and the track vets were observing the transfer. "All right with me," he said and slipped the bridle off Base Blood. Annie moved quickly to put her halter on him and attach the shank. As she did so, Base Blood lifted his head to smell her hand.

"You got a real fine horse, ma'am," the groom said. "I know he's a wind sucker, and he's sore, but if you could just find a way to get him around that, he's got more heart . . . He never stops trying for you." Embarrassed because he had revealed his affection, the groom started to walk away.

"Thanks," Annie called. "We'll take good care of him."

"Can I tell you something else?"

"Sure," Annie said, removing her sunglasses. If anyone was going to recognize her, she wanted that kid to know who she was.

"When Base Blood was four days old, they took his dam away," he said, unwilling to look directly at Annie. "She had to wet-nurse a weanling with better blood lines whose own dam had died dropping him. They was going to put Base Blood down, but somebody liked him and let him out to find a broodmare who'd accept him. None did, and one kicked him up pretty bad. So he was fed out of bottles until he was fat enough to sell as a weanling. My owner bought him for fifty dollars."

Annie moved away, presumably to turn on the hose. She could not talk. Frank Carney said, "Then he should be real happy, making all that profit."

"Oh, he will be, for sure," the groom answered, and gazed at Base Blood. "I sure liked that colt. Good luck with him."

Frank raised one hand in acknowledgment, and the boy wandered slowly out the gate. No one spoke. Annie put her sunglasses on a ledge of the barn. The water splattered and Frank watched, picking Annie's sunglasses off the ledge and putting them in his pocket.

When Annie finished washing Base Blood, she started to walk him. She avoided eye contact with Frank. It usually took about twenty minutes to cool a horse down before it was ready to pass urine. Annie needed the time.

As she came around the spit barn for the fifteenth time, Frank said, "He's ready." Annie led the colt into a stall where a catcher joined her. She and Frank waited outside the closed

stall while the catcher whistled softly. Both had attended the
ritual hundreds of times. Nevertheless, it was still slightly ridiculous and eased the tension. Annie took advantage of the
change in mood.

"I know the meeting's over today, but I think it'd be a
mistake to ship him right away."

Frank did not respond. She reminded herself that she had
not asked him a direct question. "You agree, Frank?"

"Yep."

"Can we use your empty stall?"

"That'd be fine," he said, "but I don't want any of your
fancy trucks pulling up to my tack room door."

"I'll have them park off the backstretch," she said, "and
we'll walk the colt away when we leave. A groom's coming
along, so he'll take care of it."

Frank handed her the sunglasses. The stall door opened; the
track vet inserted a needle in Base Blood's neck and drew out
a vial of blood. The colt did not react, but again studied Annie. Annie led him out of the enclosure toward Frank's barn at
the other end of the backstretch.

She was eager for medical work to begin on Base Blood
right away: X-rays, an endoscopic analysis of the lungs, and
blood tests. She needed advice on his toeing-out and his cribbing. She started to ask Frank, but stopped on the first word as
she saw him looking at Base Blood. A thin trickle of blood was
coming out of the colt's nose.

Annie held the lead as Frank looked up Base Blood's nose
and then down his throat. She saw the number tattooed inside
of the colt's upper lip, as was required for identification of
each new runner. Another race was being run on the track,
but Annie and Frank took no notice as the pack of horses tore
past them next to the service road.

"Can't see nothing," Frank said. "You'll have to 'scope
him."

Annie took the opportunity to do what she had been itching
to do all day. She gave the lead to Frank and bent down to run
her fingers over the joints of the horse's hind legs, feeling for
heat. She found a lot of it in both hocks.

"My Lord," she said, and looked up at Carney.

"He's young. If you rest him good, there isn't anything here he can't get through."

Annie was kneeling next to Base Blood's off leg, her hand still resting on the hock joint. "Frank, am I crazy?"

Carney stepped to one side and glanced down at Base Blood's front legs, chest, and head. "Not about the horse."

Annie laughed and stood up. She tucked a wisp of hair back under her hat. Without a word, Frank led the horse toward his barn, leaving Annie to follow. She let him have that. When she caught up with him, she walked along beside him silently, wondering if she could ask him to help her ice Base Blood's legs. She was ready to make her request when he suddenly spoke.

"How's Hank?"

He might as well have hit her in the stomach with a two-by-four. Annie usually walked around with a ready response to that question, and a hard grip on her emotions. However, she could not answer Frank Carney in the same way she would anyone else.

He looked over at her and saw such pain on her face that he said, "Sorry."

Her eyes filled and overflowed so suddenly that the tears were caught on the bottom of her sunglasses and she had to take them off. Wiping her face on her sleeve, Annie knew the question had not been asked to punish. Frank Carney had loved her son.

"I heard he got married last month . . . I haven't seen him in years." Her voice thickened and she fought against crying. Annie kept walking and put her sunglasses on again. She looked at Base Blood and realized how much she needed to hope.

"Did he ever tell you he came to see me in jail?"

"No. When did he do that?"

"He had his leg in a cast, run off from school."

"Was he angry at me?"

"Real angry."

Annie walked quietly, then said, "I should have told him about his father before anyone else did."

"You should have told both of us," Frank said, old anger starting to flow.

"Who his father was was none of your business. It was over, in the past." Her voice had wobbled; she knew Frank had heard it.

"The boy's daddy was still walking around, as I recall. Still is. How the hell can you say it was over? Good God Almighty, Annie . . ."

"I started out telling you just about everything, Frank, and you know it. But you don't tell things like that to a drunk."

She heard him exhale hard, as if he had been punched in the stomach. Annie wanted to grab the lead out of his hand but knew that would have been childish.

"Hank called you a liar," Frank persisted. "I said you'd never lied in your life. Probably just stayed quiet about the truth. I told him a lot of people stay quiet about things they aren't lying about, particularly if it's painful. He said something like you being his mother had become the lie. I told him he was—"

"Give me my horse," Annie said, trying to keep from crying again. "I'll ship him out of here today. I don't want to hear any more of this."

He handed her the lead and said dispassionately, "That's dumb, Annie." She knew he was right. They stood in the road with Base Blood between them, glaring at each other.

Then Annie heard the familiar low grind of Limiteen Farm's tractor-trailer and the quick beep of its air horn as it turned off the state highway. Her six-horse van was up at Belmont Park, so Annie had ordered the twelve-horse tractor-trailer. She and Frank turned to watch the huge customized sixteen-wheeler pull through the backstretch gate. She saw Orin, her driver, lean out of the cab to ask the guard for directions. Hartley, the groom she wanted, was sitting next to him on the front seat. They had made good time, having left Limiteen that morning in response to her call. The stable's yellow and white colors covered the truck, and under the rows of tinted windows on both sides of the trailer LIMITEEN FARM was painted large and clear. Annie knew that her time of anonymity was over.

Frank started off in the opposite direction, leaving Annie and Base Blood behind.

"Frank," Annie called.

He kept walking, saying, "I told you I can do without the attention. You got the horse; I'll send his papers along after the thirty-day waiting period."

"Frank, wait." She watched him until he stopped. "I'll get that truck out of here. Will you please walk Base Blood to your barn?"

He stared off at nothing for a moment, then came back and took the lead, looking at her again with hard anger. "I'll ice his legs," he offered, trying to make it sound like a fact and not a favor.

Although she had a groom who could do it, and an ice machine in the horse trailer, she said, "Thanks. That'd be great."

Base Blood turned back twice as Annie watched him follow Frank Carney down the road. Annie smiled, knowing the colt's sight was good enough to see her expression. She wanted Base Blood to know that she was not leaving him. Then she heard the tractor-trailer gear up. She hurried toward it in hope of getting it off the backstretch without too much notice being taken.

But it was too late. By the time she reached the truck's cab, a small group of gawkers was already speculating about the truck and its purpose. Several of the more confident observers admired the truck's massive machinery and chrome-embellished detail. Then, seeing Annie approach, even in her hat and sunglasses, they knew who she was and called out, "Hey, Countess, you buying or selling?" "Does Limeteen want to hire the best hotwalker 'tween here and Tampa?" "You got any Belmont winners in the back there?"

It was all friendly badinage. Annie answered each question with practiced bravado as Hartley helped her climb up into the cab. While Orin turned the huge truck around, the original group of observers grew, and word of Annie's identity spread. In spite of not feeling ready, she tucked in strands of hair casually and played the Countess of Limeteen Farm with a habitual openness. Hartley and Orin were glad to see her, and carefully avoided expressing any curiosity about her where-abouts for the past ten days. She asked the requisite questions about their trip and what was going on back at the farm. Then she warned them not to expect too much from the colt they had driven all day to pick up.

Annie paid the owner of the Dixie Motel to allow the trac-tor-trailer to be parked in a field behind his establishment. In the oak-paneled trailer, she helped Orin and Hartley set up a box stall. Then they returned in the station wagon to Frank Carney's barn with six bales of straw.

A group of men was waiting outside Base Blood's stall. One of them had a camera; two of them wore neckties. Representa-tives of the track, all of them were as friendly as old dogs when Annie greeted them on her way into Base Blood's stall. The colt was alert, his ears and nostrils busily twitching to interpret the activity around him. As Annie approached him slowly, she noticed that his two front legs stood in a tub of ice, and that both hock joints were wrapped in bandages oozing with one of Frank Carney's poultices.

A flashbulb popped, startling the colt and Annie. She con-trolled her irritation and calmed Base Blood, talking quietly to reassure him. The colt nickered as Annie stroked him. Hartley went to work with Orin's help, mucking out the stall and re-placing the straw with the bales they had brought with them. Annie went out to deflect some of the attention. After a few pictures and answers to questions, she excused herself to go to the tack room at the end of the barn.

If Frank was still there, she wanted to thank him. The door was open. Looking in, she saw his back. He was standing in front of an open wall cabinet. From among the collection of liniment bottles and jars of ointments, he took out a quart bottle of Jack Daniel's. Stuffing it inside his old denim jacket, he started for the door. When he saw Annie, he barely hesi-tated a step. "No lectures."

"Thought you couldn't afford Jack Daniel's," Annie said with disgust.

His look was one of deep loathing. "I keep this for special occasions," he said, "and today was a real special occasion."

He walked past her and disappeared around the corner of the barn.

Annie stared after him, then returned to Base Blood's stall.

"Hartley, you're going to have to spend the night here, all right?"

"Yes, ma'am."

"Orin and I will bring you dinner." She did not trust herself to say any more for fear of revealing her anger. She paced back and forth outside the stall as the two men finished their work. When she turned once, she saw Base Blood watching her, and went over to pat his cheek.

"I don't know anything about anything else in my life," she said quietly, "but I know about you."

Later that night, she again lay naked on her back in the Dixie Motel, unable to sleep, still sweating, listening to the insects outside crashing into the screen door. So much had changed since that morning, and she realized how often in her life a hope for order came by way of a horse.

She had left the wooden door open and the bulb burning under the eaves of the cabin's small porch. Rolling onto her side, she let the air cool her moist back, then restlessly swung her legs over the side of the bed. She stared at a thin line of light that came in around the window's frayed curtain and cut across her naked thighs.

Sitting on the bed, Annie remembered how the jockey had whipped Base Blood that afternoon and felt angry again. Her underwear and work shirt were still damp from having been washed earlier in the sink. Nevertheless, within two minutes she was dressed and in the station wagon, driving onto the state highway. As she drove, she combed her hair with her fingers.

She had seen plenty of hope in her thirty years around the track, and knew how crazy it was. She thought of an old trainer she once had met who put everything he had into training a single colt. Annie had asked him, "How can you believe so much in a horse?" His cryptic reply was "Beats God, don't it?" His colt lost five times in a row, and both horse and trainer disappeared into the nether world of fair racing and bush tracks. Annie was driving to just such a track, where she had found *her* horse, her toed-out, wind-sucking, two-year-old hope. That sort of hope was inspired by desperation; Annie knew it, but would not give up believing.

When she arrived at the barn, Hartley was asleep in a chair tilted against the wall outside Base Blood's stall. The groom heard her approach and woke up with a start that almost tipped him over. He and Annie exchanged smiles, followed by whispered questions and answers about the colt. Hearing them, Base Blood rolled up from where he was lying and stood with ears flicking as he watched from behind the webbing of his stall.

"He's real curious, Mrs. Carney, that's for sure," Hartley said. "Been checking on us all night."

Held back by a cribbing collar around his neck, Base Blood extended his head as far as he could over the webbing and nickered at Annie. She stepped near to let him snuffle her hand; then she slowly stroked his neck. The lightning-bolt blaze zigzagged down his huge face. Suddenly Annie felt as if her grand hopes had no chance against reality. Base Blood shuddered and changed footing, nickered appreciatively, then rolled down to sleep again. The horse seemed so accepting and trustful, she could do no less than believe in him.

With a side glance, she noticed that the lights were on in the tack room at the end of the barn. Her stomach tightened. She had no desire to see Frank Carney drunk again, or for her groom to witness such a meeting.

"See you in the morning, Hartley," she said as she walked toward the station wagon. "We'll ship early, be home for supper."

"That'll be fine, ma'am."

When Annie reached the car, she already had decided to go around the back of the barn. She reasoned with herself that she just wanted to be sure of what she suspected. What she saw as she stood in the shadows outside the tack room window was the bottle of Jack Daniel's unopened on a table. Frank was pacing back and forth beside the table from one end of the room to the other, his hands stuck in the back pockets of his jeans, his shoulders hunched, his gray hair falling over his forehead, his eyes staring at the floor as he took each slow step.

Her eyes filled and overflowed. She blinked and turned away, looking into the dark spring night. No, she thought, someday I may be able to forgive myself about Jimmy Lee, about Helena, and Henry, but never about Frank.

"What're you doing, Annie?" he called from the tack room door.

Quickly, Annie wiped her sleeves over her eyes and stepped into the light. "I couldn't sleep. Came over to see Base Blood."

"And in passing, you wanted to make sure I was drunk." He gave her a hard stare.

There was no point in denying it, so she nodded.

"Sorry to disappoint you," he said.

They stood awkwardly; Annie started to leave. After a step she turned back. "You know, there are some things we never talked about."

"Probably just as well."

"Aren't you curious about what happened?"

Without a moment's consideration, he replied, "No, I'm not."

His lack of interest made her all the more determined to make him talk. "Really? You must have wondered why or when Sam and I got back together. It didn't happen right away, you know. It was almost two years . . . I know I've wondered exactly when you started drinking again."

She could sense his body tighten with anger.

"Goddamn you, Annie! I have my answers to all that, and you have yours. There isn't any point in digging up the details. This day's going to pass, and I'd like to get through it without much more damage or dead history."

"You may be hating me for all the wrong reasons. For instance, after I shot Glorious Girl and Jimmy Lee, Sam Cumberland got to Limeteen before you did—"

His hand passed over the front of his face. Then he looked at her with a rigid contempt.

"I'm sorry, Frank. Let's forget it." Annie stood quietly, not knowing exactly what to do.

He asked, "Did you call him, or what?"

Annie spoke as evenly as she could, as if telling a story, avoiding any defensive tone. "A lot of people who worked at Limiteen had friends at Caernarvon. When all that happened, they naturally got on the phone. Sam heard and came right over to help. The police stopped him at the gate, and he asked for you, Frank. I know that; they called me to check. When they let him through, he drove down to the barn. He wanted to see you first and he looked for you. When he came up to the house, Henry and I were in pretty bad shape. The police and FBI were all over the place. Sam took over; I needed him to do that. And that's about when you showed up. But we weren't lovers until a long time after you moved out."

Frank's hands had slipped into his back pockets as he listened. He did not look at her, staring instead at his boot tracing the dirt. He took in a deep breath and let it out before he started to talk. "When I got there that morning, I was too tired to think. I drove up and the goddamn news people out front crowded around, yelling out questions, telling me things I couldn't handle. Glorious Girl was dead, your brothers were the kidnapers—I'd never even heard about them—and they'd hurt her so bad you had to put her down." He paused, and Annie thought he might not be able to continue. "And then, that you'd shot one of them. The policemen got me through the crowd on the porch. As soon as I closed the front door, I heard Sam Cumberland. He was on the phone in the library, giving orders like he owned the place." He looked up at Annie and shrugged. "It was his kind of house. I never was comfortable there."

"I know."

He traced the dirt with his boot again. "You want to walk?"

"Sure," she said.

They started off, trying to stride casually, but finding it awkward as they rounded the barn toward the track. The night was almost comfortable, because the gnats and flies were down. On the backstretch at that hour, no one was awake. A mist made whorls of light around the few bare bulbs along the shedrow.

"I had to walk in there and ask him where my wife was,"

Frank continued. "The phone kept ringing. He tried to explain things, but you know Sam. Once you're his employee, you're never much else, and he kept slipping into that high-snoot charm he uses with servants. I finally told him to answer the phone, which he didn't like too much, and he pointed straight up at the ceiling, knowing just where your bedroom was. That made me crazy enough to imagine some pretty fancy episodes over the next few months."

Annie remembered it all. "And when you came upstairs," she continued, "you found a woman angry with you for not being there when she needed you most . . . which I believe I told you about pretty hard."

He walked several steps before saying, "I remember you were loud. But that didn't bother me, because after all I'd just learned, anger was almost a relief. What really hit me was Hank. He wouldn't look at me . . . never looked right at me again. Always kind of looked off to one side like he was nervous or embarrassed. That hurt more than anything. He just never was the same again with me."

"No," Annie agreed. "Not with anyone. That's when I lost him. He and I just didn't realize it until later."

They walked away from the barns. Trees loomed through the dark mist. Annie tried not to think of Henry, but failed. She remembered him as a baby, in France, at the Haras de la Poire, at Limeteen with Speed Oliver and Glorious Girl, and then when everything began to collapse.

"You said you didn't know when I started drinking again," Frank said. "It wasn't right away, except I'm damn sure I was looking for my excuse from the moment I saw Sam. I stayed around working hard enough not to think too much, sleeping up in that room on the third floor, but I was losing you, losing Hank, losing everything. We were finished, Annie. We didn't know it, but it was too much for the two of us—maybe for any couple—to handle. We already had a lot going against us, the owner-and-trainer business, me being a drinker, and you having so damn much money."

She did not answer, but kept walking until they reached the track. Both leaned on the outside rail, feeling more comfortable at the familiar place.

"Sam was my excuse to drink, not you," Frank said. "That crazy little psychiatrist lady in the penitentiary showed me that. I didn't take a drink until I convinced myself he was your lover again, whether he was by then or not, I don't know. I blamed it on you, but it was really about Sam Cumberland getting what he wanted one more time.

"I grew up watching him get everything, without even having to try, for no other reason than his being born lucky. And here he comes again, taking what's mine . . . or was once. It seemed hopeless enough to convince myself that I might just as well drink." Even in the darkness, Annie saw how hard his hands were gripping the rail. "I didn't really hate you until you told me about the baby."

He managed to say this as a careful statement of fact, without any anger in his tone. Annie said, "I didn't realize it at the time, but I've come to think that I knew I'd lost my son, so I wanted another child . . . to have another chance. Of course, as Helena proved, it never works out as neatly as that."

"She should have been our child."

Annie heard the change in his voice, a yearning and a bitterness. "You'd moved out, Frank, a long time before that happened."

"You gave her my name."

"For her sake. I was married to you at the time."

"You're not trying to tell me you were fooling anybody. God Almighty, everybody knew . . ."

"I wasn't trying to hide anything. By then, it was nobody else's business and I didn't care."

The two of them stared out at the empty track.

"Frank, let's not blame each other anymore. Both of us had reasons. Not good ones, maybe, but strong ones. Too strong to figure out at the time. There aren't any excuses, and we've paid—Lord, have we paid—for the mistakes we made." She wanted to admit something without having it sound as if she were asking for any forgiveness from him. "I know that I was the worst thing that could have happened to you; I've said it to myself a hundred times. So go ahead and hate me, but don't blame me anymore."

She heard him shift uneasily and saw that he was looking

down at the ground, his arms stretched out on the rail. He said nothing, which once again irritated Annie. As she had so many times, she waited for him.

"When are you planning on shipping out?" he asked.

"As soon as I can get the truck over here in the morning."

"I'll have your colt ready." He pushed himself back from the rail and Annie anticipated his walking away in silence, but instead he stood straight and slowly looked up into the overcast sky. "Annie," he said, his voice a gasp, "I never said this to anyone, but we've hated each other long enough for me to want you to hear it. I'm so . . . awful sorry for what I did to Certainty." He did not move.

Annie's eyes were on the dying oak tree in the infield. "I've known that all along. Everyone did."

He bowed his head slowly. "Not everyone. There were a few who enjoyed yelling, 'Horse Killer Carney.' "

"To hell with them," Annie said softly. "No more blame, Frank."

He shook his head. "No blame, but there's no forgetting either. Is there?"

"No," Annie agreed, "no forgetting."

They walked back toward the barns.

"Something else you ought to know," Frank said. "While I was in prison, that Angel guy wrote me."

Annie stopped. "When?"

"I'd been in about a year. It was five or six weeks after your brother Fungo got killed in the riot. Right out of the blue, there's a letter with a hundred-dollar bill in it, saying he and I had something in common, hating you and wanting to get back at you."

"Is that all?"

"Two more letters came, each one with another hundred, offering to fix it up for me to work at the New York tracks when I got out, then promising me some horses if I'd 'cooperate' with him. That's all. I never answered, never heard from him again."

"Good Lord," Annie said, and started walking again to cover the trembling her fear had brought on.

"Are you surprised?" Frank asked. "Rot don't stop, you know."

"I know. He came after my daughter instead." She shook her head. "I thought he'd done enough to me after Glorious Girl to satisfy him."

"That kind doesn't satisfy. Still bothers the hell out of me that he got off. The FBI ought to be reamed out for letting him turn state's witness. If I got five years, Phil Angelo deserved as much, instead of that dumb Fungo getting it all and then getting himself killed." He looked over at her. "I heard you went to Europe."

"I had to campaign over there until I could get my owner's licenses back in America." Once again, she knew what she was going to ask Frank to do before she thought out the reasons. This time, it was no oversight; she did not dare to consider reasons. Instead, she decided to let him know what no one else did.

"You want the whole story, Frank? It took me twenty years, but I spent it all. I came up with a great stable, mainly due to you, just like I said I would. But right now, I'm just as broke as you are, living off loans and sinking right down to my chin in debt."

He stopped and looked at her. For the first time, Annie saw that Frank was shocked. "Limiteen bred two Belmont Stakes and a Derby winner," he said. "You were outbidding the Arabs at Keeneland for yearling stock."

"We bred them, but had to sell them to syndicates and partnerships. Our shares went right to the banks, and those winners haven't paid off too well in the breeding barn. I never outbid the Arabs, but they drove prices through the roof, and that's where the last of my money went. It won't be long before Limiteen'll be the most successful bankrupt in the horse business." She looked back into the barn. "And here I am, claiming a broken-down two-year-old colt with the idea bouncing back and forth in my head that he can save me." She shook her head. "Oh, yes, I'm just as crazy as hell."

At the front of the barn, Annie was no longer worried about being seen with Frank. Hartley was stretched out in his chair, snoring heavily. Stopping in front of Base Blood's stall, they silently stared at the sleeping animal. As they watched, the colt tossed in its sleep, woke up, rolled over, and rose on his legs. He saw them at the stall door but did not move, holding up his head, alert and imposing, oblivious of the cribbing collar.

"Frank . . ." she began.

"Don't even offer, Annie. You and I have too many scars."

"Listen, I don't *have* anything to offer, remember? All I'm saying is, that's a great horse and you're a great trainer. There'll be room in the truck for you tomorrow morning. I'm sure it would be a hell of a lot easier on both of us if you just stayed here and I went off, with all our old scars and excuses. But the truck leaves at six-thirty."

She spoke intensely. Base Blood let out a piercing whinny. Annie smiled at the colt, then turned and, for once in her life, walked away from Frank Carney without looking back.

THIRTY-TWO

ANNIE WATCHED from the station wagon as Frank Carney led Base Blood out of the trailer toward the Limeteen barn. Hartley walked along with them, waiting to be helpful. Without the slightest acknowledgment of his own return to the farm, Frank gave the groom the lead and stood back. He watched the colt's legs as Hartley walked the animal around to get the kinks out after the long drive.

Farther down the farm road, George Oliver was coming over from the stallion barn. Annie saw him do a double-take and stop when he saw Frank standing there, gray-haired, his hands stuck in the back pockets of his jeans as usual. George approached him slowly and spoke his name. The two men shook hands wordlessly and then watched Base Blood as if it were just another day and just another horse.

The colt was still sore, and would be for some time. Annie could see him favor his hind legs, his feet toeing out at a pronounced angle. The farrier would work on that the next morning, gradually reshaping the hoofs, then fitting new shoes with built-up sides. There would be the blood tests, 'scoping of the lungs, and X-rays of the ankles, along with the vet's examination. Soon, Annie would know something about what she had claimed for her five thousand dollars. Remembering that she had instructed the farm manager to get Base Blood's pedigree from the Jockey Club's computer service, Annie felt a sharp eagerness to get to the office. She walked over to Hartley and took the colt's shank, leading him around in a circle as George and Frank continued to watch.

Several farmhands and grooms came by, stopped, and took a look at the new colt. Most of them were too young to recognize Frank Carney; fourteen years had passed since he left Limeteen. His story, however, would be all over the farm by sundown and all over the Bluegrass the next day. Annie wondered whether he could manage the inevitable half-met eyes and half-knowing questions. She was accustomed to them, but Frank had never handled attention well.

Early that morning, as Hartley had rubbed Base Blood down in preparation for the trip, Annie found Frank outside the stall watching. By the tack room door was his old duffel bag and wooden box filled with his grooming tools, poultices, and medicines.

"I'll ride in the van with the horse," he had said, the first of his conditions. "If a room's available, I'll live above one of the barns at Limeteen. Pay me what you pay your best groom until Base Blood wins something. I won't offer advice about anything other than this colt unless I'm asked, and I will *never*, for any reason, go into Limeteen Hall."

Annie agreed just as the colt whinnied and frisked in the early morning light. Hartley laughed and pulled his shank. "He's been eating like he never tasted second-cut alfalfa before."

"Probably never has," Frank said; then, to Annie, "I'm going to groom him for a while. You still have that small paddock next to Barn Two?"

"Yes," she answered, realizing how little had changed at Limeteen since he had left.

"I want to turn him out, but I don't want him to have enough room to run. We shouldn't even think about putting tack on him for a while."

She tried not to react to the "we." "That's fine," she said. During the ride back to Limeteen, he groomed the colt from head to foot.

The colt already had changed. Whether from rest after his race, or oat-and-molasses mash with vitamins, or the sudden interest in new faces, Base Blood was an excited animal.

"Let's take him in," Frank called, and Annie led the colt over to Barn Two. The special stall was prepared with a thick blanket of straw. At Frank's insistence early in his days at Limeteen, that stall had been custom-built for cribbers. The walls were metal, with no sharp edges or protruding surfaces for a horse to grip with his teeth. Frank had worked with cribbers and believed that real potential was often overlooked because of the nervous habit.

On the other hand, the habit was usually incurable. Once Frank had told Annie of a cribber he had trained for Caernarvon Farms. After several months of hard work, he broke the colt of the wood-chewing, wind-sucking addiction. The colt won five allowance races in a row. He went on to win his first stakes race, by which time the bad habit was forgotten. Then, as the colt approached the winner's circle, he stopped directly in front of the clubhouse to chomp on an extension of wooden rail.

A rich mix of bran and oats waited in Base Blood's stall. A portable manger would be removed when the cribber finished his meal. The two-year-old spotted his dinner and went in willingly. Annie unsnapped the shank, patted him, and for a moment Frank stood watching with her.

"I listened to him breathe during the trip," Frank said. "I think he's got something in his throat he shouldn't have."

Annie felt her stomach tighten. "How bad?"

"We'll ask the vet when he 'scopes him . . . You know which room I'm in?" He did not look at her.

"Upstairs, south side. Hartley's across the hall."

He nodded and walked away. Annie knew she could do no better than to imitate his forbearance.

547

Base Blood's pedigree revealed nothing. Annie had not even heard of several progenitors in the colt's sire line. She went back to the Jockey Club's computer service to order up these unknown progenitors' pedigrees. When they came, there was nothing on which to hang her hopes or to justify what she saw in her colt. His immediate sire had the unfortunate name of Broadbent, had appeared only three times on Ohio tracks, never won a race, and never earned a dime. Similarly, Base Blood's dam had never raced, being herself the offspring of an unremarkable stallion and an unknown broodmare.

Annie knew that the odds, not to mention the smart money, were against her. Like anyone who fell for a horse, she thought of flukes like John Henry, the $25,000 gelding that won $6.5 million. She knew the power of such delusion, but reminded herself that the hopeless pedigree "by Nothing out of Less" was once applied to Derby winners like Carry Back and Canonero II. As she stared at Base Blood's bare genealogy, Annie gave up any thought of his pedigree's validating her dream. She folded the colt's papers into a file, holding to the conviction that what she had seen would have to be enough to last her until he ran again.

By necessity, that time was slow in coming. The vets, using a fiber-optic endoscope, discovered a membrane in Base Blood's throat that seemed to keep the colt's epiglottis from opening completely. A hinged valve in the throat that covers the passageway to the lungs when an animal swallows, the epiglottis must open fully to allow air into the lungs when the creature exerts itself. Base Blood had been in training, such as it was, without this basic advantage. The vet conjectured that the membrane had formed like a callus in reaction to the steady irritation from the colt's habit of sucking air. The membrane had to be removed surgically. Whether the cribbing habit had caused the growth or vice versa was only speculation. But if the callus had come first, causing the wind sucking and cribbing, then perhaps the habit would diminish when the obstruction was removed.

The operation took place at the New Bolton Center of the University of Pennsylvania. An equivalent of the Mayo Clinic for horses, New Bolton was one of the foremost centers of equine research and veterinary medicine in the world. Standing in a hallway, Annie and Frank watched through small windows on the operating room's doors as Base Blood fell to his knees and rolled to his side in a deep anaesthetic sleep. He was then cranked onto an immense tilt-top table, which was leveled off in the center of the operating room. The surgical procedure could last only two hours, the outer limit of the anaesthetic. Even under the powerful influence of the drug, Base Blood's palate kept dropping nervously, blocking the surgeon's access to the epiglottis. Finally the membrane was severed, and the doctor held it up for Frank and Annie to see as if it were a prize.

"Looks like a chaw of tobacco," Frank said, glancing at her quickly.

Since arriving at Limeteen, Frank's eyes had not met Annie's. Whenever they spoke, he managed to be watching something else, as if it needed his attention. She was often irritated by the mannerism, but let it pass, accepting his need for avoidance. On being alone with him in the hallway, however, Annie decided to take advantage of the situation.

"Frank, I'd like your advice about Limeteen."

He stayed quiet for a few moments, watching the surgical team, then said, "I haven't seen your books, so I don't know exactly what you're up against there. Seems, though, that you're stuck right in the middle of all the change."

He stopped, as was his habit, waiting for a further prod, another request for communication.

"Just go on, Frank. Don't make me have to squeeze every word," she said with irritation.

As if admitting being caught at his own game, he said, "It's all changed, Annie. There's no sport anymore. With racing, it used to be that horses meant as much, if not a hell of a lot more than money. The rich *had* money; they didn't need to think about it. Now it's pretty much all business and showing off. You did fine, both with the sport and the business. Limeteen's probably one of the best ideas for a stable in the world . . . for ten, fifteen years ago."

Stung, Annie reacted too fast. "You mean since about when

you left it." She immediately regretted the remark. "Forget I said that, Frank. I know that's not what you meant. Go on."

"I just don't know what's happened to racing, and I'm not sure exactly when it changed. Maybe when you were away in Europe and I was in jail. But it seems to have happened with everything in the country. Money went crazy and everyone went along with it. All I know is that now there isn't a tradition or a principle that isn't for sale, and horse racing's a fine example. You hold out for a principle, people think you're kind of dumb."

Annie was surprised by his anger. He seemed to be embarrassed by it as he turned from the glass window and looked straight at her.

"What I'm getting around to telling you is that a horse farm like Limeteen can't survive today. You don't have the crazy amount of money to compete with these monster national or international stables, like the Arabs or Sangster or Wayne Lukas. You're spreading yourself too thin, running broodmare operations in Ireland and France and a breeding and racing stable here. It used to work that way, before prices went up, when good bloodstock was affordable. Now it isn't unless you're a sheik. Between the three farms, you have three hundred and some horses. You should consolidate and keep thirty."

"Thirty!" Annie exclaimed.

Frank said, "You tell the banks you're doing that, and they might not take you over in six months. You sell two hundred fifty head and maybe one of the farms, and you'll have some cash to fool around with, buy the stallion shares you need, and pay off some debt."

"That's one step away from giving up everything and being a paper stable."

"Maybe so, but the way things are going now, you won't even have that one step before too long. Annie, no matter how good you are, no matter how hard you work, unless you have a whole lot of money, Limeteen, as it's going now, will bring you down."

The surgical team was moving Base Blood off the operating table onto a huge gurney. The colt still rested peacefully, and the head surgeon looked toward the doors and gave a thumbs-up sign of success.

"Which thirty?" Annie said, nodding gratefully at the surgeon.

"Let me do some homework."

"Would Base Blood be one of them?"

"Yep."

His answer was surprisingly certain. Annie snapped around to face him. "He would?"

Watching the recumbent colt, Frank said, "You found yourself a fine horse. Maybe even a great one. He has the equipment, likes to run, and showed us a lot of courage in that race we saw. But he won't win anything if he isn't healthy."

"Well, that's your problem," Annie said, "so I'm not too worried about it."

Frank smiled.

"Give me your list, Frank. I'll compare it with mine. I'm not saying I'll do exactly what you say; I have to do some homework of my own on the books. But if I take your advice, I'll want a private trainer again. I don't know how it's been for you, being back at Limeteen. I do know it's good for the farm. Most everyone's glad you're back, though you're wasted on one horse."

He was already shaking his head. "We've gotten away with it so far, Annie. I've only seen a couple of smirks, overheard a couple of dirty jokes about us. But my being your private trainer'd get too much attention, the bad kind. That you just don't need, and neither do I."

The surgeon was waving at them to come into the operating room. Frank started to open the door for her, but she put her arm out and held it closed. "We don't have that choice, Frank. Listen, I can sell out, and you can go back to the bush tracks. Then nobody'll pay any attention to us at all! Just remember one thing. Whatever they say about you, they say it worse about me. That's the price we pay, and Limeteen's worth it. For that, I can take some attention, and so can you."

He stared at her hard, and Annie did not know whether he was going to push her aside or put his arms around her.

"I'll get this colt home and do my homework," he said.

"You bring your daughter home and do yours. Then we'll see. But we're asking for more than you think, so don't tell me you know how much you can take. I still hate you, Annie; I doubt if I'll change. And I don't know how much damage that'll do if that kind of attention comes."

" 'Then we'll see,' " she said quoting him. He opened the door and they went in to congratulate the surgeon.

That night on the train to New York, Annie tried to separate Frank's suggestions from his hatred. What he had said about Limeteen was devastatingly accurate. Hearing it was hard even if it was true. She also admitted that in the moment when she had thought Frank was about to embrace her, she wished he had.

As the train roared into the tunnel under the Hudson River, Annie looked at the window. Her face was reflected almost as clearly as in a blackened mirror. She idly touched the feathered lines around her eyes and smiled sadly, wondering if she had reacted to Frank because it was so long since a man had caused such a feeling. As the train pulled into Pennsylvania Station, the image of Glynn came into her mind, as well as the question of where Sam might be that night. Carrying her overnight bag, she hurried off the train and took a cab to her town house.

She had come back to pick up Helena, whose treatment at the Connecticut clinic was ending. Successful in withdrawing the girl from her physical dependence on crack, the process had left her psychologically desolated and vulnerable. Annie drove out the next day and waited in the reception area. When she saw her mother, Helena silently began to cry. Head bowed, she walked into Annie's arms.

They drove back to Manhattan together, and in her bedroom, Annie held her daughter as she slept intermittently through the night. The next day, they flew together to Lexington. When she entered Limeteen Hall, Helena was silent. She smiled and responded politely to the staff as they greeted her, but she seemed anxious. Annie had prepared the room next to her own for Helena, which the girl seemed to appreciate. Then Annie went to unpack. When she came out, she saw that

Helena had already changed into jeans, boots, and a work shirt. Walking down the stairs, she smiled hesitantly at Annie. "I want to meet Frank Carney," she said in a small echo of her formerly assertive self.

"Barn Two," Annie said before her own trepidation could halt her. "Do you remember where it is?"

"Second on the right." Helena gazed affectionately at her mother. "I love you, Mummy, and I don't really . . ." She did not finish the familiar phrase about not needing a father, but shrugged and smiled before she continued down the stairs.

As she went back to her room, Annie wondered if Helena's therapy at the clinic had made it clear to her that she probably did need a father. When she had told her daughter the previous night about Frank Carney's return and about the painful situation with Sam, Annie was surprised that Helena's questions concerned only Frank: how long he had been in prison, what he did when he was released, how Annie had run into him. On the other hand, Sam's conduct elicited only one statement: "Mummy, it was bound to happen," a fatalistic truth with which Annie could only grudgingly agree.

Frank was in Base Blood's stall, rubbing his coat and, as he had done since their return from New Bolton, listening to him breathe. Moving around the colt, he saw the girl leaning against the stall door with her arms crossed. He knew who she was, nodded, and went on with his work. Base Blood sensed the new presence and turned his head to look. He pivoted around in the stall and walked over to her, his head extended and ears flicking.

Helena pressed back against the stall opening. "What's he going to do, bite me?" she asked.

"Just wants to take a look at you," Frank answered. "Bring your hand up under his nose and let him smell you. That's how they recognize things."

Hesitantly, she followed his instruction. The colt nuzzled her hand and nickered softly.

"They're just so big," Helena said. "I've always been scared of horses."

"He knows that, but he won't take advantage. He figures

you're probably good for a carrot now and then, so he'll try to win you over."

She gave a short laugh. "I really doubt if he's that intelligent. I mean, they're really dumb animals."

When she looked over at Frank, he was watching her. He said, "And you and I are so smart, aren't we?"

Chagrined, she pulled her hand away and crossed her arms again, staring down at the thick bed of straw. Frank took Base Blood's halter to turn him back into the stall and continued rubbing the colt's hind legs.

Angrily, Helena shifted her weight from one foot to another. "What's it like when there's a daughter running around with your name who isn't really yours?" After asking, she looked up quickly, watching for his reaction.

He showed none, but kept rubbing, finally saying, "I got through it, and I'm glad to meet you."

"What do you mean, you got through it? How do you know? You're still the same person, aren't you? You could do the same thing all over again. I know I could."

Frank stood up and looked over Base Blood's withers at the girl. She was trying to be tough, but she could not cover her fear. He ran his hand down the colt's back. "Sure I could. I've had that nightmare for years."

She stared at him, frowned, then looked down at the straw again. "I don't think I can stand that."

Frank watched her for a moment. "You want to bring that curry brush over here?"

The girl looked around, saw Frank's rack of grooming paraphernalia, and bent down. "Which one is it?"

"The metal one with teeth."

She handed it up to him, but he did not take it.

"You start at the withers," Frank said, "working in circles, not too hard, but enough to get old hair and dirt off him . . ."

"Me?"

"Might as well."

"Oh, more therapy," she muttered contemptuously.

"Well, I just don't like working alone, but it sounds like you could use some."

She glared at him over Base Blood's back, then awkwardly started to stroke over the colt's shoulder as if the curry brush were a feather duster.

"You can go harder. That's horse leather you're getting down to."

He watched until she was doing it right, then stooped and continued rubbing Base Blood's hind legs, helping the circulation to flow through the soreness.

"I've always *hated* horses," Helena said as she brushed harder.

"How could you do that?"

"What do you mean?"

"Did you ever get to know a horse?"

"No."

"Not even one?"

"No."

"Then how can you go to the trouble of hating them?"

"You know what I mean. I had to watch them when I was a little kid, all the time."

"Oh, well, you just hated the watching, not the horses." He rubbed carefully over the hock and cannon bone of the off leg, which seemed to have taken much of the weight from the colt's sore stride. "A lot of people think horses are dumb, just like you do. But horses have taught me more about a lot of things than people have."

"Like what?"

"Like not giving up. Ever."

He heard the curry brush stop, then start again. He kept going over the hock joint; the heat was less every day, and the bones were growing together perfectly. In a few weeks, the colt would have to be ridden or he would break down his paddock.

"Of course, to learn anything from them," Frank continued, "you have to work with them. This one, for instance."

"Is this my mother's superhorse?" she asked with teenage disdain.

"There you go again. Let me tell you, a horse notices a lot of little things, like that sneer in your voice and your bothered way of coming into the stall. This is a good colt, just about

555

your age in horse years. He's been through a lot. They took him away from his mother right after he was born, to kill him. When he was old enough to run, they fed him drugs so he didn't feel pain, and then ran him in a race that could have blown out his lungs.''

She stared at Base Blood, then slowly lifted the curry brush and continued the circular motion down his flanks. She continued on the other side as Frank changed the colt's stall bandages, feeling the fetlock and the pastern on each leg for possible calcium spurs, bone chips, or heat. They all felt clean and cool. Frank sensed a flow of anticipation he had not experienced for a long time. When he stood up, Helena was finishing the colt's hip.

"What's next?" she asked, not admitting anything.

"Tomorrow morning, five-thirty. You really get to know a horse when you muck out his stall."

Her mouth opened to object, but she clamped it shut.

From that day on, Helena joined the grooms and exercise riders at Barn Two every morning at five-thirty. By the time Base Blood was ready for a rider, Helena was mucking his stall and setting his bandages. At first, she was overly conscious of being the owner's crazy daughter and stayed to herself, the third Carney character at Limeteen Farm. As the mornings passed, however, Helena learned a basic rule in the thoroughbred world: who you are depends on who your horse is. Once a few stories went around about her, the only thing that really mattered to anyone about Helena was the bay colt named Base Blood.

Early in July, Frank put the colt's tack on him and dared Helena to get in the saddle. Terrified, she did it, and Frank and Annie took turns walking Base Blood first around the barn, then around the farm. Both were pleased by what they saw. There were no signs of the soreness, the hind off leg still toed out slightly but seemed not to throw his stride, and he breathed effortlessly.

When it was time to begin working the colt, Frank picked an experienced exercise rider for the job, but Base Blood would have none of it. He shied and turned away from the boy to nuzzle up to Helena.

"Okay, Helena," Frank said with a shrug, "I'll give you a leg up."

"No!" she said. "I can sit there while he walks around, but I don't know how to ride."

"I'll pony him the whole time," Frank said. "Besides, it's time you learned. All you have to do is hang on to him. He just told you he'll take care of you."

For two weeks, they rode over the long Limeteen gallops together, Helena stoically enduring first her terror, then her bone-deep soreness. Often, Annie rode along, pleased by her daughter's progress and the colt's. Frank instructed Helena continually on balance, position, and the feel of the horse. When she asked her mother to buy her a pair of chaps and a set of ten-pound weights to strengthen her arms, Helena was all business. The day that Frank unsnapped his lead line and let the girl ride Base Blood on her own, Helena came back to the barn happier than Annie had ever seen her. By the beginning of August, after weeks of longer rides on the gallops, they were ready to start work on the training track.

The summer heat in central Kentucky was so oppressive that only the dawn hours were tolerable. The rest of the day was too hot and too damp. The weather made both horses and people fractious. The first morning that Base Blood went to the training track, a number of Limeteen runners were already on their works with their exercise riders, eager to finish their sets as early as possible. Not having ridden on the track in front of others, Helena was nervous. Annie was there; she had flown back from Europe the previous night. Frank gave Helena a leg up and led the colt out of the barn to the gap in the training track's rail. As they approached it, Base Blood began to prance sideways and nickered his own excitement.

Frank yanked the lead taut and said to Helena, "Well, I guess he knows where he's going. He wants to run, but you're not ready for that yet. Don't let him get away from you. Just take him around a couple of times, nice and easy." Then he unsnapped the lead.

Helena nodded intently as she gripped the reins and then walked the colt through the gap. He pranced again, but she pulled him in. Talking to him, she kept him at a walk. Gradually, she let out her reins, and Base Blood began an easy rolling gallop around the half-mile oval. Several exercise riders yelled greetings as they went past her.

Annie stepped up to the rail next to Frank. Without looking at her, he said, "How was the trip?"

"A week of jet lag, no sleep, airplane food, a win and a show at Newmarket, a place at Deauville. The usual, except I showed a buyer the Irish stud. He offered a good price."

They glanced at each other. "So," Frank said.

"Yes, 'so,'" Annie replied. "I'm taking most of your advice."

"When?"

"I want to announce selling the stud and a dispersal sale a week before the bankers' deadline. I hope we'll win a few races before that so it won't look like a panic sale. I want to keep fifty horses, not just thirty. Then we—"

"Watch out, girl!"

They both saw Base Blood leap forward from his gallop and start running flat out. Helena fought him at first by pulling on the reins, but then she crouched down and held on. Horse and rider came flying past. Even though she feared for her daughter, Annie could not help noticing the stunning power in Base Blood's easy, long, pain-free stride. Going into the tight turn of the small track, the colt changed his lead leg with ease and charged into the far straightaway. After three furlongs, Helena exerted herself, pulled hard on the reins, and leaned back in the stirrups. Base Blood responded, easing down into a relaxed gallop.

Annie and Frank said in unison, "Thirty-five," then looked at each other, amazed.

"Don't tell anyone," Frank said, "and don't even think about it."

But Annie was already thinking. August, September, October. There were good two-year-old races in November. If Base Blood could win an impressive race before the bankers' deadline . . .

"Don't blame him," Helena said as she walked the colt up to them. "It was my fault. I got out there, and all of a sudden I really wanted to let him run. I didn't do anything; he just knew it as soon as I thought it and took off. I'm sorry."

"I don't care about sorry," Frank said angrily. "You ever let him get away from you again, you won't get on him again! Now get him back to the barn and walk him down."

Tight-lipped, Helena led Base Blood out of the gap toward Barn Two. Frank looked out over the training track.

"Frank . . ."

"Yeah, I know, you're ready to put him in the Breeders' Cup Juvenile in November to show those bankers how lucky they are to have you as a customer."

"Well, I sure wouldn't mind doing that. Except that his sire didn't have the nomination paid, and the previous owners didn't pay any foaling fees. It'd cost me about two hundred and some thousand dollars to supplement him into the Breeders' Cup. But my Lord, Frank, he—"

"Too bad," Frank said. "I've been hearing a lot about a Caernarvon two-year-old that's been running this summer. Royal Blessing. Favored in the Hopeful at Saratoga next week. It'd be real nice to beat him."

Annie did not respond. She had heard about Sam's colt, Royal Blessing, ever since he was foaled. Even Bernard Dolby had mentioned him when she saw her old friend at Newmarket. She read an interview in a racing magazine in which Sam was quoted as saying, "I've never had a Kentucky Derby winner, as my father and grandfather did. I'm hoping that Royal Blessing will allow me to continue the family tradition in his three-year-old year. His pedigree is as perfect as one could hope for."

Annie had to agree; Caernarvon had some of the best broodmare lines in the world. Along with the tradition of Caernarvon and the Cumberland name, they provided access to the world's best bloodstock. Royal Blessing's dam was by Nijinsky, the great champion son of Northern Dancer. She had been bred to Mr. Prospector, the leading sire in the United States, thus uniting Northern Dancer and Native Dancer, the two most prepotent classic lines in thoroughbred racing.

"We're getting ahead of ourselves," Annie said, "but I'm glad we're thinking alike."

"Give me two weeks," Frank replied. "Then I'll know if he'll be ready to run in anything. And then we'll have to see if he's a sprinter or a router."

"Don't feel you have to rush. If he isn't ready, we'll wait until next year." She tried to stop there, but could not. "If he is, I want to keep it nice and quiet. We'll train him here, get up early so even the farm help won't know what's going on. If training goes well, we'll get Speed Oliver to come down. He'd do that for us, and he's become a fine jockey. We'll ask Churchill Downs for one stall on Breeders' Cup Day, but not for the big races; I can't afford them. We'll ship over there the day before—"

"I know what you're thinking," Frank interrupted, an uncharacteristic indication of his own excitement. "The Breeders' Cup has those seven TV races. The track fills out the day's card with three other races. The Iroquois Stakes, right?"

Annie smiled. "An ungraded race for two-year-olds, on a day of million-dollar races, a measly fifty-thousand-dollar purse, which I need. Nobody will pay any attention unless one hell of a horse comes along. Then they'll run the film over and over so everyone at the Breeders' Cup will see it."

Frank went on, "And they'll compare it to whatever happens a couple of hours later when the Caernarvon colt runs the same distance in the Juvenile. Funny how 'everyone' is always the same one or two people."

They looked at each other, acknowledging who "everyone" was. "Besides," Annie continued, "that race is the Saturday before I have to meet with the bankers."

Frank added, "The thing I like best is that after the race we can cool Base Blood out, ship him, and get out of there before the press can leave off watching the Breeders' Cup races."

Annie waved away the gnats around her head.

"They'll find us, Frank, sooner or later. If Base Blood's anything like what we think he is, he'll drag us right into it at the end of that mile and a sixteenth. You and I have to be ready for everything they'll throw at us."

Frank gave one nod, gritted his teeth, and walked away with hands in his back pockets.

THIRTY-THREE

WHEN SPEED OLIVER received the phone call from the Countess at Limeteen Farm, he was hustling to get mounts at Laurel Race Course in Maryland. His career as a jockey had suffered from the usual instability of the trade. Starting with a promising first season, he was a success as an apprentice in California riding for Limeteen and other stables. When he came east, he lost his apprentice bug along with its weight allowances. A hard several years followed as he tried to find good mounts to ride.

His being black was inevitably noted favorably in the press on those occasions when he rode winners; otherwise, Speed faced the daily manifestations of prejudice, usually subtle but sometimes painfully overt. Some Southern owners, still shut off from the outside world by the strange feudalism that the track allows, simply did not want their hallowed silks on a "nigger," a word still in common use at turf clubs and stables.

There was also resentment on the part of his black colleagues who exercised, hotwalked, and groomed on the backstretches; they too sometimes behaved as if he were forgetting his place. The jockey room presented its own problems. The Spanish-speaking contingent was bound by culture, language, and blood. No matter the color of their skin, they did not look on Speed as a brother. The white riders tended to be loners, single-minded in their ambition. Fellowship seldom developed. As a result, Speed made few friends. After winning a share of purses, he found himself a good jockey agent, agreed to his twenty-five percent fee, and together they made their own way around the tracks of the eastern seaboard.

Over the phone, Mrs. Carney seemed to indicate something special. Speed had heard from his parents the rumors around the farm; they reported that the colt was trained in near darkness, before anyone else was awake. On his first night back at Limeteen, Speed wandered over from the Olivers' house to Barn Two and greeted Frank Carney. When the jockey first saw Base Blood, he was a little disappointed. Frank said nothing more about the colt except "You ride him, Speed; then we'll talk about him."

The next morning, Speed stood at Base Blood's stall and watched as Helena Carney put on his tack in the darkness. He looked good but was nothing special, just a big red bay with a white sock on his front off leg, and that strange lightning-bolt blaze dividing his face. The girl had rubbed him so that he shone even in the dark, but Speed had seen many horses. The only one that could impress him on first sight would have had wings. As a jockey, he had learned not to trust his eyes. He judged with his ass.

"Hey, Helena, you got this colt shining so bright, I can hardly look at him."

She smiled as she finished buckling the cinch but said nothing. Speed was sensitive to what the girl was feeling. She had been grooming and riding the colt, but when the race came along, she would have to watch from the rail.

"Can you tell me about him?" Speed asked.

"What do you mean?"

"He's your horse. How does he like to go? What do you say

563

to him; what kind of mouth noises do you make? What's he do when you use the whip, and will you please be real friendly to me so he won't think I'm taking him away from you?"

She laughed softly as she led the colt out of his stall and took Speed's arm so that Base Blood could see them walking together. "I've never even had to show him the whip," she said. "It's a hand ride every time. When we start, I say, 'Okay, Base Blood,' real quiet; then I kind of shout, 'Let's fly!' He understands it's time! You just know he does." They walked out of the barn. Annie and Frank were waiting, but before reaching them, Helena said quickly, "If anybody else has to ride him, Speed, I'm glad it's you."

"Thanks. I am, too," Speed said. "Morning, Mrs. Carney."

Annie smiled. "Speed, it's so good having you back here."

"Lots of memories around here," he said pleasantly, then wished he had not.

"I see some headlights coming up to the back gate," Frank said. "Let's get going."

Frank legged Speed up into the saddle before Base Blood knew what was happening. Seeing Helena holding the lead in front of him, Base Blood pulled his head around to see who was on his back, and started to jump.

"It's all right, Base Blood. There. Take it easy. He's our friend," Helena said with easy assurance, controlling him with the lead, yanking it firmly until the colt settled down.

When Base Blood was calm, Annie said, "You all right, Speed?"

"Yes, ma'am. I'm sitting chilly up here."

"Warm him up and get him used to you," Frank Carney ordered quietly, "then work him for a mile. We know he has speed; what I want to try is his stamina. Hold him back and see if he can finish well."

Helena unclipped the lead and watched Base Blood walk away. Annie and Frank followed as the trio made its way to the training track. Having turned over so many of "her" horses to others, Annie sympathized with Helena.

The morning was still and cool; the air felt weightless without its daytime humidity. The first light outlined the eastern hills, but they could not see clearly to the other side of the training track. They heard the rhythm of Base Blood's hoofs as they pranced and trotted over the soft cushion of sandy loam. Even phrases of Speed's easy chatter to the colt were audible as they circled the track. "Hey, now, easy now . . . I know you're the star here, baby. But you can't be a star without someone on your back . . . So, listen, it might as well be me. I mean this is a team sport, you know . . . Easy now. Easy. All right, let's go. A little faster . . . Oh, well, you like that. Well, I heard you did . . . Okay, Base Blood, LET'S FLY!"

The three spectators leaned into the rail. They could just see horse and rider at the end of the straightaway coming toward them. As the colt came by, Helena saw the fluid motion of Speed's ride and the steel of his arms and hands holding the reins. Frank saw the colt's stride, his speed, his rhythm of running. Annie saw both, and let out a yell, not a word, just a sound.

The horse and rider swept around the first turn, the rhythm of the hoofs barely changing as Base Blood changed his lead. The rhythm continued as they began to fade into the darkness. The colt went into the far turn, came around without faltering, and completed the four furlongs in forty-eight seconds. Then they went around the training track again, Speed controlling the colt from going flat out, but letting him continue and finally increase his pace for a mile, finishing well and strong.

They saw Speed rise in his stirrups and start laughing. Frank and Annie looked at each other. Annie muttered, "A minute thirty-seven." Frank nodded. Speed gave his falsetto yodel as he passed them. Gradually the colt slowed and Speed trotted him back. He pulled Base Blood up in front of them and asked, "What kind of time was that?"

"Well, Speed," Frank said, "at the moment, we aren't talking any numbers. Time only matters when you're in prison."

"Well, I got a number in my head that I just can't believe, so I'll forget it. Helena, this is one beautiful horse you've been exercising, and he sure likes what you've done. You and I are the lucky ones, you know; everybody else has to watch. But I gotta say this right here this morning. I got a long way to go before I'll ever deserve to be up on something like this one, but even so, I'll do anything to ride this colt."

Annie smiled as Frank said, "Take him on back, and, Helena, walk him out real easy."

Speed guided the colt through the gap and Helena hurried to walk along with them. Annie and Frank stood watching the colt walk eagerly toward his bath and breakfast. A number of farmhands had arrived and shouted greetings to Speed and Helena.

Annie saw Frank shake his head; she asked, "What?"

He let out a deep breath. "There's always a morning like this. It's the one you have to remember. The colt's ours, just the four of us. After Saturday, he'll be theirs."

On that still morning, the crowds, the questions, and the public performance were distant shadows. Frank was right. The private joy they had just experienced would not return. Even if they made the winner's circle, it always would be too crowded. Annie could barely wait to show Base Blood to the world, but already she knew what would be lost and what it would cost them.

"Are you ready for it, Frank?"

"Nope," he said as he started walking. "Never will be, but I'll be there."

That afternoon, it started to rain. Two days later, when the weather reports promised no let-up, they changed their plans. Base Blood was shipped to Churchill Downs a day early to give him a chance to work in the slop. The colt had worked well on wet gallops and on the muddy track at Limeteen during his training, but the unknown factor was how he would respond, not only to crowds, a new track, and the heightened tension of the backstretch, but to having mud kicked in his face from the race's front runners.

On the two-hour drive between Lexington and Louisville, Annie and Frank considered blinkers and mud caulks, deciding against the former and for calling the farm's farrier to be on hand when they saw the condition of the Downs. Annie second-guessed herself, wishing out loud that they had run Base Blood in one or two other races before exposing him to the Breeders' Cup crowd.

"He needed the time," Frank said. "Besides, if he loses,

nobody'll notice. It's when he wins, and how he wins, that we have to worry about."

The rain continued, and on Friday morning Base Blood worked well in the mud of Churchill Downs. Because most of the horses who were on the track sported Breeders' Cup saddlecloths with their names emblazoned on them, no one paid any attention to the big red bay who wore no stable cloth and had an unfamiliar black exercise rider. Many people recognized Annie, but few took any notice of Frank. Limeteen's shedrow was a single stall at the far end of the backstretch, away from barns reserved for the Breeders' Cup runners, as well as from the journalists who followed the famous trainers, jockeys, and owners.

The *Daily Racing Form*'s clockers did not note Base Blood's work in the special Saturday morning issue. The colt's past performance chart listed only his one second in a claiming race. There were eight horses in the race; Base Blood had drawn the number 3 post position in the starting gate. By the time Helena led him over to the paddock, the colt was a forty-five-to-one long shot.

Because of the rain and the relative unimportance of the early contest on a day of million-dollar races, the paddock observers were few. Annie and Frank shared an umbrella until Speed's valet, an old black retired groom hired by the track, arrived with his saddle. Frank made sure the saddlecloth and cinch were right. When Speed appeared in Limeteen's yellow and white silks, Annie distributed $100-to-win boot tickets to Speed and Helena, gave one to Frank, and kept one for herself. An old custom, the boot ticket was a favor from an owner, given in the paddock and kept for luck in one's boot.

"This is my little tradition," she said.

"Speed," Frank instructed, "the tractors have been floating the track all morning, squeezing the rain out of it. I think the base is solid, but keep him free of flying mud. Go to the front and keep him there, but don't let him get away from you and spend everything. He's never gone this distance before, but don't worry. He's got it in him. If it's going well in the stretch, don't wait for company. Let him show himself."

"Riders up" was called by the paddock judge, and Frank

legged the jockey into his saddle. Helena patted the colt's neck and released the bridle. For a moment, Base Blood stood motionless, calmly looking at Annie. She stepped up to him and slowly put her cheek against his. "You're the best thing that's happened to me," she said quietly. "Go on and run."

"Number three!" came the call, and Speed guided Base Blood into line as the eight colts circled the paddock and entered the tunnel through the grandstand for the post parade. Helena followed with the other grooms, shooting an excited, nervous smile back to her mother and Frank.

As part of their strategy to avoid attention, Annie had not requested owner's seats. From long experience at Churchill Downs, Frank knew a vantage point near a clubhouse stairwell where they could stand and not be noticed. The crowds were filling in the seats. While the colts warmed up and were loaded into the gate, Annie and Frank said nothing to each other.

The starter's bell rang and the gates sprang open. Base Blood broke to the front and was just off the rail by the clubhouse turn. He settled in to his easy long stride for the length of the backstretch, and, one by one, the rest of the field fell back. The track announcer called the race with little excitement until he noted the first two quarter-mile fractions. Suddenly his voice took on an urgency that caught the attention of the mingling, unconcerned crowd.

At the far turn, Base Blood led by five safe lengths and started to leap ahead. Through her binoculars, Annie saw Speed's mouth move but not his whip. The thousands in the crowd seemed to interrupt themselves and turn collectively toward the top of the stretch, where the unknown horse appeared, splashing through rain and mud, apparently running alone. And yet he was not coasting to an easy win. He was closing fast on the finish line as erratic cheering burst out of the grandstand when he passed. The voice of the track announcer was bellowing the name "Base Blood . . . Base Blood!" His closing strides were long and firm, and when Speed rose in the stirrups, the colt kept running flat out for almost another furlong before easing down.

"Let's go," Frank said, moving quickly down the stairs. Annie followed, not responding to the win but, instead, reacting with awe to what she had seen. They reached the winner's circle as the track announcer intoned the fact that Base Blood had broken by two fifths of a second the Churchill Downs track record of 1:41 3/5 for a mile and a sixteenth, and in the mud. The colt returned, blowing easily. As usual, Frank watched the approach, saw he was fine, then signaled to Helena. She attached her shank, Speed removed his tack, and went to the scales to be weighed out. The jockey returned quickly, and Helena let the track photographer take two pictures, both of which Frank avoided.

Then the girl led the colt around the track to the backstretch spit barn. Annie and Frank followed, she answering the questions of the few photographers and journalists who had hurried down to report on the unexpected story. Ill prepared for the deep mud of the track, they were left behind. When she walked in front of the clubhouse boxes, Annie hoped that Sam had arrived in time to watch her colt break the record.

As they moved off the track to the spit barn, rain fell heavily. The threesome waited without a word until Base Blood's urine and blood samples were taken. Then they walked through the backstretch to his stall. The news had already reached the Breeders' Cup connections, some of whom called congratulations from their shedrows, most of whom watched the colt walk by and silently appraised him. Still in his Limeteen silks, Speed was waiting with his mother and father in Base Blood's stall. Helena had contained herself well, but when she saw Bruna Oliver with tears in her eyes, and Speed matching his father's broad smile, she started laughing and crying. Unable to release her shank to hug someone, she hugged the colt. The Olivers hurried into the rain to shake hands with Annie. After the initial excitement, Speed started describing the race and everyone listened. Frank stood alone on the other side of Base Blood. When Annie looked over at him, his face did not soften, but he said quietly, "Thanks."

She did not trust herself to reply. At that moment she believed again that, in spite of all that had happened, Frank was undoubtedly the best man she had ever known. At the same time, she felt a familiar fury for having loved Sam Cumberland so much for so long.

"Let's walk him out and ship the hell out of here," Frank was saying. "We can celebrate at Limeteen."

Even though the seven Breeders' Cup races overwhelmed the press with their excitement and glory, considerable notice was taken of Base Blood's record-breaking run. His name entered public speculation, and he was listed in the winter book in Las Vegas as one of the many early contenders for next spring's Kentucky Derby. The Caernarvon Farms colt Royal Blessing was already the favorite, having won the Saratoga Hopeful and Belmont Futurity, as well as the Breeders' Cup Juvenile, although at three fifths of a second slower than Base Blood had run the same distance earlier in the day. A fifth of a second equals one length; the time difference represented a hypothetical three-length win by Base Blood.

Royal Blessing nevertheless was voted the two-year-old of the year. In campaigning for the Eclipse Award, Sam Cumberland was quoted by one source as saying, "I don't want to take anything away from the Limeteen colt, but a one-race record breaker who had no competition and has no pedigree doesn't necessarily make a champion. It might make Base Blood a fluke. I can assure you that Royal Blessing, having won the major two-year-old races, is no fluke."

Annie met with her bankers and almost laughed at their changed attitude, particularly when she paid down the $3.2 million she had received for the stud farm in Ireland. A month later, after the dispersal sale of 255 Limeteen horses, she paid off a million more and bought stallion shares with the rest. Limeteen was solvent, though financially less than sound. The banks were indeed very pleased to have Base Blood in the barn and on the books.

People called Limeteen who had never previously spoken to Annie. Track owners and trainers had always been courteous but never quite so eager. She even heard from several of Lexington's fanciest breeding farms; their managers chattered effusively about their special skills with stallions and syndication. When Frank decided which of the fifty remaining Limeteen horses were to race over the winter in Florida or California and with whom, Annie had no trouble placing them with the best trainers in the country. Each trainer, of course, was aware of the possibilities of getting the unknown record breaker into his barn. They all knew that Frank Carney had reappeared at Limeteen, but, given his past, they regarded his status as insecure. Fifteen Limeteen horses were sent to other public trainers. Under normal circumstances, Frank would have taken them to Hialeah and trained them himself, but he was determined to keep away from publicity. Instead, he took fifteen two-year-olds, including Base Blood, and some older horses to the training center at Aiken, South Carolina. Annie remained at Limeteen to look after the twenty broodmares, some of whom were descendants of the lines she had inherited from Winnie Sumner. They were in foal to some of the best bloodstock from both sides of the Atlantic; as part of the consolidation of Limeteen Farm, a half dozen had been shipped to Kentucky from Ireland and the Haras de la Brise.

Helena stayed with her mother and worked in the barns when she was free from school and studies. At a local private school, she had survived the initial gossip about her heritage and begun to make a number of friends. Some of her impish glee returned, and her laughter was heard more often through Limeteen Hall. But the damage done by Phil Angelo left scars of fear. Helena suppressed them during her busy day, but they emerged in terrifying nightmares. There were many nights when Helena's screams brought Annie running to her daughter's bed, so Annie was never away at night. If there was an important race in Florida or California, Annie either took Helena with her or made sure she would be able to return to Lexington by bedtime.

In December, Helena was fourteen. For a special gift, Annie presented her with a choice of foals from the broodmare band. Both mother and daughter knew the gift was a gamble. A foal, no matter what the pedigree or how vigilant the care, could be misformed, untalented, or even born dead. Nevertheless, the offer delighted Helena. Already a student of pedigrees, she wanted more time to study, so she asked her mother to give her until Christmas to make her selection.

Less of a gamble but more difficult to handle was the birthday present that arrived from Sam Cumberland: a set of skis, boots, and a handsome outfit complete with goggles and skin moisturizers. With them was a birthday message. Without a mention of his parenthood, Sam managed to be humorously affectionate and touching. He concluded with an invitation to Helena to fly with him in the Gwydian to Gstaad over the holidays. All this plus ski lessons, if her mother approved.

Clearly intrigued by the invitation, Helena asked for advice. Annie believed that Sam, in his way, was struggling with how to fulfill, at least in part, his role as a father. Helena had survived a nearly fatal crisis; Sam had never been a real presence in her life. For her part, Helena did not wish to leave her mother; also, the unknown, even on such luxurious terms, was still frightening to the girl. At the same time, the idea of learning to ski in Switzerland greatly tempted her.

What settled the issue was Frank's far more simple birthday present. At dawn on the Saturday morning after her birthday, Helena and Annie arrived at the Aiken training center's barn where the Limeteen horses were boarded. It was a regular biweekly trip and Frank was waiting for them in front of Base Blood's stall.

"He's got something for you in there," Frank said to Helena.

As usual, the colt greeted Helena with nuzzles and nickering, and she had to take time to respond. Then she saw, in the corner of the stall, a new pair of handmade cowboy boots. She went over and picked them up. Carved and stamped into each one was HELENA CARNEY.

She stared at Frank for a moment, then struggled to say, "I feel . . . it's like the first time in my life it's really my name. No, I mean that . . . you've just given it to me." Still unsatisfied, she looked down, embarrassed.

Annie watched Frank as her daughter, with tears in her eyes, stumbled over to him and stretched up to kiss him on the cheek. He allowed it, but kept his hands in his back pockets.

"Well, I've got something to talk to you about," he said with a seriousness that gave him an escape from the emotion of the moment.

"Let me put these on first," Helena said and sat happily on the ground to pull on the new boots. "Perfect fit," she said.

"Let me get the first set out, then we'll talk some," he said, turning to the group of exercise riders who approached. Annie and Helena went in the stall with Base Blood and looked him over until his groom arrived. By then, Frank was ready to watch the first set, so the three of them walked over to the center's training track.

"Base Blood's been off his feed," Frank said, "doing some stall walking and chewing on his manger."

"Oh, no," Annie said, alarmed. "What's the problem?"

"Changes make horses nervous; they're creatures of routine. I think it's Helena."

"Me?" the girl asked, surprised.

"I think he misses you. He sees you every couple of weeks; then you disappear. He's lonely. It's hard to explain to a horse that you have to go to school."

"What have you tried?" Annie asked, an edge of anxiety in her voice. If Base Blood started to regress and took up his bad habits again, particularly wind sucking, he could seriously damage his ability to run.

"I put a radio in there, a loud-ticking clock, a cat, and then a goat."

Helena laughed. Annie did not. "What should we do about him?" she asked.

"Give him what he wants," he replied and tilted his head toward Helena.

"I can't take Helena out of school," Annie said, trying not to sound upset. "She has to be at home."

"Well, you two have to decide that. I'm just telling you what's wrong with the horse." They reached the training track, and no one said anything until Frank continued. "Of course, I ought to tell you that the house I rent here has an extra bedroom, and I've been talking to this real nice retired college professor who's looking for some tutoring work."

Both mother and daughter were amazed. Helena reacted faster.

"Mummy?" she said, asking permission.

Annie was startled by her daughter's instant acceptance. "What?" she retorted.

"Well, what do you think?" Helena asked.

"I think about a couple of long nights we've had. What do *you* think?"

Helena stood up very straight. She was looking at the ground as she started to talk, but gradually brought her eyes up to meet her mother's. "I think I have to deal with that, but I'm ready to. If Frank will put up with me, maybe it's a good time. Besides, the track at home will freeze; we can't bring Base Blood back there. If I'm what he needs, I ought to be here."

Annie was aware that she envied her daughter for being wanted by Frank Carney and needed by Base Blood. "Let me think about it."

"You feel like riding this morning?" Frank asked the girl.

"Sure," Helena responded happily.

"Then why don't you take off those fancy new boots and get on something you can work in. Then you can gallop Base Blood in the next set."

Helena ran back toward the barn. Several Limeteen colts in the first set went by, and Annie tried to concentrate on them. Frank yelled to one of his exercise riders but otherwise was quiet.

"I can't let her do it, Frank. My Lord, she's fourteen; she's still having trouble with what happened to her. You just don't know."

"Annie, I'm training your horse," Frank said. "I told you what I think he needs and a way to give it to him. The decision's yours." His voice hardened as he went on. "But don't tell me about what I don't know. I've been through some things, too, and Helena knows that. She also knows that I'm not her father, but I might have been. I'm pretty damn sure I could be a good one, at least until the Derby. After that, well, who knows what'll happen?"

"The Derby?" After the win on Breeders' Cup Day, she and Frank both had known that they would be pointing Base Blood for the Kentucky Derby; but whether from superstition or a wary resistance to fantasy, they had not discussed it together. Of course, everyone else who spoke to either of them about Base Blood had Derby ideas and suggestions.

"If we can keep him fit, Annie, he'll beat any horse running."

Frank had never been one to overstate anything. His quiet conclusiveness on that December morning about a race on the first Saturday in May startled Annie. He was saying that out of a foal crop of nearly fifty thousand thoroughbreds of Base Blood's year, and of the twenty best that might get into the Kentucky Derby, her orphaned wind-sucking toed-out claimer with the lightning strike on his face would win. Annie tried to swallow, but her throat stuck.

Frank shifted his feet and leaned on the rail. "Ever hear of a California stable called Pearbreeze Farm?"

Annie shook her head, not yet ready to talk business.

Frank told her, "They're campaigning a mysterious two-year-old colt out there named Exwhyzee. Won a few big races. I hear they're pointing him for the Triple Crown."

Someone, Annie could not remember who, had mentioned the colt on her last trip to California.

"You might like to know that Pearbreeze Farm is owned by a company called Dynagen, which I'm pretty sure you've heard of."

Haras de la Brise, Haras de la Poire: breeze and pear. As soon as Annie heard who owned the California farm, she understood its significance. Henry's time in France had been his happiest years. Once again, Annie pictured the solemn little boy walking across the Deauville auction pavilion to speak with the new owner of "his" colt, Moonshot, then shaking hands with Sam Cumberland, his father. Annie believed that moment had been the end of Henry's innocence, leading directly to their coming to America and his involvement in the many tangles of her life. She did not even know him anymore, and once again blamed herself for bringing him back to what she had left behind.

And now Henry, having turned his trust money into millions, had a colt that might run against Base Blood, as did Sam and probably a thousand others. Everyone in America who thought he had a good two-year-old in the barn had the same dream. Annie pushed back from the rail and, without interrupting Frank's concentration on the first set, started walking back to the barn to see her dream.

THIRTY-FOUR

ON RACE DAYS, Annie could not sleep. She would arrive at Base Blood's stall before he was awake, and when the colt stirred, she would be sitting in the straw beside him with her legs drawn up and her back against the wall. He snorted, rolled up on his knees, and stood expectantly, knowing that he was going to run. Alone together, as Annie silently brushed out his coat, tail, and mane, they calmed each other. To Annie, the quiet dark of the early morning was a time of forgetting the concerns in the rest of her life. For Base Blood, it seemed a gathering of resources, not only from his training, but from whatever vestiges of his heritage remained in his meager pedigree. Nothing else mattered and nothing else quite touched them during those hours. So effective was their time together that Frank never sent the colt out for a race-day work. If she had had the choice, Annie would have gladly traded away the moments in the winner's circle for the hour before dawn in the stall. That spring, she never had to choose. Each time he ran, Base Blood gave her both.

Derby Day was like no other, for horse or human. The race held at Churchill Downs for a hundred and fifteen years was mythic in the American equine tradition, an annunciation of the winner's potential greatness, even though the race took place too early in the year and too early in a three-year-old's life. Inevitably, there were too many horses entered, some with only their owners' egos to recommend them. It was a crowded race of heavy and often dangerous traffic. The winner of the Kentucky Derby was honored from that day on with the equivocal glory of being the horse to beat. Once won, the race obliged the winner to attain greatness, an expectation seldom realized. Only eleven times in the eighty-year history of the spring races making up the Triple Crown—the Derby, the Preakness, and the Belmont Stakes—had one horse taken them all.

Outside Base Blood's stall, the Derby phenomenon had begun. A crowd gathered, flashbulbs popped, and television floodlights glared. Daily, as the colt walked to the track for his work, a noisy pack of reporters and gawkers went along. Base Blood accepted most of the annoyance, having become accustomed to such intrusions earlier in the spring, when he had his four wins. After his first two races in Florida, the Hutchinson Stakes and the Florida Derby, the attention had been merely bothersome. When he won the Flamingo Stakes at Hialeah, and then the Bluegrass Stakes at Keeneland, each in near record time by five lengths or more, the journalistic vigilance became insistent.

"Morning, Mummy," Helena said quietly as she and Frank entered the stall. The girl patted Base Blood. "Did you get any sleep?"

"The usual," Annie said as she handed the brush to her daughter and glanced at Frank. His face was heavy with fatigue, but his eyes were alert with anticipation. He had remained distant and taciturn throughout the spring, training his horses, advising on Limeteen, and ministering to the complex needs of his Derby candidate. Helena had continued to stay with him, first in his rented house in Aiken, then in motel suites after Base Blood was shipped to Florida. She and Frank were a good pair, Annie had to admit, even as she regretted the void the girl left at Limeteen Hall. Frank made Helena study and put her on such a strict schedule that she was done with her year's schoolwork before the first Saturday in May. She in turn kept him company, an important luxury during the pressure of a Derby campaign. In time, they began to trust each other enough to talk about their separate "hassles," a word that Helena used and Frank adopted. Annie saw the relationship grow and was glad of it, but envied them both its intimacy. Helena remained just as loving to her mother, but Annie sensed certain boundaries in their conversation that apparently did not exist between her daughter and Frank.

"Morning, ma'am. Frank," Speed Oliver said as he appeared at the stall door. "Helena, you better rough up that colt a little. He looks too good."

She laughed. "What are you doing here so early? I figured we'd have to drag you out of bed again."

Speed shook his head. "Every time I shut my eyes, I ran this race in my head."

"Did you win?" Annie asked.

"Never got that far. I dreamed about every mess you can think of—heavy traffic, a track made out of taffy, the starting gate opening for everyone but us . . . My favorite was the circus truck breaking open out by the final turn and us running into a crowd of penguins."

Speed had ridden Base Blood in all the colt's races, thus becoming a hot jockey and getting other first-class mounts. Success nurtured a pleasant confidence in the young rider, who became that phenomenon of American publicity, a "first black," as in the first black astronaut, the first black quarterback, the first black billionaire. The first black jockey to ride in the Kentucky Derby since 1911, Speed was proud of the accomplishment. On every possible occasion, he reminded the press that before and after the Civil War, black jockeys had dominated American tracks. Between 1875 and 1895, however, the white backlash began against Negro accomplishments during Reconstruction. Nevertheless, black jockeys rode eleven Derby winners in those years, including three ridden by Isaac Murphy, the man regarded as the first great black athlete in America. Speed had studied Isaac Murphy's life and gave the press a great deal of copy about his idol. Considered one of the greatest jockeys who ever lived, Murphy rode in 1412 races and won 612, a forty-four percent average. Speed kept a picture of Murphy prominently displayed on his locker in the jockeys' room.

When asked why there had been no black jockeys since that time, Speed had a ready answer. "Well, after Reconstruction, the Jockey Club stopped giving blacks licenses to ride on the tracks they controlled. Besides, black boys weren't trusted with the white man's horses anymore. Today, most boys want to play basketball. I wanted to play basketball because you don't get killed playing basketball. But can you imagine? They said I was too short."

The first press people began to arrive outside Base Blood's stall while it was still dark. "Ah, Countess? . . . Hey, Frank, could I just get a word . . . ?" Frank moved to the stall door and closed both the upper and lower halves, explaining, "Excuse us. This is when we talk to the horse."

Alone in the stall with Base Blood, the four stood quietly. Helena finished brushing him down and changed his stall bandages. Frank ran his hands over the legs one more time, which Annie wished she could do just to be doing something. Instead, she stood next to Speed in a corner of the stall, listening to the crowd outside get larger and noisier. Base Blood heard it, too, and began tossing his head.

"All right, let's take him for a walk," Frank said. "I'd like him to have twenty minutes, but bring him in if the crowd gets too thick. Speed, you open the doors, and Helena, when you take him out, turn him right away so that their flashbulbs don't blind him forever. Annie . . . ?" He hesitated to instruct her.

"I'll go out with him," she said, reassuring Frank of her willingness to be the press's lightning rod. "Just don't stop for anyone, Helena. If I have to stop, forget about me. Keep him walking right along. And keep an eye out for the Caernarvon or Pearbreeze colors. They're all just dying to get the family together."

Helena smiled grimly as she snapped her lead to Base Blood's halter. The Derby runners were stabled together in three special stakes barns, which only added a personal intensity to the many pressures of a Derby morning. Speed swung open the door, and for a moment there was a pause of recognition by those outside. Then came a barrage of questions, flash equipment started bursting, and a television crew's floodlights lit the shedrow. Helena led the colt out and established a brisk pace. As Annie started to follow, she looked over at Frank, who was backing into the shadows of the stall. He saw her watching him and shook his head disgustedly. She hurried out and was immediately surrounded. Setting her smile, Annie followed the colt and answered questions.

The regular racing press were thorough professionals, content with queries about the race and the horse. The Derby, however, brought a different kind of journalist to the backstretch. Oblivious of the need for quiet and calm around thoroughbreds, they came looking for more than a horse story. Annie attracted them as honeysuckle draws ants. Having learned early that anger and rebuttal only stimulated their reportorial zeal, Annie confronted them with her smile, frequent flashes of humor, and, when the questions got rough, distraction. But it was thin armor.

"Mrs. Carney, is it true you're not only going after the win here, but you want to break the Derby record?"

"Sure. We'd love to break the record, but it won't happen. When Secretariat set it, there were thirteen horses coming out of the starting gate. Today there'll be twenty. That's too crowded for records. We'll just be real happy to win."

"Who's your main competition?"

"The other nineteen." She got her laugh, but the spokesman persisted.

"No, but really, the morning line puts the Caernarvon colt at nine-to-five odds, the Lukas four-horse entry at four-to-one, and the California colt at six-to-one. Base Blood's at two-to-one."

"The morning line has never been a religion I believed in."

"Countess, you're running against your son and your former lover . . ."

Annie glanced at the woman who had been hovering around the barn throughout Derby week. She was always overdressed for a reporter on the backstretch.

"I'm not running," Annie countered. "My horse is." She saw that the woman was wearing open-toed shoes; she also noticed a pile of horse manure ten yards ahead. As the reporter marched along, she kept shoving a small microphone into Annie's face.

"Annie, let's be frank! I know about those men in your life. Isn't this race more a contest between you and them?"

"No, you're wrong. And look, I can't be Frank . . . He's my trainer."

A few members of the racing press laughed at the pun and hurried to ask their own questions, but the woman loudly went on, "Yes, he certainly is, and is he your husband or not, and is he really the father— Oh, shit!" She stopped and looked down at the manure, gingerly raising her left foot out of it.

Annie kept walking, and the rest of the press followed her jovially. Only one query diverted her.

"What does Limeteen do about horses and drugs? Do you use them?"

"You bet we use them. Every day in the barns, but not on race days."

"Then it's only hay, oats, and water?"

"That'd be like saying people can't go to hospitals. You can use drugs as either medicine or dope. We use a lot of medicine at Limeteen; I'll show you my vet bills sometime. But we don't use drugs just to get a horse to the starting gate. If a horse isn't sound, it doesn't race."

"You mean, if Base Blood was a bleeder, you wouldn't run him today on Lasix?"

Annie knew what they were getting at and tried to be careful. "No, I wouldn't, not him or any other Limeteen horse. I've said that ever since they made Lasix legal."

"How do you feel about Caernarvon's colt using it today for the first time?"

She wanted to say that she was appalled that Sam would

allow such a thing, but she knew how much he wanted to win a Derby.

"That's their business," she responded noncommittally.

"They say a colt running on Lasix for the first time runs faster than usual."

"That's what they say."

"Don't you think it gives Royal Blessing an unfair advantage?"

Annie gave in to her irritation. "Don't try to put a shank on me to lead me into saying what you'd like to hear. The rules are that if a horse is a bleeder and a vet says so, the horse can be given Lasix, at least here in Kentucky. Royal Blessing passed some blood this spring . . ."

"But they didn't use Lasix in his next races until today. Why do you suppose that is?"

Annie refused to take the bait. "You're asking the wrong person. Talk to Sam Cumberland about that." She knew the group would not drop the subject of Sam, so she tried to divert the conversation.

"Look, the biggest problem about drugs is that there's no consistency. How many horses will be running here with Bute and Lasix in them? But five weeks from today, they can't use it in New York for the Belmont Stakes. It's crazy. We're just asking for a nice, big federal bureaucracy if the states don't get together on this thing . . . Excuse me a minute."

Another colt was being led toward them. A dark brown chestnut with a black mane and tail, white stockings on his front legs, and a large star on his face, the colt was already familiar to Annie. She once again noted the beauty of the woman walking along with him as she recognized Henry in his wire-rimmed glasses. "Helena," Annie called, "let's take him back."

Turning Base Blood scattered the group around Annie, and she took the opportunity to walk along with Helena.

"I saw him, too," she said, "just as you called."

"We'll get together sooner or later," Annie told her. "This just wasn't the right time."

Helena said, "Did you see his wife? She's gorgeous."

Annie concurred. She had not heard from Greta since her

note, telling of the wedding and returning Winnie's ring. She had tried but failed numerous times to reply. Of course, she had received no communication from Henry. All she knew was what she read in *The Blood-Horse:* the Pearbreeze colt, Exwhyzee, had won or placed in four races as a two-year-old at Bay Meadows, south of San Francisco. He then went to Santa Anita as a three-year-old and ran third in the San Vicente, won the San Rafael, placed in the San Felipe, and in April won the Santa Anita Derby.

More amazing than his successes were the mishaps the colt had survived. After his Bay Meadows campaign, he bucked his shins but came back in time for his three-year-old debut. A week before the San Felipe Stakes, he came down with a virus and a fever that ordinarily would have caused a horse to be scratched. Yet Exwhyzee shook the infection in time to place, though he was cut down in traffic by another runner, which produced a gash on his near front ankle. It was healed in a week, and the colt was back in training.

"We pin-fired it a couple of times," Henry was quoted as saying, "and we have an old Indian groom working in our barn who uses a secret eucalyptus poultice. Some people think eucalyptus is poison, but it worked for Exwhyzee."

Henry's colt had an expensive pedigree. The sire, a son of Nijinsky, had been bought for $1.8 million by an agent at the Keeneland yearling sale the day after Barky Cumberland had tried to shoot Annie. The dam, a granddaughter of Native Dancer, was hammered down for another million a year later at a Saratoga broodmare sale. Oddly, the sire, named Ballroom, had never raced. Pearbreeze's explanation was that the colt had fractured his sesamoid in the farm's paddock and had never recovered sufficiently. Whatever happened to the sire had not affected his get; Exwhyzee was an extraordinary colt. Annie saw that in one quick look.

Without any warning, Sam appeared, wearing a camel-hair overcoat and a brown felt trilby; he was followed by a number of stylish-looking people carrying binocular cases and talking animatedly. Sam was, as always by the first Saturday in May, deeply tanned. His pre-race exuberance was effusive, and his friends, to whom he spoke in French, responded to his excitement. He saw Base Blood before he saw Annie or Helena, and instantly recognized the colt as well as the clutch of journalists. They in turn spotted a dramatic opportunity and spread out for camera angles. Sam snapped on his devastating public smile, which almost made Annie laugh. He approached, all surprise and delight, arms out, ready for a demonstrative greeting.

Annie too had a smile, and as cameras clicked and floodlights blazed, she held out her hand, thus halting his advance. "Hello, Sam," Annie said graciously. "Join the party."

On the other side of the colt, Helena muttered, "I don't believe this."

With perfect ease, Sam changed leads to take Annie's hand and fell into step beside her. "Good morning," he said. Then he turned to the girl. "Hello, Helena. Your colt looks splendid."

"Yes, well, he's wound tight, ready to go," the girl replied, trying to sound airy. "And since we're all being so civilized, how's yours doing? Had his Lasix yet?"

Annie slid her hand away as Sam deftly replied, "Oh, you know, all the problems he's had, still sore, off his feed, a little washy this morning . . ."

"That must mean"—Annie smiled—"that you figure he'll take it by twenty lengths."

Sam laughed, just a little too loudly. Annie glanced at his elegant friends, who were following as best they could through the flashing cameras. She did not see Glynn.

When the journalists pushed forward with questions, Sam peeled off from Base Blood's procession. He called a breezy "Good luck!" Shedding reporters with a cool smile, he led away his French contingent.

Annie knew his performance so well, as he knew hers. She wondered what he really felt. What would they have said to each other at a bar or on a backstretch with no one else around? Did he even slightly regret what Annie regarded as his total betrayal? The hurt had been dulled by the intensity of Base Blood's promise, and, strangely enough, by the flinty presence of Frank Carney. Having him in her life again, despite his silent loathing, was at least a calming constant. She could never again trust Sam; of that, she was certain. But seeing him, she did wonder what he, and she herself, really felt.

As a three-year-old, Royal Blessing had more than lived up to his Eclipse-winning promise. Starting off the year with a solid win in the Fountain of Youth Stakes at Gulfstream Park, he was pointed toward the Florida Derby, where he would have run against Base Blood. The Caernarvon colt came down with a bad virus, however, and was scratched. In early April, he came back to run a close second in the Gotham Stakes at Aqueduct. After the race, the Caernarvon vet 'scoped him and found blood in his lungs. Nevertheless, two weeks later, without benefit of Lasix, he won the Wood Memorial on the same track. His time was near the track record for the nine-furlong race, and his jockey ran him the extra furlong to give the colt a taste of the Derby distance. The *Racing Form* clockers reported a time of 2:02 3/5, three seconds off Secretariat's Derby record.

When Annie and Helena returned Base Blood to his stall, it had been mucked out and a new pillow of straw had been laid in and clipped. Frank was nowhere in sight; they led the colt in and closed the webbing, as much to keep the press out as the horse in. As Helena started to curry the colt, however, several reporters began to call questions again. Annie moved over to the door to answer, hoping to give them enough so that they would eventually move on. She again told the story of finding Base Blood, and expressed her appreciation that in the draw for post position that day, he was in the middle of the gate rather than at either end.

Then a man Annie had not seen previously, but who had a press credential hanging around his neck, called beyond her to Helena.

"Young lady, ah, *Miss* Carney, which of your fathers are you pulling for today?"

Annie, turning toward Helena, saw the other members of the press glance at their colleague, appalled. Helena held her brush, caught in midcircle, and slowly bowed her head. Annie unsnapped the webbing and walked toward the man, who smiled at her spitefully. Without warning, Annie stepped into him with a full swing and smacked him across his face. He caught part of the blow on his arm, but the force sent him stumbling backward.

"Save the dirty questions for me," Annie said, following him. "I'm used to them."

"Listen, Countess, juicy feelings are my story," the man said, holding his jaw. "Also, I'm no chauvinist. Man or woman, I fight back."

True to his word, the man shoved Annie hard so that she fell to the ground. Other members of the press grabbed him, and he staggered back to fall in a bath puddle.

A tense silence followed as the man got to his feet and brushed off his clothes. Annie, stunned, held her bruised side. Suddenly Frank appeared, carrying a shovel in his hands like a baseball bat. People lurched out of his way as Annie saw flood-lights and flashbulbs.

"Frank, no!" she yelled.

Helena pushed through the sizable crowd and grabbed Frank. He looked down at the girl, let the shovel touch ground, and brushed her hair with one hand. Then he turned to the journalist and said, "These two women can take care of themselves. But if I ever see you around my barn again, you'll have to deal with me."

"Gracious," the man said in mock alarm, "and next time you might have an ax."

Frank dropped the shovel and started for him, but Helena and a large photographer held on to him as the offending journalist was shoved and dragged away. As he went, he yelled, "Round two, tomorrow's papers!"

Annie reached out for Helena. Frank yelled at the Limiteen grooms to close Base Blood's stall doors. Several security guards arrived and, though not knowing exactly what had happened, blocked the press's access inside the barn as Annie and Helena hurried into the tack room.

Frank shut the door. The three of them looked at one another.

"You all right, Mummy?"

Annie reassured her, then said, "We'll pay for it; I'm sorry for that. But my Lord, it felt good to hit him!" In spite of the pain in her side, she was elated. "And he came back at me, so he can't sue. There ought to be a law that as soon as you become a public figure, you get to fight any journalist who asks the really rotten question."

Helena started to the door. "I'm going back to Base Blood."

"Better stay awhile," Annie said. "They're still hovering."

Helena shrugged. "Mummy, they'll always be there. It doesn't matter about us. I have to finish grooming Base Blood." She opened the door, then turned her head and gave them a confident smile. "Besides, I'm ready for it now. Earlier, I just didn't know it was coming." She went out, closing the door behind her.

As soon as Annie looked over at Frank, he pushed his hand through his hair and walked over to the corner beside the tack room's window. "We really did it," he said. "They'll dig up everything and smear it around on anything it'll stick to."

"Not if Base Blood wins. He'll be their story then, not us."

He looked at her in surprise. "Annie, winning a race gets a headline in the sports section. You, me, Helena, *and* Hank, *and* Sam"—the muscles in his face tensed and he faced back to the window—"get pictures on the front page and in those damn gossip columns." He shook his head. "That'd be the only good part if Base Blood ran last."

"He won't run last," she said.

He started pacing slowly, hands in his back pockets, looking at his feet. "Helena's right. It doesn't matter about us . . ."

He stopped and stared at the door where the girl had left. "She's the best there is." Then he looked around at Annie, the skin of his face drawn so tightly that Annie thought it would split. "Goddammit, I wish she were my—" He could not finish the sentence.

Annie did not avoid his eyes and her own grew angry at his blame. "Why don't you, for one damn second, stop hating me long enough to realize that, at the moment, if anyone is that girl's father, it's you! And she'd tell you the same thing if she had the chance. My Lord, what you've done for that girl, for *all* of us." She stopped herself, feeling her voice begin to break. Seeing his expression change to one of baffled yearning, she started backing up, into a table, knocking off a sweat scraper, which fell to the floor. "Frank, I didn't mean . . ." She did not know what she meant.

"What?" he said impatiently, stepping toward her.

She almost shouted. "I'm *grateful* to you."

"Anything else?" He was still coming.

"No!"

He stood directly in front of her, watching her with the look she had seen before of wanting to hit her or hold her. "You're lying," he said.

His hands were on her neck and he drew her into a deep, long kiss. Her arms went around him, and pressing her body into his, she kissed him again.

A boy opened the door, rushed in, then hesitated and said, " 'Scuse me." Picking up the sweat scraper, he hustled out, closing the door behind him.

Still holding her, Frank scanned her face. Annie's anxiety was obvious.

"We can just forget this," Frank said.

"No, we can't, and I don't want to. What happens now?"

He ran his hand hesitantly over her hair as he used to do, then took it away. "We run a horse race," he said. "After that, maybe we can talk"—he allowed a slight smile—"or start throwing bricks at each other."

Annie laughed softly, took his head in her hands, and kissed him again gently. "No promises."

"It's a big day," Frank said, "and everybody's a little crazy with it. Even so, you and I know better than to make promises."

Annie, without chancing a look, let go. Frank opened the door, and they went out.

Base Blood took the day in stride, eating his racing mix of oats at noon and, shortly after, rolling down in the stall for a two-hour nap. In the station wagon, Annie fought her way back across Louisville to her motel to change and supposedly rest. Traffic was heavy with the crowd of a hundred thousand, all interested in either the day's card or just going to the track's party. Whether headed for Millionaire's Row, the air-conditioned cushy suites with balconies overlooking the clubhouse turn at five thousand dollars for the day, or aiming for the track's infield with two dollars, a lawn chair, and suntan oil, people were saturated by the uncommon heat and by the mint, bourbon, and Dixieland atmosphere of the day.

Limeteen had no other runners on the card that day, and everyone connected to Base Blood wished that there had been such a distraction. Waiting for the announcement over the backstretch loudspeakers calling the eighth-race runners to the paddock was worse than watching a puddle dry. When the call finally came, the Limeteen crew moved with relief and dispatch. Helena, still in her work clothes but wearing a short dark riding jacket in deference to the Derby, attached her lead to Base Blood's halter and led him out of his stall. Frank stood nearby in his race-day outfit, an old linen coat and a tie. The Limeteen grooms and stable help watched respectfully as the colt walked by, sharing in his chance at fame. Frank walked along with Base Blood, as always with his eyes alternating from the colt to the ground in front of him. To the many greetings shouted from backstretch workers, he said, "Thank you, we appreciate it." He meant the words deeply, remembering where he and the horse were a little more than a year ago.

As they approached the gap and walked onto the track, the wall of noise from the stands hit them. Other colts were behind and ahead of them. Helena recognized the Caernarvon colors on the groom's jacket just ahead of her. Frank kept his head down, letting the horse lead him around the clubhouse turn to the tunnel, then through it into the paddock. He had prepared himself to absorb surprises, but in his first glance around the paddock he saw Sam Cumberland, then Hank Sumner, and finally Annie, standing near the Number 7 saddling stall.

Wearing a pale yellow-and-white silk dress and flat-brimmed straw hat, Annie looked as lovely as he had ever seen her. She gave him a smile, which he could not return. The crowd was jammed on three sides of the paddock and on the stand's balconies and walkways above them. As Helena led Base Blood into the enclosure, the horse nickered at Annie. She went in with him and took the lead while Helena and the jockey's valet put on the saddlecloth and saddle. Annie ran one hand down the colt's neck and felt not one tremor of nerves. Worrying that her own would travel through her hand, she took it away. She had seen Henry and Greta as well as Sam and Glynn in the paddock. All of them avoided one another's eyes. The colt reached out and nuzzled her; for that, she was grateful.

As the jockeys came into the paddock, the crowd reacted with noisy expectation. Speed came to the enclosure as Frank was testing the saddle's cinch. Speed had ridden in two previous races that day, and placed first in one.

"How's the track feel, Speed?" Annie asked.

"The rail seems a little cuppy. Don't know why. The other jocks are staying off it."

Frank said, "I think you want to be a little bit off the rail. He likes to go out in front, but in this crowd, he might not be able to. So the main thing, Speed, you know . . ."

"Traffic," the jockey replied.

"Stay clear of it; don't get boxed in. Go wide if you have to; your colt's got the distance. That California colt is a speedster; let him go. One of Lukas' entries is a front runner, so they'll set the pace. The one to watch is the Caernarvon colt. He's a stayer and can go the route. Never let him get away from you. Other than that, win the race."

"Good luck, Speed," Annie whispered as she handed him his boot ticket.

"Riders up" was called, and Helena led the colt into the paddock. As Frank was giving Speed a leg up, Helena said, "Speed, you're the luckiest person in the world to be riding this colt today."

Base Blood pranced with the weight on his back, finally giving some sign of his own excitement. The crowd reacted with hoots and yells. "Don't you think I know that?" Speed called back to Helena as he led the colt into line and around the paddock. The crowd applauded their favorites. The horses disappeared into the tunnel, and the people surged back toward the stands.

For a moment, Annie, Frank, and Helena waited, letting the other owners go ahead of them to avoid any unnecessary greetings. They glanced at one another, but there was nothing to say.

"See you later," Frank said, and went into the crowd. Helena nodded tensely and, looping her lead over her shoulder, went through the tunnel, following the other grooms to the track. Alone in the paddock, Annie made sure that Sam and Henry had gone, then went with other owners toward their boxes.

She arrived at hers and was greeted by Chigger Beasley and his wife and by Archibald Delansig and his wife. Just as the track announcer was heard requesting all to stand in order to sing "My Old Kentucky Home," Annie heard Henry say, "Hello, Mother."

She turned and saw him standing with Greta. He was unsmiling in a dark summer suit and an open shirt; she beamed in a bright red polka-dot maternity dress. People started singing all around them, including Annie's guests, who realized the significance of the encounter and gladly avoided it.

From the look on Annie's face, Greta knew that her surprise had worked. "I'm so glad no one else told you," she said. "We wanted to do that." She looked up at Henry for his agreement. He only stared at his mother and said flatly, "Good luck."

Annie was almost unable to speak. "Thank you," she said warmly in spite of his reticence. "When is it due?"

"October fifteenth, about," Greta offered quickly. Then, "Maybe we'll see you after the race." The slightest frown clouded her face, as if acknowledging the awkwardness of the meeting, which she so obviously had demanded.

Henry looked blankly at his mother, then took Greta's hand and led her down the aisle toward their box.

". . . We will sing one song for the old Kentucky home . . ."

When the crowd finished the anthem, Annie lifted her binoculars to cover her eyes. She focused on Base Blood as he and the other horses broke away from the post parade for their warm-up. Her guests respected her silence, and she kept her glasses up until the horses were being loaded into the gate, watching through tears the yellow and white stripes float over the royal blue, crimson, and gold of Caernarvon and the three intersecting black circles on a white field of Pearbreeze.

Then the gates banged open; they were off. The crowd bellowed and Annie saw Base Blood break and leap ahead. The colt in the next gate position veered out and bumped Base Blood so hard that he faltered and stumbled badly. Speed pulled up hard on his reins as Base Blood regained his footing but lost his advantage. The pack thundered by the stands on their way into the clubhouse turn, but the yellow and white silks were tenth in the field. As they entered the backstretch, the colt's stride lengthened and he began to gain ground. By the half-mile pole, he had reached the leading pack.

A cheer went up when the fractions appeared, but Annie did not look at the tote board to see what they were. The pace was too fast, and silently she urged Speed to lay back. The leaders were a long shot and one from the Lukas entry, followed closely by Exwhyzee, then another from the Lukas entry, and Royal Blessing. Two colts and a length back was Base Blood. He continued at his pace as the two horses in front of him faded. He was just behind Royal Blessing as they went into the final turn.

Several colts ran up, their jockeys asking them early to keep them in the race. The turn was crowded as several of the leaders began to tire. Exwhyzee was in the lead, dueling hard with the Lukas colt, when Royal Blessing made his move, and Base Blood moved right along behind him. Within the space of a few square yards, a dozen half-ton colts, going at forty-five miles an hour, were fighting for inches. As they came around the turn, the leaders centrifugally swerved out from the rail, making an opening. Royal Blessing's jockey saw it and whipped his mount in front of Base Blood, cutting him off. Speed snatched Base Blood up sharply, losing momentum, and, as other colts rushed up from behind, boxing him in behind the Caernarvon runner.

They swept around the final turn. Clearly lagging, the Lukas colt and Exwhyzee started to fall back, thus compacting the traffic even more. Base Blood had no room to run. In front was a wall of horses, Royal Blessing punching through to take the lead on the rail, Exwhyzee and others fading back, and yet another Lukas horse made his move, keeping the box around Base Blood. When the front runners reached the top of the stretch, however, they spread out.

Speed shouted, "Okay, Base Blood, let's fly!" and showed him space to the outside. The colt charged into it. Speed saw Exwhyzee suddenly falter, but the California colt kept going under left-and right-hand whipping from his jockey. Base Blood passed him as his stride lengthened at the sixteenth pole. Three colts, then two, remained to be beaten, the Lukas colors and Caernarvon. The yellow-and-white-striped silks edged past the Lukas colt. With a hundred yards to the finish line, Base Blood went stride for stride with Royal Blessing. In the final yards, Speed pushed his colt's head forward, and they won by a neck.

Pandemonium broke out. Chigger Beasley got Annie to the winner's circle, where the TV people took over, leading her to the right spot. She had glimpsed Sam in his box. The pain of his disappointment distorted his face, but when he saw her, it had softened momentarily. Frank waited on the track for Base Blood to return. As photographers swarmed around him, Helena hurried out to wait with him, and spontaneously she hugged him. Never taking his eyes from the approaching winner, he put an arm around the girl. Speed's smile was visible from a great distance, and his salute to the stewards had an imposing pride. Then they were all hurried together in the winner's circle.

The famous blanket of roses was placed over Base Blood's withers. Flashbulbs were so ubiquitous that there was nowhere safe to look. Annie and Helena managed only to touch hands. Base Blood, still blowing, awash in sweat, propped his chin on Annie's shoulder. "You're the best thing that ever happened to me," she said quickly. "Thank you."

She heard Frank yell, out of the picture as usual, "The colt has to start walking." Then Helena was gone and Base Blood was gone. Earnest TV personnel urged the winning party across the track to the infield pagoda for the presentation ceremonies. The governor managed to mention "Kentucky" nine times in his congratulations as the Derby trophy was handed to Annie. The television host, a warm puppy of a man, asked questions about how they all felt and what it all meant, arduously trying to keep emotions fully stimulated for the viewers' pleasure. When he asked Frank if he was proud of his daughter, Frank's face clouded until he realized the question was an honest one, innocently based on erroneous assumption. He gave a wry smile and said, "I couldn't be prouder." Then, to his relief, Speed was asked to give a commentary as the race was played back. When asked the inevitable question "How does it feel to be the first black jockey to win the Derby in this century?" Speed replied, "There's no black or white about it. It's the best."

The questions were harder when the three of them appeared immediately after the presentation ceremony in the press box six stories above the track. Some three hundred journalists from all over the world asked first about the horse, then about their Triple Crown plans, and ineluctably about the fight that morning. This led to personal queries about family relationships. Frank finally shoved his way out of the crowded room. Annie and Speed tried to turn the questions back to the race, but it was hopeless, and they too excused themselves and hurried to the backstretch to Base Blood's stall.

Two weeks and a few days later, Phil Angelo was sitting in a trattoria in San Fratello, a village at the foot of Monte Soro on the island of Sicily. He was eating three scoops of stracciatella gelato, the only thing he liked about Italy. As required, he had lived in the village for a year, in a dark room owned by a classic old *strega,* a word Phil translated to the woman's face as "cunt."

When he carried raw heroin around Europe as a messenger, Phil was allowed to work his own drug deals and had saved some money. Not that he was allowed to do much with it: hookers in Munich, a suit in London, a night of roulette at the Casino in Monte Carlo. But then he always had to return to San Fratello, and sit, and wait for his next delivery job. The heat had started early that year. Phil hated the heat. He hated Sicily and he hated to wait.

As he let a cold bite of the gelato slide down his dry throat, a copy of the *Daily Racing Form* dropped onto his table.

"Guess who won the Preakness," Juko said, and took a seat opposite him. He was Phil's "guardian," his contact with the Genovese family, who had arranged his extended Sicilian vacation. Juko was responsible for Phil's safety and behavior, and was supposed to kill him if he tried to leave the island without permission. They had to meet each day at the trattoria. He liked Phil and enjoyed talking about the horses with him. Phil regarded Juko as a dumb wop unworthy of his responsibility. A heavyset thug with a sledgehammer head and small eyes, Juko always seemed to pant as he spoke, a habit that annoyed Phil.

"What's this?" Phil asked, pushing his dripping dish to the side.

"You'll see. You owe me ten thousand lire."

Phil opened the paper and read the headline.

Base Blood Survives Fouls to Take Preakness

FAVORED TO WIN TRIPLE CROWN

Juko said, "Seems that Royal Blessing tried to run Base Blood through the rail."

Phil ignored him. "Oh, no, bitch," he muttered. "You've had enough. No Triple Crown for you." Then he grinned at Juko, reached in his pocket for a ten-thousand-lire note, balled it up, and threw it at him.

"Double or nothing for the Belmont Stakes?"

THIRTY-FIVE

ANNIE HURRIED OUT of the taxi and into the Mineola Holiday Inn. During the three weeks before the Belmont Stakes, Helena and Frank were staying at the motel in order to be near the track. Annie would have preferred to stay there with them, but there was too much daily business for her to be away from her office in town. It was almost midnight. She had left her Manhattan house an hour before in response to Helena's alarming phone call. As Annie crossed the lobby, she heard loud music from the bar. Entering the dark, blue-lit room, she saw Frank sitting in a booth with a bottle and a shot glass on the table.

Annie slid into the booth opposite him. Frank nodded as if he expected her, and finished off the jigger. "Helena call you?" he asked.

"She's pretty torn up," Annie said.

He stared at the jigger. "I thought it was time you both

knew. I was tired of hiding up in my room." He looked at her. "It was getting to be too big a lie."

"When did you start?"

He shrugged. "I don't know exactly. Sometime after the Derby, when they started calling me 'ax man.' It seemed those pictures were all over the place."

"Those pictures weren't real, Frank. That scummy paper staged them with some old dead horse. They even acknowledged it."

"It sure did remind a lot of people about what I did." He tipped the bottle and poured. "Including me."

Annie grabbed the neck of the bottle. "Frank, stop now. Please."

Some bourbon spilled on the table. Frank held on to the bottle until she released her grip. Then he too let it stand.

"Don't worry, Annie," he said bitterly, "this won't get in the way of your colt's winning the Triple Crown. And after the Belmont, I'll be gone, I promise you."

"What are you saying?" Annie asked angrily. "Base Blood isn't *my* colt; he's ours. Yours, mine, and Helena's." Frank blinked and looked across the room. "And what do you mean, you'll be gone? Do you think I could ever send him to some other trainer?"

"That's up to you. You're the owner."

Annie sat back in the booth. He glanced at the bottle but did not reach for it. She started to say something, hesitated, then went on.

"Frank, after the Derby, we talked about getting together that night at our motel." He looked away, as embarrassed as she was. "Why didn't you show up? I was waiting; you knew that."

"Because that would have been a bigger lie than pretending I wasn't a drunk."

"You're not a drunk if you don't want to be, and that night we could have been together. After that, you were different, cold and mean. When those pictures came out . . . Look, I understood what you were going through. Don't forget, I had to deal with the old pictures from the Latin Quarter and of all my so-called Mafia friends. Then the whole mess at the Preakness. But that night"—she did not know what she was going to say—"we might have . . ."

"What?" he blurted angrily, then spoke quietly. "Jumped on each other in the sack? Played at being lovers again while we campaigned another great horse? We did that once, remember? I sure as hell wasn't going down that road again."

Annie sat up straight. "You can't believe that. I loved you when I married you. I thought you were the best, the strongest man I'd ever known. I still believe it."

He stared at her. "If you believe that, you're lying to yourself as much as I was." Then he looked down at the empty jigger and began to turn it around in his hand. "I began loving you that day when you were sitting on Chigger's paddock fence deciding whether to hire me. I've never stopped . . . even while I hated you, strange as that may sound."

"Then on Derby Night, why didn't you—"

"Because when I walked down the hall toward your room, which I did cold sober, I recalled what I've known for too damn long. I knew that you loved Sam Cumberland, Annie, and always would. I stood there in the hall knowing that, and I couldn't bring myself to knock on your door. After a while I left."

He quickly poured. After one swallow, the jigger was empty, and he poured again.

Annie did nothing to stop him. "You're wrong," she said. "I don't love Sam. I loved you once, Frank. I think I could have loved you again. But not now."

She started to slide out of the booth, but he reached across the table and grabbed her arm. "Just a minute," he said. "Since you're here, I have something to tell you about Hank's horse."

"I want to go."

He held on to her as he said, "The Exwhyzee colt that ran in the Preakness wasn't the same one that ran in the Derby."

He let her go and she sat back in the booth. If anyone but Frank had made such an outrageous statement, Annie would not have listened. Even drunk, Frank would not have made the accusation without reason. "What do you mean?"

"I can't prove it yet. I'm not exactly in a position to ask an official to help. But I saw those two races, and I'm damn sure. Exwhyzee was two horses.''

She watched him, knowing how much he had been drinking but unable to ignore his opinion. "Frank, the lip tattoos, all the film. In the Preakness, there was all that trouble; it's probably the most thoroughly reviewed race in years. Somebody would have spotted a ringer.''

"Now you listen," he said angrily. "I've watched every foot of that film, probably more than anyone. Everyone else was looking at the fouls. Royal Blessing's jockey lugged in on the stretch, trying to drive Base Blood into the rail. Exwhyzee punched through and took the lead. He got a lot of clear film coverage. I can't put my finger on exactly what's different. They look the same; they almost run the same. But when Base Blood ran him down in the Pimlico stretch, I knew that California colt wasn't the same horse that ran in the Derby. I made a point of checking with the identifier; he was sure that the lip tattoo he saw in the paddock before the race was the right one. So I don't have anything to go on. Yet. But I'm damn sure, Annie. And I'm not looking through a bottle, either.''

He watched Annie for her reaction, and did not raise the jigger.

"If there were two horses that looked exactly the same," she said, "one would get his lip tattoo the first time he raced. It wouldn't be that hard to forge the same tattoo number on the second colt back home.''

Frank nodded. "And then there's an idea that occurs when you consider what Hank's company does.''

Annie stared at him, trying to remember what she had read, thinking as fast as she could to keep up with his theory. "Genetic engineering.''

"Right. I've been reading up on it, between drinks." Frank spoke slowly, struggling with the unfamiliar terminology. "So supposing seven to ten days after Exwhyzee's dam was in foal, they flush out a clump of cells and divide them under a microscope. Then they put one embryo back in the dam and the second in another mare.''

Annie nodded. Frank went on. "They've already done it with Herefords and jumpers. There've been some real nervous articles in *The Blood-Horse* about it. Start fooling around with artificial insemination or transferring embryos in thoroughbreds, and the breed explodes. You get twenty Secretariats and forty Slews, and every bloodstock value gets turned upside down. Hank could be in some deep trouble. Nothing bred artificially is allowed on a track or in the stud book; and running a ringer can send a fella to jail." He turned the shot glass in his hand but still did not lift it.

"It wouldn't work," Annie said. "The Jockey Club is blood typing foals. We send samples in from every foal that's born. I don't think it can go that far, Frank."

"The blood type is no fingerprint yet. And even so, it's possible to match two mares' blood if you're careful. But here, it doesn't matter. The second broodmare is nothing but an incubator. Genetically, she'd have no connection to the embryo she carried. When the foals were born, their blood types would be exactly the same, along with everything else."

Frank seemed as sober as if his bottle were untouched. Annie believed him. "Having two identical colts sure would explain how that colt recovered so fast and so often out in California." What the theory meant about Henry was another reminder of how little she knew her son. "How can we prove it, Frank? We can't exactly go in to the Belmont stewards and say we've got this crazy idea."

"When I figure that out, I'll let you know." He lifted the jigger in a mock toast, and this time took a long easy swallow.

Annie could not watch him. "I'm going up to see Helena. I'll watch the Derby and Preakness on film tomorrow, though I doubt I'll be able to spot anything . . . I wish I were wise enough or tricky enough to do something that'd get you to stop. It's awful, Frank. It's as if you've left us already."

He carefully filled the jigger again.

She slid out of the booth. "If it were anyone else . . . I have to say this, Frank. We have a week before the Belmont. If someone on the backstretch sees any sign of your drinking, you're no longer Limeteen's trainer."

"It doesn't show unless I want it to, remember?"

"If for no other reason, you should stop because of what this'll do to Helena. She loves you . . . very much."

He stared at the jigger. "That's close, Annie, but it's not quite wise or tricky enough."

Annie walked out of the bar to the elevator. Even as she was knocking softly on Helena's door, she hoped that her daughter was asleep. She was not. The girl's eyes were swollen from crying.

"Oh, Mummy, what are we going to do?"

Annie held her daughter. "We're going to have to be ready to go on without him."

Helena pulled away from her. "Did you fire him?"

"No. We're too close to the Belmont. It wouldn't be fair to him or Base Blood. But if the liquor shows, I'll have to. He says he's leaving after the race."

"We can't just give up on him."

"We'll never give up on him, Helena. Ever. I promise you that. But you have to know this: if *he* gives up, there's nothing we can do to change that."

"Do you love him, Mummy?"

"Yes," Annie answered firmly.

"More than Sam Cumberland?" Helena watched carefully.

Annie smiled and walked across the room to look out the window. "Falling in love with Sam was the easiest thing I ever did in my life. It took about one second. But from that time on, it's never been right."

"Do you still love him?"

Annie gave her daughter a quick glance. Then, glimpsing herself in the wall mirror, Annie unclipped her earrings. She answered the question carefully. "There've been too many times that I've been sure I didn't love him, and then found out I was wrong. So I won't say what's absolutely certain anymore. At the moment, the only thing I know I feel about him is that I *love* Base Blood for beating his fancy horse on the track."

Helena smiled as Annie put her jewelry down on the chest of drawers. "You want a roommate tonight? We've got to be up in four and a half hours."

Quickly they undressed and slipped into the twin beds. Then Helena said, "Can I come over with you, Mummy?" Annie held her daughter in her arms and hoped once again that the girl's life would be easier than her own. Helena would be fifteen in December; three times five, the same age Annie was when she ran away from the shack and went to New York.

"Sam sends me all those presents," Helena said, "but I don't feel like I really know him. Frank's been the only one like a father I've ever had. But you know, I want to love Sam, and I really want him to love me. I guess it's biological or something . . . When I saw him in the paddock at the Derby and the Preakness, I wanted him to notice me, be proud of me, show me off to that fancy woman he was with. Well, she's not so hot. Just . . . fancy. That's what he likes, obviously. I hate her.

"Oh Mummy, what are we going to do about Frank? Those newspaper pictures were so gross; that's what did it. I . . . ."

"We're going to sleep now, Helena."

"I love you, Mummy."

"And I love you," she answered, holding Helena's head comfortably on her shoulder, stroking a hand through her daughter's short black curls. Soon the girl was asleep, breathing heavily. Annie kept moving her fingers through the curls, remembering her own mother as best she could. She had no photograph, for none was kept in the shack after her death, but Annie tried once again to picture her. She could remember only the sad, fixed smile on her lips as she lay dying. Rolling her head to the side, Annie kissed Helena on top of her head, then looked down at her, letting the girl's face fill in the faded details of her mother's features.

The next morning, Frank was waiting for them in the lobby when they came down. As he had predicted, nothing of his drinking showed which fatigue could not excuse. During the drive to Belmont, no one spoke. Speed was waiting at the Limeteen barn. The jockey was riding every afternoon in the Belmont meet, but was eager to get up early to work Base Blood. While Helena went to work in the stall, and Frank sent the Limeteen sets out for their works, Annie met with her equine insurance agent at the backstretch rail.

A week before each of Base Blood's races throughout the spring, the two women had met to arrange new policy terms; the policy then took effect the second Base Blood passed the finish line, winner or loser. Annie had trusted Vanessa Blor for years. An attractive blonde who willingly admitted to never having ridden a horse in her life, her insurance estimates were sophisticated evaluations of a horse's transitory worth on the race track.

"He's insured at one million now," Vanessa stated. "If he places in the Belmont, his worth doubles. If he wins, it triples."

"Is that all?" Annie asked. "I read that Caernarvon is carrying twenty-five million on Royal Blessing, and we've beat him twice."

Vanessa smiled and shrugged. "That colt is running with probably the best pedigree on American tracks. They could syndicate him today for thirty million, even with the losses. They need a win in the Belmont, but they're already safe in the stallion barn. You see, Annie, pedigree is the insurance I don't sell."

"How long do we have to keep beating him to prove we're as good as he is?"

Vanessa cocked her head to one side. "Probably for three or four generations."

Annie looked at the agent, then turned toward the track. "I guess I'll have to live longer than I thought," she said, "but we'll keep beating him just for the fun of it. What's the premium on a three-million-dollar policy?"

"The standard three-point-eight percent of the policy's value, unless you want a guarantee of fertility."

"We'll take our chances on that. What's that come to?"

"A hundred and fourteen thousand."

"Good Lord!"

"That's why they give you five million if you win the Triple Crown, to pay your faithful insurance agent!"

The women laughed. Annie said, "That's all-risk, for a year."

Vanessa said, "Yes, that's all-risk for a year or until the next race, if there is one. Then we ought to talk again."

Annie recognized the agent's subtle inquiry about what was going to happen if Base Blood won the Triple Crown. Both she and Frank had ideas about the future, but they never mentioned them. They believed in taking one race at a time.

"Fine. Place it," Annie said.

"I'll go call London right now."

Annie greeted several trainers and owners who were leaning on the rail farther down the track. As soon as the insurance agent left, a group of journalists who had been waiting approached for a few early morning questions. Since the Derby, Annie's reaction was to feel a smile on her face and a rock in her stomach. First, she acknowledged the man from the television network who asked to change the time of the interview that was to be recorded for showing during the Belmont broadcast. Next, a tweedy couple from a national weekly magazine approached, he with his crinkled forehead and pipe, she with her perfect lacquered hairdo and tape recorder. Since the Derby they had been trying to insinuate themselves into an earnest personal friendship with Annie, an effort that grew stronger when the possibility developed of a Triple Crown and therefore a cover story. Several columnists and photographers gathered, and Annie did her best to respond to all of them. Pictures were taken; questions were asked carefully, because Annie had made it clear that she would walk away if questions became personal.

As she turned to watch a Limeteen colt breeze by, she saw another familiar face. Lyle McCracken was standing patiently nearby, obviously waiting to speak with her.

She excused herself and went over to him. "What do you want now?"

Her angry tone had no apparent effect on him. "Mrs. Carney, we've learned that Phil Angelo is back in New York."

Annie's irritation turned to dread. "I see. Are you going to try to ruin me again?" she asked, trying not to reveal her true reaction.

McCracken did not respond. "We thought you'd like to know."

"Thanks for the favor."

"You could do us a favor."

"Really? How wonderful. What could it be?"

"If the Angel contacts you, try to set up a meeting with him, and then call us." He held out his card. A special number had been written on it.

"Why do you think he's going to contact me?"

"I think you'd agree that over the years he's revealed a rather intense, even irrational interest in you. If it's still there, we want to protect you . . ."

"And use me as bait."

He did not reply but only watched her.

"Mr. McCracken, he's one of a thousand drug pushers and child molesters. Why is the FBI so interested?"

He hesitated, making his pause obvious to her. Then he said, "He was living in Sicily, where he was used often as a courier, moving opium from Turkey to the heroin factories in Marseille, then delivering the finished product throughout Europe to contacts who brought it into the States. He knows the network of something we're working on. He might fill in some holes. There are also several indictments outstanding involving your daughter."

"Yes, I remember," Annie said as she started to walk away. Then she stopped. "But since we're talking about favors, I'll trade you for one."

McCracken watched her impassively and said, "We don't necessarily get into trades, but tell me what you want."

"My son, Henry Sumner, has a stable called Pearbreeze and a company called Dynagen. His farm's in California and he has six colts, including one called Exwhyzee, here in Barn Twelve with Vlad Greer, his trainer. I want to know if he's renting some kind of stabling anywhere nearby."

The agent blinked languidly. "I found a needle in a haystack once, you'll be happy to hear. When do you need this information?"

"Last night."

"Why not just ask your son?"

"Well, *you* know, there are things a son won't tell his mother."

Annie put his card in her pocket and walked back to the rail.

After the races that afternoon, Annie returned to her town house in New York. She made her usual calls to Limeteen, then spoke with Delansig about what McCracken had told her. Several ladies had left messages urging Annie's attendance at the Belmont Ball, stressing the charitable nature of the event. She agreed to attend. She had a late dinner alone, and afterward, while in her bath, she heard the doorbell ring. A moment later, Bridey brought her an envelope, marked URGENT. Inside was a message written on the cover of Belmont's program.

Try Black Jacket Farm in Roxbury, Connecticut, off Route 67. Dynagen bought it in January. And remember that one good turn deserves another.

Annie dried herself and put on a robe. Using the phone by the bed, she called Frank Carney's room at the motel, but there was no answer. When she called Helena, her daughter was again upset.

"He said he had to go back to the track, Mummy. There were problems at the barn because the plumbers had to turn off the water. We had to haul buckets all afternoon. He drove me here after the races and we had a wonderful dinner together. We really talked. But then he put me on the elevator. I came right back down and saw him carrying a bottle out the front door."

"I'll try to find him, and I'll call you back. Try to get some sleep."

Annie called several barns on the backstretch at Belmont, but eventually gave up, figuring that Frank had simply made an excuse to Helena in order to be alone with his bottle. She found a map and located Roxbury, Connecticut. After changing into a dark blue sweater, jeans, and tennis shoes, she was about to call the car rental garage when the phone rang.

"Hello?"

"Hiya, Annie. How ya doin'?"

For a moment, her loathing superseded her fear.

"So the scum comes up to the surface again."

"I knew you'd be glad to hear from me."

"What are you doing back? Looking for six-year-olds now?"

"Hadn't thought of it, but you know of any?"

"Where are you, Phil? I'd really like to see you."

"Yeah, I can hear from the tone of your voice. Listen, I

really enjoy this, but I got something important to tell you. I don't know if your friends are listening in, but I get nervous with long chats on the phone, dig?"

"Do you have a toothpick in your mouth?"

"No, I quit, cold turkey. Why?"

"I'm just trying to remember what you look like. Go on."

"You remember me, Annie. I've known you longer than anyone else in your life, except Sam Cumberland, right?" He snickered. "Well, you ain't any Countess to me. I know who you are and where you came from. We started out together, and we could have made a fortune together. But you fucked me over, Annie. You liked the rich guys, and there you are with your stable and your money and your rich lover. Well, you know, I could be there too, if I had a hole in the middle of me to use like you do. Now shut up and listen! I'm in a hurry."

"What do you want?"

"Just to let you know I'm back, hear your voice . . . and tell you that you don't have a right to any of it. I want mine, Annie, and I'm going to take yours. For starters, there's a fire out at Belmont. In the Limiteen barn, as a matter of fact, and the sprinklers aren't on because somebody fooled around with them today. So kiss your Triple—"

Annie slammed down the receiver and yelled for Bridey. She could barely concentrate as she dialed Belmont security. They already knew there was a fire; they had no details. Annie called McCracken; after listening a moment, he interrupted and told her to meet him at the East Side Heliport as fast as she could. Annie told Bridey to go out and get her a cab. Then she called Helena.

Frank had returned to the backstretch, not because of the water problem at the barn, and not to have an easy place to drink, although he had brought his supply with him. He was leaning up against the dark side of a brick dormitory across from the Peartree shedrow, where he had an easy view of Exwhyzee's stall. He had no specific idea of what he expected to see, but was ready to watch all night on the chance that something might happen to validate what he knew was true.

Fire on the backstretch changes every intention, and when he heard the yelling and the sirens start, he ran to help. When he was close enough to realize it was Limeteen's barn, he yelled something unintelligible and ran faster, knowing that in spite of sprinkler systems and fire regulations, there was always enough straw and wood in a barn to fuel a conflagration.

He heard the horses as he saw the flames shooting up from the roof. When he ran around the corner of the opposite barn, the fire looked like a wall behind the people who were trying to hold horses, several with manes and tails singed and smoking. In that moment, he saw that the sprinklers were off, Base Blood was not out, and the flames were at his stall. The colt shrieked from behind the stall's metal gate as the shedrow's overhang started to crash down at the burning end of the barn.

The bottle of bourbon was still in Frank's hand. He dropped it, grabbed a blanket from the opposite shedrow, dunked it in a muck bucket someone was filling with water, and ran through the flames to Base Blood's stall. He smelled hair burning and realized it was his own. Covering himself with the wet blanket, he struggled with the metal gate of the stall, scorching his hands. Finally getting the latch open, he approached the terrified animal just as the straw cushion covering the floor began to flare from the heat. Base Blood was trying to turn, then rear. Frank reached for his halter and tried to talk, but the heat was too intense. He threw the blanket over the colt's head and spread it over as much of his back as he could. Without the damp protection, Frank felt his clothes ignite. He pulled on Base Blood's halter, but the colt would not move. Frank yanked the blanket farther over Base Blood's eyes as his own hair caught fire again. He brushed at it with one hand and pulled on the colt's halter with the other. Without warning, Base Blood bolted toward the door. Losing his balance, Frank was carried several steps and crashed head first into the side of the stall door, falling unconscious to the ground as Base Blood careened out. Seconds later, the overhang outside the stall crashed down, sealing the doorway.

When Helena arrived in a taxi, the guards refused to let it through. She ran from the backstretch gate. Hoses wove from fire trucks to the shedrow, and firemen sprayed the flames on the skeletal smoldering half of the Limeteen barn. Immediately she saw an ambulance crew working tensely over a man on a stretcher. Helena rushed through the temporary line set up by the Pinkertons and local police. When she was close enough to see him, she stopped and almost vomited.

"Helena," he gasped.

They had covered his body, but the skin of his charred head was split open. His hair was gone, his ears were stumps, and his eyelids were burned away. Hypodermic needles were in both arms as the paramedics spoke to one another with a calm urgency. Before Helena could start to cry, Frank's eyes fixed on her. When he started to move what was left of his lips, Helena moved closer and bent down to hear him. One of the ambulance crew yelled at her to get away, but she yelled back, "He's my father," and bent down closer, her ear to his mouth.

"The horse," Frank barely whispered, "needs you now."

Helena pulled back and nodded as the ambulance crew carried the stretcher quickly to the open doors of their vehicle. A paramedic said, "We're going to the infield. A Medevac helicopter's on its way to take him to the burn center. Do you want to come?"

Before Helena could answer, Frank let out a groan of objection and shook his head. "No. Base Blood!"

"I have to stay here," Helena answered as Frank was lifted into the ambulance and the doors were shut.

When Annie's helicopter landed, the paramedics thought it was the Medevac plane and unloaded Frank from the ambulance. He was the first person Annie saw as she, McCracken, and two other FBI agents climbed out and hurried under the rotors. The ambulance driver switched on his emergency lights, signaling the now identified helicopter to clear off, which it did as Annie knelt beside Frank's stretcher. He stared at her until the noise of the helicopter's rotors was faint enough for him to be heard. Then he started to talk, and Annie bent to his lips to hear him.

He could only slur one word into another, but she understood him. "Base Blood, okay. All that matters. Helena . . ." Alarmed about her daughter, Annie straightened up to look at him. ". . . called me"—the cracked split remains of his lower lip struggled to meet his teeth so that he could say, "father."

As the other helicopter began to descend on the infield, Annie looked up at one of the paramedics. Her question was obvious from the expression on her face. The paramedic, used to avoiding such queries, glanced away but then leveled his eyes on Annie and shook his head once.

Frank began talking and Annie put her ear to his lips again. "Don't let anyone else train him," he said. "You do it; doesn't like strangers." Annie saw the Medevac helicopter touch down as she listened. Barely she heard him say, "Annie . . . thanks again."

She kissed him, not knowing whether he knew or felt it. As her lips touched his cheek, there was a rush of breath. His eyes turned toward her and then they saw nothing. The ambulance crew lifted the stretcher and moved it to the helicopter. Annie followed, trying to watch Frank's eyes as the stretcher was secured inside. Someone yelled at her, asking if she were next of kin and wanted to get aboard. She shook her head and backed away carefully under the rotors. Standing in the infield, she watched the helicopter ascend into a night sky that glowed dully from the surrounding city lights.

Someone came up beside her. It was McCracken. "I sent the agents ahead to find Helena," he said.

Annie looked at him, thinking that he knew from experience how to shift grief into action with such alacrity. Together they hurried across the infield, over the track, and to the site of the fire. Annie walked through the destruction, following an FBI agent who guided them to a nearby barn. Next to it, a number of horse trailers had been moved into a row as temporary stalls. The Limeteen crew members who lived in the backstretch dormitory were busy settling the horses as best they could. Because of his status, Base Blood was in one of the few available vacant stalls. Annie saw Helena rubbing him, and took the opportunity to check the other horses. Miraculously, none had been seriously hurt, although some had spot burns and had lost most of their manes and tails. Several vets had arrived to minister to them, and Annie made her way back to Base Blood's stall. McCracken met her there.

"I'm assigning agents to guard you and your daughter. I'm going back to the fire; the investigators are already there. Before you leave, we have to talk."

Annie went quickly into the stall, snapping the webbing closed behind her as Base Blood whinnied. Helena glanced to see who it was, but kept brushing while Annie stroked the colt's neck and spoke softly to him. Energy came through his coat like electrical charges into her hand.

"I think Frank's going to die," Helena said softly but with no quaver in her voice.

"He died," Annie said. "I was with him." Without interrupting her stroke, she stood to see her daughter over Base Blood's withers. Helena stared at her, her blue Cumberland eyes devastated, but her ingrained awareness of the colt's need for calm keeping her from showing any other sign of her grief. She kept brushing, even as her tears fell silently on the thin cushion of straw in the temporary stall.

"You called him father," Annie said.

Helena thought for a moment. "I guess I did. Did he tell you that?"

"Yes, and that Base Blood was all right, which he said was all that mattered."

"It's *not!*" Helena replied. "Frank mattered more than—" She shook her head and did not finish.

Annie looked down at the colt's stall bandages. They were charred and shredding. "You made him very happy, Helena." Stooping down, Annie unwrapped and pulled off the bandages, carefully examining each ankle as she did so. "And to Frank, his horses always mattered more than anything."

"Except you," Helena said, "and maybe except me. He and I talked about 'the family' just tonight. He loved . . ." She could not continue, and Annie's throat was so tight that she was unable to respond. Mother and daughter quietly worked on the colt for another half hour, then stood outside until Base Blood pawed at the straw and let himself roll down to sleep.

The response of the racing community to the fire was instantaneous. Everyone at the track offered support, and many others, hearing of the fire, arrived to lend a hand. Sam Cumberland had been awakened with news of the fire by the chairman of the track's board of trustees. He drove out immediately, arriving on the backstretch at four in the morning. Within the hour, eight of his runners were shipped to Caernarvon on Long Island to make room in his barn for some of Annie's horses. It was a much needed courtesy, because the Belmont backstretch was always overcrowded. Without asking, he supervised the collection and distribution of tack, blankets, supplies, and feed to each of the Limeteen horses. When Annie came across him, Sam was washing out an old Caernarvon muck bucket in front of one of the Limeteen stalls.

"Are you and Helena all right?" he asked without interrupting his work.

Annie said yes. "She's coming back to town with me."

"I hope you don't mind my doing this," he said.

"No. Thanks," she replied, so tired that her reactions were numbed.

"I hear it was arson."

"Yes."

"If there's anything more I can do, please ask."

"I will."

"I expect there'll be a memorial ceremony. Frank and I weren't friends, but would you mind if I said something?"

"That'd be fine," she answered, walking away with Mc-Cracken.

The FBI established a round-the-clock watch over Annie and Helena at the house and the track. The Limeteen horses at Belmont were distributed between two trainers for whom both Annie and Frank had respect. Because she herself had no trainer's license, Annie asked one of them to be listed as trainer to Base Blood through the Belmont Stakes. He immediately agreed to let her and Helena work the Triple Crown candidate any way they wanted.

Belmont Park lowered its flag and organized a small ceremony to take place three days before the Belmont Stakes. Previous to the first race, the stands were filled with horse players. The infield near the finish line was crowded with backstretch employees. Neither Annie nor Helena trusted herself to speak. A microphone was set in the winner's circle, and after the chairman of the New York Racing Association and several fellow trainers spoke, Sam walked up as a representative of the Jockey Club. He had sent a note suggesting to Annie the order of the ceremony, and she had agreed to it. As he began to speak, the crowd in the stands saw Base Blood, with Speed Oliver up, wearing the Limeteen silks, come through the gap onto the backstretch and start to gallop alone around the far side of the track.

"I fired Frank Carney once," Sam began. "Within a month, I knew that I'd made a colossal mistake. For Frank was that rare human who could sense almost everything about a horse by just looking at it. Most of us here know about Frank's skill, either from watching him work or betting on his winners. Those of us who knew him personally admired his extraordinary skill as a trainer and saw how, as a man, he suffered for the mistakes he made, and how he survived and prevailed. His death is a terrible loss to the racing world, to its finest character and spirit. It is not surprising that Frank Carney gave his life to save a horse . . ."

Base Blood came around the far turn and into the stretch. Sam continued.

"That deed alone will always be remembered here, not only as an act of heroism, but for the conviction it exemplifies. A man who lives and dies for something more than himself has a purpose in life and in death that most of us will never understand. Frank had his purpose and it was total. If he were here today, he'd be embarrassed, as he always was by any praise or attention. He'd start walking away from us about now with his hands in his back pockets. But what he'd stop to see would be a horse, coming down the stretch, reaching for the wire, fulfilling itself as it had been bred and trained to do. Here he comes, Frank. You'll be here with us as long as horses run."

In the stands and in the infield, the crowd stood to see the lone horse. In a sudden burst of speed, Base Blood stretched out his stride, lifted his neck high, and thundered past. Annie did not dare watch him. Instead, she looked at Sam, who met her eyes with a look of longing.

Annie remembered standing outside that very winner's circle when Certainty had won the Belmont. Frank had avoided

the winner's circle; then Sam told her that he had been searching for her for weeks. Annie thought that nothing seems to
change. When Base Blood thundered by, Sam turned to
watch. She saw Sam's deep-set eyes follow Base Blood. As
always, he was perfectly tailored, his face tan, his thick black
hair giving way to the spreading gray of his temples, his body
erect and thin. Even in the dirt of the winner's circle, his shoes
looked polished.

The crowd applauded when Base Blood reached the backstretch gap and disappeared from the track. The day's card was
about to begin and the ceremony was complete. Then Henry
appeared, and without warning walked over and spoke into
the microphone. "I wasn't asked to say anything today," he
said. "I feel that I should speak because Frank Carney was
more of a friend, more of a father, more of a parent to me than
anyone in my life . . ."

Annie saw Greta nearby, leaning toward Henry as if she
wanted to hold him back. The crowd, confused to hear another speaker and no longer interested in the ceremony, made
enough noise to cover his speech. Henry's face was contorted
with emotion, however, a reaction Annie was amazed to see.

"So I wish to honor him, too. Frank Carney never lied, to
himself or anyone else. He never tried to fool anyone . . ."

Sam stepped next to Henry, put an arm around his shoulders, and said something with a sympathetic smile. Henry
lurched away from him, knocking over the microphone stand.
Greta hurried to Henry's side and pulled him away. Their
path led directly past Annie and Helena.

"It's not true!" Helena stood in front of her brother. "You
have a mother. You just want to stay angry. That's *your*
choice!"

Startled, Henry stared at his sister. "Helena," he finally
said, "there's a great deal you don't know."

"Then why don't you just tell me about it," Helena said
contemptuously, "instead of blaming anything you want on
her?" indicating her mother.

Greta pulled on Henry. "Please, come with me," she urged,
and the two of them hurried away.

As the group in the winner's circle broke up, Sam came over but did not speak.

"Great speech," Helena offered.

"Thank you. Sorry about what Henry—"

"It's all right," Annie said.

There was an uneasy pause; then the three of them, accompanied by a contingent of FBI agents, followed the others out of the winner's circle.

"If I don't see you, good luck in the Belmont," Sam said graciously.

"And to you," Annie returned, wishing they could get away from each other as she became aware of the couple from the magazine bearing down with a photographer.

"We're going to beat you again," Helena said provocatively, which elicited only an appreciative smile from Sam.

"Oh, you think so? Want to bet on it?"

"I've heard that ladies and gentlemen don't bet on a sure thing," she replied.

"The hell they don't," Sam answered. "You can take it from me."

"We'll wave to you from the winner's circle," Helena called as she and her mother rounded a corner.

Sam hesitated there. Annie glanced back and their eyes met, but she looked away as she raised her hand in a wave.

The next days were consumed by Annie's new role as Base Blood's trainer plus the extraordinary demands made by the press and the stringent requirements of security, both for the colt as well as for her and Helena. The FBI agents stayed in the town house, and the Pinkerton guards stood by the Limeteen barn. In addition to them, Annie retained a private security company through the running of the Belmont Stakes.

Lyle McCracken was convinced that Phil Angelo would call again, but there was no contact. The Angel's picture was issued to all track personnel in case he showed up at Belmont. Inevitably, the picture appeared in the press, and Annie's past was again reviewed. She warned Helena and Speed about Phil Angelo's return and the possible danger they faced. She also assigned security to Speed; the price of such round-the-clock protection came to $22,000 a week. Winning the five-million-dollar bonus for the Triple Crown became even more imperative.

The only relief that Annie knew from her fear and sorrow during those days was working with Base Blood. The colt looked around each morning for Frank's familiar presence, but seemed to disregard the absence when Helena led him out of his stall and he saw Annie with Speed ready for the morning work. Annie legged Speed up as she used to do for Helena when her daughter first rode the young colt. Before he started for the track, Base Blood would look carefully from mother to daughter, nostrils flaring and ears twitching, as if in an effort to understand what had changed.

As soon as he turned toward the track, however, he sensed his purpose, and often pranced and snorted his anticipation. Annie and Helena would lead him, accompanied as discreetly as possible by FBI agents and personal bodyguards. When Base Blood was working on the track, Pinkerton guards approached and checked any strangers around the rail or sitting in the stands. Yet it was impossible to protect a horse running on an open track. Base Blood's irregularly scheduled works made every trainer, exercise rider, groom, and hotwalker alert to any unfamiliarity or sudden move. Annie tried to concentrate on the colt's way of going, legs, style, attitude. She listened to him breathe, and she never thought he would do anything but win.

On the morning of the Belmont Stakes, she and Helena were both sitting quietly in his stall when he woke up. He sprang up on his legs and whinnied his readiness. After that, the long wait until post time for the featured race again seemed interminable. When they led him to the paddock, the crowds were oppressive, and the security people grew more wary. Six guards were dressed and credentialed for the paddock, trying to do their job and to remain unobtrusive, an impossible assignment. By the time Speed was in the saddle, a nervous wash had formed on Base Blood's flanks. Annie talked to him and held him back from the paddock circle to stroke his neck, hoping to calm him. Then he was away, prancing, sidestepping away from the crowd pressing in on all sides.

Annie avoided looking at anything else, except Henry's colt, Exwhyzee. She had not had time to watch the film of the previous two Triple Crown races nor to visit Black Jacket Farm. That particular problem would be investigated after the Belmont Stakes. There was no proof that Henry was running a ringer, and she could not simply accuse him. Whenever she watched the Pearbreeze colt, she saw no difference from the colt who had run in the Derby and Preakness.

Exchanging smiles with Helena before she and her security contingent followed the runners through the tunnel, Annie left for her box. After greeting the Beasleys and the Olivers, whom Annie had flown from Lexington to watch their son, she adjusted her binoculars to focus on Base Blood. He was washing out heavily as he broke from the post parade for his warm-up. Annie held her eyes on the tote board as the colt passed it. Base Blood, in post position four in a field of six, was the heavy favorite. The smart money as well as the sentimental betting placed his odds at one-to-two.

The warm-up seemed to help; Base Blood went into the gate calmly and had little time to wait. Looking over her glasses, Annie scanned the track. As always, the size of the mile-and-a-half oval awed her. The gate opened, and in refocusing her glasses, she happened to see Lyle McCracken standing down at the rail with his back to the race, watching the crowd. In that second, Annie forgave him everything.

Base Blood broke from the gate, and Speed took the length of the stretch getting the colt to the rail. Going into the club-house turn, Base Blood was fourth behind a new Lukas speed-ster, one of his other colts, and Royal Blessing. Exwhyzee was right behind them. Down the backstretch, Royal Blessing took the lead. There were cheers from the crowd as the fractions went up on the tote board: 23 seconds for the first quarter, 46 for the second, then 1:10 2/5 for the third. They were potential record-breaking times, but they were too fast for Annie. She held her breath, once again willing Speed to lay back.

Going into the far turn, the jockeys asked their mounts and made their moves. Suddenly the crowd responded with an angry roar. Annie saw the reason. Exwhyzee charged to the inside of Base Blood, and as they swung around the turn, the

Pearbreeze colt drifted out while he kept stride with Base Blood, forcing him to go wider and wider, losing ground with every stride. By the time they reached the top of the stretch, Exwhyzee began to falter from his effort. Base Blood was a dozen widths out from the rail, in fifth place.

The Belmont stretch is one of the longest in racing, and at that moment Base Blood had a huge distance between him and the finish line. The colt began to drive, blowing past four competitors in a furlong, then stretching his stride and moving up to the leader, Royal Blessing, with the final quarter mile to go. And then the Caernarvon colt, in spite of a punishing whipping by his jockey, flattened out in a tight-muscled struggle to keep pace. Base Blood shot ahead, running through deafening noise that came cascading down from the stands as he sailed by, increasingly alone. It seemed to Annie that he crossed the finish line in one of those flying strides portrayed in old sporting prints, with all four of his legs horizontal to the ground.

She quietly uttered, "Oh, Frank." Then she started out of the box, accepting the unrestrained congratulations of her party. She urged the Olivers to come with her. At the same time, she noticed the track's Pinkerton guards form a phalanx to escort her through the crowd to the winner's circle. The private security people she had hired moved with them, adding an element of professional menace to the turmoil of the winning moment.

"Congratulations, Mother," Henry said flatly as Annie passed her son's box. He stood, smiling acidly, holding Greta's hand.

"Thanks, Henry," she said carefully, without a hint of emotion.

"We'll be at the Travers," Henry said as a challenge, "then maybe at the Arc and the Breeders' Cup. Ours is the better horse, as time always tells." He turned away dismissively. Greta smiled sadly in the brief moment before she too turned back to their guests.

"That's fine, Henry," Annie said. "But which horse will you bring?"

Henry whipped around; the question had been ambiguous

enough, but as he stared at Annie, he seemed to understand what she knew.

She walked on, thinking of broodmares who, when they finally accepted that they had given birth to dead foals, simply could walk away.

As she passed through the crowd, people cheered her and yelled congratulations to "the Countess." She smiled as she knew she had to, but remembered an easier time, when enjoying a race came with winning it.

The couple from the national magazine approached sleekly, assured by Base Blood's victory in the Triple Crown of their cover story. They were joined by a television assistant director, who urged everyone to hurry along to the winner's circle so that his network's broadcast would conclude on time.

"This'll do it!" the magazine writer yelled exuberantly to Annie.

"Do what?" she said, amused by his childlike tone.

"Make him the Horse of the Century!" he gushed. "We'll put that right on the cover!"

"Don't call him that," Annie countered quickly, but no one listened. They were already fabricating their story. The simplistic title irritated her.

The track's uniformed Pinkertons led the escort to the winner's circle. The private security guards of neatly suited, dark-glassed, and ear-stoppled men, along with the women who accompanied Annie and Helena discreetly into ladies' rooms, filtered smoothly through the crush, keeping their unseen eyes on the crowd. Annie wondered where Sam was, and if Phil Angelo was watching somewhere, or, as the FBI had warned her when they tried to convince her not to go to the winner's circle, if he was focusing the cross hairs of a gun sight on her or Base Blood. As she stepped onto the track, she hugged a silent but joyful Helena. Neither spoke until Helena said, "Frank . . ."

Annie hugged her again.

Abruptly aware of the crowd's swelling roar, she looked down the track, thinking it was for Base Blood's arrival. But the winner, as usual, had continued running a long way past the finish line. She looked up into the stands and realized that the response was for her, that the crowd was standing, clapping, yelling, and stamping as loud as they could in her honor.

Annie knew how seductive and shallow such adulation was, particularly when it was stimulated by scandal and bereavement. The story of Base Blood and of Annie Grebauer Brown Sumner Carney, the Countess of Limeteen Farm, recently had moved horse racing from the sports section to the front page, just as Frank had predicted. Annie acknowledged the crowd with a wave before turning her gesture to the track and her horse.

As he loped gracefully back to the winner's circle with a beaming Speed Oliver on his back, Base Blood ignored the spectators. He saw Annie and Helena standing there, and, as he always did, he pranced for them. His face was still spattered with dirt, his coat gleaming with sweat, but his eyes were on Annie, and his ears cocked up. She smiled as he came to her and rested his massive head on her shoulder.

As nearly a hundred photographers fought for the best angle, Helena attached her shank's swivel snap to his bridle. Annie stroked his neck and said, "You're the best damn thing in our lives, Base Blood." Immediately he began to prance again, causing Speed to grab the colt's mane and forcing the two men carrying the blanket of white carnations to lurch and duck.

Then Base Blood took notice of the crowd, and of the strangers in the winner's circle. The six security men in Limeteen jackets were there to guard the colt. Several television people in blazers with their network's logo on their breast pocket were bellowing at Annie, gesturing toward the presentation stand, where the cameras, lights, and the Belmont Cup all were waiting.

As if he did not want their moment interrupted, Base Blood kept prancing around Annie, making everyone back away to a safer radius. Helena handed her mother the shank. Annie was too delighted to halt the colt's pleasure. Speed threw his unused crop to his valet, and, laughing at what Annie and Base Blood were up to, managed to jump free and run over to greet his parents. The crowd was still cheering happily, but the photographers and television crews were yelling for their privileged access.

Base Blood kept prancing slowly around, looking at Annie and finally whinnying softly. She laughed as they danced around, the center of momentary acclaim. For a few moments, they forgot the future, the danger, the next races, and the many different ways that the Horse of the Century could be beaten or destroyed.

THIRTY-SIX

IN THE BAR of a steak house on Manhattan's East Side, Phil Angelo watched the television image of Annie and Base Blood dancing around the winner's circle. The dark room was air conditioned, but Phil was sweating through his English suit. During the previous year, he had been sent to London on business, and the suit was made for him on Savile Row for $2,200. He spent the money gladly. To Phil, the Italian style of shapeless, wrinkled clothes was a conspiracy of faggot guinea designers to make clothes that looked as if a cheap awning company made them.

Combined with the beard he was letting grow and the tinted glasses he wore, the suit made a good disguise. The picture they had printed in the newspapers was old. He had a lot more hair then. Nobody would recognize him, FBI or otherwise. Instinctively, he looked toward the front door and the bright light of the street through the front windows, then back at the other patrons in the booths of the bar. The FBI would not be looking for him as hard as his former employers, not after what he had done to Juko.

Phil smiled to himself. All prison guards should get such a death, and Juko had been his jailer as much as any fat pig at Attica. But there would be no more prisons for Phil, either the legal kind or the one his mob family had put him in, with no walls but enough fear to keep him from crossing a Sicilian street without permission. Now he was walking around Manhattan, carefully, but going where he wanted, and doing what he wanted, with a little money in his pocket and the idea of getting a lot more.

Once he stopped being afraid, it was easy. Phil had no idea what had changed him, but he had a theory. It was based on justice. When he read about Annie's colt winning the Preakness and going into the Belmont favored to win, something shifted in his mind. He remembered making jokes with Juko, but he was already planning to kill him. What was happening to Annie was so totally wrong that it freed him to put it right any way he wanted. Juko had been easy. The fire at the Belmont barn was a little more tricky, but it worked. Maybe not her horse, but her trainer ex-husband. And best of all, she knew who had done it, and knew he was going to come again.

That was justice. Phil had done her a lot of favors. What if he had not picked her out that morning at Belmont and fed her breakfast? What about her first job on the backstretch, the introduction to Charlie Dell, and the rescue from Blimpie? His return on those favors was nothing but grief, and then she withheld the best chance, the only chance he had ever had to make the kind of money he deserved. While she was marrying more money than he had ever thought of, Phil was scrabbling for pennies, running, hiding, getting caught, grilled, beat up, and used. He had caused her some damage, with Glorious Girl, with Helena, but he had paid too big a price for the pleasure, becoming nothing more to anyone but a delivery man, living like an obedient dog obeying his master, and in Sicily!

At that moment on the television set, the commentator announced that Base Blood had broken the Belmont Stakes record set by Secretariat in 1973. Phil watched as Annie stepped up on the platform to receive the Belmont Cup and an over-size dummy check for five million dollars. She looked good, but did not smile.

"That's all mine, Annie Greb-ower," he muttered, "and so are you." He remembered how she had looked onstage at the Latin Quarter, walking around with nothing on. He went to see the show four times before he told Charlie Dell she was there. Phil had always regretted not having her that day in the garage apartment; then every time he recalled holding her breasts in his hand, he thought of finding the list and losing out on what he habitually projected to be at least ten million dollars.

On the TV, they were handing Annie the August Belmont Memorial Cup. She did not take it but said into the camera, "Limeteen Farm accepts this honor in memory of Frank Carney." In spite of the pressing enthusiasm of the commentator, she declined to say more. Applause broke out, which was joined by many of the patrons in the bar.

"Who the fuck do you think you are?" Phil muttered, this time a little too intensely, for several people watching next to him turned to look.

One of them said, "Buddy, your horse wins the Triple Crown, you know who you are." He received a laugh of agreement from the other patrons as they turned back to the tube.

Phil smacked a bill down on the bar, grabbed a toothpick, and walked out into the bright sunlight. He knew who she was, too, a nobody Kentucky hick who didn't know how to walk a horse around in a circle when he found her in that coat with the lining falling out. She should have stayed with him. She started running with the rich guys and forgot who she was, and him. But now, she would never forget him again. "You're mine, Annie," he muttered as he threw away the un-used toothpick, aware that it might give away his disguise. Then he crossed the street to get back in the shade.

After the presentation of the cup and the check on television, Annie spent half an hour in the Belmont press box, then hurried to the backstretch to join in the celebration at Limeteen's section of the Caernarvon barn. Owners, trainers, more members of the press, and other backstretch colleagues came by Base Blood's stall to offer congratulations and to stare at the colt. Annie lost track of how many people said that they would be telling their grandchildren about this day. As many wished that Frank Carney could have seen the race.

She and Helena stayed close to Base Blood. Lyle McCracken hovered patiently nearby; decisions had to be made about security, provided by both the private agents and the FBI. Annie and Helena had not fully mourned Frank. Now that the Triple Crown campaign was over, Annie planned to ship Base Blood to Lexington by air and rest him at Limeteen. She and Helena would rest, too, away from the emotion and strain of any track. Then they would make their plans.

Just as Annie began to feel a slight anticipation, she saw Sam and Henry standing together, watching her, back from the crowd that mingled around the shedrow. Neither looked congratulatory. Sam gestured for Annie to come over. He was obviously disturbed. As casually as possible, she joined them.

"Henry's asked us to have dinner with him," Sam said. "He's been telling me about his breeding experiments. It seems he's shipped Exwhyzee, and—"

"Shipped him? Already?" Annie's anger at what the Pearbreeze colt had tried to do to Base Blood came out before she had a chance to control it. "After your colt tried to run mine off the track, he flattened out badly and came back limping. He shouldn't be shipped anywhere."

"He's not going far," Henry said, a cool smile fixed again on his face.

"Black Jacket Farm?" Annie asked.

Henry's smile turned bitter. "Yes, Mother. He'll get there about the same time we do. I hired a helicopter. It's taken Greta on ahead and it'll be back by the time we get out to Brookhaven . . . if you care to join us."

"I can't leave Helena," Annie said.

Henry said caustically, "Oh, bring her along. It'll be one big happy family."

Annie told McCracken where they were going, and asked if

they could discuss business the next day. He hesitated, warning her that she might be in greater danger now, though he gave no details. Noting the FBI agent's unusual vagueness, she tried to reassure McCracken that no one could follow them or know where they were going, and promised that she would consult with him the next morning. Then she quickly made certain of Base Blood's security.

On the drive to the Brookhaven airport, no word was spoken among the four except when Helena commented on an FBI car following them. Annie wondered what Henry had told Sam, but did not ask. When they transferred to the helicopter, Henry took his place next to the pilot and let the three others sit in the back. As the aircraft rose and headed north over Long Island Sound toward Connecticut, Annie recalled the flight she had taken from the same airport when she and Winnie had left for the Bahamas. She looked over at Sam, sitting on the other side of Helena.

"I may as well tell you this," Henry said above the loud whine of the helicopter. "I don't think I've done anything wrong. All of the Exwhyzee winnings are in escrow, ready to be sent to whoever would have won if Exwhyzee hadn't run. I didn't do this for money, believe me."

Sam responded instantly and angrily. "Money's beside the point, so don't try that rationalization. The presence of your colt, whichever one it was, in any race changed the variables of that race. Also, the fact that you falsely won such prestigious stakes before the Derby wrecked the strategy of any number of other horses. It was an enormous deception! And *wrong* any way you look at it."

Henry's eyes widened behind his glasses, and he laughed contemptuously. "I learned deception from experts." He turned around in his seat and looked straight ahead.

Sam leaned forward so that Henry could hear. "Shall we agree that, from this point on, we'll discuss this situation as horsemen and horsewomen, and not indulge in accusation and breast beating about personal matters? Otherwise we may as well turn back."

After a moment, Henry said over his shoulder, "The Jockey Club speaketh."

Helena said, "It sure will be nice to know what you all are talking about."

The helicopter descended in a Connecticut field outlined by landing lights. The sun had just set, but they could still see a rambling white and green-shuttered Colonial house as well as several red barns nearby. Next to one of them was an unidentified horse trailer. After the passengers left the helicopter, Henry led the way into the barn.

"Bring them out one at a time," he said to the grooms in the barn, "Ex first, then Why, and then Zee." As each of the three identical colts was led out of his stall, Henry spoke proudly, explaining his ideas.

"What you're seeing is a pretty extraordinary scientific accomplishment. Genetic twins are relatively simple, but triplets are very hard. The embryo has to be removed from the mare, split and cultured, then split and cultured again. Then the three new embryos have to be surgically implanted into the surrogate mares. The purpose of all this was to reveal something of the future to the thoroughbred world, and, I admit, to show my company's expertise. We could have used rats, dogs, or cows, but I felt a certain sentimental attachment to horses, so I chose them. Besides, it's a spectator sport.

"When all of this comes out, and I assure you that I assumed it would from the beginning, we'll get much more attention than rats would have got us. I'd have preferred to run the colts through the season, but Mother discovered the secret . . . How'd you do that?"

Annie could not take her eyes off the colts. As they walked by, she tried to discover a difference but saw none. Conformation, markings, everything was exactly the same.

"Frank Carney spotted it," she said. "He knew that two different horses ran in the Derby and the Preakness. As far as I know, he was the only one who noticed. He told me the day before he died. I didn't have time to find out about it for sure, or I would have kept you out of the Belmont."

"Oh, I'm sure you would have, Mother."

"Henry!" Helena blurted, finally understanding what she was seeing. "You're really crazy."

"Why?" he responded, amused by the accusation.

His patronizing attitude angered Helena as much as did the evidence she was being shown. "Because you really think it's so neat to use three animals," Helena said, "and cheat everyone in racing, just to prove what a genius you are."

"Well, a lot of people use racing to prove one thing or another," Henry shot back. "Look around, Helena. You're too young to be so righteous, and old enough not to be so innocent."

"I'd say that's getting personal," Sam said, "and we agreed . . ."

Henry raised his hands in mock submission. "Just protecting myself from my wrathful sister," he said pointedly.

Sam overlooked it. "A breed can be preserved only by order. You've done something that could be almost impossible to control. Did you match the surrogate broodmares to the blood types of the original dam?"

"As a matter of fact, we did, but only for the science of it, not with any idea that we'd sell these colts with a provable pedigree. As I said, I intended to reveal—"

"Yes, I heard that," Sam said with disgust, "and even if you go to jail only for conspiracy to commit fraud for racing three colts under a single name, Dynagen will get a great deal of attention, which, as we read in the *Wall Street Journal*, it needs desperately. Every genetic engineering outfit in the country, obviously including yours, is running out of capital and selling out to the drug companies. For new funding, you were willing to show people less high-minded than you believe yourself to be how to destroy the breed."

Henry smiled. "Your analysis of our cash flow is quite exact, but I'll never go to jail. My lawyers are too good for that, believe me."

The last of the identical colts was led back into his stall. It was clear from his sore walk that it was he who had run in the Belmont that afternoon. Henry dismissed the grooms. Standing in the barn, Sam and Annie exchanged looks. Helena's arms were folded in front of her as she observed her brother and his blatant self-assurance.

"I should tell you," Henry offered, "that I don't give a damn about the breed. You and your Jockey Club friends do because it's all tied up with your heritage. I'm sure you'd admit that, Sam. But this branch of your family isn't exactly involved with heritage, is it? Sorry, getting personal I guess.

"Well, I believe that the thoroughbred breed needs all the help it can get. The gene pool's getting tighter. I think that thoroughbreds have reached their peak of genetic potential."

Helena rolled her eyes, but Henry went right on. "There's nothing new coming into this breed to give the gene pool any variation to improve itself. Yes, Mother's freak superhorse broke a record today, but by two fifths of a second, after *sixteen years.* And that's not going to mean anything to the breed, which Mother will find out when Base Blood tries to establish himself as a sire. With no pedigree, there's not much stamp for the get, is there?" He paused to smirk, looking at each of them.

"Not one of your ideas," Annie said slowly, "gives you the excuse to steal. You stole a lot of people's chances by running a fresh colt each time in those California races."

At that moment, Greta came into the barn. She did not go to Henry, but stood apart and said, "Someone from the FBI called to find out if you had arrived safely and when you'd be returning."

Sam stepped over to Greta. He had not spoken to her since she was about to marry Barky. "Good evening, Greta," he said. "We've been discussing Ex, Why, and Zee. You no doubt are familiar with the situation."

Everyone else watched her reaction. "I heard about the three colts two weeks ago, when we moved up here after the Preakness," she said. From her tone, it was clear that she was disturbed, but she said nothing against Henry.

"I disagree totally with your conclusions, Henry," Sam said calmly. "I assure you I've read every genetic study that you have, at least about thoroughbreds. As far as I'm concerned, there's still plenty of genetic diversity in the breed. But even if you're right, why not argue your case openly instead of wrecking an entire season of racing?"

The smirk disappeared from Henry's face. "Well, remember that I don't care about the breed; it means nothing to me. My lie was just like your lies, and I enjoyed watching my colts give yours some problems. But that's personal, and we're not supposed to talk about that, are we? Let's just say that arguing theories wastes time. I simply proved this one. And you know why? Because this is what's going to happen. Embryo transfers will be legal in five, six years; the Jockey Club and Breeders' Cup, Limited, will fall all over themselves, justifying and promoting it."

He stood rigid, staring at Sam, who said, "Go on."

"There are about a hundred tracks in this country," Henry said didactically. "Over eighty thousand races each year. The foal crop has stayed constant below fifty thousand in each of the last five years. There aren't enough quality thoroughbreds to fill cards now, and new tracks are being built in four new racing states. That's maybe forty-five hundred more races to fill. The fans don't like races with three and four second-rate horses. The tracks will be forced to bring in other breeds to fill the day's cards—quarter horses, Arabians.

"Do you think thoroughbred owners and breeders are going to let that kind of competition take over their tracks when they can produce three or four—or who knows how many— quality horses for the stud fee and in the same time it takes to breed one?"

Sam did not reply. No one moved. Henry, sensing he had made his point, went on. "Let me tell you something. There's nobility in horses, but damn little in humans. They'll legalize genetic tinkering as fast as they came around to race-day drugs. And when that happens, I'll be there waiting for them."

"Assuming you're not in jail," Sam said. "You know, you have every right to be angry with your mother and me, though by now it seems that you're hanging on to your anger a bit long. We're both deeply aware that your need to hurt us is not without cause. But you have no reason to damage others, which you've done. Your theories about the breed are nothing more than excuses for your angry behavior."

"Do you say that as a horseman," Henry asked snidely, "or as a father?"

Sam blinked, but that was the only reaction. In the same careful tone, he asked, "Is that helicopter still here? I'm afraid I won't be staying for dinner."

Henry scowled at the well-bred tone. "Going off to blab to the stewards? Gosh, Sam, I remember that for your *real* son, you threw your influence all over Kentucky to get him out of an attempted murder charge. Remember that, Maman?"

"Henry!" Greta shouted. "Stop! What are you doing?"

Henry turned to her with irritation, but Annie stopped him, saying, "What you don't understand, Henry, is that anything you do or say can't punish us any more than we've punished ourselves. I'm sure that we'll do everything we can to keep you out of jail so that your child . . . our grandchild"—she hesitated but did not dare look at Sam— "will have a father at home. In the meantime, talk to your lawyers and have them work this out to your best advantage. We'll wait for forty-eight hours. Will you agree to that, Sam?"

He nodded; Annie went on. "Greta, someday I hope we'll all have dinner together, but tonight isn't the time."

"No," Greta said. "I understand that." She walked across the barn and took Henry's arm. He looked not at her but at his mother.

Annie returned the look and said, "I've waited for years for you to call me Maman again, but not the way you did just now. It hurt me a lot, if that pleases you." Sam followed her out of the barn.

"Henry, can I stay?" Helena asked. "I'd have to get back tomorrow morning to look after Base Blood, but I'd like to have dinner with you."

"Sure," Henry said, surprised but wary. Greta smiled. Then Helena quickly followed Annie and Sam.

"I think I know where Henry is," Helena said with an authority beyond her fourteen years. "I was there for a while."

"Maybe," Annie answered. "But don't be disappointed. I'll be at the house."

"I'll meet you at Base Blood's stall tomorrow morning."

As the helicopter rose above Black Jacket Farm, Annie watched her daughter wave and join Henry and Greta walking toward the main house. Then the helicopter banked and headed south. Annie and Sam sat on opposite sides of the rear seat, each looking silently out a window. As she thought of Henry and Greta, of their baby, of Frank dying, of Phil Angelo, she gave up her hope for any kind of order in her life. When she felt Sam's hand touch her hair, she leaned into his arms. Without speaking, they held each other while the aircraft flew toward the sunset.

The helicopter descended, approaching the East Side heliport. They sat side by side without saying a word. After they got out, the wash from the helicopter's take-off enveloped them and they hugged each other again. Finally they stepped back.

"I'll go get myself a cab," Annie said as a statement of parting.

"Fine," he answered, acknowledging it. The look on his face mixed affection and despair. "Congratulations, Annie."

"Thanks, Sam. I . . ."

She turned and walked to the small terminal. At the door, she almost looked back but did not allow herself that sentiment or admission. She walked through the terminal, hailed a cab, but then saw McCracken step out of an unmarked sedan.

"There are some things we need to tell you, Mrs. Carney," he said as they were driven back to Annie's house. "Until the fire, we didn't really know if they were true. After that, we didn't want to interfere with the race and took some pretty extraordinary precautions. I thought tonight you deserved a little celebration before I told you."

"What is it?" Annie demanded.

"We have an informer in the crime family Phil Angelo worked for. They're looking for him, too. They want him dead, but we need him alive. Apparently he killed a man who was guarding him abroad. They believe Phil Angelo is close to insane and seem to be worried that he might go after them. We're worried about you for the same reasons. I planned to tell you as soon as I could after the race. I called Black Jacket Farm . . ."

Annie was exhausted with fear, but something was missing. "Killing a guard doesn't mean he's crazy—" The look on McCracken's face made her stop.

"He shot the man in the face at close range with a shotgun. He then hung him by the ankles from a rafter in an old barn. He hung a dead dog between his legs, an obscene message to his employers. And then, with a carving knife, he cut the number 'five million' across the man's back.'' McCracken turned to her to see the effect of his description. "That's why we want you to be more careful now than before."

"Please," she said, "my daughter . . . Black Jacket Farm . . .''

"Our people were on their way there as soon as I heard she wasn't coming with you.''

"Thank you.''

McCracken did not respond.

THIRTY-SEVEN

"YES?" Archie Delansig said into his phone.

"Someone named Angelo?" his secretary informed him.

"I'll take it. Turn on the recorder." There were several clicks, then the attorney said, "Mr. Angelo?"

Phil laughed. "Nobody's called me that in my life."

"What can I do for you?"

"You recording this?"

"I was about to inform you."

"Yeah, sure. Well, I'll try to give everyone a couple of laughs. I want a divorce." He laughed again.

Delansig let him enjoy himself, then said, "I'm afraid I don't understand."

"Sure you do, Delansig. You know the story. Annie and I've been together a long time, not in any way legal, but, say, spiritually, you know? We go way back, and she's made a lot of money, had a lot of success, big stable, Triple Crown a couple of days ago—all because of me. So I say there's a lot of community property involved, dig? Not legal; spiritual, like I say. Well, I want to get out of this relationship. And I bet Annie feels the same way. But to do it so I'm comfortable, so I can live in the manner that I ain't accustomed to yet"—he laughed, still having a good time—"I'm going to need a lot of money, and that's why I called you, because you're going to get it for me."

"How much?" Delansig asked.

Phil was momentarily surprised by the fast response. "I want to feel like I won the Triple Crown."

"Five million?"

"You got it."

"That should be easy enough."

There was silence. "What?" Phil exclaimed. "Easy?"

"Very. The hard part is how you guarantee you won't come back for more. Ever."

"Hey, that ain't hard. I don't guarantee it. What I guarantee is that if I don't see five million in five days, I'll feel free to start destroying assets again, one by one, and nobody'll know what I'm after. And that includes people."

"That's not divorce, Mr. Angelo; that's extortion."

"You call it anything you want. I want five million."

Delansig paused, indicating consideration. "When and where?"

Phil began to snicker. "Come on, Delansig, I'm smarter than that. Listen, I'd have pulled off that horse kidnaping if it hadn't been for Annie's dumb brothers. It's three-thirty. I'll call you in exactly five days at this number. Have the money and be ready to move. Don't have any company. Okay?"

"No."

"What?"

"Your proposal isn't even worth passing on to my client. I think that you know how stupid it is, and that you must be setting up something else. She and the FBI—and we shouldn't forget the Genovese family—they're already expecting you to try your worst, are prepared for whatever you try, and anticipate in one way or another stopping you. If I were a gambling man, I'd say they have better odds than you do. But I'm not;

I'm just a lawyer, so I'd have to say your scheme is a distraction. If it's not, well, you have to offer a better deal."

"You son of a bitch, you're playing with murder."

"Call it anything you want, Mr. Angelo. It's still a dumb deal, like something those brothers would have thought up. If you get any better ideas, give me a call, just for laughs."

Then Delansig hung up.

The recording of the conversation included a lengthy expletive at the end from Phil Angelo.

The technique was one Delansig often used in court: make people angry, and they often made mistakes. He waited a few moments for his own anger to subside, then called Annie and played her the recording. From the office in her town house, she listened silently, except for a quick groan near the end when Phil Angelo mentioned "murder."

To break the silence when the recording was over, Delansig said, "I assume the FBI will be furious that I didn't accept the offer, thinking they could have followed me without being detected. I would have done that gladly if I thought it would do any good. But I don't think Phil Angelo is quite that careless. I hope I did some other subtle damage."

"Me too," Annie said. "What do I do if he calls me?"

"Your phones are wired both here and in Lexington. He'll know that, but try to keep him talking. Agree to do anything that will keep the contact."

There was a long pause. Delansig wondered if she was still on the line. "How do we keep living like this? Do you give advice on that, Mr. Delansig?"

"No. But from personal observation over many years, I can say that, without exception, there's no one I know but you with the guts to get through this."

"Thank you. Do you always say the right thing?"

"Phil Angelo doesn't think so."

"No," she agreed. "Goodbye, Mr. Delansig."

"Goodbye, Mrs. Carney."

Within a week, Annie, Helena, and Base Blood were back at Limeteen Farm in Lexington, along with their security guards and FBI agents. Offers came in immediately from the major

637

tracks of America and Europe, inviting the Triple Crown winner to run in their meetings. Annie already had a campaign for Base Blood in mind. After a long rest, he would be pointed toward the Travers in August, sent to Europe to run against Bernard Dolby's Epsom Derby winner at the St. Leger in England in September, then in October, with the ninety-year-old Madame Pichon as a spectator, would challenge the Prix de l'Arc de Triomphe at Longchamp. If all went well, Annie would pay to supplement Base Blood into the Breeders' Cup Classic in November. If he won all of those, a nearly impossible expectation, he would deserve a title as grandiose as Horse of the Century.

The Exwhyzee scandal broke, brilliantly manipulated by Henry's lawyers. He made a sincere public confession and returned all of his winnings. While acknowledging his mistake, he made his genetic theories well known and expounded on Dynagen's accomplishments even as he cooperated with the racing authorities, the grand jury, and the media. Even after he was indicted for fraud, the three identical colts who had campaigned with such notable success in the races for the Triple Crown became the subject of intense scientific scrutiny and public curiosity. Dynagen stock subsequently rose throughout the summer, in spite of its chairman's legal problems. As one trial date after another was postponed by legal technicalities, investment capital began to flow in again. Henry was getting exactly what he wanted.

At Limeteen, Base Blood thrived. Annie kept tight security at the farm, and FBI agents came by each day. In spite of the threat, the public clamored for access to the colt. A few carefully screened visitors were allowed to visit Barn Two on a daily basis. Base Blood began to look forward to his audience; often when Helena led him out of his stall to a paddock, he would stop for the first camera he saw and pose, his nostrils flaring with magnificence.

One day late in June, as Helena was leading Base Blood to his paddock, a groom was walking a filly from the farrier back to her stall. The filly was in season, and Base Blood responded instinctively. About two hundred yards separated them when he jerked his shank loose from Helena's grip. He closed the distance in about twenty seconds. The filly saw him coming and surprised her groom with her own set of instincts. Before anyone could interfere, the filly whinnied, stood trembling in expectation, and without any of the usual resistant kicks, welcomed Base Blood's formidable advance. As the colt mounted her, the groom had little choice but to hold her head steady. A nearby exercise rider hurried over to grab her tail and hold it away so that a loose strand would not be caught and cause physical damage to the sire. Someone ran to get George Oliver in the stallion barn, but by the time he and Helena arrived, Base Blood had dropped off the filly and was strutting away, whinnying his pleasure.

Ten days later, the vet announced that the filly was in foal to Base Blood. The situation was nothing to brag about. Around a first-class stable such uncontrolled mating was never supposed to happen. Helena suffered some embarrassment, as did Annie; but after accepting the inherent problems of a birth due late in the thoroughbred year, they found themselves amused and eager at the prospect. The filly came from a strong broodmare line, and although the match was not ideal, it was surely a good one.

Six weeks before the Travers Stakes, Annie began a training routine to get Base Blood back to his edge for the million-dollar race at Saratoga. She had a record-breaking Triple Crown winner, but she had the audacity to try to improve him. The age-old routine around American tracks of keeping a racing animal in a twelve-by-sixteen-foot stall for twenty-three hours a day, with a work, a bath, and a walk making up its one hour of freedom, had always seemed illogical to her. Annie thought of the gallops at the Haras de la Poire and the training routine at the great French training center at Chantilly. Carefully maintained paths went for miles through the forests, and horses were regularly sent out on them for long runs as part of their conditioning. She remembered Madame Pichon remarking, time and again, "A thoroughbred cannot be kept a prisoner!"

When his training began again in earnest, Base Blood was out of his stall for five hours every day. Annie alternated the usual morning work on the Limeteen training track with an afternoon ride of sometimes five miles of breezes and walks. In preparation for his European races, she also began to run him clockwise on the Limeteen training track. On several occasions, she sent him by van to Keeneland. Although the race track was closed for the summer, the management generously allowed him to work on their turf course. Base Blood responded to each variation with considerable excitement and skill. The challenges of the new routine stimulated him, and his works reflected renewed energy.

Anticipating Saratoga, Annie filed for her New York trainer's license, passed the required written test, and received her papers from the New York Racing and Wagering Board with an alacrity unusual for a bureaucracy. By the time she watched Helena load the colt on the plane for the flight to Albany, Annie had the feeling—clear and distinct; it was not just the child of the wish—that he was about to amaze the world once again. Over the previous weeks, she had not revealed the times of his works to anyone; they were too hard to believe.

Annie timed their arrival on Saratoga's backstretch so that most of the stable help would be at the rail to watch the day's feature race. The strategy did not work. Near the Limeteen shedrow, a crowd waited quietly for a glimpse of the Triple Crown winner. As Helena led Base Blood down the van's ramp to walk him, there was a respectful silence. Then a deep voice called out, "If that's base blood, sure makes mine look good!" Laughter and a few hoots followed, which made Base Blood prance for his public.

Annie looked around at the many familiar faces. Almost thirty-five years had passed since she began working there. Memories flipped over in her mind and broke through her horsewoman's hardened exterior. She made herself busy in the stall, hoping that Saratoga would never change, no matter what happened in the rest of the world. What better place for America's deepest racing traditions? To have started there as a hotwalker, and to return with a Triple Crown winner who was poised to further his way into history, made an extraordinary circle of Annie's career. She refused to let the threat of Phil Angelo spoil the experience.

• • •

It was Travers week. The weather played to the popular will with cool misty mornings, sunny dry days, and comfortable nights. The many levels of the track's glistening white grandstand were blazingly outlined with red geraniums. Each day the track dried out to a fast, easy surface. The early morning breakfast crowd in the clubhouse swelled with people waiting to watch Base Blood work, even though, for safety reasons, he ran in company, with his companion between him and the crowd.

Since Frank Carney's death, Annie had avoided the many social obligations of a great winner's owner, but she decided to attend the Travers Ball because the woman who headed it had made a point of inviting Helena, too. It had been a long time since mother and daughter had dressed up. Wearing long summer dresses with bare shoulders would feel odd after so many months in boots, jeans, and work shirts. Upstairs in the old frame house that Annie had rented a few blocks from the track, they gave each other advice and helped with makeup, hair, zippers, and hooks. Knowing their bodyguards were waiting downstairs, they tried to contain their steady laughter.

"Do you think Sam will be there?" Helena asked as she bent into a mirror, applying eyeliner.

"He might be," Annie answered. "But I doubt it. The Cumberlands usually don't go unless they won the previous year and their colors are used." Standing behind Helena, Annie twisted and arranged her amber hair on top of her head.

"Have you seen him?" Helena asked, examining one eye and then the other in her mirror.

"Not since the day of the Belmont. Have you?"

Helena shook her head, dipped a tissue into a jar of cream, and wiped the eyeliner off. "I went over to the Caernarvon barn one morning to see Royal Blessing, checking out the competition. But Sam wasn't there." Then she looked at her mother to watch for a reaction. "You know, that fancy woman he was with ran off and married someone else."

Realizing that she was being observed, Annie chuckled. "I suppose you're looking to see if my heart stopped or something. Sorry. It didn't miss a beat."

Both of them worked silently. Annie slid in her hairpins and

641

wondered when Sam had lost Glynn, but did not ask her daughter for any details. She felt no triumph, no sympathy.

"Well, if he's there tonight," Helena said, "he'd better dance with me." She filled the sink with water.

Annie smiled into the mirror at her daughter and said, "I'm sure he will. He's a very good dancer."

"Yeah, I bet. Very smooth, very old-fashioned. It'd be like Fred Astaire dancing with Madonna. Mummy, I'm not going to wear any eye makeup. It looks really dumb on me." With that, she began to wash her face.

Annie smiled and went into her room to finish dressing. She decided not to wear any jewelry, but then she happened to glimpse Winnie's wedding ring in her case. She remembered the Travers Ball when he had asked her to marry him. She slipped the ring on her finger. Then, in keeping with the evening's nostalgia, she pulled out the string of pearls that Charlie Dell had given her and carried them into Helena's room.

The sight of her daughter in a pale blue strapless gown of silk taffeta made Annie catch her breath. She put the pearls around Helena's neck and fastened the clasp.

"Oh, Mummy, where did these come from?"

"From someone who wanted to give me a childhood, but he couldn't, so he gave me these. He would have loved you to have them."

Helena hugged her mother and said, "Come on, let's go to this ball!"

Sam Cumberland was one of the first people they saw when they arrived at the old brick bath hall. He greeted them both with his easy charm, which caused Helena to roll her eyes at her mother. At the chairwoman's table he helped Annie into her seat next to the star of a television detective series that she had never seen, a fact that—as soon as he learned it—left the actor with little interest in her. On her other side was the head of Japan's racing ministry, who spoke very little English.

Helena sat across the table between Sam and a handsome, tall senior at Andover who regarded his dinner partner with obvious delight. As Annie watched, for she had little else to do, Sam had both the young people laughing in no time, and Helena joined his banter with undisguised affection. At the first opportunity, Sam asked Helena to dance. Reaching the floor before it was too crowded, they put on a display of happy spins and glides that attracted some attention and certainly was the focus of the young man left alone at the table.

Annie could not remember exactly when Helena had learned to dance. She thought it must have been at school, but was surprised that her daughter was so good. Annie also noticed when Sam executed a little hitch step she and he used to do. Helena got it on the second try and, seeing her mother watching, gave a "not bad" shrug. Sam turned to look just as the actor, with an obvious sense of obligation asked Annie to dance.

As the dinner and the music progressed, Sam danced with every woman at the table except Annie. Helena's attention was claimed by her young dinner partner, to whom she responded at first with shyness then with animated curiosity. Annie went through several courses attempting to converse with the Japanese gentleman in a few careful phrases. She liked him, and he managed to extend an invitation for Base Blood to run in the Japan Cup in November. Before she could adequately respond, Sam came to her side and said, "Annie?"

She looked up and saw that he was apprehensive about her reply. Excusing herself from the Japanese gentleman, she walked to the dance floor, where she let Sam take her in his arms. She danced close to him because any other way would have seemed artificial. It was exhilarating in its familiarity.

"Did you set up this evening?" she asked.

"What do you mean?"

"When we all ended up sitting so cozily at the same table, it occurred to me that you may have arranged the seating."

"Well, Millie did ask my advice about how to get you here, so I decided to take advantage of it. Was it all right?"

"Sure. The actor would have preferred a mirror, and the nice man from Japan and I have been playing charades. Just don't tell me that the young man next to Helena is going to go to Princeton."

She heard Sam's laugh, and they danced without speaking until he said, "I love you, Annie."

For a few steps, she did not respond. "No. You're lonely, Sam."

He leaned back to look at her. "You heard about Glynn?"

"Only that she married someone else."

He smiled cheerlessly. "A guy four years younger than she is."

Annie offered no comment. Then Sam pressed her close to him again.

"What would it mean to you," he said, "if I told you that it's not because I'm lonely, that Glynn's leaving was as much a relief as a blow to my ego, and that I've known for some time —and believe me, before Glynn left—that if there's any chance for me to be with someone for the rest of my life, it can only be with you."

"I'd be very sorry," Annie replied without rancor.

He missed a step but recovered adroitly. "Then what did holding each other in the helicopter mean to you? And what do you feel now? What does all that mean?"

"That we've loved each other," she answered, "and shared a lot, and hurt together for some mistakes we made. But it's all about the past, Sam, not the future."

"Mummy"—Helena had danced up beside them with the young man—"Charlie wants to ask you something."

"Mrs. Carney," he said, "I understand Helena has to be up pretty early tomorrow, so I was wondering if I could drive her home."

Annie hesitated as Sam interjected, "I've known Charlie Todd since he was born. Straight A student, perfect driving record, doesn't drink because he's the Massachusetts junior state tennis champion. The only problem that I can see is that he knows nothing about thoroughbreds."

"But I'm willing to learn," Charlie said, giving Annie a beguiling smile.

"All right," Annie said. "But straight home. I'll be there soon."

"I thought I'd take him by to meet Base Blood," Helena said. "Just for a minute."

Annie agreed and Helena kissed her. Then the young cou-

644

ple hurried back to the table, and Sam and Annie continued to dance.

"Where were we?" Annie asked.

"Nowhere," Sam replied.

"Oh, Sam, what did you expect?"

"Nothing. I just hoped. Still do."

"Don't. If we've learned anything, it's that when we get too close, something goes wrong. I don't know why, maybe because we were too different to begin with."

"Trust me, Annie."

"I do. You believe in what you say. And there's a lot of me that'll always love you. But I know we can't be together."

They danced without speaking, neither eager to let the other go despite what had been said.

"Do you remember the Travers Ball," Sam said, "when Belinda told Mother about us?"

"Yes," Annie said. "Winnie asked me to marry him that night." Behind Sam's neck, she touched the ring with her thumb.

"I never knew that," Sam said. "Here?"

Annie nodded. "You and your parents had just left. We were still dancing, right over there."

"Did you say yes right away?"

"I don't think I actually said yes. We just did it."

"Yes, I remembered all that when we caught the helicopter at Brookhaven."

"So did I."

"Well, I'm going to ask you, too, and let me finish. I've heard everything you've said tonight, and I remember that when you learned about Glynn, you said you'd never take another chance on me. But I want to marry you. I will want to marry you anytime you change your mind. I agree that we weren't exactly made for each other, but you might consider that just because of that, we probably needed all this time and struggle and pain to understand how to be together. I say we can be together anytime we want."

"I don't agree with you," Annie said softly, "but thanks for the offer." She held Sam's hand affectionately as she stepped out of his arms. "And please don't wait for me to change my mind."

"That's my business," he said, the crooked smile spreading over his face.

Hand in hand, they returned to the table. Sam helped Annie into her chair and thanked her for the dance. Soon after, she excused herself from the party, receiving best wishes and good luck from everyone but Sam.

"Remember that the Travers is famous for upsets," he said loud enough for those around to hear; they laughed and applauded.

Annie smiled and called back, "The Travers has always been full of surprises. Maybe we'll have one for you." Then she left the ball and was driven home.

Helena and her escort, Charlie Todd, drove to the track in his Jeep, both talking spiritedly. They were followed by Helena's security guard in another car. Helena learned that Charlie had been orphaned when he was a child and brought up by a series of uncles and aunts. They exchanged reactions about parents and families and what each hoped to do. Charlie parked the Jeep at the end of Base Blood's barn, and, still talking, they walked down the shedrow toward the colt's stall. He saw them coming and nickered a greeting. As they approached, another of the private security men stepped forward, but when he saw who it was, he let them pass. Three of the track's Pinkerton uniformed guards were also standing nearby, and it was only by chance that Helena saw that one of them, wearing thick horn-rimmed glasses and a scruffy beard, was Phil Angelo. He quickly turned away.

Without a second of consideration, Helena grabbed a pitchfork and ran toward the Pinkertons. The other two saw her coming and reacted just in time for Phil to put his arm up for protection. Two of the pitchfork's tines went through his forearm and jabbed into his cheek. He yelled as Helena pulled the pitchfork out to lunge at him again, but Charlie and a security man grabbed her. Base Blood whinnied in alarm and half reared in his stall. While Helena fought to get free, Phil ran off into the dark.

She shouted. "Get him! Let me go!"

Charlie released her, but the security man held on. The guard who had followed Helena from the ball rushed up with a revolver in his hand.

"Go find him!" she yelled. "That's Phil Angelo!"

The remaining Pinkertons looked at each other, then dumbly back at Helena. The two security men, however, reacted instantly. One of them went with the Pinkertons, who blew their whistles for assistance. Helena went to Base Blood to calm him, at the same time shooting questions at the security man who had met them.

"How long was he here? Did he get into the stall?"

"He just arrived. The Pinkertons introduced me, a new guy they said, but I didn't recognize . . ."

"Did he get near the stall?"

"I . . . I don't think so."

"That's not good enough. Get to a phone. Call security and get more guards here. Tell them about Phil Angelo and say we need a vet to take a blood test. Then call my mother and tell her what happened. She's either at the ball or home."

As the security man ran off to find the nearest phone, Helena saw Charlie staring at her, and realized that her strapless dress was torn so that she was almost exposed. She lifted up the top and held it in place with her arm. Blood had spattered on her shoulder. Charlie took out his pocket handkerchief and wiped it off.

"Who was he?" he asked.

"An old enemy," Helena answered. "Base Blood seemed to recognize him. I wonder if he saw him before the fire. He was probably trying to fix Base Blood so that he can't run, maybe kill him."

"How would he fix the horse?"

"The colt, you'd say. The easiest way would be to give him a shot of some kind of depressant, some new designer drug that's one step ahead of the chemists. I'm going to have to stay here, Charlie. I'm sorry."

"Can I stay, too?"

In a barn not far away, Phil Angelo was in a stall, stripping off the Pinkerton uniform as quickly as he could. Helena had punctured his arm badly. He cursed the girl while he wiped the blood off his face and struggled with the shirt, careful to avoid the sleeping horse in the stall. He had worn other clothes under the uniform in case of an emergency, but had not expected to be wounded and bleeding. When the uniform was off, he remembered the glasses. He dropped them in the straw bedding as he left the stall and tried to walk casually toward the hole in the backstretch perimeter fence. He realized that the hypodermic needles would be found in the uniform, but they made no difference now. He had to shave the beard and find someone to fix his arm. As he felt for the revolver that had been part of his Pinkerton costume, he cursed Helena again, wondering why she had showed up. The gun was still secure in his waistband. He checked the safety again. With his luck that night, he would not have been surprised if the .38 fired and blew his balls off.

Reaching the chain-link fence, Phil found the spot he had cut the previous night. The heavy wire gave way and he rolled under it, groaning as his punctured arm hit the ground. When he stood up, he felt faint, but continued walking away from the track as normally as possible. He crossed Union Avenue. His dark blue shirt concealed the blood until it began dripping from his fingers.

Two police cars sped silently past him on their way to the track's main entrance. After walking another hundred yards, he saw his car in a pizza joint's parking lot and hurried to it. He opened the front door and collapsed into the seat.

"We go to plan two," Phil said out loud, "soon as I get a Band-Aid on my arm."

He started the car and pulled out of the lot. Driving downtown on Union, he hoped maybe his luck would show up. Five million was a big gamble; luck owed him. He parked the car in the Grand Union Supermarket lot, got out, and waited for the dizziness to pass. Then he walked away in the cool, starlit night.

THIRTY-EIGHT

COMPOSITE PICTURES of Phil Angelo with and without glasses, with and without a beard, were distributed to all employees of the Saratoga track. Lyle McCracken had arrived in the middle of the night with a new group of twelve FBI agents who were supervising security. Base Blood's shedrow was blocked off to everyone except the identified crew tending the horses.

As usual, Annie and Helena were in the colt's stall when he woke up realizing it was a race day. His reaction of snorting excitement was the same as it had always been. Mother and daughter stayed in the stall with him as long as possible, able to enjoy for the last time that day the simple elation of preparing the colt to race.

McCracken's first suggestion was to scratch Base Blood and get him, Annie, and Helena away from the Saratoga track. He argued hard and was explicit about the dangers they might face. When Speed Oliver arrived, they shared McCracken's dire warnings with the jockey, who had the same response as Annie and Helena: Base Blood runs. Once McCracken understood their intransigence, he demanded certain restrictions, to which they agreed.

Base Blood's race-day routine was not altered. When the Travers was called over the backstretch loudspeakers, Helena led him around to the tree-shaded paddock, where Annie met them. Each was accompanied by appropriately clad bodyguards, Limeteen grooms' jackets for Helena's, coats and ties for Annie's. By that time, word of the threat to Base Blood had spread among those in the paddock, including Sam Cumberland. As soon as he had a chance, he came over to Annie and Helena, who were in Base Blood's saddling stall.

Noticing the number of security guards, Sam said, "I came looking for you this morning, but they wouldn't let me through. Did Henry find you?"

Surprised, Annie shook her head. "When did he call?"

"He and Greta arrived last night. Probably couldn't reach you. He seems to have had quite a change of heart. They came by the barn this morning. They'll be sitting in my box. I assume all these people are taking good care of you."

Annie reassured him. Sam turned to Helena. "Your colt looks fine, but we'll beat him today, I think."

"Want to bet?" Helena challenged.

"Anything you want," Sam dared.

"Another dance sometime."

"You're on," Sam said, cheerily trying to relieve the stress. "By the way, you made quite an impression on Charlie Todd."

The girl's face flushed as she held Base Blood's lead. "Not as good as the one I made on Phil Angelo," she said proudly to change the subject. "If I'd had another second, he wouldn't have been able to run away." Involuntarily, all three of them looked out at the thousands of faces watching the saddling from behind the white paddock fence. Then Sam said, "You two be careful," and to Annie, "I meant what I said last night."

The jockeys came into the paddock, and Sam strode back to the numbered tree around which Royal Blessing was being walked by a Caernarvon groom. Speed Oliver was followed by two of his own enormous bodyguards, who joined the others in watching the crowd as the jockey conferred with Annie.

"Speed, I don't have to tell you anything."

He smiled and said, "Then I'll tell you. Hey, that's a switch! I'll break right out to the front and keep him there. I want him to show off all this fancy training we've been hearing about. With only four other colts running, I don't see any traffic problems. But if Royal Blessing tries anything, we'll run him down!"

Speed looked at Base Blood and grinned. "The colt's lucky," he said. "Even with all these guards running around, he thinks it's just another race. Well, that's the way I'll ride him."

Annie legged him up, and Helena led the colt out of the enclosure to his place under the trees. The crowd began to yell and applaud, inspiring Base Blood to do his usual sidestep prance. The paddock judge called the numbers, and the five colts fell into line and circled the paddock. The shouts of admiration and encouragement for Base Blood swelled, and he tossed his head in acknowledgment.

Suddenly, he stopped, his eyes on the crowd, his nostrils and ears working, looking at something, trying to understand. Helena, who was leading him, pulled at the lead, then jerked at it. Base Blood, still looking into the crowd, gave a loud whinny. The paddock judge ordered Helena to get the colt moving. Speed talked to him and patted him, but he would not move.

Annie walked quickly across the paddock as the judge gave a second warning. She touched Base Blood's neck and gently stroked him, feeling a different kind of reaction coming from him. In spite of it, she said, "Base Blood, Base Blood, listen. Come on, now. Run. It's time."

Base Blood tossed his head and turned to her, nickered briefly, then put his head on her shoulder. The crowd responded with laughter and more cheers. The colt instantly began to prance, and Helena, followed by the contingent of bodyguards, led him quickly toward the track and the post parade.

Annie waited, as she had agreed to do, while the crowd in the paddock walked at a leisurely pace to their boxes. The fans and handicappers hurried to return to the clubhouse, the grandstand, or their lawn chairs under the nearby trees, in which television monitors were placed. Rubbing the fingers of her hand together, Annie tried to decipher what she had felt from Base Blood.

"Mrs. Carney." Lyle McCracken stood next to her. Surrounded by her security men, she started for the Trustees' Room, where she had agreed with McCracken to watch the race, and where, if Base Blood won, she would receive the trophy. Then she heard a familiar voice.

"Maman."

Annie had not been looking at the people still standing along the paddock fence. Henry and Greta were there, she as lovely as ever and noticeably more pregnant, he with the recognizable smile of the son Annie had not seen for so long. She walked over to them, gave Greta a kiss on the cheek, then looked at Henry. "I'm so glad you came," she said.

"Wouldn't miss it," Henry said. "Greta seems to have convinced me that I've not only been a felon; I've been a real jerk. I'm hoping you can start to forgive me after the race."

Annie could only nod. Then Henry said, "Nice ring you've got there." Greta saw it, and the three of them awkwardly embraced over the rail. McCracken moved closer, and Annie continued on her way to the Trustees' Room.

Phil Angelo moved his wheelchair as fast as he could through the crowd on the grandstand apron. Perversely imitating the pride of the handicapped, whom he had seen so often at tracks, he wore shorts to allow his leg braces to catch the eye, as well as a wide-brimmed straw hat to shield him from the sun and careful observation. His beard was shaved down to a mustache, and he had shaved his legs to make them look more pallid. The braces cut into his legs, and the cotton balls stuffed under his lips and cheeks distorted his face uncomfortably. Nevertheless, the disguise had worked. Depending on the sympathy of people when they saw the braces, he gradually moved directly to the rail across from the pole that marked the last furlong from the finish. He was right where he wanted to be.

What he could not believe was that the colt had seemed to spot him, stopped dead in the paddock, and looked right at him. That scared Phil; he had moved out of there as fast as he could propel the wheelchair through the crowd.

He looked across the track to the infield. Nobody was there except a couple of photographers checking their cameras, which were taped to the rail. Nervously, he felt the straps of the braces, figuring how quickly he could get them off after the race began when no one would be paying attention. He thought his chances of getting away by running back through the crowd were pretty good. He had a different shirt and shorts under the ones that showed. There would be a lot of confusion; he planned to get lost in it.

Base Blood's pony rider in the post parade was an armed state trooper, dressed in the track's uniform of breeches and jacket. He kept Base Blood on the infield side of his pony, away from the crowd. Speed talked his usual easy banter, worked a handhold in Base Blood's mane in case he needed it, and started thinking the race. At the furlong pole, the colt stopped again, halting the pony rider. Base Blood did not look around, but Speed felt a deep tremble under him. He urged the colt forward, as did the pony rider. The other horses in the race broke past them in their warm-up run. Base Blood stood a moment, then lifted his head high, gave a piercing whinny, and leaped away from the pony rider. Speed was glad he had the mane to hold. He let the colt run, hoping that whatever had bothered him would be expelled, and by the time they returned to the starting gate, Base Blood seemed his normal self, ready and determined.

Annie watched the TV monitor in the small white room on the ground floor of the clubhouse. She sat at one of the tables with Lyle McCracken. Standing behind them were two other FBI agents, one with a walkie-talkie.

"Helena?" Annie said to McCracken, who glanced at the agent. He spoke into the walkie-talkie and replied, "In place."

Several other trustees and their guests were in the room, avoiding the crowds and enjoying the air conditioning. The steady roar from the stands above them sounded like a hollow echo. There was a constant cracking of stressed wood as the old structure adjusted to the weight of the record crowd.

The starting bell rang; the five colts vaulted out of the starting gate. Speed sent Base Blood to the lead and guided him to the rail ahead of the pack. Royal Blessing's jockey apparently had instructions to stay close to the leader to press him into too fast a pace. Speed had no concern. Base Blood was going coolly.

On the backstretch, Base Blood lengthened his lead to four lengths. None of the other horses could keep up. At the final turn Royal Blessing's jockey was already using his whip—to no avail. Base Blood leaped forward and entered the stretch alone.

As usual, Speed yelled out, "Okay, Base Blood, LET'S FLY!" But it seemed unnecessary. Speed glanced around to see if anyone was coming. As he turned forward, he saw someone in shorts leap over the grandstand rail. Nearby, someone else jumped onto the track, a policeman. The jockey felt the colt react and plunge ahead faster. The man in shorts ran out to the middle of the track. Two others chased after him. Sprinting away from them, the man lurched toward the inside rail and pointed a gun. Speed tried to turn Base Blood, but felt two jolts under him and saw two puffs of smoke from the gun. The jockey prepared for a fall. The colt shuddered but plunged on, suddenly roaring from his lungs as the screams and yells from the crowd tore over them. The man on the track jumped back and tried to aim the gun again, but before he could fire, Base Blood ran over him. For an instant, Speed saw a look of unbelieving terror on the familiar face as Base Blood's lead hoof tore open the top of his head.

The colt charged on. Speed could see blood coming from his mouth and thought of trying to ease him, but dared not interfere with the force that was driving him to the finish line. He knew the colt was dying; as tears came to his eyes, he shouted again, "Fly, Base Blood, fly!" The colt lunged, faltered once, but Speed pulled him up. He saw the finish line and sat firmly on the colt to get him there. Ten strides to go, then five, and Base Blood started to crumple. Yet he managed to plunge on, his last steps lurching forward, keeping the momentum of his body going, passing the finish line, then, after two more strides, crashing down on his off side, throwing Speed from his back to roll over and over down the track. For an interminable moment, Base Blood's legs continued to run in the air. Then they were still.

Annie was on her feet, heading for the door of the Trustees' Room before the second-place finisher crossed the line. McCracken was there first and held the door shut.

"Mrs. Carney, that may have been only part of the plan," he warned.

"That doesn't matter!" she replied. "Did you notice that he never hesitated? Base Blood knew." The look on her face changed to cold resolve. "Mr. McCracken, get me to the track."

The agent hesitated, then beckoned to the other agents. There was pounding on the door. When it opened, Annie followed the wedge of men, who moved quickly through the shocked crowd standing on the clubhouse apron. Annie's private security people, the Pinkertons, and several other agents joined them before they reached the winner's circle. Annie saw Helena kneeling by Base Blood, then Sam and Henry pushing through the crowd. She reached toward them; McCracken let the two men through to her.

The three hurried out to the track, where guards were trying to sort out the track officials and the press. Down the stretch, the lumbering square-shaped horse ambulance passed the cordon of police and FBI agents who surrounded Phil Angelo's trampled, bleeding body. The ambulance that followed the race was already beside Speed Oliver, who was standing in obvious pain. When he saw Annie, the jockey shook loose of the paramedics and limped toward her, one arm dangling at an unnatural angle.

Helena was stroking the colt's cheek. There was blood on her hands. Annie hurried to her and stooped beside her. "He's . . ." the girl said, her face about to break open with grief.

"Helena," Annie began, but at the sound of her voice, Base Blood shuddered and his front leg moved, pawing the air. He lifted his head to look at Annie, nickered, then choked, and his head crashed lifelessly onto the track. Her hand was already to his lips. Knowing he was dead, she said softly, "You're the best thing that . . ."

Then she stood, and her arm encircled Helena. Sam came up beside them; Henry and Speed stood together nearby. The track vet was listening through a stethoscope for the colt's heartbeat. When he heard none, he stood and regretfully shook his head. The men from the horse ambulance were about to stretch their canvas to prevent the crowd from observing the removal of Base Blood's carcass.

Sam, however, stepped forward and shouted, "Wait a minute! Everyone back away. Just for a minute, get the ambulance out of here and stand back."

At first, the track officials did not understand, but then they obeyed Sam. The horse ambulance was driven down the track. Everyone moved back, leaving Base Blood lying alone on the track. Within a half minute, the entire crowd of sixty thousand was silent.

THIRTY-NINE

THE WEANLING broke away from his mother, and on his disproportionately long legs, each of which seemed to have a tentative will of its own, he scampered across the paddock, then stopped so suddenly, he almost fell back on his haunches. Bobbing his head, then extending his neck so far that he lost his balance, he tried to understand what Annie was holding in her arms. Used to the woman, the weanling came close enough to smell. When the baby reached out to grab at him, he took off, whinnying his alarm.

Annie held her granddaughter so that she could see the weanling scamper and frisk back to his mother. The baby yelled, trying to get the little horse to return.

"That's who I wanted you to meet, Kate," Annie said to the five-month-old girl. "His name's Base Line. Can you say that?"

Annie had been looking after the baby for almost a week,

and had enjoyed it. She was going to miss having her grand-daughter at Limeteen Hall when Greta and Henry returned from their vacation. Henry had been released after giving up his defense, pleading guilty, and serving six months in prison.

The farm station wagon drove past Limeteen Hall and down the farm road to the paddock where Annie held the baby. Helena rolled down a window. The car was full of her friends from school in tennis outfits.

"Mummy, can everyone stay and have some snacks? I'll make them."

"Sure, but make some for me, too. We'll be up in a while."

Helena had never returned to the backstretch after Base Blood was shot. In the following months, she had continued to help around the farm before and after school, and often went riding with her mother, but only to keep her company. Soon her interests in other activities became apparent, and after Charlie Todd arrived at Christmas, having arranged with Sam a visit to Caernarvon Farm, Helena took up tennis with fierce purpose. At first, Annie was saddened by her daughter's rejection of what Annie believed was most important in her life, but she accepted it when she realized that the girl's experience with a colt like Base Blood had been too ideal, too much a fairy tale.

Holding Kate up in order to pique the weanling's curiosity once again, Annie thought of her past and wondered if there were any more mistakes to catch up with her. She remembered lying in Sam's arms several months after Base Blood's death and, for the first time, allowing herself to express grief.

"I feel as if it was my past that killed him," she had said. "Base Blood had nothing to do with that. It was going to catch up with me sooner or later, and it killed him."

Sam held her for a long time, letting her cry. When she grew quiet, he said, "You can forget the guilt. When you were lucky enough to find him, it's because of your past that you could see what he was. You gave him his life." He kissed her gently. "The past doesn't catch up with us, Annie. It rides us every day like a glue-seated jockey. The best we can do is run with it, and take the whip when it comes."

Remembering the carrot she had brought for the occasion,

Annie held it out to Base Line, who was again bobbing his way toward them. Kate Sumner squealed with pleasure at the weanling's approach. The colt, born on the last day that Annie was fifty—five times ten—would have to be broken and trained later than the rest of her foal crop.

Annie had already decided that Base Line would not race as a two-year-old. But when he was three . . .